D1175363

THE WESLEYAN EDITION OF THE
WORKS OF HENRY FIELDING

THE TRUE PATRIOT
AND
RELATED WRITINGS

HENRY FIELDING

The True Patriot
and Related Writings

EDITED BY
W. B. COLEY

Wesleyan University Press
Middletown, Connecticut

Published in the United States by Wesleyan University Press

Published simultaneously in Great Britain by Oxford University Press copyright © 1987 by Oxford University Press.

LIBRARY OF CONGRESS CATALOGING-IN-PUBLICATION DATA
Fielding, Henry, 1707–1754.
The true patriot and related writings.
(The Wesleyan edition of the works of Henry Fielding)
Includes index.
1. Great Britain—History—George II, 1727–1760—
Pamphlets. I. Coley, W. B., 1923– . II. Title.
III. Series: Fielding, Henry, 1707–1754. Works. 1983.
[DA503 1745.F54 1987b]   941.07′2   86–18463
ISBN 0–8195–5127–9

All inquiries and permissions requests should be addressed to the Publisher, Wesleyan University Press, 110 Mt. Vernon Street, Middletown, Connecticut 06457.

Distributed by Harper & Row Publishers, Keystone Industrial Park, Scranton, Pennsylvania 18512.

First American Edition

PREFACE

THE Wesleyan Edition of the works of Henry Fielding has as its primary aims a fuller definition of the canon and the establishment of a reliable text according to modern bibliographical standards. In addition, its editors aim to supply the reader with whatever is relevant to the immediate context and essential meaning of their respective texts. They are not asked to supply interpretations or 'readings' of the materials they edit.

So much by way of reminder, a reminder made necessary in part by the unfortunate lapse of time between volumes. In the case of the present volume, however, a word must be said concerning the General Introduction. Like the others in this edition it sets forth such things as the evidence for attribution, circumstances of composition, biographical contexts, printing and publication details. Unlike some of the others it treats in considerable detail the political circumstances in which the writings appear to have been produced. For these are writings with a political purpose somewhere behind them. Fielding may not have liked writing about politics—there is evidence that he was uncomfortable doing so—and it can be argued that he did not write terribly well about politics. But it is a mistake to deny the importance of political considerations in the case of such writings as are collected here. Far from being politically neutral, as previous editors have said, the *True Patriot* in particular can be fully understood only against a rather detailed background of the political purposes and activities of those 'true patriots' with whom Fielding was closely associated at this time. Much the same is true of the pamphlets as well. The General Introduction, therefore, should not be construed as an attempt to interpret Fielding's own politics, whatever they may have been, but rather as an attempt to suggest how he came to write what he wrote when he wrote it. In that sense the introduction simply extends the effort to place these writings in a relevant context of personal circumstances.

The bibliographical principles followed in preparing the texts of this volume, as well as the specific procedures and decisions which went into the establishment of these texts, are set forth in the Textual Introduction, which, as readers of my earlier volume in this edition will recognize, I have based on the one which Fredson Bowers wrote for that earlier volume. It is a pleasure to record my indebtedness, just as it is necessary to note that any deficiencies, either of formulation or application, are my responsibility. Certain of the appendices here record editorial emendations to the copy-text as well as bibliographical descriptions of the various states or editions of the writings being edited. Because the texts in the present volume have had to be conservatively handled in the absence of any clear authorial revision or even super-intendence, the interested reader is once again invited to read Professor Bowers' Textual Introduction to either *Joseph Andrews* or *Tom Jones* for a fuller sense of how the bibliographical principles of the Wesleyan Edition affect the handling of more sophisticated problems.

The reader is further reminded that the Wesleyan Fielding attempts to combine chronological with generic coverage, wherever this is prac-ticable. With the plays, the novels, and in its own way the *Miscellanies*, chronology and genre take care of themselves. In volumes like the present, however, it should be noted that the primary principle is generic. This is a collection of Fielding's political writings which can be shown to constellate around the *True Patriot*, the principal undertaking from the period in question. Were the plan of the Wesleyan Fielding strictly chronological, the *True Patriot* might have had to be grouped with, say, the satirical *Charge to the Jury* of 1745 or with *The Female Husband* of 1746, neither of which bears any generic resemblance to the writings the paper is grouped with here.

Of the material in the present volume a considerable proportion has not been republished since the originals of Fielding's own lifetime. The Murphy–Millar *Works* of 1762 printed none of the three pamphlets and only ten issues of the *True Patriot* itself. The so-called Henley edition of 1903 follows Murphy–Millar in both what it excludes and what it includes. In 1934 Ifan Kyrle Fletcher published what he called a line-for-line reprint of the *History of the Present Rebellion in Scotland*. However, for reasons given in an appendix here, Fletcher's text seems of dubious accuracy, and he provides no substantive annotation. In the case of the *True Patriot* we have been luckier. I have had the benefit of two earlier editions, one published, the other not. Robert Dudley French provided substantive annotation of the leading essays but no textual editing in his unpublished Yale dissertation of 1920. I have cited him wherever I found him useful. In 1964 Miriam Austin Locke, who does not seem to have made use of French, published a reduced photo-facsimile edition, also with substantive annotation of the leading essays only, but no textual editing. My sense of the *True Patriot* differs radically from hers, but I have had occasion to cite her edition a good deal, because it reprints the entire *True Patriot*, not just the material which can be attri-buted to Fielding. The difference between our editions is worth insist-ing upon. Locke, though she annotates only the leader material and does not consider matters of attribution outside of that leader material, does offer the convenience of an unemended text of the entire paper. The Wesleyan Fielding, on the other hand, extends its annotation beyond the leader essays—all of which are included here—to all items which can be arguably assigned to Fielding. Because it is an edition of Fielding and not of the paper as a whole, it does omit items which do not seem to be his. In an appendix I have reprinted material in which Fielding *may* have had a hand, either as compiler (from other sources) or as commentator.

The early preparation of this edition was undertaken at the same time as I began work on my edition of the *Jacobite's Journal*. Therefore, I have many of the same people to thank, and I do so now. In addition I have benefited from the generosity of Peter Hemingson, who allowed me to read his unpublished Columbia dissertation editing the three pamphlets included in the present volume. The fact that my habits of annotation and some of my conclusions differ considerably from his in no way diminishes my sense of that act of kindness. My editorial colleagues Hugh Amory, Martin C. Battestin, Bertrand A. Goldgar, Michael Harris, and Malvin R. Zirker, Jr., have proffered information, advice, and assistance of various kinds. I have been helped, too, by communications from Thomas R. Cleary, Thomas Lockwood, Michael Treadwell, and Simon Varey. In trying to trace a possible connection between Fielding and the Marine Society I sought help from Hew Joiner and James Stephen Taylor. Dr R. Hope and R. M. Frampton of the Society welcomed me to the facilities at Lambeth Road and suggested a number of leads. When I first began the task of editing, I paid a visit to Rupert C. Jarvis, whose writings on Fielding and on the Forty-Five have made important clarifications of the canon. His advice and encouragement came at a critical time.

For various reasons the remarkable collaboration between the two presses responsible for publishing this edition has become more complicated and even precarious of late, so much so, in fact, that this volume, completed in 1982, has been languishing while new arrangements were slowly hammered out. John Holland has been primarily responsible for resolving matters at the Wesleyan end, and I am deeply grateful to him and Karen Barrett for dealing with the impasse.

Institutions as well as individuals have been supportive. My own university has continued to provide both research funds and a generous leave schedule. The John Simon Guggenheim Foundation awarded me a fellowship which materially assisted me in getting started. I regret the Foundation has had to wait so long for its support to bear fruit. The Lily

Foundation enabled me to have extended access to Yale's important eighteenth-century holdings. I should also like to thank, and not for the first time, the staffs of the British Library, the Bodleian, the Cambridge University Library, Durham University Library, Edinburgh Public Library, the National Library of Scotland, and King's College Library (Aberdeen). Nearer home, the Sterling and Beinecke libraries at Yale have been tolerant beyond the call, as have my friends in the Olin Library of Wesleyan University. The Houghton Library (Harvard) and the New York Public Library have extended courtesies.

As a reading of the list of the Advisory Board will show, the Wesleyan Fielding has suffered the loss of some of its most loyal supporters. I should like to pay my personal respects to the memory of Richard L. Greene and James M. Osborn, close mutual friends, whose support went far beyond the mere giving of advice. The former persuaded Wesleyan to undertake the edition in the first place, and Osborn effected the unusual collaboration between his alma mater and Clarendon. I wish they had lived to see things completed.

I have dedicated this volume to my mother, who did not live to see it completed. She was a Macdonell of Glengarry, and her roots, I discovered, went back pretty much to the jacobite times. In fact, one of the unexpected benefits of my work on this volume was a deeper understanding of her person through her history. She would not have recognized the Latin epitaph with which I have saluted her, and she might not even have approved of it. It comes from Dr William King, the Oxford jacobite, who thundered it out six times during his famous speech at the opening of Radcliffe's Library in 1749. King, of course, was invoking the return of the Pretender, the jacobite Messiah. My use of it here, though not jacobitical, is equally hopeless.

W.B.C.

Middletown, Connecticut
December 1982; January 1985

LIST OF CONTENTS

ABBREVIATIONS

Baker	*A Catalogue of the Entire and Valuable Library and Books of the Late Henry Fielding, Esq; . . . sold by Auction by Samuel Baker*. London, [1755].
Blaikie, *Itinerary*	*Itinerary of Prince Charles Edward Stuart*. Ed. Walter Biggar Blaikie. Publications of the Scottish History Society, vol. xxiii. Edinburgh, 1897.
CGJ	*The Covent-Garden Journal*. By Sir Alexander Drawcansir, Knt. Censor of Great Britain. London, 1752. Ed. Gerard Edward Jensen. 2 vols. New Haven, 1915.
Champion	*The Champion; or British Mercury*. By Capt. Hercules Vinegar, of Hockley in the Hole. London, 1739–41. Volume and page references are to the collected edition of 1741 (2 vols.); otherwise reference is by date to the original issues.
Charge	*The Charge to the Jury: or, The Sum of the Evidence, on the Trial of A.B.C.D. and E.F. All M.D. For the Death of Robert at Orfud*. London, 1745.
Coxe, *Pelham*	William Coxe. *Memoirs of the Administration of the Right Honourable Henry Pelham*. 2 vols. London, 1829.
Cross	Wilbur L. Cross. *The History of Henry Fielding*. 3 vols. New Haven, Conn., 1918.
DA	*The Daily Advertiser*. London, 1731– .
Dialogue	*A Dialogue between the Devil, the Pope, and the Pretender*. London, 1745. Text and pagination are from the present volume.
DNB	*Dictionary of National Biography*. London, 1885–1901.
Dudden	F. Homes Dudden. *Henry Fielding, His Life, Works, and Times*. 2 vols. Oxford, 1952.
Egmont Diary	HMC Report: *Manuscripts of the Earl of Egmont: Diary of Viscount Perceval Afterwards First Earl of Egmont*. Vol. iii. *1739–1747*. London, 1923.
EHR	*The English Historical Review*. London: Longman, 1886– .
Elcho, *Short Account*	David, Lord Elcho. *A Short Account of the Affairs of Scotland in the Years 1744, 1745, 1746*. Ed. Evan Charteris. Edinburgh, 1907.
Forbes, *Lyon in Mourning*	*The Lyon in Mourning, or a Collection of Speeches Letters Journals . . . by the Rev. Robert Forbes, A.M.* 3 vols. Ed. Henry Paton. Publications of the Scottish History Society, vols. xx–xxii. Edinburgh, 1895–6.

Fortescue, *History* The Hon. J. W. Fortescue. *A History of the British Army*. Vol. ii (First Part: *To the Close of the Seven Years' War*). London, 1910.

French   '*The True Patriot* by Henry Fielding.' Ed. Robert Dudley French. Unpublished Ph.D. dissertation. Yale, 1920. University Microfilms: 72–3, 290.

Gentleman &   *A Dialogue between a Gentleman from London . . . and an Honest*
Alderman   *Alderman of the Country Party*. London, 1747. Text and pagination from *The Jacobite's Journal and Related Writings*. Ed. W. B. Coley. Oxford and Middletown, Conn., 1974.

GM   *The Gentleman's Magazine*. London, 1731– .

Henley   *The Complete Works of Henry Fielding, Esq. With an Essay on the Life, Genius and Achievement of the Author, by William Ernest Henley, LL.D.* 16 vols. London, [1903].

History   *The History of the Present Rebellion in Scotland*. London, 1745. Text and pagination are from the present volume.

HMC   Historical Manuscripts Commission.

Jarvis, *Collected*   Rupert C. Jarvis. *Collected Papers on the Jacobite Risings*. 2 vols.
Papers   Manchester, 1972.

JJ   *The Jacobite's Journal*. London, 1747–8. Ed. W. B. Coley. Oxford and Middletown, Conn., 1974.

Joseph Andrews   Henry Fielding, *Joseph Andrews*. Ed. Martin C. Battestin. Oxford and Middletown, Conn., 1967.

Journals of . . .   *Journals of the House of Commons*. Vol. xxv [17 October 1745–22
Commons   November 1750]. London, 1803.

Jowitt, *Dictionary*   *The Dictionary of English Law*. Ed. Right Hon. the Earl Jowitt and Clifford Walsh. London, 1939.

Locke   *The True Patriot: and the History of Our Own Times*. Ed. Miriam Austin Locke. University of Alabama Press, 1964.

Loeb   The Loeb Classical Library.

Lodge, *Private*   *Private Correspondence of Chesterfield and Newcastle 1744–46*.
Correspondence   Ed. Sir Richard Lodge. London: Office of the Royal Historical Society, 1930.

London Stage   *The London Stage, 1660–1800*. Part 3: *1729–1747*. Ed. Arthur H. Scouten. 2 vols. Carbondale, Ill., 1961. Part 4: *1747–1776*. Ed. George Winchester Stone, Jr. 3 vols. Carbondale, Ill., 1962.

Malmesbury   *A Series of Letters of the First Earl of Malmesbury . . . from 1745 to*
Letters   *1820*. Ed. Right Hon. the Earl of Malmesbury. 2 vols. London, 1870.

Marchmont Papers   *A Selection from the Papers of the Earls of Marchmont*. Ed. Sir George Henry Rose. 3 vols. London, 1831.

Memorials	*Memorials of John Murray of Broughton*. Ed. Robert Fitzroy Bell. Publications of the Scottish History Society, vol. xxvii. Edinburgh, 1898.
Miscellanies I (1743)	*Miscellanies, by Henry Fielding, Esq; Volume One*. Ed. Henry Knight Miller. Oxford and Middletown, Conn., 1972. References to vols. ii and iii are to the Andrew Millar edition of 1743.
MLN	*Modern Language Notes*. Baltimore, 1886– .
MLR	*Modern Language Review*. Cambridge, Eng., 1905– .
N&Q	*Notes and Queries*. London, High Wycombe, 1850– .
OED	*The Oxford English Dictionary*. Oxford, 1888–1986.
OP	James Francis Edward Stuart, the Old Pretender.
Owen	John B. Owen. *The Rise of the Pelhams*. London, 1957.
Parliamentary History	*The Parliamentary History of England, from the Earliest Period to the Year 1803*. Vol. xiii: A.D. *1743–1747*. T. C. Hansard: London, 1812.
Plomer, *Dictionary*	*A Dictionary of the Printers and Booksellers . . . in England, Scotland and Ireland from 1726 to 1775*. Ed. H. R. Plomer *et al.* Oxford, 1932.
PQ	*Philological Quarterly*. Iowa City, 1922– .
Proper Answer	*A Proper Answer to a Late Scurrilous Libel*. London, 1747. Text and pagination from *The Jacobite's Journal and Related Writings*. Ed. W. B. Coley. Oxford and Middletown, Conn., 1974.
Rat	*An Attempt towards a Natural History of the Hanover Rat*. London, 1744.
Spectator	*The Spectator*. Ed. Donald F. Bond. 5 vols. Oxford, 1965.
Statutes at Large	*The Statutes at Large, from Magna Charta to . . . 1761*. Ed. Danby Pickering. Cambridge, 1762.
Stephens, *Catalogue*	*Catalogue of Prints and Drawings in the British Museum*, Division I: *Political and Personal Satires*. Ed. Frederic G. Stephens, Vol. iii, part I. London, 1877.
Tom Jones	*The History of Tom Jones, A Foundling*. Ed. Martin C. Battestin and Fredson Bowers. Oxford and Middletown, Conn., 1974.
TP	*The True Patriot*. London, 1745–6. Ed. W. B. Coley. Oxford and Middletown, Conn., 1987. Text and pagination are from the present volume.
Yale Walpole	*The Yale Edition of Horace Walpole's Correspondence*. Ed. W. S. Lewis. New Haven, Conn., 1937–83.
YP	Charles Edward Stuart, the Young Pretender.

GENERAL INTRODUCTION

THE writings comprised in the present volume of the Wesleyan Edition are the products of what may be called the second period of Fielding's intensive political journalism. They are four in number and they are not all journals or newspapers in format. Three in fact are pamphlets—the *Serious Address*, the *History of the Present Rebellion*, and the *Dialogue between the Devil, the Pope, and the Pretender*, all from 1745. These are informed by the same political purpose as the journal or newspaper which is included—the *True Patriot* of 1745-6—namely, to deal with the crisis represented by the jacobite uprising known as the 'Forty-Five' and the implications this event was perceived to have for the Pelham adminis-tration in general and for its new 'patriot' allies in particular. The pattern of a paper preceded by a cluster of pamphlets is typical of Field-ing's activity in this field. It is repeated, for example, in the third period of his political journalism, culminating in the *Jacobite's Journal* of 1747-8, and it is not unlike the pattern of his first such period, his anti-Walpole activity centered around the *Champion* (1739-41).

The present volume does not include everything Fielding is known to have published during the period under consideration: for example, the *Charge to the Jury . . . on the Trial of A.B.C.D*, which appeared in July 1745. The *Charge* is mainly a satire on the medical incompetence alleged to have hastened the death of Walpole. Although hardly very respectful of the former prime minister, it is not at bottom a political piece and on that ground alone would perhaps not merit inclusion in the present volume. However, because it represents a kind of coda to Fielding's long-lived preoccupation with the man, it will be grouped with the other, more political pieces which share that preoccupation, in the volume devoted to the *Champion* and related anti-Walpole writings.

In this connection, the reader is reminded of the policy of the Wesleyan Edition to arrange the canon, as far as is convenient, chrono-logically by genre. There are obvious exceptions, of course. The *Miscel-lanies* of 1743 will be kept intact, despite the mix of genres represented in its three volumes, because Fielding presumably wanted it that way. And certain works such as the novels stand on their own—with the exception of *Jonathan Wild*—and raise no problems of editorial arrangement. In the case of the present volume, then, Fielding's writings from the period under consideration are included or excluded according to whether or not they were informed by roughly common political purposes. Strictly speaking, perhaps, the political pamphlet might be assigned to a different genre from that of the political newspaper, but it seemed more sensible to subsume them both under the heading of political writings. And that is the principle adhered to in the present volume and others like it in the Wesleyan Edition.

Readers who come to the less familiar 'true' patriotism of 1745–6 from the egregious delights of the unqualified 'patriot' opposition of the *Champion* days will be surprised at the outset by one major difference. In 1745–6 Fielding is no longer an opposition writer, no longer a champion of the politically excluded against those who would keep them out. Now he can be called—indeed he was called[1]—with some (if not complete) justice a ministerial writer. Still very much a political writer, of course, but with a somewhat different set of obligations and tasks. It could be said of Sir Robert Walpole, from the literary standpoint at least, that if he hadn't existed, it would have been necessary to invent him. By the autumn of 1745 Walpole no longer existed, and although Fielding tried to replace him, so to speak, with Granville, with the loss of the original something went out of it. In 1745 the prime minister was Henry Pelham, notoriously a creature of Sir Robert's and busily implementing many aspects of the latter's political program. As Fielding himself noted ruefully,[2] Pelham, unlike his master, did not put much stock in hiring ministerial propagandists. And for a writer who wanted to sign on in that capacity it would not have been tactful to resurrect exactly the fervencies of the old anti-Walpole days. Conditions, in other words, had changed.

It is easy—and misleading—to exaggerate the changes, to write Fielding off as a mere political opportunist or turncoat. To some minds—including at times his own, apparently[3]—he was those things. But the subtleties of the political context require us to hedge on such an

---

[1] By *GM*, xvi (1746), 260, whose condensation of *TP* no. 29 (13–20 May 1746) begins: '*This writer*, who is become a strenuous advocate for the ministry ...'. The *GM* remark is almost certainly ironic, reflecting an awareness that formerly 'this writer' was an opposition writer.

[2] In *TP* no. 14 (28 January–4 February 1746), below, p. 209, where Fielding says he has been assured by those who know the prime minister that he 'hath the utmost Contempt for any Good or Harm' that political writers can do him.

[3] To judge from the defensiveness with which he treats the connection between writing and politics. See *JJ* no. 17 (26 March 1748), pp. 214–15, where he defends his former colleague James Ralph from such charges: 'Why is an Author obliged to be a more disinterested Patriot than any other? ... I do not think a Writer, whose only Livelihood is his Pen, to deserve a very flagitious Character, if when one Set of Men deny him Encouragement, he seeks it from another....' The *TP* itself justifies changing one's politics under certain circumstances; see 'The Present History of Great Britain', no. 25 (15–22 April 1746), Locke, p. [205], which is almost certainly not by Fielding. For the possibility that Ralph had taken over that department, see below, p. lxiii *n.* 1.

outright denomination. A close reading of the contents of this volume will go a long way toward supplying that context. However, in addition, it will be helpful to consider briefly Fielding's nonpolitical history during the time that intervened between the first period of his political journalism and the second.

Paradoxically, the fall of Walpole in February 1742, an event which Fielding had been laboring long to assist, can be said to mark the symbolic end and failure of the first period of his political journalism. In actual fact, *The Opposition: A Vision* (December 1741) is the last writing which fits unexceptionably into his anti-Walpole period. The two works which follow it are not really political. The 'Defence' (as he calls it in his 'Preface' to the *Miscellanies*) or vindication of the duchess of Marlborough (April 1742), though it had some political overtones, was in the first instance mercenary: Fielding hoped to be rewarded by her and was not.[1] And the joint effort (with William Young) of *Plutus, God of Riches* (May 1742) is political only in that it is dedicated to the patriot peer, Lord Talbot, who at the Strand Tavern meeting of the opposition on 12 February 1742, had joined Argyll, Bedford, Lyttelton, Dodington, and others in condemning the 'narrow bottom' or exclusionary ministry formed by Carteret and Pulteney. Talbot later subscribed to Fielding's *Miscellanies*, perhaps out of gratitude, but there was no known political issue from the event.

And, reasonably enough, there could not have been. For after the fall of Walpole the next administration, under the nominal direction of Wilmington, managed to reward Carteret (secretary of state) and Pulteney (a peerage [Bath] as the price for the end-of-session preferment of his friends; he himself had been denied the office of lord privy seal) and a sufficiency of their adherents, without taking in the rest of the patriot opposition, in particular without taking in any of Fielding's political connections—Dodington, Chesterfield, Lyttelton, or Pitt.

All things considered, it was a masterful operation, designed in no small way by Walpole from behind the curtain. The objective was to form a ministry that was both stable and acceptable to the king. Some members of the opposition had to be detached and brought in to augment the 'old' whigs with whom the king felt comfortable. But the acceptable choices were not broad. The king hated his son, the prince of Wales, and all the latter's associates, among whom at one time or another Chesterfield, Lyttelton, Pitt, and Dodington could be numbered. The king also disliked

[1] In the 'Apocrypha' of *TP* no. 6 (10 December 1745), below, p. 374, Fielding records the death of a man 'supposed to be a Pensioner of the late Duchess of Marlborough', with the comment, 'He is supposed to have been poor'.

the tories as a group, for he judged them to be anti-Hanoverian at bottom. Convinced that opposition mistrust of Carteret and Pulteney would prevent their effective leadership in the commons, the king contrived to get Wilmington nominated as head of the treasury board without actually disaffecting the Carteret–Pulteney bloc. Wilmington was a shrewd choice. He was widely thought to be an unthreatening nonentity in a crucial office. He had not been guilty of association with the hated Walpole. Friendly to Argyll and Dodington, he was acceptable, if perhaps only marginally, to the opposition. And the king judged him loyal to the king. With the main lines of the ministry established, Newcastle, speaking as an influential 'old' whig, persuaded Pulteney to admit the impracticability of making too many changes in the administration during the present session. Since whatever augmentations there were came mainly from the ranks of the Carteret–Pulteney adherents and not from the 'patriot' opposition, the court could be said to have engineered the disintegration of the crucial anti-Walpole opposition— and the defeat of Fielding's hopes of enjoying what in another context he was to call the 'purposed Recompence'.[1]

The adroit political exclusion of his 'patriot' mentors in 1742 produced disarray, not an immediate renewal of resolve. Before the fact there had been considerable propaganda aimed at heading things off. After the fact there did not seem much that could be done. Given the political situation in which he and his friends found themselves, it could hardly have been surprising if Fielding had decided to give up political writing as a bad job. This in effect is what he says he will do, in the 'Preface' to the *Miscellanies* of April 1743.

The modern view of the *Miscellanies* has been put by Aurélien Digeon, who called the work 'une liquidation de son passée littéraire'.[2] A more recent scholar appears to draw the inference even more emphatically, arguing that the publication represented Fielding's decision to abandon literature for the law.[3] This may be so, but Fielding's remarks in the 'Preface' do not entirely support such an inference. What he says there is that he will abandon a certain kind of literature, not literature itself. After denying that he had contributed 'one Syllable' to the *Champion* or any other public paper since June 1741, after denying authorship of an anonymous scandal on a private person or family, after denying that he

---

[1] In his 'Preface' to the second edition of his sister's *David Simple* (July 1744), where the recompense was to have been the reputation of a diligent lawyer who was above writing political scurrility. See below, p. xxiv. In the present instance Fielding had clearly hoped to be recompensed with either place or pension for his journalistic efforts on behalf of the patriots.

[2] *Les Romans de Fielding* (Paris, 1923), p. 118.

[3] Martin C. Battestin, 'General Introduction', *Tom Jones*, pp. xx–xxi.

had ever libeled anybody (he insists on the distinction between ridicule and scurrility, between jesting at the expense of a public character and 'murder' of a private individual), after denying that he ever inserted a single word in the opposition paper, the *Gazetteer*—after all these denials, he makes a promise: 'I will never hereafter publish any Book or Pamphlet whatever, to which I will not put my Name.' And he adds that this is a promise he will 'sacredly keep'. The line between ridicule and scurrility, between public jest and private 'murder', is a fine one, and he will not try to tread it anonymously.

The 'Preface', then, seems less like a repudiation of literature in general than a repudiation of the kind of literature which conventionally masked itself in anonymity, that is, political satire and polemic. The 'law' certainly played a part here. After only three years of study Fielding had been admitted to the bar in June 1740, a fact which does not seem to have prevented him from activities on the *Champion* for another year. But if we accept the testimony of Arthur Murphy and the anonymous anecdotalist of the *Annual Register* account,[1] Fielding worked hard at the law, at least at first. Later, according to Murphy, his application became more intermittent, owing to reasons of health. Whatever the assiduity with which he was lawyering in 1743, the evidence of the *Miscellanies* indicates Fielding was taken seriously by many members of his new profession. He himself draws attention, proudly, to the fact that 'more than half the Names which appear to this Subscription [to the *Miscellanies*]' are associated with the law ('Preface', p. 13). As he had earlier noted also, however, lawyers do not look kindly on colleagues who write satires. In *Joseph Andrews* (1742), when Mr Wilson asks an attorney to hire him as a legal copyist, the attorney refuses, because 'he was afraid I should turn his Deeds into Plays, and he should expect to see them on the Stage' (III. iii. 217). Fielding clearly had no wish to offend, particularly as this kind of writing had not satisfied what in the 'Preface' to the *Miscellanies* (p. 7) he calls the 'much more urgent Motive' that made him allow *The Wedding Day* to be acted, namely, his need of money.

Whatever the intended extent of his decision, Fielding did not break literary silence for approximately fifteen months. Perhaps many of the reasons for this silence had little to do with the sacred promise he had made in the *Miscellanies*: preoccupation with the law, his own deteriorating health, his wife's terminal illness (she died in early November 1744

---

[1] 'Essay on the Life and Genius of Henry Fielding, Esq;' in *Works* (London, 1762), i. 37–8; 'Some Account of the late Henry Fielding, Esq;' *Annual Register . . . for the Year 1762*, 6th ed. (London, 1805), p. 18*n*.

after both had spent considerable time at Bath in hopes of arresting it).
In any case, the mode of his breaking silence was a bit peculiar.

On 13 July 1744 his sister brought out the second edition of *David Simple*, with a preface by Fielding himself. Since the preface was signed, it did not constitute a violation of his promise to forgo anonymity. But why break silence in this way? The first 'reason' he gives is that he had been identified, wrongly, as the author of the main work. Since *David Simple* was published anonymously—the title page said simply that it was 'by a Lady'—Fielding could argue that to attribute it to him was to imply that he had broken his sacred promise. More telling, perhaps, is his second 'reason', namely, that such an attribution 'may have a Tendency to injure me in a Profession, to which I have applied with so arduous and intent a Diligence, that I have had no Leisure, if I had Inclination, to compose any thing of the Kind' (p. iv). The issue up to this point, let it be noted, is not one of anonymous scurrility. *David Simple*, though certainly anonymous, was in no way personal or scurrilous. The issue is one of diligence. Fielding does not wish to be seen as anything but a lawyer. To appear to be diluting his energies by writing is to appear a less serious lawyer, and he adds that he is 'very far from entertaining such an Inclination [to write such things as *David Simple*]' because he knows the paltry value of the rewards which fame bestows upon authors.

Whatever the seemingly innocuous attribution of *David Simple* may have meant, Fielding goes on to say that other, more scurrilous works had been laid to his charge, notably the *Causidicade* (1743), a virulent attack on Lord Hardwicke, chief justice Willes, and other legal lights, for their supposed machinations in the appointment of William Murray as solicitor-general. As Fielding puts it, to accuse him of writing the *Causidicade* was to accuse him of 'down-right Idiotism, in flying in the Face of the greatest Men of my Profession'. The issue is no longer one of mere diligence in the profession.[1] It is one of professional ethics. Mr Wilson's attorney friend was right to be afraid.

After noting the thanklessness of the Muses and his detestation of them, after pointing to the dangers facing him as a lawyer who is thought also to write satire, in the 'Preface' to *David Simple* Fielding goes on to declare that he now feels 'at full Liberty to publish an anonymous Work, without any Breach of Faith' because 'there is no Reason why I should be under a Restraint, for which I have not enjoyed the purposed Recompence'. The

---

[1] Apparently careful to ensure that his supposed connection with this scurrilous poem did not survive, Fielding takes up the authorship question in *JJ* no. 11 (13 February 1748) and no. 15 (12 March 1748), pp. 161, 197–9.

recompense in this case was not money or place, but the reputation of living up to contracts, the reputation of being a serious lawyer, not the author of libels on his profession.

There is something odd about this repudiation of his earlier promise. Logically, of course, it hardly behooves one who has just declared he detests the Muses to press for the liberty to write anonymously if he likes. If one does not intend to exercise the liberty ('probably I shall never make any Use of the Liberty'), why make such a big thing out of claiming it? And what has happened to his professed fear of flying in the face of his profession? Is he no longer worried that his legal colleagues will mistrust him? Or does he feel that such irreparable damage has been done to his reputation that he may as well press on if the opportunity presents itself? Does he perhaps perceive that such an opportunity may indeed be about to present itself in the form of journalistic assistance to his 'patriot' friends, now trying once more to mount a coherent program for getting into place?

In the present state of the evidence, such questions are largely unanswerable. But they arise naturally. It seems legitimate, even necessary, to ask them. And though unanswered, they suggest a good deal: a beleaguered mind, financial distress, a curious ambivalence toward the profession of law (or the uncertainty of success in it), a desire to leave open some options in case things, in particular political things, should change. In 1744, perhaps even as early as the second edition of *David Simple*, Fielding was at Bath. An unpublished letter from him to James Harris, bearing the partly undecipherable dateline of Bath —— 10 1744, asks Harris for a loan and says that Mrs Fielding's illness obliges him to take lodgings there, although he has scarcely any hopes for her recovery. His prognosis was correct. She died in Bath in early November—the exact date is not known—and was buried in St Martin-in-the-Fields on 14 November 1744. Nine days after her burial there appeared, anonymously, *An Attempt towards a Natural History of the Hanover Rat* (1744), a satirical attack on the hiring of Hanoverian mercenaries and on the pursuit of a 'Hanoverian' (rather than an English) foreign policy. The *Rat* is not a work which has been traditionally associated with Fielding. The title is nowhere listed in the various advertisements or announcements of his works. Nor is there any unequivocal reference to it in the canon itself or in the privileged contemporary commentary on the canon. Murphy asserted that 'a large number of fugitive political tracts, which had their value when the incidents were actually passing on the great scene of business, came from his Pen' (*Works* [1762], i. 29). The *Rat*, if it is in fact Fielding's, must be of that number.[1]

However, if we are to believe the testimony of two of his contemporaries, the *Rat* could not have been composed at a more difficult time. According to Murphy, the death of Fielding's beloved wife—she died perhaps less than a fortnight before the *Rat* was published—'brought on such a vehemence of grief, that his friends began to think him in danger of losing his reason' (*Works* [1762], i. 38). Fielding's cousin, Lady Mary Wortley Montagu, seems to have thought, as her daughter put it, that 'the first agonies of his own grief ... approached to frenzy'.[2] Modern readers who admit the *Rat* to the canon are apparently willing to make allowances for the presumed hyperbole of this contemporary testimony. Certainly Fielding's grief had its limits. In an unpublished letter to Harris, from the Malmesbury archive and dated from Old Boswell Court on 11 January 1745[6] he can say that he is prevented from writing further by the company of 'the woman in the world whom I like best', presumably alluding to his deceased wife's maid, Mary Daniel, whom he would take as his second wife on 27 November 1747. But even when the necessary allowances have been made, particularly for the duration of his grief, to have produced and published such a controlled parody, such contrived satire, as the *Rat* is, and only a fortnight after his wife's death, seems unduly heroic.[3]

Whatever the continuing state of his mind and body during this period, there is direct evidence that Fielding was working at the law—perhaps with frequent intermissions, as Murphy says; perhaps with diligence, as the 'Preface' to *David Simple* says; but almost certainly in ways that were new to him, ways that did not require him, for a time at least, to be well enough or undistracted enough to be able to ride the circuit in pursuit of business. According to the 1762 commentator on Murphy's 'life' of Fielding of that year, 'the gentlemen of the western circuit' had a 'tradition' that after attending the judges for 'two or three years without the least prospect of success' Fielding published some

---

[1] The attribution was first proposed by Gerard E. Jensen, 'A Fielding Discovery', *Yale University Library Gazette*, x (1935), 23–32, and is now widely accepted.

[2] 'Introductory Anecdotes by Lady Louisa Stuart', *Letters and Works of Lady Mary Wortley Montagu*, ed. W. Moy Thomas (London, 1861), i. 106.

[3] The timing of the *Rat* is odd in other ways as well. Its concern for the Hanoverian mercenaries, who had not been debated in parliament since January 1744, and its failure to single out Granville (Carteret) as the major obstacle in the way of the patriot coalition about to be concluded, mark the pamphlet as more appropriate to the earlier period of, for example, Chesterfield's contributions to the mercenary issue, that is, late 1743 or early 1744. The present editor, whose responsibility the *Rat* is, considers that as of the moment the case for Fielding's authorship of it is still open. It will be addressed in the volume comprising Fielding's 'opposition' writings.

'proposals' for a new law book, the news of which stimulated a temporary upturn of business for him.[1] Such a book seems never to have been published; indeed, as late as 1748 his journalistic adversaries were twitting him on its continued nonappearance. Nor have any 'proposals' as such been identified. However, beginning in late February 1745 a series of advertisements in the London papers announced that two folio volumes on crown law, by Henry Fielding, 'shortly will be publish'd'.[2] Even if, as his enemies later charged, these volumes were largely based on the notes of his maternal grandfather, Sir Henry Gould, their imminence in late February 1745 strongly suggests that Fielding must have been working on them in November 1744, that is, during his wife's final illness, and probably a good deal earlier. Whatever their true provenance these volumes could have been worked on by someone who, for whatever reason, was confined to Bath and hence kept from the circuit or the term in London. Their existence, even unpublished, helps explain why Fielding published nothing for eight months after the *Rat* appeared.

Why the two law volumes were not published as promised, is not known. Murphy says Sir John Fielding told him that at Fielding's death they were 'deemed perfect in some parts' (*Works* [1762], i. 29). Perhaps many other parts were far from perfect and further research proved difficult; perhaps Fielding's interest flagged; perhaps his advertisements were merely 'ghosts', advertisements for nonexistent works, though it is difficult to imagine Andrew Millar consenting to have his name listed as publisher in such a case. In any event, sometime early in 1745, possibly as early as the advertisements for his law book, Fielding began his slow and somewhat interrupted return to the Muses. According to his most recent editor, it was shortly after the turn of the year that he began work on *Tom Jones*, and before the news of the jacobite rebellion became common knowledge in London, that is, by early August 1745, he had completed at least the first six books.[3] In dedicating the finished product to Lyttelton, Fielding states that it was owing to the former 'that this History was ever begun', that it was 'by your Desire that I first thought of such a Composition' (p. [3]). Such statements are flattering, and open to interpretation, to be sure, but their truth has never been challenged

[1] *Annual Register...for the Year 1762*, ed. cit., p. 18 n.
[2] See William B. Coley, 'Henry Fielding's "Lost" Law Book', *MLN*, lxxvi (1961), 408–13; 'General Introduction', *The Jacobite's Journal and Related Writings* (Oxford, 1974), pp. xix, lxxvii, identifies the salient attacks on his failure to produce the book.
[3] Battestin, 'General Introduction', *Tom Jones*, pp. xxiv, xxxv–xxxix. But for a sense of the complications in this hypothesis, see Hugh Amory, 'The History of "The Adventures of a Foundling": Revising *Tom Jones*', *Harvard Library Bulletin*, xxvii (July 1979), 177–303.

seriously. Thus it seems safe to conclude that at a critical time for him Fielding was 'restored' to literature by an enlightened patron, by one, furthermore, who had been a political mentor as well and who would not have counseled a risky return to the Muses if there had been at that time a likely need for the writer's more political talents. In early 1745 the 'patriot' friends or 'new allies' were still getting used to being 'in place'.[1]

Given the presumed distraction of a two-volume law book which had been publicly promised but not completed; given the likely commencement in early 1745 of the *magnum opus* that was to become *Tom Jones*; given the apparent lack of encouragement to resume writing on behalf of his 'patriot' friends—given all these things, it would hardly surprise if Fielding had not published anything 'occasional' during the rest of that year. The fact of the matter is, he did.

In March 1745 his sometime nemesis, Sir Robert Walpole, died, dosed to death, it was commonly alleged, by squabbling surgeons and physicians, who could not decide whether it was a kidney case or a bladder case. Shortly after Walpole's death, Fielding's surgeon friend John Ranby published a 'narrative', as he called it, of the events and disagreements of the last months of the case. Stimulated in part by the notoriety of the patient and in part by the fact that parliament was at the time considering a bill to grant the Surgeons independent (and elevated) status as a company separate from their longtime associates the Barbers, a veritable rash of pamphlets on the case broke out in the spring and summer of 1745. One of these, entitled *The Charge to the Jury: or, The Sum of the Evidence, on the Trial of A.B.C.D. and E.F. All M.D. For the Death of one Robert at Orfud*, a Cooper pamphlet first advertised as published on 2 July 1745, is listed as Fielding's in Millar's advertisement inserted in the second edition (1758) of Sarah Fielding's *Cleopatra and Octavia*.[2] The *Charge* meets the most stringent requirements of the *hath–doth* stylistic and in addition makes use of Fielding's favorite illustration of the medical mind at work, the controversy over whether the heart is on the left and the liver on the right side of the body ('The Colledge had now altered all that' [pp. 4–5]).[3] It seems pretty clearly his work. Remarking

---

[1] For the so-called broad bottom of November 1744 and the inclusion of some of Fielding's political mentors in the government thereby constituted, see below, pp. xci–xciv.

[2] R. C. Jarvis, 'The Death of Walpole: Henry Fielding and a Forgotten *Cause Célèbre*', *MLR*, xli (1946), 113–30, provides the relevant medical and journalistic background, as well as the case for Fielding's authorship. See also Battestin, 'General Introduction', *Tom Jones*, p. xxv and *n*.

[3] This point, hitherto unremarked in discussions of the case for Fielding's authorship, is strengthened by the fact that in *TP* no. 1 (5 November 1745), below, p. 105, he uses the same illustration (differently worded) to show the fashion of change in medical matters.

on the public sale of a copy of the *Charge*, the *Times Literary Supplement* ('Notes on Sales') of 4 March 1926 asserts, 'There was no other literary man of the period who could have written this "Charge".'

Perhaps. But it is doubtful that an attribution would have been made so confidently without the authority of Millar's advertisement. For why should Fielding break silence—if we exclude the *Rat* as not certainly his, and the 'Preface' to *David Simple* as merely a contributed 'puff' doubling as an advertisement for himself, then nothing by Fielding had been published since April 1743, a period of over two years—and, what is more, turn aside from *Tom Jones* and whatever may have been going on with the law book? Money, that 'more urgent Motive', say the modern commentators,[1] taking note of the fact that in June 1745 one Tristram Walton brought suit to recover a debt of £400 (plus costs) from Dr Arthur Collier of New Sarum, Wiltshire, a family friend of the Fieldings' from Salisbury days, as well as a subscriber to the *Miscellanies*. When Walton demanded special bail in the case and got it, Fielding and his friend James Harris became pledges for Collier, their 'lands and chattels' to be security in case Collier did not pay.[2] Fielding's management of it notwithstanding, the case ultimately went against Collier and, presumably, his pledges, for he does not seem to have paid. In a letter from Lisbon near the end of his life Fielding refers bitterly to Margaret Collier and the 'obligations her family have to me, who had an execution taken out against me for 400 l. for which I became bail for her brother'.[3] Early in 1745, however, the Collier case could have seemed but a cloud no bigger than a man's hand on Fielding's financial horizon. In addition, it may be wondered how much money a shilling pamphlet of 22 pages was expected to bring in, even granting the popularity of the topic, unless, of course, it was to be the opening shot of a campaign to reenter 'occasional' writing. But as far as is known, the *Charge* was the first and only shot until the onset, nearly three months later, of the real shooting at Prestonpans, an event hardly predictable at a time when the Young Pretender had not yet landed.[4]

---

[1] For example, Jarvis, *Collected Papers*, p. 121; Battestin, 'General Introduction', *Tom Jones*, p. xxiv.

[2] For details of the case, see J. Paul de Castro, 'Fielding and the Collier Family', *N&Q*, twelfth series, ii (5 August 1916), 104–6.

[3] Ibid., p. 105. In an unpublished letter to James Harris (in the Malmesbury archive), dated 13 May 1746, Fielding appears to be trying to shift financial responsibility for the bail onto Harris.

[4] Although Fielding was habitually impecunious, it seems more likely that his primary motive in writing the 1745 *Charge to the Jury* was to defend Ranby, who had been a subscriber to the 1743 *Miscellanies*. Ranby's Walpolean *contretemps* was evidently on Fielding's mind. He alludes to it in *Tom Jones* (II. ix. 111–13), where he also praises Ranby's competence (VIII. xiii. 468; XVII. ix. 911).

2. *A SERIOUS ADDRESS TO THE PEOPLE OF GREAT BRITAIN*

During the summer of 1745 the Pelhams' position *vis-à-vis* the king worsened considerably. Almost nothing they advocated or performed seemed to escape the royal censure. They clashed with the king on matters as different as the need to accommodate Prussia and Austria and the proposal (which the king endorsed) to marry his second son to princess Louisa of Denmark. During the royal absence in Hanover the regency board bickered obstructively in a foretaste of what would occur when the principals returned home and parliament was in session.[1] In Flanders, Germany, and the Italian theatre the military campaigns were going from bad to worse. Hardwicke called it 'the most disagreeable summer that I have ever spent in my life'.[2] Although the Pelhams themselves were taking most of the heat, the precariousness of their tenure (and the implications of that) was not lost on their 'patriot' allies.[3]

On 25 July 1745 the Young Pretender set foot on the mainland of Scotland. He did not come, as he would have in February 1744, with the resources of the French fleet and units from the French armed services. Instead he had only the followers whom tradition calls the seven men of Moidart. Even the larger ship which was escorting him had to put back to France without landing the money and arms he had raised on his own initiative. Hardly an auspicious beginning, and yet, paradoxically, its very inauspiciousness caused much of the initial political embarrassment in England.

The first sketchy reports of the YP's landing seem to have reached the ministry in London about 1 August 1745. On that date Newcastle wrote Argyll, summarizing government intelligence in the matter and the steps already taken, concluding with a reference to 'one letter that says, the Pretender's son is actually landed in the Isle of Mull'.[4] To cover themselves, the lords justices had issued a proclamation on 1 August, offering a £30,000 reward for the arrest of the YP, but according to Lady Hardwicke, 'a certain Earl [Bath], who was at the ordering of it, went out of town before signing it',[5] and London papers reported later that certain

[1] John B. Owen, *The Rise of the Pelhams* (London, 1957), p. 278, cites Pelham to Devonshire, 9 July 1745, to show the depressing effect of the regency bickering on the administration.
[2] To Joseph Yorke, 23 August 1745, *Life and Correspondence of Philip Yorke Earl of Hardwicke, Lord High Chancellor of Great Britain*, ed. Philip C. Yorke (Cambridge, 1913), i. 439.
[3] For a narrative of the political uncertainties of 1745 and the 'patriot' awareness of them, see below, pp. lxxx–lxxxix.   [4] Quoted from Coxe, *Pelham*, i. 255.
[5] *Life of Hardwicke*, i. 436. This is confirmed by Horace Walpole, who wrote Hanbury Williams on 6 August 1745 that Bath 'went to Tunbridge the day he should have signed the proclamation'; *Yale Walpole*, xxx. 92. Walpole later (22 November 1745) wrote Mann that Bath 'absented himself when any act of authority was to be executed against the rebels'; *Yale Walpole*, xix. 167.

elements represented the proclamation of 1 August as premature, based on insufficient evidence, and undertaken 'with Views and Designs quite foreign from an Invasion'.[1] At least as late as 8 August officials in London were disinclined to believe what their Edinburgh sources were telling them.[2] Newcastle wrote Argyll on 14 August as if the matter was only 'now put out of all doubt'.[3]

The first public notice of the YP's landing to appear in the official *London Gazette* was in the issue of 13–17 August, in the form of a report based on Edinburgh letters dated 11 August, which stated that seven persons had landed between Mull and Skye, one of whom, 'there is reason to believe', was the pretender's son.[4] The result of this kind of reportage was widespread incredulity. On 20 August Pelham wrote Argyll that he was 'not so apprehensive of the strength or zeal of the enemy, as I am fearful of the inability and languidness of our friends'.[5] Five days later Philip Yorke wrote Joseph Yorke that 'it is fashionable in town [London] not to believe a word of the matter', and on 31 August Hardwicke wrote archbishop Herring, 'There seems to be a certain indifference and deadness among many, and the spirit of the nation wants to be raised and animated to a right tone.'[6]

Under the circumstances such 'languidness', at least among the public, seems hardly surprising. Certainly the king's continued absence had something to do with it. The public could be excused for not thinking there was an emergency as long as the king himself sojourned in Hanover. In 'high places', however, such languidness was politically motivated, as indeed almost all initial reactions in government were. The Pelhams, by this time verging on paranoia and nervously aware of their vulnerability in the event of a domestic crisis while the king was away, were 'believers'. That is, they were the most disposed to take the rebellion seriously. Not because they had better intelligence than their colleagues did, and not just because they were more vulnerable to the king's disapprobation. The Pelhams saw in the rebellion a legitimate excuse to recall British troops from Flanders, thereby reneging on Granville's more belligerent foreign policy and perhaps conducing to an early end of the war. The point was not long lost on Chesterfield, who

---

[1] See, for example, *General Evening Post* of 5–8 October 1745.

[2] SP Scot. 25/24 and 58, and HMC 42, Fifteenth Report, Appendix vi (Carlisle MSS), p. 200; as cited in Jarvis, *Collected Papers*, i. 230 and 247 n.

[3] Coxe, *Pelham*, i. 257.

[4] As for the subsequent military movements of the jacobites, no official mention was made of them in the *Gazette* until 10–14 September, barely a week before the battle of Prestonpans (21 September), when it was reported merely that the clans were gathering.

[5] Coxe, *Pelham*, i. 258.

[6] Yorke, *Life of Hardwicke*, i. 436, 442–3.

from his post in Dublin had been offering Newcastle professedly 'disinterested' advice as how best to manage the new 'patriot' allies and to
defeat Granville. On 12 September 1745 he wrote Newcastle that the
rebellion must be handled in such a way as to strengthen the Pelhams'
domestic game even if Granville still prevailed in foreign matters, and he
urged the Pelhams to find some way to 'brand' Granville and his followers before the first meeting of parliament, after which time the latter
might gather strength.[1]

Granville himself was with the king in Hanover until the end of
August, but he had several warm adherents in the cabinet, notably his
son-in-law Tweeddale, secretary of state for Scotland, and Earl Stair.
According to the somewhat posterior testimony of Thomas Birch,
Tweeddale represented the rebellion as no more significant than the
desertion of a highland regiment [the 43rd, later the 42nd] that had tried
to march back to Scotland in the summer of 1743,[2] and he and Stair led a
strong opposition in council to a resolution calling for the return of all
English troops from Flanders. As a result of their opposition the resolution seems to have been watered down to a recall of but half the troops in
Flanders.[3] Moreover, in his capacity of secretary of state for Scotland,
Tweeddale was not exactly expeditious in seeing to it that the much
needed arms found their way northward to Sir John Cope for distribution to the well-affected clans. Some of the infighting over arms for Scotland was undoubtedly the result of jealousies among the Scottish peers,
notably Argyll, who arrived in London on 2 September without having
tried to raise a single soldier for the government, though it was said of
him that if he had wished to, he could have raised more than the government itself could have done.[4] But the struggle to see who would be
uppermost in Scottish politics does not fully account for the 'languidness' within the administration. After Granville arrived back in England,
he and his adherents continued to treat the rebellion as a fiction 'of no
other importance than to give a handle to their antagonists in the
ministry to draw off our troops in Flanders, and by that means defeat the
great schemes which might be executed on the Continent'.[5]

---

[1] *The Letters of Philip Dormer Stanhope, 4th Earl of Chesterfield*, ed. Bonamy Dobrée (London, 1932), iii. 664; Lodge, *Private Correspondence*, pp. 67–8.

[2] Birch to Philip Yorke, London, 28 September 1745, in Yorke, *Life of Hardwicke*, i. 460.

[3] Walpole to Mann, 7 August 1745, *Yale Walpole*, xix. 90–1; Coxe, *Pelham*, i. 261.

[4] See Jarvis, *Collected Papers*, i. 104. For a contemporary account by a participant in the squabbles among the Scottish peers, see 'Diary of Hugh Earl of Marchmont', *Marchmont Papers*, i. 98–176. Jarvis, pp. 102–4, sketches the effect of the factional differences in London on the administrators in Edinburgh.

[5] Thomas Birch to Philip Yorke, 14 September 1745, Yorke, *Life of Hardwicke*, i. 450–1. A week later (21 September) Birch wrote Yorke that Granville's friends were sanguine that he would recover his

One other cause of 'languidness' in the administration itself was insecurity. Almost as soon as the 'broad bottom' of November–December 1744 was formed, the Pelhams began having doubts of its tenure. On 30 December 1744 Andrew Stone wrote Hardwicke of Newcastle's fears that there would be an early [end of March 1745] dismissal when the business of the session was done and that the Pelhams would be replaced by Granville and associates.[1] Having heard the same rumors indirectly from Granville himself, Chesterfield, with the courage that comes of detachment, repeatedly urged the Pelhams to threaten resignation, thereby forcing the king's hand with Granville.[2] Whatever they may have thought privately of Chesterfield's assumption that Granville lacked the necessary support in parliament, the Pelhams resisted his advice, apparently judging that the king, if need be, could form a government without Granville, a view shared by the modern historian.[3] Philip Yorke thought that when the king returned from his summer in Hanover, he would be resolved to change ministers,[4] and Pelham wrote Devonshire on 17 September 1745 that he did not expect to be left in office, apparently voicing this belief often enough for Horace Walpole to record it as common knowledge.[5]

The predictions were not without substance. On 17 September the king offered Harrington a free hand if he would desert the Pelhams and undertake an independent administration. Although the royal offer stipulated that only Pelham and Newcastle need go—the rest might remain—Harrington refused, and Newcastle reported Harrington's notion that Granville 'will be sent to' but that he will not risk it.[6] Assuming the patriotic stance, Newcastle told Chesterfield that as soon as the danger from the rebellion was over, he and his brother would resign. Chesterfield's not unexpected reply was that the Pelhams should make

ministerial post and treated the rebellion with contempt and the recall of British troops from Flanders with dislike, as tantamount to abandoning the allies; ibid., i. 457.

[1] BL Add. MS 35408, f. 110, as cited by Owen, p. 269. The point is that, despite a fairly comfortable parliamentary majority on the divisions, the Pelhams had failed to win over the king's support. Walpole's letters to Mann for this period make frequent (and disparaging) reference to the perceived precariousness of the new coalition.

[2] For example, Chesterfield to Newcastle, 13 April 1745, *Letters*, ed. Dobrée, ii. 596; Lodge, *Private Correspondence*, p. 45. Chesterfield records hearing the rumors, in a letter of 23 March; Lodge, p. 30.

[3] Owen, p. 273, thinks the king could have formed such a government only if it excluded both Granville and Bath.

[4] BL Add. MS 9224, f. 2, cited by Owen, p. 279 *n.*

[5] Devonshire MSS, cited by Owen, p. 280; Walpole to Mann, 13 September, *Yale Walpole*, xix. 105, says, 'Mr Pelham talks every day of resigning'.

[6] BL Add. MS 33073, f. 228, cited by Owen, p. 282. Chesterfield wrote Stone, 30 September, that Harrington's refusal 'to undertake the administration of affairs exclusively of the two Brothers' [Pelham and Newcastle] confirmed him in his opinion that 'those two Brothers have the game in their hands'; Lodge, *Private Correspondence*, p. 71.

an immediate stand, should demand that the remnant of the 'new' whigs
be dismissed and that the king's confidence in his two ministers be
restored—all this as a *sine qua non* of their continuance in office.[1] Fielding's sometime patron, the duke of Richmond, counseled sticking it out,
arguing that the consequence of Granville's replacing them would be
the destruction of government, either by rashness or by design for the
pretender's interest.[2] All in all, September was a cruel month for the
Pelhams.

Although the rebel successes in Edinburgh and at Prestonpans
produced a public disposition to be more serious about the rebellion (in
addition these events discredited the political optimism of Tweeddale
and Granville), on the parliamentary level whatever loyalty was bred of
the crisis was counterbalanced by disillusionment over the Pelhams'
continued failure to take effective measures and to establish credit with
the king. The 'old whigs' and their 'new' patriot allies remained strongly
averse to the alternative of Granville, but they were dispirited by the
Pelhams' ineffectiveness. Things got so bad that shortly after the publication of Fielding's three pamphlets on the rebellion Lord Strange said
in debate (23 October 1745) that since the house seemed unable to give
the king any coherent advice, it should stand adjourned for three months
until the rebellion was over.[3] And in the commons, during the first three
months of the session, on only two divisions were there as many as three
hundred members in attendance.[4] The king's address on the subject of
the rebellion was well received, but Dashwood, seconded by Philips and
Sydenham, tried to attach a clause to the thanks entreating shorter parliaments and a diminution of government influence in elections. On the
division, it is worth noting, two of Fielding's political mentors, Lyttelton
and Pitt, voted against the clause, thus evincing a certain 'patriot' loyalty
to the government that had only partly accommodated them.[5]

A writer who wished to make himself useful to the Pelhams and their
political allies at this time could not have expected to contribute very
directly to a resolution of the *parliamentary* dispiriment, but he might
well have thought he could contribute in the area of public relations. He
could, that is, make the *public* case for taking the rebellion seriously. To
do so would be patriotic, in the larger, more conventional sense. It
would also be politically helpful to the Pelhams and their new allies in

---

[1] Newcastle to Chesterfield, 21 September; Chesterfield to Newcastle, 30 September; Lodge,
Private Correspondence, pp. 70, 71.

[2] BL Add. MS 32705, f. 187, Richmond to Newcastle, 16 September 1745, cited by Owen, p. 283.

[3] Devonshire MSS, Hartington to Devonshire, 24 October 1745, cited by Owen, p. 284.

[4] The computation is from Owen, p. 284.

[5] For the speeches of Lyttelton and Pitt against the clause, see *Parliamentary History*, xiii. 1343–51.

the struggle against Granville. By late September the appropriate time for such a contribution was fast approaching. After Edinburgh and Prestonpans the case for seriousness was easier to make. It remained mostly to emphasize the implications. Furthermore, with the exception of some published sermons and some editorializing in the newspapers, there was not a great deal yet in print, though much was about to be.

Of what was in print prior to the end of September perhaps the most notorious item was the speech given by archbishop Herring at the 24 September meeting of the Yorkshire association, where, it was reported, over £40,000 was raised. Herring's speech was widely reprinted, and his likeness appeared in the popular prints as 'The Mitred Champion', an allusion to newspaper reports that he had gone to the lengths of appearing in 'a lay military Habit' at the head of his inferior clergy so as to inspire his diocese and countrymen.[1] There is some evidence that Herring, not previously noted for militancy or outward zeal, was gradually worked up to such a pitch by the influence of lord chancellor Hardwicke. As early as 31 August Hardwicke wrote Herring to suggest the latter might draw 'the secular, as well as the spiritual sword' so as to rouse and animate 'the spirit of the nation . . . to a right tone', and adumbrated the reasons: 'Is it not time for the pulpits to sound the trumpet against popery and the Pretender?'[2] On 12 September Hardwicke even proposed the line such an admonition might take: 'One thing I have always observed:—that representing the Pretender as coming (as the truth is) under a dependence upon French support; I say, stating this point, together with Popery, in a strong light, has always the most popular effect.'[3] Hardwicke's advice was not exactly original; the French and Romish connections had been a perennial theme of anti-jacobite propaganda for years. But original or not, it seems to have taken, for Herring's speech places the two points in a very strong light.

From the published evidence, it is not clear whether Hardwicke's exertion of his influence on Herring was merely a personal expedient, dictated by their churchly connection, or part of a larger, informal effort by the Pelhams to once more use the established clergy to offset any perceived tendency among their rural, less whiggish colleagues to be 'soft' on jacobitism.[4] Whatever the reason, the pulpits were among the first to

[1] Stephens, *Catalogue*, III. i. 508–10, nos. 2634, 2635; *General Evening Post* of 28 September–1 October 1745.

[2] Yorke, *Life of Hardwicke*, i. 442–3. The correspondence between Hardwicke and Herring in 1745 is collected in *EHR*, xix (1904), 528–50, 719–42.

[3] Ibid., i. 450.

[4] For Fielding's possible role in such an effort in 1747–8, see 'General Introduction' to *Jacobite's Journal and Related Writings*, pp. lxvii–lxviii.

sound, in Hardwicke's words, 'the trumpet against popery and the Pretender'. If the government was in fact cultivating expressions of concern for the implications of the rebellion, Fielding, with a number of connections 'in place', might well have been apprised by some of them of the opportunity to be useful, presuming, of course, that he had not already figured it out for himself. And if the apparently familiar language of his reference—in an unpublished letter to James Harris, dated 5 October 1745—to sharing the lord chancellor's views of the Prussian military successes can be taken to mean there was some sort of connection between the two lawyers, then Fielding may have had additional, hitherto unsuspected encouragement to take up his pen.

The preceding is of course conjectural. What is fact is that on or about 3 October 1745 there was published, under the Cooper imprint, an anonymous shilling pamphlet of some forty-five pages, sounding the trumpet against popery and the pretender much as Hardwicke had suggested to Herring. Entitled *A Serious Address to the People of Great Britain*, it may confidently be attributed to Fielding, since he makes the attribution himself.[1] With the possible exception (as noted) of the *Rat*, it is the first political piece known to have been composed by Fielding since *The Opposition: A Vision* of December 1741.

For a pamphlet of its type, the *Serious Address* was widely advertised, and its publication date seems precisely inferable from the unanimity of the earliest 'this day is published' advertisements: for example, *DA* and *General Advertiser* of 3 October, *General Evening Post* and *London Evening Post* of 1–3 October 1745. The 3 October date is further confirmed by several anticipatory advertisements: 'next Thursday [3 October] will be published'.[2]

The case for attributing the *Serious Address* to Fielding rests chiefly on five interlocking pieces of external evidence: (1) It is listed (item no. 15) among 'Books Printed for A. Millar ... by Henry Fielding, Esquire', in an advertisement inserted in the 'Second Edition Corrected' (1758) of Sarah Fielding's *Lives of Cleopatra and Octavia* [N3ʳ], where it is referred to somewhat inexactly by its running-title ('The Certain Consequences of the Rebellion in 1745').[3] (2) The Cooper advertisement in *TP* no. 4

---

[1] Although its attribution to Fielding is of long standing—see Cross, iii. 310—the *Serious Address* has never previously been printed in an edition of Fielding's works.

[2] For example, in *General Advertiser* of 30 September, and *General Evening Post* and *London Evening Post* of 28 September–1 October 1745. The earliest advertisements read 'People of England' for 'People of Great Britain', but such discrepancies were by no means uncommon and the more detailed advertisements go on to give the correct running title as eventually printed.

[3] The presence of the *Serious Address*, which is a Cooper imprint, on a list of Millar's books presents no real difficulty. Millar was billed by the printer (Strahan) for all known Fielding pamphlets

(26 November 1745) states that the *Serious Address* and the *Dialogue between the Devil, the Pope, and the Pretender* are by the same author; the latter title (item no. 17) is also among the Fielding books listed by Millar in the 1758 edition of *Cleopatra and Octavia*. (3) Fielding's own note (p. 79) in his *Proper Answer to a late Scurrilous Libel* (1747) reads: 'See the serious Address published in the Time of the late Rebellion, and the Dialogue between an Alderman and a Courtier, published last Summer; both by the Author of this Pamphlet.' (4) Fielding's own note (p. 58) in his *Dialogue between a Gentleman from London . . . and an Honest Alderman of the Country Party* (1747) reads: 'See the serious Address to the People of *Great Britain*, written by the Author of this Pamphlet.' (5) The title page of the so-called 'Second Edition' [state c^2] of the preceding *Dialogue* reads: 'By the Author of the *True Patriot*, and *A serious Address to the People of Great-Britain*'; to which the title page of the revised printing of the above [state *e*] adds, 'Both published at the Time of the late *Rebellion*'.[1]

In addition to the five pieces of external evidence, the *Serious Address* meets the necessary (but not 'sufficient') internal test for style by using *hath* and *doth* in place of the more usual *has* and *does*.[2]

William Strahan printed the *Serious Address*, as he did Fielding's other pamphlets for Cooper during this period. To judge from the evidence of Strahan's ledgers, as well as the relatively heavy advertising of the pamphlet, the *Serious Address* must have been one of the most widely distributed of Fielding's political writings on behalf of the Pelhams. Strahan's ledgers record a first printing of 3,000 copies.[3] This is the second largest first printing afforded any Fielding pamphlet of the

which appeared under Cooper's imprint during this period. Millar seems to have had some sort of arrangement with Mary Cooper whereby he remained Fielding's 'primary' publisher and she was allowed to imprint and distribute the 'minor' works.

[1] For the various 'states' of the 1747 pamphlets here cited, see *The Jacobite's Journal and Related Writings*, Appendix iv, pp. 437–40. With reference to the attribution of the *Serious Address* it should be noted that on the title page of the National Library of Scotland copy (Rosebery 1. 5. 229) what appears to be a late 18th-century hand records 'by Warburton of Nottingham'. Given the important, almost certain, reference to Warburton in *TP* no. 1 (5 November 1745), below, p. 109, this is not a bad guess. Warburton may have had some sort of loose connection with Fielding at this time.

[2] For more on this 'test' for style, first proposed by one of Fielding's contemporaries, see Appendix VI, below, pp. 331–2.

[3] 'The Strahan Papers', BL Add. MS 48800, f. 38ᵛ [51ᵛ], which reads: 'For printing a Serious Address to the People of Great Britain 3 sheets English octavo N.º 3000 @ £1: 17 p Sheet'. Total charges came to £5. 11s. The fact that Strahan listed these charges under Millar's account for October 1745 led de Castro to conjecture that the *Serious Address* bore Cooper's imprint, not Millar's, because the latter, a Scot with a father still living in Paisley, found it prudent not to involve himself with Fielding's attacks on the Scottish rebels; 'The Printing of Fielding's Works', *The Library*, Fourth Series, i (1920), 259–60. But Strahan continues to bill Millar for Fielding pamphlets bearing the Cooper imprint in 1747 and containing nothing of possible offense to Scotland. Probably Mary Cooper is not listed among Strahan's accounts for this period because of an arrangement with Millar which did not accord her the status of a publisher of first instance. See p. xxxvi *n.* 3, above.

period for which we have evidence, being exceeded only by the *Gentleman & Alderman* of 1747, which had a first printing of 3,500 copies.[1] A little later in his accounts for the same month (October) Strahan records: 'For printing the 2ᵈ Edit. of the Serious Address, 3¼ Sheets No. 1000.'[2] The total charge for this work is originally given as '2:19:6'. However, the 6 is struck through and the 19 shillings seems to be emended to 11. Immediately beneath this second entry concerning the *Serious Address* the ledger reads: 'For overruning a Sheet of Dᵒ for the 1st Impression, No. 500', with a computed charge of 10s. Then yet another entry, directly beneath the third, records a charge of 5s. 9d. 'For half a Ream of Paper for Dᵒ'.[3]

The relatively large first printing—his other two pamphlets of October 1745, the *History of the Present Rebellion* and the *Dialogue between the Devil, the Pope, and the Pretender*, had first printings of 1,000 and 500 copies respectively—not to mention the rather large second printing, raises the hypothesis of subsidy, ministerial or other. Aside from the size of the printing, however, there is no evidence to support such a hypothesis—no snide references in hostile pamphlets, no gossip in the press, no private letters which mention it, no published records of government disbursements which could be connected with the pamphlet or its author. Perhaps it was just a case of the publisher's taking a chance on the timeliness of the appeal, as well as the growing urgency of the crisis to which the appeal addresses itself. If the merits of the *Serious Address* seem hardly to account for the popularity implied by the large printings, the fact remains that it was published in at least four formats, two of which have very much the look of piracies. And piracies indicate that somebody thought the work would sell.

The first format or 'state' of the *Serious Address* is of the pamphlet by itself, bearing the Cooper imprint. The title-page is reproduced here, on page 1. In this state (*a*) the pamphlet appeared *c.*3 October 1745. What may have been the next format to be published is a 26-page octavo, bearing what professes itself to be the Cooper imprint (but lacking the determinative printer's device), the date (1745), but no price. The type used for this 26-page format is quite unlike that used for Cooper's other pamphlets of the period and quite unlike that used by Strahan for work

---

[1] For more detailed comparisons of the printing runs of Fielding's pamphlets of 1745 and 1747 as recorded by Strahan, see 'General Introduction', *The Jacobite's Journal and Related Writings*, p. 1 n.

[2] BL Add. MS 48800, f. 38ᵛ [51ᵛ].

[3] de Castro, 'The Printing of Fielding's Works', p. 261, suggests that these last three entries concern the 'edition' in which the *Serious Address* was coupled with another work, entitled *A Calm Address*. For a bibliographical description of this and other states of Fielding's pamphlet, see Appendix IV, below.

he was doing for either Cooper or Millar at this time.[1] Cooper would hardly have authorized an unpriced (and shorter) reprint by another printer when she either had or was about to have a competing version printed by Strahan. The text of the 26-page piracy—for this is almost surely what it is—does not incorporate any of the changes and additions (the footnote references) of the second 'authorized' edition. On the assumption that it would have done so had these been available, the 26-page version should probably be placed second in the chronological sequence of four formats in which the *Serious Address* appeared.

The second authorized state (state *b*) announces itself on its title-page as 'The Second Edition Corrected, with Additions'. It too bears the Cooper imprint, but in this case the type and other physical features resemble not only those of state *a* but also those of other Cooper–Fielding pamphlets printed by Strahan. The so-called second edition does have a fair number of corrections, many of a largely cosmetic or at most semisubstantive nature, and one or two involving the omission of as much as two consecutive sentences. The additions include two identifications of source and some lines specifying the treatment accorded protestants by catholics in France and Ireland. What most prominently distinguishes state *b* from state *a* is the fact that in state *b* a second, shorter work is subjoined to the *Serious Address* to produce a format of 47 pages. Entitled *A Calm Address to All Parties in Religion, Whether Protestant or Catholick, On the Score of the present Rebellion*, the shorter work is printed separately in *DA* of 3 October 1745 (reprinted in the issue of 16 October) and is advertised as separately published, in *DA* of 5 October 1745, where its price is given as 1*d*. or 5*s*. per hundred.

The title-page of *A Calm Address* further states that it is 'Printed and Sold by J. Oliver, in Bartholomew-Close'. John Oliver, who was publisher to the Society for the Promotion of Christian Knowledge, also published largely for the Methodists and other nonconforming bodies. Almost entirely a religious publisher, Oliver is not likely to have been the primary publisher of anything of Fielding's. How his publication *A Calm Address* came to be subjoined to Fielding's *Serious*

---

[1] A slip enclosed with the Yale copy (Fielding Collection 745sa) cites the Elkin Matthews Catalogue no. 81 to the effect that this may be the first edition and that it is the only recorded copy. Neither statement is true. There is at least one other copy of the 26-page format, in the New York Public Library (CK p.v. 304 [no. 9]), and the claim that it may be the first edition seems absolutely invalidated by the fact that it does not appear to have been printed by Strahan. The possibility that the 26-page format was pirated from manuscript or from the printer's copy with which Strahan's shop was working—and hence might have preceded the 'authorized' first edition into print—seems so remote as to preclude speculation.

Address is not known, but evidently it got around. The *General Evening Post* of 19–20 November advertises a 'new edition' of it, to which is added *The Drapier's Letter to the Good People of Ireland*, and *GM*, xv (1745), 541–4, reprints it in the October issue.[1] Its association with the *Serious Address* has led some scholars to attribute *A Calm Address* to Fielding, even though it does not meet the *hath–doth* test for style.[2] This and the fact that it was separately (and almost certainly earlier) published by John Oliver tell overwhelmingly against the attribution.

Although the Strahan ledgers make no reference to anything beyond the 'second edition', the *Serious Address* did appear with a title-page announcing it as a 'Third Edition' and professing a Cooper imprint. This format also includes *A Calm Address*, but the pagination differs from that of the 'second edition' (state *b*) and the type and certain other physical features do not resemble either those of state *b* or Strahan's other work for Cooper. Since it is unlikely that Cooper would have switched printers at such a late stage, it may be concluded that the 'Third Edition' is another piracy. Support for such a conclusion can be derived from the title-page, which gives the price of this format at 6*d.*, not the original shilling which states *a* and *b* announced. Such a reduction in price is more apt to be owing to a piracy than it is to a lowering of the price of an apparently active item by its original publisher.

All this activity, licit or illicit, surrounding the *Serious Address* suggests popularity more than subsidy, but in the absence of better evidence the latter possibility cannot be entirely ruled out. What can be said, however, is that all signs point to the *Serious Address* as the most widely distributed pamphlet of the three reprinted in the present volume.

As to the date or facts of its composition, once again there is little hard evidence. The presence of anticipatory advertisements in the papers of 30 September can probably be taken to mean that copy was in (or about to go into) the printer's hands by the end of that month. The text itself contains little that permits useful dating. The admonitory reference to the 'Progress' of the rebellion, given at the outset of the pamphlet, consorts best with a date sometime after the news of Edinburgh and perhaps Prestonpans reached London (*c.* 24 or 25 September). To judge from the

---

[1] Jarvis, 'A Rare Fielding Tract on the Jacobite Rebellion', *Manchester Review*, iii (1942–4), 234–6, notes its appearance in *GM* and refers generally to advertisements in 'the news-sheets of the period'. See also *Collected Papers*, ii. 174–6.

[2] Cross, ii. 15, and iii. 310, noting the association, neither clearly affirms nor denies the attribution. But Jarvis, *Collected Papers*, ii. 176, asserts that Cross 'unequivocally' attributes it to Fielding. On external and internal grounds alike, Jarvis rejects the attribution. The argument for Fielding's authorship is made most fully by Peter Harold Hemingson, 'Fielding and the '45: Henry Fielding's Anti-Jacobite Pamphlets' (unpub. diss., Columbia University, 1973), pp. 169–82.

London papers, public apprehension seems to have begun around the middle of September but to have intensified markedly after the fall of Scotland's capital and the government defeat in the field. In other words, the last week of September.

After some warmed-over reminders of Stuart intransigencies during the reigns of Charles II and James II, Fielding remarks that the Old Pretender has just moved from Rome so as to more easily take possession of his son's conquests. The remark is satirical, in part, but it is not without precedent. From Italy Mann wrote Walpole of such rumors as early as 24 August 1745 NS, and a week later added details of monies from the Pope preliminary to such a departure.[1] The 'inspiration' for Fielding's remark came undoubtedly from the papers, not from private correspondents. Under a Paris dateline *DA* of 16 September 1745 reports advices received from Italy that 'the Chevalier himself will likewise leave Rome in a short Time and come to our Court'. And in its issue of 25 September 1745 the same paper reports the substance of a letter from Paris which states that the Old Pretender is expected there shortly but will not go public till he receives 'certain' news that his son is making progress in Scotland. In fact, of course, the Old Pretender never left Italy, but by the last week in September there were enough rumors about to suggest he was going to follow up his son's expedition.

There are three additional references in the *Serious Address* to contemporary events which can be dated somewhat precisely. On page 28 Fielding alludes to the blow dealt 'lately' to French trading interests, presumably by the taking of Cape Breton. However, that 'blow' fell in June 1745, more than a month prior to the arrival of the Young Pretender in Scotland and is of no help in determining dates of composition. On page 30, very near the conclusion of the *Serious Address*, Fielding purports to quote or at least to paraphrase from the Pretender's 'Declaration now publish'd in Scotland'. Because Fielding's quotation or paraphrase is such a distortion of the various manifestoes issued by or in the name of the Pretender, it is not quite clear which one he had particularly in mind.

According to the parliamentary resolution (7 November 1745) to burn them publicly, there were six printed papers or declarations to be distinguished. Two were signed by James, both dated from Rome as of 23 December 1743 NS. One of these concerns itself entirely (and briefly) with nominating Charles Edward as prince regent. It is not the 'Declaration' Fielding alludes to here. The other condemns the Hanoverian 'usurpation', refers to the Union between England and Scotland as

---

[1] *Yale Walpole*, xix. 94, 96.

'pretended', offers to pardon 'all Treasons' except for those who 'wilfully and maliciously oppose us', proposes to call a 'free Parliament' and to act by its advice, proposes further to safeguard property and the religious liberties of persons and institutions as per the law of the land, offers to reward all those who were helpful in the Stuart restoration, and promises to redress all grievances and in particular to take off the malt tax. Despite the fact that this 'Declaration' makes no direct mention of being above the laws with respect to property, despite the fact that it does not make the proposals with respect to neutrals or inactives which Fielding claims it does, it is probably the manifesto or declaration to which he alludes.

Of the remaining four, all signed by Charles Edward, dated respectively 16 May 1745 NS (Paris), 22 August 1745 (Lochiel), and 9 and 10 October 1745 (Edinburgh), the last two postdate the publication of the *Serious Address*, and the Lochiel declaration limits itself to offering a counterreward for the apprehension of George II. The YP's declaration of 16 May 1745 NS reiterates and clarifies many of the proposals in his father's long declaration of 23 December 1743 NS. It is perhaps a little clearer about extending the royal pardon to those who make the effort to 'accept of it' and hence, by implication at least, about excluding from it 'neutrals' who did not make such an effort.[1]

However, for the purpose of dating the *Serious Address* it is not important to narrow Fielding's allusion any further. The OP's long declaration of 23 December 1743 NS and the YP's recapitulation of 16 May 1745 NS were often printed together, at least in England, and they both seem to have been in the public domain there early in September. Walpole wrote Mann on 6 September 1745 about two published manifestoes: 'By one he [the Pretender] promises to preserve everybody in their just rights; and orders all persons who have public monies in their hands to bring it to him.'[2] *DA* of 5 September 1745 extracts from an Edinburgh letter dated 27 August, which speaks of 'a Manifesto publish'd here, but few Copies of it to be met with, by the Pretender's Son Charles'.[3] *GM*, xv (1745), 504, lists *The Pretender's Manifesto* among its September books. In short, Fielding could have made his allusion any time after early September.

---

[1] The actual printing of it probably took place in Scotland in June or July, under supervision of Murray of Broughton; see *Memorials*, pp. 158–9; also Andrew Henderson, *The Edinburgh History of the late Rebellion*, 4th ed. (London, 1752), p. 22. However, public distribution does not appear to have been widespread until late August–early September.

[2] *Yale Walpole*, xix. 103.

[3] *DA* of 13 September advertises the publication of 'A Letter from a Gentleman at *Edinburgh* to his Correspondent at *London*', said to contain 'a genuine Copy' of the Pretender's declaration.

The third and final reference to contemporary events which might help to date the composition of the *Serious Address* occurs in the closing paragraph, a somewhat tacked-on peroration exhorting Englishmen to 'unite in Associations' to repel the invaders. If getting the nation to take the rebellion seriously was the first order of business for the Pelhams, the second order, closely related to the first in its political ramifications, was to determine quickly how to raise an effective military force to do the job. Such a determination was made doubly difficult, of course, by the split within the administration as to the seriousness of the rebellion. But it was difficult in its own right as well. After the suppression of the 'Fifteen', various acts (1 Geo. I, stat. 2 [1715], cap. 54, sec. 1; 11 Geo. I, cap. 26) had been passed to disarm the highlands. At the outbreak of the 'Forty-Five' the government, whose predecessors had disregarded Cope's suggestion to lodge arms in the highland forts, had somehow to get arms in a hurry to the well-affected clans, which had generally abided by the disarming laws, before their jacobite opposite numbers, who had not so generally abided, could take advantage of their relative defenselessness. For a number of reasons, at bottom mostly political, delivery of such arms was much delayed. One reason was that at the out-break of the rebellion a number of the lieutenancies, especially in Scotland and the northeast counties of England, were not filled. The lord lieutenant was the principal military officer of the crown within the geographical limits of his constituency, most commonly the county or shire. Himself appointed by the crown, the lord lieutenant was responsible for recruiting the militia, mustering, equipping, and training it, and for appointing the officers who would lead it in the domestic emergencies for which it was mostly called up. Lieutenancy appointments, therefore, were of considerable political importance, and in Scotland particularly the squabbling for power among Argyll (now tending toward persistent opposition), Tweeddale (Granvillean in politics), and the Marchmont connection had much impeded the appointment process. For those wishing somehow to obstruct the arming process, the absence, in many areas, of the responsible crown officer provided a convenient excuse.[1]

In England itself, arms and the lieutenancies to distribute them were not quite so problematic as manpower itself. Of the two conventional sources of military manpower, one, the regular or 'standing' army, was largely preoccupied with the Flanders campaign. Some units of it had been sent for by this time, but over considerable resistance (including the king's), and they were slow in arriving. Since the regular army was

---

[1] For the state of the lieutenancies in the northeast counties and Scotland at this time, see Jarvis, *Collected Papers*, i. 97–119.

still considered part of the royal prerogative, the Pelhams must have worried about how large a recall the king would easily permit them to make. The other conventional source of manpower was that perennial political football, the militia.[1] As a result of the continuing process of disarming the general population, the militia had been allowed to deteriorate badly, its function as an instrument of domestic repression reduced and assigned to the combination of standing forces and foreign mercenaries characteristic of mid-century England. At the outbreak of the 'Forty-Five' the militia were not in a state of readiness.

Furthermore, there were serious doubts whether the militia could even be legally mustered or equipped. The existing laws required that whenever the militia was called into active service, one month's pay, on the scale laid down by statute, had to be provided and then refunded from the public revenue before any further charge could be made for this service.[2] An act of 1734 (7 Geo. II, cap. 23) had removed the legal stop and empowered the king to place the militia in active service notwithstanding the fact that the month's pay formerly advanced had not been repaid. But this act had expired in its terms in 1735, and George II, away in his beloved Hanover during the summer of 1745, had steadfastly refused to delegate to the council of regency the power to convene parliament in his absence. So, as of the publication of the *Serious Address* there was no parliament in session to vote either the refund of a first month's pay or the setting aside of the existing legal provision concerning it. The militia, which in the north had been ordered by the council to be readied for immediate service, was bogged down by legal and political difficulties.

The most immediate way out of this impasse was to find legally and politically defensible alternatives to the whole lieutenancy procedure. Two in particular received considerable publicity: (1) local 'associations' made up of persons who 'subscribed' monies to raise and maintain units of volunteers, often under the informal auspices of the lieutenancies themselves, more or less for strictly local service; (2) the so-called 'new' regiments, initiated at their own expense by various noblemen friendly to the government or anxious to ingratiate themselves with it, these regiments to be on the same footing as the regular army except that the private men were enlisted for a short term only. Opponents of the noblemen's regiments argued that the whole scheme was

[1] On the considerable 'political' importance of the militia question, see John R. Western, *The English Militia in the Eighteenth Century* (London, 1965), especially chs. iv–v.
[2] By the terms of 14 Car. II [1662], c. 3, s. 6. Jarvis, *Collected Papers*, i. 97–101, 120–9, discusses the legal problems.

a political 'job', pointing out that the officers of these regiments were for the most part appointees of the noblemen themselves and hence beneficiaries of an enlargement of political patronage, and that they would, if given permanent rank, displace a number of career officers.[1] The chief proponent of the 'new' regiments was the duke of Bedford, to whom Fielding would begin to pay court during this period. Walpole wrote Mann on 20 September 1745, recording Bedford's plan to ask leave of the king to raise a regiment, and recording also Bedford's extreme impatience with the failure of the ministry to take active military steps.[2] The question of rank in particular heated up the debates in parliament. Pitt, perhaps somewhat connected to Fielding for the moment and certainly mindful of the Bedford connection, defended the regiments in the commons.[3]

With such endorsements, why weren't the 'new' regiments cited by the *Serious Address* in some loyal connection or other? There can be only one answer to this question: at the time Fielding was composing the *Serious Address* the regiments were no more than a gleam in the eyes of Bedford and a few choice associates. *DA* of 26 September reports that as of 'Tuesday last' [24 September] upwards of one hundred men had entered the duke of Bedford's service and the duke himself had set out on 25 September for Woburn Abbey to raise the *posse comitatus*. But Parliament, whose authorization was required, would not meet until 17 October; estimates for the proposed regiments were not presented to the commons until 29 October; and the regiments themselves were not voted till 4 November, a full month after publication of the *Serious Address*. In late September, then, the political future of the 'new' regiments was decidedly uncertain. The king, for one, disliked the idea, and there were other doubters as well. It would not have been politically tactful for a 'patriot' pamphlet to press too hard on an issue with such potential for creating political divisiveness.

Which leaves only the 'associations' and raises again their relevance to the dating of the composition of the *Serious Address*. To judge from the London papers the association does not seem to have been publicly perceived as a viable method of raising necessary manpower until after the highly publicized success of archbishop Herring and Lord Malton at York on 24 September 1745. By 3 October *DA* prints a 'Plan for a Military Association in the City of London for the Defence of his Majesty',

---

[1] See, for example, the speech by Hume Campbell in the debate in commons on the motion to disallow permanent rank to the officers appointed to the 'new' regiments; *Parliamentary History*, xiii. 1382–7.　　　　　　　　　　　　　　　　　　　　　[2] *Yale Walpole*, xix. 110.

[3] For his speech opposing Hume Campbell, see *Parliamentary History*, xiii. 1387–91. Pitt's possible connection with Fielding is raised below, pp. lxxxvi–lxxxvii, and in *TP* no. 8 (24 December 1745), below, p. 158 *n*. 1.

and by 15 October it was publicly proposed that every county and city should raise troops to be paid for by subscription money. Fielding anticipates such later, more general awareness of the 'association'; indeed the *Serious Address* may have contributed to such awareness. Fielding in his turn would not have been likely to confer his praise on associations, whatever their 'old English Spirit', if he had not had the example of Yorkshire before him. The York meeting was on 24 September. The London papers carried news of it as early as 28 September, although Herring's actual speech does not appear to have been printed until 30 September. Perhaps the earlier of these two dates provides the safer *terminus ad quem*. Given what Murphy says about Fielding's celerity in composition (*Works* [1762], i. 14, 26, 29), given the somewhat spatch-cocked appearance of the *Serious Address*, with its chunks of quotation and looseness of argument, the reference on the final page to the 'Associations' may have been written on the very day Yorkshire was in the news, and the pamphlet itself, which gives no evidence of revision, sent to the printer almost immediately.

3. THE HISTORY OF THE PRESENT REBELLION

Among the 'Books Printed for A. Millar . . . Written by Henry Fielding' in the advertisement on the fly-leaf [N3^r] of the second edition (1758) of Sarah Fielding's *Cleopatra and Octavia* there is one (item no. 19) described as 'History of the Rebellion in Scotland, 1745. Price One Shilling'. Since Millar's advertisement also lists the *Serious Address* and the *Devil, Pope, Pretender* from this period, the attribution has commanded considerable respect. Cross (ii. 56 *n.*) conjectured that the item Millar's advertisement so described was identical with a Cooper pamphlet advertised among the October 1745 books in *GM*, xv (1745), 560, under the title *The History of the Present Rebellion in Scotland*. However, Cross had never actually seen a work by that title and so could not confirm his conjecture.[1] The Strahan ledgers record a charge to Millar's

---

[1] Cross, ii. 54–6, also attributes to Fielding a 1747 Cooper imprint entitled *A Compleat and Authentick History of the Rise, Progress, and Extinction of the late Rebellion*, and is more than a little ambiguous about its supposed relation to the 'lost' 1745 work. Cross argues that the 1747 *Compleat and Authentick* 'is based upon the detailed account of the rebellion which Fielding had published piecemeal in the "True Patriot"'; that the absence of Fielding's characteristic *hath–doth* mannerism was part of a deliberate disguise; and that the concluding paragraph, 'No one needs to be told', was 'by the hand that wrote the last leader of the "True Patriot"'. This attribution is supported and elaborated by Mabel Seymour, 'Henry Fielding', *London Mercury*, xxiv (June 1931), 160, and 'Fielding's History of the Forty-Five', *Philological Quarterly*, xiv (1935), 105–25. Jarvis refutes the attribution in 'Fielding, Dodsley, Marchant, and Ray', *N&Q*, clxxxix (July–December 1945), 90–2 and 'Fielding and the "Forty-Five"', *N&Q*, cci (January–December 1956), 479–82. Although Jarvis somewhat misrepresents Cross and in addition makes some factual errors of his own, his refutation is persuasive and is accepted by the present editor.

account in October 1745 'For printing the History of the Rebellion', and evidence like this and Millar's 1758 advertisement kept the attribution alive despite the fact that no copy of the title was publicly noticed for some time. Then, in 1934, Ifan Kyrle Fletcher issued what he described as a 'line-for-line and page-by-page' reprint of the 'original',[1] and copies began slowly to come to light.[2] Neither Murphy (1762) nor Henley (1903) reprints the *History* in his edition; the present volume marks its first appearance in an edition of Fielding's works.

The publication of the *History* was advertised in the *London Evening Post* of 3–5 October, the *General Advertiser* of 7 October, the *St James's Evening Post* of 5–8 October, and the *DA* of 8 October 1745. The spread of three days among the 'this day is published' advertisements cannot be accounted for, but such a spread was by no means unprecedented. A legitimate conclusion would be that the *History* appeared on or about 7 October.[3] The Strahan ledgers, which list printing jobs by the month, not day of the month, and apparently in the order in which the jobs were finished, lists the *History* directly under the first entry for the *Serious Address* in Millar's account for October and above the entry for the *Devil, Pope, Pretender*, a chronological sequence which the newspaper advertisements confirm.

Prior to the appearance of the customary 'this day is published' advertisements, there was some 'puffing' of the *History. DA* of 5 October, for

[1] Fletcher's reprint, entitled *The History of the Present Rebellion in Scotland, by Henry Fielding* (Newport, Monmouthshire, 1934), certainly hastened the attribution process, but it has confused the bibliographical picture. As he acknowledges, Fletcher corrects eight typographical errors in his 'original'. But there are a number of other, unacknowledged differences in the accidentals from those of any known state of the *History*. Either Fletcher's reprint was carelessly made, its professions of accountability notwithstanding, or else Fletcher was indeed reprinting from a state of the text not otherwise known. The present editor's inquiry of the Fletcher firm elicited the answer that the 'original' from which Fletcher reprinted could not be traced. Until that 'original' is traced, or until a state of the *History* much more closely resembling Fletcher's reprint is observed, his reprint must be considered to be without textual authority.

[2] The fact that the running title of the *History* claims it was taken from the relation of one 'Macpherson' led some important research libraries to catalogue it under that name only, thereby evidently misleading a number of Fielding scholars.

[3] This conclusion is confirmed by an undated note (in the Malmesbury archive) written by Dr John Barker to accompany a letter dated 5 October 1745 from Fielding to James Harris. Barker's note tells Harris that at the beginning of next week (5 October was a Saturday) there will be a history of the invasion taken from the relation of Mr James Macpherson, a refugee from the YP's army, and that the history will be published by authority. Although Barker attributes this news to the public prints, it is not likely they were his only source. The anticipatory 'puffs' for the *History* do not give Macpherson's first name, whereas Barker does, correctly. In addition, the earliest 'this day is published' advertisements refer to Macpherson as 'Captain', whereas Barker and the actual running title of the *History* refer to him as 'Mr.' John Barker (1700–48), a writer on medical matters and at that time a practicing physician in Bath, was a friend of Fielding's and a subscriber to the *Miscellanies*. He may have known more about the *History* than he lets on to Harris, but there is no other evidence to support his contention that the work would in fact be published by authority.

example, has the following item: 'We hear that Mr. Macpherson, who lately escap'd from the Pretender, hath made some curious Discoveries relating to the Methods which he took on his first Arrival in Scotland.'[1] Those who subscribe to the *hath–doth* test for style, even in limited samples such as this, will conclude that Fielding himself wrote the 'puffs', which differ slightly in form from paper to paper but which all meet the *hath–doth* test.

About the actual composition of the *History*, as is so often the case with Fielding's 'fugitive' pieces, there is almost no hard evidence. If there were a 'real' or historical James Macpherson who escaped from the YP's army, then the date of his escape or rather the date of his arrival in London to give his account, would provide an approximate *terminus a quo*. But no such Macpherson seems to have existed. The *Caledonian Mercury* of 28 October, taking note of the publication of the *History*, asserts, 'there never was an Officer of the Name of Macpherson in the Prince's Army', and this assertion is supported by the fact that no such person appears in the standard listings of participants in the rebellion. Furthermore, there are some difficulties in the pamphlet's treatment of Macpherson. For a Macpherson to have had a hut in the heart of Macdonald country, as the text tells us he did, is extremely unlikely. The running title, which Fielding may not have written, but of which he must surely have been cognizant, speaks of Macpherson as a captain, holding his commission in the YP's army. That such a high-ranking commission was bestowed upon such a chance acquaintance, especially outside the clan structure, is again unlikely, and it is worth noting that the text proper makes no reference to such a commission and no reference to the rank of captain, either. In fact, the text states that after the YP learns Macpherson is a presbyterian—and he learns this almost immediately upon meeting him—he never speaks to him again. The running title also states that Macpherson was forced into the YP's service, whereas the text itself shows him entering eagerly, upon invitation, and being rewarded for so doing. At one point in the text (p. 54) he is described as pulling guard duty outside the YP's quarters, which is a most unlikely duty for a captain, not to mention an unspeakable presbyterian. In sum, Macpherson is a fabrication and his 'escape' will not help in dating the composition of the *History*.[2]

Another equally insubstantial figure does provide some help, how-

---

[1] This item appeared also in the *General Advertiser* of 3 October, *London Evening Post* of 3–5 October, *Penny London Post* of 4–7 October 1745.

[2] Some of the preceding points are made by Jarvis, *Collected Papers*, ii. 125–7, in dismissing Macpherson as a fiction.

ever. Among the persons who, the *History* claims, set out from Rome
with the YP 'in the Beginning of Summer' is 'one *Patrick Graham*, his
Confessor'. Like Macpherson, Graham seems to have been a fiction. No
such name is listed among those who were involved in the rebellion and,
more tellingly, no person of that name or capacity is mentioned in any of
the accounts written by those persons who did actually accompany the
YP to Scotland. As it did with Macpherson, the *Caledonian Mercury*
emphatically denounced the imposition: 'It is therefore solemnly
declared, as well as notoriously known, that there neither is nor ever
was, in the Army or Retinue of his Royal Highness, any such Person as
Father Graham, the pretended Author of the Letter in question. . . . In
fine, the whole Series of the Letter is one continued palpable Lie.'[1]
Unlike Macpherson, however, Graham had a life before Fielding, so to
speak. On or about 23 September 1745 there appeared a Cooper imprint
entitled *A Genuine Intercepted Letter, from Father Patrick Graham, Almoner
Confessor to the Pretender's Son, in Scotland, to Father Benedick Yorke, Titular
Bishop of St. David's, at Bath*, and selling at 3*d.* Although at least some of
Cooper's early advertisements (for example, *Daily Gazetteer* of 21 September 1745) claim the pamphlet was published by authority, the
absence of such a claim in the later advertisements, not to mention the
title-page itself, suggests the claim was false. In any event, the pamphlet
scored one of the first propaganda successes of the rebellion and was
reprinted in a number of the London papers (for example, *General
Evening Post* of 21–4 September, *General Advertiser* of 24 September, and
St James's Evening Post of 24–6 September 1745).

Lie or not, authorized or not, the *Letter* was clearly Fielding's source
for the name and function of Patrick Graham and possibly for a number
of other touches in the *History*. The *Letter* describes the YP kneeling and
kissing the earth, wearing a religious amulet about his neck, frequently
professing his great zeal for the catholic faith and his hatred of heretics.
In Fielding's *History* the YP does things which resemble these. The
Letter also refers to religious conversions in large numbers, to the
restoration of abbey lands and catholic churches; it denounces as for-
geries the claims of toleration supposed to have been made on behalf of
the Stuarts; and it declares that the national debt will be 'sponged' away
because it has been illegally contracted under Hanoverian usurpation.
These are all commonplaces of anti-jacobite propaganda, of course, and

[1] In listing the *Letter* among the September publications, the *Scots Magazine*, vii (September 1745),
448, adds: 'A note was published in the Edinburgh newspapers, by order, importing, That the whole
of this letter is one continued lie; that it is notoriously known, there never was such a person as
Father Graham in the army or retinue of the Chevalier.'

their presence in the *History* is not proof positive that Fielding was reminded of them by his reading of the *Letter*. But he did read the *Letter*—the fiction of Patrick Graham could have come from nowhere else—and may have been stimulated by a number of its familiar features as well.[1] Since Graham is first mentioned at the beginning of the *History* and since the pamphlet gives little evidence that Fielding went back over it to insert names or new characters, it is quite likely that the *History* was not begun until at least 23 September, and probably somewhat later.

The latest datable allusion to be found in the *History* is to the battle of Prestonpans or, more accurately, the arrival of the news of it in London along with lists of the killed and wounded which Fielding reprints. The battle itself took place on 21 September, and *DA* of 26 September reports that a list of the killed and wounded had come to London 'Yesterday', although the paper does not in fact print such a list. By the end of that week, however, just two days later, some of the London papers had published lists, none of them conformable to the lists Fielding gives in his *History*. In a note subtended to the list of rebel wounded which concludes his treatment of Prestonpans in the *History*, Fielding states: 'This Account is taken from the *Caledonian Mercury*, printed since Mr. *Macpherson* left them' (p. 70). Such an unequivocal-seeming assertion by the author should take care of the source question, but in this case it does not. The *Caledonian Mercury* is not the source of the entire preceding 'Account'. In its issue of 23 September it gives, not a conflated list (like that in the *History*) of killed *and* wounded on the king's side, but simply a list of the killed. Five names are on this list. Three can be found in the *History*'s conflated list of killed and wounded; two are not to be found anywhere in the *History*, which itself prints three names not in the *Caledonian Mercury* list. For that part of the 'Account' which pertains to the casualties among the king's forces, Fielding (or perhaps his 'source') is indebted to the *London Gazette*.[2] In its issue of 24–8 September, under dateline 'Whitehall, September 28', the *Gazette* prints a sequence of names, descriptions of condition, and regimental designations which are identical to those in the *History*, with three curious and unaccountable exceptions.[3] The *Gazette*

---

[1] The *Letter* asserts that Graham converted a 'Mr. Cameron', which may have given Fielding the hint (and part of the name) for the episode involving 'James Cameron', who is said to have embraced the faith after the confessor read a letter of absolution and indulgence from the pope, and in consequence thereof was commissioned an ensign, getting, in the words of the *History*, 'Heaven and a Pair of Colours both in an Hour' (p. 53).

[2] The *Caledonian Mercury* of 4 October 1745 reprints this *Gazette* list of 24–8 September as 'the most exact . . . of the Officers killed and wounded'.

[3] Instead of the *History*'s 'Whitmore' the *Gazette* has, apparently correctly, 'Whitney'; and under Leigh's regiment the *Gazette* lists Bremer and Rogers before Whiteford, whom it describes as only 'slightly wounded'.

listing of killed and wounded officers on the king's side was widely reprinted in the London papers—for example, by the *Daily Post* and *General Advertiser* of 30 September 1745—and it is possible that one of these reprintings provided Fielding with his source. In the absence of more determinative evidence, however, about the most that can be said of this material is that it could not have been available to Fielding before 28 September at the earliest.

Besides its list of officers killed and wounded on the king's side the *History* provides a list of officer prisoners as well as lists of the rebel killed and rebel wounded. None of these latter three categories appears in the *Gazette* of 24–8 September. Two of them derive from the *Caledonian Mercury* of 23 September. The *Mercury*'s list of officer prisoners on the king's side closely resembles that given in the *History*, in a number of significant ways. The names and the sequence in which they are given collate exactly except for one omission (in the *History*) and two pairs of switched regimental assignments. The regimental designations and their sequence collate exactly. Colonel Whiteford is accurately (and knowledgeably) denominated a 'Volunteer' in both accounts, and Major Griffith, Master-Gunner of Edinburgh Castle, is so described in both accounts.[1] The *History*'s list of officer prisoners, then, must have come from the *Caledonian Mercury* of 23 September, which did not reach London readers until about 28 September, that is, until the date of the *Gazette* from which the list of killed and wounded was taken.

Right after its list of prisoners and before its lists of rebel killed and rebel wounded the *History* estimates (p. 70) the number of private men on the king's side who were killed, wounded, or made prisoner. The source of this estimate has not been found. The *Caledonian Mercury* concludes its account with a computation of 'enemy' dead at 'about' 500, wounded at 900, and prisoners at 1,400, making no distinction between officers and private men in these categories. The London papers published a number of estimates which varied widely. None of them gives Fielding's figures, which in their neatly ascending centenary character seem almost improvised.

The *History*'s list of rebel killed, four names in all, resembles exactly, as far as it goes, the list printed in the *Caledonian Mercury* of 23 September, even as to the regimental designations and the format of entry. The Edinburgh paper can be confidently confirmed as Fielding's source for this material. However, the *History* concludes this category with the computation 'Together with about 50 Men' (p. 70), whereas the *Caledonian Mercury*

---

[1] Although Griffith does not seem to have actually held a major's commission, contemporary accounts generally so designate him.

estimates 'about 30 private Men'. The source of Fielding's computation has not been found. Again, the London papers published a number of widely varying estimates, none of them corresponding exactly to Fielding's.

The *History* concludes (p. 70) its account of Prestonpans with a list of rebel officers wounded (two) and an estimate of the wounded private men. Fielding's own note at the end of this segment credits the 'Account' to the *Caledonian Mercury*. However, this particular segment of the account cannot derive from the *Caledonian Mercury*. The Scottish paper has no separate category for rebel wounded and lists only 'Capt. James Drummond, alias Macgregor mortally wounded, of the Duke of Perth's Regiment' as the fifth name in its list of officers dead. The *History*, on the other hand, omits Drummond altogether and gives the names of the duke of Perth and Captain David Narlack as the wounded rebel officers, neither of whom appears anywhere among the *Caledonian Mercury* lists. Fielding's authority for listing these two among the wounded is not known. The early reports in the London papers, if they mention Perth at all (some do not), list him (erroneously) as killed.[1] The name 'Narlack' is a mystery. No such name appears either in the newspaper lists of the day or in the later compilations of those who took part in the rebellion. Possibly, it was garbled from a more familiar Scottish name or else misread from Fielding's hand by the printer. It is not likely that this name (or any of the other, minor deviations from published sources) is owing to privileged or 'inside' information such as Fielding might have been able to get from his friends within the ministry. The same is true of the *History*'s concluding estimate that 80 rebel private men were wounded (p. 70). The *Caledonian Mercury* estimates '70 or 80 wounded', and Fielding may well have settled on the latter figure as giving a more favorable picture of the activities of Cope's army.

To sum up the evidence, what can be traced in the way of 'public' sources for his treatment of Prestonpans indicates that Fielding could not have written about the casualties of the battle until he had seen the *London Gazette* of 24–8 September and the *Caledonian Mercury* of 23 September. If the advertisement of the *History* in the *London Evening Post* of 3–5 October 1745 is taken as premature and indicative only of transmission of copy to the printer; if Dr Barker's note can be taken to mean that

---

[1] For example, *DA* of 26 September and *St James's Evening Post* of 24–6 September 1745. James Drummond (1713–46), titular third duke of Perth, with the YP at Perth by 4 September and a lieutenant-general in his army, does not appear to have been wounded, much less killed, at Prestonpans. Possibly the report of his wound/death arose from a misunderstanding of the *Caledonian Mercury* listing of Captain James Drummond in Perth's regiment. Perth died, after Culloden, on shipboard for France in May 1746.

copy was in the printer's hands by 5 October; then a *terminus ad quem* of *c.* 4 October seems possible, if not certain.

How popular was Macpherson's sordid fiction of rebel activities? Despite the rather extensive advertising accorded it—there was a second flurry of advertisements early in November[1]—and despite Dr Barker's 'hearsay' evidence that the *History* was to be published 'by Authority', less circumstantial evidence suggests that the pamphlet did not have unusually wide circulation, at least in England. Strahan's ledgers record a charge to Millar's account in October 1745 'For printing the History of the Rebellion 2¾ Sheets N.° 1500 @ 22. Sh', the total charge for the job being £3. 6s.[2] But there is no further record of the *History* in Strahan's ledgers, which means that the number of authorized London copies should stand at 1,500, a middling number compared to that for the *Serious Address* (4,000, in two printings) and the *Devil, Pope, Pretender* (500, in one printing). The implications of but a single entry in Strahan's ledgers are supported by the fact that the copies the editor has observed exhibit variants which appear to be stop-press corrections in a single impression. If Dr Barker's statement that publication was to be by authority were true, one would expect a larger initial printing or at least a second printing. Neither seems to have been the case. Nor is there any evidence that the *History* circulated in unauthorized London piracies. At home, so to speak, Macpherson's story was not notably successful.

Outside England, however, it may possibly have had considerable additional circulation. There were reprints in Dublin and Belfast, both of which appear to have been set from unrevised copies of the London issue, not from manuscript.[3] In Dublin at least, there was a certain amount of prepublication activity. Faulkner's *Dublin Journal* of 22–6 October quotes from the *DA* of London (5 October): 'We hear that Mr. Macpherson ... hath made some curious Discoveries....' And the issue of 26–9 October states that 'Macpherson's History of the Present Rebellion (who made his escape from the young Chevalier) is read by everyone, and hath changed the tone of many disaffected people.' In view of such blatant puffery it is not surprising to find a 'this-day-is-

---

[1] In, for example, *DA* of 5, 7, and 8 November, and *London Evening Post* of 5–7 November 1745, where the advertisements contain the following statement: 'As the Facts told in this History set this young Pretender in a true Light, the Enemies of our Constitution have used the utmost Endeavours to decry and suppress it.' Statements of this kind were sometimes made to generate reader interest. In the present case Mary Cooper may have had unsold copies she was trying to dispose of. There is no other evidence that antiministerial elements made any effort to suppress the *History*, and Strahan's ledgers do not record a second printing (for which renewed advertising would be appropriate).

[2] BL Add. MS 48800, f. 38ᵛ [51ᵛ].

[3] For this reason the numerous variants, mainly accidental or semisubstantive in nature, cannot be accorded any authority. For bibliographical descriptions, see Appendix IV, below.

published' advertisement of the *History* in the *Dublin Journal* of 2–5 and 7–10 November. The advertisement puts the reprint's price at 3*d.* That price, which is not on the title-page of inspected copies (their title-pages carry no price) is low enough to suggest one of two possibilities: either the reprint received some sort of subsidy, possibly from Fielding's quondam patron and fellow 'patriot', Lord Chesterfield, then taking a stern view of the rebellion from his governor's post in Ireland, or else there were extraordinary reprint arrangements, possibly amounting to piracy.

The date of publication of the Belfast reprint is not known, nor is its price, though the latter was not likely to be higher than that of its Dublin counterpart. The mere appearance of a Belfast reprint lends support to the hypothesis that the Irish reprints may have been dictated, at least in part, by political considerations. Certainly the *History*'s publication record in England does not of itself appear to justify such Irish coverage. As no records exist of the number of copies of either the Dublin or the Belfast reprints, it is useless to speculate how many Irish readers actually read Macpherson's 'curious Discoveries'.

4. *A DIALOGUE BETWEEN THE DEVIL, THE POPE, AND THE PRETENDER*

The third and last of the political pamphlets reprinted in the present volume is the *Dialogue between the Devil, the Pope, and the Pretender*. The earliest known advertisement of this title appears in the *General Advertiser* of 12 October 1745. No further advertisements are known to have appeared until 15 October, which suggests that the advertisement in the *General Advertiser* did not necessarily signal actual publication or public availability. The *Dialogue* begins to get what might be called intensive advertising on 15 October,[1] and this has recently been taken as the true date of publication.[2]

The *Dialogue* was published anonymously by Cooper—the early advertisements proclaiming only that it was 'by an Eminent Hand'. The evidence for attributing it to Fielding is similar in kind to the evidence which links him to the other two pamphlets reprinted in this volume. Millar lists the *Dialogue* among Fielding's works, in the flyleaf advertise-

---

[1] For example, in *DA* of 15, 16, 17, and 18 October; *General Evening Post* of 15–17 and 17–19 October; *London Evening Post* of 12–15 and 15–17 October 1745.

[2] Among others by Martin C. Battestin, 'General Introduction', *Tom Jones*, p. xxv *n.* 2; and Jarvis, *Collected Papers*, ii. 186 *n.* 8. Cross, ii. 15 and iii. 312, dates its publication as 5 November 1745, apparently on the basis of the advertisement for it in the first number (5 November 1745) of the *TP*. Dudden, i. 521, and ii. 13, follows Cross.

ment in the second edition (1758) of Sarah Fielding's *Cleopatra and Octavia*. In *TP* no. 4 (26 November 1745) a Cooper advertisement states that the *Dialogue* and the *Serious Address* are 'both by the same Author'. The *Dialogue* also passes the *hath–doth* test for style, and there is no internal evidence which would dispute Millar's attribution.[1]

Like the two other Cooper pamphlets reprinted here, the *Dialogue* is entered under Millar's account for October 1745 in the Strahan ledgers. Two items unrelated to Fielding intervene between the entry pertaining to the *Dialogue* and the earlier entry pertaining to the *History*, which suggests that Strahan did the job of printing the *Dialogue* somewhat later than the job of printing the *History*. Strahan's entry reads in part as follows: 'For printing Dialogue betwixt the Devil Pope and Pretender $2\frac{3}{4}$ Sh N$^{\circ}$ 500 ... For $2\frac{3}{4}$ Reams of Paper for D$^{\circ}$ 11/6.'[2] The total charge for the printing was £2. 2s.; for the paper, £1. 11s. $7\frac{1}{2}d$. As there is no record in Strahan's ledgers of further work undertaken with respect to the *Dialogue*, it must be assumed that the initial run of 500 copies was the only authorized run. Moreover, no piracies or reprintings in combination with other texts have been discovered. A run of only 500 copies would make the *Dialogue* the least 'popular' of Fielding's pamphlets during the period under consideration.[3]

As to the date of composition of the *Dialogue* there is no external evidence other than that suggested by the sequencing of the Strahan ledger and by the early advertisements of the pamphlet in the newspapers. If the advertisement in the *General Advertiser* of 12 October can be taken to mean that copy was at (or expected at) the printer's by that date, then a *terminus ad quem* of *c.*10–12 October may be inferred for composition. Such an inference presumes that copy went directly to the printer upon completion, and although there is no evidence one way or another on this matter, it seems unlikely that Fielding sat on so topical a work for any length of time.

Internal evidence is hardly more helpful. On page 82 the Pretender refers to the jacobite 'Victory over the *Heretics*' at Prestonpans (21 September 1745), news of which reached London *c.*24 or 25 September. Unless it can be assumed that Fielding revised the early portions of the pamphlet so as to include such a reference, the presumption must be that he began it sometime after that date. There is no evidence of any

[1] However, Jarvis, *Collected Papers*, ii. 123, while accepting the attribution, maintains that the *Dialogue* is 'certainly not in Fielding's characteristic vein'.

[2] BL Add. MS 48800, f. 38^v [51^v].

[3] Of the other Fielding pamphlets of this period for which printing figures exist, only the *Proper Answer* (1747) had so small an initial printing, but even it had a second printing of 500 copies in January 1748. See BL Add. MS 4880, f. 58^v.

such revision, however, and the assumption seems groundless. Given the fact that the *Serious Address* and the *History* also belong to the post-Prestonpans period, and given the further fact that they were published prior to the *Dialogue* and probably in the order in which they were completed, the allusion to Prestonpans in the *Dialogue* is not likely to indicate even the commencement of composition.

On page 88 the pope begins to recite the curse he proposes to lay upon England, 'that damn'd heretical Country'. The Pretender interrupts him before he gets very far, but what the pope does utter bears a spiritual (if not verbal) resemblance to the formula curses of excommunication which were being reprinted in the autumn of 1745 to stimulate anticatholic sentiment. The so-called 'Curse of Ernulphus', found in the Textus Roffensis traditionally attributed to Ernulf, bishop of Rochester, had been recently reprinted as 'The Pope's Dreadful Curse' in the sixth volume of the *Harleian Miscellany*, which was advertised as published in the *General Evening Post* of 12–15 September 1745. The 'Curse' was later published separately at 3*d.* a copy[1] and then reprinted in a number of London papers,[2] some of which later noted the purchase, by a 'Patriot', of 500 copies for public distribution.[3] The *General Evening Post* of 1–3 October reprinted, as did some other London papers, the 'Ceremony of Cursing by Bell, Book, and Candle', the text taken from Foxe's *Acts and Monuments*, Bk. viii (Henry VIII), *sub anno* 1533. The formula of the pope's curse in the *Dialogue* differs from these published curses, to be sure, and is certainly not indebted to them verbally. However, it seems likely that the 'idea' of having the pope curse was stimulated by the wide publicity given such things in late September and early October.[4]

In his catalogue of the debilitating luxuries which the English permit themselves the pope cites, *inter alia*, 'a large Equipage, *French* Cook, and *French* Wines, imported in diametrical Opposition to the Interest of the Public' (p. 97). At times of intensified rivalry with France English social commentators commonly ridiculed the English affectation of things French, especially French wines and French servants. On 5 September 1745 the king issued a proclamation 'For putting the Laws in Execution

---

[1] According to advertisements in, for example, *DA* of 27 September and the *Daily Post* of 26 September 1745.

[2] For example, *General Evening Post* of 19–21 September; *Penny London Post* of 25–7 September; *Old England* of 28 September 1745.

[3] For example, *General Evening Post* of 28 September–1 October and *DA* of 2 October 1745.

[4] The next datable allusion in the text of the *Dialogue* is that by the Pretender to his 'Declaration' or manifesto (p. 86), which seems to have been commonly known in England by early September, well before Prestonpans, and hence of no particular help in dating the composition of the *Dialogue*. For the details of the various publications of the Pretender's manifesto, see above, pp. xli–xlii.

against Papists and Nonjurors' (*London Gazette* of 3–7 September 1745). The proclamation stirred things up briefly—the papers carried numerous reports of searches, accusations and the like—and apparently stimulated a revival of requests that those who employed French servants dismiss them in accordance with the spirit (if not the letter) of the proclamation. One French servant in particular seems to have become something of a *cause célèbre*. He was Cloué, the duke of Newcastle's French chef, popularly known as 'Cloe', by informed consent the most distinguished practitioner in England.[1] A popular print of the day entitled 'The Duke of N——tle and his Cook' depicts Cloué in his kitchen indicating displeasure with the proclamation to Newcastle, who is wringing his hands and crying: 'O! Cloe if you leave me; I shall be Starv'd by G—d.'[2] The *Westminster Journal* of 5 October 1745, taking note of the large numbers of French servants retained by persons of quality, emphasizes the disloyalty of such behavior. In reprinting the *Westminster Journal* essay, *GM*, xv (1745), 544–5, notes: 'Many *French* servants are also not turn'd off, among whom is the famous cook to a noble duke.'[3] Fielding's reference to a French cook rather than to the class of French servants in general suggests he may have been responding to the fuss over Cloué, which is difficult to date exactly but seems to have been in the air as late as the first week in October.

The pope concludes his catalogue of English profligacy with the example of their toleration of 'one single impudent Buffoon', who for many years has 'gone on with Impunity, in Defiance not only of Law but of common Decency, to vilify and ridicule every thing solemn, great and good ... once a Week, in the public Papers, and once in a public Assembly (if any be so infamous to frequent it) to traduce the Persons and Characters of Nobles, Bishops, and even of the King Himself' (p. 98). This oblique (and heretofore unnoticed) reference is certainly to John 'Orator' Henley—Fielding will make a number of clearer references to him in the *True Patriot*—and happens to yield a proximate dating.

---

[1] Cf. *Tom Jones*, I. i. 33 and *n.* For more on Cloué and his productions, see Romney Sedgwick, 'The Duke of Newcastle's Cook', *History Today*, v (1955), 308–16.

[2] Stephens, *Catalogue*, III. i. 543–4 (no. 2684). Stephens dates the print by associating it (erroneously) with the later royal proclamation of 6 December 1745, which was specifically directed against Jesuits and 'Popish Priests'.

[3] Horace Walpole's *MS Political Papers*, f. 1, state that Cloué had been turned away, at the insistence of the duke of Grafton, for whom he was to dress a dinner in honor of Marshal Belleisle commemorating his imminent return to France. The dinner in question appears to date from 29 July 1745, and Cloué is said to have excused himself from the duty because he was tired out 'with playing at bowls'; *Yale Walpole*, xxx. 92. If Newcastle did in fact turn Cloué away in August, the dismissal must have been temporary, else the *GM* comment and the popular print are pointless.

As Fielding's reference asserts, Henley had been haranguing the public in advertisements, letters, and weekly lectures 'for many Years'. However, in the autumn of 1745 his efforts caused a temporary flare-up of attention.[1] According to his own advertisement for it (*DA*, 28 September 1745), his Sunday lecture of 29 September at the 'Oratory-British-Chapel' included a number of topics which in their titles at least sounded disloyal, or at least disparaging: the religion and valor of Sobieski [the Young Pretender], St Michael and the Dragon, or the Dragoons routed [referring to the precipitous retreat of Cope's dragoons], Horse-Race of the Generals [the abject retreat of Cope and the other officers to Berwick], regiments raised by Geomancy [referring to the proposed 'new' regiments to be formed by various noblemen], Paper War at the Bank, French near London, stocks falling and the king dining on two poached eggs, reason of troops not fighting, and so forth. *DA* of 30 September prints an advertisement in the form of a letter calling for a meeting of those who disapproved 'the scurrilous and treasonable Discourse made last Night [Sunday] to a numerous Audience', so as to show their 'Abhorrence and Detestation of that audacious, insolent, and dangerous Abuse of Liberty'. Henley responded with a signed advertisement in *DA* of 1 October (repeated in the next issue) threatening to indict the authors of the hostile letter for conspiracy and citing the Toleration Act and its protections. *DA* of 2 October prints a letter in its editorial columns which, without naming him, singles out Henley from among the many rumormongers in the time of crisis and charges him with traducing the king, glorifying the Pretender, reproaching the French for not supporting the rebellion, declaring that 'we should soon be call'd back from the Desertion (his own Phrase) of the Chevalier's Father', and fostering general despair at home over the supposed folly and villainy of the government's actions. The letter concludes with a recommendation that this 'Enemy of Religion' be silenced.[2] In *DA* of 4 October Henley countered again with an advertisement claiming that critics of his lecture attempted to raise an uproar at various coffee houses, that he was threatened with 'pistolling and stabbing in the Pulpit', and that he was innocent of all charges against him. And his next Sunday lecture (6 October) according to the

[1] As early as 24 August 1745 Henley had run an advertisement in the *DA* announcing that in his Sunday lecture he would remark on 'the coming of Messiah the Prince', that is, the Young Pretender, son of God.

[2] *DA* of 8 October prints an unsigned letter-advertisement requesting that the writer of an anonymous letter which was delivered to Justice De Veil's house discovering some 'very great Misdemeanours' against the government by 'a certain noted Person', 'make out the Accusation' in the public interest. The context makes clear that Henley is intended.

advertisement of it in *DA* of 5 October, began with a defense of the liberty of the pulpit.[1] Although Henley was not actually taken up during the Forty-Five—he was a year later, 4 December 1746[2]—his notorious practices provoked an unusually strong public reaction *c.* 28 September–8 October 1745 and undoubtedly prompted Fielding to potshot him in the *Dialogue*.[3]

There is one final reference in the text of the *Dialogue* which can be dated approximately. To counter the pope's optimism with respect to the rebellion, the devil asserts (p. 98) that 'the heretic Army will be sent for home', that is, recalled from Flanders to fight the jacobite rebels. When the pope says that God will forbid such things, the devil replies (p. 99), 'this will happen and hath happened even at this Time'. It is not entirely clear whether the Devil is referring to the order which sent for the troops or to their actual arrival in England. On the assumption that the latter meaning is more likely, the reference may be dated no earlier than 23 September 1745, which was when the first contingent (three battalions of foot) actually landed back in England.[4] The Devil's passing reference to the increased popularity of associations (p. 98) probably requires that the date be adjusted slightly more toward the end of the month, perhaps even into October.[5]

In sum, then, internal evidence, such as there is, requires a date of composition no earlier than the last week in September. The Henley allusion in particular suggests that the latter part of the *Dialogue* was written sometime in the first week of October. Once again the underlying presumptions are that Fielding wrote the *Dialogue* quickly, without much (if any) revision, that he sent it to Strahan immediately upon

[1] Henley's *DA* advertisement of 5 October also lists among his lecture topics 'The Pr——r annihilated by an Author'. If this can be taken as a reference to Fielding's *Serious Address*—the date does not give Henley much time to puzzle out the authorship—then it is further evidence that the two men had their eyes on each other's activities at this time. In *DA* of 4 October 1745 a hostile letter-advertisement signed 'Philopatrius' refers to Henley as 'an audacious Buffoon', language which is interestingly close to that of the *Dialogue* (p. 98). For Fielding on Henley, see also the index to this volume.

[2] See *GM*, xvi (1746), 666.

[3] Henley's holograph notes for his sermons of October 1745 are in BL Add. MS 23743; his MS addresses to the public 'in 1745–6' are in BL Add. MS 2298, of which ff. 33ᵛ and 34ʳ record his criticism of the exaggerated fears and cowardice exhibited toward the jacobite 'chimera'. That Henley became aware of the dangerous line he was pursuing is indicated by his holograph draft dated 20 October 1745: 'Whereas a Clamour has been artfully rais'd and malitiously propagated, that I am inclin'd to Popery and the Pretender, built on some Minutes in my advertisements & on unconnected parts of Sentences in my Discourses . . . I think it necessary to declare that I am Humbly at the devotion of his most Gracious Majesty . . . that the Nature of my Oratory is misunderstood or wilfully mistaken'; BL Add. MS 10349, f. 223ʳ.

[4] As reported in *DA* of 24 September 1745.

[5] For the public notoriety accorded to these military associations and its use in dating composition, see above, pp. xlv–xlvi.

completion, and that Strahan kept it in his shop for no more than a couple of days. Of such presumptions the most that can be said is that although the evidence supporting them is circumstantial, there is no known evidence that would refute them.

5. *THE TRUE PATRIOT*

The *London Evening Post* of 2–5 November 1745 carries a 'This Day is publish'd' advertisement for a weekly paper entitled 'The True Patriot. And, The History of Our Own Times'. As far as is known, this is the first reference to what was to be Fielding's most extended 'political' undertaking during the period of the Forty-Five. Furthermore, the *London Evening Post* advertisement seems to have been the only one published, a modest advertising program indeed and one which suggests Fielding's project may have lacked financial support even at the start. There are no references to the *True Patriot* before the fact by any of Fielding's friends or contemporaries, and very few after the fact as well. Fielding himself refers to it obliquely in an unpublished letter to James Harris, but not until after the first of the year 1746 and even then not by name. Both the advertisement in the *London Evening Post* and the *True Patriot* itself come as something of a surprise.

The initial number of the *True Patriot* appeared on 5 November 1745, the anniversary of the Gunpowder plot, Guy Fawkes' day. It is difficult to believe that Fielding and his associates in the undertaking did not have their eye on that earlier attempt to subvert the government so that the catholics might rise up in safety. But the fact is, neither the *True Patriot* itself nor any other known commentators on the paper mention the anniversary and its appositeness for a journal undertaken nominally in defense of the existing government. The paper ran for thirty-three numbers, the first thirty-two of which survive intact in the Burney Collection of the British Library. The final number does not appear to have survived in its original form. It is reprinted here in the version that appeared in the June 1746 issue of the *London Magazine* (xv [1746], 298–9) under the title 'Substance of the Author's Farewel to his Readers'.

In format the *True Patriot* adheres rather closely to the conventions characteristic of the weekly papers of the time. Printed on a large half-sheet folded so as to make four pages, it ran three columns of print per page, the central column divided from its neighbors by vertical lines. Unlike Fielding's *Champion* and *Jacobite's Journal*, but like his *Covent Garden Journal*, the *True Patriot* dispensed with a headpiece or illustrative cut at the head of the initial page of each issue. According to its modern editor, the paper has a total page size of 15 × 10⅜ inches, the printed matter on each page running to 12⅞ × 9¼ inches.[1] The initial letter of each leading essay is set in ornamental block of constant design. The price of the paper is centered and bracketed beneath the center column of each first page, and the fourth and last page of each issue carries the customary colophon, which happens to vary somewhat over the run of the paper.

The *London Evening Post* advertisement describes the *True Patriot* as 'undertaken on a new Plan', apparently meaning that the intelligence secured for the paper by its privileged authors will be conveyed in 'a digested and agreeable Method to the Reader'. And for a time the two 'historical' departments of the paper, devoted to foreign news and domestic news respectively, do differ from the conventional itemizations of the other papers by presenting their news in a more expanded narrative form. Substantively, however, the *True Patriot* is a fairly typical representative of the weekly 'journal' of its time, a hybrid species which had evolved to meet the exigencies of the stamp duties by combining the leader essay of the more literary periodicals of the *Tatler–Spectator* tradition with the short 'news' items and 'historical' features characteristic of what might be called the *news* paper. Each number of the *True Patriot* begins with a lead essay, generally prefixed by a motto from a classical author. These leader essays almost always take up the entire first page of the paper and not infrequently run onto the second page. Next come the two 'historical' features, 'The Present History of Europe' and 'The Present History of Great Britain'. For approximately the first half of the *True Patriot*'s life these two features are based, substantively, upon the *London Gazette* or, occasionally, upon another London paper, the *General Advertiser*. The 'true and material Intelligence' so derived is recast by Fielding into a fuller, more discursive, more narrative form than it appeared in originally. Thus, though the paper does not seem to have had a news-gathering apparatus of its own (in the first number Fielding implies that it has), it does convey its derivative material in a more 'digested and agreeable' form than did the newspapers of record, something more like a 'History of Our Own Times' promised in the *True Patriot*'s running title. Furthermore, the fact that it was a weekly obviously saved the *True Patriot* from some of the inaccuracies characteristic of the diurnal papers and helped Fielding resume his satire of contemporary journalism (in no. 1, he asserts that 'there is scarce a Syllable of TRUTH' in any of the contemporary papers).

[1] Miriam Austin Locke (ed.), *The True Patriot: and The History of Our Own Times* (University of Alabama Press, 1964), p. 13.

In the first seventeen numbers the department which customarily followed the two historical departments (it is omitted from no. 13) is entitled: 'Apocrypha. Being a Collection of certain true and important WE HEARS from the News-Papers'. 'Apocrypha' includes a number of 'straight' items taken from the *London Gazette* and other London papers and credited to these sources by a system of initials which is set forth in the third number (19 November 1745). In addition this department prints a number of items from the same sources (also credited) to which it subjoins brief ironic commentary by the 'True Patriot' himself. Since much of this satiric commentary meets the *hath–doth* stylistic, and since the department is discontinued at almost exactly the time other changes in the paper suggest Fielding may have lessened his editorial attention, it is reasonable to conclude that he was in charge of 'Apocrypha' and wrote its commentary (reprinted in Appendix VII, below). Taken collectively, the two categories of reprinted material which make up 'Apocrypha' provide the reader with enough 'news' to satisfy somewhat that motive for buying a paper and with enough satire and political 'point' to amuse and instruct the reader who might be looking for those things along with his news. Also subjoined to the 'Apocrypha' is a number of categorical lists with such conventional titles as 'Ships taken', 'Casualties', 'Preferred', 'Committed', 'Married', and the like. As far as can be determined, these items were mostly derived from other sources, but without credit. Occasionally the 'True Patriot' will add comments on particular items in these categories too, comments which either satirize the journalistic conventions governing the presentation of such material or which praise and notice individuals presumably known to the editor (these items with comments are also reprinted in Appendix VII, below). Even after the disappearance of the 'Apocrypha' itself, the categorical lists continue to appear to the end of the paper, but there are no editorial comments after no. 20 (11–18 March 1746), further indication of Fielding's lessening interest in the undertaking.

There are other signs that the *True Patriot* underwent some sort of mid-life crisis. Beginning with issue no. 17 for the 'Present History of Great Britain' and no. 18 for what had become simply 'Foreign History', the two historical departments undergo considerable change. After an energetic start, during which their discursive and narrative form shows signs of marked editorial attention, the two departments rely more and more on verbatim reprintings credited to the *London Gazette* and other papers. Then suddenly, in late February–early March 1746, they take on the form of editorial commentary—some might call it analysis—on the foreign and especially the domestic scene. The change is striking.

Instead of a narrative of events or compressed items of news, the departments emphasize ideology and a pronouncedly judgmental attitude towards policies and the political implications of events. The 'Present History of Great Britain' in particular undertakes to define what can only be called a kind of watered-down Bolingbrokeism, which it calls, repeatedly, the new patriotism. Opposition is faction and faction is odious. The extinction of parties altogether is what is called for; 'mere' politics is contemptible and ultimately self-interested; the country needs 'statesmen', not politicians; and 'patriots' and 'courtiers' are not only compatible, in such a view of government, but 'necessarily conjoined' (no. 17). There are frequent references to abstractions like public service, common cause, liberty, the voice of the people, the constitution.

As a set, these abstractions seem to be posing some sort of alternative to the pragmatic political process as practiced, say, by Sir Robert Walpole (interestingly, he is not mentioned by name, presumably for fear of alienating his protégé, Henry Pelham, in 1745–6 the principal minister). Practical politics has turned out to be private and selfish, not public and disinterested. England has a glorious constitution. It is sufficient to have it implemented by the prince, the patriot king, assisted by those trusted by the prince, on account of their natural talents as leaders, and obeyed by the commonality, who perceive both the trust and its basis in the nature of things. The failure to achieve such a patriot politics till now has helped to corrupt the country, and the corruption makes governmental solutions that much more difficult. Luxury, Idleness, Extravagance, Contempt of Ordinances, Want of Regard for Commonwealth—the progression implicit in these abstractions (no. 24) reveals the anticapitalist bottom line of the 'patriot' myth—the root of all evil is the defeat of Land by Money. Neither Fielding nor anybody else writing leaders for the *True Patriot* deals with the ideology at quite so exalted a level.[1] But Luxury is one of the topoi of the paper's leader essays, and

---

[1] It is generally thought that the marked differences in the editorial direction of all but the leader material beginning with no. 18 (25 February–4 March 1746) were due to Fielding's legal obligations; see, for example, Locke, ed. cit., p. 24. According to the calendar published in no. 16 (11–18 February 1746) the Lenten assizes of the western circuit opened at Southampton on 4 March and commenced final sittings at Worcester on 29 March. And the Easter term sittings of the King's Bench for London and Westminster are noted in no. 23 (1–8 April 1746) as beginning on 18 and 22 April respectively and finishing their after-term business around mid-May. Although there is no published evidence that Fielding actually attended the Lenten assizes in 1745—or the King's Bench Sittings (at which Locke, p. 24, says his presence was 'necessary')—on the evidence of the *True Patriot* changes it seems likely that he did both these things. They would account for the lessening of his involvement in the paper.

The editor of Fielding's own writings is perhaps less obliged than the editor of the *True Patriot* materials as a whole to identify the writer who took over the two historical departments, for example, but it might be worth considering the candidacy of James Ralph, Fielding's former colleague on the *Champion* and Dodington's literary man-of-all-work. If the *True Patriot* was indeed undertaken by

later in his career Fielding will deal with it in terms that are compatible with the more politicized terms often employed by the mid-century opposition.[1]

So much for the more or less regular departments of the *True Patriot*. On an irregular basis the paper printed 'letters' on various topics. The letters sometimes appear between the leader essay and the first of the historical departments, sometimes after the categorical lists which conclude the 'Apocrypha'. In the first three numbers the paper concludes its editorial matter with a column and a half entitled 'Observations on the Present Rebellion', counseling against overzealous and wholesale condemnation of the Scots and the catholics simply because some members of these two groups appeared to be involved with the rebellion. This particular feature is singled out for mention in the colophons of nos. 2 and 3, and in no. 3 it takes the form of a letter replying to the preceding installment and purporting to have been contributed by 'a Person of very high Eminence'. Declared to be postponed in no. 4, it never reappears. In no. 9 a lengthy, unsigned letter ('from a Person of great Property') proposes the formation of a regular militia as the best way to achieve national security. The next issue commences a series, the installments of which bear varying titles, on the militia scheme, considering its historical and political background, the alternatives, constitutional problems, and a plan for implementation. The series runs through no. 15, where a continuation is promised. Number 16 announces a postponement, but the series is never resumed.

In two numbers (1 and 17) the paper prints occasional poems ('A Loyal Song' and 'An Epilogue, Design'd to be spoken by Mrs. Woffington') which are models of their kind. Both are reprinted elsewhere, the latter earlier than its appearance in the *True Patriot*, and neither can be safely attributed to Fielding.

Dodington and the kind of patriot grouping implied by the leader of no. 1 (see below, pp. lxix–lxxi), and if such a group needed to bring in somebody to take up the editorial slack, Ralph, with his extensive 'patriot' experience, was an obvious candidate. The *hath*–*doth* usage found in the early historical departments gives way, with no. 18, to the more common *has*–*does*, which Ralph used. More significantly, perhaps, the heavy use of italic for rhetorical emphasis, which begins also with no. 18, is very like that found in the 'Lilbourne' essays of the *Champion*, essays generally and plausibly assumed to be Ralph's. Finally, the greater emphasis on political ideology and what may be called a more professional historical perspective recall the Ralph of the Lilbourne' essays, the first volume of the *History of England* (1744), and, later, the *Remembrancer* (1747–51) more than they do Fielding or any other identifiable candidate. The case for Ralph is certainly not proved. However, given Fielding's failure to produce anything like a systematic political ideology in the leaders, his legal distractions may have provided the undertakers of the *True Patriot* with just the sort of excuse they needed to bring in some one who might remedy that defect.

---

[1] See, for example, *A Charge to the Grand Jury* (1749), and especially *An Enquiry into the Causes of the late Increase of Robbers* (1751) and *A Proposal for Making an Effectual Provision for the Poor* (1753).

On the fourth and final page of each issue appear the advertisements.[1] They seldom take up more than one column and often considerably less. In both scope and source they suggest the paper must have subsisted on revenues other than those brought in by advertising. As is perhaps quite to be expected, there are none of the social, political, and commercial advertisements which are so much a staple of the daily papers. The advertisements in the *True Patriot* are solely for books, except for two that seem more like notices: one for help for a poor family (no. 9), and another, patently satirical, requesting the services of a skilled 'undertaker' (no. 11). Many are standing advertisements, left pretty much without alteration for number after number. Furthermore, there are no ads at all after no. 25 (22 April 1746)—no ads, that is, for the last two months of the paper's life. The overwhelming majority of the advertisements comes from two sources—Mary Cooper and Andrew Millar—with Robert Dodsley a distant third. According to the modern editor of the *True Patriot*, of the 235 distinct items advertised (the figure includes repeaters), 44 were published by Cooper, alone or with others; 6 by Dodsley alone; 6 by other publishers; and 179 by Millar (mostly in standing ads).[2]

At the bottom of the fourth and final page of each issue (the canonical location) appears a colophon, which takes slightly varying forms over the existing thirty-two numbers. The colophon declares the paper to be 'Printed for M. Cooper', and she is the only person named in those of the first eighteen numbers. Beginning with no. 19 the colophon adds, 'And sold by George Woodfall'. The headnote inserted beneath the dateline on the first page of nos. 17 and 18 gives Millar's name and address and urges persons who have knowledge of attempts to suppress the *True Patriot* to so inform him. This headnote also gives the names and addresses of Ann Dodd and [Henry] Chappelle, in addition to that of M. Cooper, as persons with whom subscriptions to the paper may be entered.

The curiously restrictive pattern of advertisements in the *True Patriot* raises questions concerning the ownership and management structure of the paper. Who in fact were the undertakers? And what might have motivated them to start up a new paper at just this time? Once again there is no hard evidence. No lists of partners or shareholders, and hence no evidence of any transactions in shares. No minutes of shareholders' meetings like those for the *Champion*, available apparently to G. M. Godden but now seemingly lost.[3] No references, even gossipy

---

[1] Locke, ed. cit., pp. 14–16, analyzes these in some detail.   [2] Ibid., pp. 14–15.

[3] See her *Henry Fielding: A Memoir* (London, 1910), pp. 100, 115–16. They seem to have been those once owned by Isaac Reed, who wrote Boswell *c.* November 1792: 'I have the minutes of the partners

ones, to the project in the journals and pamphlets of the period. Nothing in the correspondence or memoirs of Fielding's known friends who might have been associated with the venture (such as Dodington, Lyttelton). And nothing explicit in the surviving letters from Fielding himself to James Harris.

In the absence of harder evidence the pattern of advertisements in the *True Patriot* encourages consideration of the hypothesis that the management of the paper's non-editorial aspects was in the hands of publishing and bookselling professionals like those cited in the colophons and headnotes, that is, Millar, Cooper, Dodsley, Woodfall, Dodd, and Chappelle. Without giving his evidence, Cross (ii. 18–19) suggests that the paper was the enterprise of booksellers 'as anti-jacobite as the editor, with whom patriotism counted much, and money somewhat less at just that time'. The hypothesis may be plausible, but the assigned motive is not. Undoubtedly all concerned in the paper's management were patriotic enough. But by November 1745, well after the fall of Edinburgh and the defeat at Prestonpans, there was no untapped market for patriotism of that sort. Even the opposition papers were professing their loyalty. And the country was sufficiently, if ineffectively, alarmed by the rebellion. Given the distinctive political slant of the *True Patriot*, other motives are more likely.

By the middle of the eighteenth century, if not a little earlier, most of the principal London papers were in the control of booksellers. The commonest form of newspaper ownership was a stock company or shareholder group, in which the actual authors or 'projectors' were not likely to have held a major portion of the shares.[1] For the weekly papers it has been estimated that there was an average of ten shareholders per company, with booksellers predominating in most cases.[2]

There appear to have been two major reasons for the bookseller takeover of the newspaper business. A paper offered the prospects of long-term income in return for a moderate outlay. More importantly, perhaps, newspapers were the cheapest medium of mass advertising, made even cheaper for shareholders, who customarily got reduced rates on their own advertisements, provided there was room. Whoever

of that paper [the *Champion*] in my possession by which it appears that James Ralph succeeded Fielding in his share of the paper ...'; *The Correspondence and Other Papers of James Boswell Relating to the Making of 'The Life of Johnson'*, ed. Marshall Waingrow (New York, n.d.), p. 497.

[1] According to Godden, *Henry Fielding*, p. 100, the minutes of the meetings of the partners in the *Champion* undertaking record that Fielding himself 'did originally possess Two Sixteenth Shares of the Champion as a Writer in the said paper'.

[2] The account here and below is based on Michael Harris, 'The Management of the London Newspaper Press during the Eighteenth Century', *Publishing History*, iv (1978), 95–112.

controlled the papers controlled to a considerable degree the feasible advertising outlets and could thereby ensure continued exposure for their own books while being able to restrict the outlets for their less well-placed competitors. Control of the papers was in turn made easier by the fact that the booksellers also had considerable control over the existing means of distribution. The *National Journal* of 29 March 1746, for example, noting a combination among the proprietors of the daily papers designed to obstruct their new competitors, alleges that 'most of the Pamphlet Shops, etc. are by Necessity or Choice become such Slaves to them [the newspaper proprietors], as to deny selling any Paper which has not the good Fortune to be licensed by these Demagogues'.[1] In 1740 the *Champion*, then still under Fielding's editorial direction, professed to be having trouble from the repressive tactics of bookseller shareholders of more established papers. And the 'Apocrypha' of *True Patriot* no. 11 (14 January 1746) prints a 'We Hear' reporting that several coffee-houses have lost customers because they refused to take in the *True Patriot*, a suppressive measure which may be reflected also in the headnote to nos. 17 and 18.[2]

Granted, then, that the evidence of bookseller involvement in mid-century newspapers is considerable; granted, too, that the pattern of advertisements in the *True Patriot* is not inconsistent with bookseller management—the question of motive remains a nagging one. In the event, the *True Patriot* turns out not to have been a financial success, at least judging from its relatively short life and the paucity of its advertising. But could any group of presumably practical professionals have seriously believed that a weekly paper of pronounced political cast would make it in the marketplace at that time? It seems unlikely. And if booksellers comprised the management (or most of it) of the *True Patriot*, why did they cease to advertise at all after no. 25, that is, with almost two full months to go before the paper ceased publication?[3] Had the voting power of management rested with the bookseller-advertisers, it seems likely that when the ads went, the paper would have gone too.

---

[1] As quoted by Harris, p. 97.

[2] For the 'Apocrypha' reference, see below, p. 402. Harris, p. 97, who does not mention the 'Apocrypha' reference, does take the headnotes of nos. 17 and 18 to indicate bookseller opposition. However, suppression on more political grounds must not be dismissed as a motive, particularly in the case of a paper as political as the *True Patriot*. The refusal of coffee-houses to take in a paper was apt to be on grounds more political than merely mercenary, and the headnote reference to 'some who are concerned in imposing on the Public, by propagating Lies and Nonsense' is certainly susceptible to a political interpretation as well.

[3] Even on the hypothesis that there may have been what amounted to contractual reasons for continuing until a specified date, whether or not the undertaking showed a profit, one would still assume that the lure of 'cut-rate' advertising would have attracted at least some of the bookseller management, if indeed there was any.

It has been suggested that perhaps the paper was begun with the understanding that the government would provide a subvention of sorts by 'taking off' a certain number of copies, at the prescribed price, for judicious free distribution.[1] There is absolutely no evidence to support this hypothesis. In fact, what evidence there is suggests that, whatever may or may not have been promised or 'understood', the government did nothing at all to help the paper. And no contemporaries even suggested that it did. The charge of governmental support was several times raised against Fielding's *Jacobite's Journal*, but never against the *True Patriot*. It is perhaps not surprising that no such charge was made during the crisis of the Forty-Five. Opposition journalism was keeping a low profile, for obvious reasons. But if in fact the government had supported the *True Patriot* by taking off copies, surely Fielding's enemies would have felt free to air the charges in later, less critical times. As far as is known, they did not.

Even more telling against the hypothesis of government subvention is the marked tone of unrequitedness that can be heard in the later issues of the *True Patriot*. The disillusioned tone of Fielding's leader in no. 14 (28 January–4 February 1746) would be more than tactless in a writer who was being supported by the very minister he said was so indifferent to him. It is one thing to disclaim ministerial support. It is quite another to assert of the principal minister that 'he hath the utmost Indifference for all Writers, and the greatest Contempt for any Good or Harm which they can do him'. Fielding was likely correct in what he wrote here. Pelham spent less for political propaganda in particular and for secret services generally than his predecessor (Walpole). But it could hardly have been ingratiating—or intended to be ingratiating—to add that Pelham's contempt for writers 'may proceed from a Consciousness of his own Rectitude, and I presume doth so'; or later, that 'it is the Flattery of Ministers, and the Support of their iniquitous Measures, which recommends to their Countenance'.[2] The heightened, self-pitying tone of unrequitedness in the final two numbers of the *True Patriot* almost certainly results from Fielding's failure to gain either a place or a pension for his labors on the paper—'Whatever therefore may be my Fate, as I have discharged my Duty to my King and Country . . . I shall now retire with the secret Satisfaction which attends right actions, tho' they fail of any great Reward from the one, and are prosecuted with

---

[1] Cross, ii. 18, thinks it 'probable' that the government did purchase copies. Robert Dudley French, '"The True Patriot" by Henry Fielding' (unpubl. diss. Yale University, 1920), p. 20, and Locke, p. 5, merely note the possibility.

[2] For the three quotations concerning Pelham and the ministers, see below, pp. 209, 209, 211.

Curses and Vengeance from the other'.[1] But the interesting omission of any reference to ministers in his farewell peroration and his tactless description of Pelham's indifference to writers (in no. 14) do not give much comfort to the hypothesis of ministerial subvention.

There was of course another kind of newspaper to be found in London during this period. Undertaken for different reasons from those of the essentially commercial bookseller enterprises and on the whole occasional and shorter lived, this was the 'political' paper. As a rule its prime movers were members of the political opposition or of a faction whose views differed to some degree from those of the ministers in power. Not much is known about the management of these political papers, possibly because their members viewed themselves more as subscribers than as shareholders and hence did not feel required to keep records in the fashion of more purely commercial enterprises. Fielding's friend and sometime political mentor, Dodington, alludes briefly in his 'Diary' to the circumstances and method of starting up just such a political paper. The sudden death of the prince of Wales in March 1751 upset a good many carefully nurtured political expectations, including Dodington's. In the immediate fallout from that event some of the prince's bereft adherents pressed for a clarifying decision: either form a regular 'party' as soon as possible, or abandon opposition altogether. A corollary of any decision to form a party, according to Dodington, would have been 'to fix the subscription for a paper by Mr. Ralph, supported by about twenty of us at 10 guineas each, and what else we can get'.[2] Dodington's statement is tantalizingly brief, and the projected paper seems not to have been undertaken. But Fielding's colleague Ralph, under the pseudonym 'George Cadwallader', had already edited what must have been just such a political paper, the *Remembrancer* (1747–51), on behalf of the prince of Wales and presumably under Dodington's direction. Booksellers may indeed have seen commercial possibilities in certain 'political' papers—anti-Walpole sentiment, for example, had sold very well[3]—but in some cases they may have undertaken the professional management at the instigation of the politicians who wanted publication, and they may have done so with an understanding that they would be indemnified for possible prosecutions and even for certain losses.[4] And Dodington's 'Diary' entry implies that private subscription

---

[1] From no. 33 (17 June 1746), as reprinted in the *London Magazine*, xv (1746), 299; see below, p. 307.

[2] *The Political Journal of George Bubb Dodington*, edd. John Carswell and Lewis Arnold Dralle (Oxford, 1965), p. 111.

[3] It should be noted here that according to the *Champion* minutes available to Godden, the listed partners in that decidedly political paper were all booksellers, except Fielding; *Henry Fielding*, p. 115.

[4] Harris, pp. 105–6, considers briefly indemnification from prosecution.

to the founding of a 'political' or 'party' paper was no new thing. Furthermore, although the 'Diary' figures are clearly approximate, a start-up funding of £200 plus, shared out among as many as twenty persons, shows that the difficulties of getting started were by no means beyond the capacities of persons of substance. If in its politics the *True Patriot* seems a little too occasional, even opportunistic, to have been the brainchild of booksellers acting solely in their own commercial interests, it most certainly was not beyond the interest or the capacities of a 'patriot' grouping in search of a public outlet with which to make some political points. Very possibly the *True Patriot*'s equivalent of Dodington's twenty subscribers put the practical management of the paper, for the time being at least, in the hands of professionals like Millar, Cooper, Woodfall, Dodd, and Chappelle,[1] with the understanding that the editorial direction would be up to the editor the subscribers had chosen.

If, on balance, the initial push behind the *True Patriot* would appear to have been political, not commercial, the question of motive must still be raised. What objectives would a 'patriot' subscription expect to achieve by undertaking a paper in November 1745? Before the question can even be attempted, the participants must be more clearly identified, and this cannot be done with much assurance. In his opening leader Fielding takes the conventional rhetorical step of establishing his editorial persona. He is, first of all, a 'Gentleman'. There may be genteel, not to say snobbish, implications lurking in that emphasis. With his often remarked fondness for 'Esq' (which lawyers affected) and a certain confidence of social attitude, Fielding struck some of his contemporaries as considering himself a cut above them socially,[2] and there are probably traces of this attitude in the persona of *True Patriot* no. 1. Certainly Fielding is quick to assert that he is no mere journalistic hack from Grub Street, that indeed he is not even acquainted with any such. But granting that he found this particular distinction easy to make for himself, in the present instance the application seems more than merely personal. Not only will the 'Gentleman' editor refrain from the characteristic scurrility of political papers; he will also, by virtue of his station, be privy to more

---

[1] It may be noteworthy that at least three of the 'professionals' whose names appear in the head-notes or the colophons of the *True Patriot* had been previously involved with political journalism. In 1744 Mary Cooper had been examined by the authorities concerning the publication of *Old England*; PRO, State Papers, Domestic, George II, Entry Book 134 (sec. letter book), ff. 37–8, as cited by Herbert M. Atherton, *Political Prints in the Age of Hogarth* (Oxford, 1974), p. 7 n. Ann Dodd had been one of the sellers of an edition of the *London Evening Post* and was examined by the government in regard to it; PRO, State Papers, Domestic, George II, General, vol. 50, ff. 272–3; as cited by Atherton, p. 13 n. Henry Chappelle, one of the partners in the *Champion*, had bid successfully for the rights to the 1741 collected edition (two volumes) of that paper; Godden, *Henry Fielding*, pp. 115–16.

[2] For the evidence, see 'General Introduction', *The Jacobite's Journal and Related Writings*, p. lxxxi.

reliable news from the precincts of power. And the social connects even more firmly with the 'literary' when the editor considers his identity. He might be Bolingbroke, an unnamed bishop (probably Hoadly), Chesterfield, Warburton, Dodington, Lyttelton, Fielding, or Thomson—'or indeed any other Person who hath distinguished himself in the Republic of Letters'.

The rhetorical fiction implicit in such a catalogue of eminences does not presume that the reader will take all the possibilities equally seriously. However, an ideological orientation of sorts is intended. The writer, whoever he may in fact be, is *like* these eminences in some way or other—more like them than like, say, Granville or Bath or even the 'old corps' members of the Pelham administration. And the way he will be like them is in respect of the two characteristics they commonly share: distinction in the republic of letters, and a certain political stance or ideology, which at one time was known and identified, often disparagingly, as 'patriot'.

To a reader contemplating the availability of a new, unheralded weekly these names signal that the *True Patriot*'s political genealogy comes in a direct line from the *Craftsman*, *Common Sense*, the *Champion*, from the literary efforts of the old Leicester House opposition, nominally led by the prince of Wales but for practical purposes managed first by Dodington and then by Lyttelton, with Chesterfield on the sidelines and Bolingbroke dispensing doctrine behind the scenes.

Those who define Fielding's attitude towards Bolingbroke in terms of his hostile 'Fragment of a Comment on Lord Bolingbroke's *Essays*' (1754; 1762), will wish to insist on the irony of Bolingbroke's being named here in the *True Patriot*.[1] Actually there is no irony except that of pretending to attribute to him what of course he did not write. Fielding's posthumous 'Fragment' attacks Bolingbroke's antitheology in no uncertain terms, it is true, but the 'metaphysical' Bolingbroke, so to speak, came late and was a Bolingbroke many of his political friends found disconcerting.[2] Undoubtedly his irreligious views had always been implicit in his political writings as well as in his conversations with friends, but he does not seem fully to have developed these views until the frustrations of the 1740s over his continued alienation from the centers of favor.

---

[1] This is not the first time Fielding invokes the name of Bolingbroke in a literary connection. In the *Champion* of 1 March 1740 the editorial *persona* recalls that his bookseller asked him to go to the coffee-houses and say that Bolingbroke wrote the *Champion*—a successful 'Scheme'. See collected edition (1741), i. 325.

[2] Chesterfield wrote Lyttelton from Lyons on 11 September 1741 NS that he had just spent three days with Bolingbroke and found him 'plunged in metaphysics' and speaking of nothing else; *Letters*, ed. Dobrée, ii. 473–4.

The Bolingbroke whom Fielding flatters himself with here is the Bolingbroke whose introduction in 1738 to the prince of Wales and his opposition grouping led to 'The Idea of a Patriot King' (1738) and the later addressing of the essay on 'The Spirit of Patriotism' to Lyttelton; the Bolingbroke who, during the 1744 negotiations between the Pelhams and the patriot opposition which led up to the broad bottom, was regarded even by Chesterfield as the principal architect of the patriot strategy for coming into power: get rid of Carteret and establish a coalition with the Pelhams.[1] Both parties to the coalition agreed as to the desirability of the first of these two objectives. But the notion of a coalition between the Pelhams and the patriots struck many of the 'old corps' as threatening; they looked upon the patriot leaders (Chesterfield and Dodington in particular) as running with Bolingbroke and the tories. Hence the patriot need to detach the important discontented whig (Bedford) and tory leaders (Gower) and to force the recalcitrant remainder into the position of looking like jacobites. As late as 18 November 1745 Bolingbroke was in correspondence with Hardwicke, an 'old corps' mainstay of the Pelham administration, the 'great and glorious' man to whom Fielding pays so particular (and flattering) attention.[2] According to his son, Hardwicke was 'rather reserved about his intercourse' with Bolingbroke, which was indeed somewhat enigmatic and provoked a suspicious jealousy in Newcastle among others.[3] Mainly Bolingbroke offered information about French affairs, but every so often he advised Hardwicke how to cope with the party intrigues at home. A letter of 14 January 1745 warns of the effect on the Pelhams' new allies of continued party intrigues, apparently referring to Cobham's persistent demands, and recommends moving ahead with a bill to reinforce the qualifications required of justices of the peace so as to meet tory objections that the qualifications had been lowered to favor whigs.[4] Failure to thus quiet tory objections and to detach key figures elsewhere will lead, he fears, to 'a schism even this session'. Bolingbroke here sounds the same note Chesterfield sounds with Newcastle. Both undertake a cautious but insistent prodding of the Pelhams to accept the fact that if they want an impregnable coalition in parliament, they are going to have to do a little more than they have done for the patriots. Neither names nor numbers are mentioned out loud, but the advice is clear: 'As you [the Pelhams] have to do with some ill men, and some weak ones, you have to

---

[1] See, for example, 'Diary of Hugh Earl of Marchmont', *Marchmont Papers*, i. 10–12, 15, 19–20, 38, *et passim*.

[2] In the leader of *TP* no. 33 (17 June 1746), below, p. 308.

[3] George Harris, *The Life of Lord Chancellor Hardwicke* (London, 1847), ii. 213–14.

[4] Ibid., ii. 114–15.

do with others that have sence & virtue & courage.'[1] In other words, some additional patriots will have to be dealt with.

Fielding may have been told of Bolingbroke's continued presence behind the patriot front, but he need not have been. Bolingbroke is named in *True Patriot* no. 1 because he provided the ideology of the original patriot grouping around the prince of Wales, an ideology which, *mutatis mutandis*, had filtered through Chesterfield and Dodington among others and was still informing, with Bolingbroke's persistent presence, the program of the later 'true' patriots in 1745–6. The emphasis on the need to suppress all faction, indeed all parties as such; the emphasis on the king and the constitution, with the corresponding depreciation of politicians, ministers, and the intervening political 'process'; the elitist acknowledgment that some men (like Pitt) had innate natural superiority and that these innate qualities of natural superiority, not their party standing, are what should qualify them as statesmen;[2] the implication that the country had sunk into degenerate luxury and had acquired in the process a politics appropriate to this despised state, as manifested by a creeping tendency to buy and sell even places and power and by the consequent triumph of the exchequer over the prerogative—these are some of the themes of Bolingbroke's earlier writings on politics. In the main they are also the themes sounded by the *True Patriot*.

That Bolingbroke was himself a man of letters as well as a political ideologue, like the others Fielding names in *True Patriot* no. 1, is not without significance. One of the reasons the political opposition during Walpole's years and after was successful in recruiting so many important writers lay in the sustenance the latter found in the conservative myth. Perhaps in part because Walpole himself seemed so unflatteringly pragmatic about what he expected of writers, so mercenary in his relations with them, many of the more talented men of letters came to believe (and to proclaim) that the world of 'every man has his price' was not a world friendly to literature. As Fielding's friend James Ralph put it, there were really only three things open to the contemporary writer: to write for the booksellers, to write for the stage, or to write for a faction.[3] The first was intolerable; the second, Fielding had tried; the third was risky and often unpalatable. In the *True Patriot* Fielding puts this third option into bitter personal perspective: 'The Fate of such Persons

[1] Ibid., ii. 115.

[2] Cf. *TP* no. 8 (24 December 1745), below, pp. 161–3.

[3] *The Case of Authors by Profession or Trade* (London, 1758), p. 19. In Ralph's opinion, the third, though restrictive in many respects, was 'the most flattering of all these Provinces' (p. 29).

[political writers] is only Neglect from the Party they espouse, and sometimes Hanging from that which they oppose. It is the Flattery of Ministers, and Support of their iniquitous Measures, which recommends to their Countenance.'[1] The patriot utopia, on the other hand, envisages a world without ministers, without factions, and without the selfish manipulations of political infighting. King and country would be more congenial themes for literature than the 'iniquitous Measures' of scheming ministers. And implicit in the 'pure' visions of the patriot ideology was the promise that if the patriots got in, they would reward the writers they had been cultivating. With the restoration of older, higher virtues would come the restoration of literary values as well, made possible by an aristocratic system of patronage that would be, it was argued, far more stimulating of the talented writer than the grub-street emphasis on 'every man has his price'. That is, the 'natural' elite who would be the 'statesmen' (not the 'ministers'—the difference in denomination is insisted upon) of the patriot myth would have an affinity for their counterparts among the men of letters, and both groups would work together to restore the lost values, literary as well as political. A familiar Augustan myth, to be sure, but a close reading of the *True Patriot* reveals how much the paper implicitly endorses its entropic view of the contemporary scene and the antidote offered by Bolingbroke's ideology.

The other identities hinted at in the first leader are less surprising. The unnamed bishop is probably Benjamin Hoadly (1676–1761), controversialist low churchman and bishop of Winchester (1734). By 1745 Hoadly was mostly inactive, but his reputation as an anti-jacobite, pro-Hanoverian divine lingered on. The author of 'The Subject. No. III', reprinted in the *General Advertiser* of 19 October 1745, lists Hoadly (ahead of York and Worcester) first among those uniting the people behind a protestant king. Hoadly had been a subscriber to Fielding's *Miscellanies* (1743), and Fielding may have known him and his sons from the years (1723–34) when Hoadly was bishop of Salisbury.[2] In defining the concept of 'true Greatness', which knows no profession, party, or place, but lives only in the 'noble Mind', Fielding had cited the example of Hoadly, 'blazing' among the divines, in a passage which goes on to exemplify that curiously 'patriot' concept with a number of opposition figures, including Chesterfield and Dodington.[3] Theologi-

---

[1] *TP* no. 14 (28 January–4 February 1746), below, p. 211.
[2] Cross, ii. 112.
[3] 'Of True Greatness' (1741), vv. 251–62, in *Miscellanies*, i. 28–9. Hoadly is also praised in *Tom Jones*, ii. vii. 105.

cally speaking, Hoadly was a minimizing divine, and his stress on the primitive simplicity of such sacraments as the eucharist (when freed from the encumbrance of later, self-seeking interpretations) is interestingly compatible with the patriot stress on a return to the older, simpler virtues freed from the selfish privatism of the political and monetary processes.[1] Of the dignitaries hinted at here Hoadly is the only one who did not actually belong to the tight little circle of patrons and writers who were actively engaged in the patriot cause, but Fielding seems to have perceived Hoadly's role in the religious factionalism of the time as analogous to the role of the patriots in the political factionalism.

Chesterfield, who is alluded to next, did belong to that circle, though by the autumn of 1745 his membership was, so to speak, nonresident. As part of the broad bottom worked out in late 1744 he had, after a brief assignment as plenipotentiary to The Hague, taken up his place as lord lieutenant of Ireland. Like many of his colleagues Chesterfield had gone over into serious and protracted opposition as a result of the fallout from the Excise Bill of 1733. He came under Bolingbroke's ideological influence sometime prior to the latter's return to France in 1735. In 1734 Fielding dedicated to him his *Don Quixote in England*, which is commonly taken to be the author's first public overture to the opposition.[2] During Bolingbroke's absence in France the task of trying to implement his metapolitics fell principally to Chesterfield, whose role in the defeat of Walpole was crucial. Excluded from the post-Walpole administration, thus confirming his inveteracy toward Carteret and Pulteney, Chesterfield persevered in opposition.[3]

On the death of Wilmington in July 1743 Pelham bested Bath in the competition for treasury. From behind the scenes Orford (Walpole), who disliked Carteret, Bath, and the new whigs generally, counseled the Pelhams to get 'recruits from the *Cobham* squadron, who should be persuaded, now Bath is beaten, it makes room for them, if they will not crowd the door when the house is on fire, that nobody can go in or out'.[4] Actually the Pelhams seem to have opened negotiations with Gower and Cobham as early as July 1743, but alterations to the administration were

---

[1] Cf. Parson Adams' suggestive summary of Hoadly's *Plain Account of the Nature and End of the Sacrament of the Lord's Supper* (1735), in *Joseph Andrews*, I. xvii. 83.

[2] For example, by Cross, i. 159–60.

[3] Chesterfield to Stair, 6 January 1743: 'The nation sees with uneasiness that the change of a few men has not produced the least change of domestic measures, but rather the contrary; and those very men are the avowed screens of former men and measures which they so much condemned'; *Letters*, ed. Dobrée, ii. 529.

[4] Orford to Pelham, 25 August 1743, as quoted in Coxe, *Pelham*, i. 91–3; see also Owen, p. 172.

minimal. Carteret retained office, and Chesterfield remained in opposition. Over the summer, the royal failure to follow up the victory at Dettingen (Stair resigned his command in consequence and was firmly supported by Cobham), complications arising out of the treaty of Worms (September 1743), and Carteret's tendency to negotiate without consulting his administration colleagues—these charged even further the anti-Hanoverian atmosphere in what was a rather independent commons and provided opposition propagandists with just the kind of divisive issue they wanted. With Dodington, Chesterfield laid plans for a special meeting of the opposition prior to the opening of parliament. The meeting, which took place at the Fountain Tavern on 10 November 1743, produced a 'whip' alerting the opposition members of Commons to the possibility that the bill authorizing Hanoverian mercenaries might be brought on by 'surprise' at the opening of session. Among the signers of the 'whip' were Dodington, Pitt, and Lyttelton.[1] In the meantime the protracted negotiations between the Pelhams and the Cobham–Gower axis broke down over the Hanoverian issue. On 8 December Gower resigned the seals and Cobham resigned his regiment.[2]

Despite their preparations for dealing with the Hanoverian issue in parliament the opposition could not agree on the attitude to be taken toward the war itself. Pitt and Lyttelton, with the support of Chesterfield and Dodington, were inclined, though somewhat reluctantly, to approve the war in Flanders and to favor coalition with the Pelhams as the means of ousting Carteret. Cobham and the Grenvilles, on the other hand, wanted to condemn the war entirely, hoping to force its abandonment and thereby the overturn of the entire ministry.[3] This cleavage in the opposition made a concerted attack on the government policies more than usually difficult, and the invasion scare of February 1744, followed a month later by the official declaration of war with France, produced a widespread inclination to support the administration on matters of national concern. In addition the exertions of Orford had persuaded a great many of the old corps who were wavering on the Hanoverian issue that the mercenaries should be continued in British pay. By the end of session on 12 May 1744 the administration in theory still enjoyed the same overall majority of one hundred that it had enjoyed the previous session, though on any particular division it could be frightened.[4]

[1] Owen, pp. 197–8.

[2] *Egmont Diary*, iii. 278. For the Cobham–Gower demand that any new coalition include some tory leaders, see *Marchmont Papers*, ii. 295–6. Even Orford came to think that an accommodation with the Cobhams might be worth inclusion of a limited number of tories; Owen, p. 194.

[3] Richard Glover, *Memoirs of a Celebrated Literary and Political Character*, 2nd ed. (London, 1814), p. 19.   [4] Owen, p. 221.

Once again the disasters of summer intensified the Pelhams' difficulties with the king and Carteret. The pragmatic army took the field with serious deficiencies in the manpower promised by the Dutch and Austrians. The French made rapid progress in the Netherlands, capturing many of the barrier fortresses almost without a fight. An Austrian army under Prince Charles of Lorraine saved matters temporarily by entering Alsace, a move which forced the French to detach nearly half their troops from Flanders. Pleading financial distress and the need to reduce her armies unless subventions were forthcoming, Maria Theresa pressured the British government to grant her an additional £150,000 to ensure the Austrian presence in Alsace. Dissension in the allied high command prevented the pragmatic army from exploiting its temporary numerical superiority in Flanders. Frederick II of Prussia reentered the war in August and took his armies into Bohemia, whereupon Austria withdrew, in self-protection, from Alsace, thus rendering the British grant futile and even more unpopular than it had been. The Austrian withdrawal from Alsace also enabled the French to return their detachments to Flanders, and the pragmatic army quickly retreated into winter quarters. Prague fell in mid-September, and shortly afterwards the Austrians were driven from Bohemia. In the Italian theatre Charles Emmanuel, badly beaten by the Spanish, was once more threatening to treat with the Bourbon powers because Austria had not lived up to her military obligations under the Treaty of Worms.

This series of disasters brought relations between the Pelhams, on the one hand, and Carteret and the king, on the other, to a critical point. Frederick II had communicated his personal views of the Hanau negotiations (1743) to the leaders of the opposition, as did Prince William of Hesse,[1] and Chesterfield and the other opposition leaders planned to provoke a crisis over the matter as soon as parliament convened. By the end of August things were so bad in the Closet that both Newcastle and Pelham had decided to resign if the king did not dismiss Carteret.[2] To save Carteret the court tried first to detach Harrington from the Pelhams by offering him the secretary of state in room of the former, who quite obviously could not do his business thus opposed by the Pelhams. Harrington refused and Dorset evaded a similar invitation. Having failed to divide the old corps by such tactics, the king and the prince of Wales (temporarily united in their common deference to Carteret) went to work on the opposition. The prince sent a message to

---

[1] For the meetings between their ministers in London and Bolingbroke, Chesterfield, and Marchmont, see *Marchmont Papers*, i. 20–69.

[2] See Owen, p. 232, for the evidence.

Chesterfield, Cobham, and Gower offering complete removal of the old corps and a new broad bottom 'without reserve'.[1] Their joint reply was to the effect that the opposition could not serve in a ministry with Granville on any basis.

Their prompt and somewhat self-righteous refusal may have been easier to make because they had already almost come to terms with the Pelhams. As early as August 1744 William Murray, then solicitor-general and the chief medium of communication between the Pelhams and the patriot opposition, was stressing to Bolingbroke the need for an alliance between the two groups if Carteret was to be brought down. Such an alliance, in Murray's opinion, could only come about if the patriots abandoned their habit of treating the administration as a homogeneous and indivisible entity. On its side, the opposition seems to have elaborated its old 'anti-ministerial Cabinet', designed mainly to concert parliamentary activities, into a 'junto' of nine leaders, so as better to deal with the Pelhams' attempts at conciliation.[2] The junto included Bedford, Chesterfield, Cobham, Gower, as peers; and Cotton, Dodington, Pitt, Waller, Lyttelton, as commoners. By early November 1744 Pelham himself was in direct negotiation with Chesterfield, and by *c.* 20 November agreement had been reached as to the general removal of Granville, Bath, and their adherents, and as to the outlines of a more systematic, less 'Hanoverian' war policy. Four days later Granville resigned and the broad bottom began forming.

In the ensuing discussions places and honors were seen as the price the administration had to pay, not only to secure the necessary working majority in parliament, but also to make certain that the new allies would support even a more limited continental war now that Granville had been ousted. On 1 December 1744 Chesterfield wrote Newcastle that he, Gower, and Cobham had prepared and were ready to submit a list of 'our necessary people'.[3] Among those 'necessary' people was Chesterfield himself. A member of the junto, he had played a prominent role in the late stages of the negotiations, and although the king still disliked him personally, he got the safely remote post of lord lieutenant of Ireland.[4] All in all, fifteen former members of the opposition got into place, including some tories,[5] and the parliamentary gain

---

[1] *Marchmont Papers*, i. 88; Owen, p. 236.

[2] Glover, *Memoirs*, ed. cit., p. 27. [3] *Letters*, ed. Dobrée, ii. 541.

[4] Although the king's continued dislike of him meant that he could not yet be admitted to the inner cabinet, Chesterfield was commonly regarded by the Pelhams as the most significant of the 'new' acquisitions. See Lodge, *Private Correspondence*, p. xiii *n.*, citing HMC, Fourteenth Report, Appendix, Part ix (London, 1895), 'The MSS of Buckinghamshire', p. 110.

[5] Mostly at the expense of the Granville–Bath squadron, which lost thirteen, Tweeddale

to the administration, in Chesterfield's somewhat sanguine estimate, was 'a hundred head of Tories'.[1]

Supposed parliamentary gains notwithstanding, the Pelhams were uneasy about their new broad bottom. Some of the new allies did not always vote with the administration. Granville may have been out of office, but he retained the king's ear, and the king continued to resent and frustrate the Pelhams whenever possible. At their February 1745 meeting the Independent Electors of Great Britain chose Cotton (new in place) and Wynne (he had refused a peerage) among their stewards for the year, and Andrew Stone, Newcastle's secretary, reporting on the meeting, said the opposition planned 'much heat, and opposition' toward the end of session. Stone later wrote Hardwicke of Newcastle's fears that there would be an early dismissal at the end of the parliamentary session, with the ouster of the Pelhams and the restoration of Granville.[2] And from The Hague in March 1745 Chesterfield wrote Newcastle that he had been approached by Granville to know if he would serve in a new administration, should one be formed.[3]

Such an offer (if indeed it quite came to that) would not have been inconsistent with Granville's politics. In both 1743 and 1744 he was reported to have made overtures to the tories with respect to forming a ministry exclusive of both the old corps and the 'patriots'.[4] Given the king's pronounced and public dislike of the tories, Granville's overtures seem quixotic, but they were a measure of his desperate need to circumvent the Pelhams' inveteracy and that of Chesterfield, Bolingbroke, and their circle. The tories, for their part, may have seemed 'broken' as a party by the defection of Gower and 'family', as Chesterfield professed to believe, but Newcastle wrote the latter on 26 March 1745 that the duke of Beaufort had been set up in Gower's place as tory chief, that the

remaining as secretary of state for Scotland. The prince of Wales's followers were left intact so as not to antagonize him unduly. In general the formula was to replace 'new whigs' with 'new allies', leaving the old corps in place or with compensation for losses; Owen, pp. 243–50, summarizes the shuffling.

[1] To Newcastle, 10 March 1745 NS, *Letters*, ed. Dobrée, ii. 573; Lodge, *Private Correspondence*, p. 22.

[2] Stone to Hardwicke, BL Add. MS 35408, f. 110, cited by Owen, p. 269. Stone's report on the meeting of the Independent Electors is in BL Add. MS 35602, f. 76, as quoted in Owen, p. 263. Newcastle's fears may have been typically exaggerated, but it is worth recalling the modern judgment that the king could have formed an alternative government, provided he did not try to include in it either Granville or Bath. See above, p. xxxiii.

[3] Chesterfield to Newcastle, 23 March 1745 NS, *Letters*, ed. Dobrée, ii. 582; Lodge, *Private Correspondence*, p. 30. He mentions the Granville overture again, in a letter dated 13 April 1745; Lodge, p. 45.

[4] The 1743 overtures are recorded in a communication from Philip Yorke to Coxe; BL Add. MS 9224, f. 2, cited by Owen, p. 190. For those of November 1744, see *Marchmont Papers*, i. 88, and above, p. lxxviii. The invitation to Gower indicated that despite the royal mistrust of them the detachment of at least some tories was contemplated.

tories had excluded Gower from the early negotiation with the ministry over the bill to better regulate the justices of the peace, and that Cotton, Wynne and 109 other tories had vented their displeasure with the way the justices of the peace negotiations were going, by voting against the government on the £500,000 to be given for extraordinary services of war.[1] Although the government majority was well over one hundred, and although he expressed great satisfaction with the steadfastness of Gower, Pitt, and Lyttelton on particular divisions, Newcastle continued to worry about how further to satisfy the new allies without offending 'that old corps which must be the principal support of us all'.[2]

Uncertainty as to the future of the coalition was not restricted to the Pelhams. The 'patriot' allies shared many of the same misgivings. Parliament had been prorogued on 2 May 1745 without any major setbacks for administration programs, but once again summer brought its peculiar set of problems. The Pelhams clashed openly with the king on three of them: the appointment of the allied commander-in-chief in Flanders; the retention (stipulated by the Dutch as part of the price for their support in the campaign) of 8,000 Hanoverian mercenaries, now on the king's payroll; and the proposal, strongly supported by the king, that Cumberland marry Princess Louisa of Denmark. Particularly infuriated by the Pelhams' obstruction of the marriage proposal—they considered it expensive and unnecessary now that Denmark no longer wished to supply England with mercenaries—the king accused them of deceit. In the Closet he and Granville privately concerted measures for selecting a suitable candidate for the recently vacated imperial title. As far as the Pelhams were concerned, Granville may have been out, but he was far from down.

In May 1745 Saxe defeated Cumberland at Fontenoy, and the French went on to overrun Flanders. Frederick was once again mastering the Austrians. In the Italian theatre the Franco-Spanish armies were invading Lombardy. Then, in late July, the Young Pretender landed in Scotland, bringing with him the threat of a supportive French invasion. At home the regency (the king was summering in Hanover) bickered endlessly over the proper posture to take towards the rebellion. Tweeddale, Bath, and Stair in particular were at loggerheads with their fellow regents, insisting that the rebellion was a mere trifle, that certain persons wished to exaggerate its importance so as further to restrict British efforts on the continent or to score political points at home.[3] In

---

[1] Lodge, *Private Correspondence*, pp. 40–1.   [2] Ibid., p. 41.
[3] As early as 9 July 1745 Pelham wrote Devonshire complaining of the enervating effects of such bickering; Owen, p. 278. For the struggle among the Scottish peers and members to exploit the situation, see 'Diary of Hugh Earl of Marchmont', *Marchmont Papers*, i. 98–170.

an effort to concentrate allied forces in Flanders and Italy the Pelhams had proposed (June 1745) forcing some kind of accommodation between Austria and Prussia. Such was George II's hatred of his nephew of Prussia that he strenuously opposed any such accommodation even while he was abroad in Hanover and remote from the negotiations. The royal objections were fueled by the not unexpected support of Granville and his adherents, who asserted that the deadlock between king and ministry was owing to the Pelhams' mismanagement. When the king, against his will, finally signed (15 August NS) a secret treaty with Prussia, by which England undertook to arrange a peace between Prussia and Austria on the basis of the treaty of Breslau, the consensus among the Pelhams was that their diplomatic victory had been purchased at the cost of their own survival.[1]

Nor did the jacobite rebellion itself yield any great parliamentary advantages to the administration. On 23 October Pitt, who had voted with the government against Dashwood's motion to attach a clause to the address of thanks, unexpectedly moved the recall of all British troops from Flanders. Since all but about 2,000 horse were already under orders to return, it seems likely that Pitt was courting popularity in the house and putting the ministers on notice.[2] The Pelhams evaded Pitt's motion by moving the previous question, which they carried by a majority of only twelve. Among the 'new' allies Dodington, Lyttelton, and George Grenville joined Pitt in voting against the government.[3] Faced with such signs that their coalition might prove unstable, the Pelhams renewed their efforts to bring Pitt into the administration.

Part of the difficulty in doing this lay in the old corps' perception of Cobham and his connection. Whereas Bedford and Gower had impressed with their steadfastness and loyalty, Cobham and Pitt, in particular, were still suspect.[4] In November Bedford and Gower arranged a meeting of principals. Once again the sticking point was foreign policy. Pitt continued obdurate in his demand that all support for Maria Theresa be withdrawn and support for the Dutch drastically curtailed. For the Pelhams to concur in such an extreme version of

---

[1] For the opinions of Hardwicke and Pelham in particular, as well as the king's subsequent initiatives with Harrington, see above, p. xxxiii, and Owen, pp. 281–2.

[2] The inference is Owen's, p. 284. For the motion and the vote on it, see *Journals of Commons*, xxv. 10.

[3] The earl of Shaftesbury to James Harris, 24 October 1745, *Malmesbury Letters*, i. 7–8.

[4] Bolingbroke himself had deplored Cobham's factious behavior as far back as 14 January 1745; Bolingbroke to Hardwicke, BL Add. MSS 3558, f. 7, cited by Owen, p. 285 *n.* In a letter of 4 November 1745 Walpole told Mann that in parliament Pitt 'has alternately bullied and flattered Mr. Pelham'; *Yale Walpole*, xix. 155. Pitt's unnerving tactics did little to reassure the old corps of his reliability.

anti-Hanoverianism would have jeopardized their standing with the old corps, not to mention the king, and so the talks broke off.[1] The inclusion of Pitt remained a 'patriot' objective.

To understand better what further political objectives might have prompted the founding of the *True Patriot*, it is necessary to understand the patriots' perception of their role and their prospects during this period of ministerial uncertainty. Some understanding can be got from Chesterfield's surviving correspondence with Newcastle. Although he was neither a major ideologue like Bolingbroke nor a powerful and persistent leader like Pitt, Chesterfield was clearly regarded by the Pelhams as the major 'catch' of the broad-bottom coalition.[2] In their correspondence Newcastle cultivates him carefully as a link between the ministry and its new allies. Chesterfield, on the other hand, writes under a double obligation: to bolster his new colleague with reassuring advice and at the same time to impress him with the importance to the ministry of their new coalition. It is not surprising therefore that the Newcastle–Chesterfield correspondence is revealing of, among other things, the patriot strategy for survival. For whatever sternly optimistic face he may have put on for Newcastle's benefit, Chesterfield was well aware that the coalition was endangered. Back in London briefly, in May 1745 he writes Robert Trevor: 'At home things stand now on the foot of six months' warning; and at the return from Hanover we are to know our fate, and to be really in, or really out, we are now neither.'[3] Earlier, from The Hague, he had advised Newcastle to conciliate Gower and his friends so as to break the tory faction by making the excluded remnant seem not only inconsiderable but jacobite.[4] As a corollary of their intention to drive a wedge between the two other factions within the ministry (old corps and 'new' whigs) the patriots were more than willing to keep clear of as many tories as was feasible for a safe parliamentary majority.[5]

---

[1] For Newcastle's detailed account of the meeting, see his letter to Chesterfield, 20 November 1745, in Lodge, *Private Correspondence*, pp. 78–86. Pitt reacted by seconding Hume Campbell's motion (28 October 1745) to form a select committee to inquire into the causes of the rebellion and the subsequent management of it; *Marchmont Papers*, i. 143–7. Pitt may have intended the motion to be without hostility to the administration, but in debate matters heated up; *Parliamentary History*, xiii. 1363–82. The motion lost by 82; *Journals of Commons*, xxv. 10. The king subsequently pointed out that since the two most recent motions Pitt had supported were beaten down, Pitt's parliamentary assistance was not worth bargaining for; Owen, p. 286.

[2] See above, p. lxxviii, *n.* 4. For the view of his own colleagues Stair and Bolingbroke that he was a timorous, vacillating leader, see *Marchmont Papers*, i. 11.

[3] 27 May 1745, in HMC, Fourteenth Report, Appendix, Part ix (London, 1895), p. 113.

[4] Letters of 9 March and 13 April 1745 NS; Lodge, *Private Correspondence*, pp. 20, 44. Fielding employs something like this strategy *vis-à-vis* the 'Opposition' in the *True Patriot* and, later, in the *Jacobite's Journal*.

[5] In his letter of 13 April 1745 NS Chesterfield tells Newcastle that skillful management could strip the 'new' tory opposition of Watkin Williams Wynne and Lord Oxford, the only two 'significant' people in it; *Letters*, ed. Dobrée, ii. 594–6, and Lodge, *Private Correspondence*, p. 44.

On the matter of Granville himself, Chesterfield's advice, though it may have derived considerably from his sense of betrayal at the former's desertion to the exclusionist ministry of 1743, strongly resembles Bolingbroke's: 'You must mark out Lord Granville by exterminating without quarter all who belong to him.'[1] And the Pelhams, he insisted, must force the issue by threatening to resign *en masse* if the king continued to favor Granville. No matter that the Pelhams had decided to soldier on for the summer, not wishing to resign 'after we had raised all the supplies'.[2] The point is made, and will be made again: only by dismissing more 'new' [Granvillean] whigs—*all* the 'new' whigs if possible—can the appropriate places be made for certain important malcontents among the patriots.

From Dublin, in the knowledge of the changes wrought by the jacobite rebellion, the advice is even sterner: 'Some publick brand should surely be put upon Lord Granville and his followers before the meeting of Parliament, that people may know where the power at least if not the favour is lodg'd. Finches turn'd out, Garters properly dispos'd of, would be the true signs where the best power is to be found.' And in case Newcastle has forgotten how important it is to preserve his coalition, Chesterfield recalls the parliamentary imperative: 'If you cannot show a very great majority in Parliament and hinder the forming of a party of various denominations which will then be called a Nationall Party, I need not mention the necessary and obvious consequences of such a situation.'[3] Whatever else they may do, the Pelhams must try to preserve their parliamentary majority at least at the levels they enjoyed in the preceding session. To do less is to convey an appearance of weakness, which could be exploited by their parliamentary enemies.

[1] To Newcastle, 13 April 1745 NS; Lodge, *Private Correspondence*, p. 45. Ten days later Chesterfield buttresses his argument by reporting to Newcastle that he has heard the prince of Wales is negotiating a reconciliation between Granville and the old corps, and he warns Newcastle to be on the alert against this Trojan-horse scheme; 23 April NS, *Letters*, ed. Dobrée, ii. 601, and Lodge, *Private Correspondence*, p. 47. The Trojan-horse metaphor is Chesterfield's. Little more than six months later Newcastle will report overtures from the prince of Wales to form a ministry *excluding* Granville and the patriots as well. See below, p. lxxxiv.

[2] Newcastle to Chesterfield, 26 April 1745; Lodge, *Private Correspondence*, p. 53.

[3] 12 September 1745; Lodge, *Private Correspondence*, p. 68. William and Edward Finch, younger brothers of the earl of Winchelsea, held the offices of vice-chamberlain of the household and groom of the bedchamber respectively. The opposition suspected the Finches of serving as conduits between Granville and the king, but the Pelhams were reluctant to press for removal of two officers so personal to the king, and the Finches were not in fact removed. The reference to a 'Nationall Party' is suggestive. 'National' was a term the patriots were fond of affixing to whatever political configuration they happened to be projecting; as when, for example, Stair urged Pelham in August 1744 to support a 'national government according to the constitution . . . in which project every honest man would join him'; *Marchmont Papers*, i. 11. Here, however, Chesterfield apparently alludes to some sort of patchwork coalition which would support the court program in the name of the country as a whole but would exclude the Pelhams and, possibly, some of their patriot allies as well. See below, p. lxxxvi.

By this time Newcastle had already written Chesterfield how 'a new method is now taken up, to cajole and flatter almost every member of the administration at the expense of the two Brothers',[1] and Chesterfield lost no time in feeding his correspondent's paranoia: 'The cajoling of individuals may in time have effect, and I doubt [suspect] will.' To counteract any such effect the Pelhams must exert their full force now: 'They have friends who will stand or fall with them.'[2] The allusion here to the patriot 'friends' makes a quiet point that should not be lost in evaluating the praise devoted to the ministry by the *True Patriot*: given the inveteracy of their leaders towards Granville and Bath, most patriots had no viable alternative to the Pelhams.

Newcastle seems to have picked up on the point rather quickly. His often quoted letter of 20 November 1745 underscores the second of Chesterfield's implied alternatives for the patriot friends of the ministry. He reports, possibly with some satisfaction, that the Pelhams received 'Broad hints' of an accommodation with the prince of Wales and his followers, specifically excluding Granville himself, 'if we would part with those that were lately taken in and replace those who had been lately removed'.[3] On condition, that is, if they would renege on the broad bottom and replace the patriots with 'new' whigs of the type included in 1742 and excluded in 1744, that is, Granvilleans. Although Newcastle carefully and immediately reports the Pelhams' negative response, to thoughtful patriots the condition of acceptance by itself must have been a salutary reminder of their own expendability. For all Newcastle's reassuring talk about a 'union so essentially necessary . . . both for the publick and ourselves',[4] the possibility had been raised that Granville or the prince might try to split the broad bottom in much the same way the patriots had split the old corps from the 'new' whigs.

Chesterfield disposes quickly of the 'Broad hints'. He reduces the question to one of power: 'The Prince and Lord Granville and company neither can nor will support you: they want the power as well as the places, whereas my friends in the opposition only want the places, without being, or meaning to be, your rivals in power.'[5] Inasmuch as one of Chesterfield's friends in opposition was William Pitt, who wanted to be secretary at war, the statement seems somewhat disingenuous. Moreover, up till then patriots had been reluctant to manifest publicly such an

---

[1] 21 September 1745, at which time he also complains to Chesterfield that the doctrine of the 'king in toils' is being vented at every opportunity; Lodge, *Private Correspondence*, p. 69.

[2] To Andrew Stone, 30 September 1745; Lodge, *Private Correspondence*, p. 71.

[3] Ibid., p. 79.   [4] Ibid., p. 83.

[5] 25 November 1745, Lodge, *Private Correspondence*, pp. 87–8. 'Want' here carries the force of 'require'.

appetite for places, preferring instead to affect a kind of 'tory' indifference to such things.[1] But if Chesterfield's statement is excessive, his 'point' is not without interest. From the Pelhams' perspective the patriots should be the preferred partners. As relative johnnies-come-lately they could hardly expect the most exalted offices, at least at first. The prince and Granville, on the other hand, could—the former because he was laying the groundwork for his own presumed succession to the throne, the latter because anything less was clearly inapposite to such a talent. Union with the prince or Granville would involve the Pelhams in a considerable sharing, perhaps even a surrender, of real political power. Better to settle for the parliamentary 'support' offered by the Cobham connection.

Time was running out—it was already late November and pressures on the Pelhams were building once again—as Chesterfield was quick to emphasize: 'If you had fix'd your scheme with the opposition some time sooner, I think you would have done it easier, for they now see that you want them, as much as they want places, which I can assure you is not a little. You must make the best bargain you can with 'em.'[2] Pitt, who was clearly the major stumbling block, turned cold and reserved toward the ministers, according to Newcastle; and Lyttelton, though 'warm, eager, well inclined', was 'partial in the greatest degree to Mr. Pitt and his opinion'.[3] Soon both parties to the coalition were considering dumping Pitt in the interests of getting on.[4] On 6 January 1746 Newcastle writes Chesterfield that Gower told him he 'really thought we could form an administration, if the King desired we should, exclusively of those whom we wished to have but could not have, Mr. Pitt, etc.'[5] Newcastle also professes to have broached Gower's scheme to the king himself, whom he reports pleased, and to have added that in his own opinion Chesterfield 'would not hurt this scheme when he came over'. In reply, Chesterfield confirms Newcastle's opinion—he reports having heard that Pitt has 'reconnected' with the prince of Wales in opposition—and

[1] Privately, to be sure, their posture was different. Writing to Hardwicke on 28 November 1745, Chesterfield, having asserted that nothing could be done in foreign affairs until the domestic uncertainties were settled via a firm political connection with certain malcontents, admits 'with shame' that 'places only can (I see) form that connection'; *Letters*, ed. Dobrée, ii. 215. He goes on to urge the use of whatever force is necessary to 'extort' those places.

[2] To Newcastle, 25 November 1745; Lodge, *Private Correspondence*, p. 87.

[3] To Chesterfield, 30 November 1745; Lodge, *Private Correspondence*, p. 90. However, there were pressures on Lyttelton to dissociate himself from Pitt, and other observers noted his distinct uneasiness. See below, pp. lxxxvi, xcvi–xcvii.

[4] On 6 December 1745, for example, Chesterfield admitted to Newcastle the unreasonableness of Pitt and Cobham in trying to connect what they called 'constitutional' bills with their own private demands; Lodge, *Private Correspondence*, p. 93.

[5] Ibid., p. 97. In the quoted matter 'exclusively of' means 'excluding' or 'which excludes'.

thinks the scheme 'very possible too'. However, the price of excluding Pitt must be 'breaking considerably into the opposition and hindering it from being reckon'd a national opposition'.[1] In particular Chesterfield would hope Lyttelton ('after some convulsions', presumably the result of his loyalty to Pitt) and the Grenvilles might be retained, and Barrington 'got', presumably from the Cobhams, to whom he had attached himself after the formation of the broad bottom of November 1744.

The merit of attaching such people, Chesterfield points out, is that they 'would cripple Pitt's opposition extremely'. As for Pitt himself, Chesterfield professes bewilderment at his 'unaccountable conduct' and presumes on his own knowledge of the man to advise the Pelhams 'to avail your selves to the utmost, in the Closet, of his opposition, and to have no other regard or management for him than what mere decency absolutely requires'.[2] By early 1746, in other words, much of the patriot leadership had come round to the view expressed over a year earlier by Bolingbroke, namely, that Pitt's recalcitrance imperiled the coalition. Pitt's abuse of Pelham during the debates on the proposed augmentation of the navy was particularly unsettling, and before the Christmas recess he dominated the debate over Lord Cornbury's motion to thank the king for his announcement of the arrival of 6,000 Hessians in England, but not for the Hessians themselves. Cornbury and Pitt lost by 146, Dodington ('for fear of going out') and Gower voting with the government, Lyttelton ('silent and uneasy') and the Grenvilles voting with Pitt.[3] It was the opinion of Horace Walpole that such behavior in parliament was 'pretty certain' to produce a 'dismission of the Cobhamites', an opinion he repeats shortly after the new year, noting that Pitt 'has driven Lyttelton and the Grenvilles to adopt all his extravagances, but then they are at variance again within themselves'.[4] In short, the coalition was in danger of falling apart, or at least losing its effectiveness.

L'affaire Pitt did not really heat up until after the *True Patriot* began

---

[1] 11 January 1745[6]; Lodge, *Private Correspondence*, pp. 100–1. Chesterfield's source has not been identified, but there was much unsubstantiated (and contradictory) rumor at the time concerning possible political realignments. Walpole wrote Mann (29 November 1745) that 'the prince hates him [Pitt] since the fall of Lord Granville'; *Yale Walpole*, xix. 175. For the significance of Chesterfield's use of the term 'national' opposition, see above, p. lxxxiii *n.* 3.

[2] Lodge, *Private Correspondence*, pp. 101, 100.

[3] Owen, pp. 290–2. The characterization of Dodington and Lyttelton is that of Henry Fox, in a letter to Ilchester, 21 December 1745.

[4] To Mann, 20 December 1745 and 3 January 1746, *Yale Walpole*, xix. 188–9, 194. In the second letter Walpole asserts that Lyttelton's wife hated Pitt for dominating her husband 'so at present it seems he [Lyttelton] does not care to be martyr to Pitt's caprices'. In time even Cobham came round to the view that Pitt was 'a wrong-headed fellow, that he had no regard for'; *Marchmont Papers*, i. 176, in the 'Diary' for 1 May 1746. In the autumn of 1745, however, a permanent breach between these two is not so clearly indicated.

publishing (5 November 1745), and when the paper raises the issue editorially, it does so only once and then by indirection, without naming names, apparently so as not to exacerbate matters.[1] But the Pitt problem had appeared potentially troublesome to the 'patriot' leaders even before the formation of the first stage of the broad bottom in November 1744. During the negotiations with the Pelhams in the late summer of that year, Bolingbroke, who found Pitt supercilious and inclined to mix emotions with business, urged that the only way around the difficulties presented by Pitt's behavior was to adopt the 'pathetic style' toward the ministry—that is, to try to soften up the old corps by acting moderately, laying aside all particular personal bargains (such as Pitt's), and pressing gently for foreign policy laid out on a more 'English' plan than Carteret's.[2] And although the Cobhams quite naturally seem not to have found the 'pathetic style' congenial, the more moderate among the patriot leaders (Chesterfield, Bedford, Gower, Dodington) generally adopted Bolingbroke's advice and adhered to it even during the 1745–6 attempts to enlarge the broad bottom so as to include some of the Cobhams. The *True Patriot* itself adopts the 'pathetic', not the confrontational, style.

As the Newcastle–Chesterfield correspondence implies, however, the coalition was beset by many more uncertainties than those caused by Pitt's behavior. Any newspaper undertaken on behalf of the patriots in the autumn of 1745 would have easily found other tasks to address itself to. Some of the new allies did not always vote with the government on the divisions,[3] and there was always the risk that powerful malcontents like Pitt and Cobham would work to increase that parliamentary instability. Since the only counterweight to Granville's superiority in the Closet was the Pelhams' superiority in the commons, anything that seemed to threaten their parliamentary superiority had to be taken seriously. If their majority was in fact weakened badly by defections among the new allies, the Pelhams and the old corps would have had every reason to reconsider the price they had paid for what turned out to be unreliable advantages. Given the highly charged atmosphere and the rumors of shifting political alignments in late 1745, there was always a chance that the king (perhaps with the help of the prince of Wales) could form an alternative ministry which would either exclude the Pelhams and restore Granville or exclude both. Since these options were

---

[1] See no. 8 (24 December 1745), below, pp. 158–63.

[2] *Marchmont Papers*, i. 70–1.

[3] On 4 November 1745 Walpole wrote Mann that 'at least twice a week all his [Pelham's] new allies are suffered to oppose him as they please'; *Yale Walpole*, xix. 154.

threatening to the patriot leadership, for one reason or another, it was therefore appropriate for a patriot paper to bolster the Pelhams as strongly as possible while at the same time stressing the importance to the latter of retaining their recent coalition and the parliamentary advantages it theoretically brought. The Pelhams should be shown to be vital to the patriots; the patriots should be shown to be vital to the Pelhams.

For this reason it was necessary to define carefully the 'true' patriots as distinguished from the 'false' patriots like Granville and Bath, who had deserted the common cause of the anti-Walpole days and squeezed themselves into the narrow-bottom administrations of the immediate post-Walpole period. Such a definition had to do two things in particular. It had to make a strong but not threatening case for the old Bolingbroke ideology of metafactionalism.[1] And it had to single out Granville as the apostate and archenemy of good government. On the face of it, the latter objective would seem the easier to achieve. Granville and Bath were reported to have told the king that despite their dislike of the Pelhams they would never go over into formal opposition.[2] But contemporary observers were skeptical. As long as Granville and Bath enjoyed the king's favor in the Closet and obstructed the Pelhams in so many ways, they had the same political effect as an opposition, even though they never formally declared themselves as such. And in times of emergency like the rebellion, it could be argued, to act like an opposer is to act like a jacobite, an enemy of the country. The syllogism implicit in all this was easier to make in Granville's case because so much of his foreign policy struck people as favoring 'Hanoverian' rather than 'English' concerns.

The foreign-policy issue was a very touchy one with the king, of course, and had to be dealt with tactfully. Here the antifactionalism or metapolitics of Bolingbroke came in handy. With its emphasis on the primacy of king and constitution, it permitted a kind of high-minded reassurance of the king and his family that could be made to seem consistent with a gentle emphasis on the need to keep the country and its interests foremost in one's thoughts, a kind of patriotism, in other

---

[1] It should be emphasized once again that although Fielding deprecates party and faction in his leaders, the most extended or analytical treatment of Bolingbroke's ideas occurs in the 'Present History of Great Britain', beginning with issue no. 18 (25 February–4 March 1746). By that time Fielding was not writing the 'Present History'. For the possibility that it was then Ralph's department, see above, p. lxv, *n.* 1.

[2] BL Add. MS 35408, f. 80, cited by Owen, p. 240 *n.* Actually Granville proffered the 'strong assurances' shortly after his enforced resignation in November 1744 and appeared to limit them to opposition to necessary war measures; Owen, p. 246.

words. Patriotism in this larger sense—contrasting with the narrower patriotism of a 'country' party conceived as made up of tory squires who represented the landed interest and opposed the central government— was made easier to define and defend by the fact that the country was faced with a rebellion at home. Inasmuch as Granville, Tweeddale, and others were at first inclined to minimize the importance of the rebellion, it was relatively easy to stigmatize them as unpatriotic on that account without harping unduly on the more controversial and divisive issue of their 'allemanick' foreign policy. For the patriots the rebellion was a doubly useful issue. It permitted them to argue strongly that the 'country' (not politics or politicians or party) ought to come first. It also appeared to legitimize and encourage a partial withdrawal from the continental land war which many of them disliked. And in their support of the Pelham ministry the rebellion permitted coalition patriots to argue that at such times of crisis it was not wise to change horses in midstream and that the motives of those who proposed such a change resembled motives which could be stigmatized as jacobite. The rebellion, in other words, might bind some people to the coalition out of loyalty to their country and thereby make it easier to isolate the recalcitrants.

There is absolutely no reason to suppose that Fielding and his colleagues would not have been loyally concerned about their country's future if it had not also suited their politics of the moment to be so. It is worth noting,however, that to take the rebellion seriously did very much suit their politics. The 'patriots' had found an historical moment when their somewhat self-serving ideology fitted in usefully with patriotism of the larger, less controversial kind. They were ready to take political advantage of that moment.

If the situation facing the patriot coalition in the autumn of 1745 is most broadly illuminated in the figures of Bolingbroke and Chesterfield, the other, lesser eminences mentioned as possible authors of the *True Patriot* sustain in a quite remarkable way the pattern of patriot involvement. William Warburton (1698–1779), the first of the lesser eminences to be hinted at,[1] had been appointed chaplain to the prince of Wales in 1738. Although he was later to insist that he 'never was of any Party except the Love of my Country be called Party', he did concede that he found himself 'thrown pretty much amongst the Anti-ministerial Men'.[2] Since the prince of Wales at that time had become the center of a loose association of anti-Walpole patriots, it is not difficult to think Warburton's concession disingenuous. In 1738 Lyttelton was secretary to the

[1] For the identification, see *TP* no. 1 (5 November 1745), below, p. 109, *n.* 3.
[2] See *The Correspondence of Alexander Pope*, ed. George Sherburn (Oxford, 1956), iv. 238 *n.*

prince and although the earliest extant letter between him and Warburton is dated 10 June 1740, Lyttelton's biographer finds it 'reasonable' to date their acquaintance roughly from the date of the chaplaincy.[1]

Whatever circle of antiministerial men Warburton's chaplaincy may have thrown him among, his friendship with Pope, which dates from *c.* 1740, must surely have enlarged it. Pope tried, with unhappy results, to connect him with Bolingbroke. A connection with Chesterfield was more successful: in a letter of 12 August [1741] Pope appears to allude to an effort by Chesterfield to procure a living for Warburton.[2] Although the living turned out to be unavailable, Warburton evidently kept up the connection. On 15 May 1742 Chesterfield wrote thanking him for sending a copy of the revised 'Commentary' on Pope's *Essay on Man*.[3] And in a letter of 4 June 1745 Chesterfield, about to take up his lord lieutenancy, invites Warburton to be one of 'my Domestic Chaplains in Ireland'.[4] Warburton turned down the invitation, according to Chesterfield, for reasons of 'filial duty and friendship',[5] but Thomas Birch believed the real reason was Warburton's engagement to be married to Gertrude Tucker, Ralph Allen's favorite niece and major beneficiary.[6] Pope had introduced Warburton to Allen in 1741, and the connection took. Warburton dedicated his 1742 'Commentary' on the *Essay on Man* to Allen, referring to him as patron and worthy friend. The engagement to Allen's niece seems to have been public knowledge by September 1745 and bespeaks a certain constancy of attendance at Prior Park. In November Warburton preached at the chapel there a sermon 'Occasioned by the Present Unnatural Rebellion', which at Allen's suggestion was published. If Fielding had not already made Warburton's acquaintance during the latter's early chaplaincy to the prince of Wales, he almost certainly would have made it at Allen's.[7] The two men were undoubtedly never intimate, but the somewhat 'private' compliment to him here

[1] Rose Mary Davis, *The Good Lord Lyttelton* (Bethlehem, Pa., 1939), p. 70. For the 1740 letter, in which Lyttelton acknowledges receipt of one of Warburton's books, see Warburton's *Works*, ed. Francis Kilvert (London, 1841), xiv. 196, cited by Davis, p. 70 *n.* In the letter Lyttelton remarks, 'But as you write to flatter no party, or sect, you must expect to displease all violent men, for the same reason as the candid approve of you.' The remark indicates how Warburton's argumentative method and rhetorical posture might be easily reconciled with a patriot 'metapolitics'.
[2] *Correspondence*, iv. 356–7 and *n.*
[3] *Letters*, ed. Dobrée, ii. 498–9.
[4] Ibid., iii. 628.
[5] To Warburton, 20 June 1745; *Letters*, iii. 632.
[6] BL Add. MS 35396, f. 320, as cited by Benjamin Boyce, *The Benevolent Man: A Life of Ralph Allen of Bath* (Cambridge, Mass., 1967), p. 165 *n.*
[7] For Fielding's connection with Allen, one of his great benefactors, see *Tom Jones*, 'Dedication', p. 4 *n.* Boyce, p. 127, conjectures that Fielding may have met Allen as early as 1741, perhaps through Lyttelton or Chesterfield.

suggests Fielding had no difficulty in placing Warburton in a friendly, 'patriot' context.[1]

The next two eminences to be hinted at were well-known 'patriot' politicians, with opposition credentials dating back (in one case with intermissions) to the previous decade. In addition, both were among the most important and lasting influences on Fielding's literary and 'political' life. Dodington, the first, began as an opposition whig, was soon taken up by Walpole and given a place in the treasury (1724).[2] While retaining that place, he supplanted Lord Hervey as the chief political adviser to the prince of Wales, who was then (1732) contemplating, under outside direction, a more formal program of opposition. By 1734 Dodington was completely supplanted in the prince's favor by Lyttelton, who at Cobham's direction persuaded the prince to replace Dodington, still technically a place-holding member of the government, with Chesterfield, a leader of the declared opposition.[3] Dodington then seems to have run more or less straight for five years, resisting strong pressure from the prince to vote for the motion (1737) to increase the latter's royal allowance. By the spring of 1740, however, he had gone over into declared opposition once again, attaching himself to the duke of Argyll and resuming some sort of relationship with those around the prince of Wales. He busied himself especially with the 'patriots' who were trying to prevent Pulteney and Carteret from forming an exclusionist ministry on the old Walpolean model. In 1742 Dodington proposed to Dorset and Wilmington that the latter offer to form an administration on an 'extensive bottom', this administration to include, quite naturally, Dodington himself. The proposal was fruitless. Pulteney and Carteret prevailed, even upon the prince of Wales, and for the next two sessions Dodington remained in active opposition. He was a member of the so-called antiministerial cabinet drawn up by the opposition in the autumn of 1743 to concert their parliamentary strategies.[4] He was a member also of the 'junto' of nine (with Bedford, Chesterfield, and Lyttelton) which replaced the antiministerial cabinet for the purpose of negotiating with the Pelhams for Granville's defeat and the formation of a more inclusive ministry. When the Bath–Granville contingent resigned in November

---

[1] By complimenting Warburton in the *TP* Fielding may also have intended to please Allen, 'by stealth', which raises the interesting question, was Allen a financial contributor to Fielding's paper? The fact that Allen still held government contracts need not have been a deterrent in the case of a paper which counted support of the Pelhams among its political strategies.

[2] For a synopsis of his connection with Fielding, see *TP* no. 1 (5 November 1745), below, p. 110 *n*.

[4] See Lord Hervey, *Some Materials Towards Memoirs of the Reign of King George II*, ed. Romney Sedgwick (London, 1931), ii. 385–8.

[4] *Parliamentary History*, xiii. 146.

1744, Dodington was one of ten opposition leaders in the Commons to whom Pelham offered places, Dodington taking the lucrative treasurership of the navy, which he retained until 1749.[1]

Although Dodington may have had something to do with the founding and direction of the *Remembrancer* (1747–51), an opposition paper in the service of the prince of Wales and edited by Dodington's man-of-all-work, James Ralph, and although Ralph negotiated his employer's formal reengagement with the prince of Wales's opposition in 1749,[2] there is no real evidence that in the autumn of 1745 the tergiversant Dodington was anything more than nervously in place and reckoning the extent of his allegiance to an administration which looked increasingly unstable. With the possible exception of Pitt, in 1745–6 the patriots considered themselves distinct from the prince of Wales and his bloc, a distinction made easier by the fact that the prince was trying out a connection with Granville.

Strictly speaking, Dodington's qualifications for being listed among persons distinguished in the 'Republic of Letters' are rather oblique. He did write occasional verse, much of it unpublished, and he does seem to have been behind a number of political pamphlets and papers of his time.[3] But as far as *bona fide* members of the republic of letters were concerned, his main claim to literary distinction lay in his being one of the last of the patrons, the 'British Maecenas', as Thomson called him. He was fed with soft dedication by, among others, Young, Thomson (*Summer*, 1727), and Fielding (*Of True Greatness*, 1741). Lyttelton once addressed an eclogue to him. 'Leonidas' Glover was his friend. Fielding's colleague James Ralph worked for him for years. Even after the political unpleasantness between the *Remembrancer* and the *Jacobite's Journal* in 1748 Fielding was a frequent recipient of Dodington's hospitality.[4]

Politically, the two may not have been unreservedly compatible until

---

[1] Except where noted, the preceding sketch of Dodington's political career is based on *The House of Commons 1715–1754*, ed. Romney Sedgwick (London, 1970), i. 500–3.

[2] See *The Political Journal of George Bubb Dodington*, edd. Carswell and Dralle, p. 3. Ralph had been confidential secretary to Dodington from about 1743, and his possible role in the *True Patriot*, coupled with its citation of Dodington among the exemplars of its genealogy, suggests that the paper may have to be included in the 'succession of journals advertising the view of Dodington and his friends'; the quoted phrase is from the 'Introduction', *Political Journal*, p. xiii. The suggestion itself originates with the present editor of the *True Patriot*.

[3] According to the *DNB*, which gives neither authority nor details, misdates the *Remembrancer*, and calls its editor 'Rudolph' [Ralph?]. A contemporary attack on Dodington asserted that he had written an essay on financial matters for the *Remembrancer*; see *The House of Commons 1715–1754*, ed. Sedgwick, i. 503.

[4] See *Political Journal*, pp. 67, 130, 132, 134, 143, 148–9, 163.

Dodington accompanied Argyll into formal opposition in 1740.[1] When Fielding signaled his conversion (or availability) to opposition by his dedication of *Don Quixote in England* (1734) to Chesterfield, Dodington was on his way out of his connection with the prince of Wales and entering a period of relative detachment from opposition politics. In 1745, however, he and Fielding were still politically compatible. The compliment in *TP* no. 1 confirms that fact. Given what is known of his later experience in such undertakings, Dodington may well have been a prime mover in setting up the *True Patriot* under the editorship of his friend. The compliment here suggests that, too.

The next and last 'political' eminence to be alluded to in *TP* no. 1 is Fielding's friend and patron, George Lyttelton. The fact that he will dedicate *Tom Jones* to Lyttelton suggests Fielding's sense of their long relationship as well as anything.[2] In that dedication Fielding says it was by his patron's 'Desire that I first thought of such a Composition', adding, 'I partly owe to you my Existence during great Part of the Time which I have employed in composing it.'[3] Exactly how and when Lyttelton contributed to Fielding's existence during composition is not known. But if it is also a fact that about a third of *Tom Jones* had been written before the outbreak of the 'Forty-Five', then the present compliment resonates in ways not indicated by the immediate context.[4]

Tom Jones or not, Lyttelton belongs on the list of eminences. For one thing, his 'patriot' credentials were impeccable, not so lofty as Chesterfield's, but more consistent, certainly, than Dodington's. Shortly after he got back from his Grand Tour in 1730 Lyttelton was introduced to the prince of Wales by Dodington. Four years later he had so far advanced his case with the prince that he was able to persuade him to dismiss Dodington as chief political adviser. In 1735 Lyttelton entered parliament (for Okehampton) on the interest of his brother-in-law, Thomas Pitt, with whose brother William and his own cousins the Grenvilles he acted at the direction of his uncle, Lord Cobham, in a family grouping known variously as 'the Cousinhood', 'the Nepotism', and 'Cobham's Cubs'. With this small but vocal grouping he maintained a violently

[1] It should be noted here, however, that the January 1741 'Preface' to *Of True Greatness*, an epistle addressed to and highly laudatory of Dodington, says, 'This Poem was writ several Years ago'; that is, possibly as early as 1739, when Argyll (and Dodington?) was showing signs of going into formal opposition.

[2] For the salient features of that relationship, see *TP* no. 1, below, p. 110 n. 2.

[3] *Tom Jones*, ed. cit., pp. 4, 5.

[4] It is tempting to surmise that Lyttelton may have helped get Fielding the editorship of the *TP* and may even have been one of the undertakers of it, but there is no real evidence one way or the other and the likelihood of Dodington's presence makes such a surmise unnecessary. On the composition of *Tom Jones*, see above, pp. xxvii–xxviii.

antiministerial posture in the commons, and his subsequent appointment as the prince's secretary (1737) was judged by the latter's more
moderate followers to be a sign that the prince intended to go into formal opposition, 'as there was nobody more violent in the Opposition
[than Lyttelton], nor anybody a more declared enemy to Sir Robert
Walpole'.[1] After Walpole's fall (1742) the Cobhams detached themselves
from the prince—he supported the new ministry, which had excluded
most of the 'true' patriots—and continued in active opposition. When
the first stage of the broad bottom was accomplished (November 1744),
Lyttelton, who in the fashion of the times had managed to retain his
secretaryship with the prince, was appointed lord of the treasury, whereupon the prince dismissed him. Although two of them had places—
Lyttelton and George Grenville (on the admiralty board)—the Cobhams
united with Pitt, who had not got in, 'in opposing the measures of [the]
Government' during the 'Forty-Five'.[2]

Thus, by the time the *True Patriot* began publishing (5 November
1745), Lyttelton was in effect a member of the administration who often
voted against it. Loyal to Cobham, who was a violent and factious man,
and obviously dominated by Pitt's overbearing force, Lyttelton must be
differentiated in this respect at least from the other, more 'moderate'
politicians on Fielding's list—Bolingbroke, Chesterfield, even Dodington. Numerically insignificant in themselves, the Cobhams were perceived by Pelhams and moderate 'patriots' alike as threats to the
working majority in parliament. Pitt in particular seemed capable of
stirring up the malcontents of all persuasions. As Chesterfield noted to
Newcastle, in an atmosphere of such divisiveness and instability a
'national' opposition might form out of elements of the Bath–Granville
squadron, the prince of Wales's followers and, possibly, Pitt and his
people.

As one of Pitt's people, what is Lyttelton doing on a list, even a
rhetorical fiction of a list, of putative authors of the *True Patriot*? Does
the inclusion of his name signify that the paper was covertly Cobhamite?
The answer must clearly be no. Pitt and his people voiced very strong
positions with respect to three important issues facing the administration in 1745: the inclusion in the government of Pitt himself, the
handling of the jacobite rebellion, and foreign policy with respect to the
continental war. On the first of these issues the Cobhamite position was

---

[1] Hervey, *Memoirs*, ed. Sedgwick, [iii]. 850.
[2] The quoted phrase is George Grenville's; *The Grenville Papers*, ed. William James Smith (London, 1852), i. 427. The preceding sketch of Lyttelton's political career is based on *The House of
Commons 1715–1754*, ed. Sedgwick, ii. 232–3.

that inclusion of Pitt was a *sine qua non* of further cooperation with the Pelhams. On this issue, however, the *True Patriot* adopts the moderate or 'pathetic' style advocated by Bolingbroke. Although one leader (no. 8) does urge the inclusion in government of all men whose talents were disposed by nature 'for the Purposes of Society',[1] Pitt is never mentioned by name, and the issue can hardly be said to have been pressed editorially.

To raise the issue of inclusion but never to name the man himself is certainly cautious, even nervous, editorial policy. But it is not hostile, either. It falls considerably short of Chesterfield's advice to Newcastle to dissociate the coalition from Pitt altogether, the strong tone of which was at least partly owing to the fact that Chesterfield was addressing it to a minister whose confidence in the coalition needed stiffening. Furthermore, it must be noted that Chesterfield's advice came later. In early November 1745, when the *True Patriot* began publishing and the patience of the negotiators was not yet so strained as it would become, such editorial policy was simply moderate, reflective perhaps of the centrist position among the patriots—conciliatory of Pitt, on the one hand, but unwilling to sacrifice the coalition for his sake.

Pitt also accused the Pelhams of mismanaging the measures taken to put down the jacobite rebellion and, what is more, of covering up their mismanagement. To judge from George Grenville's testimony and some of his own votes as well, Lyttelton seems to have concurred in this position.[2] The *True Patriot*, though it concedes certain difficulties, indeed even stresses them, puts the blame squarely on the obstructionist tactics of the Bath–Granville squadron. The Pelhams, so the paper suggests, are doing the best they can, given the disarray in the closet and the consequences of Granville's foreign policy. It is the 'Opposers', both in and out of government, who are to blame. This is not quite the view that Pitt and his people were putting forward.

On the almost paralyzing question of what to do about the continental war—the failure to resolve which had caused the 1745 negotiations

[1] See below, p. 159.

[2] Lyttelton presumably voted, with Pitt, against Dashwood's motion to amend the address of thanks to the king; his speech is in *Parliamentary History*, xiii. 1344–8. He voted for Pitt's motion to recall the rest of the British troops from Flanders; earl of Shaftesbury to James Harris, 24 October 1745, *Malmesbury Letters*, i. 8. Though his vote is not specifically recorded, he concerted with Pitt in the negotiations preliminary to Hume Campbell's motion for a select committee to inquire into the causes of the rebellion; *Marchmont Papers*, i. 143, 147. And Pitt's unexpected motion to consider an augmentation of the navy, of which Lyttelton appears to have been apprised beforehand, was defeated after abusive debate by forty-five votes, a failure which Walpole characterized as leaving Pitt with nothing 'but his words, and his haughtiness, and his Lytteltons and his Grenvilles'; to Mann, 22 November 1745, *Yale Walpole*, xix. 169. Owen, p. 291, concludes that with respect to Pitt's various motions the Cobham group was acting pretty much 'in unison'.

between Pitt and the Pelhams to be broken off—the *True Patriot* once again eschews any Cobhamite emphasis. Editorially speaking, no judgment at all is rendered as to the appropriate conduct of the war until the 'Present History' of no. 17 (18–25 February 1746), which urges that those who use the war issue to undermine the ministry be treated with contempt, because now that the administration is truly national—the failure of the Bath–Granville stopgap in early February had made some room for Pitt and other malcontents—to oppose the administration is to oppose the commonweal.[1] The 'Present History' of no. 19 (4–11 March 1746) even speaks of the war as 'just' and 'necessary', necessary because to enjoy domestic security the country must exert itself abroad.[2] But these judgments of the war come relatively late in the newspaper's life, at a time when Cobham's people had won some places and Pitt had moderated his attitudes. When the war issue was in hot dispute, however, the *True Patriot* kept a tactful silence, concentrating instead on the less equivocal issue of the rebellion at home.

In sum, then, there is nothing in the *True Patriot*'s handling of the crucial issues of 1745 which would have put off any but the most intransigent Cobhamite. And indeed there were signs of disunity within the Cobham grouping itself. George Grenville, in his narrative recollection of this period, cites a serious indisposition between Pitt and Cobham resulting from the ministerial shuffles of November 1744. Grenville, who was then being offered a place on the admiralty board, was at first unwilling to accept it, out of friendship for Pitt, who was not offered anything. Cobham, whose breach with Pitt appears to have widened over the latter's *volte-face* on the issue of involving British troops in Flanders (January 1745), countered Grenville's objections, and the latter reluctantly went into place. Although by his own admission Grenville joined Pitt 'in opposing the measures of [the] Government' during the rebellion crisis, he recorded later that 'all this time' he felt his support for Pitt was met by indifference, coldness, and slights of every kind from the latter.[3]

Like Grenville, Lyttelton appears to have been politically loyal to Pitt in 1745, and like Grenville he appears to have felt driven by the stronger man. The evidence for Lyttelton's discontent—his wife's dislike of Pitt, Walpole's testimony that he was showing public signs of discontent, Chesterfield's sense that he could be detached, 'after some convulsions'[4]

---

[1] See below, pp. 227–8.   [2] See Locke, p. [169].
[3] *Grenville Papers*, ed. Smith, i. 424, where he also records that Pitt's turnabout in parliamentary behavior after getting the lucrative post of paymaster-general of the forces (May 1746) 'gave the last blow to all intercourse between Lord Cobham and him'.
[4] See above, p. lxxxvi.

–dates from just after the turn of the year, but the discontent must have been building. As the government's negotiations with Pitt dragged on into 1746, Lyttelton became so fed up with political infighting that he recorded a wish to retire from political life altogether and to take up a diplomatic post in some quieter sphere.[1] Whatever the exact state of his feelings in November 1745—and as his friend, Fielding may have been privy to them—Lyttelton was not likely to have been much offended or even inconvenienced by the compliment to him in the opening leader. Ideologically, so to speak, he and the paper stood pretty much for the same things.

Lyttelton also qualifies for the *True Patriot* list because he was a person of some distinction in the republic of letters. In 1745 his literary reputation rested mainly on his *Letters from a Persian in England* (1735), but he was commonly supposed also to have written a good deal of anonymous political material. Like Dodington, though in a rather different style, Lyttelton was an active literary patron. It testifies further to the almost 'familial' nature of the list of supposed authors of the *True Patriot* that the final two names, those of Fielding and Thomson, are those of literary men who had not only been active in the patriot cause but had also been beneficiaries of Lyttelton's patronage, as well as of Dodington's.

Thomson was a Scot, and Millar was his publisher. He seems to have come early to the notice of Dodington, to whom he dedicated *Summer* (1727) and who seems to have set up the poet's connection with the prince of Wales's circle. Thomson's first government sinecure (secretary of briefs) was bestowed upon him by Baron Talbot, the lord chancellor (1733–7), for whose son Charles Richard he had been traveling tutor.[2] In 1734 Dodington passed Thomson on to Lyttelton, who persuaded the prince of Wales to confer upon the poet a pension of £100 a year (1737) after his earlier sinecure had expired at the death of the lord chancellor. In the period 1737–40 the author of 'Rule Britannia' (1740) seems to have done a certain amount of 'patriot' writing for Lyttelton and the prince. The former, upon becoming one of the lords of the treasury in the broad

---

[1] BL Add. MS 32707, f. 92; Lyttelton to Newcastle, 24 April 1746; cited by Owen, p. 302.

[2] Cross, i. 363–4, inadvertently blurs Thomson's 'patriot' connection by identifying Charles Richard, who died in September 1733, with the dedicatee of Fielding's and Young's *Plutus, the God of Riches* (1742). In fact the lord Talbot of 1742 was William, eldest and surviving son of the lord chancellor, who 'repaid' the compliment of a dedication by subscribing to Fielding's *Miscellanies* (1743). A discontented whig with political connections to Bedford, William Talbot had a reputation as a patriot—Horace Walpole later called it 'a very free-spoken kind of patriotism on all occasions'; *Memoirs of the Reign of King George the Third* (London, 1845), i. 36. In 1747 Talbot was commissioned by the prince of Wales to assist in getting the tories to unite with the prince; *The House of Commons 1715–1754*, ii. 463. Talbot may well have been one of the 'patriot' influences on Thomson.

bottom of November 1744, procured for Thomson the sinecure of surveyor-general of the Leeward Islands at £300 a year. To the prince Thomson dedicated *Liberty* (1734–6) and the 1744 edition of *The Seasons*. After a period of lessened activity in the early 1740s he returned to 'patriot' themes in his penultimate play, *Tancred and Sigismunda*, which opened at Drury Lane on 18 March 1745, with Garrick and Susannah Maria Cibber in the leads.[1] The printed play is dedicated to the prince of Wales.

To modern readers the 'patriot' strain in Thomson's *œuvre* seems so lofty, so high-minded, that it is difficult to imagine it having enough political 'point' to warrant subsidy from any political faction. But the high-mindedness was compatible with a similar strain in Bolingbroke's metapolitics, and on the boards at least the plays apparently generated considerable political feeling. According to a hostile letter in the *Daily Post* of 26 April 1745 a 'very remarkable new Lord of the Treasury' [Lyttelton] had attended the public rehearsals of *Tancred and Sigismunda* and was 'proud of appearing its Foster Father'.[2] The letter also states that on opening night 'this celebrated *Person*, and his Friends in the Box with him (all very lately most flaming Patriots!) were seen clapping their Hands' at a speech in II. iv, urging renunciation of 'those Errors and Divisions; | That have so long disturb'd our Peace'. Among Lyttelton's friends 'in the Box', according to Victor, was Pitt, credited by another historian of the theatre with having assisted Lyttelton in 'the direction and influence' of the play during rehearsals.[3] Evidently such collaboration with the 'patriot' *literati* was not without its drawbacks. In a letter of 31 May 1745 Thomson wrote that 'not entirely trusting to the Broad Bottom, I will try to subsist on the narrow but sure one of Self-Independency'.[4] However, independence did not come easy. Thomson's letter goes on to say that he is writing a new play on Coriolanus, a subject he seems first to have worked on three years earlier, and that Lyttelton and Pitt, 'now reconciled' to the subject, are reading the manuscript and will shortly proffer their advice. How much 'direction and influence' they finally exerted is not known—the play appeared

---

[1] For a reading of the play that perceives a number of its passages to be susceptible to a 'jacobite' interpretation, see John Loftis, 'Thomson's *Tancred and Sigismunda* and the Demise of the Drama of Political Opposition', in *The Stage and the Page: London's 'Whole Show' in the Eighteenth-Century Theatre*, ed. Geo. Winchester Stone, Jr. (Berkeley and Los Angeles, 1981), pp. 34–54.

[2] The letter is reprinted as his by Benjamin Victor, *Original Letters, Dramatic Pieces, and Poems*, 3 vols. (London, 1776), i. 101–4. It may also be consulted in Alan Dugald McKillop, *James Thomson (1700–1748): Letters and Documents* (Lawrence, Kansas, 1958), pp. 178–80. An excerpt is in *London Stage*, Part 3: *1729–1747*, ii. 1160.

[3] Thomas Davies, *Memoirs of the Life of David Garrick, Esq.* (London, 1780), i. 79.

[4] Reprinted in McKillop, p. 181.

posthumously (1749) with a prologue by Lyttelton[1]—but if they were now reconciled to the subject, as Thomson says, they must have seen some 'patriot' possibilities in its treatment. For Thomson, then, the patriot connection was still very much alive in 1745, a fact to which Fielding's compliment in the *True Patriot* indirectly testifies. In all likelihood Thomson did not contribute a syllable to Fielding's paper, but it would not have been out of place for him to have done so.

Thomson's name comes last on the list of supposed authors of the *True Patriot*. Preceding it is Fielding's own, 'disemvowelled' like the other seven. The ordering is curious. One might expect that the name of the 'real' author should conclude the list, as a kind of complimentary anticlimax to the other, greater names. It is possible that Fielding intended to conclude his list in just this way. The printed text assigns two prefixed courtesy titles to Fielding—'Mr. Mr. F——g'—and none at all to Thomson, a discourtesy of which Fielding would surely not have wished to be guilty in a context of compliment.[2] The point is hardly important unless the sequence can be held to tell against Fielding's authorship and for Thomson's. Which raises the not uninteresting question, what in fact is the evidence for Fielding's authorship of the *True Patriot*?

His name was not associated with the paper in any public way—excepting of course its playful and tantalizing appearance, in the first leader, among those of the 'possible' authors—for several years. The *London Evening Post* advertisement, the only one that has been located, does not name him. Nor do the contemporary pamphlets and newspapers, at least not right away. No material in the *True Patriot* is signed with his name or even with an initial which might be identified as his. Andrew Millar does not list the *True Patriot* among Fielding's works in any of the advertisements which have proved so helpful in confirming other attributions.[3] With one exception, there is no explicit reference to Fielding's editorship of the *True Patriot* in either the correspondence or the printed works of contemporaries who knew him and the publishing scene well enough to comment as the paper was appearing.

The one exception is the unpublished Fielding correspondence with James Harris, his Salisbury friend and financial supporter. In a letter dated 2 January 1745[6] Fielding writes of receiving some some 'Wit'

---

[1] As Thomson's literary executor Lyttelton was instrumental (with Quin) in getting the play performed, Rich taking it for Covent Garden. See *London Stage*, Part 4: *1747–1776*, i. 90.

[2] See below, p. 110 and *nn*.

[3] Locke errs in stating (p. 16) that the *True Patriot* is listed in Millar's advertisements in the 1754 edition of *Jonathan Wild* and the 1758 edition of Sarah Fielding's *Cleopatra and Octavia*. Millar lists no papers by Fielding in his advertisements, presumably because he was not their publisher.

from Harris, which the public will undoubtedly relish a week from Tuesday. Although no name is given, this is clearly a reference to something Harris wished to contribute to a periodical paper, and Fielding's manner of expressing pleasure at its receipt is clearly that of the principal editor. Nine days later Fielding writes Harris that the public's reception of his 'Wit' increased the sale of the paper and prompted a transcription by another paper. In short, then, the evidence from the correspondence with Harris confirms that Fielding was editing a weekly periodical in January 1746 and that Harris contributed at least one piece to it,[1] but neither letter gives the title of the periodical in question.[2]

The actual title itself is not publicly associated with Fielding until 1747, and then only in an indirect attribution. The title-page of the so-called second edition of Fielding's anonymous electioneering pamphlet, *A Dialogue between a Gentleman ... and an Honest Alderman* (1747), states that it is 'By the Author of the *True Patriot*, and *A serious Address to the People of Great-Britain*'.[3] There is a further clue to Fielding's authorship in the *Jacobite's Journal* no. 5 (2 January 1748). A letter signed 'HA! HA! HA!' welcomes 'old Trot [editorial *persona* of the *JJ*] ... under whatever Title thou dost please to appear; Champion, Patriot, Jacobite, any thing'.[4] It is by no means certain that Fielding wrote this letter of ironic praise, but the printing of it indicates he wished neither to withhold nor contradict the attributions contained in it. Although as of 1748 all references associating Fielding with the *True Patriot* were, in a manner of speaking, self-references, it is hard to believe that the people who followed such things did not know who the principal writer of the *True Patriot* was. However, in the case of political journalism public identification of the man behind the mask, so to speak, was usually made by journalists unfriendly to the writer in question. During the 'Forty-Five' it may not have seemed prudent to attack so 'patriotic' a journal as the *True Patriot*. Perhaps it was not worth anybody's while to do so. Whatever the reasons, they clearly did not obtain during Fielding's tenure as editor of the *Jacobite's Journal* in 1747–8. Before that paper reached its twentieth

---

[1] Additional evidence that Harris was helping in some way with the *True Patriot* comes from a letter to him from his cousin the fourth earl of Shaftesbury, dated London, 25 January 1746. Remarking on the defeat of Hawley's army by the rebels at Falkirk (17 January 1746), Shaftesbury concludes: 'The affair turns out another Preston Pans *almost*, but don't quote me for your author'; *Letters of the First Earl of Malmesbury ... from 1745 to 1820*, ed. Right Hon. Earl of Malmesbury (London, 1870), i. 30. The 'author' is certainly Fielding, and Shaftesbury's remark indicates that Harris was transmitting opinion (and probably 'news' as well) to him for his paper.

[2] For evidence that Fielding's friend Harris supplied the leader of *TP* no. 10 (7 January 1746), see below, p. 171 *n.* 1.

[3] For a facsimile of the title-page, see Wesleyan Edition, p. [2], and for a bibliographical description, pp. 437–8. Fielding's authorship of *A Serious Address* is discussed above, pp. xxxvi–xxxvii.

[4] Wesleyan Edition, p. 120.

number, he wrote, 'A heavier load of Scandal hath been cast upon me, than I believe ever fell to the Share of a single Man.'[1] Much of this 'Scandal' has survived and been identified. What is surprising about it is the continued absence of any reference to Fielding's earlier work on the *True Patriot*. In 1748 his enemies may attack him for his plays, his work on the *Champion*, *Joseph Andrews*, his legal career, and his political connections. But they do not attack him for the *True Patriot*. Given the very detailed knowledge some of the scandalmongers profess about his private life, it seems almost inconceivable that they did not know about Fielding and the *True Patriot*. Given the fact that in 1748 there was no compelling crisis like the jacobite rebellion to mute hostile voices, it is difficult to account for the silence.

Indeed, the silence does not appear to have been publicly broken until 1752, when Fielding, under the *persona* of 'Sir Alexander Drawcansir', had enlisted his *Covent-Garden Journal* in a lucrative newspaper war. One of his principal adversaries, Bonnell Thornton's *Drury-Lane Journal*, includes in its first number (16 January 1752) a mock advertisement of works 'proper to be bound with the Lucubrations of Sir Alexander Drawcansir', proper because they are by the same author. The advertisement reads in part: 'Where may be had, The Works of Hercules Vinegar, Esq; ... John Trotplaid, Esq; The True Patriot'.[2] Thornton, who works up a certain rhetorical energy from attacking Fielding's activities as a political writer, will make the connection one more time. In a journal purporting to come from 'Drawncansir' himself, he has the latter saying, 'Having once blunder'd into Politics, 'twas the same thing to me, what cause I espous'd: so I e'en call'd myself honest John Trotplaid, and laid about me pellmell among the Jacobites: I was a *True Patriot* every inch of me.'[3] Shortly after the first of Thornton's two references to the *True Patriot*, the *Gentleman's Magazine* also found occasion to mention it. Under the heading 'Literary News for January 1752' the magazine begins its extended notice of the *Covent-Garden Journal* on a note of unusual asperity: 'Mr *H—y F—ld—g*, after having failed in the *Champion*, the *True Patriot*, and the *Jacobite Journal*, has this month made another attempt to establish a news-paper.'[4] Why it took so long for his adversaries to make public the *True Patriot* connection is not clear.

The capstone is put on the building case for Fielding's authorship by

---

[1] No. 20 (16 April 1748), ed. cit., p. 235.

[2] *Have at You All: or, The Drury-Lane Journal* (London, 1752), p. 24. Thornton's 'little Threepenny Pamphlet' appeared weekly and was later bound in a continuously paged volume. The quoted description is from p. 215.

[3] No. x (19 March 1752), ed. cit., p. 237.

[4] *GM*, xxii (1752), 25–6.

Andrew Millar's edition of the _Works_ (1762), which reprints ten of the original thirty-three leaders of the _True Patriot_. The 1762 _Works_, presumably because Arthur Murphy contributed a long prefatory essay, is commonly referred to as the 'Murphy edition'. Murphy actually knew Fielding during the latter's final years and is in fact the only 'editor' so privileged. Since Millar was Fielding's principal publisher and close personal friend, it has always been assumed that he must have known the last word in matters of attribution, copy text, authoritative revisions (if any), and the like. Or if Millar didn't, Murphy did. The 'insider' status of the two identified participants in the 1762 _Works_—whether real or mostly imagined—has had the effect of conferring upon that edition an importance in excess of its merits. In fact, almost nothing is known of the actual editorial arrangements. Who determined the canon, particularly the anonymous works in it? What was the nature of the copy-texts? Were any of these marked up by Fielding (or under his direction) so as to distinguish them authoritatively from the first printed versions? In the case of the four newspapers, none of which is reprinted in anything like its entirety, who made the decisions about what to reprint? And on what basis?

Not all of these questions can be answered with respect to the _True Patriot_. However, two things may be pretty confidently asserted. First, the selections reprinted in the 1762 edition do not appear to derive from copy-text marked up by Fielding or by any person privy to his final intentions.[1] Second, the principal of selection, whatever it may have been, does not settle the case for attribution. Many of the leaders excluded in 1762 manifest signs of Fielding's hand which are just as strong as those manifested by leaders included in 1762. In other words, inclusion may constitute a strong argument for attribution, but exclusion does not constitute even a minimal argument for disattribution. Some sort of personal judgment—perhaps influenced by economic considerations as well—seems to have been at work in narrowing the selections to ten. The fact that they reprinted anything at all, however, shows that one undoubted authority (Millar) and one possible authority (Murphy) knew Fielding to be the editor and principal writer of the _True Patriot_. This 'knowledge' caps the argument from external evidence.

The argument from internal evidence is, in its own way, equally diffuse. It does not lend itself to convenient summary. Comprising matters of (among others) substance, tone and attitude taken toward substance,

---

[1] For the textual differences between the original leaders and those reprinted in the 1762 _Works_, see Appendix V, below. Murphy's marked-up text for the _Covent-Garden Journal_ exists, but no equivalent for the _True Patriot_ is known.

habits of allusion and exemplification, and of course style, the argument from internal evidence finally becomes audible to the trained or experienced ear. In abstracted form, however, it is not easily communicable to the less experienced, and the editor should not be too easily faulted for preferring alternative forms. Thus, the kind of annotation given to the materials of the present volume, particularly the *True Patriot* materials, should be seen as constituting much of the detailed argument for Fielding's authorship. The annotation tries to show that the substance of these materials is substance Fielding would have been concerned with, given his concerns of the time as well as his other treatment of it; that the tone and attitude taken toward that substance resemble the tone and attitude taken by Fielding in similar contexts; that there is a reservoir of allusion and exemplification which Fielding draws from, not invariably, but often enough to suggest a recognizable mind set; that the verbal style is consistent with the style of works where there can be no question of Fielding's authorship. Style, of course, has proved grudgingly resistant to quantified analysis. In many cases it is still most persuasively examined by a kind of intuitive particularity. In Fielding's case, however, there is one stylistic mannerism which may alert us to his possible presence, namely, his strong tendency to use *hath* and *doth* for the more familiar *has* and *does*.[1] Given the lack of determinacy in so much stylistic analysis, it should hardly surprise that the beguiling simplicity of the *hath*–*doth* 'test' brings a sigh of relief to the scholar struggling with nominations to the Fielding canon. Obviously such a test, though it may generate a 'necessary' proof of Fielding's authorship, does not generate a 'sufficient' proof of it. *Hath* and (less commonly) *doth* were still in some use among Fielding's contemporaries. Nevertheless, with appropriate safeguards the test can be very helpful, and it has been silently invoked, along with other supporting evidence, in the case of the *True Patriot*. It confirms what the other kinds of evidence suggest, namely, that Fielding wrote most of the leaders and, for a time, a good deal of the other material as well.[2]

The preceding long account must now be summarized. In 1745 Fielding took up once again the third of Ralph's alternatives for a writer—writing for a faction. He became the editor and principal writer of the *True Patriot*, a paper very likely underwritten by patriot politicians like Dodington and Lyttelton in some sort of commercial arrangement with

---

[1] See Appendix VI, below.

[2] In the case of nonleader material, it shows 'negative' at precisely the time when Fielding should have been attending the western circuit and hence less able to keep abreast of the more topical matters customarily dealt with in that material.

publishing professionals like Millar and Cooper. Now that most of Fielding's political mentors were in place, there are marked changes in the tone with which he treats a number of subjects, particularly that of the Pelham ministry, and his attitude is no longer 'opposition' in nature. However, the transition from 'out' to 'in' must not obscure the fact that the faction Fielding is writing for in 1745–6 is composed more or less of the same people with whom he had been running, politically, that is, since the mid-thirties—Dodington, Lyttelton, and Chesterfield in particular. Furthermore, the transition from 'out' to 'in' should not obscure the fact that the basic ideology, whenever it shows, is still watered-down Bolingbroke.

It is easy to charge Fielding, and the men he was writing for, with being political turncoats, with changing their tune the minute they came into place. Contemporaries made these charges all the time, and there is substance in them. But in 1745, before the patriot coalition felt firmly in place and secure from the vagaries of the shifting political scene, a case had to be made for the importance of the patriot position. To the Pelhams the case had to be made that their security depended on acquiring and keeping new friends from the patriot grouping. Such a case rested on some privately communicated assumptions, the most compelling being that which promised that the new patriot friends would be satisfied with places and not the power, whereas other possible allies of the Pelhams would want the power as well. Publicly, more or less the same point could be made by asserting that the metapolitics which underlay the patriot position was consistent with a disclaimer of power, with the idea of a coalition of parties, even though their political enemies charged them with mere political greed.

A case had also to be made to the patriots themselves, the included as well as the excluded, if these were to hold together sufficiently to constitute a desirable acquisition in the eyes of the Pelhams. To make this case for unity the editor of a patriot paper had to stress the intolerability of the Granvillean alternative, which must not have been difficult for one so experienced in making use of the 'Great Man' concept as Fielding. Walpole translated into Granville easily, if not entirely effectively. But the editor had also to stress the power and purity of the patriot 'ideology', to remind readers of the 'faith', in other words, at the same time that he pointed out how the 'faith' actually encouraged the notion of a coalition with nonpatriots so as to replace narrow-gauge party politics.

There is evidence that the *True Patriot* did not succeed in its tasks. The various signs of editorial change beginning with no. 18 (25 February–

4 March 1746) may point to nothing more than Fielding's inability to give the paper his fullest attention while trying to attend the Lenten assizes of the Western Circuit and the ensuing sittings of the King's Bench in London. But there may have been more to it than that. Ralph, or whoever took over the twin departments of foreign and domestic history, conducts those departments along very different lines. The 'Present History of Great Britain' in particular becomes far more of an apology for the patriot politics than it had been previously. Compared to the political analysis offered by this department beginning with no. 18, Fielding's leaders seem relatively simplistic, almost reluctantly political, offering readers nothing very systematic to hold on to. Even with Ralph's[?] more historical and analytical contributions, the paper may have had difficulty in conveying just what editorial position it stood for. Excusing the patriot politicking on the grounds of some vague metafactionalism cannot have been an easy job. In no. 30 (20–7 May 1746), near the end of the paper's life, the writer of the 'Present History of Great Britain' reports hearing from the coffee-house politicians that 'they cannot tell what the Patriot would be at, or what the Frame is into which he would mould the Minds of his Countrymen'.[1] There is a ring of truth in this report. The paper ceases publication three issues later. And as the paper ruefully notes on several occasions, neither Pelham nor the king seems to have paid any attention.

From a more personal view the *True Patriot* must also be regarded as a failure. Fielding's motives for undertaking it have been divided, by the commentators, between patriotism and a need for money. Neither appears quite to cover the case. The paper was patriotic mostly in the political sense, and the editor's salary can hardly have been sufficient to detach him from the law. Almost certainly Fielding resumed writing for a faction because he figured there was likely to be some sort of long-range reward in it—a pension, a place, or even a ministerial subvention. None of these things happened. Perhaps the paper was not thought good enough. Certainly Pelham saw in it no reason to adjust his low opinion of political journalists. The patriot politicians, Fielding's old political mentors, either would not or (more likely) could not do anything for him at the time. Lyttelton, as a Cobhamite and follower of Pitt, did not yet have enough clout with the ministry. Dodington probably did not, either. Chesterfield was above it all, or at least distant from it all. The Bedford connection was in the future. Fielding had not been on board long enough for Hardwicke, the titular head of his profession, to want to move on his account. The king, to whom Fielding makes a kind

---

[1] See Locke, p. [239].

of rueful farewell bow, though he kept up on what the press attacked him for,[1] was probably unaware of Fielding's editorial existence. At any rate, it was too early for the king to be easy with the new recruits from the patriots.

Whatever the reasons, the rewards were not forthcoming. Fielding would have to resort one more time to the third of Ralph's alternatives. Not until after the *Jacobite's Journal* activity of 1747–8 would he reap what he had sowed: possible (but temporary) subvention from the Pelhams, vicious character assassination by opposition journalists, and, finally, a chance to spend what turned out to be the not very considerable remainder of his life as a Westminster justice, earning some of 'the dirtiest money on earth'.[2] In 1746 even this hung fire.

---

[1] That George II was in the habit of reading some newspapers at least, especially those unfriendly to his government, is indicated by Hardwicke's memorandum of a private audience to discuss the consequences of Granville's resignation and the formation of the broad bottom late in the previous year. After noting that swarms of 'libels' usually attended political events of such magnitude, Hardwicke remarked, somewhat disingenuously, that 'scarce any material of that kind has appeared this winter', to which the king replied, 'I, myself, have seen twenty'. The chancellor then suggested that the king had perhaps seen these 'in the weekly papers', that is, in papers of a more political cast than the dailies, papers not unlike the *True Patriot*. See George Harris, *Life of Hardwicke* (London, 1847), ii. 110.

[2] 'Introduction' to *The Journal of a Voyage to Lisbon* (London, 1755), p. 26.

TEXTUAL INTRODUCTION

THIS edition offers a critical unmodernized text of *A Serious Address to the People of Great Britain*, *The History of the Present Rebellion in Scotland*, *A Dialogue between the Devil, the Pope, and the Pretender*, and *The True Patriot*. The text is critical in that it has been established by the application of analytical criticism to the evidence of the various early documentary forms in which the materials appeared. It is unmodernized in that every effort has been made to present the text in as close a form to Fielding's own inscription and subsequent revision (if any) as the surviving documents permit, subject to normal editorial regulation.

I. THE COPY-TEXT AND ITS TREATMENT

No manuscript is known for any of the material in the present volume; nor is any formal assignment of copyright from Fielding to the publisher extant which would permit us to assert flatly the authoritative nature of the manuscripts sent to the press. In the case of the three pamphlets, however, the evidence of the Strahan ledgers demonstrates that Strahan printed pamphlets with these titles, and so we may properly infer that the earliest impression at least was set from holograph. No known record of the printing of the *True Patriot* survives, but the presumption is surely strong that a periodical would have been set from holograph.

With the exception of the *Serious Address* there is no evidence that Fielding ever revised any of the texts in the present volume. We cannot tell, indeed, whether he even read proof on them. If he did so, he left no clear trace of the fact. Contemporary political ephemerae of the sort represented by Fielding's three pamphlets do not in general show much sign of careful supervision by their authors. In the case of his periodical, Fielding is not likely to have had time to revise or perhaps even to read proof consistently, assuming that he would have been concerned to do so.

For an unmodernized edition such as the Wesleyan Fielding the most authentic form of what are known as the 'accidentals' of a text—the spelling, punctuation, capitalization, word-division, and such typographical matters as the use of italicized words—can be identified only in the document which lies nearest to the lost holograph, that is, in the first edition, the one printing which was set directly from manuscript. An editor will understand that the first edition by no means represents diplomatic reprint of the manuscript and that in most respects the accidentals are a mixture of the author's and the compositor's. But whatever its relative impurity, the first edition stands nearest to the author's own characteristics and represents the only authority that has been preserved for the texture in which his words were originally clothed. For these reasons the editor has adopted as his copy-text the first edition of the *Serious Address*, the only text in the present volume which was editorially emended (probably, but not quite certainly by Fielding himself), reset, and reimpressed. One of the Yale copies of the *History of the Present Rebellion* exhibits one different press figure and an uncorrected turned letter, two differences which appear to indicate that this copy was produced earlier in the press run than the other observed copies, all of which are in other respects typographically identical with the Yale copy and are presumably products of the same (interrupted) impression. For the sake of principle, this Yale copy (described in textual Appendix IV) was selected as copy-text. The *Dialogue* and the *True Patriot* both appear to have been produced in a single impression.

In the absence of evidence that Fielding supplied much more than the original holograph, the treatment of the texts has been essentially conservative. Changes—even those which seemed desirable as restoring Fielding's supposed stylistic habits—have been made cautiously, in part because on the evidence of copy-texts, at least, Fielding's journalistic practice seems less conformable or consistent than that of his prose fiction. Furthermore, the printing-house styling in the copy-texts themselves is by no means consistent, most notably in the matter of capitalization. In the surviving specimens of his holograph Fielding often makes no distinction other than size between a capital letter and an uncapitalized one, a practice which probably acounts for much of the inconsistency in capitalization in the copy-texts.

With few exceptions, all accidental as well as all substantive alterations have been recorded in the textual apparatus so that the interested reader may reconstruct the copy-texts in detail as well as the substantive variations from them. In a few essentially formal matters, however, the following editorial changes have been made silently. (1) Typographical errors such as turned letters or wrong font are not recorded. (2) The heading capitals and small capitals which in the originals begin each pamphlet and each number of the *True Patriot*, as well as some of the departments within the journal, have been ignored. (3) Throughout, necessary opening or closing quotation marks have been supplied silently, as have closing parentheses. Moreover, running quotations marks in the left margin have been omitted and the quotations indicated according to the modern custom. This necessary modernizing of an eighteenth-century text for a modern critical edition extends also to the silent removal of closing quotation marks at the end of a paragraph when the quotation, in fact, continues without interruption in the next paragraph, marked as usual by opening quotation marks. (4) Single quotation marks have been normalized to double, as is the common (but not entirely consistent) practice of the copy-texts, wherever quotation is primary and direct. (5) When the apostrophe and roman 's' follow an italicized name, the roman is retained only when it indicates the contraction for 'is' but is silently normalized to italic when the possessive case is required. (6) The font of punctuation is normalized without regard for the occasionally variable practice of the original. Pointing within an italic passage is italicized; but pointing following an italicized word that is succeeded by roman text is silently placed in roman when it is syntactically related to the roman text. (7) The ampersand and other standard abbreviations (*e.g.*, *viz.*, *i.e.*, *vid.*) have been placed in the font opposite to that of the matter to which they pertain. (8) Speech assignments, wherever contracted, have been silently expanded. (9) Final periods have been additionally supplied between true independent and syntactically complete sentences where copy-text originally prints only the long dash; periods thus supplied have been placed after the last word of the sentence and before the long dash, as is the common practice of the copy-text where both sorts of punctuation are present. (10) The variable and unsystematic treatment of the long dash, particularly in the *True Patriot* in connection with Latin quotations, has been normalized. When the quotation itself is not syntactically complete, in headings or when used within Fielding's own sentence which continues following the quotation, only the dash appears in the present edition and any irrelevant periods are silently omitted. When such a syntactically incomplete quotation ends a Fielding sentence, the period is placed after the dash, silently, without regard for the copy-text positioning. (11) The conventional form of address which opens letters to the editor in the *True Patriot* is normalized to italic and conventional capitalization (*Sir*). (12) In the mottoes, and in Latin quotations generally, the ampersand is silently expanded to *et*; the contracted suffix *-q* is expanded to *-que*; titles have been expanded and italicized; authors' names have been expanded; the period customarily used after the author's name has been changed to a comma where there is following matter; designations of such things as book, epistle, and verse have been englished and expanded; and in the case of Greek, modern lettering and accenting have been adopted.

A few procedures for dealing with the text may be mentioned briefly even though they involve matters which are recorded in the apparatus. In their method of dealing with interjections within quotations or directly quoted speech, the texts in the present volume are more consistent or at least less confusing to the reader unfamiliar with eighteenth-century practice in such matters than were the texts comprising the volume which included the *Jacobite's Journal* and related writings. In the latter volume not only the inconsistency of method but certain ambiguities of method persuaded the editor to normalize this textual situation by consistently adopting the compromise but acceptable method at the time, of enclosing all such interjected material in parentheses, and then recording such alterations of the text in the appropriate appendix. In the present volume, however, such normalizing has been eschewed except in the few cases where copy-text practice might confuse the modern reader. In such cases normalizing is recorded in the apparatus. The *Dialogue* is not consistent in the way it treats parenthetical stage directions, indicators of asides, and speech directions, particularly with respect to internal punctuation and the choice of square brackets or parentheses. On the assumption that Fielding would have assented to the principle of consistency, had he been concerned to make thorough editorial corrections himself, the editor has normalized such matters and recorded same in the textual apparatus.

2. THE APPARATUS

All the textual apparatus is placed in appendices where it may be consulted by those who wish to analyze the total evidence on which the present text has been established. In the first appendix appears the List of Substantive Emendations. All verbal variation has been recorded here, and to the substantives have been added variant readings in the accidentals when these have influenced meaning in a strongly semisubstantive manner. Since the purpose of this list is to present at a view the major editorial departures from the copy-text, only the earliest source of the approved variant is recorded, together with the history of the copy-text reading up to its accepted emendation in the earliest source. Certain emendations not found in the collated early texts have been assigned to W, that is, to the present edition, whether or not they actually originated here or with some preceding editor. By their nature they cannot be authoritative, even though they have proven to be necessary corrections, and hence a more precise record would serve little purpose, especially since minimal independent emendation has proved necessary in the substantives themselves. The basic note provides, first, the page–line reference and the precise form of the emended reading in the present text. Following the square bracket appears the identification of the earliest source of the emendation in the texts collated. A semicolon succeeds this notation, and following this appears the rejected copy-text reading with the sigla of the texts that provide its history up to the point of emendation. In these notations certain arbitrary symbols appear. When the variant to be noted is one of punctuation, a *tilde* (~) takes the place of the repeated word associated with the pointing. An inferior caret ∧ calls attention to the absence of punctuation either in the copy-text or in the early text from which the alteration was drawn. Three dots indicate one or more omitted words in a series; *omit* means the matter in question was omitted.

The List of Accidentals Emendations (Appendix II) follows on the record of substantive and semisubstantive emendation, and conforms to the same rules. The list includes all other changes made in the copy-text except for those described as silently normalized. A list of word-divisions (Appendix III) holds information about hyphenated compounds that will permit an accurate reconstruction of the copy-text from the modern print. The reader may take it that any word hyphenation at the end of a line in the present text has been broken by the modern printer, and that the hyphenation was not present in the copy-text unless it is separately listed and confirmed here. Correspondingly, when a word is hyphenated at the end of a line in the copy-text, the editor has been charged with ascertaining whether it is a true hyphenated compound or else an unhyphenated word that has been broken; the facts are then recorded in this list. Although certain of the editorial decisions with respect to these copy-text readings approach the level of emendation, no record has been made of their treatment in editions other than the copy-text.

In all entries in the accidentals list the forms of the accidentals to the right as well as to the left of the bracket accord with the system of silent normalization adopted for the edited text. Moreover, no record is made of variation in the accidentals that is not the matter being recorded. That is, if a punctuation variant alone is the question, the lemma of the word to which the pointing refers will take the form of the accidentals of the Wesleyan text regardless of the spelling or capitalization of the word in the text from which the punctuation variant was drawn. In this respect, then, the *tilde* to the right of the bracket signifies only the substantive and not its accidentals form in any edition other than the copy-text.

Because there are, strictly speaking, no true *editions*, other than the first, of any of the texts in the present volume, with the exception of the

Serious Address, there is no Historical Collation in the textual apparatus of the present volume.

3. COLLATION

The copies which were observed and collated in preparing the various texts comprising the present volume are listed in Appendix IV by place of deposit and by call number. They will not be relisted here. As a matter of editorial policy, ineligible for such listing are copies in private hands or in collections which do not grant ready access to the public. There has been some attempt to list copies with an eye to geographical distribution in Great Britain and the United States, so that scholars from various parts of those countries may more conveniently check the bibliographical decisions of the present editor.

W. B. COLEY

Opposite: Title-page, first edition. The Beinecke Rare Book and Manuscript Library, Yale University: Fielding Collection 745s. The motto is from Sallust, *Bellum Catilinae*, ii, 5–7: 'In the name of the immortal gods I call upon you, who have always valued your houses, villas, statues, and paintings more highly than your country; if you wish to retain the treasures to which you cling, of whatsoever kind they may be, if you even wish to provide peace for the enjoyment of your pleasures, wake up at last and lay hold of the reins of state. Here is no question of revenues or the wrongs of our allies; our lives and liberties are at stake.' (Loeb.)

Mary Wolryche

A SERIOUS
ADDRESS

TO THE

People of GREAT BRITAIN.

In which the

CERTAIN CONSEQUENCES

OF THE

PRESENT REBELLION,

Are fully demonstrated.

Necessary to be perused by every LOVER
of his Country, at this Juncture.

---

*Per Deos Immortales, vos ego appello, qui semper Domos,
Villas, Signa, Tabulas vestras, pluris, quam rempublicam
fecistis: si ista cujuscumque modi sint, quæ amplexemini,
retinere; si voluptatibus vestris otium præbere, vultis:
expergiscimini aliquando, & capessite rempublicam. Non
nunc agitur de vestigalibus, non de Sociorum Injuriis;
Libertas & anima nostra in dubio est.*

SAL. BEL. CATALIN.

LONDON:

Printed for M. COOPER, at the *Globe* in *Pater-noster-
Row.* MDCCXLV.

[Price One Shilling.]

A SERIOUS

ADDRESS

TO THE

People of GREAT BRITAIN.

In which the

CERTAIN CONSEQUENCES

OF THE

PRESENT REBELLION,

Are fully demonstrated.

Necessary to be perused by every LOVER of
his Country, at this Juncture.

---

*Per Deos Immortales, vos ego appello, qui semper Domos, Villas, Signa,
Tabulas vestras, pluris, quam rempublicam fecistis : si ista cujusque
modi sint, quae amplexamini, retinere ; si voluptatibus vestris otium
praebere, vultis ; expergiscimini aliquando, et capessite rempublicam. Non nunc agitur de vectigalibus, non de Sociorum Injuris ;*
LIBERTAS et ANIMA NOSTRA in dubio est.

SAL. BEL. CATILIN.

LONDON:
Printed for M. COOPER, at the *Globe* in *Pater-noster-Row*.
M DCC XLV.

Title-page of the 26-page piracy of the first edition. The Beinecke Rare Book and
Manuscript Library, Yale University: Fielding Collection 745sa.

A SERIOUS
ADDRESS

To the PEOPLE of

GREAT BRITAIN.

In which the

Certain CONSEQUENCES of the

PRESENT REBELLION,

Are fully demonstrated.

Neceſſary to be peruſed by every LOVER of
his COUNTRY, at this Juncture.

The SECOND EDITION Correƈted, with Additions.

Per Deos Immortales, vos ego appello, qui ſemper Domos,
Villas, Signa, Tabulas veſtras, pluris, quàm rempublicam
feciſtis: ſi iſta cujuſcumque modi ſint, quæ amplexamini,
retinere; ſi voluptatibus veſtris otium præbere, vultis:
expergiſcimini aliquando, & capeſſite rempublicam. Non
nunc agitur de veƈtigalibus, non de Sociorum Injuriis;
Libertas & anima noſtra in dubio eſt.

SAL. BEL. CATALIN.

LONDON:

Printed for M. COOPER, at the *Globe* in *Pater-noſter-*
Row. MDCCXLV.

[Price One Shilling.]

A SERIOUS

ADDRESS

To the PEOPLE of

GREAT BRITAIN.

In which the

Certain CONSEQUENCES of the

PRESENT REBELLION,

Are fully demonstrated,

Neceſſary to be peruſed by every LOVER of
his COUNTRY, at this Juncture.

The THIRD EDITION Corrected, with Additions.

Per Deos Immortales, vos ego appello, qui ſemper Domos, Villas,
Signa, Tabulas veſtras, pluris, quam rempublicam feciſtis: ſi
iſta cujuſcumque modi ſint, quæ amplexamini, retinere ; ſi volup-
tatibus veſtris otium præbere, vultis : expergiſcimini aliquando,
& capeſſite rempublicam. Non nunc agitur de vectigalibus, non
de Sociorum Injuriis ; Libertas & anima noſtra in dubio eſt.
SAL. BEL. CATALIN.

L O N D O N:
Printed for M. COOPER, at the *Globe* in *Pater-noſter-Row.*
MDCCXLV.

[Price Sixpence.]

The Beinecke Rare Book and Manuscript Library, Yale University: Fielding Collection 745sc. For this spurious 'edition', possibly a Scottish piracy, see Appendix IV.

A SERIOUS

ADDRESS

TO THE

PEOPLE of GREAT BRITAIN

GENTLEMEN

The Rebellion lately begun in *Scotland*, under the Banner of *a popish Pretender*,[1] encourag'd and assisted with the Counsels and Arms of *France* and *Spain*, is no longer an Object of your Derision. The Progress of these Rebels is such, as should awaken your Apprehensions at least, and no longer suffer you to neglect the proper Methods for your Defence.[2] The Cause, indeed, is of such a Nature, that the *least* Danger is sufficient to *alarm* us; but the *highest* (was it possible to arrive at such an Height) should not *dishearten* or *terrify* us from engaging in it.

I am unwilling to think there is a Man in this Kingdom, Papists excepted, *weak* enough to wish well to this Rebellion. I am as unwilling to believe there is one, who desires to preserve our present Constitution, *base* enough to decline the Hazard of his Life, and of his Fortune, in its Preservation. Is any *Englishman* so ignorant, as not to know the Happiness of our present Constitution? So insensible, as not to perceive the total Destruction with which it is threatned? Or *so mean, so inglorious a Coward*, as patiently to submit to this Destruction?

To what Opinion, or to what Principle, must any Man sacrifice himself and his Country, who inclines to the Pretender's Side on this Occasion? The old, obsolete, absurd Doctrine of Hereditary Right, if admitted, would not justify him: The Right of his present Majesty is much stronger and clearer, even in this Light.[3] The suspicious Birth of

[1] James Francis Edward Stuart (1688–1766), known as the Old Pretender, was the son of James II and Mary of Modena. See 'General Introduction', above, pp. xxx–xxxi, xli–xlii.

[2] The Pretender had been proclaimed at Perth in early September; Edinburgh capitulated to the rebels on 17 September, without a fight; and on 21 September 1745 the YP's forces defeated the king's army under Cope at the battle of Prestonpans, the first pitched battle of the rebellion. See 'General Introduction', above, pp. xliii–xlvi, and, for the battle itself, *History*, below, pp. 63–6.

[3] On the assumption, which Fielding makes in the next sentence, that the OP was not the true son of James II, then George II has the clearer hereditary right. The Act of Settlement, 12&13 Will. III, c. 2, enacted (1701) after Mary's death and that of the Duke of Gloucester, Princess Anne's son, upheld the hereditary right by going back in the Stuart pedigree to the daughter of the exiled Queen

the Pretender was attended with such glaring Evidence of Fraud and Imposture, that no Jury would have suffered him to have succeeded, even to a private Right descended from *James* the Second, could his Pretensions have been fairly and impartially tried before them.[1] I shall not, however, insist upon this Point. The Doctrine itself of such an indefeasible Right to the Crown hath been justly exploded; the Legislature of the Kingdom have unanimously declared against any such Principle:[2] The Reverse of it is Law, a Law as firmly established as any other in this Kingdom; nay, it is the Foundation, the Corner-Stone of all our Laws, and of this Constitution itself; nor is the Declaration and Confirmation of this great Right of the People one of the least of those Blessings, which we owe to the Revolution.[3] Whatever, therefore, tends to the Shaking of this fundamental Right, doth of itself introduce an opposite System of Government, and *changes not only the King, but the Constitution.*

Admitting, therefore, this Pretender to be the Son of *James* the Second, the stronger is the Reason for rejecting him. *Shall we return like a Dog to his Vomit?*[4] Shall we bring back that Family which we have expelled, together with the Principles *for which* we expelled them; and which, with the Restoration of the same Family, must be also restor'd? Shall we pronounce, as this insolent Man hath dared to do in his Declaration, *that we have been under an Usurpation these fifty Years?*[5] That

of Bohemia (herself the child of James I), the Electress Sophia of Hanover. By the terms of the Act, succession, after Princess Anne and her descendants and William's, was limited to the Electress and her descendants, 'being protestants'. *Statutes at Large*, x. 357–9.

[1] When after fifteen years of marriage and a history of gynecological problems Mary of Modena gave birth to a son in June, 1688, the whigs claimed it was an imposture, a supposititious child brought into the labor room in a warming pan. Although the charge was later dropped because it implied the Stuart exclusion was owing to a fact of birth, not parliamentary legislation, it was revived during the Forty-Five. See, for example, *A Particular Account of the Pretender's Birth* (1745), *Some Farther Proofs, Whereby it appears that the Pretender is truly James the Third* (1745), *Bp. Burnet's and Bishop Lloyd's Account of the Birth of the Pretender* (1745); *OE* of 16 November 1745. Fielding alludes satirically to the warming-pan episode in *JJ* no. 6 (9 January 1748), p. 125, and no. 32 (9 July 1748), p. 331 and *n*.

[2] By the Revolutionary Settlement of 1689, most particularly by the Bill of Rights (1 Will. & Mar., sess. 2, c. 2) and, later, the Act of Settlement (12&13 Will. III, c. 2); *Statutes at Large*, ix. 67, and x. 357. Although parliamentary exclusion of catholics from the throne was clearly at the expense of the divine-right theory, monarchy was still to be hereditary, if not indefeasibly so.

[3] Prior to the establishment of a *bona fide* parliament (which itself required the establishment of a monarch) the parliamentary convention of 1689 drafted a 'Declaration of Rights', which, after William and Mary accepted the throne, was 'confirmed' by being turned into the Bill of Rights, 'An Act for declaring the rights and liberties of the subject and settling the succession of the crown'.

[4] Proverbs 26: 11: As a dog returneth to his vomit, so a fool returneth to his folly.

[5] In a 'royal declaration' dated from Rome, 23 December 1743 NS, and proclaimed on various occasions in Scotland by his son, the OP denominated the post-Revolutionary government of Great Britain as 'a foreign usurpation' and George II as 'the usurper'. For a text, see James Browne, *History of the Highlands*, iii (Glasgow, 1843), 20–3; *Historical Papers Relating to the Jacobite Period, 1699–1750*, ed. Colonel James Allardyce, i (Aberdeen, 1895), 177–80. Like many of his anti-jacobite contemporaries,

Lords and Commons, and the whole *English* Nation, have been Traitors so long?[1] That the Bill of Rights, the Act of Succession, and the Act of Union, were *High-Treason*?[2]

Let us look back to the History of that Prince, from whom this Pretender claims. It was not only the Difference of his Religion from that of this Country, which made him unfit to be King of it; he was unfit to govern even a Catholic Country, which had Liberties to defend, because his Mind was strongly tainted with all the Notions of absolute Power. Passive Obedience, and Non-resistance on the Part of the Subject, and a *dispensing Power* in the Crown, with an indefeasible Hereditary Right, *Jure Divino*, were as much Articles of his political Creed,[3] as the Supremacy of the Pope, or Transubstantiation, were of his religious one: Upon the former he acted thro' his whole Reign; nay, in the Reign of his Brother; whose Indolence gave him a great Share of the Royal Authority, and this it was which chiefly occasioned the Weakness and Faults of that Reign, at home and abroad. By his Instigation, did King *Charles* the Second make War with the *Dutch*, against the Interest of *England*, only *because they were a free State, and likely to assist this Kingdom in maintaining its Liberties.*[4] By his Instigation, did he nurse up the Power of *France*, that *France* might assist the two Royal Brothers *in enslaving the People of* England. By his Instigation, did the same *Charles* the Second dissolve those Parliaments that press'd the Bill of Exclusion.[5] By his Instigation, did he take away, by *Quo Warranto's*,[6] the Charters of all

Fielding goes to great lengths to impugn the credibility of this and other Stuart declarations. See 'General Introduction', above, pp. xli–xlii, and below, p. 91.

[1] Fielding's emphasis differs markedly from that of the declaration: 'We do therefore . . . absolutely and effectually pardon and remit all Treasons, and other Crimes hitherto committed against Our Royal Father or Ourselves; from the Benefit of which Pardon We except none; but such as shall, after the Publication hereof wilfully and maliciously oppose us . . .'; Allardyce, i. 178; Browne, iii. 21.

[2] Of these three, only the Act of Union (1707) is mentioned in the OP's declaration: 'We see a Nation always famous for Valour, and highly esteemed by the greatest of foreign Potentates, reduced to the Condition of a Province, under the specious Pretence of an Union with a more powerful Neighbour'; Allardyce, i. 177; Browne, iii. 21. By the terms of the Act of the Union Scotland accepted, among other things, the Hanoverian succession as provided by the Act of Settlement ('Succession').

[3] Cf. Fielding's satirical analyses of these doctrines in *Gentleman & Alderman* (1747), pp. 8–14, and *JJ* no. 3 (19 December 1748), pp. 104–6.

[4] The so-called third Dutch war, 1672–4, led up to by the secret Treaty of Dover (1670) with France, designed to disrupt the Triple Alliance. James claimed to have opposed this war on the grounds that 'it would quite defeat the Catholick design'; *Life of James the Second*, ed. J. S. Clarke, i (London, 1816), 450, 455.

[5] Bills of exclusion were introduced in the Commons in 1679, 1680, and 1681, for the purpose of disabling James duke of York from inheriting the crown. Charles II dissolved the three parliaments (the third, fourth, and fifth of his reign) which were considering them.

[6] 'A Writ which lies against any Person or Corporation, that usurps any Franchise or Liberty against the King, without good Title; and is brought against the Usurpers to shew by What Right and Title they hold or claim such Franchise or Liberty. . . . The Statute of *Quo Warranto* is the 18 Ed. I . . .

Corporations that had oppos'd the Crown in Elections.[1] By his Instigation, did he shed some of the *best and noblest Blood* in this Kingdom,[2] *against Law*, and by *Form of Law*, which is the worst of all Tyranny.[3] It was *James* Duke of *York*, who whetted the Axe which beheaded *Algernon Sidney*,[4] for writing a Book in Defence of our Liberties,[5] and the good Lord *Russel*, for promoting the Bill of Exclusion, *as a Member of Parliament*.[6] When in spite of that Bill he ascended the Throne, he fully justified the Caution of Parliament, and of those worthy Patriots, in their Design of excluding him, both as a Bigot and as a Tyrant; and this in direct Contradiction to the strongest and most solemn Promises of maintaining both our Religion and Liberties;[7] Promises which he again

And the Attorney General may exhibit a *Quo Warranto* in the Crown Office against any particular Person, Body Politick or Corporate, who shall claim or use any Franchises, Privileges or Liberties, not having a legal Grant or Prescription for the same'; Jacob, *New Law Dictionary*, 4th ed. (London, 1739), *s.v.*

[1] Under the Corporation Act of 1661 (13 Car. II, sec. 2, c. 1) a corporation, the civil authorities of a borough or incorporated town or city, was required to acknowledge the regal supremacy and to abjure resistance to the king; in addition, the commissioners appointed to administer the act were empowered to remove civil officials at their discretion. After the lapse of the commissioners' powers (1664) the crown, by issue of *quo warranto* for alleged malfeasance or technical irregularity in the incorporation of charters, continued to remodel or even invalidate charters of those corporations deemed hostile to it. In 1681 the crown stepped up its attack on corporation charters, which culminated in the successful action against the charter of the City of London. See Gilbert Burnet, *History of My Own Times* (London, 1724), i. 568; J. R. Jones, *The First Whigs* (London, 1961), pp. 199–206.
[2] Cf. *Proper Answer*, p. 69: 'For this Purpose were the Laws perverted, to shed some of the best and noblest Blood in the Nation.' Fielding may have taken the epithet from James Ralph, *The History of England . . . With an Introductory Review of the Reigns of the Royal Brothers Charles and James*, i (London, 1744), 752, where in a similar context the historian writes: 'nor do these Men want Advocates . . . for having doom'd to death one of the best and noblest of their Fellow-Subjects'.
[3] Cf. Burnet, *History of My Own Times*, i. 561: 'Killing by forms of law was the worst sort of murder.' Burnet is here quoting indirectly from Russell's deathbed 'paper', in which he seems to have had a considerable hand. See *The Speech and Last Behaviour of William late Lord Russell* (London, 1683), p. 4: 'For to kill by Forms and Subtilties of Law, is the worst sort of Murder.' For Russell, see below, *n.* 6.
[4] Theoretical republican or 'real Whig', member of the so-called Council of Six, Sidney (1622–83) was implicated in the Rye House plot, which was alleged to have planned the murder of the king and the duke of York. At his trial one of the major charges brought against Sidney was that he was the author of treasonable opinions expressed in some unpublished papers found in his study. Judge Jeffreys presided, and Sidney was executed on Tower Hill, 7 December 1683. Cf. Fielding's own note in his *Proper Answer*, p. 69: 'Lord *Russel*, *Sydney*, &c. murdered by Form of Law, for having been the Champions of Liberty, and of the Protestant Religion.'
[5] The posthumous (1698) *Discourses concerning Government*, reprinted in 1740. Baker, item no. 278, lists a 1751 edition among Fielding's books.
[6] William, Lord Russell (1638–83), son of the first duke of Bedford and ancestor of Fielding's 'princely' benefactor, whig exclusionist and anticatholic, member of the Council of Six. Also implicated in the Rye House plot, Russell was tried for premeditating rebellion, was sentenced, and executed at Lincoln's Inn Fields on 21 July 1683. During the so-called Oxford parliament of 1681 Russell seconded the exclusion bill.
[7] In his first speech to the privy council James II promised to maintain the liberty and property of his subjects, and 'to Defend and Support' the church of England. For a text, see *An Account of what His Majesty said at His first coming to Council* (London, 1684 [1685]). According to Burnet, *History*, i. 620, 'the

repeated, when he thought his Crown was in Danger,[1] and again broke, when he thought himself in the least delivered from that Danger. Besides his avowed Design of establishing Popery, besides all those Acts of arbitrary Power, enumerated in the Declaration of Rights, *which struck at the very Root of Liberty, and the Fundamentals of our Constitution*, there are many Instances of wanton Cruelty and inveterate Revenge, where neither the Interest of the Priest or Tyrant were concern'd, (and which could proceed only from that cruel Disposition, which he had before discovered in *Scotland*, by the Delight he testified in the Groans and Skreams of Wretches under Torture*;)[2] witness the inhuman and unparallel'd Butchery committed in cold Blood, by his immediate Order, on *Monmouth's* conquer'd People in the West;[3] for which his wicked Instrument, *Jeffreys*, was at his Return immediately rewarded with the Seals:[4] The

* *Vide Burnet's* History of *Charles* II. *Vol. I. p.* 583.

common phrase was, We have now the *word of a King, and a word never yet broken*.' In his own notes on the occasion James described his speech as giving 'unspeakable satisfaction to all persons, but especially to those who by the malicious insinuations of his enemies were in some doubt what might become of their liberties and religion'; *Life of King James the Second*, ed. J. S. Clarke (London, 1816), ii. 3–4.

[1] See *His Majesty's Most Gracious Speech to both Houses of Parliament, On Friday the 22nd of May, 1685* (London, 1685). Burnet, *History*, i. 620, inferred James's fondness for the speech from his having 'repeated it to his Parliament, and upon several other occasions'. According to *Great Britain's Memorial against the Pretender and Popery*, 9th ed. (London, [1745]), p. 3: 'He afterwards confirmed this Declaration to his first Parliament, and renewed it again upon *Monmouth's* Invasion.' James himself asserted that although he made the speech without notes and 'without much premeditation . . . he thought it necessary not to vary from it [Heneage Finch's transcript] in the declarations or speeches he made afterwards, not doubting but the world would understand it in the meaning he intended'; *Life of James the Second*, ed. Clarke, ii. 4. Cf. *Proper Answer*, p. 71 and *Tom Jones*, VIII. xiv. 477.

[2] By order of the king, James was 'exiled' to Scotland from October 1680 to March 1682 as Commissioner to the Estates. His nominal mandate was to conclude remodeling of the militia and to secure the peace after the Covenanters' rebellion under Cameron and Cargill. During that time, according to Burnet, *History*, i. 583, 'When any are to be struck in the boots [a Scottish torture involving the placement of the prisoner's legs in iron boots and the driving of wedges between the boot and the leg], it is done in the presence of the Council: And upon that occasion almost all offer to run away. . . . But the Duke, while he had been in *Scotland*, was so far from withdrawing, that he looked on all the while with an unmoved indifference. . . . This gave a terrible idea of him to all that observed it, as of a man that had no bowels nor humanity in him.'

[3] After the failure of Monmouth's rebellion at Sedgemoor in July 1685 a special commission was issued to five justices of the high court to try those who had been taken up as rebels. Known as the 'Bloody Assizes', the hearings of this commission on the western circuit convicted some 1,381 persons of treasonable participation, of whom perhaps 200 were hanged and 800 transported. See G. W. Keeton, *Lord Chancellor Jeffreys and the Stuart Cause* (London, 1965), p. 329. James II's harsh treatment of the rebels is again alluded to in *JJ* no. 37 (13 August 1748), p. 365; and in *Tom Jones*, VIII. xiv. 478–80, the Man of the Hill describes his own flight after Sedgemoor.

[4] George Jeffreys (1648–89), first baron Jeffreys, lord chief justice and presiding judge of the 'Bloody Assizes'. On his way back from Bristol, the last town on the assizes, Jeffreys stopped off at Windsor, where he was rewarded by James II with the appointment of lord chancellor, 28 September 1685. According to Burnet, *History*, i. 648, 'that which brought all his excesses to be imputed to the King himself, and to the orders given by him, was, that the King had a particular account of all his proceedings writ to him every day. And he took pleasure to relate them in the drawing room to

unmanly,[1] as well as illegal Murder of *a poor old Woman*, in the Case of Lady *Lisle*;[2] and that ever-memorable Removal of Lord Chief Justice *Herbert* from the King's Bench, *in order to hang a private Soldier contrary to Law*.[3] These are Facts which bespeak not only a bad Prince, but a bad Man; not only an arbitrary and wicked, but a base and contemptible Mind: Facts which would have glar'd in the History of a *Dionysius*,[4] or of any the most abhorr'd Tyrants of Antiquity.

But it may be said, that though this Pretender derives a Right, he ought not to derive any Infamy from his supposed Father, since *He* may possibly protect that Religion and Liberty, which the other endeavoured to extirpate.

Upon what these Hopes are founded, is not easy to conceive; on the contrary, without allowing the Legitimacy of his Birth, of which, however, the Temper he hath always disclosed, is the strongest Evidence, we might be allowed to draw some Apprehensions from the Education

foreign Ministers, and at his table, calling it *Jefferies*'s campaign.' Cf. G. W. Keeton, op. cit., p. 324: 'there can be no question that both [Sunderland and James II] regarded Jeffreys and his colleagues as the official instruments of a policy decided upon in council'.

[1] Rude, undecent, irregular behaviour, such as no ways becomes a man (Dyche-Pardon); unbecoming a human being; unsuitable to a man, effeminate (Johnson).

[2] Alice Lisle (1614?–85), widow of the regicide John Lisle, who was a lord of parliament and later lord president of the High Court of Justice under Cromwell, was charged with harboring rebels after Sedgemoor, knowing them to be rebels. Jeffreys presided at her trial at Winchester on 27 August 1685. He conducted severe cross-examination of witnesses and, according to Burnet, *History*, i. 650, and the whig historians of the next generation (Oldmixon, Kennet, and Ralph, *inter alia*), threatened a reluctant jury with attainder until it returned a verdict of guilty. The sentence was for burning, but the king remanded it to beheading, and that sentence was carried out on 2 September 1685. See *State Trials*, edd. Cobbett and Howells (London, 1809–26), xi. 354–74; G. W. Keeton, *Trial for Treason* (London, 1959), pp. 103–34. The king's own posterior notes mention the Lisle case as one of those which brought 'great obloquy' upon him; *Life*, ed. Clarke, i. 43.

[3] Edward Herbert (1648?–98), titular earl of Portland, succeeded Jeffreys as chief justice of the King's Bench in 1685, upheld the dispensing power in the Hales case (1686), and in April 1687 was asked to grant execution against a deserter, condemned at the Reading assizes, so he could be shot before his regiment at Plymouth. Herbert ruled against the crown and was then ordered to change places with Sir Robert Wright, chief justice of Common Pleas, who at once found for the crown. Although 7 Henry VII, c. 1, and 3 Henry VIII, c. 5 had made desertion from the colors a felony and hence punishable at common law, the legal question was still open; W. S. Holdsworth, *History of English Law* (London, 1922–64), vi. 228ff. Herbert is reported to have said he 'could never concur to award execution for a man to die upon an offence which the law did not condemn him for'; Dr Williams's Library, *Morrice Entring Book*, 2, ff. 98–100, as quoted by F. W. Kenyon, *The Stuart Constitution, 1603–1688* (Cambridge, 1966), p. 440. See also Alfred F. Havighurst, 'James II and the Twelve Men in Scarlet', *Law Quarterly Review*, lxix (1953), 534.

[4] Probably Dionysius I (*c.* 430–367 BC), tyrant of Syracuse and opponent of the Carthaginians, whose government offended Plato and has been traditionally considered oppressive. For Augustans he was a 'type' of the tyrant; in *Spectator* no. 508 (13 October 1712) Steele writes of the head of a certain club as one 'whom for his particular Tyranny I shall call *Dionysius*'. However, the reference in *JJ* no. 8 (23 January 1748), p. 135, to 'the famous *Sicilian* Tyrant of Old' may be to his son Dionysius II, also a literary practitioner, who was reported to have spent his final years in exile working as a school-teacher.

which he had in his Infancy, under this very Person, and which was afterwards compleated in the Courts of *France* and *Rome*.[1]

These Circumstances alone would justify our Fears, had his own Conduct given us none: But when of all the Professors of that cruel Religion, he is known to be the most bigotted; when without Power, without Dominions, he hath in the little Circle of his mock Court exhibited the strongest Picture of a Tyrant, affecting every Opportunity to express his Resolution of being arbitrary, what further, what stronger Assurances can we want; nay, what could we possibly have of the *Misery*, the *Perdition*, which such a Choice must entail on ourselves, and our Posterity?

His Bigotry is so well known to the whole World, that it requires no Instances. His whole Life is one constant Act of Superstition. A single Example, however, is too glaring to be passed by, as it shews an Abhorrence to our Religion scarce to be parallelled. When he was in *Scotland*, in the Year 1716,[2] he absolutely refused to admit Dr. *Lesly*,[3] a Protestant Divine, to say Grace at his Table; but ordered a Roman Catholic Priest to perform that Ceremony.[5] This Dr. *Lesly* was a *Non-juror*, one who had

---

[1] For the social and educational regimen which James II drew up for his son at St Germains in 1696, see HMC, *Stuart Papers*, i. 114–17. This directive appointed the duke of Perth (fourth earl and first titular duke), a convert, 'to be Governor to our dearest son', and William Dicconson and Dominick Sheldon, both catholics, to be undergovernors; i. 119, 151.

[2] To lend the support of his presence to the jacobite uprising of 1715 the OP landed at Peterhead (Aberdeenshire) on 22 December 1715, by which time the enterprise was hopeless, and withdrew for France on 4 February 1716.

[3] Charles Leslie (1650–1722), prominent nonjuror and controversialist divine, with a record of Stuart affiliation going back to James II. In 1701 Leslie was sent to St Germains by the English nonjurors to signify their acknowledgment of James III and to proffer a set of 'Instructions' to which they wished James to give his assent; HMC, *Stuart Papers*, iv. 3–4. In 1711 Leslie again visited the OP at St Germains, with a memorial on the state of parties in England, urging the jacobite cause and an armed landing in England. Two years later he accepted the OP's invitation to 'officiate to the protestants in the [royal] family' at Bar-le-Duc, where he said he was graciously received and given marks of special favor; 'A Letter from Mr. Leslie to a Member of Parliament in London' (1714), reprinted in *Somers Tracts*, 2nd ed. (London, 1815), xiii. 673; George Hilton Jones, *The Main Stream of Jacobitism* (Cambridge, Mass., 1954), p. 90.

[5] The story of the OP's refusal of Leslie while in Scotland appears to be a fabrication. En route to his embarkation for Scotland the OP wrote to Abbé Inese (Innis) from St Malo on 1 November 1715: 'Mr. Lesley will either go to Scotland, or joyn the Duke of Ormonde in England, as his age and health will permit him, he knows very well how much I shou'd have desired to have him along with myself, but the secret was to be prefer'd to all'; HMC, *Stuart Papers*, i. 457. There is no clear evidence that Leslie ever made the trip. Cf. the OP's paper entitled 'Reasons for not assisting at the *Te Deum* at Perth', dated January 1716: 'As to myself, since my coming here [Scotland] everybody knows I had not so much as a priest with me nor have not now any living constantly at this place'; HMC, *Stuart Papers*, iv. 13. However, the anti-jacobite tradition preferred a view of greater bigotry. Cf. the letter from the duke of Montrose to Lord Stair, London, 26 January 1716, in John Murray Graham, *Annals and Correspondence of the Viscount and the First and Second Earls of Stair* (Edinburgh, 1875), i. 301: 'I am assured, from very good hands in Scotland, that the Pretender's behaviour is exceedingly disgusting even to his friends. He pushes his bigotry so far that he won't allow a Protestant minister so much as to say grace to him: an instance of this they give, when he was at Brechin, where my lady Panmure had a parson ready before supper, but he was not allowed to lift up his hands.' See also Alistair and Henrietta

embraced his Party, and was by him made a Bishop.[1] He was a *Scotch-man*,[2] refused this little Favour in the Face of his Countrymen, who were to expose their Lives and Fortunes in order to set this Popish Bigot on the Throne of *Great Britain*: All these Men he ventured disobliging, rather than he would shew the least Countenance to that Religion, which some simple Protestants have been weak enough to flatter themselves, that he would better defend than a Prince of our own Religion.

Nor is the Civil Tyrant less apparent in this pretended King, than the Religious: His little Court at *Avignon* was compared by the late Lord *Mar*,[3] who was at it, to that of *Lewis* XIV. in the absolute Demeanour of its Sovereign;[4] (for indeed it could resemble it in no other Instance;) where this mock King strutted about with a kind of theatrical Pomp, and, though conquer'd, banish'd, deserted, without a single Smile of Fortune to swell his Ambition, he retained all those Principles of Pride and arbitrary Power, with which Flattery and Success inspired the Mind

Tayler, *1715: The Story of the Rising* (London, 1936), p. 128, which quotes an unidentified 'news-letter of the period' as saying that when the OP passed Aberdeen, 'he wowld not conforme so far as to allow a Protestant chaplin, having Father Innise along to direct his conscience'; and Peter Rae, *The History of the Rebellion*, 2nd ed. (London, 1746), p. 360: 'But as he never attended any Protestant, though Episcopal Worship, nor heard any Protestant so much as to say Grace to him; but constantly employed his own Confessor, Father *Innes*, to say the *Pater Noster* and *Ave Marys* for him.' It is note-worthy that none of these contemporary sources identifies Leslie with any rejected protestant clergyman.

  [1] Cf. Peter Rae, *History of the Rebellion*, 2nd ed. (London, 1746), p. 355: 'we are told ... he [the OP] made several Lords, and Bishops of which the famous Mr. *Lesly*, his Chaplain, was said to be one; tho' we could never hear to what Place he was design'd'; the unidentified 'news-letter of the period' quoted by Alistair and Henrietta Tayler in *1715: The Story of the Rising*, p. 128: 'He [the OP] has created some peers, as Ogilvie of Powrie, Mr. Leslie a bishop and some others'; and John Oldmixon, *History of England During the Reigns of King William* ... (London, 1735), p. 624: 'In Prosecution of the Farce he was playing, he made several Lords, Knights, and Bishops; one of the latter was said to be *Lesley*, the *Libeller*, whose Seditions and treasonable Practices had drawn him out of *England* from the Pursuits of Justice.' There are no records of such creations in the Scots peerage, and the entire episode seems an anti-jacobite fabrication. See also *Secret Memoirs of Barleduc* (London, 1715), p. xxi, and [Abel Boyer], *The Political State of Great Britain*, xi (London, 1716), 24.

  [2] Leslie was born and educated in Dublin.

  [3] John Erskine (1675–1732), sixth (22nd) earl of Mar, in the reign of Anne had been a member of the privy council, keeper of the signet, and as secretary of state for Scotland (1705) had strongly sup-ported the Act of Union (1707). Known as 'Bobbing John' for his political shiftings, Mar appears to have become a committed jacobite upon his dismissal by George I at the latter's accession. Mar raised the standard for the OP (without authority) at Braemar in September 1715 and was *de facto* commander of the rebel armies in Scotland during the Fifteen. Created jacobite duke in 1715 (attainted 1716), Mar left the failure in Scotland with the OP in February 1716, living briefly in Paris and environs before proceeding to Avignon in April, where he was made a knight of the Garter. Later Mar removed to Rome as manager of jacobite affairs for some years. See HMC, *Report on the Manu-scripts of the Earl of Mar and Kellie* (London, 1904), p. 511; and *Supplementary Report on the Manuscripts of the Earl of Mar and Kellie* (London, 1930), p. 255.

  [4] Fielding's authority for attributing such views to Mar has not been identified. As preserved in the *Stuart Papers*, Mar's letters for the period in question and later uniformly make the opposite point, namely that the exiled court was noteworthy both for its austerity and its toleration of protestants.

of *the Grand Monarch*.[1] This is a Fact publish'd by many, who, from Detestation of his Principles, abandoned the Cause of a Man who thus tyranniz'd over voluntary Slaves, whom Rebellion alone had subjected to his Authority.

And shall we be cheated with so gross an Imposition, that it is not under the Banner of this Pretender, but of his Son, that the *Highlanders* have now taken up Arms? What is the Son but the Tool of the Father? Doth he not act by Commission from him?[2] Hath he not taken upon himself the Title of Regent only, during the Absence, and in the Name of his Father?[3] Is not his Father now actually removing from *Rome*,[4] to come and take Possession of his Son's Conquests, were we either so weak, or so miserable as to be conquer'd by such an Invader?

This is the Person who is now to be obtruded upon us; this is he for whom we are to exchange a Prince, who, during a Reign of eighteen Years, hath not stain'd a Scaffold with a single Drop of *English* Blood; (an Instance not to be parallel'd in any one Reign since the Conquest.)[5] Nor can his Enemies shew any one Example in his whole Reign, where any, even the lowest Subject, hath been oppressed in his Person, or deprived of his Property, by Means unauthoriz'd by the known Laws of this Realm.

But if the Sins of this Pretender's Forefathers, the Religion and

[1] A popular anglicism for the French king, in particular Louis XIV. See *TP* no. 1 (5 November 1745), below, p. 104.

[2] Alluding to the proclamation dated Rome, 23 November 1743 NS, under the OP's sign manual, which designated the YP as regent: 'We therefore esteem it for Our Service, and the Good of Our Kingdoms and Dominions, to nominate and appoint, as we hereby nominate, constitute and appoint, Our dearest Son Charles Prince of *Wales*, to be sole Regent of our Kingdoms of England, Scotland, and Ireland, and of all other Our Dominions during Our Absence'; text from *Historical Papers relating to the Jacobite Period*, ed. Allardyce (Aberdeen, 1895), i. 180–1; see also Browne, *History of the Highlands*, iii. 20.

[3] The YP's own declaration, dated Paris, 16 May 1745 NS, but printed at Edinburgh in July 1745 for Murray of Broughton, who distributed it, begins: 'By Virtue and Authority of the above Commission of Regency, granted unto Us by the King our Royal Father; We are now come to execute His Majesty's Will and Pleasure . . . We do therefore in His Majesty's Name, and pursuant to the Tenor of his several Declarations, hereby grant . . .'; text from *Historical Papers*, i. 182; Browne, iii. 65–7.

[4] London newspapers circulated reports that the OP was expected in France to lend more direct personal support to his son's undertaking; for example, *DA* of 25 September 1745. Such reports notwithstanding, the OP never left Rome. See 'General Introduction', above, p. xli.

[5] The stress on George II's lenity resembles that given by archbishop Herring in his speech at the formation of the Yorkshire Association on 24 September 1745: 'We are now bless'd with the mild Administration of a Just and Protestant King, who is of so strict an Adherence to the Laws of our Country, that not an Instance can be pointed out during his whole Reign, wherein he made the least Attempt upon the Liberty, or Property, or Religion, of a single Person'; first printed in the *London Gazette* of 24–8 September 1745, probably at Hardwicke's suggestion, and then widely reprinted (e.g., *DA* of 30 September 1745; a convenient text is in *GM*, xv (1745), 472. Herring had uttered similar sentiments in his *Sermon Preach'd at . . . York, September the 22d, 1745* (London, 1745), pp. 13–16. Fielding will repeat this praise of the king in *Gentleman & Alderman* (1747), p. 15, and *Proper Answer* (1747), p. 81. See also 'General Introduction', above, p. xxxv.

Principles in which he hath been educated, the popish Bigotry and civil Tyranny, which he hath always profess'd and practis'd, be not sufficient to raise our Terror and Detestation of his Name; there is yet another Reason behind, one more conclusive, if possible, against his Cause, than any I have yet urged. This Firebrand is not only the Instrument of *Rome* and *Spain*, but of *France* too: He brings not only papal Bulls, and *Spanish* Inquisitions, but *French* Gallies[1] and Bastiles[2] along with him.

If Popery and arbitrary Power, if the Destruction of our Religion and Constitution cannot alarm us, still the Apprehensions of *French* Government must be surely sufficient. Whatever the highest Degrees of Wickedness or Folly might prompt us to submit to under an absolute popish Monarch of our own, there is not, I hope, a single Person so base, as patiently to see his Country betrayed to be a *Province of France*, the certain, the inevitable Consequence of the Pretender's Success. True it is, that neither of these Powers have been yet able to land any Forces in this Kingdom; a happy Circumstance, for which we are only obliged to the excellent Disposition and Care of our Fleets:[3] For are they not known to have both Transports and Men ready for this Purpose?[4] Nay, was not that *French* Man of War, which was

---

[1] Like the 'Bastiles' and the Inquisition itself, an emblem of supposed catholic cruelties to protestants. Cf. the 'Postscript' of *A Faithful Account of the Cruelties Done to the French Protestants, On Board the French King's Gallies, On Account of the Reformed Religion* (London, 1700), p. 34: 'This Account was lately printed in Holland, and is confirmed by ... many Letters ... representing the worse than *Pagan Barbarities* done to our renowned Brethren in the *French Galleys*, who after the most cruel Persecution of 15 years remain glorious Confessors of the *reformed Religion*.'

[2] If meant in its extended sense of fortified 'prisons', this nominal usage antedates the earliest *OED* example by forty-five years.

[3] Contemporary estimates of the navy were by no means so laudatory, and Fielding's compliment here may have its political elements. His friend and sometime political mentor Dodington was treasurer of the navy, and the duke of Bedford, soon (if not yet) a 'princely' benefactor, was first lord of the admiralty and hence nominally responsible for the appointment in August of Admiral Vernon to command the Western Squadron. Vernon, celebrated by Fielding in *The Vernoniad* (1741) as the hero 'who greatly bore | Augusta's Flag to Porto Bello's Shore', had come up with a scheme for guarding the coasts with Folkestone cutters and other small ships, an expedient which some found serviceable and others, desperate. See Walpole to Mann, 20 September 1745, *Yale Walpole*, xix. 109–10. Fielding's praise notwithstanding, even in sympathetic quarters Bedford's task was described as 'to redress the infamous practices of our navy'; Leicester to Bedford, 2 August 1745, in *Correspondence of John, Fourth Duke of Bedford*, ed. Lord John Russell, i (London, 1842), 33. Among opposition politicians, including Pitt, it was commonplace to charge that the navy was being ruinously neglected in favor of the expensive land war. Alderman Heathcote, for one, called it 'a neglected, dishonoured, and ruined fleet'; letter to Marchmont, 6 September 1745, in *A Selection from the Papers of the Earls of Marchmont*, ed. Sir George Henry Rose, ii (London, 1831), 342.

[4] Cf. Walpole to Mann, 6 September 1745: 'Notice came yesterday, that there are ten thousand men, thirty transports and ten men of war at Dunkirk'; *Yale Walpole*, xix. 103. Throughout the autumn there were intermittent 'reports' in the London papers that the French were readying invasion forces.

providentially defeated by one of ours,[1] filled with both Men and Arms for his Service?[2]

Is *English* Liberty, or is *French* Slavery so little known, that it is necessary to expatiate a Moment on either? Shall I even be permitted to remind you of the Security, with which the Freedom, the Life, the Property of *Englishmen* are guarded by the Law? Can the greatest Man among us, even the King himself, take one of these from the poorest? Can any Man be imprisoned wrongfully, without present Redress, and future Satisfaction? Can he be punish'd without a Trial, without an unanimous Conviction, by twelve Men of his Equals, having been first accus'd on the Oaths of a Grand Jury of the like Number?[3] Is he then liable to any other Sentence, than that to which the express Letter of the Law adjudges him, a Sentence which the King can neither aggravate or alter?

Is his Property less safe than his Life? May he not enjoy it how he will, and give it to whom he pleases? Can any Man take from him an Acre, or a Shilling, but by a due Course[4] of Law, in which his Cause is to be determined by the same Jury of his Equals?

Perhaps the Slavery of *France*, though *too nearly our Neighbour*, may be less known, and her *Lettres de Cachet* may be a Word less understood than the *Habeas Corpus* Act.[5]

Give me Leave, therefore, to inform you, that the Person of a *Frenchman* is so far from being protected by their Laws from Imprisonment,

---

[1] The *Elizabeth*, an old ship that had been captured from the English in Queen Anne's reign, currently chartered from the ministry of marine by Walter Rutledge of Dunkirk, an Irish merchant and privateer. She was escorting the light frigate (*La du Teillay, La Doutelle*) which was carrying the YP to Scotland when they met up with the British man-of-war the *Lyon* (*Lion*) on 9 July 1745 off the Lizard. In the ensuing fight both the *Lyon* and the *Elizabeth* were heavily damaged, and the latter had to put back to Brest. The encounter was 'officially' described in the *London Gazette* of 20–3 July 1745; see also *DA* of 23 July. The early reports did not know either the identity or the mission of the ship which the *Elizabeth* was escorting. See also 'General Introduction', above, pp. xxx–xxxi, and *History*, below, p. 37.

[2] Contemporary estimates of what the *Elizabeth* was carrying differ widely. See *History*, below, pp. 36, 39, for Fielding's. *DA* of 3 August 1745 claimed she had on board £40,000 and arms for 'several thousand Men', as well as a company of volunteers ('Grassins de Mer') from the French navy; according to Bishop Forbes's sources, the *Elizabeth* carried a thousand stand of arms and 500 men; *Lyon in Mourning*, i. 284. Cf. also Mann to Walpole, 17 August 1745 NS, *Yale Walpole*, xix. 88. For a modern account, see John S. Gibson, *Ships of the '45* (London, 1967), pp. 7–16.

[3] Cf. *A Charge Delivered to the Grand Jury* (1749), p. 8: 'The Institution of Juries, Gentlemen, is a Privilege which distinguishes the Liberty of *Englishmen* from those of all other Nations . . . an Advantage, which is at present solely confined to this Country.' See also *TP* no. 3 (19 November 1745), below, p. 130 and *n.* 4.

[4] i.e., a judicial or justiciary proceeding. See *JJ* no. 29 (18 June 1748), p. 308.

[5] Fielding will define *lettre de cachet* in the next paragraph. The comparison of it to *habeas corpus* may have particular political point. The Habeas Corpus Act (31 Car. II, c. 2) had been suspended during the invasion scare of 1744 and was to be suspended again on 21 October 1745 (by 19 Geo. II, c. 1), shortly after publication of the *Serious Address*. The opposition viewed its suspension as a form of political repression; see Coxe, *Pelham*, ii. 348–9; and *Gentleman & Alderman* (1747), p. 16.

that they are every Day liable, without any Crime, nay, *without any Accusation*, to be seized by the Authority of a *Lettre de Cachet*, (a Warrant under the King's Signet, backed by a Secretary of State)[1] and conveyed not only to Prisons, but *Dungeons*, where their Friends and Relations neither know the Places of their Confinement, nor if they did, would they have any Method of obtaining their Discharge, (however innocent) nor even of procuring Access to them.

And as they may be sent to these Prisons without any Accusation, so may they be detained there without any Trial, often for many Years, and sometimes to the End of their Lives, however long Nature may be able to struggle with all the Miseries, Wants, and Inclemencies of a noisome Dungeon.

Nor is this Cruelty exerted *rarely*, on *high Exigencies of State*, or *against dangerous and traiterous Persons only*; but on the slightest Occasions, and to satisfy the private Resentment of one Man against another. Lettres de Cachet (says a celebrated *French* Writer)* sont les Armes que certaines Gens emploient en France contre leurs Enemies.[2] *These Letters are the Arms which several[3] Persons in* France *employ against their Enemies*. The Jealousy of an amorous Intrigue hath frequently brought on this Mischief: This an *English* Gentleman, well known in the World, experienced; who was confined seven Years in the *Bastile*, by one of these Letters, on Account of an Amour.[4] Nor need this be the Jealousy of a Minister of State, a Prince of the Blood, or of any great Man; that of a *Valet de Chambre* to any of them will be sufficient; nay, or of any other Person, who by Interest or Money can purchase one of these Letters; which may be had from the lowest Court-Dependant: So common are they, that in the Administration of Cardinal *Fleury*, the gentlest and mildest Prime Minister which *France* ever knew,[5] no less than FORTY-

* *Richelet*.[6]

---

[1] Cf. Pierre Richelet, *Dictionnaire de la langue françoise, ancienne et moderne* (Amsterdam, 1732), ii. 256, *s.v.* 'cachet': 'C'est une lettre du Roi, contresignée par un Secrétaire d'État.' That Fielding's definition comes from Richelet is made clear by the references to him below.

[2] Richelet, *Dictionnaire*, ii. 256, prints 'ennemis' for 'Enemies'.

[3] Fielding mistranslates here: *certaines* means 'some' or 'certain'.   [4] Not identified.

[5] André-Hercule de Fleury (1653–1743), bishop of Fréjus (1698), preceptor to the Dauphin Louis XV, cardinal (1726), was *de facto* prime minister from 1726 to 1743. Cf. *Memoirs of the Life and Administration of the late Andrew-Hercules de Fleury* (London, 1743), pp. 90, 99: 'But perhaps the Cardinal's capital Fault was, his desiring to engross Power. ... The late Cardinal *Fleury* was undoubtedly as absolute a Minister as ever govern'd *France*'; also *The Perseis: or, Secret Memoirs for a History of Persia*, 2nd ed. (London, 1745), pp. 28–31, 173–5. It was more common for Englishmen to praise Fleury for his pacific diplomacy and his honesty. See Pope, 'The First Satire of the Second Book of Horace', l. 75, and 'Epilogue to the Satires ... Dialogue I', l. 51.

[6] César Pierre Richelet (1631–98), French poet, translator, editor, and grammarian, published his dictionary in 1680.

EIGHT THOUSAND of these Letters were granted,[1] which were sold by his Officers and Servants to any who would pay for them; so that well may the abovementioned Writer say of them, *That they make the* Abbés *and* Courtiers *tremble*.[2]

Nor are the Lives of these miserable People more secure than their Liberties. As to all the lower Sort, they hold their Lives in a manner at the Will of their Masters; who, if they think proper to kill them, are seldom in more Danger than of a moderate Mulct; it being inconsistent with *French* Politeness to hang a Gentleman for the Death of a Slave or a Peasant.

As to their legal Method of destroying Persons, take the following Instance. A *Gascon*, in the Year 1713, killed an Officer of the Finances. It appeared on the Evidence, that it was done in the Defence of his Wife, who was assaulted and very rudely treated by the Officer; on this he was acquitted. Upon Application of the superior Officers of the Finances, (the Craft being in danger) the Cause was try'd over again before other Judges, by the King's special Mandate; and the poor *Gascon*, notwithstanding he made the same good Defence, was convicted and executed.[3]

Inferior Punishments (the Gallies for Instance) are inflicted often in a summary Manner, without any Form of Trial; and many are condemned to them for Life by Order of the King, or of the Secretary of State.

Nor is it only in civil Matters, from Jealousy of State, that these Severities are exercised; the Clergy are allowed the Use of them against the *Jansenists*; that is, against those of their Countrymen who dare to maintain the Liberties of the *Gallican Church, in Opposition to the illegal Claims of the Pope*.[4] Such a wicked League will there always be in Roman Catholic Countries, between ecclesiastical and civil Tyranny.

[1] The authority for this figure has not been identified. It may in fact be low; see below, *n.* 4. For the quite varied and not altogether repressive uses to which *lettres de cachet* were put in the 18th century, see Frantz Funck-Brentano, *Les Lettres de Cachet à Paris . . . Suivie d'une Liste des Prisonniers de la Bastille, 1659–1789* (Paris, 1903), pp. ix–xxx.

[2] Richelet, *Dictionnaire*, ii. 16: 'Les Lettres de cachet font trembler les Abez & les courtisans.'

[3] Not identified.

[4] Cf. Richelet, *Dictionnaire*, ii. 103, *s.v.* 'lettres fermées': 'Si tu es Janseniste, tu auras bientôt une lettre de cachet.' A recrudescence of anti-Jansenism was set off by the papal bull known as 'Unigenitus' (1713), in which Clement XI condemned the basic Jansenist doctrines, and culminated in the temporary registering of the bull as a *loi d'état* (1730) and in the activities of the *convulsionnaires* at the tomb of François de Paris in the early 1730s. Of the liberation of prisoners after the death of Louis XIV Saint-Simon wrote, 'Presque tous ces prisonniers l'étoient sous prétexte de jansénisme ou de la Constitution'; *Journal du Marquis de Dangeau . . . avec les Additions Inédites du Duc de Saint-Simon*, xvi (Paris, 1859), 171 *n.*, dated 10 September 1715; also *Mémoirs de Saint-Simon*, xxix (Paris, 1918), 43. Cf. Davy de Chavigné, 'Projet d'un monument sur l'emplacement de la Bastille' (1789): 'il suffit de rappeler que la Bastille n'a cessé d'être remplie, pendant la douce administration du cardinal de Fleury, et que plus de cinquante mille lettres de cachet ont été expédiées pour la seule affaire de la bulle "Unigenitus"'; as quoted in Fernand Bournon, *La Bastille*, Histoire Générale de Paris (Paris, 1893), p. 178. See also Georges Hardy, *Le Cardinal Fleury et Le Mouvement Janséniste* (Paris, 1925), 'Introduction' and chs. iii and v.

If their Lives and Liberties are so insecure, we ought not to suppose their Properties to be in a better Situation. And first, no Man in the Kingdom (of what Quality soever) dares cut his Corn, when ripe, till the King's Officers have chosen what Part they will receive for his Service, and this at their own Price:[1] A Restraint of the utmost Inconvenience to the poor Farmer, who is obliged to bribe these Officers to do their Duty, which, in order to exact Money of these Wretches, they will often neglect till the Corn becomes rotten on the Ground.[2]

And how easy it is to deprive them even of this precarious Property, may be gathered from the Conduct of their Courts of Judicature; which, whenever a Cause is to be tried between a great Man and his Inferior, are always filled with the Nobility, who never fail by their Presence (as their Intent visibly is) to influence and awe the Judges by whose Voices the Cause is determined.

Instances of this kind happen almost every Day; indeed they are as common there in Decisions of private Property, as Examples of Corruption in *England* at Elections in the most corrupt Borough of the Kingdom.[3]

Lastly, as to their Taxations: The Method is in all their Provinces, that whereas a certain Sum is arbitrarily demanded by the Court of the Province, the *Intendant* (an Officer appointed by the Court) hath Power to levy it in what Manner he pleases; a Power which is always exercised with the greatest Oppression and Partiality.[4] Such are the Cruelties with which the levying these Taxes are attended in this present War, that there is scarce a Peasant in *France* who hath a Bed left to lie upon; and to such Miseries are they reduced, as I am assured by a Gentleman just come over from thence, that by Filth, Famine and Grief, *they have almost lost the human Countenance*.[5]

---

[1] Since by 1745 royal tithing (*dîme royale*) and nonecclesiastical imposts in kind (*en nature*) had been abandoned in France, and since he reserves comment on French 'Taxations' for later, Fielding may refer here to royal regulations of the grain trade by compulsory sales and price-fixing. Contemporary economic theory made much of the grain trade as a basis for comparing the workings of regulated and nonregulated economies. See Louis-Paul Abeille, 'Réflexions sur la Police des Grains en France et en Angleterre' (1764), reprinted in *Collection des Économistes et des Réformateurs Sociaux de la France* (Paris, 1911), pp. 104–6.

[2] This was in fact a common complaint. See Marcel Marion, *Histoire Financière de la France depuis 1715*, reprint ed. (New York, n.d.), i. 87.

[3] Cf. *Gentleman & Alderman* (1747), p. 28: 'As to the Corruption practised at Elections, it is so known and certain, that I should think no Man deserved the least Credit who denied it.'

[4] Although the intendants did have considerable fiscal autonomy, it was common to exaggerate their power. See Henri, comte de Boulainvilliers, *État de la France*, 'nouvelle édition' (Londres, 1752), 'Préface de l'Auteur', pp. lxxi–xc. Baker, item no. 81, lists a 1736 Paris publication with this title among Fielding's books but makes no attribution.

[5] Not identified. The curious stress on the 'human Countenance' might suggest Hogarth, whose 'Autobiographical Notes' do describe a later trip to France. But Hogarth is not known to have made a trip there in 1745.

And this, Gentlemen, is the Constitution, this is the Government now endeavoured to be obtruded upon us, and which is to rage here with all the Aggravation with which the worst Governments exercise their Tyranny over a dependant Province.

This then being the Civil Exchange we are to make, let us now examine the Religious. And here I shall omit the Advantages which, in a spiritual Sense, our Religion hath over popish Heathenism and Innovation; that Task hath been often executed by much more able Pens: It is sufficient for my present Purpose to set before you the Horrors of Popery in a temporal Light only.

On this Head, I may be excused from an unnecessary Panegyric on that Freedom with which all Men in this Nation are suffered to enjoy their own Consciences, and to serve their God in what Manner they please.

How different from, indeed how opposite to this is the Temper of Popery, even in *France* itself, where the Malignity and Fury of that Religion rages with somewhat less Violence than in those Countries from whence the religious Model brought over to us by the Pretender must be derived. Hear a learned and ingenious Writer*, speaking of *Marseilles* in the Year 1686, at a Time when *James* II. was attempting to introduce this very Religion into *England*.

"The Instances (says he) I saw, are so much beyond all the common Measures of Barbarity and Cruelty, that I confess they ought not to be believed, unless I could give more positive Proofs of them than are fitting now to be brought forth; and the Particulars that I could tell you are such, that if I should relate them, with the necessary Circumstances of Time, Place, and Persons, these might be so fatal to many that are in the Power of their Enemies, that my Regard to them restrains me. In short, I do not think that in any Age there ever was such a Violation of all that is sacred, either with relation to God or Man: And what I saw and knew there, from the first Hand, hath so confirmed all the Ideas that I had taken from Books, of the Cruelty of that Religion, that I hope the Impression that this hath made upon me, shall never end but with my Life. The Applauses that the whole Clergy

* Dr. *Burnet*.[1]

---

[1] Gilbert Burnet (1643–1715), bishop of Salisbury and 'whig' historian, of whose work Fielding seems to have made frequent use. Upon the accession of James II, Burnet, who had fallen into disfavor, left England and traveled through France, Italy, and Switzerland, publishing (1686) an account of these travels in a series of letters to Robert Boyle, under the title *Some Letters, containing an Account of what seemed most remarkable in Switzerland, Italy, &c*. The aim of the work, according to Burnet, was to expose the tyranny of popery subsequent to the revocation of the Edict of Nantes (1685).

give to this Way of Proceeding, the many Panegyricks that are already writ upon it, of which, besides the more pompous ones that appear at *Paris*, there are Numbers writ by smaller Authors in every Town of any Note there; and the Sermons, that are all Flights of Flattery upon this Subject, are such evident Demonstrations of their Sense of this Matter, that what is now on foot may well be termed, The Act of the whole Clergy of *France*; which yet hath been hitherto esteemed the most moderate Part of the *Roman* Communion. If any are more moderate than others, and have not so far laid off the Human Nature, as to go intirely into those bloody Practices, yet they dare not own it, but whisper it in secret, as if it were half Treason; but for the greater Part, they do not only magnify all that is done, but they animate even the Dragoons to higher Degrees of Rage: And there was such a Heat spread over all the Country upon this Occasion, that one could not go into any Ordinary, or mix in any promiscuous Conversation, without finding such Effects of it, that it was not easy for such as were touched with the least Degree of Compassion for the Miseries that the poor Protestants suffered, to be a Witness to the Insultings that they must meet with in all Places."[1]

Again, a little afterward:

"I must take the Liberty to add one thing to you, that I do not see that the *French* King is to be so much blamed in this Matter, as his Religion, which, without Question, *obligeth him to extirpate Hereticks, and not to keep his Faith with them*; so that, instead of censuring him, I must only lament his being bred up in a Religion that doth certainly oblige him to *divest himself of Humanity, and to violate his Faith, whensoever the Cause of his Church and of his Religion require it*; or if there is any thing in this Conduct, that cannot be entirely justified from the Principles of that Religion, it is this, that he doth not put the Hereticks to Death out of hand, but forceth them, by all the Extremities possible, to sign an Abjuration, that all the World must needs see is done against their Consciences; and being the only End of their Miseries, those that would think any Sort of Death a happy Conclusion of their Sufferings, seeing no Prospect of such a glorious Issue out of their Trouble, are prevailed on, by the many lingering Deaths, of which they see no End, to make Shipwreck of the Faith. This Appearance of Mercy, in not putting Men to Death, doth truly verify the Character that *Solomon* giveth of the *tender Mercies of the Wicked, that they are cruel*."[2]

---

[1] Taken from 'The Fifth Letter', *Some Letters* (Rotterdam, 1687), pp. 254–6, dated 'Nimmegen', 20 May 1686. Baker, item no. 77, lists the 1687 Rotterdam edition among Fielding's books.

[2] Proverbs 12: 10: but the tender mercies of the wicked are cruel. The preceding paragraph is a quotation from *Some Letters*, p. 257, with some italics added and some omitted.

But what is the State of Popery in *Italy* and *Spain*, where the Inquisition flourishes, that Inquisition which we are to expect here, could this *Italian* Pretender, by the joint Assistance of *Spain*, succeed in his Attempts: For it is the only Interest (as we shall prove by and by) that *Spain* can propose from the Enterprize wherein she is embarked.

I will here present you with a very short Sketch of this Inquisition, every Word of which I have extracted from the famous History of *Philip à Limborch*,[1] after having recommended the Book at large to the Perusal of such as are able to procure it.[2]

The Judge of this hellish Court, who is called the Inquisitor, is appointed by the Pope, and is always a Person duly qualified for the Exercise of such a Power, which is almost totally arbitrary: For though (says *Limborch*)[3] he is bound to certain general Laws, yet many things are left to his Pleasure. Besides, the very Application of the Laws to particular Cases which come before the Inquisition, and also the Method of Proceeding and drawing a Confession from the Prisoners, depends very much on their Will.

In order to bring any Person before this Court, no direct Charge is necessary; it is sufficient, that the Accuser relates to the Inquisitor, that there is such a Report, and that it hath frequently come to the Ears of the Inquisitor from grave and reputable Persons, that such a one hath done or said some Things against the Faith; and by this Means (says he) the Process is carried on.[4] Now, as to the Witnesses against these Criminals, in favour of the Faith, all Persons, even such as are not allowed in other Tribunals, are admitted; nay, even perjur'd Persons, who having taken an Oath before the Inquisition to speak the Truth, have forsworn themselves by concealing it, and would afterwards correct themselves, and swear back again; nay, all other infamous Persons whatsoever.

The Method of examining these Witnesses is as iniquitous as the admitting them; for at this Examination none are present but the Witness himself and the Judge, the Writer, and two Assistants to the Inquisitor; nay, sometimes these two are omitted at the whole Examination,

---

[1] *The History of the Inquisition. By Philip à Limborch, Professor of Divinity among the Remonstrants. Translated into English by Samuel Chandler*, 2 vols. London, 1731 [1732].

[2] Cf. the 'Preface' of *A Brief Representation of the Cruel and Barbarous Proceedings against Protestants in the Inquisition. Extracted from The History of the Inquisition, written by . . . Philip à Limborch* (London, 1734), pp. v–vi, speaking of the original *History*: 'but the Unhappiness is, that both the *Bulk* and the *Price* of it is so great, that the *meanest People* are little, if at all, the better for it: They cant spare so much Time, as it will necessarily require to read six or seven Hundred Pages *in Quarto*; nor fifteen or sixteen Shillings for the Purchase of it; if they cou'd.'

[3] The remainder of this paragraph is quoted, with minor modificiations, from Limborch's *History*, ed. cit., ii. 107 (Bk. iv, ch. i).

[4] To this point the paragraph is a mixed periphrasis and quotation of Limborch, ii. 130 (Bk. iv, ch. vi). The remainder of the paragraph derives similarly from ii. 136, 139–40 (Bk. iv, ch. ix).

and are only call'd in to attest the Witness's signing his Deposition. And how doth their Presence (says my Author) make any thing to the Defence of the Criminal? Or what doth it avail him, that his Accusers are known to Persons whom he himself knows nothing of, and who are forbidden to discover any thing after?[1]

The Prisoner having been kept in Dungeons and in Irons, and having been accus'd as above, is at length brought before his Judge, where being under all the Circumstances of Horror, he is privately examin'd before his Judge, and a Notary only: Here every Art is made use of to entrap and ensnare him into a Confession,[2] by which, if they do not prevail, they have usually Recourse to Torture, the last and greatest Argument on the Side of Popery. Of the Manner of this Torture, as it is very singular, I shall give a short Account from the aforesaid Author, after having premis'd, that the slightest Proof imaginable renders the Criminal liable to undergo it.

The Place of Torture in the *Spanish* Inquisition is generally an underground and very dark Room, to which one enters thro' several Doors: There is a Tribunal erected in it, in which the Inquisitor, Inspector and Secretary sit; when the Candles are lighted, and the Person to be tortured, brought in, the Executioner, who was waiting for the Order, makes an astonishing and dreadful Appearance; he is cover'd all over with a black Linen Garment down to his Feet, and tied close to his Body; his Head and Face are all hid with a long black Cowl, only two little Holes being left in it for him to see through. All this is intended to strike the miserable Wretch with greater Terror in Mind and Body, when he sees himself going to be tortured by the Hands of one, who, thus, looks like the very Devil.[3]

The Torture being prepar'd, the Criminal, having been exhorted, or rather insulted over by the Priests, is delivered to the Torturer to be stript.

This[4] Stripping is perform'd without any Regard to Humanity or Honour, not only to Men, but to Women and Virgins, though the most Virtuous and Chaste, of whom they have sometimes many in their Prisons; for they cause them to be stript, even to their very Shifts, which

---

[1] Paraphrased and quoted from ii. 144–5 (Bk. iv, ch. xi).

[2] To this point the paragraph is a compression of ii. 154–61 (Bk. iv, ch. xiv). The remainder is Fielding's comment.

[3] This paragraph is quoted fairly exactly from ii. 217–18 (Bk. iv, ch. xxix), where Limborch himself is quoting one of his authorities, Gonsalvius Montanus, *Sanctae Inquisitionis Hispanicae Artes* (Heidelbergae, 1567), pp. 65–6.

[4] This paragraph quotes, with some excisions of references to the *pudenda*, from ii. 219–20 (Bk. iv, ch. xxix), where Limborch quotes from Gonsalvius, op. cit., p. 67.

they afterwards take off, and then put on them straight Linen Drawers, and make their Arms naked quite up to their Shoulders. As to the Torture (which they call Quassation)[1] it is thus perform'd: The Prisoner hath his Hands bound behind his Back, and Weights tied to his Feet, and then he is drawn up on high, till his Head reaches the very Pully; he is kept hanging in this Manner for some time, that by the Greatness of the Weight hanging at his Feet, all his Joints and Limbs may be dreadfully stretched, and on a sudden he is let down with a Jerk, by the Slackening the Rope, but kept from coming quite to the Ground, by which terrible Shake, his Arms and Legs are all disjointed, whereby he is put to the most exquisite Pain; the Shock which he receives by the sudden Stop of his Fall, and the Weight of his Feet stretching his whole Body more intensely and cruelly.

There are many other Kinds of Torture, too tedious to be transcribed here: Two, however, for their singular Cruelty, should not be omitted.

The first is this:[2] There is a wooden Bench, which they call the wooden Horse, made hollow like a Trough, so as to contain a Man lying on his Back at full Length, about the Middle of which there is a round Bar laid a-cross, upon which the Back of the Person is plac'd, so that he lies on the Bar, instead of being let into the Bottom of the Trough, with his Feet much higher than his Head; as he is lying in this Posture, his Arms, Thighs and Shins are tied round with small Cords or Strings, which being drawn with Screws at proper Distances from each other, cut into the very Bones, so as no longer to be discerned. Besides this, the Torturer throws over his Mouth and Nostrils a thin Cloth, so that he is scarce able to breathe through them, and in the mean while a small Stream of Water, like a Thread, not Drop by Drop, falls from on high upon the Mouth of the Person lying in this miserable Condition, and so easily sinks down the thin Cloth to the Bottom of his Throat; so that there is no Possibility of breathing, his Mouth being stopp'd with Water, and his Nostrils with the Cloth; thus the poor Wretch is in the same Agonies, as Persons ready to die, and breathing out their last. When this Cloth is drawn out of his Throat, as it often is, that he may answer to the Questions, it is all wet with Water and Blood, and is like pulling his Bowels through his Mouth. The other Torture, which my Author says is *peculiar to this Tribunal*, is called the Fire; and this is, by holding a large Chafing-dish of Charcoal close to the

---

[1] Chandler's translation (ii. 219) has 'Squassation'.

[2] The subsequent description of the two tortures (the bench and the fire) is quoted fairly exactly from ii. 222–3 (Bk. iv, ch. xxix), which is based on Gonsalvius, pp. 76, 77.

tortur'd Person's Feet, being first greas'd with Lard, that the Heat may more quickly pierce thro' them.

I now proceed to their Punishments, (for what you have hitherto heard, is only their Method of Trial) and these are in Number seven:[1] First, Confiscation of Goods; and this is so extremely severe, not only on the Criminals, but on their Relations and Heirs, that even a Daughter's Portion, tho' paid before, is to be revok'd and confiscated; the second is the Corruption of Blood, and disinheriting their Heirs; third, they are render'd infamous; fourth, they are deprived of all natural Right; fifth, they are imprisoned; sixth, they are laid under the Bann, *i.e.* put out of the Protection of the Law, and any one may kill them with Impunity; seventh, and last Punishment, is Death, and that by burning, or indeed sometimes rather roasting them alive; for all these Punishments are inflicted with the utmost Severity. Nay, sometimes (says my Author)[2] this Punishment of Burning is heightened by another Kind of Cruelty. In *Spain* and the *Netherlands*, lest they should speak to the Spectators, when brought to the Stake, and piously testify their Constancy, they were gagged with an Iron Instrument; so that in the Midst of their Torments they could utter only an inarticulate Sound. And if they could invent any thing more terrible, they would not fail to use it against Hereticks: This *Carena* testifies,[3] affirming, that the Custom of punishing Hereticks with Fire is most reasonable, *because Burning is the most terrible Death, and therefore the most grievous of all Crimes ought to be punished with it; so that if any Punishment more terrible than this could be found out, it ought to be inflicted on Hereticks; and also because by this Means the Heretick and his Crime is more speedily blotted out from the Remembrance of Mankind.*

My Author concludes his Chapter of their Punishments in the following Words.[4]

"Thus we see, that there is no Kind of Punishment that can possibly be invented, but is enacted against Hereticks, and that greater Gentleness is used towards Thieves, Traitors and Rebels, those Enemies of Mankind, than towards miserable Hereticks; who, endeavouring to worship God with a pure Conscience, and regulate their Lives by the Gospel Rule, *yet oppose some Doctrines of the Church of* Rome, *which they are*

---

[1] The descriptions of the seven punishments are extracted and condensed from Limborch, ii. 15–27 (Bk. iii, ch. ii).

[2] The remainder of this paragraph is taken directly from Limborch, ii. 27 (Bk. iii, ch. ii).

[3] Caesar Carena, *Tractatus de Officio Sanctissimae Inquisitionis* (Lugduni, 1669), *tit.* 13, 1. *Num.* 7, as cited and quoted by Limborch, ii. 27. In the 'Catalogue of Authors' prefixed to his *History* Limborch identifies Carena as 'Auditor of Cardinal *Camporeus*, Judge Conservator, Counsellor, and Advocate Fiscal, of the Holy Office' (p. xii).

[4] The quotation is from Limborch, ii. 27 (Bk. iii, ch. ii). The italics are Fielding's.

persuaded are contrary to the Gospel; and that it is a much more grievous Offence in that Church, to oppose certain Opinions by the clear Light of the Word of God, and to reject certain Pharisaical Superstitions, than openly contemn the Divine Commands by an impious and profane Life, and vilely to dishonour the most Holy Name of God."

This is the Temper of Popery! Of that Religion in which the Pretender was educated, which he hath always profess'd, to which he is the most devoted Bigot! This is the Religion now practised in those Countries, where he hath been bred, by whose Assistance he now invades these King-doms! And this is the Religion, which by their Assistance is to be intro-duced here: A Consequence which would so certainly attend his Success, that it is almost capable of Demonstration; first, from the Nature and Temper of the Religion itself, which regards the Professors of all other Religions to be in a State of Damnation; that no Faith is to be held with them; that they are to be extirpated with Fire and Sword; Methods which have not only been prescribed, but practised in the most barbarous and violent Manner, against the most binding Laws, and the most solemn Agreements; witness the two famous Massacres in *France* and in *Ireland*, the first of which was executed in Consequence of a Treaty made to no other Purpose, than to decoy the *Hugonots* to their Destruction;[1] the other in the midst of profound Peace,[2] when the Papists enjoy'd the private Exercise of their Religion, and all the civil Protection that could be given to any Subjects. In one of these, no less than a Hundred thousand, in the other at least Forty thousand *unhappy Protestants were in the dead of Night surpriz'd in their Sleep, and murder'd without Mercy or Exception, for the Sake of Religion only**. And this not by Thieves and Robbers, but religious

* *Thuanus, Mezeray, Rapin* and *Whitlock*.[3]

[1] The so-called St Bartholomew's Day massacre of 24 August 1572, assented to by Charles IX under pressure from his mother (Catherine de Médicis) and the Guise faction. According to *A Rela-tion of the Barbarous and Bloody Massacre of about an Hundred Thousand Protestants, Begun at Paris, and Carried on over all France by the Papists, in the Year 1572* (London, 1745), p. 10: 'the King was advised to set on foot a Treaty of Peace; not so much out of a Design to quiet Matters . . . as to ensnare the Protestants into some fatal Trap, in which they being catched, might be safely and easily destroyed'. The treaty had as its 'first Bait' the marriage of the king's sister, Marguerite de Valois, to the huguenot Henry of Navarre, an event which attracted many leading huguenots to Paris. The *Relation* was advertised as published, by *General Advertiser* of 10 October and *London Evening Post* of 8–10 October 1745, which might possibly suggest a *terminus a quo* for the 'second edition' of the *Serious Address*. However, the *Relation* derives from at least as early as 1678 (it is often attributed to Burnet), and there were of course many other sources for the imputation of planned treachery.

[2] On St Ignatius' Day, 23 October 1641, to use the somewhat overprecise dating cited in *Great Britain's Memorial against the Pretender and Popery*, 9th ed. (London, [1745]) p. 16, where it is also estimated that 'forty or fifty thousand *English* Protestants' were killed on that day alone. In *TP* no. 3 (19 November 1745) Cooper advertised Sir John Temple's *The Irish Rebellion: Or, A History of the Attempts of the Irish Papists to extirpate the Protestants in the Kingdom of Ireland; together with the barbarous Cruelties and bloody Massacres which ensued thereupon.*

[3] Thuanus (Jacques Auguste de Thou [1553–1617]), *Historiarum Sui Temporis . . . Libri Centum*

Cut-throats, who thought that by spilling the Blood of Heretics they wash'd away their own Sins. Secondly, The extreme Bigotry of this Pretender, who must consequently hold all these Tenets in the highest and strongest Degree. Thirdly, From the Parties who espouse his Cause, particularly from the Cabals of the Court of *Rome*, where the Restoration of this Family hath been the favourite Scheme ever since their Expulsion; nay, why else should the Catholics themselves, in this Country, have ever ventur'd their Lives and Fortunes in his Cause? Why should they even wish well to it, since all, who have any Understanding among them, know they are sacrificing their Liberties? As to a bare Toleration of their Religion, they have it already in the fullest Manner by Connivance.[1] The absolute Establishment of their Religion, and Extirpation of Heresy, is and must be their only Motive; and we may trust to the Assurances they have of effecting it. Lastly, from Experience; for what greater Security, what Promises more solemn, can this Pretender give, than his Father did before him? How he kept those Promises, hath been mention'd already.

If we want more Instances,

Can this Nation hope for better legal Securities for the Toleration of its Religion under a Catholic Prince, than the *French* Protestants had for the Toleration of theirs by the Edict of *Nantz*?[2] And yet did not *Lewis* XIV. revoke that Edict, though it was the Act of his Grandfather, a Prince whom he always affected to make his Model and Example in Government?[3] Can

---

Triginta Octo . . . , ed. S. Buckley (London, 1733), iii. 145: 'proditumque a multis, plus xxx hominum CIↄ toto regno in his tumultibus varia peste extincta; quamvis aliquanto minorem numerum credo.' François Eudes de Mézeray, *Histoire de France, depuis Faramond jusqu'à maintenant* (Paris, 1643–51), ii. 1107, states that in two months no fewer than 25,000 persons were ravaged. Paul Rapin de Thoyras, *History of England*, trans. Nicholas Tindal (London, 1732), ii. 385, cites an estimate that 'above forty thousand *English* Protestants were massacred by the *Irish*'. Bulstrode Whitelocke, *Memorials of the English Affairs* (London, 1682), pp. 45–50, describes the alleged atrocities without estimating casualties. These four works, in the editions cited, are listed among Fielding's books by Baker, items nos. 439, 640, 308, and 430, respectively.

[1] Fielding here takes note of the fact that except during periods of perceived emergency civil authorities were reluctant to implement the considerable body of anticatholic legislation which had accumulated since Elizabethan times. On 5 September 1745 George II had signed a proclamation for putting into effect the laws against papists and nonjurors; *London Gazette* of 3–7 September 1745. Another royal proclamation, dated 6 December 1745, 'For putting the Laws into Execution against Jesuits and Popish Priests', noted the earlier proclamation and said it was not being enforced; *London Gazette* of 3–7 December 1745. See also *Dialogue*, below, p. 97 and *n*.

[2] The Edict of Nantes (1598), promulgated by Henry IV, guaranteed to French protestants freedom of conscience, rights of public worship in restricted places, social and political equality, retention of fortified towns at that time in their possession, and certain state subsidies of their religious costs.

[3] The revocation (1685) abrogated the residual religious and civil liberties of French protestants, whose political rights had already been annulled by Richelieu and Louis XIII in 1629. For English protestants of its time the revocation seemed as if it might bear on the challenge James II was mounting against the Anglican exclusivity.

any Prince be laid under stronger Restraints by the freest Subjects, than the Emperors of *Germany* have been by their Capitulations, and by the Treaty of *Munster*?[1] And yet how ill have these Capitulations been kept with regard to the Protestants! The Genius of Popery will break thro' all Restraints; the most watchful Care cannot prevent it; and yet, were that the only Evil, what a terrible Misfortune is it in Government, for a Nation to be always distrusting its Sovereign! But Instances are numberless, that no Precautions can save a People under this Circumstance. It is but lately, that the Palatinate, by the Failure of the Protestant Line, hath come under a Popish Prince. Have we forgot how many *Palatines* were forc'd to take Refuge here against the Rage of popish Persecution, no longer ago than in the Reign of Queen *Anne*?[2] How cruelly, how perfidiously, were the *Bohemian* and *Hungarian* Protestants used by their Sovereigns,[3] almost to the Ruin of the *Austrian* Family. And I pray God, that the great Services they are now doing the present Queen,[4] may not

---

[1] As part of the peace of Westphalia concluding the Thirty Years' War, the treaty of Münster (1648) provided that the chief imperial institutions were henceforth to be composed on a footing of religious equality; that religious disputes were to be decided by arbitration and not by simple majority rule; that Calvinists were to be admitted to the religious peace of Augsburg (1555); that the citizens of a state were no longer required automatically to adopt the religion of their ruler (*cujus regio ejus religio*); that dissidents in religion should be allowed the right of private worship; and that protestant administrations would be admitted to the imperial Diet with full voting rights.

[2] In the years 1708-9, particularly after passage of the general naturalization bill (7 Anne, c. 5; *Statutes of the Realm*, ix. 63) in March 1709, more than 10,000 Palatine Germans emigrated to England. The Elector Palatine, Duke William of Neuburg, was a catholic and anxious to convert his protestant subjects. Anne had earlier (1702) responded to an appeal from electoral princes and imperial states of the protestant religion to protect the Palatines from religious persecution. *A Brief History of the Poor Palatine Refugees, Lately Arriv'd in England* (London, 1709), pp. 23-5, reprints 'The Palatine Case', which emphasizes the devastation caused by French incursions into their lands. The modern assessment is that poverty, not persecution, was the major motive for Palatine emigration, and that they chose England because they were promised resettlement in the colonies. See H. T. Dickinson, 'The Poor Palatines and the Parties', *EHR*, lxxxii (1967), 464-85.

[3] Referring to the deprotestantization of these estates resulting from the counterreformation and, in particular, the Habsburg encroachments in the 17th century. In the reign of James I the Bohemian 'question' provoked great popular excitement in England, largely because Frederick V, Elector Palatine and James's son-in-law, was widely perceived as a protestant champion. When Frederick yielded his newly acquired crown in Bohemia (1620) in the face of Spanish military intervention, parliament urged James to go to war if necessary. Pym sounded the popular note when he spoke of the 'religion which is being martyred in Bohemia' (quoted in J. V. Polišensky, *The Thirty Years War*, trans. Robert Evans [London, 1971], p. 163). James demurred, and according to a contemporary satire, for each health drunk to the king in the taverns, there were ten drunk to the protestant princes abroad; 'Tom Tell-Troath, or a free Discourse touching the Manners of the Time', reprinted in *Somers Tracts*, ed. Scott (London, 1809), ii. 472.

[4] Maria Theresa (1717-80), archduchess of Austria, queen of Hungary and Bohemia (1740-80), titular head of the Habsburgs, and a catholic. Earlier in its intermittent war with Austria, Prussia had overrun most of Bohemia and had even sacked Prague itself. The Hungarian Diet of 1741 had pledged a *levée en masse* in support of Maria Theresa, and Hungarian forces had been instrumental in expelling Prussia from its Bohemian conquests of 1744. During May and June 1745 English newspapers carried reports of considerable Hungarian military activity; see, for example, *DA* of 25 June 1745. Fielding's vehemence in this case comes from the fact that in the war of the Austrian

be forgot hereafter, as those of the *Vaudois*[1] were by the Duke of *Savoy*, if the Jesuits ever regain that Ascendant over her Councils, as they had over those of that Prince, though he was otherwise a very wise Man![2] But how much more certain will be the Infraction of any legal Restraints, under a Prince coming in by Force of Arms, by the Assistance of popish Powers, who will consider this Nation as a conquer'd Country, conquer'd not only for him, but for his Lord and Protector the Pope. To dream of Security under such an Invader, is like setting open our Doors to a Highwayman, and trusting to his Honour and Conscience not to rob us. Nay, it is more absurd; for a Highwayman is not bound in Honour or Conscience to rob us, whereas the Pretender is bound by both, to destroy our Religion and Liberties: His Conscience tells him he must do the one, his Engagements with *France* oblige him to do the other. For till we are enslaved, *France* very well knows she cannot be Mistress of *Europe*, and therefore she uses this Tool to do that Work for her, which all her own Power cannot perform.

But should this great Work be once effected, let us never hope for another Deliverance.[3] If we give up these great Purchases of our Ancestors, our Posterity will never be able to regain them. It will, indeed, put a final End to the Protestant Religion, as well as to Liberty, in *Europe*.

In what Light, therefore, can we see this Measure of our Enemies to introduce such a Government and such a Religion, but as the highest

Succession Maria Theresa was an ally of England, which was paying her increased (and unpopular) subsidies to maintain an active posture in the coalition against France. When the Pelhams became convinced of the seriousness of the rebellion in Scotland, Maria Theresa came under increased English pressure to make peace with Frederick II of Prussia, whose victories at Hohenfriedberg (4 June 1745 NS) and Soor (Bohemia) on 30 September 1745 NS had effectively consolidated his prior conquest of Silesia from the corporation of Bohemian estates.

[1] Also known as the Waldenses or Waldensians, a primitive protestant sect claiming apostolic origin and regarded by many protestants of the time as the sole Christian church to have preserved the primitive faith. Although they had a long history of persecution, their symbolic importance for European protestantism dated mainly from 1655, when the duke of Savoy attempted to exterminate them, an event commemorated in Milton's sonnet 'On the late Massacre in Piedmont'. Frequently dispersed among protestant European countries, the Vaudois were concentrated in the Piedmont and the Cottian Alps. Since the 15th century they had been governed by the House of Savoy.

[2] His emphasis on ingratitude suggests that Fielding here refers to Victor Amadeus II (1666–1732), duke of Savoy (1675–1730) and king of Sardinia (1718–30). His treatment of protestants varied as he came under greater or lesser pressure from his cousin, Louis XIV, to consolidate the latter's revocation of the Edict of Nantes. After the duke joined the Grand Alliance, the Vaudois helped him fight the French, eliciting thereby religious and civil privileges, which were soon evaded. Similarly, in the war of the Spanish Succession, when the duke deserted France for the allies (1703), he invited the Vaudois to make military contributions, which they did, and which, under resumed pressure from Louis XIV, the duke 'forgot'.

[3] Another deliverance, that is, like the 'glorious revolution' of 1688. Some contemporary writers also cited the reign of Queen Mary; see, for example, *The Question Consider'd, whether England can be otherwise than miserable under a Popish King?* (London, 1745), an October book abridged in *GM*, xv (1745), 522–6.

Insult on our Understanding, as an open Declaration that they suppose us to be Fools, as well as intend to make us Slaves. This is indeed a pregnant Example of that Contempt for *English* Wisdom, which *France* hath of late particularly affected.

Could the Instability of human Nature, or that Satiety which the Possession even of Happiness too often induces; nay, could the Sense of any Grievance incline us to a Desire of Change, yet surely the Colours under which this Invader comes, are sufficient to make the most fickle, the most simple, or the most angry Man reject him. Was the Throne vacant and elective, would it be possible to give a stronger Reason against the Pretensions of any Candidate, than that he was recommended by those two Crowns, under whose Protection, and by whose Assistance, this Pretender now disturbs these Kingdoms? One of these Crowns, divided from us by incompatible Interests, the natural Enemy and Rival of our Trade, and which hath long regarded us as the principal Obstacle to that Ambition, whose Views extend themselves all over *Europe*, and which in this last Campaign, hath by many Instances of Cruelty exerted an unwonted and an unwarranted Fury towards us.[1] The other, naturally less an Enemy perhaps to our Power, but more to our Religion, and both at present making War on our Trade with the most violent and implacable Rage.

Were therefore the Views of our Enemies less apparent on this Occasion, were the Advantages which they propose in this Measure to acquire to themselves, or the Destruction which they will necessarily bring upon us, less manifest; yet, surely, if that known Line,

Hoc Ithacus velit et magno mercentur Atridæ,[2]

may ever be quoted with any Force of Argument, it is on this Occasion. If *France*, if *Spain* would chuse this Man to reign over us, common Sense cries aloud to us, *reject him*. If it be their Interest to support, it is that of *Britain* to oppose him. If he will strengthen them, he must ruin us. Nor are the particular Views of each Crown less obvious. What can be

[1] After the sanguine ambiguities of Fontenoy (May 1745), the dismal opening of a dismal campaign for the allies, there were claims that French artillery had discharged 'such irremediable missiles as the laws of war disavow' and that their treatment of English prisoners and wounded was 'merciless'; *GM*, xv (1745), 422, 304. The French did in fact refuse to release English and Hanoverian prisoners until England released Marshal Belleisle, who had been taken prisoner under ambiguous circumstances at Elbingerode in December 1744 and confined in England since February 1745. To effect the prisoner exchange, Belleisle was released in late July 1745 and left England on 13 August.

[2] *Aeneid*, ii. 104: 'this the Ithacan would wish and the sons of Atreus buy at a great price' (Loeb). The line concludes the first of three speeches by Sinon designed to delude the Trojans about the Trojan horse. Sinon is here posing as the vengeful enemy of Odysseus, one whose death at the hands of the Trojans would bring great joy to the 'man of Ithaca' and to the House of Atreus. For another sounding of the Trojan-horse theme, see the title-page of *Dialogue*, below, p. [76].

plainer than the Advantage which *France* must gain in her two grand Views of extending her Dominions and her Trade, than by placing a Lieutenant (for he would be absolutely and really no more) to reign over that People who are the most capable of obstructing her in both; and who, in all Ages, have had the greatest Share in clipping the Wings of her Ambition, and since in checking the Growth of that Commerce to which her late most prudent Ministers have so vigorously applied themselves;[1] well knowing that in that alone, and not in vast Tracts of Land, consist the Riches, and consequently the Power of a Kingdom.[2] In this Branch she hath lately felt the Force of *British* Opposition,[3] and is at present thoroughly sensible how dearly she hath bought her Success on the Continent, by a War which hath almost totally ruin'd her Trade,[4] and which must have effectually destroyed it, had she not found this Way of distressing us at Home, and of confining our Naval Force to the Defence of our own Coasts.

And what can the Views of *Spain* be, other than to settle here that Religion which is profess'd and practis'd in her own Realm, with a Cruelty and Persecution in which she out-does even *Rome* herself? In a political Sense, it cannot be the Interest of *Spain* to subject this Nation to a Dependance on the Councils of *France*, which must be the necessary Effect of the Pretender's being establish'd here. Such a Design can be espoused by that Court on no other Motives than the Desire of propagating their Religion, even at the Expence of their Civil Interest; and to that bigotted View they have at all times sacrificed every other; witness,

[1] Referring to the pacific (hence 'prudent') administration of the recently deceased (1743) Cardinal Fleury, the latter part of whose tenure as prime minister coincided with a pronounced commercial expansion by France; Paul Vaucher, *Robert Walpole et la politique de Fleury, 1731–1742* (Paris, 1924), ch. iv, sec. 5. For the British view that France, prior to her active involvement in war (1744) had achieved marked commercial superiority, see Arthur McCandless Wilson, *French Foreign Policy during the Administration of Cardinal Fleury, 1726–1743*, Harvard Historical Studies, vol. xl (Cambridge, Mass., 1936), ch. x.

[2] Cf. William Douglas, *A Summary, Historical and Political, of the . . . British Settlements in North-America* (London, 1760), i. 3: 'In this present war [of the Austrian Succession], the French court seems to neglect their colonies, trade, and navigation, the principal care of their late good and great minister Cardinal Fleury; and run into their former romantic humour of land-conquests.' This section of the *Summary* appears to have been written in 1747. After the French land successes in Flanders during 1745, d'Argenson gave signs he feared France was becoming overextended in Europe.

[3] Most notably by the capture of Cape Breton in June 1745, widely perceived as a heavy blow to French fishing and trading interests in North America. In addition, there were considerable naval successes in the East Indies; see the *London Gazette* of 6–10 August 1745.

[4] Among the English it was a commonplace that since she had declared war on England, France had suffered great commercial losses. Cf. *General Evening Post* of 3–5 October 1745: 'We hear that a curious Gentleman has made a Calculation of the Value of our Ships taken by the French and Spaniards since the Commencement of the War, as likewise the Value of the Prizes taken by our Men of War and Privateers, and makes the Balance to be upwards of 4,000,000 l. on our Side.' See also *Daily Gazetteer* of 19 September and *General Evening Post* of 24–6 November 1745; reprinted in *GM*, xv (1745), 428, 525.

among many other Instances, their Conduct in the *Low Countries*, in the Reign of *Philip* II.[1] This therefore must be her Purpose, in abetting the Enterprize now carrying on with *France* against our establish'd Government; and the Zeal with which she hath engaged in the Cause, shows the Assurances she hath received from this her Agent of fulfilling her Design.

As to our Loss by this detestable Exchange, what would it be less than of every thing dear and valuable, of our pure and excellent Religion for Popery and abject Superstition? Of our inestimable Liberties for *French* Slavery; and of the Trade, Wealth and Commerce, of a powerful, a free and a flourishing People, for the Misery and Poverty of a subjected dependant Province?

And what are the Pretences with which this Invasion is colour'd over? What is the Creed imposed on our Minds, by our more impudent than powerful Enemies, but that a popish Pretender, educated in all the Tenets of Bigotry, will maintain a Religion to which he is a proffess'd Foe; and which he cannot even tolerate, according to the Faith in which he is bred, under Pain of Damnation? That one nursed up in hereditary Principles (for I may justly so term them) of absolute Power, will protect our Liberties? And that the Creature, the mere Instrument of *France*, will secure us the Possession of those Blessings which to deprive us of is the Interest, and hath been the principal Aim of that Crown? God be praised, as these things are gross and visible, so they are seen and felt. It is not, therefore, with a Purpose of correcting an ignorant, a supine, or a perverse People, that the Friends of our Religion and Liberties have taken up their Pen; but with the more pleasing Intention of encouraging and animating Men already resolv'd to continue to themselves and their Posterity those Blessings they enjoy, and chearfully to hazard their Fortunes and Lives,[2]

---

[1] Philip II (1527–98), who had married Mary I of England and ruled as joint sovereign from 1554 to 1558, had received the Spanish Netherlands from his father Charles V, Holy Roman Emperor. In 1567 Philip sent the duke of Alba (Alva) as captain-general to extirpate the protestant and separatist elements in those provinces. To the English, not the least significant result of Alba's bloody repressions—nearly 20,000 killed, 100,000 forced to emigrate—was the almost complete disruption of the Dutch machinery of commerce and industry, and a crippling trade war with what was then England's principal overseas market. Philip's repressive program for the Netherlands singled out for favor the English catholics refuged there, and was perceived as a threat to Elizabeth and the protestant succession.

[2] Cf. Walpole to Mann, 4 October 1745: 'The good people of England have at last rubbed their eyes and looked about them, a wonderful spirit is arisen in all counties among all sorts of people'; *Yale Walpole*, xix. 125–6. Walpole, like many others, particularly cites archbishop Herring, the text of whose 'Speech . . . at Presenting an Association, Enter'd into at the Castle of York, Sept. the 24th, 1745', was made publicly available in the *London Gazette* of 24–8 September 1745; reprinted in *DA* of 30 September and elsewhere. By the latter date Herring had published separately his 'Sermon Preach'd at . . . York, September the 22d, 1745. On the Occasion of the Present Rebellion in Scotland'.

rather than submit to render those precarious, or these worthless, under popish and arbitrary Power.

I will not on this Occasion descend to consider particular Interests: I will not remind all those who are possessed of Abbey-Lands or forfeited Estates,[1] or who are interested in the Funds,[2] how much they are concerned to oppose a Torrent which threatens to overwhelm their Fortunes. The Whole is at Stake. We have the Pretender's own Word for it, in his Declaration now publish'd in *Scotland*, that he is above our Laws; that he will regard none of them, not the most antient, upon which the Security of every Man's Property rests, nay, even the Security of their Lives, and of the Bread, the Inheritance of their Children. For even *Neutrals are to be included in his Resentment, and all those who do not take Arms in his Cause subjected to the Penalties of* High-Treason.[3] A most detestable and bloody Declaration! Which may raise a Doubt, whether its Inhumanity flies more in the Face of natural Justice, or of our Law; by which, even as long ago as the Reign of *Henry* VII. it is declared that any Man may support the King *de facto*,[4] without incurring those Penalties which this

---

[1] It was a commonplace of anti-jacobite propaganda that a Stuart restoration would bring with it a restoration, to the abbeys and churches, of the lands dispersed among lay owners during the reign of Henry VIII and confirmed by statute in 1 & 2 Phil. & Mar., c. 30 (*Statutes at Large*, vi. 40). For other references to the possibility, see index, *s.v.* 'Church lands'.

[2] The stock of the national debt, considered as a mode of investment (*OED*). It was widely rumored that the OP intended to wipe out the national debt, and hence the private investment in its stocks, as obligations contracted under an unlawful 'usurpation'. The issue was perceived as so disturbing to Englishmen that the YP's second declaration, dated 10 October 1745 and thus too late for the *Serious Address*, stated emphatically that the OP 'is resolved to take the Advice of his Parliament' with respect to the Funds; text in Andrew Henderson, *The Edinburgh History of the Late Rebellion*, 4th ed. (London, 1752), p. 38; Browne, *History of the Highlands*, iii. 104–7. See also index, *s.v.* 'Funds' and 'Debt, National'.

[3] Fielding once more distorts the 'literal' meaning of the OP's declaration dated Rome, 23 December 1743 NS. The declaration said nothing about the Pretender's being above the law, although it did describe the Hanoverian tenure as 'a foreign usurpation' and called for a 'free' parliament to help repair 'the breaches caused by so long an usurpation'. Far from disregarding property rights, the declaration promised that the restored monarch would pass, with the advice of his 'free' parliament, whatever legislation was necessary to secure the liberty and property of the individual. Finally, the italic passage, which some contemporary readers may have taken as direct quotation, apparently derives from the declaration's somewhat ambiguous statement that the Pretender would exempt from his general pardon none 'but such as shall, after the publication hereof, wilfully and maliciously oppose us, or those who shall not appear or endeavour to appear in arms for our service'. As spelled out in the YP's declaration dated Paris, 16 May 1745 NS, the requirements for a pardon seem less tolerant of neutrality: either join the jacobite army, or set up the Stuart standard in new places, or openly renounce 'all pretended allegiance to the usurper'. Texts from Browne, *History of the Highlands*, iii. 21–2, 65–6; *Historical Papers Relating to the Jacobite Period, 1699–1750*, ed. Allardyce, i (Aberdeen, 1895), 177–8, 182–3.

[4] The statute 1495, 11 Henry VII, c. 1, said by some writers to be only declaratory of the common law, was traditionally held to distinguish between *de jure* and *de facto* monarchs and to protect the allegiance of subjects to the latter from later charges of treason, such as those which Fielding professes to find implicit in the OP's declaration. See *Statutes at Large*, iv. 54–5; *The Tudor Constitution*, ed. G. R. Elton (Cambridge, 1965), pp. 2, 4–5.

wicked, insolent, incensed Tyrant hath denounced against the whole People of *England*, (some few Rebels only excepted.)

Good God! Is this a Bait to allure us? Nay, can such a Curse be imposed on us by any Force, unless what is capable of conquering the whole Kingdom, and extirpating its Inhabitants? But with what less than such an Extirpation (if the Strength of our Enemies could equal their Rage) are we actually threatned by this Incursion of Barbarians? Shall we open our Gates to a Banditti, a Rabble of Thieves and Outlaws, who have already exercis'd the most barbarous Methods on those who have yielded to their Force? What are they indeed but Savages, who, as they inhabit as barren a Country, have the barbarous Manners of *Huns* and *Vandals*; and, like them, would by their Swords cut their Way into the Wealth of richer Climates. What are we to expect but Rapine and Massacres, from a Gang of Wretches whom the Desire of Plunder and an innate Love of Rebellion and Civil War have animated to this Undertaking.

Let us therefore unite in Associations;[1] let us call forth the old *English* Spirit in this truly *English* Cause; let neither Fear nor Indolence prevail on one Man to refuse doing his Duty in the Defence of his Country, against an Invader by whom his Property, his Family, his Liberty, his Life, and his Religion are threatned with immediate Destruction.

---

[1] Units of volunteers for localized military service, often raised and trained under the informal auspices of the county lieutenancies, but financed and maintained by voluntary local subscriptions of private citizens. For the political significance of this alternative to the militia, on the one hand, and to the unpopular use of foreign mercenaries (notably Hanoverians), on the other, see 'General Introduction', above, pp. xliv–xlvi. It may be significant that Fielding says nothing here in praise of another alternative measure for raising troops, namely, the noblemen's regiments, undertaken at private expense by, among others, Fielding's 'princely' benefactor-to-be, the duke of Bedford. The formation and authorization of such regiments had been in the public news before publication of the *Serious Address*. However, the Pelhams may have been less than happy with this means of raising troops because it conferred power on people who might not always be amenable to ministerial control. George II had misgivings about it because the officers of these regiments were to receive rank in the regular military establishment, thereby displacing 'career' officers.

THE

HISTORY

OF THE

PRESENT REBELLION

IN

SCOTLAND.

[Price One Shilling.]

Half-title, first edition. The Beinecke Rare Book and Manuscript Library, Yale
University: Fielding Collection 745h.

THE

HISTORY

OF THE

PRESENT REBELLION

IN

SCOTLAND.

From the Departure of the Pretender's Son
from *Rome*, down to the prefent Time.

In which is

A full ACCOUNT of the Conduct of this Young
Invader, from his firft Arrival in *Scotland*;
with the feveral Progreffes he made there;
and likewife a very particular RELATION of
the Battle of *Prefton*, with an exact Lift of the
Slain, Wounded, and Prifoners, on both Sides.

Taken from the Relation of Mr. JAMES MACPHER-
SON, who was an Eye-Witnefs of the Whole, and
who took the firft Opportunity of leaving the Rebels,
into whofe Service he was forced, and in which he
had a Captain's Commiffion.

——— *Ne pectora vano*
Fida Metu paveant. OEtaeas fpernite flammas.
OV. METAM.

LONDON:
Printed for M. COOPER, at the *Globe* in *Pater-nofter-
Row.* MDCCXLV.

Title-page, first edition. The Beinecke Rare Book and Manuscript Library, Yale
University: Fielding Collection 745h. The motto is from Ovid, *Metamorphoses*,
ix, 248–9: 'Let not your loyal hearts be filled with groundless fear. Scorn the
Oetaean flames!'

THE

HISTORY

OF THE

PRESENT REBELLION

IN

SCOTLAND.

THE present Rebellion is a Matter of such Consequence to this Country, and must so seriously engage the Attention of every *Briton* who hath the least Regard either to his own real Good, or the Welfare of his Posterity, that I shall make no Apology for the present Undertaking; in which my Reader may be assured, that as the utmost Pains have been taken to procure the best Intelligence, so he may safely rely on the Truth of the Facts related.[1]

The Pretender's eldest Son *Charles*, who is now in the twenty-fifth Year of his Age,[2] having, in the Beginning of the Summer, taken a solemn Leave of his Father at *Rome*,[3] and in the Presence of the Pope and Cardinals, having made a solemn Vow that he would never forsake his Religion; set out with one *Patrick Graham* his Confessor,[4] the Marquis of *Tullibardin*,[5]

[1] For similar claims of privileged intelligence, see *TP* no. 1 (5 November 1745), below, p. 108.

[2] Charles Edward Louis Philip Casimir, eldest son of James Francis Edward Stuart and Princess Maria Clementina, daughter of Prince James Sobieski, was born at Rome on 20 December 1720 NS.

[3] Not true. The YP left Rome, clandestinely, early in January 1744 so as to take part in the projected French invasion of that year. By the son's account, the father did not know in advance of the project of 1745; see *The Stuart Papers at Windsor*, edd. Alistair and Henrietta Tayler (London, 1939), p. 120. For the YP and the earlier project, see 'Memoria Istorica per l'Anno 1744', reprinted in *A Jacobite Miscellany*, ed. Henrietta Tayler (Oxford, 1948), pp. 10–28.

[4] For evidence that no such person accompanied the YP, see 'General Introduction', above, p. xlix.

[5] William Murray (1689–1746), styled marquis of Tullibardine, oldest surviving son of the first duke of Athol, attainted for his part in the rebellion of 1715 and excluded from succession to the dukedom (it passed to his 'whig' younger brother James in 1724), created (1717) jacobite duke of Rannoch, was in fact one of the original 'seven men of Moidart' who landed with the YP in Scotland. He

General *Macdonell*,[1] and some other Attendants, amongst which is one Mr. *Fisher*, a Person who some Years ago murdered his Friend Mr. *Darby* in the Temple, for which he hath a Pardon under the Pretender's Sign Manual, and is advanced to the Post of Major in the Highland Army.[2]

Having past through *France* by Land, and visited the *French* King in his Camp,[3] from whom he obtained five Independant Companies, besides a large Quantity of Arms,[4] and a Ship of War,[5] together with

was to die in the Tower in July 1746. The contradictory reports in the newspapers of his role at the siege of Carlisle are ridiculed in the 'Apocryphal History of the Rebellion' in *TP* no. 4 (26 November 1745) and no. 5 (3 December 1745), below, pp. 356, 363.

[1] Sir John Macdonald, somewhat obscure soldier of fortune and another of the 'seven men of Moidart' who accompanied the YP to Scotland. Although claiming to be of the clan Macdonald, Sir John is usually described by contemporaries as Irish. *The Caledonian Mercury* of 22 August 1745 refers to him as 'General Macdonel, Uncle to the Earl of Antrim'; cited in *General Evening Post* of 27–9 August 1745. Lord Elcho called him a captain in the 'Carbineers', presumably his rank in the French service from which he came. In the jacobite army Macdonald was a general and 'Instructor of Cavalry'; see Forbes, *Lyon in Mourning*, i. 283, and ii. 312 n.; *1745 and After*, edd. Alistair and Henrietta Tayler (London, 1938), p. 6. His MS account of the expedition to Scotland is reprinted in *A Jacobite Miscellany*, ed. Henrietta Tayler (Oxford, 1948), pp. 45–67. In 1745 Macdonald was at least sixty years old.

[2] A curious mix of fact and inspired fabrication. On 10 April 1727 Henry Fisher, an attorney, shot to death and then robbed his friend Widdrington Darby, clerk of the Prothonotary's office in Hare-Court, Inner Temple. On 17 May 1727 Fisher escaped from Newgate and fled to the continent. *London Evening Post* of 12–14 December 1747 cites a letter from Fisher to his father, which describes the former's retirement to Florence, his embrace of catholicism, and his desire to pursue the religious life. *General Advertiser* of 4 February 1747 lists Fisher, apparently facetiously, as having been in the YP's retinue in Scotland. But there is no evidence that Fisher played any part in the Forty-Five. The Fisher-Darby case interested Fielding; he mentions it in *Tom Jones*, VIII. i. 402. Whatever his religious inclinations, Fisher did not neglect Mammon. According to the 'Memoirs of Thomas Jones', *The Thirty-Second Volume of the Walpole Society, 1946–1948* (London, 1951), pp. 71–2, in 1778 'this old shrivel'd assisin' was a banker in Rome and paid Jones, the Welsh landscape painter, £40 on behalf of his client, the Bishop of Derry.

[3] Neither the passage through France nor the meeting with Louis XV took place in 1745. Although the YP had earlier sought such a meeting, after the failure of the French invasion scheme of 1744 the French government, on the higher levels at least, seems to have lost interest in the YP. Just prior to embarking for Scotland, the YP wrote the king, informing him of the project and asking support for it. O'Sullivan, one of the 'seven men of Moidart', noted the difficulties of getting the requisite shipping without letting the French in on the secret; *1745 and After*, p. 46.

[4] Contemporary estimates of both arms and men differed widely. *London Evening Post* of 15–17 August 1745 reports the YP's landing near Fort William, 'which to be sure he is to take with his *three hundred well-dress'd Men*'. *DA* of 16 August 1745 puts the figure at 300, 'part of them very well drest'. *DA* of 20 August and *St James's Evening Post* of 17–20 August file reports of 2,000 men. The estimates may derive, respectively, from the *Caledonian Mercury* and the *Edinburgh Evening Courant* of 13 August 1745. In a letter to James Edgar, his father's secretary, dated 12 June 1745 NS, the YP estimated he had 1,500 muskets, 1,800 broadswords, 'a good quantity of powder, Balls, flints, Durks, Brandy, etc. . . . and twenty small field pieces two of which a mule may carry'. See *The Stuart Papers at Windsor*, edd. Alistair and Henrietta Tayler (London, 1939), p. 126. The YP wrote his father on 2 July 1745 NS that he would rendezvous with a 'man of war of 67 guns, and 700 men aboard as also a company of sixty volunteers all gentlemen whom I shall probably geat [get] to land with me, I mean to stay, which tho' few will make a shew, they having a pretty uniform' (ibid., p. 132). Cf. Forbes, *Lyon in Mourning*, i. 285, 292. Whatever the correct figures, the men and perhaps

[*See opposite page for n. 4 cont. and n. 5.*]

further Promises of future Assistance,[1] he departed for *Brest*; where the aforesaid Soldiers and Arms being put on board, in the Beginning of *August* they sailed out of that Harbour;[2] the Pretender's Son himself, together with those Attendants who accompanied him from *Rome*, being embarked in a small Vessel.[3]

They had not been long at Sea before they met with one of our Men of War,[4] between whom and the *Frenchman* a very sharp Engagement ensued; in which both Ships suffered extremely, and the latter was so entirely disabled, that she was obliged to put back into *Brest*.[5]

During this Engagement, the small Vessel which carried the Pretender's Son escaped, and made immediately for the Western Coast of *Scotland*. No *English* Man of War being at that Time in those Seas, they cruized for some Days off the Islands of *Bara* and *Ust*, and at last stood in for the Coast of *Lochaber*, and on the 10th of *August* in the Evening landed between the Islands of *Mull* and *Skie*.[6]

much of the armament were on the escort ship, which was driven back to France without landing its cargo. See below, p. 39.

[5] The *Elizabeth*, an old man-of-war captured from the English in Queen Anne's reign and presently chartered from the ministry of marine by Walter Rutledge of Dunkirk, one of a group of wealthy Franco-Irish privateer-merchants who stood to profit from any diversion of the British navy. See John S. Gibson, *Ships of the '45* (London, 1967), pp. 7–16. The *Elizabeth* was variously estimated as carrying 64 or 67 guns.

[1] On 31 August 1745 the YP did receive letters dated 1 and 10 August NS from Campoflorido, the Spanish Ambassador to France, and the duc de Bouillon, respectively, promising him arms, money, and troops from France and Spain; Blaikie, *Itinerary*, p. 11; David, Lord Elcho, *Short Account of the Affairs of Scotland* (Edinburgh, 1907), pp. 247–8; *Jacobite Epilogue*, ed. Henrietta Tayler (London, 1941), pp. 251–2. But prior to his embarkation even such indirect promises seem to have been lacking.

[2] The *Elizabeth* did sail from Brest, but not 'in the beginning of August' and not with the YP on hand. The *Elizabeth* sailed in early July to rendezvous off Belle-Île with the light frigate carrying the YP and his immediate followers. The latter, who had foregathered at Nantes, sailed on the 'small Vessel' from St Nazaire on 3 July NS. After considerable delay the two ships set sail for Scotland on 16 July NS.

[3] *La du Teillay* (*La Doutelle*), frigate of 16 guns, supplied by Antoine Vincent Walsh of Nantes, another Franco-Irish merchant-privateer and associate of Rutledge's. See *Stuart Papers at Windsor*, p. 126; Forbes, *Lyon in Mourning*, i. 284; Gibson, *Ships of the '45*, pp. 7–16.

[4] On 20 July NS, off the Lizard, they met the *Lion* (*Lyon*), 64 guns, commanded by Capt. Peircy Brett (1709–81), later lord commissioner of the admiralty 1766–70, admiral 1778, MP Queenborough 1754–74. The *Lion* was on her way from Spithead to join Admiral Martin's fleet in the Bay of Biscay; Gibson, *Ships of the '45*, p. 11.

[5] The 'Engagement' was described in the *London Gazette* of 20–3 July 1745. For eyewitness accounts by O'Sullivan, Macdonald, Abbé Butler, and Captain Darbé of *La du Teillay*, see *1745 and After*, pp. 50–1; *Stuart Papers at Windsor*, pp. 136–7; and Winifred Duke, *Prince Charles Edward and the Forty-Five* (London, 1938), pp. 47–9. The earliest public accounts did not make explicit the connection with the YP's expedition.

[6] Under dateline 'Whitehall, August 17', the *London Gazette* of 13–17 August 1745 cited letters from Edinburgh, dated 11 August, describing a French ship off the west coast of Scotland, which, 'after having cruized for some Days off the Islands of Bara and Uist, stood in for the Coast of Lochaber; and had there landed, betwixt the Islands of Mull and Skie, several Persons', among them, it was reported, the Pretender's son. Fielding's wording here clearly derives from the *Gazette* account, and his impressively precise (but highly inaccurate) '10th of *August*' may have been calculated by

One *Macpherson*, whose Hut stood about a Mile from the Sea-shore,[1] seeing these People land, had the Curiosity to advance towards them, and was told by one of his Countrymen that came with them who they were, and particularly, that the young Man was the Prince of *Wales* and the Son of his King. *Charles* presently came up to him, and giving him a *French* Pistole,[2] asked him if he would not bear Arms for his King and Country, to which *Macpherson* readily answered he would, and then *Charles* very graciously held forth his Hand for him to kiss, which he accordingly did.[3]

The young Pretender then threw himself on the Ground, and kiss'd it, after which his Confessor cut a Turf and presented it to him,[4] saying, *In the Name of the most holy and infallible Pope, I present thee this as Regent for thy Father,*[5] *and do hereby, by virtue of the full Powers to me delegated, invest the most puissant* James III. *with the Possession and Rule of the Kingdom of* Great Britain; *which he is to hold at the Will and Pleasure of the Holy See. Dost thou therefore, in his Name, accept the Government of these Realms, on the Condition of fighting the Cause of our holy Mother the Church, to the utter Extirpation of the Persons of Heretics; and wilt thou persevere manfully in the same, till the Blood of Heretics shall be washed away from the Face of the Earth?*

The Young Pretender on his Knees received the Turf from the Hand of his Confessor, and faithfully promised in his Father's Name to fulfil all that had been enjoined him.

backdating from the date of the Edinburgh letters cited by the *Gazette*. See 'General Introduction', above, p. xxxi. In fact, the YP landed first at Eriska (Eriskay) in the western isles on 23 July NS, and two days later on the mainland at Loch nan Uamh (Inverness-shire); Blaikie, *Itinerary*, p. 2.

[1] Fielding's invention. On the extreme unlikelihood of a Macpherson in the heart of what was Macdonald country, see 'General Introduction', above, p. xlviii.

[2] Originally a Spanish gold coin (two escudos), it had been introduced to France as the *louis d'or* in the 17th century and was thereafter widely and variously used in Europe. The combinative term 'French Pistole' recalls the two major enemies which anti-jacobites insisted were behind the YP's expedition.

[3] But cf. the running title, above, p. [34], where it is stated that Macpherson 'was forced' into rebel service; Jarvis, *Collected Papers*, ii. 126.

[4] Not only the name and function of the YP's supposititious confessor, but also some of the ceremonial kissings of hand and earth, as well as the papist and antiheretical bias of the confessor's presentation, can be found in *A Genuine Intercepted Letter, from Father Patrick Graham, Almoner and Confessor to the Pretender's Son, in Scotland, to Father Benedick Yorke, Titular Bishop of St. David's, at Bath* (London, 1745), a Cooper pamphlet which claimed to be 'Published by Authority'. It appeared *c.* 23 September 1745 and was widely reprinted in the London papers. See 'General Introduction', above, p. xlix, and Jarvis, *Collected Papers*, ii. 130–2. Patrick Graham was the name of the first archbishop of St Andrews under James III of Scotland and had opposed the latter over the question of papal influence in prelatical and parliamentary appointments.

[5] In a declaration and a supporting 'commission', both dated Rome, 23 December 1743 NS, the OP had appointed his son regent 'of all Our Dominions'. By the time the *History* appeared, the commission of regency had been proclaimed on several occasions in Scotland and had been noted, along with other declarations from the same source, in the London papers. For texts, see *A Full Collection of All the Proclamations and Orders published by the Authority of Charles Prince of Wales* (n.p., 1745), pp. 1–2; *The History of the Rebellion in the Years 1745 and 1746*, ed. Henrietta Tayler (Oxford, 1944), pp. 363–5.

Then he and his Confessor fell both on their Knees, and continued in a devout Posture several Minutes, invoking the Assistance of the Saints, and repeating each several hundred *Pater Nosters*, and *Ave Mary's*.

This Ceremony being ended, in which all present assisted, the Marquis of *Tullibardin*, and five other *Scottish* Chiefs took their Leave of their Commander, and having kiss'd his Hands, set out to disperse themselves among the Clans.[1]

Charles then asked *Macpherson* how far they were from a House, and was told that he was full seven Miles from any Town, or indeed from any House, unless some few bad Huts, such as his own, which were scattered here and there, and were inhabited by Highlanders.

Charles behaved with great Curtesy to this Highlander, and asked him several Questions concerning the State of the Country, till the Confessor having enquired his Religion, was told by him that he was of the Presbytery. After which Answer the young Man grew immediately reserved to him, and speaking something to his Confessor in a Language which he did not understand,[2] but which the Confessor answered with a Smile, turned away from him. Nor did he ever afterwards speak to him.

Charles spent three Days in visiting the several Huts of these Highlanders; amongst whom he distributed his Money very liberally, so that by the End of the third Day, he had enlisted upwards of 70 in his Party. He delivered them Arms, (for he had Arms with him for 500 Men only) a sufficient Number for 6500 having miscarried in the *French* Man of War.[3]

On the 14th of *August* the Marquis of *Tullibardin*, and two other of the *Scotch* Chiefs returned with a Body of above 300 of the Clans,[4] who were immediately disposed into a Regiment, and called, *The Royal Regiment of Highland Guards*.[5] The Command of which was given to the Marquis,

---

[1] According to contemporary accounts, Tullibardine was too infirm to leave the ship immediately upon arrival; Forbes, *Lyon in Mourning*, i. 288. Too infirm, also, to 'disperse ... among the Clans', Tullibardine was present at a meeting between the YP and three (not five) of the chiefs—Ranald Macdonald of Clanranald, Donald Macdonald of Kinlochmoidart, and Macdonald of Glenaladale; 'An Account of Proceeding, from Prince Charles' Landing to Prestonpans', *Miscellany of the Scottish History Society*, ix (Edinburgh, 1958), 203–16.

[2] Fielding loses no opportunity of stressing the French connection and its implacable hostility to protestants.

[3] For contemporary estimates, see above, p. 36 and *n.* 4

[4] Fielding may have been led to invent an active early role for Tullibardine by the frequency with which the latter's name was reported in connection with raising the men of Athol during the march to Perth in late August and early September. *DA* of 7 September, for example, reported that Tullibardine, at the head of 500 men, had taken over his brother's house at Blair. On 14 August the YP was at Kinlochmoidart; Blaikie, *Itinerary*, pp. 6–7. Lochiel and Keppoch were out gathering their men at this time, but did not arrive until the raising of the standard at Glenfinnan on 19 August.

[5] Probably a garbled reference to the guard of Clanranalds who attended the YP on the march to Glenfinnan. 'An Account of Proceeding . . .', *Miscellany of the Scottish History Society*, ix (Edinburgh,

one *Mackay* was made Lieutenant Colonel, and Mr. *Fisher* Major. The Captains and inferior Officers were chosen out of the Clans.

This Regiment was no sooner formed, than the utmost Diligence was made use of to discipline them, and instruct them in the Use of Arms. Nor was much less Diligence used by the Confessor, assisted by another Priest whose Name was *Fraser*,[1] to instruct them in the *Roman* Catholic Religion, and this with such Success, that upwards of 200 of these ignorant People were converted in less than a Fortnight.

The Government no sooner received Advice of the landing of the Pretender's Son in *Scotland*, than immediately a Proclamation was published, with a Reward of *L*.30000 for the apprehending him.[2] And at the same Time, an Order was issued for all the Officers of his Majesty's Land Forces in *Great Britain* to repair to their respective Posts.[3]

The Regiments which at that Time lay in the North were Colonel *Gardiner's* and *Hamilton's* Dragoons,[4] together with the Regiments of Foot of *Lascelles*, *Murray*, *Guise*, and *Lee*.[5] These were ordered to

1958), 207, states that the YP took pleasure in teaching the Clanranalds their exercise and that they were pleased with him, 'calling themselves his Guard of Safety'. O'Sullivan estimates them at 'about two hundred' as of 20 August (*1745 and After*, p. 59). But these men were raised from one clan only and were under the command of the chief's son Ranald, not the officers Fielding will mention. O'Sullivan remarks the difficulties of organizing the Highlanders in regular units—'they must go by tribes' (p. 61)—and this fact alone tells heavily against Fielding's account.

[1] Not identified; probably, like Graham, a fiction. The subsequent charge of proselytizing was commonly made, but without evidence. Most of the western clan members were already catholics. In *TP* no. 3 (19 November 1745) and no. 4 (26 November 1745), Cooper advertised *The Artifices of the Romish Priests in making Converts to Popery*.

[2] The chronology flatters the ministry, perhaps unintentionally. Under dateline of 1 August 1745 the lords justices issued a proclamation offering the reward for the apprehension of the YP 'in case he shall land, or attempt to land, in any of His Majesty's dominions'; as printed in the *London Gazette* of 3–6 August. The proclamation mentions receipt of intelligence that the YP had embarked from France so as to land 'in some Part of His Majesty's Dominions'. Official evidence suggests that as late as 8 August the ministry in London did not believe reports of an actual landing; SP Scot. 25/54 and 58, and HMC, *Fifteenth Report*, Appendix vi (Carlisle MSS), p. 200, as cited in Jarvis, *Collected Papers*, ii. 247. For the political implications, see 'General Introduction', above, pp. xxxi–xxxii.

[3] Cf. *London Gazette* of 10–13 August, under dateline War Office, August 13: 'It is their Excellencies the Lords Justices Directions, that all Officers belonging to His Majesty's Land Forces serving in England or Scotland, do immediately repair to their respective Posts.'

[4] Colonel James Gardiner (1688–1745), veteran of Marlborough's campaigns and sometime aide-de-camp to the second earl of Stair, had succeeded General Humphrey Bland in 1743 as colonel of the regiment of light dragoons, later known as the 13th hussars, quartered near Stirling. General Hamilton's dragoons, later the 14th hussars, were at grass at Haddington until called in to Leith and Edinburgh. Averaging about 300 men apiece, these two units were the only cavalry in Scotland at the time and neither had seen actual service. See Jarvis, *Collected Papers*, i. 25–47.

[5] The 47th foot, later the Loyal North Lancashire regiment; the 46th foot, under command of Lt.-Col. Clayton; the 6th foot, later the Royal Warwickshire regiment; and the 44th foot, later the Essex regiment, only five companies of which, under Lt.-Col. Halket, marched to Cope at Stirling. See Jarvis, *Collected Papers*, i. 30.

march directly towards *Stirling*, where they were to encamp under the Command of Lieutenant-General Sir *John Cope*.[1]

Had some of the well-affected Chiefs had it in their Power, in the Infancy of this Rebellion, to have armed their Clans, it might most probably have been crushed in the Eggshell; but there being a Provision by a very severe Law against this,[2] without an Order of Council, and there being some Time as well as Difficulty required to obtain this Order,[3] the Rebels had unfortunately, an Opportunity to form themselves, before any such Step could possibly be taken against them.

By the 20th of *August*, before which time the two other Chiefs were returned with their Clans,[4] the Army of the Rebels was increased to the Number of 1200.[5] They then proceeded to form two other Regiments, one of which was commanded by General *Macdonell*,[6] and the other by the Pretender's Son himself.

[1] Sir John Cope (1690–1760), MP Queenborough 1722–7, Liskeard 1727–34, Orford 1738–41; major general 1739, lt.-general 1743, KB 1743, commander-in-chief in Scotland 1745. After the failure at Prestonpans (21 September 1745), although he was cleared by the board of inquiry, Cope was not employed again.

[2] The clans had been legally disarmed by 1 Geo. I (1715), c. 54, 'An Act for the more effectual securing the peace of the *Highlands* in Scotland', later enforced (1724) by 11 Geo. I, c. 26; *Statutes at Large*, xiii. 306–12, and xv . 246–54. The latter had empowered the lords lieutenant of the Highland counties to convene the clans 'from time to time' for the surrender of all weapons.

[3] Certain exceptions in the disarming legislation had been made for the lords lieutenant of the counties for the purpose of raising the militia. But the militia legislation itself was judged to have been rendered technically inoperable by this time, and many politicians agreed with the duke of Argyll, the most powerful figure in Scotland, that 'it was not lawful for any person in the Highlands to defend the Government, or his own Home, family or goods, though attacked by Robbers or Rebels'; Jarvis, *Collected Papers*, i. 104. Because parliament had been prorogued, a bill to enable the raising of the militia did not receive the royal assent until 2 November 1745; *Journals of Commons*, xxv. 12–19. For the politics behind the reluctance to issue an order of council to arm the well-affected clans, see 'General Introduction', above, p. xliii.

[4] Lochiel, with 700 Camerons, and Keppoch, with 300 Macdonalds, joined the YP on 19 August, just after the standard had been raised at Glenfinnan, an event which Fielding dates (below, p. 43) as 22 August. See Blaikie, *Itinerary*, p. 8.

[5] A figure not attained until after the acquisitions at Glenfinnan, it is confirmed by the historians; Blaikie, *Itinerary*, p. 8, where it is broken down into 200 Clanranalds, 700 Camerons, and 300 Macdonalds; *1745 and After*, pp. 59–60.

[6] Fielding's error here may result from his confusion of General Macdonell, whom he has earlier identified (p. 36) as having accompanied the YP from France, with one of the Highland chiefs. Regimental commands among the clans were jealously retained by the chiefs or their representatives: the Clanranalds by Ranald Macdonald, sixteenth laird; Glengarry by Colonel Aeneas Macdonald; Keppoch by Alexander Macdonald of Keppoch; and Glencoes by Alexander Macdonald of Glencoe. See Elcho, *Short Account*, pp. 241–5; Blaikie, *Itinerary*, p. 91. Although technically none of the Highland chiefs bore the title of general, the London press occasionally so designated them; for example, *DA* of 26 September 1745 refers to a 'General Macdonald' as dangerously wounded at Prestonpans, apparently meaning Captain Archibald Macdonald of Keppoch; and for a similar confusion, see Walpole to Mann, 27 September 1745, *Yale Walpole*, xix. 116 and *n.* But Sir John Macdonald, the YP's old companion, played almost no active military role, and his honorary title of 'Instructor of Cavalry' was not conferred until Perth in early September.

On the 22d,[1] having made themselves Tents, they marched a few Miles, and encamped on a Hill, (for before this Time they kept in separate Companies, at some Distance from each other, in order to avoid Discovery;) a Stratagem which had so good an effect, that whoever recollects the Accounts which the News Papers gave us of the first landing of the Pretender, must remember with what Incertainty they spoke of a few Men being landed in the West of *Scotland*, who were sometimes Gentlemen from *Ireland* hunting, and sometimes were quite vanished, every subsequent Account actually contradicting the former;[2] so that few, except the most credulous, gave any Belief to it, imagining it was rather a Story devised by some Persons for particular Purposes which need not be mentioned.[3] This Infidelity was of very pernicious Consequence, especially as it prevailed in some measure even among the greater People: Nay, so accustomed were they to treat this Rebellion as imaginary, that even when it was impossible to doubt longer of its Reality, they made it still the Subject of Contempt and Ridicule;[4] saying it was only a Company of wild Highlanders got together, whom the very Sight of a Body of Troops, however small, would infallibly disperse: Nay, one great Man is reported to have asked, with a contemptuous Air, Why they did not read the Proclamation to them?[5] This induced

---

[1] Fielding appears to lose track of his chronology here. When, after a short digression, he refers again (p. 43) to this same encampment on a hill, he dates it as of the 21st, which makes better sense, inasmuch as he then goes on to say that 'On the 22d they erected their Standard' (p. 43).

[2] As late as 22 August the *DA* asserted that the alarm was set off by Irish ships sailing among the western islands to load meal and by a group of Irish gentry landing on the islands to hunt and hawk, one of them 'personating' the YP; also *Penny London Post* of 21–3 August and *Old England* of 24 August. Cf. *General Evening Post* of 31 August–3 September 1745: 'As to what you mention of being alarmed with odd Stories from our Country, we were for about twenty Days as oddly alarmed ourselves, without coming to any Certainty whether there was any landing or rising in our Highlands or not, one Account always contradicting another.'

[3] Cf. *General Evening Post* of 5–8 October, in a letter entitled 'The Briton': 'These, and many other Stories, were propagated by wicked and designing Men, with a View to lull the Nation into Security, and prevent them whom it most concerned, from knowing the Designs and Strengths of our Enemies until it should be too late to oppose them.'

[4] Cf. Pelham to Argyll, 20 August 1745: 'I am not so apprehensive of the strength or zeal of the enemy, as I am fearful of the inability or languidness, of our friends. I see, the contagion spreads in all parts; and, if your Grace were here, you would scarce, in common conversation, meet with one man who thinks there is any danger from, scarce truth in an invasion, at this time'; Coxe, *Pelham*, i. 258. For the politics of the various reactions, see 'General Introduction', above, pp. xxxi–xxxiv.

[5] Cf. Lady Hardwicke to Colonel Joseph Yorke, 1 October 1745: 'Lord Charles Hay had, shall I call it by so mild a name as imprudence, to say in the Drawing-Room a few hours before the news of Cope's defeat came, that there was nothing necessary but to read the Proclamation'; *Life and Correspondence of Philip Yorke Earl of Hardwicke*, ed. Philip C. Yorke (Cambridge, 1913), i. 463. The Proclamation, which was integral to the Riot Act of 1715 (1 Geo. I, st. 2, c. 5), 'chargeth and commandeth all persons, being assembled, immediately to disperse themselves, and peaceably to depart to their habitations . . . upon the pains contained in the act made in the first year of King George, for preventing tumults and riotous assemblies'; see *English Historical Documents, 1714–1783*, edd. D. B. Horn and Mary Ransom (London, 1957), pp. 271–5. The Riot Act singled out offenses committed in Scotland,

a Supineness in our Councils, and gave the Rebels Time and Opportunity to grow more formidable than they could ever have become from such a Beginning, had the Report of it met with more Credit at first, and afterwards with less Contempt than it did. However, we may learn the Truth of that old Observation, That it is never safe to despise the most contemptible Enemy too absolutely. A Lesson which, I hope, our future Politicians will learn from the present Case.

But to return to our History: The Rebels being now upwards of 1200 strong, grew somewhat bolder, and began to place greater Confidence in their Strength.

On the 21st, therefore, as we have said, they came to a Rendezvous on an open Hill, where they encamped in the Sight of the Country.

On the 22d, they erected their Standard with great Solemnity: The Priests first washed it all over with Holy Water, and blessed it; then a certain Number of *Ave Mary's* and *Pater Nosters* were said, besides Prayers to the Saints; in all which Acts of Devotion, *Charles* distinguished himself with greater Zeal (if possible) than the Priests themselves.[1] In the Afternoon of this Day in which they erected their Standard, they were reinforced by a Body of 200 Highlanders,[2] who brought them an Account that the King's Forces were marching towards *Stirling*.[3]

The chief Care of the Rebels began now to be the procuring Provisions, as their Mouths grew very numerous; in order to which they sent out a Party, who, on the 22d in the Evening, drove a Herd of black Cattle into the Camp, which were receiv'd by them with great Joy.[4]

and its 'pains' included death and confiscation of movables. Fielding might have heard of Hay's gaffe from one of his more highly placed friends in the administration.

[1] The standard was erected at Glenfinnan on 19 August 1745 by Tullibardine. According to Murray of Broughton, the YP made 'a short but very Pathetick speech'; *Memorials*, ed. Robert Fitzroy Bell (Edinburgh, 1898), pp. 168–9, summarizes it. There is no responsible contemporary evidence to support Fielding's characterization of the religiosity of the ceremonies. However, the standard does appear to have been blessed by Hugh Macdonald, consecrated Bishop of Diana *in partibus* (1731), vicar-apostolic of the Highlands; *The Forty-Five: A Narrative of the Last Jacobite Rising by Several Contemporary Hands*, ed. Charles Sanford Terry (Cambridge, 1922), p. 195. For a unique account of the ceremonies, see the untitled MS reprinted in *Miscellany of the Scottish Historical Society*, ix (Edinburgh, 1958), 209.

[2] Presumably the recruits brought by Lochiel and Keppoch on the afternoon of 19 August at Glenfinnan. See above, p. 41 and *n*.

[3] The YP did learn of Cope's marching on 22 August, but at Kinlochiel, not Glenfinnan, and from Glenbucket, not the Highlanders who joined at the raising of the standard. Furthermore, the intelligence was of Cope's marching by Dalwhinnie to Fort Augustus. See Blaikie, *Itinerary*, p. 8; *1745 and After*, pp. 62–3.

[4] A fictional episode. Of the feasting at Glenfinnan O'Sullivan wrote, 'there were so many Cows given them likewise'; *1745 and After*, p. 60. Jarvis, *Collected Papers*, ii. 129, notes in this connection that *La Du Teillay*, on her way back to France, ran into three grain ships off the isle of Skye and, as ransom, required them to distribute their cargo at Kinlochmoidart, where the YP made use of it. In

On the 23d, a Party of 400 of the Rebels, chiefly belonging to the Royal Regiment of Highland Guards, attacked and defeated a small Party of the King's Forces, under the Command of Capt. *Scott*. The Captain himself was wounded in the Arm; and a Serjeant, even after the Battle, was cut all to Pieces;[1] which Fate all the rest had shared, had it not been prevented by one *Stewart*, a Captain of the Highlanders.[2] These Fellows had already so well profited under their popish Instructor, as to learn the Language of *Heretic Dogs!* and the true Arts of propagating Religion with Fire and Sword.

The Rebels began now to encrease considerably, and by the 28th, they were full 2000 strong.[3] At this Time they added a Battalion to the Regiment of Guards,[4] and likewise formed a third Regiment, of which the Duke of *Perth* was declared Colonel.[5]

O'Sullivan's words, 'It was a Vast Soccor in that jouncture, for the poor people had not a Scrap of meal for above six months before'; *1745 and After*, p. 58. 'An Account of Proceeding, from Prince Charles' Landing to Prestonpans', *Miscellany of the Scottish History Society*, ix (Edinburgh, 1958), 208, puts the number of ships at six.

[1] On 16 August at Loch Lochy, Macdonald of Tiendrich (Keppoch) and some Glengarry men attacked two companies of the Royal Scots (Sinclair's regiment) marching from Perth, at Cope's order, to reinforce the garrison at Fort William. Their captain, John Scott, was wounded in the shoulder, according to Murray of Broughton, and 'a Serjeant and three or four men killed'; *Memorials*, p. 166. See also *GM*, xv (1745), 443, 497; *Lyon in Mourning*, i. 36; Blaikie, *Itinerary*, p. 7; John Home, *History of the Rebellion in the Year 1745* (London, 1802), pp. 59–60. The charge of mutilation after the battle is unfounded. In fact, Lochiel paroled Scott to Fort William so that he might have better medical treatment; Jarvis, *Collected Papers*, ii. 136.

[2] Not elsewhere so identified and therefore probably an invented person. When the standard was raised at Glenfinnan on 19 August, Alexander Stewart of Invernahyle was there to report that the Stewarts of Appin would join shortly; 'An Account of Proceeding, from Prince Charles' Landing to Prestonpans', *Miscellany of the Scottish History Society*, ix (Edinburgh, 1958), 209; Major A. McK. Annand, 'Stewart of Appin's Regiment in the Army of Prince Charles Edward, 1745–46', *Journal of the Society for Army Historical Research*, xxxvii (1960), 15. There is no record of such an intervention by him in the Loch Lochy skirmish on 16 August. Colonel John Roy Stewart, formerly a British cavalry officer, joined at Athol on 31 August and became one of the more active military leaders; *Letter-Book of Bailie John Stewart of Inverness 1715–1752*, Scottish History Society, second series, ix, ed. William Mackay (Edinburgh, 1915), 455, *n.* 3; Blaikie, *Itinerary*, p. 11. But there is no record of his having attended the YP as early as 16 August.

[3] This estimate had appeared in various London papers; *London Evening Post* of 31 August–3 September 1745, under dateline Edinburgh 26 August, and *DA* of 7 September, under dateline Edinburgh 31 August. Murray of Broughton, *Memorials*, p. 175, puts the figure as of this date at less than 1,800. He counts deserters.

[4] There is no evidence of either the unit or the mode of augmentation. At approximately this time the YP was joined by units of Glengarry Macdonalds, Macdonalds of Glencoe, and Grants of Glenmoriston; Blaikie, *Itinerary*, pp. 9–10; 'An Account of Proceeding . . .', *Miscellany of the Scottish History Society*, ix. 211. Fielding is presumably reflecting intelligence of such augmentations in his own way.

[5] James Drummond (1713–46), sixth earl and titular third duke of Perth, joined at Perth on 4 September and was made lt.-general; Elcho, *Short Account*, pp. 248–9; Blaikie, *Itinerary*, p. 12. 'Chevalier' de Johnstone, *Memoirs of the Rebellion in 1745 and 1746*, 2nd ed. (London, 1821), p. 15, asserts that Perth joined the 'day after' the YP arrived at Perth and brought with him 'a part of his vassals', estimated as 150 strong by O'Sullivan (*1745 and After*, p. 69) and 200 by Elcho (*Short Account*, p. 248). It is evidently Perth's detachment that Fielding constitutes here as 'a third Regiment'.

General *Cope* had now assembled a pretty considerable Body of the King's Forces near *Stirling*;[1] but the Ways towards the Rebels were such, that it would have been impracticable to come at them without the utmost Hazard of losing the whole Army in the Attempt: Nor had he indeed any other Way of attacking them, than by taking a vast Scope round; which he declined, as he chose rather to keep himself posted between them and the City of *Edinburgh*; well knowing, that could the Capital of *Scotland* be preserved, any Success they might have of assembling a Body in the Highlands, where they must soon be starv'd, would be in the End fruitless and ineffectual.[2]

However, the Alarm of their Success daily encreasing in *England*, and the Numbers which from time to time joined them giving a very just Cause of Uneasiness to our Ministry here, the General receiv'd peremptory Orders to march forwards,[3] which he did; and in the mean Time the Rebels gave him the slip,[4] and on the 29th march'd towards *Perth*, the Duke of that Name leading the Van, *Charles* marching in the Centre, and General *Macdonell* in the Rear. This Evening they were joined by Lord *Geo. Murray*, Brother to the Duke of *Athol*,[5] and by three other Gentlemen, one of whom is Brother to an Earl.[6]

[1] When Cope marched north from Stirling on 19–20 August, he had, according to *Scots Magazine*, vii (1745), 398, between 1,500 and 2,000 men, an estimate which conforms approximately to that of most contemporary accounts. Jarvis, *Collected Papers*, i. 32, puts the figure at 1,740. For Cope's dispirited reckoning before the board of inquiry (1746), see *Report of Proceedings . . . in the Examination into the Conduct . . . of Lieut-General Sir John Cope* (London, 1749), p. 16.

[2] Fielding may have been privy to the fact that Cope intended to alter his original design of taking a large force north and investing the forts in the Highlands. Cf. Cope to Tweeddale, 17 August 1745: 'He had upon serious consideration resolved to send a Detachment of 300 Men to support the Garrisons in the North, and to awe the People in their Neighbourhood. This resolution I took not thinking it safe to leave the Capital of this Part of the Country exposed to a second landing'; SP Scot. 27/79, quoted in Jarvis, i. 11–12, 22. The approbation implicit in 'well knowing' suggests that Fielding is tactfully preparing the case against the lords justices, in particular Granville and Tweeddale, whose opinion was that the rebels need only be confronted with force and their effort would collapse; Tweeddale to Cope, 22 and 24 August, in *Report of Proceedings*, pp. 129–31.

[3] Tweeddale to Cope, 15 and 22 August 1745; *Report of Proceedings*, pp. 122–3, 129–30. Jarvis, ii. 132, calls Fielding unique among contemporary observers in noting these peremptory orders and the change of plan they required. Fielding may have had a ministerial source, perhaps Lyttelton.

[4] A widely held view, even though some London papers noted Cope's reluctance to confront the rebels at Corrieyarrack pass; for example, *General Evening Post* of 10–12 September 1745. By declining the Corrieyarrack gambit and choosing instead the northeast, lowland route to Inverness, Cope in effect 'slipped' by the rebels, thus opening their way to Edinburgh. Jarvis, i. 15–20, cites evidence for the view that the rebel design of closing with Cope before he reached Inverness was thwarted by the latter's forced marches.

[5] Murray (1694–1760), younger brother of James, the loyal second duke of Athol, and of Tullibardine, did not in fact join until shortly after the YP reached Perth on 4 September 1745. Out in both 1715 and 1719, Murray had recently been appointed sheriff-deputy by the government and had visited Cope on 21 August. Upon joining the YP, Murray was made lt.-general. See Blaikie, *Itinerary*, p. 12; 'Chevalier' de Johnstone, *Memoirs*, 2nd ed. (London, 1821), p. 16; *Report of Proceedings*, pp. 16, 132; Winifred Duke, *Lord George Murray and the Forty-Five* (Aberdeen, 1927), ch. v.

[6] William Murray (1696–1756), third earl of Dunmore (1752), brother of John Murray, second earl

On the 30th, they marched no more than three Miles, on Advice that the King's Forces, under the Command of his Excellency Lieutenant-General Sir *John Cope*, was marching towards them.[1] However, this afterwards proved a false Rumour. *Charles* express'd great Bravery on this Occasion; and shewing a Medal which he wore on his Right Arm, said, *he feared nothing while he had the Protection of that holy Relique*.[2] And indeed the greater Part of the Army, who were now Catholics (so well had the Priests, who were now likewise encreased in Number, bestowed their Time, and so plentifully had they bestowed their Reliques) seemed to rely more, some on an old Tooth, others on a Lock of Hair, and others on some such Bawble, for Protection, than on their Swords: Not that they neglected the human Means of strengthening themselves; on the contrary, they spent at least twelve Hours in every Day in the Exercise of their Arms, to their Instructions in which the few Officers they had addicted themselves incessantly.[3] *Charles* himself was constantly busied either in this, or his Devotions; which last occupied a full third Part of his Time: Nay, so very devout is he in his Inclinations, that General *Macdonell* one Day endeavoured, with some sort of Ridicule, to give him a gentle Reprimand; but he returned it with great Severity, saying, God knew best what might be the End of any other Journey he was taking; but this he was certain of, that whenever he was on his Knees, he was on his direct Road to Heaven;

of Dunmore, who during the Forty-Five was a general of foot under Cumberland. After Culloden William Murray surrendered, pleaded guilty to treason, and was pardoned. Walpole to Mann, 13 September 1745, notes the adherence of Lord George Murray and William Murray; *Yale Walpole*, xix. 104 and *n*. Of the other persons who joined at Perth, perhaps the two most notable were David Ogilvie (1725–1803), styled Baron Ogilvie (1731–83), eldest son of the fourth earl of Airlie, attainted for his part in the rebellion, titular earl of Airlie (1761); and William Drummond (1690–1746) fourth viscount Strathallan. According to Elcho, *Short Account*, p. 249, Ogilvie was made lord lieutenant of Angus and was 'sent to raise men'. Murray of Broughton, *Memorials*, p. 230, says that Strathallan was appointed governor of Perth and commander-in-chief of such forces as were or might be in that town. O'Sullivan places Strathallan at the head of the 'Perthshire Squadron' of horse just prior to Prestonpans; *1745 and After*, p. 75.

[1] The implication of fearfulness or caution is false. Both O'Sullivan and Sir John Macdonald testify to forced marches of 20–5 miles a day as the YP tried to come up with Cope at the Corrieyarrack pass; *1745 and After*, p. 64 and *n*. The YP then rested his forces as he awaited intelligence of Cope's movements. By 30 August, when he marched to Dalnacardoch, about six miles from Blair Castle, the YP knew that Cope had 'slipped' round him to Inverness, which the latter had in fact reached on 29 August; Blaikie, *Itinerary*, p. 11; *Report of Proceedings*, p. 47.

[2] Fielding may have taken his cue for this purely fictitious anecdote of the medal from a contemporary pamphlet entitled *A Genuine Intercepted Letter, from Father Patrick Graham* . . . (London, 1745). See 'General Introduction', above, p. xlix. The *Letter*, which is itself fictitious, carries the dateline 'Perth, September 1, 1745'.

[3] Cf. O'Sullivan: 'The stay we made at Perth, gave us some leasure to acustome our folks to a little regular duty, of mounting of guards, & occupying of postes, & vissiting of them, wch was still forming 'um'; *1745 and After*, p. 67. See also John Heneage Jesse, *Memoirs of the Pretenders* (London, 1845), i. 228.

a Road in which he was certain one Day or other to come to a happy End of his Journey.

While they remained in this Camp, *Charles* gave two Instances, the one of his exact Regard to Discipline, the other of his more exact Regard to his Religion. One of the Highland Guards had stole a Sheep; of this being accused, he was try'd by a Court-Martial, and condemned to be shot, which Sentence was accordingly executed; a Rigour, which Regard to Discipline might have excused, had it been as well exerted towards another, who having committed a Rape on an Infant of 11 Years of Age, was pardoned.[1] Nor could any other Reason be assigned for the too great Severity shewn to the one, or the too unjust Mercy shewn to the other; but that the former was a Protestant, and the other a Papist: Nay, the only Defence which the latter could be brought to make, was that the Girl was a Heretic, and *against such all things were lawful*.[2] A dreadful Religion indeed, which teaches us to divest ourselves of Humanity to our fellow Creatures, only from serving their God in a different Manner, and holding different Tenets of Religion from our own: And which horrible Zeal can be only accounted for from the worldly Interest of Priests, and the dark Ignorance in which they bury the Minds of all Lay Zealots, over whom they exercise so despotic an Authority, that however benevolent and good they may otherwise be in their Dispositions, yet when the Cause of their Religion once interferes with their Humanity, the latter is always sure of being sacrific'd to the former: So that as in the Protestant Religion, that is to say, in the pure and true Spirit of Christianity, sincere Piety always renders a Man kind, good, and charitable towards all other human Beings; so doth a violent Zeal in Popery as certainly divest him of all these amiable Principles; and the more pious the Catholic, the worse always must be the Man, in all Matters where the Interest of his Religion, or of propagating the Faith, as they call it, is concern'd: A Fact so established, that every Page almost of the Histories of popish Countries abounds with Examples of the bloodiest and most cruel Actions done, at the Instigation of Priests, by Men who on all other Occasions have shewn the very mildest and best Dispositions.

---

[1] Although the London papers sometimes hinted at acts of pilferage and even sexual abuse, no evidence has been found for either of this artful pair of anecdotes. Lord George Murray, who described himself as determined that there should be no pillaging, refers to some sheep-stealing at about the time the rebel army crossed the Forth at Frews (13 September); 'March of the Highland Army', *Jacobite Memoirs of the Rebellion of 1745*, ed. Robert Forbes (Edinburgh, 1834), pp. 33–4. Jesse, *Memoirs of the Pretenders*, i. 236, records that during the march through the lowlands Lochiel shot one of his men for plundering.

[2] A veritable topos of anti-jacobite propaganda, including Fielding's. See the index of this volume, *s.v.* 'Heretics'.

I hope my Reader will pardon this Digression, which I thought the Nature of the Fact sufficiently warranted on this Occasion. I now return to these Rebels, by whose Arms this blessed Religion is attempted to be introduced, with all the War and Massacre and Bloodshed, in which its Genius delights, into this Country.

On the 31st, they came to *Perth*,[1] which they took Possession of without any Opposition: Here Mass was celebrated publickly, and *Charles* and most of the Army assisted at it.[2] Then the Pretender's Declaration was publickly read at the Market Cross, after which he was proclaim'd with great Solemnity.[3] A Minister of the Kirk meeting with *Charles* in the Street, offered to give him Advice, not to shew so great Zeal for his Religion, and reminded him of the Fate which his Father had met with in the last Rebellion, which he attributed to his Disregard to the holy Presbytery and adhering to Popery, to which, the Minister said, he had sacrificed his Crown. *Charles* answered coldly, his Father preferred an heavenly Crown to an earthly one: Upon this, one of the common Soldiers reviled the Minister, and spit in his Face; for which Fact, without any other Merit, he was within two Days afterwards preferred to be a Lieutenant.[4]

One of the Highland Chiefs, who, tho' he had simply embraced the Party of the Rebels, was however a rigid Presbyterian, declared the highest Indignation at this Preferment, and ventur'd to remonstrate against it to *Charles* himself: He was answer'd, that his Word was not to be controuled, nor the Reasons of his Conduct to be enquired into by the Subject. And the very next Morning this poor Man was found shot in his Bed; nor was any the least Enquiry made after the Murderer.[5]

Such is the Spirit of Popery and arbitrary Power, to which the Blood of so many Millions hath been shed for a Sacrifice.

While the Rebels lay at *Perth*, they had frequent Alarms of the King's

---

[1] The rebel army did not reach Perth until the evening of 4 September; Blaikie, *Itinerary*, p. 11. Fielding could have got the correct date from the *London Gazette* of 10–14 September. On 31 August they were at Blair Castle in Athol, which Fielding mistakenly places after Perth in his version of the YP's itinerary; see below, p. 49.

[2] There is no trustworthy evidence that mass was said in public, and such a celebration was highly unlikely.

[3] Cf. 'Chevalier' de Johnstone, *Memoirs of the Rebellion in 1745 and 1746*, 2nd ed. (London, 1821), pp. 14–15: 'There he immediately proclaimed his father, James the Third, King of Great Britain; and published a manifesto, and, at the same time, the commission appointing him Regent of the kingdom: both of them dated from Rome'; also Elcho, *Short Account*, pp. 248, 251. The event was widely reported in the London papers; for example, *General Evening Post* of 14–17 September.

[4] The anecdote is apocryphal.

[5] Cf. *DA* of 16 September: 'Letters have been receiv'd from Scotland, which relate, that one of the Chiefs of the Rebels had been found shot in his Tent. He it seems was invited into their Service, and not finding Things as they had been represented to him, had made heavy Complaints thereof.'

Forces being ready to attack them,[1] on which Account the whole Army, amounting to 3600 Men and upwards,[2] and which were disposed in three Regiments, were drawn out, and lay one whole Night and Day under Arms; but no Enemy appearing, on the 2d of *September*, at Ten in the Morning, they marched back into their Camp. The same Day the Marquis of *Tullibardin*, at the Head of 500 Men, took Possession of the Duke of *Athol's* House at *Blair*,[3] whither the next Morning *Charles*, the Duke of *Athol*,[4] Lord *Asgill*,[5] Lord *George Murray*,[6] and some more, repaired, and were entertained by the Marquis, who was saluted there by the Title of the Duke his Brother.

The Duke of *Perth* summoned many of his Tenants to meet him at *Blair*, and bring with them all the Rent they owed him, on Pain of being treated with the utmost Severity. He likewise ordered as many of them as could procure Arms to furnish themselves therewith, and bring them along with them: Most of these obeyed his Summons, and produced him all the Money and Arms in their Power. But instead of discharging these

---

[1] In fact, while at Perth the YP received intelligence that Cope, realizing his blunder, had sent to Edinburgh for shipping to be dispatched to Aberdeen so that he might transport his army by sea to Dunbar and hence back to the capital itself. The rebels held a council to consider intercepting Cope on his march to Aberdeen (he reached it on 11 September), but the decision was for Edinburgh; Murray of Broughton, *Memorials*, pp. 187, 189–91.

[2] Fielding's source for this estimate has not been found; the figure is higher than that commonly given in the London papers. *General Evening Post* of 10–12 September estimates 3,000; *DA* of 3, 5, and 10 September reports a range from 1,500 to 3,000. Jacobite sources give lower figures: Elcho, *Short Account*, pp. 244–9, implies a figure of 2,150; de Johnstone, *Memoirs*, p. 15, asserts that on his arrival in Perth the YP 'had not above a thousand followers', but there were considerable augmentations at Perth; Robert Chambers, *Jacobite Memoirs of the Rebellion of 1745* (Edinburgh, 1834), p. 32 *n.*, prints a letter from the YP to his father, dated from Perth, 10 September 1745, in which he says, 'I have got together thirteen hundred men, and am promised more brave determined men.'

[3] Cf. *DA* of 7 September, reprinting a letter dated Edinburgh, 31 August: 'We have this Day Accounts that the Marquis Tullibardin has, with a strong Party of 500 Men, taken Possession of his Brother's House (The Duke of Atholl) at Blair. The Duke of Atholl was obliged to go to Edinburgh with his Family.' James Murray, the duke of Athol, who was loyal in the Forty-Five, had left Blair Castle for Edinburgh (and ultimately London) some ten days earlier; Winifred Duke, *Prince Charles Edward and the Forty-Five* (London, 1938), p. 90. The *Caledonian Mercury* of 2 September prints a story that Tullibardine had written his brother demanding that he vacate both title and estate, but the same paper later retracts the report. On the YP's itinerary Blair Castle preceded Perth by some days.

[4] There is some confusion here. James Murray, the titular duke of Athol, was no longer in his own house to be 'entertained', having fled to Edinburgh some ten days earlier. Fielding alludes to Murray's departure below, p. 50. But if the reference is to Tullibardine, now about to be 'saluted' by that title, the result is the non-sense of Tullibardine's entertaining himself. Fielding may have intended to name the duke of Perth.

[5] Not identified. Probably an error, not a fiction, though none of the names of the notables who joined the YP at this time garbles conceivably into 'Asgill'.

[6] By his own account Lord George Murray 'joined the standard at Perth the day his Royal Highness arrived there' (i.e., 4 September 1745); 'Marches of the Highland Army', *Jacobite Memoirs of the Rebellion of 1745*, ed. Chambers (Edinburgh, 1834), p. 30. There is no evidence that Murray was present for the entertainment at Blair Castle on 31 August, which Fielding mistakenly puts after Perth on the YP's itinerary.

poor Wretches, after they had delivered him their Rent (and some of
them more than was due) he insisted on their bearing Arms in the Pretender's Cause. To this likewise several submitted, (such are the Terrors
of arbitrary Power) three however resisted, declaring, that besides the
Inconvenience which the Neglect of their Affairs would subject them to,
and the Danger of the Undertaking, it was against their Conscience to
assist the Cause of Popery against the true Religion of their Country; to
which one of them had the Boldness to add, he was sorry to see his
Grace embark'd in such a Cause: Upon this, the Duke flying into a Rage,
snatch'd up a Pistol which lay in his Tent, and immediately shot the
poor Man through the Head. After which the other two made their
Escape from him, and one from the Camp, the other being pursued and
killed by one of the Rebels, who was Witness to the whole Transaction.[1]

This Duke of *Perth*, notwithstanding the apparent Cruelty of this
Action, is a Man of a good Character, and hath formerly behaved himself like a worthy and good-natur'd Gentleman:[2] But such is the Nature
of this Cause, and of the Spirit with which it is conducted; headed by a
young, rash, ambitious, fiery Zealot, under the absolute Government
and Guidance of furious, enraged Priests, who breathe nothing but
Blood and Desolation, and have so effectually breath'd their horrid
Principles into the poor wild Wretches under their Influence and
Command, that the whole Army, according to *Macpherson*, and others
who have seen it, is liker to a Legion of Devils than of Men. May God
confine them to their own Borders, or, if they attempt to overleap them,
inspire this Nation with a Spirit sufficient soon to drive them out of her
own Bowels, in which they would quickly become the most violent and
mortal Disease.

The Duke of *Athol*, who had retired to *Edinburgh* with his Family,[3] on

---

[1] In this paragraph Fielding is embroidering several reports from the London papers. Cf. *General Evening Post* of 14–17 September: 'The Duke of Perth's Tenants, who will not willingly concur in his Measures, are fled, leaving their Families and their Harvest-Work, to avoid an ill-tim'd and cruel Resentment'; also in *Penny London Post* of 16–18 September. And *Penny London Post* of 25–7 September: 'We hear from Dundee, that the Duke of Perth kill'd two of his own Farmers for refusing to raise in Arms with him, and that Lord Ogilvie has been very cruel to everyone that refus'd him'; also in *General Evening Post* of 24–6 September, and *St James's Evening Post* of the same date.

[2] For James Drummond, titular third duke of Perth, see above, p. 44. Walpole dismissed him as 'a silly race-horsing boy'; to Mann, 27 September 1745, *Yale Walpole*, xix. 118. But Murray of Broughton, *Memorials*, pp. 188 n. –189, confirms Fielding's estimate: 'full of disinterestedness, of undaunted courage, the most exemplary, humanely, and universally beloved'; and 'Chevalier' de Johnstone, *Memoirs*, 2nd ed. (London, 1821), p. 27, judged Perth to be honorable and possessed of a mild and gentle disposition.

[3] So reported in the London papers; for example, *DA* of 7 September, citing a letter datelined Edinburgh, 31 August. In fact the duchess of Athol was 'separated' from the duke; Walpole to Mann, 13 September 1745, *Yale Walpole*, xix. 106. And their children appear to have been left to the charge of the duke's jacobite brother, Lord George Murray, who mentions his responsibility in a letter to the

the first News of the Rebels Approach, had taken such Care to convey away every thing which could be either carried or drove off from his Territories, as well as his House, that the Marquis of *Tullibardin* had great Difficulty to provide a very moderate Entertainment for the Pretender's Son and his Followers: The Army therefore, (which was now grown very numerous) found very little Reason to be satisfied with the Plentifulness of their Quarters.[1] Indeed, if the Priests had consulted Policy as much as Religion, they could never have found a fitter Opportunity to proclaim a general Fast than the present. No Bull of the Pope's would ever have been more certain of finding a most exact and punctual Obedience. The whole Army therefore, which on the 2d of *September* had encamped at the *Blair* of *Athol*, on the 3d marched back again towards *Perth*.[2] In their March the Van-Guard had like to have fallen in with a small Party of the King's Dragoons;[3] upon which an Alarm was immediately spread through the whole Army of the Rebels, that Sir *John Cope* with the King's Forces was approaching; but these few Dragoons presently retiring, delivered them from their Apprehensions almost as soon as they were risen, and quickly after some more welcome Guests arrived; for on the same Day about thirty Head of Cattle were driven to the Camp, for which the Pretender's Son promised the Owners Payment, when he had got Possession of what he called his Father's Crown.[4]

On the 9th of *September*, the *Inverness* Post was stopt as he passed by *Athol*; he was immediately brought before the young Pretender, who

duke dated 3 September; Winifred Duke, *Prince Charles Edward and the Forty-Five* (London, 1938), p. 93; also Duke, *Lord George Murray and the Forty-Five* (Aberdeen, 1927), pp. 67, 70. For Athol's letters describing his plans, see *More Culloden Papers*, ed. Duncan Warrand, iv (Inverness, 1929), 23.

[1] Neither the premise nor the inference is supported by the evidence. Tullibardine had in fact written ahead to have the castle made ready, and the absent duke's factor, who had remained behind, reported that Tullibardine 'seemed much pleas'd' by the arrangements; Winifred Duke, *Prince Charles and the Forty-Five* (London, 1938), p. 91. Murray of Broughton, *Memorials*, p. 186, states that the YP's troops 'were here very commodiously quartered ... and here was the first time that the men could properly be said to have had bread from the time of their rendezvous at Glenfinnan'. Tullibardine's approbation of the 'alterations made there [Blair castle]' appear to have been known in London; Walpole to Mann, 13 September 1745, *Yale Walpole*, xix. 106.

[2] There is no evidence of such a march by 'the whole Army' from Blair back to Perth, although smaller units may have done so; see the next note, below. On 3 September the main rebel army had not yet reached Perth, resting for the night at Dunkeld; Blaikie, *Itinerary*, p. 11.

[3] Not substantiated. However, although Cope did not take the dragoons with him on his march north, some of Gardiner's had been sent to Perth in August to relieve the foot; Jarvis, *Collected Papers*, i. 36. Actual contact with the dragoons is not recorded until the YP was much nearer Edinburgh; Blaikie, *Itinerary*, p. 13. Just possibly Fielding is utilizing the report of a 'false Alarm' which appeared in several London newspapers. As an illustration of the rebels' supposed cowardice, *DA* of 17 September prints a report from Edinburgh, dated 10 September, that Tullibardine's men were returning to Perth from Athol at night with some horses and were mistaken by the rest of the rebel army for royal dragoons ready to attack; also in *Penny London Post* of 16–18 September. Both reports go on to record (in dialect) the rebels' fear of fighting the 'Tracoons'.

[4] Not substantiated.

ordered his Packets to be searched,[1] and two Priests, one of whom is made a Bishop,[2] and dignified by the Title of his Lordship, were appointed to read the Letters. Some of these Letters were detained, and the rest delivered back again to be conveyed as directed.

While the Army lay at *Blair*, Mass was constantly celebrated twice a Day in the Chapel of the Castle;[3] at which *Charles* never failed to assist, together with all the principal Noblemen, and others. Here 30 *French* Officers,[4] together with the famous General *Cameron*,[5] joined them; these were immediately dispersed in a new Regiment, the Command of which was given to that General.

These Officers, who landed in a long small Vessel in the West of *Scotland*, brought with them Dispatches to *Charles* from his Father, and, as was reported,[6] a considerable Sum of Money. The Confessor likewise read a Letter publickly, which he had received from the Pope, containing Absolution and Indulgences to all those who should embrace the Catholic Religion and the Pretender's Party:[7] And many took him at his Word, particularly one *James Cameron*, who had so well recommended himself by expressing an extraordinary Zeal against Heretics, that the Confessor procured him an Ensign's Commission: He was afterwards

---

[1] Fielding's elaboration of an event widely recorded. The *Edinburgh Evening Courant* of 5 September and the *Caledonian Mercury* of 6 September report the interception and search of the Inverness post at Blair, the former mentioning that a clergyman wearing a white cockade interrogated the postboy 'specially'. See also *DA* of 12 September and *General Evening Post* of 10–12 September, with an indication the event took place on Sunday, 1 September, which does not fit Fielding's chronology.

[2] The newspaper reports make no mention of a second priest or of a bishop.

[3] Fielding's invention. Reporting on the YP's stay at Perth, the *Caledonian Mercury* of 16 September states that 'Mr. Armstrong preached before the young Chevalier, from the Text of Isaiah xiv. 1, 2'. The service was Scottish episcopal; Robert Chambers, *History of the Rebellion of 1745–46*, p. 21; Jesse, *Memoirs of the Pretenders*, i. 229; W. Drummond Norie, *Life and Adventures of Prince Charles Edward Stuart* (London, n.d.), i. 11.

[4] Not substantiated. There were frequent rumors of foreign augmentations; for example, *London Gazette* of 10–14 September and *DA* of 17 September report that 'some Gentlemen of Distinction from the Low Countries [i.e., French from the Flanders theatre] have joined them'. Murray of Broughton wrote Lord Pitsligo from Blair castle on 2 September 1745 that 'yesterday' a gentleman arrived from France with assurances of assistance; *Jacobite Letters to Lord Pitsligo*, edd. Alistair and Henrietta Tayler (Aberdeen, 1930), p. 31. See also below, *n.* 6.

[5] Presumably Donald Cameron (1695–1748) of Lochiel, eldest son of the chief and colonel (not general) in command of his regiment of Camerons. The 'Lochiel' of the Forty-Five, he had been one of the first to come out for the YP and would be instrumental in the bloodless taking of Edinburgh later in the month. He led the advance guard into Perth.

[6] No such report has been found. In a letter to Tweeddale dated 14 September 1745 Cope enclosed copies of letters to the YP at Perth from the Spanish ambassador at Paris (dated 1 August NS) and the duc du Bouillon (dated 10 August NS) promising aid from their respective countries. Elcho, *Short Account*, p. 247, says they were brought to Blair by John Roy Stuart; see also Browne, *History of the Highlands*, iii (Glasgow, 1843), 443–4. On the same day (31 August) he received the promissory letters, the YP also received assurances from Marshall Saxe that 'he would do all in his power to prevent the English from sending men from Flanders to England'; Elcho, loc. cit.

[7] There is no record of such a letter at this time. In the *Dialogue*, below, p. 84, Fielding represents the pope as giving the pretender indulgences for this purpose.

rebuked by his Brother (who is a rigid Presbyterian) for going to Mass; upon this he swore, that he had got Heaven and a Pair of Colours both in an Hour.[1]

At this Time the Alarm grew very high in *London*. On the 9th, his Majesty published a Proclamation for disarming Papists and Non-jurors, and for commanding all Papists and reputed Papists to depart from the Cities of *London* and *Westminster*, and from within ten Miles from the same; and for confining Papists and reputed Papists to their Habitations, and for putting in Execution the Laws against Riots and Rioters.

And now Addresses of the most loyal and zealous Kind began to flock in from all corporate Bodies in the Kingdom, in which the City of *London*,[2] the Court of Lieutenancy,[3] and the whole Body of Merchants,[4] led the Way: All these were conceived in the strongest Terms of Loyalty, and expressing a true Sense of the Dangers with which these Kingdoms were threatned by Popery and arbitrary Power. All People began to think of arming themselves in the Cause of the Public; and several Noblemen, who have since put it in Execution, took out Commissions to raise Regiments for the public Service.[5]

[1] Fielding's invention. The name and rank of James Cameron and the concept of two brothers may have been suggested by the list of rebel dead at Prestonpans, which Fielding copied in this pamphlet (below, p. 70) and which contains the names of Allan Cameron and James Cameron, ensign. There is no evidence they were brothers; indeed their differing regimental affiliation makes it unlikely. For Allan Cameron, see *A List of Persons Concerned in the Rebellion . . .* edd. Lord Rosebery and the Rev. Walter Macleod, Publications of the Scottish History Society, viii (Edinburgh, 1890), 282. There is no listing for James.

[2] The addresses began to 'flock in' shortly after George II arrived back in England from Hanover, on 31 August. Temporally speaking, the 'way' was led by the City of Worcester, whose 'humble Address', dateline Kingston, 3 September, appeared in the *London Gazette* of 31 August–3 September 1745. The City of London's address, dateline Kensington, 10 September, was recorded in the name of the lord mayor and 'the rest of your Majesty's Commissioners of Lieutenancy', promising to have the City militia always in readiness; *London Gazette* of 7–10 September.

[3] The somewhat irregular convention of lords lieutenant for the City of London. The principal crown officers within the prescribed limits of their lieutenancies, they were charged with raising, arming, and employing the militia, as per 14 Car. II (1662), c. 3, s. ii (2). See *Serious Address*, above, p. 31, and 'General Introduction', above, p. xliii; also Jarvis, *Collected Papers*, ii. 97–119.

[4] Under dateline Kensington, 11 September, the *London Gazette* of 10–14 September prints the 'humble Address' of the merchants of the City of London, pledging loyalty to the present royal family and further exertions in support of public credit. Their subsequent meeting to consider raising two regiments at their expense 'for his Majesty's Service' is reported in *General Evening Post* of 10–12 September, and their opening of a subscription to raise 'upwards of a million sterling, at easy Interest, if 'tis wanted', in *DA* of 12 September.

[5] Most notably Fielding's 'princely' benefactor-to-be, the duke of Bedford, whose appointment as lord lieutenant of the county of Bedford is reported in the *London Gazette* of 17–21 September. Walpole wrote Mann (20 September 1745) he had just heard that Bedford 'will ask leave of the King to raise a regiment', that the duke of Montagu had a troop of horse ready, and that the duke of Devonshire was out raising men in Derbyshire; *Yale Walpole*, xix. 110; *DA* of 26 September. By 28 September *DA* reports that twelve peers of the realm had determined to raise thirteen regiments among them, and estimates of two regiments of horse and thirteen of foot, to be raised by thirteen noblemen,

Sir *John Cope* was now at *Inverness*,[1] with his Forces, where he received Orders to take the most immediate Road to the Rebels, even by Sea, if there were no other more expeditious Method;[2] in pursuance of which Orders, he embarked his Forces at *Inverness*, and sailed directly towards *Leith*,[3] by which means he hoped to intercept the Rebels before they could possibly arrive at *Edinburgh*.

The Rebels lay all this while in their Camp near *Perth*, where their Generals and other Officers lost no Opportunity of regimenting and disciplining them with the utmost Expedition.

One Evening (when *Macpherson* himself happened to do Duty as one of the young Pretender's Guards) a Person came to the Camp, and was, by his Desire, conducted to the Presence of *Charles*, with whom he staid in close Conference, at which only the Dukes of *Perth* and *Athol* (for so the Marquis of *Tullibardin* was now called) were present, during several Hours.[4] Soon after his Departure, it was rumoured through the whole Army that the City of *Edinburgh* was to be betrayed to them, and that they were to march in a Day or two to take Possession.[5]

Accordingly, on the 11th Instant, at Break of Day, the Army marched, and came that Day to *Dumblain*, which is 22 Miles.[6] The next Day they halted in the Morning, were drawn up and reviewed by

were finally presented to the Commons on 29 October, and voted on 4 November; *Journals of Commons*, xxv. 13, 14. For the politics implicit in this mode of raising troops, see 'General Introduction', above, pp. xliv–xlv.

[1] According to his own, later testimony before the board of inquiry, Cope arrived at Inverness on 29 August and left there 4 September; *Report of Proceedings*, pp. 33, 47.

[2] In a letter from Tweeddale to Cope 10 September, it is clear that the 'Idea of endeavouring to force your Way ... into the *Low-Country*' either by the coast road or by the sea, was Cope's own, though consonant with a previous government order to confront the rebels at the earliest possible opportunity; *Report of Proceedings*, p. 185. On the 'peremptory' nature of the earlier order and its effect on Cope's plans, see above, p. 45 and *n.* 3.

[3] In fact, Cope marched from Inverness to Aberdeen, 'with all possible Expedition, without a Halt', and there embarked for Leith; *Report of Proceedings*, p. 34. Unfavorable winds required a landing at Dunbar, too late to prevent the rebels from investing Edinburgh; *Report of Proceedings*, p. 35.

[4] No evidence for such an episode has been found. Indeed, according to O'Sullivan, the duke of Perth was absent from Perth a good deal of the time, raising his men in the countryside; *1745 and After*, p. 69. Tullibardine was similarly occupied in and around Blair; letters from Lord George Murray to Tullibardine at Blair dated from 7–10 September, printed in Winifred Duke, *Lord George Murray and the Forty-Five*, pp. 77–81. Murray of Broughton, *Memorials*, p. 188, expressly states that the YP left Tullibardine behind at Blair to raise the Athol men.

[5] There is no evidence of such a rumor at such a time. Fielding is looking ahead to the unopposed capture of Edinburgh on 17 September, which was widely rumored to have been the result of a betrayal by certain public officials. See below, pp. 56, 58.

[6] Essentially correct, though according to O'Sullivan (*1745 and After*, p. 69) and Maxwell of Kirconnel (*Narrative of Charles Prince of Wales' Expedition to Scotland in the Year 1745* [Edinburgh, 1841], pp. 32–3) only part of the army actually made it as far as Dunblane (Dumblain). Mabel Seymour, 'Fielding's History of the Forty-Five', *PQ*, xiv (1935), 111, notes the indebtedness of the information here to the *London Gazette* of 17–21 September 1745.

General *Cameron*;[1] and having been under Arms all that Day, advanced in the Evening as far as *Down*, which is only two Miles distant from *Dumblain*.

On the 13th, they again marched at Day-break, and in the Morning passed the Frith[2] at the Ford of *Frews*, five Miles above *Stirling*. Here *Charles* attempting to give an extraordinary Instance of his Bravery, by passing the Water first, and mistaking the Ford, very narrowly escaped drowning,[3] from which he was preserved by Lieutenant *Duncan Madson*, who at the Hazard of his own Life rescued him from the Waves;[4] a Service for which he would certainly have been rewarded, had not Religion and the Priests (*Madson* being a firm Adherent to the Presbytery) opposed his Promotion. Indeed so strong is this Biass in the Mind of *Charles*, that not a single Instance can be produced of any Preferment being bestowed by him, unless on those who have embraced his Religion.[5]

The Army having pass'd the Frith at this Ford, which is about five Miles above *Stirling*, halted for some Time, while a Council was held at their Front among the Generals, after which they were directed to march towards *Glasgow*,[6] and they all apprehended the Design was to

[1] Most contemporary accounts agree that there was a day's halt at Dunblane, but there is no evidence of a review by General Cameron, whose prominence Fielding appears to antedate and exaggerate.

[2] i.e., the Firth (of Forth). Seymour, 'Fielding's History of the Forty-Five', *PQ*, xiv (1935), 111, notes that the information and even the wording of this sentence derive from *London Gazette* of 17–21 September 1745.

[3] Fielding's tendentious elaboration of an event widely reported. Cf. *Caledonian Mercury* of 16 September: 'the Young Chevalier had been the first who put Foot in the Water, and waded through the Forth at the Head of his Detachment'; reprinted in *St James's Evening Post* of 21–4 September 1745. The near drowning is Fielding's invention; John Home, *History of the Rebellion in the Year 1745* (London, 1802), p. 77, and Robert Chambers, *History of the Rebellion in Scotland in 1745, 1746* (Edinburgh, 1827), i. 90, refer to the river Forth's being low as the result of dry weather. For a poem celebrating the fording, see Dougal Graham, 'Impartial History . . . of the late Rebellion . . . in the Years 1745 and 1746', *Collected Writings*, ed. George MacGregor, i (Glasgow, 1883), 93. Graham claims to have witnessed the fording.

[4] The rescue is certainly a fiction, and the name 'Duncan Madson' does not appear among those which historians have associated with the rebellion.

[5] There is a difficulty here. The running title of the *History* (above, p. [34]) states that Macpherson himself had a captain's commission, yet the text proper (above, p. 39) has him informing the YP's confessor, in the former's presence, that he 'was of the Presbytery'. Fielding may not be responsible for the running title, and it is worth noting that there is no reference in the text to Macpherson's captaincy. Indeed, his pulling guard duty (above, p. 54) tells against such a commission.

[6] There is no evidence from the likely participants either for such a council at this time or for orders to march to Glasgow. Lord George Murray, who mentions neither, did write to Tullibardine from Perth on 10 September, 'We are to be at Glasgow & Edinr'; Winifred Duke, *Lord George Murray and the Forty-Five*, p. 90. Henderson, *The Edinburgh History of the late Rebellion*, 4th ed. (London, 1752), pp. 10–11, offers an explanation without naming his source: 'They seemed to direct their Rout to *Glasgow*, which City they summoned; but receiving no Answer, they turned toward Edinburgh.' On the night of 13 September, from Leckie House, the YP did write the provost of Glasgow for a contribution of £15,000 and the surrender of all arms; Blaikie, *Itinerary*, p. 13. *DA* of 24 September prints a

make an Attempt on that City; but on the 14th in the Morning, the Posture was chang'd; they turned short towards the East, and came to *Falkirk*; and on the 15th advanced within Sight of *Edinburgh*, their Vanguard being posted about three Miles to the East of *Gogar*, and which is about the same Distance from *Edinburgh*.[1] Here they again halted, and were drawn up, in order, as they supposed, to form the Attack of the Town;[2] but were immediately surprized to see the young Pretender, with the Duke of *Perth*, &c. at the Head of the Royal Regiment of Guards only, advance directly towards the Town, where, as they soon after heard, the Gates were thrown open for their Reception.[3] General *Guest*, with some of the King's Forces,[4] some arm'd Townsmen, with the

report datelined Edinburgh, 16 September: 'The Rebels sent two of their Number last Saturday [14 September] to Glasgow, and demanded 15,000 l. Contribution, but we have not learned what Answer was return'd.' In all probability Fielding is drawing his own inferences from the *London Gazette* of 17–21 September: 'The rebels left Perth the 11th, and marched all that Day to Dumblain, twenty miles, to Down; and on Friday the 13th they passed the Forth at the Fords of Frews, five Miles above Stirling; They then seemed to direct their March towards Glasgow; but on the 14th in the Morning they turned Eastward, and marched by Falkirk, towards Edinburgh.' See also *DA* of 23 September.

[1] The *Caledonian Mercury* of 16 September reported that detachments had come as far as Kirkliston, Wainsburgh, and Gogar, 'five or six Miles distant'; as cited in *Daily Gazetteer* of 24 September. The main rebel army reached Linlithgow early on the 15th, halted there for much of the day, and encamped three miles east of town along the Edinburgh road; Blaikie, *Itinerary*, p. 14; Lord George Murray, 'Marches', in *Jacobite Memoirs of the Rebellion of 1745*, ed. Robert Chambers (Edinburgh, 1834), p. 36; Murray of Broughton, *Memorials*, pp. 192–3. The source of Fielding's further precision has not been found.

[2] Both the itinerary and the dating seem foreshortened here. There is no evidence that the army generally supposed itself ready to attack Edinburgh as early as the 15th. Indeed, Murray of Broughton, *Memorials*, p. 193, speaks of being under arms on the 16th, marching in close files and 'being ready to receive the Dragoons in case they should venture to attack'. And the YP did not send his summons to the city magistrates demanding surrender until he was at Corstorphine on 16 September; Blaikie, *Itinerary*, p. 14. Fielding could have found a more accurate itinerary in the *Caledonian Mercury* of 23 September, the issue from which he says he got his casualty figures for Prestonpans (below, p. 70).

[3] Edinburgh was in fact entered, not by the YP, who was with the main body at Slateford, but by Lochiel ('General' Cameron) with O'Sullivan, Murray of Broughton, and 900 men. The Netherbow gate was opened for another purpose, and the rebels forced their way in without firing a shot; *Memorials*, pp. 194–5; *1745 and After*, pp. 71–3. Here and above (p. 54) Fielding implies that Edinburgh was betrayed in some way. He was one of the first to do so in print. Archibald Stewart (d. 1780), MP Edinburgh 1741–7 and provost of the city, was arrested on suspicion of treason 30 November and committed to the Tower 13 December 1745; *Journals of Commons*, xxv. 22, and *GM*, xv (1745), 614. He was later acquitted.

[4] Joshua Guest (1660–1747), lt.-general 1745, deputy governor of Edinburgh Castle 1745. His retirement into the Castle 'where the Publick Offices and the Inhabitants had secured their most valuable Effects' was reported in the *London Gazette* of 17–21 September and reprinted in the London papers of 23 September. At this time Guest had no units of the regular foot with him, and the dragoons had retreated one more time, to Haddington. The reference to the king's forces is therefore to the 'new City Regiment' formed from the commissions recently sent to the city by the government in London; *Caledonian Mercury* of 16 September reports the movements of this regiment, sixteen companies of trained bands, and the city guard just prior to the taking of the city. See also Blaikie, *Itinerary*, p. 15.

Bank and most of the valuable Effects,[1] and with Provisions, as it was then said, for ten Weeks, being retir'd into the Castle.[2]

The Declaration was then read, and the Pretender immediately proclaimed at the Market Cross, as he had been before at *Perth*; at which Ceremony some Magistrates (but whether voluntarily or by Compulsion was not known) assisted, with all the Gentry and Nobles of the Rebels Army.[3] This Ceremony was accompanied by a triple Discharge of the Small Arms from the Guards, as well as from the Artillery, with most of which the Castle had supply'd the Town for their Defence;[4] and this Salute was again returned from the Army without the Walls; such, I mean, as had Fire-Arms, which did not amount to a third Part.[5]

In the Evening, some of those who had attended the Pretender's Son

[1] The removal of the two Edinburgh banks to the Castle was reported in the London papers; for example *DA* of 21 September and *London Evening Post* of 19–21 September.

[2] The source of this estimate has not been found. However, the London papers carried many reassuring reports of the castle's supposed provisions; for example, *DA* of 5 October: 'And we are further inform'd, that the Governor of the Castle has several Months Provisions, and is in no Danger.' The *Caledonian Mercury* of 30 September reported that the castle, although blocked off on the city side, was getting provisions by rope at the corner of the west port. Cf. Walpole to Mann, 27 September: 'it is scarcely victualled for a month, and must surely fall into their hands'; *Yale Walpole*, xix. 118.

[3] The *Caledonian Mercury* of 18 September reports the YP's entry into the city, his attendance at Holyrood in Highland dress, and in the afternoon the carpet spread at the Cross, with subsequent readings of the OP's declaration, the act of regency, and the YP's confirmatory manifesto. No source has been found for Fielding's definite placing of the magistrates at the ceremony. According to John Home, 'few gentlemen were to be seen on the streets, or in the windows'; *History of the Rebellion in the Year 1745* (London, 1802), pp. 101–2. But the *Caledonian Mercury* of 23 September states that 'Greater Demonstrations of Joy was never seen since the Restoration of King Charles II'. And Fielding may have been put in mind of the detail by the *Gazette* account (10–14 September) of the similar ceremonies at Perth, which took particular note of the *absence* of that city's officials.

[4] No eyewitness account mentions such a salvo, though Home does say that 'at mid-day they surrounded the Cross with a body of armed men, and obliged the Heralds to proclaim King James'; *History*, pp. 101–2. Given the rebels' clear need to conserve ammunition, this detail is probably fictitious, designed to stress further Fielding's imputation of betrayal or mismanagement; see above, p. 54. However, the rebels did acquire arms and ammunition at the taking of Edinburgh. According to O'Sullivan, 'there were a good or indifferent twelve hundred stand [of arms] found and some ammunition, wch were much wanting to us'; *1745 and After*, p. 74. Elcho, *Short Account*, p. 257, estimates a thousand stand of arms and notes that the rebels 'Stood in need of them'. At his subsequent trial provost Stewart deposed that 'the whole Arms of the City-Regiment were returned [to the castle] except those of the Men upon Guard', but the arms in possession of the trained bands were held to be the property of the burgesses and, according to Stewart, General Guest did not comply with the request that he send down troops to 'take up' these arms. According to Henderson, *Edinburgh History of the Rebellion*, p. 11, about eighteen artillery pieces had earlier been brought down from the castle and planted 'upon the Ports of the Town'. According to testimony at Stewart's trial, some of these may have been spiked on Guest's orders before the rebels occupied the city; *Trial of Archibald Stewart*, pp. 122–3, 125.

[5] The source of this particular estimate has not been found. However, prior to the news of the fall of Edinburgh the London papers carried many reports that the rebels were short of firearms. *DA* of 16 September speaks of the rebels as 'indifferently arm'd' and then (17 September) estimates, 'Not one half of them have tolerable Arms'. For a distinctly minority view, see Murray of Broughton, *Memorials*, p. 198, where it is claimed that in the whole rebel army 'there was not two hundred men without Musquets'.

into the Town, returned into the Camp, and gave an Account to the
Rebels there of the Reception which *Charles* and his Friends had met
with; and which (whether it arose from Fear or Favour I will not determine) was much more to his Satisfaction than he expected.[1] Indeed, had
the City been inclined to have made a vigorous Resistance, it would have
been very difficult, if not impossible, for the Pretender's Forces to have
taken it in any reasonable Time; especially as they daily expected a Visit
from Sir *John Cope*,[2] and who, it was said, was to have been greatly
strengthened with a Regiment from the Townsmen of *Edinburgh*.[3] This
Success, therefore, (to whatever Treachery it was owing) greatly elated
the whole Party, especially the Priests, who failed not to ascribe it to the
Favour of Heaven, as they again deriv'd that Favour from the Prevalence
of their own Prayers. These Persons little consider the horrid Impiety
they are guilty of, by attributing to the immediate Interposition of the
Supreme Being, the Consequences which are produc'd by the Iniquity
and Villany of Men; making him thus, in order to serve their vile Purposes, the Author of the blackest Treachery and Deceit; as if he would,
by his own divine Conduct, authorize and sanctify that detestable and
hellish Maxim of popish Priestcraft, to do Evil that Good may come of
it; or in other and truer Words, as if he would inspire the blackest
Principles into the Minds of Men, in order to propagate a most cruel,
impious, and idolatrous Religion, by all the Means of Treachery and
Violence. A horrid Blasphemy, by which they have made God the

---

[1] See *Caledonian Mercury* of 23 September. Elcho, *Short Account*, p. 259, estimates a crowd of 60,000
and says they 'fill'd the Air with their Acclamations of Joy'.

[2] On 17 September, the day Edinburgh fell, Cope's army had not yet disembarked at Dunbar
(not Leith, as originally planned). Home, *History*, pp. 93–4, states that on the evening of the 16th
the Edinburgh magistrates learned 'that the transports with General Cope's army were off Dunbar;
and as the wind was unfavourable for bringing them up the Frith, that the General intended to
land his troops at Dunbar, and march them to the relief of the city'. In his own defense provost
Archibald Stewart later claimed that Cope's troops 'could not get within Six Miles of it [the city]
sooner than the *Friday Evening*, near *four Days* after the City was taken'; *Trial*, p. 130. Reflecting on
Stewart's trial, Murray of Broughton, *Memorials*, pp. 195–7, judges that under the circumstances
Edinburgh would have been reduced 'in less than half a days time'. Certainly the view from
London was different: Tweeddale to Cope, 21 September: 'You may well believe, we were all much
surprized and concerned to hear, that the City of *Edinburgh* had capitulated with the Rebels, especially, when there was so near a Prospect of your coming with the Army under your Command to
their Assistance'; *Report of Proceedings*, p. 193.

[3] *DA* of 24 September carried a report that 'about 400 of the Volunteers in Edinburgh had receiv'd
their Arms before the Rebels had enter'd the Town, and as the Soldiers, &c. went out of the Town,
they also follow'd them, and had join'd Sir John Cope, whose Army is, we hear, near 4000 strong, and
the greatest Part good Troops'. The so-called Edinburgh regiment was to have been 1,000 men, paid
for by voluntary subscriptions, raised by royal commission under the king's sign manual. The commission had only reached the city on 9 September. Contemporary observers estimated the total
actually raised at between two and three hundred, and generally held the unit in low esteem; see, for
example, *A True Account of the Behaviour and Conduct of Archibald Stewart, Esq.* (London, 1748), p. 16,
which compares them facetiously to Falstaff's empressments of the dead bodies of the hanged.

Author of dreadful Massacres, *in which a hundred Thousand poor Souls, of all Ages and Sexes, have been inhumanly, in one Night, butchered in their Sleep*.[1]

The Pretender, with his principal Followers and 500 of his Guards, were lodged in the Town,[2] where he was treated with rather more Respect than Fear will well account for, though I am willing to attribute as much as possible to that Motive, as the Weakness of Human Nature will allow it, base as it is, some little Degree of Excuse preferable to those wicked Principles, which as they are more diabolical, so are likewise more voluntary and in our own Power. The rest of his Guards took up their Quarters in the Canongate:[3] And this Part of his Army found sufficient Means, notwithstanding what had been withdrawn into the Castle, to refresh themselves,[4] after the Labours of a very fatiguing and hungry March, where they had little more to comfort and keep up their Spirits, but those Hopes of Rewards which their Priests very liberally bestowed on them in another World, and these now and then sweetened with some Insinuations of temporal Preferments in this, when the Treasures of *England* shall be employ'd to reward the Loyalty and Sufferings of Highlanders.

As to the main Body of the Rebels, as soon as their several Guards and Picquets were fixed (for their Generals omit no sort of military Discipline or Precaution) the rest of them were ordered into their Camp,[5] in order to their Repose, which was very acceptable to Men who had little else besides the Noise and Smell of Gunpowder to regale themselves with for the last 24 Hours:[6] This Want, however, was somewhat remedied the next Morning, when their Friends sent a pretty large Supply of Provisions to the Camp,[7] which was nevertheless soon

---

[1] The so-called St Bartholomew's Day massacre of 1572. See *Serious Address*, above, p. 23.

[2] Fielding's source for the number of guards and their disposition has not been found. The YP himself lodged at Holyrood, in the Duke of Hamilton's apartment; Elcho, *Short Account*, p. 259. For the disposition of the guard itself, which Elcho puts at 1,000, see *Short Account*, p. 261. Apparently the majority was lodged 'in the parliament house and Assembly room' (p. 265).

[3] This detail, which is accurate as to place, does not appear in the accounts published by the London papers. Elcho, *Short Account*, p. 265, says that there were fifty guards in the Canongate. Murray of Broughton, *Memorials*, p. 198, says, 'No more men were quartered in Town than were necessary for its preservation.'

[4] Fielding probably means to imply a degree of collaboration among the citizens. But cf. O'Sullivan, *1745 and After*, p. 73, who says he 'went to the Majistrats spoke to 'um a little high' and ordered that 'there shou'd be bread & beer deliverd to the detachempt immediately as a gratification, & that every thing else wou'd be payed for'.

[5] In the King's Park near Duddingstone; Blaikie, *Itinerary*, p. 15.

[6] Fielding seems to forget that according to his account the main rebel army met with no resistance just prior to Edinburgh and that the city itself fell without a shot being fired. There was occasional cannonading from the castle.

[7] According to Home's eyewitness account, 'a great quantity of provisions, which had been ordered from the town, was brought to the Highlanders, just as he arrived among them'; *History*, p. 103. See also Murray of Broughton, *Memorials*, p. 198, and *The Woodhouselee MS*, p. 31.

exhausted by so large a Multitude; and several Parties, without asking Leave of their Commanders, detached themselves up and down the Country to provide for their own Bellies.

The Rebels (as the Guards, &c.) within the Town, were now not much better supplied than those without, the Provision which the People cared to afford them being almost totally exhausted the first Day, and the neighbouring Country having before been pretty well drained by the Prudence of General *Guest*. Some of the more violent desired to be led on to the Assault of the Castle,[1] though almost impregnable by Nature, and well furnished with Cannon, Ammunition and Men. This Attempt was too romantic and impossible, to receive any Countenance from their Commanders: And it was then with the utmost Difficulty that they were restrained from plundering the whole Town; however, the Consideration that they were their own Countrymen somewhat allayed their Fury, though it did not entirely prevent all Disorders; and many Violences were in spite of the superior Officers committed, as well on the Persons as Properties of the Inhabitants, both Men and Women;[2] for all of whom (except those concerned in the Treachery of delivering up the Town) the Reader will have a just Compassion. God forbid that any City of *England* should ever be exposed to the same Danger, to all the Rapine and Cruelty which such a Banditti of Ruffians, when let loose by their Commanders, nay, even encouraged by them, would without Mercy commit; a Scene of Misery more easy to conceive, than pleasant to describe; and of which, without my undergoing that irksome Task, the Reader may have an adequate Idea, by perusing the History of any one popish Conquest.

As it was no easy Matter to prevent the Hunger of the Soldiers from committing Outrages at this Season, so the furious Zeal of the Priests, and of their young Pretender, now elated with Success, was as difficult to be bridled: And it was not without the utmost Persuasion, backed with some strong Remonstrances from the cooler and more politic of his Party, that *Charles* was prevailed on not to have Mass celebrated, and *Te Deum* sung in the principal Kirk of the City. Nor would this prudent

---

[1] A plausible surmise, for which no source available to Fielding has been identified. After the victory at Prestonpans (21 September 1745) the question of besieging the castle was seriously debated by the rebel leaders and a halfhearted undertaking begun. Prior to Prestonpans, however, there is no evidence that the question was a serious one. According to the *Lockhart Papers*, ii. 447, a cannonading from the castle on 18 September wounded Lochiel and some of his guard, leading to a proposal that the rebels strengthen the guard around the castle so as to reduce it by famine.

[2] Another plausible surmise for which no source has been found. Most London reports of plundering and supposed atrocities refer to a later time, after Prestonpans, when even sources sympathetic to the jacobites conceded there were problems. See *DA* of 5 October 1745 and Elcho, *Short Account*, p. 281.

Council have restrained him for the present from an Act which would have incensed the whole Kirk of *Scotland*,[1] had not an Alarm of General *Cope's* being landed at *Dunbar*,[2] by threatning immediate Danger, given some Assistance and Support to their Arguments. The Reluctance with which this Design was laid aside, and indeed the whole Temper of these Men, may well be gathered by the Language of one *Callaghan*, an *Irish* Priest, who had newly joined them, and who declared, in the Hearing of Mr. *Macpherson*, that no farther Success was to be expected by those who durst not publickly celebrate the true Religion in Defiance of a Sett of Protestant Dogs; nor could they hope the Lord would fight their Cause, who suffered his Temples to be polluted by Heretics.[3]

The News, however, of Sir *John Cope's* landing, a little deadned the Joy[4] which the Encrease of Numbers,[5] want of Opposition, and the betraying the Capital of *Scotland* into their Hands, had given the Rebels; and the more, as Fame had greatly enlarged the Strength of the King's Forces, who were reported to be augmented by two *Dutch* Battalions,[6]

[1] An unsubstantiated anecdote, inconsistent both with the YP's policy of keeping a low religious profile and with his proclamation of 23 September, read upon his reentry into Edinburgh after Prestonpans, which offered protection to all ministers of the gospel and asked that they not abandon their kirks as they had previously done; see *Caledonian Mercury* of 23 September 1745.

[2] By his own posterior testimony, Cope finished disembarking the last of his forces on 18 September, which was the date Hamilton's and Gardiner's dragoons joined him after their departure from Edinburgh, and the whole unit began marching toward Edinburgh on the 19th; *Report of Proceedings*, p. 36. According to Murray of Broughton, *Memorials*, p. 198, by the evening of the 19th the YP had 'certain intelligence' of Cope's march from Dunbar.

[3] The priest, the name, and the episode are invented.

[4] According to Murray of Broughton, *Memorials*, p. 199, the YP expressed, not alarm, but 'a great deal of satisfaction' at the report. Rebel leaders frequently complained of the difficulty of keeping their forces intact when there was no prospect of meeting the enemy.

[5] Under an Edinburgh dateline of 24 September, *DA* of 1 October 1745 reports that the YP was joined by the Grants of Glenmoriston 'and some others' on 20 September; see also *Caledonian Mercury* of 23 September 1745. The Grants, totaling perhaps 100 men, joined at Duddingston; Blaikie, *Itinerary*, p. 16. Inasmuch as Fielding particularly notes the Grants, below, p. 62, he may have had in mind other augmentations which were rumored about this time. According to Home, at Edinburgh the YP was joined by MacLachan of MacLachan with 150 men and by Lord Nairne with 250 men from Athol; *History*, p. 331. Murray of Broughton, *Memorials*, p. 198, says 'a good many' joined the duke of Perth's regiment as volunteers; but cf. Elcho, *Short Account*, p. 261.

[6] Expectations of Dutch assistance were of long standing. On 3 September from Inverness Cope wrote Tweeddale: 'My information is, that yesterday Morning about four of the Clock the Rebels had an Account of Troops landed at *Leith*.... The Troops landed they reported from *Ostend*; I wish it were true'; *Report of Proceedings*, p. 184. From London Walpole wrote Mann on 6 September of his hope that 3,000 Dutch 'are by this time landed in Scotland'; *Yale Walpole*, xix. 103. *DA* of 7 September reports 'Advice, that 1500 of the Dutch Troops from Williamstadt, being the first Embarkation, are arriv'd at Leith'. The 'Advice' was premature. *DA* of 19 September reports, 'We hear that an Express is arriv'd at the Marquis of Tweeddale's Office, with the Account that one Regiment of the Dutch Forces was landed at Leith'; *DA* of 21 September: 'We hear that 2500 Dutch Troops from Williamstadt are arriv'd in Scotland.' At Cope's trial, evidence was deposed to show that the Dutch were prevented from landing at Leith, 'forced, by contrary Winds, into Burlington Bay'; *Report of Proceedings*, p. 192. By the terms of the Treaty of Utrecht (1713) the States-General were required to furnish 6,000 soldiers for the defense of the British crown. The troops sent over from Willemstadt belonged to the

and in themselves to be much more numerous, than in Reality they were.[1]

On the 19th, the whole Army of the Rebels was drawn forth, and having receiv'd a fresh Distribution of Arms from those taken in the City of *Edinburgh*, there were upwards of 4000 regularly armed, and full 3000 more, who were provided with Daggers and other irregular Weapons, the whole amounting to between 7 and 8000 Men.[2]

With 2500 of these, General *Macdonell* was commanded to keep Possession of *Edinburgh*,[3] and the rest under the Command of General *Cameron*[4] marched that Evening, and encamped at *Duddington*, in order to meet and fight the King's Forces.

On the 20th, the *Grants* of *Glenmoriston* and some others joined the Rebels,[5] who having by their Scouts received information of the March of General *Cope*, advanced that Evening to a Place called *Carberry-hill*,[6]

garrisons of Tournai and Dendermond, which had surrendered to the French on 20 June 1745 NS and released under pledge not to serve against French forces before January 1747. The French exacted the pledge in the case of the Dutch troops in Scotland and they never joined Cope in action; Blaikie, *Itinerary*, p. 88.

[1] According to Elcho, *Short Account*, p. 266, just prior to Prestonpans the YP had 'a pretty just account' of Cope's horse and foot, an opinion concurred in by Murray of Broughton, *Memorials*, p. 200, who puts the figure at 'about 2700'.

[2] Fielding's source, for either the review of the army or the estimate of its numbers, has not been identified. His figures, though high, roughly reflect those published in London. Cf. *DA* of 24 September 1745, citing a letter from Newcastle dated 20 September, which places the rebels at Haddington to the number of 5,000, with 2,000 left behind in Edinburgh itself. On 20 September Walpole wrote Mann that the rebels marching to Edinburgh numbered 5,000, a figure which corresponds to that offered by Samuel Boyse, *Impartial History of the Late Rebellion* (Reading, 1748), p. 80, who notes that only half that number actually engaged in the fighting at Prestonpans; *Yale Walpole* xix. 108 and 109 *n*.

[3] Neither Sir John Macdonald nor Macdonald of Keppoch stayed behind at Edinburgh. Fielding's figure of 2,500 soldiers in Edinburgh, though not markedly out of line with estimates published in the London papers, is high. He may have arrived at it by mediating between estimates of the entire rebel force (including irregulars, deserters, etc.) at between seven and eight thousand and the estimate (again high) of Cope and other governmental apologists that the rebels numbered 5,000 at the forthcoming battle of Prestonpans; *Report of Proceedings*, pp. 43, 59. According to Murray of Broughton, 'In obedience to the orders given on the morning of the twentieth the gaurds [*sic*] retired from the Citty and joined the Army at Duddingston'; *Memorials*, p. 199. Murray states (p. 198) that a 'small' guard was left at Holyrood. Elcho, *Short Account*, p. 262, claims that the city and the castle believed, mistakenly, that 300 highlanders had been left behind to 'cut off any Sally from the Castle'.

[4] The 'famous General *Cameron*'; see above, p. 52. Lochiel, who, according to Henderson, *History*, p. 27, was 'Governor' of the city during its initial occupation by the rebels, was not titularly a general nor was he commander of the main body. Murray of Broughton states that the YP marched at the head of his army, with the Camerons, Lochiel commanding, 'in front'; *Memorials*, p. 200.

[5] Reported in the *Caledonian Mercury* of 23 September 1745.

[6] Named in its account of the battle by the *Caledonian Mercury* of 23 September. Cf. Elcho, *Short Account*, p. 266: 'Gain'd the top of Carberry hill which goes to Tranent, where they plainly descried Gen. Cope's Army drawn up in Line of Battle in the plains below Tranent.' See also Murray of Broughton, *Memorials*, p. 200, and de Johnstone, *Memoirs*, p. 30, who puts the arrival at Carberry Hill 'about two o'clock in the afternoon'.

where they pitched their Tents.[1] Indeed they were now pretty well supply'd with the Addition they had received from *Edinburgh*,[2] with a sufficient Number for those Forces which they had with them, which amounted to upwards of 5000.[3] In the Evening the two Armies came in view of each other, and accordingly, though the Rebels had pitch'd their Tents, both of them lay that Night on their Arms.

About Three in the Morning the Rebels began to move, and turn'd at first Eastward and marched about a Mile in Length,[4] then facing about to the Left they formed themselves in five Columns;[5] in which Posture they advanced towards Sir *John Cope*, *Charles* himself taking Possession of a neighbouring Hill, from which he might survey the whole Action.[6]

It is said, he at first declared a Resolution of leading on his Army himself to the Charge, but was dissuaded from it by General *Cameron*, who told him, he would then put his own Life, on which the Success of his Father's Arms depended, on the same even Chance with that of the meanest Soldier; that it would be difficult for him to restrain his natural Ardour in the Action, and thus by exposing his Person, he might win the

[1] In the evening of the 20th the rebel army was not pitching tents but maneuvering, 'in close order of Battle', to get nearer Cope; Murray of Broughton, *Memorials*, p. 201. The *Caledonian Mercury* of 23 September reports that both sides were under arms that night. Fielding's plausible inference concerning the tents may have been stimulated by another item in the *Caledonian Mercury* of the same date, reporting a rebel demand for the city of Edinburgh that it supply 1,000 tents for the army. But see the next note.

[2] In addition to whatever arms and supplies were seized when the rebels first entered Edinburgh, Elcho reports being sent by the YP on 18 September to demand of the magistrates '1000 tents, 2000 targets, 6000 pr of Shoes, and 6000 Cantines'; *Short account*, pp. 261–2. The demand was reported by the *Caledonian Mercury* of 23 September 1745. At his trial provost Stewart dated the rebel request as of the 19th and claimed the rebels did not get the mandated equipment until 'three Weeks' after the battle; *Trial*, pp. 61, 131.

[3] The modern consensus puts the number at *c.* 2,500; Blaikie, *Itinerary*, p. 91. See also above, p. 62 and *n*.

[4] Cope later testified before the board of inquiry that his patrols first reported eastward movement at 3:00 A.M.; *Report of Proceedings*, p. 40. The movement was required by the rebel decision to attack Cope's left (east) flank, which meant marching first due east (in the afternoon) and then northeast (at night), traversing a small defile at the east end of the ditch and boggy ground which separated the two armies. See Murray of Broughton, *Memorials*, pp. 200–1; Lord George Murray, 'Marches', pp. 38–9; O'Sullivan, *1745 and After*, p. 79; de Johnstone, *Memoirs*, pp. 33–4; *Lockhart Papers*, ii. 448–9; and, for a convenient modern account of the preliminary maneuvering, Katherine Tomasson and Francis Buist, *Battles of the '45* (London, 1962), pp. 47–64.

[5] After negotiating the defile, the bog and the ditch, the rebel column faced left towards Cope, first in three main units or 'Columns' (front, rear, reserve), then, in forming for battle, into five; see Tomasson and Buist, *Battles of the '45*, p. 68.

[6] According to all contemporary witnesses, the YP posted himself with his life-guards behind the attack line and somewhat in advance of the highland reserves, nominally commanded by Lord Nairne. See O'Sullivan, *1745 and After*, p. 79; de Johnstone, *Memoirs*, p. 37; Andrew Lumsden, 'A Short Account of the Battles of Preston . . .', in *Origins of the 'Forty-Five*, ed. Walter Biggar Blaikie, Publications of the Scottish History Society, ii (Edinburgh, 1916), 408. Fielding's plausible introduction of a hill is not borne out by the topography of the battlefield, which was essentially the flat plain leading down to the sea.

Victory, and lose his Cause.[1] He added, that it would be time enough for him to engage in such a Risk, when King *George* himself should in Person oppose him; but that Sir *John Cope* was not of Consequence or Dignity sufficient to justify his hazarding himself Arm to Arm against him.

These Arguments were backed by the Priests, who declared it was Presumption; at the same Time asserting, that by Invocation of the Saints, and by *Ave Mary's* and *Pater Nosters*, he would lend more Assistance to his Cause than the Valour of Thousands could give to it.

Won, therefore, by these united Persuasions, he with his Priests ascended the Hill, where, while they devoted themselves to Prayers to the Saints, the Army proceeded to the Charge.[2]

About Four in the Morning, the Patrole brought an Account to General *Cope*, that the Rebels were in Motion in their Camp;[3] upon this the King's Forces, who had lain all Night on their Arms, were drawn up in order of Battle; the Foot being in the Center, two Squadrons of Dragoons placed on the Right, and as many on the Left, the remaining two Squadrons being drawn up in the Rear to support the Foot: The Artillery were placed in the Front to the Left.[4]

This was the Situation of both Armies, when the Highlanders marched on to the Attack; and Sir *John Cope*, whose Disposition was truly good and military, rode several times from the Right to the Left of the Line, encouraging his Troops, who all express'd great Spirit, and a Resolution of doing their Duty. This Disposition the General was afterwards obliged in some little to alter, by the Alterations which the Enemy made in theirs.[5]

---

[1] Either a brilliant inference or privileged information. Although there is no evidence for Lochiel's initiative or for the gist of his argument as rendered (plausibly) here, both O'Sullivan and Lumsden speak of the efforts made by Lord George Murray and the highland chiefs to prevent the figurehead of the rebellion from exposing himself to danger; *1745 and After*, p. 79; 'Short Account', in *Origins of the 'Forty-Five*, p. 408. Home, *History*, pp. 108–9, refers to a council of war, while the army was still at Duddingston, in which the chiefs were particularly opposed to the YP's proposal that he lead them into battle. That the YP was not involved in the fighting (which lasted only eight minutes) was widely noted in London; for example, *GM*, xv (1745), 530.

[2] The priests, their arguments, and the scene are invented.

[3] Cf. Cope, *Report of Proceedings*, p. 40: 'Then [4:00 A.M.] an Account was brought us, that they were moving northward, down towards *Seaton*, to come up by the East-end of the Plain, to attack us upon our left Flank.' This was the movement of the rebels as they passed through the defile and lined up off what was at that time Cope's left flank, requiring him to wheel his entire line about to a north–south axis.

[4] This description of Cope's battle formation is essentially accurate, except that his artillery was on the right front and the squadron of Gardiner's dragoons, lacking room on the right wing, 'formed in the Rear of the Artillery-Guard, a few Paces behind, ready to sustain it'; *Report of Proceedings*, p. 40. Before Cope wheeled his entire line around to face the rebels' new formation, his artillery had been on the left front as specified here. See Tomasson and Buist, *Battles of the '45*, pp. 63–4.

[5] Fielding's exculpatory description of Cope's 'Disposition' at this juncture is confirmed by the testimony of eyewitnesses given to the board of inquiry in 1746: 'he saw Sir *John* ride from Right to Left, giving his Orders to the Troops, and returning frequently backwards and forwards in the Front of the Line'; *Report of Proceedings*, p. 60. See also Tomasson and Buist, *Battles of the '45*, p. 64; *GM*, xv (1745), 520. In London, however, blame was not long in coming to Cope; for example, Walpole to Mann, 27 September 1745, *Yale Walpole*, xix. 117.

The extreme Column of the Rebels, which were to the Right, having advanced till they were opposite the Cannon,[1] which consisted only of six small Field Pieces,[2] immediately faced about, and ran with the utmost Violence up to the Mouths of the Cannon, which by an extreme Neglect of those whose Duty it was, not however to be in the least charged on the General, never fired on them once:[3] It was then that the brave Colonel *Gardiner* ordered his Dragoons to charge them in Flank, which Service he could not prevail on them to perform; but having given them a single Discharge of their Fire-Arms, they immediately turned about, and like Men struck with a sudden Panic, ran away.[4]

The Colonel having in vain attempted to rally them, (as did Lord *Loudon*,[5] who threw himself at their Head, and charged the Rebels) on a sudden quitted his Horse, and charged with the Foot,[6] who being

[1] Fielding's error in placing Cope's artillery on his left wing instead of the right leads here to the further error of confronting it with the rebels' right wing, the 'extreme' or farthest advanced from the bog and the ditch. It was the rebels' left wing, predominantly Lochiel's Camerons, which opposed Cope's artillery and soon overran it; Tomasson and Buist, pp. 64–7. The source of Fielding's confusion with respect to Cope's artillery is not known; the account in *Caledonian Mercury* of 23 September is correct.

[2] Cope's entire artillery consisted of six cannon (1½-pounders) and six 'cohorns' (mortars).

[3] It was fairly common knowledge that Cope had not been able to commandeer any professional gunners from Edinburgh castle; in consequence he had to make do with a volunteer (Whitefoord), the aging master-gunner of Edinburgh castle, and three invalids; *Report of Proceedings*, p. 40. However, at Cope's examination by the board of inquiry it was deposed that all of the cohorns and five of the cannon were fired once (p. 54). Elcho, *Short Account*, p. 271, and Murray of Broughton, *Memorials*, p. 203, concur in saying that the cannon only managed one firing. Some fuses had been 'damnified' by long storage in the castle and it is not known how many mortar shells actually burst; Tomasson and Buist, *Battles of the '45*, p. 64.

[4] Colonel James Gardiner (1688–1745) commanded one of the two regiments of dragoons that were with Cope at Prestonpans. Because there was insufficient room on the right wing between the artillery and the foot for both Gardiner's squadron and that of his second-in-command, Lt.-Col. Whitney, Gardiner's squadron was demoted to a position just in the rear of the artillery. After Whitney's squadron broke and the artillery with its guard was being overrun by Lochiel's Camerons, Lord Loudon ordered Gardiner to charge. According to Cope's later testimony, 'upon that Squadron's receiving a few shot from the rebels, they rein'd back their Horses, and went off likewise'; *Report of Proceedings*, p. 41; also Tomasson and Buist, *Battles of the '45*, pp. 67, 69. Only a handful of his dragoons kept the field with Gardiner, whose bravery was laconically noted in the London papers; see, for example, *DA* of 1 October 1745. For Gardiner's life and death, see below, *n.* 6 and p. 66.

[5] John Campbell (1705–82), fourth earl of Loudon (1731), governor of Stirling Castle (1741–63), aide-de-camp to George II (1743), appointed colonel (April 1745), was acting as adjutant-general with Cope at Prestonpans. In June 1745 Loudon (Loudoun) had been given the commissions necessary to raise a 'new' highland regiment, to consist of twelve companies and some 1,250 men. His new regiment, which had been recruited mostly around Inverness and Perth, was represented at Prestonpans by three companies in reserve. Although he joined Cope in the retreat to Berwick after the battle, Loudon was made commander of the highland anti-jacobite forces in October 1745. See Major A. McK. Annand, 'John Campbell, 4th Earl of Loudon', *Journal of the Society for Army Research*, xliv (1966), 22–4. In the account of the battle which he deposed at Cope's examination, Loudon said that after he ordered Gardiner to attack, 'I saw no more of what happened there, as I went directly to the Foot'; *Report of Proceedings*, p. 140.

[6] Many of the apotheosizing accounts of Gardiner's death record that after his dragoons left the field, Gardiner himself dismounted and tried to rally the foot. However, Alexander Carlyle cites cornet Ker, Gardiner's kinsman, who was posted nearby, as saying Gardiner fell from his horse after two

attacked with great Fury by the Highlanders, and seeing themselves deserted by the Horse, after having made two irregular Fires, which did very little Execution, many of them threw down their Arms, and turned their Backs to the Enemy.

All was now in general Confusion: Poor Colonel *Gardiner*, and those few brave Officers that stood their Ground, fell a Victim to the Rage of the Enemy,[1] who finding no longer Resistance, fell to the most inhuman Butchery,[2] with which having somewhat tired themselves, they proceeded to make Prisoners of all those, who survived the blunted Edge of their Swords.[3]

On the KING's Side there fell in this Action, and were wounded;[4]

Of Colonel Gardiner's Dragoons.

The Colonel himself, kill'd.
Lieut. Col. Whitmore,[5] wounded.

gunshot wounds in his right side, and, unable to remount, was cut down by an axe; *Autobiography of the Rev. Dr. Alexander Carlyle*, ed. J. H. Burton (Edinburgh, 1860), pp. 137–43.

[1] The sanguinary circumstances of Gardiner's death became something of a *cause célèbre*. According to an undated 'Letter concerning the Behaviour and Fall of that brave Officer in this unfortunate Action', after receiving initial wounds in the breast and shoulder Gardiner dismounted and was wounded three more times: by a bullet in the shoulder, by a broadsword on the forehead, and finally, from behind, by a Lochaber axe; *London Magazine*, xiv (1745), 543–4; *GM*, xv (1745), 530. Still alive, Gardiner was taken from the battlefield to the local minister's house in Tranent, where he died the next morning; Alexander Carlyle, *Autobiography*, pp. 137–43. Murray of Broughton, who insists that 'the many Storeys spread about Col¹ Gardners death were equally groundless', argues that Gardiner's shame at his regiment's behavior drove him to obstinate resistance; *Memorials*, p. 204. Later, at Carlisle, the authorities executed one John McNaughton for Gardiner's death; *List of Persons concerned in the Rebellion*, pp. 252–3, 380. But Murray of Broughton claims that McNaughton, whom he calls 'an honest inoffensive creature', was a hundred yards away from Gardiner when the latter was finally struck; *Memorials*, p. 204 n.

[2] Contemporary accounts on both sides agree that the battle was bloody. After giving a first fire, many of the highlanders threw away their muskets and resorted to the sword; Murray of Broughton, *Memorials*, p. 203. Most jacobite accounts stress the effect of the weaponry. The *Caledonian Mercury* of 25 September 1745: 'Certain it is that never were such Strokes seen given by Sword as on the above Occasion; not only Mens Hands and Feet were cut off, but even the legs of Horses'; de Johnstone *Memoirs*, p. 38: 'The field of battle presented a spectacle of horror, being covered with hands, legs, arms, and mutilated bodies; for the killed all fell by the sword.' Nevertheless, jacobite officers were sensitive to the issue of atrocities and there is evidence they were busy after the battle trying to prevent 'inhuman Butchery'; *Battles of the '45*, pp. 71–2. Henderson *History*, p. 31, attributes much of the stripping and mutilation of the bodies to 'the Boys who followed the Rebels'.

[3] Fielding may mean to imply that the rebel swords had been deliberately blunted so as to wound more atrociously. However, many of the highland soldiers carried axes, scythes, and pitchforks, in addition to the regulation broadsword. For a detailed (if dyspeptic) account of their weaponry, see *The Woodhouselee MS*, ed. A. Francis Steuart (London, 1907), pp. 26–7.

[4] Fielding's list of the killed and wounded on 'the King's Side' most closely resembles the list published in the *London Gazette* of 24–8 September 1745. The *Gazette* list was widely reprinted in the London papers; for example, by *DA* and *Daily Post* of 30 September 1745.

[5] No such name appears on any of the published lists in connection with Gardiner's regiment. Evidently a mistake for 'Whitney', which appears at this place in the *Gazette* list. Lt.-Col. Shugbrough Whitney, who commanded a squadron of Gardiner's dragoons on the right wing between the foot and

In Hamilton's Dragoons.

Lieut. Col. Wright, wounded.
Major Bowles, wounded.

In Lascelles's Foot.

Capt. Stuart, kill'd.
Ensign Bell, much wounded.

In Murray's.

Capt. Leslie, slightly wounded.
Ensign Haldane,[1] dangerously wounded.

In Guise's.

Capt. Pointz, dangerously wounded.
Capt. Holwell, kill'd.

In Leigh's.[2]

Lieut. Col. Whiteford,[3] wounded.
Capt. Bremer, kill'd.
Capt. Rogers, kill'd.

the artillery, received a disabling wound on the sword arm; *Report of Proceedings*, p. 41; *Battles of the '45*, p. 67. Appointed lt.-col. of Gardiner's regiment in June 1739, Whitney is often referred to as 'colonel' in the report of Cope's examination and is undoubtedly the 'Col. Whitney' listed below (p. 70) among the prisoners from Gardiner's regiment'; *The Whitefoord Papers*, ed. W. A. S. Hewins (Oxford, 1898), p. 91 *n*. He must have been among those captured officers who broke their parole, for he was in the battle of Falkirk (17 January 1746) and was killed.

[1] *London Gazette* of 24–8 September 1745 prints 'Haldane', as do all other known printed lists. The ensign in question is probably identical with the Ensign 'Holden' whom Fielding lists among the prisoners from Murray's regiment (below, p. 69). In the latter case *Caledonian Mercury* of 23 September 1745, Fielding's acknowledged source, prints 'Haldane'.

[2] So spelled in the *Gazette* of 24–8 September 1745, but more commonly 'Lee's', as below and in the narrative above, p. 40.

[3] *London Gazette* of 24–8 September describes 'Whiteford' as 'slightly wounded' and lists him after Bremer and Rogers. One of the few legitimate heroes in Cope's army at Prestonpans, Charles Whitefoord (d. 1753), of Cochrane's 5th Marines, was visiting relations in Scotland when the rebellion broke out. He volunteered his services to Cope, first as Commissary and later as commander of the artillery: 'At the unhappy affair of Prestonpans he acted (tho' unqualified) as Engineer, fired all the guns were discharged on that occasion, stayed, after he was deserted by the whole people were to assist him, till he expended all the powder he had, killed the Ensign and knocked down what they called their Royal Standard, was wounded, taken prisoner and lost his horses and baggage'; *The Whitefoord Papers*, p. xviii. The *Gazette* list and those deriving from it place Whitefoord with Leigh's, probably because his artillery was on the line next to that regiment and after the dragoons fled and the artillery guard was overrun, Whitefoord stood fast and was taken with the latter unit, which was a company of Leigh's. In the list of prisoners below (p. 70), he is listed separately (and properly) with master-gunner Griffith, his assistant with the artillery. According to Jarvis, *Collected Papers*, i. 279, Whitefoord was the historical Waverley, turned by Scott 'into Colonel Talbot with all the glamour of *Waverley* around him'.

The following Officers were taken Prisoners.[1]

Of Guise's Regiment.

Capt. Pointz.
Lieutenants, Cuming and Paton.[2]
Ensigns, Wakeman and Irvine.

Of Lord John Murray's.

Capt. Sir Peter Murray.
Lieut. James Farquarson.
Ensign Allan Campbell.

Of Lee's.

Col. Peter Halket.
Captains, Basil Cochran,[3] Chapman, and Tatton.
Lieutenants, Sandilands, Drummond, Kennedy, and Hewitson.
Ensigns, Hardwick,[4] Archer and Dumbar.
Mr. Wilson, as Quarter-master.
Dr. Young.

Of Murray's.

Lieut. Col. Clayton.
Major Talbot.
Captains, Reid, John Cochran, Scot, Thomas Leslie, and Blackes.
Lieutnants, Thomas Hay, Cranston,[5] Disney, Wale, Wry, and
    Simms.

[1] Although the *London Gazette* never published a list of prisoners, a number of such lists, by no means identical, were published in the London papers during the last week of September and the first week of October. Fielding's list appears to derive from *Caledonian Mercury* of 23 September 1745 as emended by at least one London paper, *Daily Post* of 3 October. In its sequence and spelling of names, as well as in regimental assignment, Fielding's prisoner list also closely resembles that in a pamphlet (without title-page) whose half-title reads: 'A True and Full Account of the late *Bloody* and Desperate Battle fought at Gladsmuir, betwixt the Army under the Command of His Royal Highness *Charles* Prince of Wales, &c. and That commanded by Lieutenant General Cope, on *Saturday* the 21st of September, 1745.' Although this account reprints (p. 8) the YP's declaration dated 30 September 1745 a reference (p. 1) to allowing 'the few following Lines a Place in your Paper' may indicate the earlier appearance of those 'Lines' and the prisoner list which follows (pp. 4–5) in a newspaper, undoubtedly a Scottish one.

[2] *Caledonian Mercury* of 23 September 1745 prints 'Patton'.

[3] Copy-text prints 'Basil, Cochran'; here emended to conform to *Caledonian Mercury* of 23 September 1745 and to all other known listings of this person.

[4] Copy-text prints 'Hadwick'; here emended to conform to *Caledonian Mercury* of 23 September 1745 and all other known listings of this person.

[5] *Caledonian Mercury* of 23 September 1745 here inserts the names of cornets 'Jacob' and 'Nash', which not only interrupts the listing by rank but, if their rank is correct, is additionally inappropriate. A cornet was the fifth grade of commissioned officer in the cavalry, not the infantry (where the corresponding grade was ensign). Fielding and *Daily Post* of 3 October 1745 list them more plausibly with

Ensigns, Sutherland, Lucey, Haldane,[1] Birnie, and L'Estrange.
Adjutant Spencer.

Of the Earl of Loudon's.

Captains, Mackay, Monro, and Stuart.
Capt. Lieut. Macknab.[2]
Lieut. Reid.
Ensigns, Grant, Ross, and Maclaggan.

Of Lascelles's.

Major Severn.[3]
Captains, Adam Drummond, Forrester, Anderson, Corbet, and
Collier.
Lieutenants, Swinie, Johnston, Carrick, Dundas, and Herring.
Ensigns, Stone, Cox, Bell, Gordon, and Goulton.
Dr. Drummond.

Of Hamilton's Dragoons.

Col. Wright.
Major Bowles.
Cornets, Jacob and Nash.[4]
Quarter-master Nash.
Dr. Trotter.

Hamilton's dragoons. However, there may have been some uncertainty about their rank. *St James's Evening Post* of 24–6 September 1745 lists them both as captains, without regimental designation. In his list of officer-prisoners Elcho lists 'Cornets' Jacob (wounded) and Nash (not wounded) with Hamilton's regiment; *Short Account*, p. 275.

[1] Copy-text prints 'Holden'; here emended to conform to *Caledonian Mercury* of 23 September 1745. He is undoubtedly the 'Holdane' whom Fielding lists above (p. 67) among the killed and wounded from Murray's regiment.

[2] *Caledonian Mercury* of 23 September 1745, which lists individually (rather than collectively) by rank, places its 'Capt. Lieut. Macnab' [*sic*] after 'Monro' and ahead of its 'Capt. Stewart' [*sic*], which is a departure from strict ranking. For the next officer on Fielding's list *Caledonian Mercury* prints 'Reed'. Reid, who was apparently one of the many captured officers who broke their parole, later played an important part in the capture (March 1746) of the men and treasure landed from the *Prince Charles* sloop, which had been chased into the Kyle of Tongue by the *Sheerness* and run aground. Reid was with Loudon's regiment in Flanders, notably at the defence of Bergen-op-Zoom, and from 1758 in the American campaigns. An accomplished flautist and composer of military music, he left money for a chair in music at Edinburgh. See Major A. McK. Annand, 'General John Reid, 1721–1807', *Journal of the Society for Army Historical Research*, xlii (1964), 44–7.

[3] *Caledonian Mercury* of 23 September 1745 lists a 'Capt. Barlow' after 'Major Severn' and before 'Capt. Adam Drummond'.

[4] *Caledonian Mercury* of 23 September 1745 lists 'Burroughs' and 'Alcock' with Hamilton's dragoons in place of cornets 'Jacob' and 'Nash', whom it puts, implausibly, with Murray's regiment of foot.

Of Gardiner's Dragoons.

Col. Whitney.
Lieut. Grafton.
Cornets, Burroughs and Alcock.
Quarter-master West.

Col. Whiteford, Volunteer.
Major Griffith, Master-Gunner of Edinburgh Castle.[1]

Above 300 private Men kill'd, above 400 wounded, and near 500 made Prisoners.[2]

Of the Rebels there fell,

Capt. Robert Stuart, *of Ardsheil's Battallion.*
Capt. Archibald Macdonell, *of Keppoch's.*
Lieut. Allan Cameron, *of Lindevra's*; and
Ensign James Cameron, *of Lochiel's Regiment.*[3]
Together with about 50 Men.[4]

The Duke of Perth, wounded.
Capt. David Narlack, wounded;
And 80 Men.*[5]

* This Account is taken from the *Caledonian Mercury*, printed since Mr. *Macpherson* left them.

---

[1] Eaglesfield Griffith (Griffiths), master-gunner of Edinburgh castle for thirty years, was 'Conductor of the Train, and Commissary of the Stores and Provisions' for Cope, in addition to assisting Whitefoord with the artillery; *Report of Proceedings*, p. 89. Griffith may also have served as Cope's brigade-major, although in the report of Cope's examination by the board of inquiry he is nowhere assigned any rank but is referred to consistently as 'Mr.' or 'Master'. Elcho, *Short Account*, p. 275, lists among the artillery and volunteers a 'Maj. Griffiths', which suggests that the rank was generally assumed. See also Jarvis, *Collected Papers*, i. 20; *The History of the Rebellion in the Years 1745 and 1746*, ed. Henrietta Tayler (Oxford, 1944), p. 40.

[2] These computations are not taken from *Daily Post* of 3 October 1745, which describes its totals differently, nor from *Caledonian Mercury* of 23 September, which concludes its listing: '"Tis computed about 500 of the Enemy were killed; and that 900 are wounded, and that we have taken about 1400 Prisoners. . . .' Computations of Cope's losses which were published in the London papers differed considerably. However, Fielding's is identical with that in *General Evening Post* of 24–6 September, although the latter's casualty lists are different from his; see also *Old England* of 28 September.

[3] To this point Fielding's list of rebel fallen is identical with those in *Caledonian Mercury* of 23 September 1745, *Daily Post* of 3 October (which appears to reprint from the former), and *General Evening Post* of 28 September–1 October (which credits 'The Edinburgh News Paper, dated Sept. 24'). After the entry for 'James Cameron' *Caledonian Mercury* of 23 September adds, 'Capt. James Drummond, alias Macgregor, mortally wounded, of the Duke of Perth's Regiment.'

[4] *Caledonian Mercury* of 23 September 1745, followed by *Daily Post* of 3 October, prints 'And about 30 private Men, and 70 or 80 wounded.'

[5] Fielding's note to the contrary, these three lines are not taken from the *Caledonian Mercury* of 23 September 1745 (nor from *Daily Post* of 3 October). The earliest reports in the London papers do list Perth as killed; for example, *St James's Evening Post* of 24–6 September, *General Evening Post* of

The Rebels, after this Action, immediately marched back again to their Camp,[1] whence they intended to proceed to *Edinburgh*, in order to call a Parliament,[2] lay Siege to the Castle,[3] and put the whole Civil Government under the Name of the Pretender; but as Mr. *Macpherson* took this Opportunity to escape from them, we cannot with Certainty declare any more of their Proceedings since.

General *Cope* finding it impossible to rally the Army, escaped after the Dragoons to *Lauder*;[4] some of these, as well as the Foot, got safe to *Berwick*, where General *Cope* is since arrived with the rest,[5] who, we

24–6 September, and *DA* of 26 September, which adds, 'and Fifty private Men killed', possibly the source of Fielding's estimate above. For Perth, who was not killed and may not have even been wounded, see above, p. 44. 'Narlack' has not been identified and Fielding's source for this name has not been found.

[1] The main body spent the night of the 21st at Musselburgh, and the YP was at Pinkie House, which belonged to Tweeddale. According to Elcho, *Short Account*, p. 277, 'the rebel soldiers were pretty busy in picking up what they Could [*sic*] find, and some of them went home . . . with their plunder'. On the 22nd the YP went back to Holyrood, where he remained till the end of the month; the main body was billeted in the suburbs, principally in Duddingston. See Blaikie, *Itinerary*, pp. 16–17.

[2] Cf. *DA* of 27 September: 'It is very currently reported, that the Rebels are gone back to Edinburgh, and that the young Pretender had issued out an Order for the Parliament of Scotland to meet at the Parliament House in that City the 7th of October.' The report was unfounded but apparently widespread; Walpole repeated it to Mann on 27 September (*Yale Walpole*, xix. 118). It may have arisen from a confusion with the YP's call of a council of his principal advisers on 22 September, which met daily at Holyrood; Blaikie, *Itinerary*, p. 17. One of the council's first bits of business was a discussion of the feasibility of an immediate march to Berwick; Murray of Broughton, *Memorials*, pp. 211–12; Elcho, *Short Account*, p. 279. de Johnstone, *Memoirs*, pp. 46–7, lists the convening of a Scottish parliament as among the unsuccessful proposals made in the council after Prestonpans.

[3] After Prestonpans there was anxious speculation in London about what the rebels would do next. On 27 September 1745 Walpole wrote Mann: 'Indeed they don't seem so unwise, as to risk their cause upon so precarious an event [immediate invasion of England]; but rather to design to establish themselves in Scotland, till they can be supported from France, and be set up with taking Edingborough Castle, where there is to the value of a million, and which they would make a stronghold: it is scarcely victualled for a month, and must surely fall into their hands'; *Yale Walpole*, xix. 117–18. In addition to the money deposited in the castle for safekeeping by the two Edinburgh banks, there was an estimated '10,000 arms'; Newcastle to Cumberland, 25 September OS, BL Add. MS 327051, f. 213, as cited by *Yale Walpole*, xix. 117*n*. Upon returning to Edinburgh the YP resumed the guard around the castle so as to prevent its provisioning, but General Guest, exhibiting orders from Tweeddale, responded with some cautionary cannonading and the blockade was withdrawn. See James Maxwell of Kirkconnell, *Narrative of Charles Prince of Wales' Expedition to Scotland in the Year 1745* (Edinburgh, 1841), pp. 48–50; Murray of Broughton, *Memorials*, pp. 217–20; Elcho, *Short Account*, pp. 291–3; Henderson, *Edinburgh History*, pp. 35–7.

[4] Cf. *London Gazette* of 21–4 September 1745, dateline Whitehall, September 24: 'and Sir John Cope, with about 450 Dragoons, had retired to Lauder; Brigadier Fowkes and Colonel Lascelles had got to Dunbar'. According to his own later testimony Cope marched south to Lauder, where he halted for an hour 'to refresh the Men' and then 'quartered that Night [of the 21st] at Coldstream and Cornwall'; *Report of Proceedings*, pp. 43, 194. In stressing that the dragoons preceded Cope in flight Fielding is not quite accurate. Cope later testified that the only way to get the dragoons 'to make a decent Retreat' was 'by keeping upon their Head in order to keep them back'; *Report of Proceedings*, p. 43.

[5] Cf. *London Gazette* of 24–8 September 1745, dateline Whitehall, September 28: 'By Letters from Berwick of the 23d and 24th we are informed, that about 500 of the Dragoons under Sir John Cope were then there; that some of the Foot had likewise got to that Place, and others were gone for

hope, will take a future Occasion to regain that Honour, at the Expence of these very Rebels, which they lost in this Action.

As to the Rebels, we have been since informed, they have been mustering their whole Force, in order to invade this Kingdom, where, we doubt not, but they will meet with a Reception becoming a brave Nation, whose All is at Stake in the Contest. And as every *Englishman*, we are confident, will exert his utmost Spirit and Force on this Occasion, so we trust in God, that the Religion, Laws, Liberties, and Lives of this Country will never, thro' the Indolence or Cowardice of its Inhabitants, be exposed to the Mercy and Disposition of a licentious Rabble and cruel Banditti.

Indeed there are already many Instances of this public Spirit, which not only Individuals, but whole Bodies of Men have shewn; witness that ever-memorable Association in Defence of public Credit, enter'd unanimously into by so large a Body of the Merchants of *London*,[1] and which hath totally defeated one of the most wicked and basest Designs to blow up the whole Nation, which was ever devised by Man. Some of the Contrivers and Abettors of this detestable Scheme are known, and must expect to be ever hereafter regarded by all *Englishmen*, as the most flagitious and profligate Enemies of their Country, and as such, to be held in everlasting Abhorrence.[2] Indeed, Crimes like this deserve the most

Carlisle.' Cope reached Berwick on 22 September, whence he sent a dispatch saying he had found there Fowkes, Lascelles, and 'not above 30' of the foot; Jarvis, *Collected Papers*, ii. 133, where it is asserted that of 'all the contemporary historians' Fielding is the only one who does not make Cope the first to arrive at Berwick with the news of his own defeat. Actually, Fielding seems merely to clarify the gist of the two accounts in the *London Gazette*.

[1] The *London Gazette* of 26–8 September 1745 prints a notice signed by many London merchants and headed as follows: 'We the under-signed Merchants and others, being sensible how necessary the Preservation of Publick Credit is at this Time, do hereby declare, that we will not refuse to receive Bank Notes in Payment of any Sum of Money to be paid to us; and we will, to the utmost of our Power, endeavour to make all our Payments in the same Manner.' A note follows the list of names: 'The Agreement was not begun to be sign'd till Thursday the 26th Instant, at Two o'Clock in the Afternoon, and was sign'd by the above Persons before Five last Night, when it was sent to the Press.' The *Gazette* of 28 September–1 October 1745 prints a continuation of the list, which has been estimated to total 1,760 names; *Yale Walpole*, xix. 128 *n*. Earlier in the month the merchants had presented their loyal address to the king, offered to raise, at their own expense, two regiments for his service and to make available a million pounds sterling 'at easy interest'; *London Gazette* of 10–14 September; *General Evening Post* of 10–12 September, *DA* of 12 September.

[2] After the news of Prestonpans reached London, there was a rash of rumor concerning the public credit, and at least the threat of a serious run on the Bank of England. Cf. *General Advertiser* of 30 September 1745: 'Among the many base Artifices employed to hurt the Publick Credit, and thereby to distress Trade, we hear that a certain noted Gentleman hath distinguished himself by drawing out the Sum of 5000 l. which he had in the Bank, carrying the Money to a Banker, changing it for Bank Notes, drawing out his Cash again, and so continuing the same Round till he was discover'd.—'Tis hoped that when he comes to be named in a proper Place, he will be treated with that Contempt which is due to his base Attempt, by all who wish well to the Commerce and Prosperity of Britain.' See also *GM*, xv (1745), 500, 504.

exemplary Punishment, and will justify a Legislature, even in going out of the common Roads of Justice to come at and punish them.

I shall conclude these Papers, with exhorting every Man in this Kingdom to exert himself, not only in his Station, but as far as Health, Strength, and Age will permit him, to leave at present the Calling which he pursues, and however foreign his Way of Life may have been to the Exercise of Arms, to take them up, and enure himself to them: Nor should this be delayed a Moment, for, I repeat it once more, HIS ALL IS AT STAKE. This is not the Cause of a Party: I shall be excused, if I say it is not the Cause in which the King only is concerned; your Religion, my Countrymen, your Laws, your Liberties, your Lives, the Safety of your Wives and Children; THE WHOLE is in Danger, and for God Almighty's Sake! lose not a Moment in ARMING YOURSELVES for their Preservation.[1]

---

[1] Cf. the call for joining in loyal associations, *Serious Address*, above, p. 31.

❀❀❀❀❀❀❀❀❀❀❀❀❀❀❀❀❀❀

A

DIAEOGUE

BETWEEN

The DEVIL, the POPE,

AND THE

PRETENDER.

❀❀❀❀❀❀❀❀❀❀❀❀❀❀❀❀❀❀❀

[Price One Shilling.]

1745

Half-title, first edition. The Beinecke Rare Book and Manuscript Library, Yale University: Fielding Collection 745d[1]. The L of DIALOGUE has been manually inked to resemble an E.

A

DIALOGUE

BETWEEN

The DEVIL, the POPE,

AND THE

PRETENDER.

—— Comes additur una
Hortator Scelerum.

VIRGIL.

L O N D O N:
Printed for M. COOPER, at the *Globe* in *Pater-noster-Row.* MDCCXLV.

A

DIALOGUE

BETWEEN

The DEVIL, the POPE,

AND THE

PRETENDER.[1]

DEVIL.

Your Servant, my old Friend, I kiss your Toe with profound Veneration.[2]

POPE.

Who breaks in upon me thus abruptly?—Ha! I ask your Mightiness's Pardon, I see your Foot, and I kiss it with the utmost Adoration.

DEVIL.

It is so long indeed since I have heard from you, I thought you had absolutely forgot me.

---

[1] J. Paul de Castro, 'The Printing of Fielding's Works', *The Library*, fourth series, i (1921), 260 *n.*, quotes John Boyle, fifth earl of Cork and Orrery, to Countess Orrery, 4 February [1744]: 'I write to you amidst the terrors of the Devil, the Pope and the Pretender; the French Fleet is said to be near our shores, the Young Pretender said to be on board . . .'; *The Orrery Papers* (London, 1903), ii. 181. The 'Infernal Triumvirate', as it was called (*General Advertiser* of 4 November 1745), figured prominently in ballads, political caricature, and anti-jacobite propaganda in the decade 1710–20 and whenever fears of jacobite activity were revived. See William Thomas Morgan, *A Bibliography of British History (1700–1715)*, Indiana University Studies Nos. xxiii–xxiv, ii. 541–2; *Political Ballads of the Seventeenth and Eighteenth Centuries*, ed. W. Walker Wilkins (London, 1860), ii. 104, 105–8, 109–12, 120–3; Stephens, *BM Catalogue*, ii, items no. 1607, 2636, 2658, 2659.

[2] The comparison implicit here is with the supposedly less debasing, less abject custom of kissing hands, as in England. See *TP* no. 10 (7 January 1756), below, p. 178.

POPE.

You are the only Person, I believe, who will think so; and if you have not heard from me of late, it is because my whole Time hath been engaged in projecting Schemes for your Service.

DEVIL.

I am heartily glad to hear it; for by the Situation of Affairs below, I began to fear the whole World were becoming Protestants.

POPE.

You will have more Reason to think, I hope, before we part, that they are all becoming Papists; but in your own Name, what Reason can you have to complain? I am afraid, Brother, there is some Truth in the Insatiability which is reported of your Temper. Can you want Souls, when all *Europe* is at War;[1] for of those slain in Battle, a Third must at an Average be supposed to fall your your Share.

DEVIL.

No Thanks to you, Brother. You will be pleased to remember this is no religious War. The Ambition of Princes will send themselves and their Subjects to me without any Assistance of yours. Indeed, Brother, you will shortly place the private Views of Men to my Account.

POPE.

Indeed, Brother, and so I shall.—Who are the Prime Ministers of these Princes? Are they not my Cardinals? Are not the Schemes of extending Dominions, and enriching one Country at the Expence and Ruin of another, often hatch'd within the Walls of the Vatican, and thence by my Instruments infused into the Cabinets and Councils of Princes? Are not those Confessors, who keep a Key to the Consciences of those Princes, mine? Do they ever insinuate, that the Designs of introducing Bloodshed and Desolation into Kingdoms, without any other Motive than that of Ambition, is wicked and unlawful? On the contrary, Do they not often promote and always encourage them in these Projects? And as for private Views, none but you yourself, (and you must be

[1] The so-called war of the Austrian Succession (1740–8), which before it concluded had embroiled England, the Dutch, Russia, Bavaria, Saxony, Poland, France, Charles Emmanuel III of Savoy and Sardinia, Marie Theresa, Prussia, and Spain. The pope's calculation, in the next clause, seems to presume that the 'heretics' or noncatholic dead will automatically go to hell.

in yourself too to do it) can deny that my Indulgences, Pardons, and Absolutions, are the best Methods to propagate Iniquity, which you could invent. And since you provoke me, I must tell you, it is to me you owe much the greater Part of the Souls in *Christendom*.

DEVIL.

Hold, Brother. [*aside*] *I must not anger this old Fellow, for he is the best Friend I have*.

POPE.

Is my Inquisition lull'd asleep?

DEVIL.

Nay, even I can't bear that. My Inquisition, if you please; I am sure I invented it, and am prouder of it than of all my other Inventions.

POPE.

True, you did; but I have encouraged it; and if none but you could have produced such an Invention, none but I would have received it; nor could I act from any other Motive in so doing, than merely a Desire to oblige you. Nay, so visible is this, if Mankind did not absolutely want Common Sense, it must have discovered the Alliance between us.

DEVIL.

Be not angry, my good Friend: I did not mean to offend you; nor do I deny the Obligations I have towards you. I own the Justice of your Remonstrances, and confess, that even I myself did not know how much you had done in my Service.

POPE.

And how much I am doing too.—There is a Scheme on Foot.

DEVIL [*eagerly*].

Ay, what?

POPE.

Don't you know it then?

DEVIL.

You know, Brother, yours are the only human Schemes, (if, indeed, they may be called human) which I cannot penetrate.

POPE.

What think you of the Propagation of your Inquisition?

DEVIL.

My Friend!—where?

POPE.

In *England*.

DEVIL.

In *England*?

POPE.

In *England*: Nay, I thought it would make you stare. Know then, since I must inform you, that under the Protection of the Kings of *France* and *Spain*, I have sent over the Pretender's Son *Charles*, in order to protect the Liberties and Properties and Church of *England*.[1]

DEVIL.

Ha, ha, ha.

POPE.

Now, do you tell me what Success it will have.

Devil shakes his Head.

POPE.

Zounds! you are enough to dishearten a Man, and to discourage him from undertaking your Cause.

[1] The Young Pretender had landed on the mainland of Scotland (25 July 1745) and by the time Fielding was writing this pamphlet had taken Edinburgh (17 September) and had defeated the king's troops under Cope in the first pitched battle of the rebellion, at Prestonpans (21 September). The early declarations or 'manifestoes' published in his father's name and in his own spoke reassuringly of the Stuart intention of safeguarding the property rights and religious liberties of both individuals and the established church.

DEVIL.

You know my Interest must make me wish well to your Enterprize; but I have always despaired of any Success of this kind in that damn'd ——I mean that not damn'd heretical Country: The Rascals have tasted the Sweets of Liberty in Church and State too long. And as for the Protection of them by a Popish Prince you know, Brother, they have had an Example.[1]

POPE.

Well, Brother, and don't you know that was a considerable Time ago. Don't you know the Inconstancy of Mens Tempers, that they love Change so well, as often to exchange manifest Good for Evil! There is no Deceit so gross, but that some will swallow it.

DEVIL.

Mum! I smell human Flesh.

POPE.

Quick! change yourself into the Dress of Cardinal *Alberoni*;[2] you are so like, there is no knowing one from t'other. There—hide this Foot.

The PRETENDER *prostrates himself at the Pope's Feet, and kisses his Toe.*

Most Holy Father, your Blessing.

POPE.

Rise, Child, you have it. Well, what News from the Army of the Church in *Scotland*?

[1] In the reign (1685–8) of James II, the Old Pretender's father. For Fielding's version of that reign, see 'Mystery the Fourth', *JJ* no. 3 (19 December 1747), pp. 106–8.

[2] Giulio Alberoni (1664–1752), cardinal 1717. Italian-born agent of the duke of Parma, he accompanied Vendôme to Spain (1711), where he became briefly principal minister to Philip V, whose marriage to Elizabeth Farnese of Parma he negotiated, and revived the inquisition. During his tenure there the queen's project of securing establishments in Italy for her two sons led to the Spanish expeditions against Sardinia and Sicily (which Byng destroyed) and to a short war with the Quadruple Alliance, of which England was a member. Before he was banished to Italy late in 1719, Alberoni played a considerable role in Ormonde's projected invasion of England and in the Spanish expedition to Scotland, which was supposed to concert with it. See William Kirk Dickson, *The Jacobite Attempt of 1719*, Publications of the Scottish History Society, xix (Edinburgh, 1895), especially pp. xxiv–xxxviii, liv–lviii. Upon hearing that Austria wished to sequester Alberoni's Italian estates because of his supposed partiality for Spain, Mann wrote Walpole 2 April 1743 N.S., 'I hope 'tis true, for I want to see him a little mortified for his late and former pranks'; *Yale Walpole*, xviii, 199 and *n*.

PRETENDER.

Excellent News! We have obtained a Victory over the *Heretics*.[1]

POPE.

I am rejoiced at it. Indeed I could expect no less Success from the constant Prayers which myself and the good Cardinal here have offered up on that Occasion: We had just finished our *Ave-Mary's* when you came in to us.

PRETENDER.

I have been constantly on my Knees, particularly to St. *Thomas à Becket*, to whose Assistance I chiefly impute our Success.

POPE.

He is an excellent Saint.

DEVIL.

Let *Tom* alone. I have not left a better Saint behind me.

PRETENDER.

I don't understand your Eminence.

DEVIL [*aside*].

Poh! I had forgot myself; but it is impossible even for me to refrain joking on such an Occasion.

POPE.

His Eminence hath not so much Regard for St. *Thomas* as for some other Saints. St. *Ursula* and the 11,000 Virgins receive his chief Devotions.[2]

---

[1] At Prestonpans on 21 September. For Fielding's description of it, see *History*, above, pp. 63–6.

[2] As the result of the conflation of 4th-century traditions concerning certain unnamed virgin martyrs at Cologne and the 9th-century Cyrmo-Breton legend of the migration of women from Britain during the reign of Maximus, St Ursula had come to be thought of as a British princess who went on a pilgrimage to Rome with 11,000 virgins and on her return was massacred with them by pagan tribesmen for refusing matrimonial and sexual relations. Although it is not necessary to postulate a source for so bare an allusion, Fielding might have read about St Ursula in Geoffrey of Monmouth's *Historia regum Britanniae*; Baker, item no. 191, lists among Fielding's books a 1718 English translation entitled *The British History, Translated into English From the Latin of Jeffrey of Monmouth*. The account of Ursula is in Book V, caps. xv–xvi, pp. 156–60; it describes the ravishment as follows: 'while they [the pagan Huns and Picts] were thus exercising their barbarous Rage, they happened to light upon these Virgins, driven on those Parts, and were so inflamed with their Beauty,

PRETENDER.

Every Man certainly hath his particular Saints; nor can any one in his Senses doubt the prodigious Power of those holy Virgins, to whom I have said 11,000 Prayers in my Time. The Reason I chose St. *Thomas* is, because he is on the Spot, and because he was a Martyr to the Propagation of your Holiness's Power,[1] in that very Kingdom where we are now endeavouring to re-establish that Power: And there is no Doubt but that holy Martyr will now exert his more than mortal Power in the Cause of the Church; and tho' perhaps he may chuse to be invisible, will head our Troops on this Occasion.

POPE.

St. *Thomas* did indeed deserve well of our holy Chair.[2]

PRETENDER.

Your Holiness is too gracious in saying so: It is a Light in which no Man can ever do Works of Supererogation; for he who hath done the most for that Chair, hath done no more than his Duty.

POPE.

My Son speaks with a Respect to that Chair, which becomes him; and while you preserve that Respect, you may depend on all the Protection which the Saints can give you.

PRETENDER.

When I think with less Reverence of the holy See, may they all abandon my Cause, and my Soldiers desert my Standard.

POPE.

You might have spared the latter Part of the Curse, as being a necessary Consequence of the former; but by the Infallibility with which we stand invested, we pronounce that neither will ever happen. On the contrary, my Son, as you are now fighting the Cause of the Church, the Arms of the Church and her Treasures too shall assist you; I will open

that they courted them to their brutish Embraces ...' (p. 159). Cf. also John Speed, *The History of Great Britaine*, 2nd ed. (London, 1627), bk. VI, cap. lix, p. 279.

[1] Becket was murdered in his cathedral (1170) by four knights of Henry II after he had refused to absolve the king's bishops unless they swore obedience to the pope.
[2] Becket was canonized by the occupant of the 'holy Chair', Pope Alexander III, in 1173.

the Treasures of our holy Chair on this Occasion, and will very bountifully bestow on you.—

The Devil laughs in his Sleeve.

PRETENDER.

Your Holiness is too generous; though I own it is what the Cause stands in need of.[1]

POPE.

I will bestow on you—One hundred thousand—Indulgences.[2]

PRETENDER.

On my Knees I thank your Holiness.

POPE.

Ay, and with full Power to be disposed of by yourself or Order on whomsoever you please.

PRETENDER.

This is Generosity indeed!

POPE.

Nor will we stop here: We will at the same Time issue forth from the same holy Treasury Two hundred thousand—Curses,[3] to be distributed in the same Manner and by the same Power amongst your Enemies.

[1] Citing Cardinal Albani as his source, Mann wrote Walpole 24 August 1745 NS that the only thing preventing the OP from going to France or Avignon so as to direct his son's expedition 'is the want of money, for which he has applied to the Pope'; *Yale Walpole*, xix. 94. In fact the OP had applied to Benedict XIV as early as 19 August NS for 'cent mille scudi pour mettre son fils en état de remonter sur le trône britannique, et d'y rétablir la religion catholique romaine'; S.P. 98/49 f. 205, as cited by *Yale Walpole*, xix. 94 *n*.

[2] Cf. Mann to Walpole, 7 December 1745 NS, reporting that Benedict XIV 'has given the Pretender 50,000 crowns, and 100,000 indulgences, nay, to as many as will pray for the success'; *Yale Walpole*, xix. 170 and *n*.

[3] To represent the supposed virulence of catholic hostility towards protestants and other heretics the London papers of September ran a number of items having to do with curses, papal and other. Two in particular, the so-called Curse of Ernulphus, and the 'Ceremony of Cursing by Bell, Book, and Candle', were widely reprinted. See, for example, *DA* of 27 September, *Daily Post* of 26 September, *General Evening Post* of 19–21 September and 1–3 October 1745; also 'General Introduction', above, p. lvi.

PRETENDER.

Prodigious Liberality! And that we may not seem altogether unworthy of it by neglecting any Means on our Part, we will pawn all our Jewels, nay our very Royal Plate, in this truly religious Cause.[1]

POPE.

You do well, my Son, such temporal Arms will do some little Service, when supported by those more powerful spiritual ones, which we have bestowed on you. And to make them the more effectual, you shall have holy Money for the Purpose. Let your Jewels and Plate therefore be sent in to us, and our own Coffers shall produce the Coin, which shall receive a particular Blessing, and be washed all over with holy Water on this Occasion: For which Use the holy Cardinal and ourself will presently prepare a large Quantity of this divine Cordial.[2]

PRETENDER.

May the holy Virgin, St. *Thomas*, St. *Ursula*, with the 11,000 Virgins, and all the other Saints, grant us Power to return this Goodness to the holy Chair:[3] Nor shall we ever be forgetful [*speaking to the Devil*] of the many Obligations we have to your Eminence, who have with such Zeal always espoused our Cause.

POPE.

We are indeed Joint-Workers therein.

DEVIL.

It is a Cause which will never want any Assistance I can give it; nor do I doubt but your Majesty will remember, the Moment you return to your Dominions, the just Judgment which fell on your Royal Father, for declining in the very Beginning of his Reign the only Method by which our Religion can be securely established in an heretical

---

[1] Extracting a letter from Rome dated 29 August NS, *DA* of 10 September 1745 reported that the Old Pretender, 'in order to contribute as much as was in his Power towards the Success of this Expedition [the rebellion in Scotland], has pawned part of his Jewels in the Banks of this City for the Sum of 100,000 Roman Crowns'. See also *St James's Evening Post* of 17–19 September and *Caledonian Mercury* of 25 September 1745.

[2] In coopting the devil for the task, the pope may be playing on the devil's proverbial aversion to holy water.

[3] Mann wrote Walpole 31 August 1745 NS that he was certain the Old Pretender had received 80,000 crowns from the bank at the Monte di Pieta on a supposed deposit of jewels, and adds, 'they assert that he has received 50,000 more from the Pope'; *Yale Walpole*, xix. 96 and *n*.

Country;[1] I mean the Inquisition, the only Means adequate to such an End.

PRETENDER.

It shall be done instantaneously.

POPE.

My Son will not have the least Pretence to the contrary; for as he will come into his Throne by Conquest, he will have no Excuse for keeping any Terms with Heretics: I shall leave it therefore to your Eminence to consider of an Inquisitor, and other Officers for the Court, which we will appoint directly.

PRETENDER *to the Devil*.

No Person can be so proper as your Eminence.

DEVIL.

I will undertake it.

PRETENDER.

Your Holiness will vouchsafe me a formal Absolution from all the Promises I have made in my Declaration.[2]

POPE.

You shall have it, Son, though you need none; for Promises with Heretics you know are *ipso facto* void: Nay, the most solemn Oath given to such is so far from binding, that it is meritorious to break it.[3]

DEVIL [*aside*].

A wholsome Doctrine, to which I owe many a good Soul.

[1] In his first speech to the council James II assured it that he would support and defend the Church of England, assurances which he repeated in his speech before the first (and only) parliament of his reign. See *Serious Address*, above, pp. 6–7.

[2] For the 'Promises' contained in the OP's declaration dated from Rome 23 December 1743 NS, see 'General Introduction', above, pp. xli–xlii. In particular, the OP promised security for the rights and liberties of all protestant subjects, as well as of all ecclesiastical and educational institutions covered by law.

[3] A stock charge of anti-jacobite propaganda, repeatedly made in connection with the Stuart declarations promising religious toleration in the event they were restored. See index, *s.v.* 'Heretics'.

PRETENDER.

I have a Suit to your Holiness, which I hope will not be denied me; it is to confer the Archbishoprick of *Canterbury* on my Confessor.

POPE.

Son, we shall always pay due Regard to your Recommendation; but am afraid we cannot grant that Request, having already partly promised that See to another; but he shall be a Bishop, and we may promote him in due Time as he merits, and we see Occasion.

PRETENDER.

I hope your Holiness will not refuse me this.

POPE.

We shall have Abbies and many other good things to favour your Friends with;[1] and you may be assured, Son, that as long as you behave with proper Duty to the Church, your Holy Mother will exert the utmost Indulgence towards you, and shall always, where our own Promise, or something urgent doth not interpose, give a very benign Ear to your Recommendations.

PRETENDER.

I wish I had not ventured to promise—

POPE.

I wish so too; but your Promise is void, and we absolve you from it: And let me tell you, Son, you did ill in promising what was not in your Power to perform. The Bishopricks of *England* are ours, we claim them, and we will dispose of them. Do you consider what it is you ask, that it is no less than appointing a Person under us to be the Head of the *English* Church?

PRETENDER.

I thought him a very proper Man.

[1] Anti-jacobite writers argued persistently that the restoration of the Stuarts would be followed by a restoration of the church lands which had been expropriated and put into lay hands during the reign of Henry VIII and later. Fielding sounds the theme repeatedly. See index, *s.v.* 'Church lands'.

POPE.

You thought! ha! you thought in spiritual Matters! Do you not know, that even thinking in such Matters by the Laity is a Crime? Do not presume, Son, on the Indulgence of a fond Parent: The Church, that tenderest Mother to dutiful Children, when provoked, is of all the severest. And if she once lifts the Rod of her Curses, where is the Child who can bear her Indignation?

DEVIL [*pulling in his Cloven Foot, which before was half out.*]

Let me beseech you, Royal Sir, immediately to submit, and do not provoke our holy Father too far.

PRETENDER.

Oh, I do, I do submit, and humbly ask Pardon for my Offence.

POPE.

Your Submission is received, but not without Penance: I must in Mercy to your Soul enjoin you some wholesome Penance for your Contumacy. I order you therefore to lay on two Dozen Lashes on your Royal base Back, repeating six *Ave-Mary's* between every Lash; this being performed, we pronounce you once more *rectum in curia*,[1] and absolve you from all further Guilt. But beware of any future Contumacy; for by all the Saints, if my Will be ever more opposed in *England*, I will lay that damn'd heretical Country under a Curse, whence it shall never be redeemed. I will curse Young and Old, Men and Women, Maids and Batchelors, Wives and Husbands, Widows and Widowers. I will curse all Degrees, Orders and Professions; nay, I will curse the Earth itself, the Houses, the Trees, the—[2]

PRETENDER.

O forbear, holy Father, on my Knees I beseech you, forbear: I cannot endure these Execrations.

DEVIL.

They are terrible indeed.

---

[1] More commonly, *rectus in curia*, right in court, a legal formula here used in its more restrictive sense as applying to one who had been outlawed but has reversed his outlawry so that he can have the benefit of the law. In Latin, *curia* may have religious connotations which are not at all out of place in the present context.

[2] See 'General Introduction', above, p. lvi.

POPE.

Rise, my Son, and praise that indulgent Lenity which hath forgiven thy Crime; but beware henceforth of giving any Offence to a Power, to whom thou owest that Crown thou art about to take Possession of, and of whom thou art to hold it, as a Fief of the holy See, in Imitation of thy Predecessor *John*, of blessed Memory.[1] Happy had it been for that wicked Nation thou art to govern, if none of his Successors had swerved from that Allegiance he vowed to us; but these things are past, and upon their sincere Repentance I shall again stretch forth my Toe for them to kiss.

PRETENDER.

It shall be my sole Endeavour to produce that Repentance.

DEVIL [*half disclosing his Foot, unobserved by the Pretender*.]

Remember, Sir, gentle Means will never effect it. First, therefore, an Inquisition must be established before they have Time to breathe; then I would advise an immediate Massacre of the Protestants;[2] the severest Methods are the wholsomest; perhaps some of them may repent and be converted, while the Knives are at their Throats; if so, a few Masses said for their Souls may redeem them; and believe me, it is a most charitable Act to preserve the Souls of Heretics at the Expence of their Blood.

PRETENDER.

I shall execute whatever the Church pleases to command, being well convinced, that however sinful an Action may appear, if it have but the Sanction of the Church, it is in Reality holy.

POPE.

That's well and dutifully spoken: It is under our Direction only that the Laity can ever be safe.

[1] After a period of excommunication precipitated by disagreements over the election to Canterbury, King John resigned the kingdoms of England and Ireland to Pope Innocent III in 1213. He received them back under a bond of fealty and homage in return for payment to the Holy See of 1,000 marks a year. In addition John gave sums to various religious foundations, and the chaplains at Chichester said masses for the soul of King John 'of blessed memory'; *Chichester Chartulary*, 40 (Sussex Record Society, xlvi [1946]), as cited by Austin Lane Poole, *From Domesday Book to Magna Carta, 1087–1216*, 2nd ed. (Oxford, 1955), pp. 428–9.

[2] It was a commonplace of anti-jacobite propaganda that if the Stuarts were restored, there would be religious massacres on the model of those in Ireland and France in earlier times. Fielding himself sounds the theme repeatedly. See index, *s.v.* 'Massacres'.

DEVIL [*stretching forth his whole Foot.*]

Sin is a Language understood by the Church only, and without her Interpretation Men no more know the Meaning of their Actions than they do of Words in an unknown Tongue. Adultery, Rape, Rapine, Treachery, Perjury, and Murder, are sometimes Sins; but at other Times, and for the Sake of Religion, they are not only innocent, but commendable, and have intitled many a Soul to Happiness—in one of my Ovens—[*aside*].

POPE.

As the Poets feign'd the Blood of the Gods not to be real Blood, but *Ichor*,[1] so the Blood of Heretics is not real Blood, but a poisonous sort of Liquor, which it is highly meritorious to spill; and at my next Promotion of Saints,[2] I shall prefer those who have shed the most: Nay, indeed we have many in our Kalendar already, who have been promoted to their Dignity on that single Merit.

DEVIL.

The Text forbids you to spill Man's Blood;[3] but that extends not to Heretics, who are Dogs, not Men.

PRETENDER.

Your Eminence says true, and Humanity to Men doth not teach us Mercy to Dogs.

DEVIL.

A noble Sentiment, and worthy of the Church of which I am Cardinal.

POPE.

I suppose our Abbey Lands will be easily discovered; if there be any

---

[1] The ἰχώρ of Homer's *Iliad*, v. 339–42, where Diomedes wounds Aphrodite in the hand as she is protecting Aeneas. Pope's note on his translation of the passage (v. 421–4) cites *Paradise Lost*, vi. 344–7, which describes the wound given Satan by Michael.

[2] A curiously apposite detail, though Fielding may not have realized it. As *promotor fidei* Benedict XIV had dealt with beatifications and canonizations under his three immediate predecessors. During his own pontificate there were six beatifications and six canonizations, and the bulk of his published work concerns itself particularly with these matters; *Yale Walpole*, xix. 171 *n*.

[3] Exodus 20: 13: Thou shalt not kill. An instance of the devil's proverbial fondness for citing scripture for his own purposes.

Doubt concerning them, you will take Care to have it decided in favour of the Church.[1]

PRETENDER.

It is the Pleasure of your Holiness to be contented with the Restoration of the Lands themselves, or will you be pleased to insist on an Account for the Profits ever since the Usurpation?[2]

POPE.

That is a Question worthy consulting your Eminence upon, and I should be glad of your Opinion.

DEVIL.

My Opinion will be guided by the Prospect of Success: I am for all that we can get. It is the Cause of the Church, and Moderation is sinful.

POPE.

Well, we will debate it hereafter.

DEVIL.

Ay! my first Advice is to secure the Land itself.

POPE.

Of that I will have no Demurrer. My Curse attend those who presume to make it a Doubt.

PRETENDER.

Let not your Holiness conceive an unkind Thought of me on that Account: I will be no sooner warm in my Throne, than they shall be restored; such shall be my Will and Pleasure; a Will and Pleasure, which in all Matters where your Holiness doth not think fit to interpose, shall be a Law.

---

[1] For the 'Care' to be taken with respect to the abbey lands, see the journal entries for 31 January, 1 and 28 February, in *TP* no. 10 (7 January 1746), below, pp. 175, 177, and index, *s.v.* 'Church lands'.

[2] 'Usurpation' is the word used in the Pretender's 'Declaration' dated from Rome, 23 December 1743 NS, in which it refers to the Hanoverian tenure on the throne of England. See *TP* no. 10 (7 January 1746), below, p. 178 *n.* 1, and *Serious Address*, above, p. 4.

POPE.

So I would have it. And the Church, while you preserve an inviolable filial Obedience to her, shall assist you to make it so. The Doctrine of Princes governing by any other Laws than those we give them, is impious and heretical. *By me* (that is by this Chair) *Princes govern*, (says the Text)[1] not by Laws made by the Subject: The very Notion of a People's making Laws to govern themselves, is absurd and unnatural. Do Children make Laws for their Parents to rule by, or Slaves for their Masters? No, I disannul every Law in your Kingdom, and absolve you from keeping them, notwithstanding any Promise you have made, or any Oath you may out of Conveniency take to the contrary.[2]

PRETENDER.

I am glad to find this Doctrine, which I have always rigidly adher'd to, hath the Sanction of your Holiness's Authority.

POPE.

O, it is most holy and orthodox; and tho' the Church is sometimes obliged a little to temporize, this is the Doctrine she always hath at Heart: Indeed it is her Interest so to think; for an absolute King and an absolute Church always stand well together, and do irresistibly support each other. And sure you are well paid for your absolute Obedience to us by our maintaining you in absolute Power over all your Subjects.

DEVIL.

If Kings have any Right from Heaven, it is to be absolute; for Heaven never gave a Power for Men to circumscribe: Hereditary Right there-fore, *jure divino*, and absolute Power, are one and the same. Now, to prove the Certainty of indefeasible hereditary Right,[3] this single Datum is only necessary, which no Man, I think, will have the Impudence to deny, *viz.* That the People are the King's Property; for if this be granted, it will surely follow, that the King (as every private Man hath) hath a Right to his Property; now this Right is derived from that Power which

---

[1] Proverbs 8: 16: By me princes rule, and nobles, even all the judges of the earth.

[2] For example, his coronation oath. By the terms of the coronation oath act of 1689 (1 Will. & Mar., c. 6) the monarch promised to govern 'according to the statutes in parliament agreed on, and the laws and customs of the same'; *Statutes at Large*, ix. 4. Fielding returns often to the theme of broken oaths. See *Proper Answer*, p. 71; *JJ* no. 2 (12 December 1747), p. 99, and no. 3 (19 December 1747), p. 104; *Tom Jones*, VIII. xiv. 477.

[3] For a satiric gloss of the concepts of kingship *jure divino* and indefeasible hereditary right, see the elucidation of the jacobite 'Mysteries' in *JJ* no. 3 (19 December 1747), pp. 103–9.

gave the Property, and no Power could give such Property, but that which made the People; thence it very plainly and naturally follows, that the Right of a King is *jure divino*.

PRETENDER.

Your Eminence hath made it most clear.

POPE.

But his Eminence hath forgot one Point, which I could not have expected he would have forgot: I mean the Tenure under which this Power is granted; for however absolute it be over the People, it is not *simpliciter* absolute, but to be holden at the Will of the Church, which hath no less absolute Power over the Crowns of Kings, than they have over the meanest of their Subjects.

PRETENDER.

It would be the utmost Impiety to doubt it.

POPE.

You say well, my good Son. The Church therefore invests thee with absolute Authority over thy Subjects, to hold nevertheless at her Will and Pleasure: Receive therefore her Blessing, and go forth and fight her Battles to the utter Extirpation of the Goods, Persons and Names of Heretics. With their Goods thou shalt endow the Church, their Persons thou shalt commit to the Fire, and their Names we will ourselves take care to see blotted out of the Records of the Book of Life.

PRETENDER.

It shall be my principal Care to fulfil your Holiness's Pleasure in all things: And now, if your Holiness pleases to grant me once more your Benediction, I will proceed to perform my Penance.

POPE.

Do so, my Child; thou hast my Blessing; and his Eminence and myself will proceed immediately to prepare the holy Water. You shall have a full Hogshead. I will likewise order the proper Officers to issue the hundred thousand Indulgences, together with the Curses, and also—the Money.

PRETENDER.

The Saints, who only can, reward such Goodness.—I humbly take my Leave, and once more kiss your holy Toe.

The Pretender is going, but is called back by the Pope.

POPE.

Hold, Son.—Remember to send the Plate and Jewels immediately; you may respite your Penance till that is over.

PRETENDER.

They shall be sent instantly.

POPE *and the* DEVIL.

Ha, ha, ha.

DEVIL.

Was ever so blind a Bigot!

POPE.

It seems you think so; for that cloven Foot was uncovered almost all the Time he was in Company: Had he once cast his Eyes on the Ground, he must have seen it.

DEVIL.

You are mistaken: Superstition would have prevented him; the same Superstition which can make Men see cloven Feet and Devils where there are none, prevents them from seeing them where they really are. But can your Holiness believe in Earnest we have any Chance of Success in this *English* Project?

POPE.

Why should you doubt it?

DEVIL.

Because if we do succeed, the Protestants there must be more silly than the rankest Ass you ever imposed Penance upon. A Mixture of *Italian*, *Spanish* and *French* Government to protect Liberty, and a

Popish Bigot to defend the Protestant Religion: Ha, ha, ha. As I hope to be sav'd, the Impudence of the Imposture almost makes me blush.

POPE.

As you hope to be sav'd! a pretty Oath for the Devil.

DEVIL.

I had forgot myself: I have not put off my Cardinal's Skin; but you know, Oaths without any Meaning come very well out of my Mouth.

POPE.

And so the Imposture would make you blush: You are a modest Devil indeed; I am sure you are a very forgetful one, and as you have more than once this Day forgot the Character you had assumed, so you seem to me to forget who are the Persons to be imposed upon. They are not Devils, Sir, but Men, weak, simple Men; and when you please to recollect what I have already done with them, I believe, what I now propose will not seem so impracticable, and you may spare your Blushes.

DEVIL.

Your Holiness, it is true, hath done a great deal.

POPE.

Am I, Sir, at the Head of Mahometanism, or of Heathenism?

DEVIL.

No, your Holiness is the Head of the Christian Church.

POPE.

Very well, Sir; and have I not unveil'd the only Religion in the World, which hath ever taught the Doctrines of Benevolence, Peace and Charity, to be the Foundation of Hatred, War and Massacres? Have I not propagated Ambition with the Doctrine of Humility? Have I not taught Men to persecute and stab and burn each other? Nay, have I not made them Executioners of some of the worst Tortures, which you your-self could supply me with, and all in Obedience to Laws which in the plainest and most intelligible Terms direct the very contrary? Doth not the Book say, *Do unto all Men, that which you would have them do unto you?*[1]

---

[1] The so-called Golden Rule, derived from Luke 6: 31 and Matthew 7: 12.

And have I not made them, in mere Obedience to this Law, do unto all Men every thing, which they would most fear to have others do unto themselves? Why do I mention a single Instance? Have I not deduced Heathenish Doctrine and Mahometan Principles from Christianity, and in a Word, turned Heaven into Hell?

DEVIL.

The Force of your Reasoning is too strong to be opposed: All you have said, is—Poh! I hate the Word, Truth; but I must confess all this you have done, and it is not easy after that to say what you cannot do.

POPE.

After what I have mentioned, I think I need give you no other Reason for my Hopes of Success, than my having undertaken it; but however, since you seem not to have been in *England* lately; tho' I must own, I thought you had been there a long Time, and had been assisting the good Work.

DEVIL.

Do not upbraid me with Idleness; tho' I have not been there myself, I have several Emissaries, and some in the Disguise of Popish Priests: But I interrupt you; and I should be glad to hear the Grounds of your Hope; for it is a serious thing, and you must know, however I may fear it, I must wish it Success.

POPE.

First, then, this Attempt is made at a Time, when the best Heretic Forces are out of the Kingdom, engaged in a foreign War.[1] 2*dly*, It is begun in a Part of *Scotland*, inhabited by Men almost Savages, whom my Priests will soon convert to their Religion,[2] and whom Poverty and Hunger will easily animate to any Undertaking when there is Hope of Plunder: And if these can find their Way into *England*,[3] they will be

---

[1] At the outbreak of the rebellion almost all the British regulars were still in Flanders. In late July, at the time when the YP landed in Scotland, Walpole estimated that the troops at home numbered 'not five thousand', an estimate which squared with French intelligence; Walpole to Mann, 26 July 1745, *Yale Walpole*, xix. 79 and *n*. For the recall of the Flanders units, see below, p. 98.

[2] Anti-jacobite propaganda insisted that wholesale conversions would accompany any military successes the YP might have, and during the autumn of 1745 'reports' of such conversions were bruited in the London papers. See, for example, *History*, above, p. 50.

[3] At the time Fielding was writing this, the YP's forces lay inactive around Edinburgh. The decision to march south into England would not be taken until the end of the month. The actual direction of march was determined on 31 October, and the advance units crossed the Tweed on 5 November; Blaikie, *Itinerary*, pp. 22–4.

presently joined by all the Roman Catholics, against whom there are Laws indeed to deprive them of Arms; but these Laws are so seldom executed, that they are of very little Validity.[1] Now, as to the Heretics, you know there are some, (tho' few) who hold that noble Doctrine of indefeasible hereditary Right, which, I could scarce keep my Countenance, while you so excellently and logically derived from Heaven. Again, there are others who will persuade themselves, though as contrary both to Reason and Experience, as you know it is to Truth, that their Religion may be safe under a Popish King; these rely on that strong Argument of WHO KNOWS BUT; an Argument which can never be answered. *Lastly*, as for the whole Body of the People, they have so little Regard to Religion itself, that they hold one Form of Worship to be as good as another: And as for the upper Part of them, they are so sunk in Luxury, and every other Vice, that the very Name of Morality is scarce left among them. Their Luxury is so great, that there is scarce a Man of Fortune without a Palace, without the most expensive Pictures, a large Equipage, *French* Cook,[2] and *French* Wines, imported in diametrical Opposition to the Interest of the Public: And to this Luxury they sacrifice without Scruple their Friends, their Relations, their Honour, and their Country. Their Immorality is so great, that as there is no Vice, which they do not practise, so there is none of which they are ashamed. As no Man is ashamed of being a Miser, a Drunkard, or a Glutton; of betraying his Friend, or of deserting him in his Necessity and debauching his Wife or his Daughter; or lastly, of sacrificing his Country to his own Interest; so neither are the Women ashamed of publickly prostituting their Chastity, the only Virtue the Men expect them to maintain. And as to every kind of Riot and Extravagance, they glory and vie with each other in it. At a Time when their Country is engag'd in a War abroad, and invaded at home, they have the Impudence to import *Italian* Singers and *French* Dancers,[3] at more Expence of their Reputation than

---

[1] Of such little 'Validity' that on 5 September 1745 the king issued a proclamation 'For putting the Laws in Execution against Papists and Nonjurors'; *London Gazette*, 3–7 September 1745. The laws on the books prohibited use or possession of arms; for other prohibitions, see Jarvis, *Collected Papers*, i. 303–25; and Robert Blackey, 'A War of Words: The Significance of the Propaganda Conflict between English Catholics and Protestants, 1715–1745', *Catholic Historical Review*, lviii (1972–3), 535 *n.*

[2] To have French servants of any kind was at this time judged by many to be at least disloyal, at most dangerous. For the possibility that Fielding here has in mind the *cause célèbre* of Cloué, the Duke of Newcastle's French chef and something of a culinary avatar to contemporary gourmets, see 'General Introduction', above, p. lvii. 'Luxury' is in effect a Fielding topos; see index, *s.v.*

[3] French dancers were judged to be the best and still active at the major theatres. Italian singers had been hired on the expectation of a full season of opera. In fact, however, the opera, beset with financial difficulties and public disapproval of its Italianate composition, did not begin its season at the King's until 7 January 1746; see *TP* no. 9 (31 December 1745), below, pp. 164–71.

of their Money. And to shew their Profligacy in the highest Light, one single impudent Buffoon hath for many Years gone on with Impunity, in Defiance not only of Law but of common Decency, to vilify and ridicule every thing solemn, great and good amongst them; and, with a Mixture of Nonsense, Scurrility, Treason and Blasphemy, once a Week, in the public Papers, and once in a public Assembly (if any be so infamous to frequent it) to traduce the Persons and Characters of Nobles, Bishops, and even of the King himself.[1]—If this be the Case, what think you of my Hopes, Brother?

DEVIL.

There is some Truth in what you have said; but by the Force of Divination which is in me, I presage the Event will not answer your Expectation. For in the first Place, the heretic Army will be sent for home;[2] and those Troops which have stood the Fury of 100000 *French* Forces, and the Thunder of 200 Pieces of Artillery,[3] will cut off your Highland Banditti with as much Ease as a Mower doth Thistles, before them. Your *Roman Catholics* are too wise to incense a Government they know it is impossible to overturn. And as for those Doctrines which you flatter yourself have their Followers, there are not 100 Men in the Nation who do not scorn and deride them. As to Religion and Morality, I am glad to say there is not much among these People, and therefore I shall be sure of them without any Assistance of yours: But yet I am afraid there is Common Sense, and even Luxury itself will prevent them sacrificing the Means of supplying it. And what would you say if a Spirit of Liberty should appear amongst them, equal to what the *Romans* ever displayed in the freest Times of the Commonwealth; if they should all unite in Associations to defend their King and Country,[4] and a Million of Men,

[1] The buffoon is John 'Orator' Henley, whose Sunday lectures and newspaper advertisements for same had become particularly incendiary in late September, early October 1745, for what many took to be jacobitical and francophile tendencies. See 'General Introduction', above, p. lviii, and, for other attacks on Henley, the 'Apocrypha' in *TP* no. 1 (5 November 1745), below, p. 338, and no. 2 (12 November 1745), p. 345, and the leader of no. 3 (19 November 1745), p. 130.

[2] After considerable ministerial infighting the Pelhams authorized a troop recall even though the king was still absent in Hanover. The first units arrived in England on 23 September; *DA* of 24 September 1745. Other units followed at intervals until December. For the politics of recall, see 'General Introduction', above, pp. xxxi–xxxii.

[3] At Fontenoy in Flanders on 11 May 1745 NS. The battle, which was bloody and protracted, ended in an orderly allied retreat from numerically superior French forces. The source of Fielding's figures is not known. Although somewhat inflated, they are in line with contemporary English estimates. See, for example, *DA* of 7, 16, and 21 May 1745. Contemporaries were unanimous in stressing the crucial efficacy of the French artillery. For the British units which took part in the battle, see Francis Henry Skrine, *Fontenoy* (Edinburgh and London, 1906), pp. 131–5.

[4] Associations were formed by local groupings of persons of substance who 'subscribed' monies to raise, pay, and maintain volunteers for military service. These volunteers were to be recruited locally

headed by the best Troops in the World, should be ready to bear Arms against your Cause?

POPE.

God forbid any such thing should happen.

DEVIL.

You need not affront me, Sir;—you might pray to me to forbid it as well; but it is not in my Power; for this will happen and hath happened even at this Time. And what is still worse, I am afraid this cursed Rebellion, like some other of your Schemes, will produce an Effect contrary to what was intended, will inspire them with a serious Mood of thinking, and put a Stop to all that Luxury and Immorality which I have been so long endeavouring to raise to its present Heighth; an Effect which if it should not produce, I shall not want your Assistance to destroy them.

POPE.

Brother, I take it ill of you, after what I have done for you, to treat me in this Manner; Consequences, you know, are more in your Power than mine. I am sure nothing hath ever been wanting on my Part for your Service; and however little I have been able to perform, I might at least expect my hearty Endeavours would be well receiv'd.

DEVIL.

That is to say, you expect Gratitude from the Devil. Is that the Wisdom of your Holiness?

POPE.

Why not! I have been told that even you are good when you are well pleas'd.

DEVIL.

Ay, so I am; but none but myself know how to please me.

and their associated service was understood to be limited to the general area represented by their association. For the politics of this alternative to more conventional means of raising troops, see 'General Introduction', above, pp. xliv–xlv, and *Serious Address*, above, p. 31, where Fielding urges loyal citizens to join in them. In late September and early October London papers ran increasing numbers of notices pertaining to the associations and their subscriptions.

POPE.

I wish I had never attempted it. I could with much less Difficulty have obtained the Favour of Heaven, and I am sure much greater would have been my Reward. Pray, Sir, what have you ever done for me, in return for all the Favours I have conferred on you, except a little Gratification of Vanity; which, perhaps, I might better have gratify'd by Acts of Goodness? What Pleasure or Profit in Reality accrued to myself from your Inquisition, or any other Scheme of yours, which I have with so much Care and Diligence cultivated? What have I got by all the watchful Nights and aching Heads which I have known in your Service, but the Hatred of Heretics, and I'm afraid of Heaven too? What solid Good have I procur'd to myself?

DEVIL [*with a Sneer*].

—The Honour of my Service: A Reward sufficient; all that I have bestowed on every Tyrant, Plunderer and Destroyer of Mankind from the Beginning of the World, and yet you see they have all been contented; for, a Word in your Ear, Brother, you have heard that Virtue is her own Reward; but this is much truer of Vice, and of no Vice so true, as of Cruelty. What other Reward have I myself from the Exercise of it in the highest Degree? Can you expect more from my Inquisition, than it produces to the Inventor himself? Is there no Joy, no Delight in seeing a Body roast as well as a Soul? Cannot you relish the one, as I enjoy the other? But as you hinted Ingratitude to me, I must retort it on you: Was not *Alexander* the Great contented, that I suffered him to live but half your Age?[1] Did not he say, he had lived enough to Glory,[2] that is, in other Words, he had done Mischief enough?[3] whereas you know what a large Lease I granted you, and yet you are not satisfied.

POPE.

Well, Sir, you will be pleased to renew my Lease.

DEVIL.

Not an Hour, Sir.

---

[1] Alexander lived from 356 to 323 BC. In 1745 Pope Benedict XIV was seventy years old.

[2] Cf. Quintus Curtius, *Historiae Alexandri Magni Macedonis*, IX. vi. 18–19: 'ego me metior non aetatis spatio, sed gloriam'.

[3] For Fielding's view of the 'Mischief' perpetrated by Alexander, see 'Of True Greatness', lines 64–98, and 'A Dialogue between Alexander the Great and Diogenes the Cynic', *Miscellanies* (1743), i. 21–3, 226–35.

POPE.

Sure your Mightiness is not in Earnest in refusing.

DEVIL.

Sure your Holiness is not in Earnest in asking!

POPE.

If but for five Years.

DEVIL.

And do you really think you can cheat the Devil? Did you imagine I was to be cajol'd into a Renewal of your Lease by this pretty trump'd up Scheme of introducing Popery and the Inquisition into *England*? None of your wild Projects for me; shew me you can do any real Service to my Cause, which another will not execute as well, and I will give you as much Time as is necessary to complete it; otherwise, as soon as your Lease is expired, I shall expect you below according to Articles: And so I kiss your Toe, and you may kiss my —.

POPE.

Impudent Rascal! but I will have my Terms of him yet, or I'll blow up his Church, and send his Inquisition back to the Place from whence it came.

The TRUE PATRIOT

AND

The History of Our Own Times

(To be Continued Every Tuesday.)

Tuesday, November 5, 1745.[1]   Numb. 1.

ILLE EGO, *qui quondam* - - - - -.[2]

Fashion is the great Governor of this World. It presides not only in Matters of Dress and Amusement, but in Law, Physic, Politics, Religion, and all other Things of the gravest Kind: Indeed the wisest of Men would be puzzled to give any better Reason, why particular Forms in all these have been, at certain Times, universally received, and at others universally rejected, than that they were in, or out of Fashion.

   Men as well as Things are in like Manner indebted to the Favour of

---

[1] The 'Present History' of this first number takes notice, without comment, of 'This Day being the Anniversary of the Gun-Powder Treason Plot' (Locke, p. [36]). Since Fielding makes no rhetorical 'point' of it, the coincidence of dates is probably just that, a coincidence. Other papers, however, suggest the possibilities: 'As *this Day*, a hundred and forty Years ago, was design'd by the *Papists* as a *Festival* of THEIR OWN, to commemorate the Return of *Idolatry*, *Bigotry*, and *Tyranny* over both the Body and Mind; in which had they succeeded, the present Generation, brought up in the *same Superstition*, had been acting the Farce of a senseless Thanksgiving for the *rivetting on our Chains*, instead of paying, as now, the Offering of a *rational Praise*, that we remain *Protestants* and *Free*: It is presum'd, that all who have a just Value for *those Titles* will not only join in the *publick Rejoicings*, but in such serious *Reflections* on what they have *escap'd*, and what they *enjoy*, as may cause a settled Abhorrence of those *detestable Principles*, that are ever CONSPIRING against *civil* and *religious Liberty*.' (*London Evening Post* of 2–5 November 1745.)

[2] The opening words of the four-line *procemium* of the *Aeneid* which, according to Donatus and Servius, was rejected by Virgil's first editors, but is often thought genuine: *Ille ego, qui quondam gracili modulatus avena | carmen, et egressus silvis vicina coegi | ut quamvis avido parerent arva colono, | gratum opus agricolis; at nunc horrentia Martis* ('I am he who once tuned my song on a slender reed, then, leaving the woodland, constrained the neighboring fields to serve the husbandman, however grasping—a work welcome to farmers; but now of Mars' [Loeb]). The lines mark Virgil's transition from a poet of peace to a poet of war. On the doubtful authenticity of this *procemium*, see R. G. Austin, *P. Vergili Maronis 'Aeneidos' Liber Primus* (Oxford, 1971), pp. [25]–27.

this *Grand Monarque*.[1] It is a Phrase commonly used in the Polite World, that such a Person is in Fashion; nay, I myself have known an Individual in Fashion, and then out of Fashion, and then in Fashion again. *Shakespeare* hath shared both these Fates in Poetry,[2] and so hath Mr. *Handel* in Music;[3] so hath my Lord *Coke* in Law,[4] and in Physic the great

[1] In English usage, most commonly applied to the French king (especially Louis XIV), with overtones, as here, of absolutism and tyranny. See *Serious Address*, above, p. 11.

[2] Fielding seems to endorse the common Augustan perception that Shakespeare's popularity had diminished during the Stuart Restoration, when fashion ran to heroic tragedy and comedy of manners, to be revived again during the 18th century. *CGJ* no. 31 (18 April 1752), i. 315, affects to know of two hundred editions of Shakespeare being prepared for press and observes, 'there is nothing in this Age more fashionable than to criticise on Shakespeare'.

[3] Handel's English reputation—he had resided there since 1712—was extremely volatile, tied as it was for so long to the social and financial vicissitudes of Italian opera. With Heidegger he put on operas for the Royal Academy of Music in the early 1720s. After bankruptcy there, they took the opera to the King's (Haymarket) for five seasons. Heidegger then leased the theatre to the competing 'Opera of the Nobility', and Handel tried leasing from Rich at Covent Garden for opera on two nights of the week. Under the complex pressures of social politics, increased competition, expensive production costs, public alternations between italophilia and xenophobia, Handel gradually switched modes (from opera to oratorio) and languages (Italian to English). But his reputation remained precarious. In a note to the four-book *Dunciad* (1742) Pope remarked Handel's having introduced a fuller chorus and a greater variety of instrumentation in the orchestra, 'which prov'd so much too manly for the fine Gentlemen of his Age, that he was oblig'd to remove his Music into Ireland' (Bk. IV. v. 54 *n.*). Walpole wrote Mann on 24 February 1743, 'Handel has set up an Oratorio against the Operas, and succeeds . . .' (*Yale Walpole*, xviii. 180). By 1745, however, Handel himself confessed, in his famous letter on English as a language for music, that he had suffered 'the Loss of the publick Favour' (*DA* of 17 January 1745). In April 1745 Mrs Elizabeth Carter wrote Catherine Talbot, 'Handel, once so crowded, plays to empty walls in that opera house, where there used to be a constant audience'; cited by Otto Erich Deutsch, *Handel* (New York, [1955]), p. 610. By the autumn of that year the Earl of Shaftesbury told his (and Handel's) friend James Harris that the composer, though better, 'has been a good deal disordered in his head'; Deutsch, p. 624. Owing mainly to the disfavor accorded such luxuries during the rebellion, Handel put on no programs until his 'New Occasional Oratorio' of 14 February 1746; see 'Apocrypha', *TP* no. 14 (28 January–4 February 1746), below, p. 414, and the leader of no. 18 (25 February–4 March 1746), below, p. 229. Jensen suggests Fielding and Handel may have been personally acquainted through their common interest in the Foundling Hospital (*CGJ*, ii. 210). But a prior and more likely connection would have been James Harris, close friend of both men. Deutsch, p. 622, writes that 'Handel may have visited the Harris family at Salisbury repeatedly'.

[4] Sir Edward Coke (1552–1634), commonly called Lord Coke, though he was not in fact a peer. As a lawyer himself, Fielding must have been well acquainted with both the substance and the authority of Coke's juridical writings, notably his 'Reports' (1600+) and 'Institutes' (1628+), both of which were fundamental to legal training even in Fielding's day. Although Coke's work had its critics (Prynne and Hobbes among them), there was never any serious diminution of its importance until after this date. Therefore Fielding probably alludes here to the vicissitudes of Coke's political career, which he himself likened to the bounces of a tennis ball (*DNB*). With Lord Burghley providing the Cecil connection, Coke rose rapidly in the reign of Elizabeth I: solicitor general (1592), speaker of the House (1593), attorney general and consultant to the privy council (1594), then adviser to the Lords. In 1603 he was knighted and for a time under James I continued to prosper, rising to chief justice of Common Pleas (1606). After the death (1612) of Salisbury, however, Coke was without the Cecil connection to protect him against the enmity of men like Bacon and, later, Buckingham. In addition Coke was beginning to intensify his opposition of common law to the absolutist doctrines of both crown and clergy. In 1613 Bacon got the king to 'demote' Coke to King's Bench and then (1616) to dismiss him from his judicial and conciliar offices. Subsequently, Coke's role in the parliamentary criticism of the court led to his imprisonment in the Tower (1621) and to charges of treason and

Sydenham:[1] And as to Politics and Religion, I am sure every Man's Memory will suggest to himself very great Masters in both, even in the present Age, who have been, in the highest Degree, both in and out of Fashion.

It is, therefore, the Business of every Man to accommodate himself to the Fashion of the Times; which if he neglects, he must not be surprized if the greatest Parts and Abilities are totally disregarded. If *Socrates* himself was to go to Court in an antique Dress, he would be neglected, or perhaps ridiculed; or if old *Hippocrates* was to visit the College of Physicians, and there talk the Language of his Aphorisms,[2] he would be despised; the College, as *Molière* says, *having altered all that* at present.[3]

But of all Mankind, there are none whom it so absolutely imports to conform to this Golden Rule as an Author; by neglecting this, *Milton*

financial irregularities, both of which were dropped. After the death of James I (1625) Coke maintained his 'perpetual turbulent carriage' towards what he took to be exaggerations of the prerogative—the Stuart prerogative, it should perhaps be noted. As member for Norfolk he attacked Charles I's foreign policy and financial measures so resolutely that the monarch contrived to exclude him from the parliament of 1626 by picking him sheriff of Buckinghamshire. However, Coke resumed his advocacy of legal and parliamentary remedies for the 'grievances' of the state and in 1628 promoted the Petition of Right. After his death (1634) Charles I ordered his papers to be seized. See Stephen D. White, *Sir Edward Coke and 'The Grievances of the Commonwealth'* (Chapel Hill, 1979), pp. 3–23, for a convenient summary of Coke's political life and thought.

[1] Thomas Sydenham (1624–89), clinician and epidemiologist, pioneered the use of quinine for fevers and a regimen of cooling in the treatment of smallpox. For these and other therapeutic innovations, he complained constantly of professional persecution; see Kenneth Dewhurst, *Dr. Thomas Sydenham 1624–1689: His Life and Original Writings* (Berkeley and Los Angeles, 1966), pp. 101–2. Andrew Broun, *A Vindication of Dr. Sydenham's New Method of Curing Continual Fevers* (London, 1700), p. 82, asserts that such hostility from his professional colleagues 'baulked' Sydenham of employment by the royal family and led to an attempt by the College of Physicians to revoke his license; cited by Dewhurst, p. 43. At first more honored abroad than at home, Sydenham later became known as the English Hippocrates, and by the 18th century his *Observationes Medicae* (1676) had become a standard medical textbook. Fielding, who suffered from gout and dropsy, quotes from the 'Dedication' of Sydenham's 'A Treatise of the Gout and Dropsy' (1683; in Latin) in the *Champion* of 3 May 1740, ii. 175–6, and in *Tom Jones*, XIII. ii. 688, on the vanity of human wishes respecting public gratitude and the permanence of fame. See *Whole Works*, trans. J. Pechey, 9th ed. (London, 1729), p. 340.

[2] Of the large, dubious corpus traditionally associated with Hippocrates the *Aphorisms* was the best-known work, from the earliest times 'regarded with a reverence almost religious'; W. H. S. Jones, *Hippocrates*, Loeb Library, iv (London, 1931), p. xxxiii. Until the breakdown of the Hippocratic tradition its authority was unquestioned. Tradition holds that Hippocrates compiled it in his old age as the summary of his life's experience; modern estimates fix the date of compilation *c.* 415 BC. Fielding here compares the aphoristic 'fashion' of style (simple, clear, propositional) with the obscurantist pedantries he so often ridicules in his treatment of contemporary physicians.

[3] *Le Médecin malgré lui* (1666), II. vi, where Sganarelle, replying to a query as to whether his diagnosis has erred in locating the heart on the right and the liver on the left side of the body, says: 'Oui, cela était autrefois ainsi; mais nous avons changé tout cela, & nous faisons maintenant la Médecine d'une méthode toute nouvelle.' Fielding is here remembering Molière *via* his own one-act ballad-opera redaction of the play, entitled *The Mock Doctor* (1732), where he renders the passage thus: 'Ay, Sir, so they were formerly; but we have changed all that. The College at present, Sir, proceeds upon an entire new Method.' The passage seems to have been on his mind about this time; he uses it again in *The Charge to the Jury* of 2 July 1745: 'The Colledge had now altered all that' (pp. 4–5).

himself lay long in Obscurity,[1] and the World had nearly lost the best Poem which perhaps it hath ever seen.[2] On the contrary, by adhering to it, *Tom Durfey*, whose Name is almost forgot,[3] and many others who are quite forgotten, flourished most notably in their respective Ages, and eat and were read very plentifully by their Cotemporaries.

In strict Obedience to this sovereign Power, being informed by my Bookseller, a Man of great Sagacity in his Business,[4] *That no Body at present reads any thing but News-Papers*, I have determined to conform myself to the reigning Taste. The Number indeed of these Writers at first a little staggered us both;[5] but upon Perusal of their Works, I fancied I had discovered two or three little Imperfections in them all, which somewhat diminished the Force of this Objection, and gave me Hopes that the Public will expel some of them to make Room for their Betters.

The first little Imperfection in these Writings, is, that there is scarce a Syllable of Truth in any of them. If this be admitted to be a Fault, it requires no other Evidence than themselves, and the perpetual Contradictions which occur not only on comparing one with the other, but the same Author with himself at different Days.

2dly, There is no Sense in them; to prove this likewise, I appeal to their Works.

[1] Here and elsewhere Fielding subscribes to the Augustan commonplace that Milton was not widely read until the Augustans themselves (credit often given to Addison) saw to it that the middle-class reader felt comfortable with his work, especially *Paradise Lost*. Cf. *CGJ* no. 19 (7 March 1752), i. 248: 'Milton himself (I am ashamed of my Country when I say it) very narrowly escaped from the Jaws of Oblivion; and . . . was like to have been bundled up with those *Ephemeran* insect Authors, of whom every Day almost sees both the Birth and the Funeral.'

[2] Cf. *JJ* no. 8 (23 January 1748), p. 138: '*Paradise Lost*, the noblest Effort perhaps of human Genius, hath its Blemishes . . .'; and the letter from 'Geoffrey Jingle' in *CGJ* no. 50 (23 June 1752), ii. 36: 'And did not the finest Poem in our Language, lie for Years neglected, for no other Reason (that I know) but its wanting that Advantage [rhyme]?'

[3] D'Urfey (1653–1723), playwright, poetaster, writer and collector of songs, was broadly popular in a number of literary genres during the later Restoration and after. Singer to monarchs, laureate of country squires, the convivial D'Urfey was said by Pope to have been the last English poet to have appeared in the streets accompanied by a page; the four-book *Dunciad* (1742), iv. 128 *n.*; see also Twickenham Edition, v. 439. From Dryden's time on, it became something of a ritual to pick on D'Urfey as the 'type' of those whose popularity could be dismissed as mere pandering to the public taste. Cf. *CGJ* no. 10 (4 February, 1752), i. 195, which attests to a lingering popularity: 'but surely it is astonishing that such Scriblers as Tom Brown, Tom D'Urfy, and the Wits of our Age should find Readers, whilst the Writings of so excellent, so entertaining, and so voluminous an Author as Plutarch remain in the World, and, as I apprehend, are very little known.'

[4] The 'fiction' of the literary *persona* by no means requires that its details be linked to those of 'real life', but it should perhaps be noted that although the *TP* colophon indicates that Mary Cooper was the bookseller of record in the present case, Fielding's friend and major publisher, Andrew Millar, may have been the silent partner in the undertaking. See 'General Introduction', above, pp. lxv–lxvii.

[5] In the 'Apocrypha' of *TP* no. 3 (19 November 1745), below, p. 348, Fielding lists the 'Marks of the Historians cited in this Work'. They are the *General Advertiser*, the *Daily Advertiser*, the *Daily Gazetteer*, the *Daily Post*, the *London Courant*, the *St James's Evening Post*, the *London Evening Post*, and the *General Evening Post*. For some reason Fielding does not list two opposition papers, the *Westminster Journal* and the *Craftsman*.

3*dly*, There is, in reality, NOTHING *in them at all*. And this also must be allowed by their Readers, if Paragraphs which contain neither Wit, nor Humour, nor Sense, nor the least Importance, may be properly said to contain nothing. Such are the Arrival of My Lord —— *with a great Equipage*, the Marriage of Miss —— *of great Beauty and Merit*, and the Death of Mr. —— *who was never heard of in his Life*, &c. &c.

Nor will this appear strange, if we consider who are the Authors of such Tracts; namely, the Journeymen of Booksellers, of whom, I believe, much the same may be truly predicated, as of these their Productions.

But the Encouragement with which these Lucubrations are read, may seem more strange and more difficult to be accounted for. And here I cannot agree with my Bookseller, that their eminent Badness recommends them. The true Reason is, I believe, simply the same which I once heard an Œconomist assign for the Content and Satisfaction with which his Family drank Water-cyder,[1] *viz.* because they could procure no other Liquor. Indeed I make no doubt, but that the Understanding as well as the Palate, tho' it may out of Necessity swallow the worse, will in general prefer the better.

In this Confidence, I have resolved to provide the Public a better Entertainment than it hath lately been dieted with; and as it is no great Assurance in an Author to think himself capable of excelling such Writings as have been mentioned above, so neither can he be called too sanguine in promising himself a more favourable Reception from the Public.

It is not usual for us of superior Eminence in our Profession, to hang out our Names on the Sign-Post; however, to raise some Expectation in the Mind of every Reader, as well as to give a slight Direction to those Conjectures which he will be apt to make on this Occasion, I shall set down some few Hints, by which a sagacious Guesser may arrive at sufficient Certainty concerning me.

And, *first*, I faithfully promise him, that I do not live within a Mile of *Grubstreet*;[2] nor am I acquainted with a single Inhabitant of that Place.

---

[1] An inferior liquor made by watering and subjecting to a second pressure the pulp left after expressing the juice for cider (*OED*, *s.v.* 'Ciderkin'). The 'Œconomist' and his family have not been identified.

[2] 'Originally the name of a street near Moorfields in London, much inhabited by writers of small histories, dictionaries, and temporary poems; whence any mean production is called "*grubstreet*"' (Johnson). It ran north out of Fore Street to Chiswell Street, in Cripplegate Ward Without. In 1830 its name was changed to Milton Street. Again, literary convention does not mandate any connection with 'real life', but at this time Fielding was paying rent on a large house in Old Boswell Court, between Carey Street and Butcher Row, near Lincoln's Inn Fields. See J. Paul de Castro, 'Fielding at Boswell Court', *N&Q*, 12th series, no. 1 (1 April 1916), pp. 264–5.

2dly, I am of no Party; a Word which I hope, by these my Labours, to eradicate out of our Constitution: This being indeed the true Source of all those Evils which we have Reason to complain of.

3dly, I am a Gentleman:[1] A Circumstance from which my Reader will reap many Advantages; for at the same Time that he may peruse my Paper, without any Danger of seeing himself, or any of his Friends, traduced with Scurrility, so he may expect, by means of my Intercourse with People of Condition, to find here many Articles of Importance concerning the Affairs and Transactions of the Great World, (which can never reach the Ears of vulgar News-Writers) not only in Matters of State and Politics, but Amusement. All Routs, Drums, and Assemblies,[2] will fall under my immediate Inspection, and the Adventures which happen at them, will be inserted in my Paper, with due Regard, however, to the Character I here profess, and with strict Care to give no Offence to the Parties concerned.

Lastly, As to my Learning, Knowledge, and other Qualifications for the Office I have undertaken, I shall be silent, and leave the Decision to my Reader's Judgment; of whom I desire no more than that he would not despise me before he is acquainted with me.

And to prevent this, as I have already given some Account *what* I am, so I shall proceed to throw forth a few Hints *who* I am; a Matter commonly of the greatest Importance towards the Recommendation of all Works of Literature.

First, then, It is very probable I am Lord *B——ke*.[3] This I collect from

---

[1] Fielding is here establishing his editorial *persona* so as to distinguish his paper from its numerous competitors, but it might be noted that here and elsewhere his references to supposedly inferior writers tend to conflate literary and social distinctions. He seems to have had a reputation for calling attention, in little ways, to his own 'genteel' status. Hostile contemporaries enjoyed contrasting such pretensions with certain 'low' features of his private life and financial condition. See *London Evening Post* of 22–5 October 1748, and *The Jacobite's Journal and Related Writings*, ed. W. B. Coley (Oxford, 1974), p. lxxxi.

[2] 'Drum' and 'Rout' were frequently used as synonyms to mean a gathering of fashionable persons, at a private house, in the evening, often for the purpose of playing cards for money. Although neither word is included in the major dictionaries of the day, they evidently lent themselves to nice social nuance. See Eliza Haywood, *The Female Spectator*, Book XII, ii (London, 1745), 269: 'She told me, that when the Number of Company for Play exceeded ten Tables, it was called a *Racquet*, if under it was only a *Rout*, and if no more than one or two, it was only a *Drum*'; cited by *OED*, *s.v.* 'Drum'. There is a satirical definition in *Tom Jones*, XVII. vi. 898.

[3] Henry St John (1678–1751), first viscount Bolingbroke, MP Wooten Basset (Wiltshire) and sometime protege of Marlborough's and Harley's, tory leader in commons during Anne's last four years, architect of the Treaty of Utrecht (1713). After Anne's death (1714) he was dismissed from his offices, impeached and attainted by Walpole's direction, and fled to France, where he renewed his jacobite connections by becoming secretary to the Old Pretender, a post he lost after the recriminations of the Fifteen. Pardoned in 1723, Bolingbroke returned to England and, after a brief flirtation with Walpole, concerted with Wyndham and Bath to unite the tories and opposition whigs against Walpole. During this decade (1725–35) he was one of the principal contributors to the *Craftsman*, where his 'Humphry Oldcastle' papers and the 'Dissertation on Parties' first appeared. After failing

my Stile in Writing and Knowledge in Politics. Again it is as probable that I am the B——p of ****,[1] from my Zeal for the Protestant Religion. When I consider these, together with the Wit and Humour which will diffuse themselves through the whole, it is more than possible I may be Lord *C*—— himself,[2] or at least he may have some Share in my Paper.

From some, or all of these Reasons, I am very likely Mr. *W——n*,[3] Mr.

to unite the opposition to Walpole, and under increasing pressure from the latter, he went again to France, returning briefly in 1738 to write 'The Idea of a Patriot King' and to advise with Frederick Prince of Wales, who was then beginning to consolidate an opposition of his own, including Fielding's friends Dodington and Lyttelton. By 1744 Bolingbroke was in England more or less for good, working behind the scenes to persuade the Pelham broad bottom to include more tories. Because of his former connections with the jacobites he kept a low profile during the Forty-Five, being reduced to providing advice, especially to Hardwicke, on foreign policy matters. Among contemporaries like Chesterfield Bolingbroke enjoyed an enormous reputation as a stylist, a fact to which Fielding indirectly attests in the *Champion* of 1 March 1740, i. 325, where the bookseller undertaking that paper asks the writer of it 'to go to several Coffee-Houses where I am little known, and assert roundly that my Lord *B——ke* was the Author of the *Champion*. . . . For that the same Scheme had been successfully tried by another.' See also 'General Introduction', above, pp. lxxi–lxxiv.

[1] Identification here is unsure. French, p. 179, and Locke, p. 43, follow Cross, ii. 20, in suggesting Benjamin Hoadly (1676–1761), at this time bishop of Winchester, who is unequivocally mentioned, in a similar context, in *TP* no. 3 (19 November 1745), below, p. 129, and *n*. Locke, p. 43, considers the possibility that the reference is to Thomas Herring, archbishop of York, whose 'Zeal' for the protestant religion was more conspicuous during the Forty-Five than was Hoadly's. Against this latter identification, however, is the unequivocal reference to Herring by his correct title (archbishop) in *TP* no. 3 (19 November 1745), below, p. 129, also in a very similar context. For Hoadly, see *TP* no. 3, below, p. 129, *n*. 2.

[2] Philip Dormer Stanhope (1694–1773) fourth earl of Chesterfield 1726, KG 1730, MP St Germans 1715–22, Lostwithiel 1722–3, held a number of posts in the royal household before serving as ambassador to The Hague 1728–32. Entering strenuous opposition over the Excise Bill (1733), he wrote numerous political pieces for opposition journals like *Fog's Weekly* and (as 'Geoffrey Broadbottom') *Old England*; with Lyttelton he seems to have been one of the undertakers of the opposition *Common Sense* (1737–9). In addition he was the anonymous author of some of the most notorious anti-Hanoverian pamphlets of Walpole's last years. Excluded (by Carteret's machinations and the king's animosity) from the Wilmington ministry which followed the fall of Walpole, Chesterfield remained in the 'patriot' opposition until the broad-bottom coalition of late 1744, which also took in Lyttelton and Dodington among Fielding's political mentors. Chesterfield accepted the lord lieutenancy of Ireland and since July 1745 had been in Dublin, where he was maintaining a delicate diplomacy between Pelhams and their 'new allies'. In October 1746 he would become secretary of state, northern department. Like Bolingbroke and Lyttelton, Chesterfield was known as a man of letters and a literary patron. He subscribed to Fielding's *Miscellanies* (1743), and Fielding pays steady court to him from the days of his own first flirtations with the opposition (he dedicated *Don Quixote in England* [1734] to Chesterfield, and there is a flattering allusion to him in the epistle dedicating *The Intriguing Chambermaid* [1733; 1734] to Mrs Clive); through the intense opposition journalism of the *Champion* (see, for example, 29 January 1740, i. 225), 'Of True Greatness' (1741), and the *Miscellanies* (1743); to 'Letter XL' which he contributed to his sister's *Familiar Letters* (1747). For the subsequent falling off in their relationship, see *The Jacobite's Journal and Related Writings*, ed. W. B. Coley (Oxford, 1974), pp. xxii–xxiii, xlix–l, lxiii.

[3] Identification is uncertain. Cross, ii. 20; French, p. 180; and Locke, p. 43, conjecture Thomas Winnington, but this seems unlikely. Winnington (1696–1746), MP Droitwich 1726–41, Worcester city 1741–6, became one of Walpole's most loyal subordinates. Lord of the admiralty 1730–6, treasury 1736–41, paymaster general 1743–6, he was described latterly as the 'confidant' of George II, who during the struggle between Granville and the Pelhams relied on Winnington to manage the crown's business in the Commons. At the king's instigation Winnington opposed the government on the

D—n,[1] Mr. L—n,[2] Mr. F—g,[3] Mr. T—n,[4] or indeed any other Person who hath ever distinguished himself in the Republic of Letters.

This at least is very probable, that some of these Gentlemen may

matter of the 'new' regiments being raised to fight the rebels, and the king was persuaded to accept the Bath–Granville attempt at a ministry in February 1746 in part because he believed Winnington could manage the Commons for them. See *The House of Commons 1715–1754*, ed. Romney Sedgwick, ii (London, 1970), 551–2. Although praised by Horace Walpole and others for his wit and 'style', Winnington was not in fact known as a writer. A more likely identification would be William Warburton (1698–1779), controversialist divine, editor (Pope and Shakespeare), and prolific writer (e.g. *The Alliance between Church and State* [1736], and *The Divine Legation of Moses demonstrated* [1738–41], which Fielding praises in his note to line 81 of his 'Part of Juvenal's Sixth Satire Modernized', *Miscellanies* [1743], i. 91). Close friend of Fielding's patron Ralph Allen, Warburton had married the latter's favorite niece in September 1745. Fielding and Warburton may have met at Prior Park as early as December 1741; see Benjamin Boyce, *The Benevolent Man: A Life of Ralph Allen of Bath* (Cambridge, Mass., 1967), p. 126. Fielding's second unequivocal reference to Warburton by name is in *Tom Jones*, XIII. i. 687, where his learning is praised. In 1738 Warburton was appointed chaplain to the Prince of Wales, in which capacity he must have appeared sympathetic to the opposition gathering at Leicester House. He was known to Lyttelton and Chesterfield, the latter offering in 1745 to take him to Ireland as his chaplain, an offer Warburton refused. His *Sermon Occasion'd by the present unnatural Rebellion . . . preach'd in Mr. Allen's Chapel, at Prior Park near Bath* is listed as published in *General Advertiser* of 9 November 1745, and Warburton was to publish two more sermons before the rebellion had run its course. See also 'General Introduction', above, pp. lxxxix–xci.

[1] George Bubb Dodington (1691–1762) MP Winchilsea 1715–22, Bridgwater 1722–54, Weymouth and Melcombe Regis 1754–61, was first taken up by Walpole, who made him lord of the treasury (1724–40). At the accession of George II (1727) Dodington gravitated toward Spencer Compton and the duke of Dorset. In 1732 he supplanted Lord Hervey as the chief political adviser to the Prince of Wales, to whom he introduced Lyttelton, who supplanted him there. After a somewhat vacillating independency Dodington associated with Argyll in 1740, following him into opposition and assisting in turning the Cornish boroughs against Walpole. After the latter's fall, and failing to implement his own idea of a broad bottom, Dodington continued in opposition and, in the unfriendly words of Horace Walpole, 'headed the young Patriots, and the needy Scotch Jacobites, and on the coalition [1744] was made treasurer of the Navy in the room of Sir John Rushout'; 'HW's MS Poems', p. 97, as cited by *Yale Walpole*, xvii. 258. At the time of writing, Dodington seems to have been loosely affiliated with the so-called Cobham faction—Pitt, Lyttelton and the Grenvilles (to whom Dodington was related). Himself an occasional versifier, Dodington was best known as a patron, helping Thomson, Young, Fielding, Whitehead, and Glover, among others. Fielding praises him in the *Champion* of 29 January 1740, i. 225, and dedicates his poem *Of True Greatness* (1741) to him. There is further praise in the 'Essay on Conversation', *Miscellanies*, i. 352; *Tom Jones*, XI. xi. 612; and *Amelia*, XI. ii. 462, where he is described as 'one of the greatest Men this Country ever produced'. On a purely social level, Fielding may have been more intimate with Dodington than with any of his other benefactors, their friendship apparently unimpaired by the hostility in 1748 between Fielding's ministerial *Jacobite's Journal* and the opposition *Remembrancer*, which was being conducted for Dodington by Fielding's friend James Ralph. See *JJ* no. 17 (26 March 1748), pp. 212–15. For Dodington's possible role in the *True Patriot*, see 'General Introduction', above, pp. lxix–lxx.

[2] George Lyttelton (1709–73), dedicatee of *Tom Jones* and unquestionably the most profound and prolonged influence on Fielding's literary and political life. MP Okehampton 1735–56, secretary to the prince of Wales 1737–44, lord of the treasury 1744–54, Lyttelton had been at Eton with Fielding in the early 1720s. In 1733 Fielding addressed to him an unpublished poem entitled 'An Epistle to Mr. Lyttelton'; Isobel Grundy, 'New Verse by Henry Fielding', *PMLA*, lxxxvii (1972), 213–45. There are further compliments in *Of True Greatness* (1741) and the *Miscellanies* (1743). The preface which Fielding contributed to his sister's *Familiar Letters* (1747) describes the 'inimitable writer' of the 'Persian Letters' as 'one who is master of style, as of every other excellence'. In *JJ* no. 18 (2 April 1748) Lyttelton is defended against the attacks on him by Horace Walpole, and in no. 33 (16 July 1748) is praised for his probity and for being 'almost the only Patron which the Muses at present can boast among the Great'. By 1745 Lyttelton had acquired a certain reputation for his *Letters from a Persian in England*

[*See opposite page for n. 2 cont. and nn. 3 and 4*]

contribute a Share of their Abilities to the carrying on this Work; in which, as nothing shall ever appear in it inconsistent with Decency, or the Religion and true Civil Interest of my Country, no Person, how great soever, need be ashamed of being imagined to have a Part; unless he should be weak enough to be ashamed of writing at all; that is, of having more Sense than his Neighbours, or of communicating it to them.

I come now to consider the only remaining Article, *viz*. the Price, which is one Third more than my cotemporary Weekly Historians set on their Labours.[1]

(1735), and the gossip of insiders credited him with writing a number of fugitive political pieces in the anti-Walpole crusade. But it was as a patron of letters that he was most conspicuously active, having assisted such writers as Thomson, Fielding, Edward Moore, Gilbert West, perhaps Mallet. In 1734 his uncle Lord Cobham had directed Chesterfield to persuade the prince of Wales to replace Dodington with Lyttelton, and in 1735 he had been brought into parliament on the interest of his brother-in-law Thomas Pitt, with whose brother William and his own cousin Richard Grenville he acted under Cobham's direction. After Walpole's fall the Cobham group detached from the prince of Wales (he tolerated the exclusionist ministry) and remained in opposition until the broad bottom of late 1744, when the prince finally dismissed Lyttelton from his secretaryship for having accepted a place in the treasury. Late in 1745 Lyttelton seems to have been restless in place, apparently because of the failure to find room for Pitt and George Grenville; see Chesterfield to Newcastle, 11 January 1746, Lodge, *Private Correspondence*, pp. 100–1; Owen, *Rise of the Pelhams*, pp. 291–3; and 'General Introduction', above, pp. xciii–xcvii.

[3] Copy-text reads: 'Mr. | Mr. F——g'. French, p. 182, suggests the typographical error resulted from Fielding's having inserted his own name 'as an afterthought while reading proof', an insertion the printer made 'carelessly'. However, there is no evidence one way or the other as to whether Fielding read proof on the *TP*, and since the error involves the end of one line and the beginning of the next, the printer's hand or eye may have been distracted for other reasons.

[4] James Thomson (1700–48), by this time author of *The Seasons* (1726–30), *Liberty* (1735–6), and a number of heroic tragedies, had been pensioned by the prince of Wales in 1737 or 1738, possibly at Lyttelton's suggestion, and although 'political' only in a rather elevated sense, must be counted among the writers (Fielding was another) recruited by the 'patriot' opposition for propaganda purposes. Still on princely pension in 1745, Thomson brought out his 'patriot' tragedy *Tancred and Sigismunda* in March at Drury Lane, with Garrick as male lead. Both Lyttelton and Pitt were said to have played important roles in the production and even the composition of this play, which when printed was dedicated to the prince; Thomas Davies, *Memoirs of the life of David Garrick, Esq.* (London, 1780), i. 79; *London Stage*, Part 3, ii. 1160; and the 'Bellario' letter in the *Daily Post* of 26 April 1745, reprinted in Alan Dugald McKillop, *James Thomson (1700–1748): Letters and Documents* (Lawrence, Kansas, 1958), pp. 178–81. Evidence of friendship between Fielding and Thomson is admittedly circumstantial, but it is persuasive. Andrew Millar was the principal publisher of both. Fielding's friend and patron Dodington performed similar functions for Thomson as early as the composition of *The Seasons*. Lyttelton went further. After getting himself into place in the broad bottom of late 1744, he got Thomson the sinecure of surveyor-general of the Leeward Islands, and in 1748, after Thomson lost his pension from the prince of Wales, Lyttelton appealed to Pelham for a governmental pension to replace it; *Letters of... Chesterfield*, ed. Bonamy Dobrée (London, 1932), i. 1119; Rose Mary Davis, *The Good Lord Lyttelton* (Bethlehem, Pa., 1939), pp. 58–61. As part of his general attack on the heroic drama, Fielding had ridiculed Thomson's *Sophonisba* (1730) in his own *Tragedy of Tragedies* (1731), but after that references to the poet are uniformly laudatory. Fielding's poem 'Liberty' (1743) echoes Thomson's poem of the same name. In *JJ* no. 27 (4 June 1748) Fielding will give *The Castle of Indolence* (1748) its earliest full critical appreciation, and Thomson's obituary, as carried in *JJ* no. 40 (3 September 1748), though not certainly by Fielding himself, seems unusually full and sympathetic.

[1] The price of the *TP*, which was a weekly, was three pence. The rationale which follows resembles that given in *CGJ* no. 1 (4 January 1752), where the 'bookseller' justifies the similar price of

And here I might, with Modesty enough, insist, that if I am either what or who I pretend to be, I have sufficient Title to this Distinction. It is well known that, among Mechanics,[1] a much larger Advance is often allowed only for a particular Name. A genteel Person would not be suspected of dealing with any other than the most eminent in his Trade, tho' he is convinced he pays an additional Price by so doing. And I hope the polite World, especially when they consider the Regard to Fashion which I have above professed, will not scruple to allow me the same Pre-eminence.

But in reality, this is the cheapest Paper which was ever given to the Public, both in Quality, of which enough hath been said already, and in which Light a Shilling would, I apprehend, be a more moderate Price than the Three Halfpence which is demanded by some others: And *secondly*, (which my Bookseller chiefly insists on) in Quantity; as I shall contain, he says, full three times as many Letters as the above-mentioned Papers; and for which Reason he at first advised me to demand Four-pence at least, for that one Ninth Part would be still abated to the Public. To be serious, I would desire my Reader to weigh fairly with himself, whether he doth not gain six times the Knowledge and Amusement by my Paper, compared to any other; and then I think he will have no Difficulty to determine in my Favour.

Indeed the prudent Part of Mankind will be considerable Gainers by purchasing my Paper; for as it will contain every thing which is worth their knowing, all others will become absolutely needless; and I leave to their Determination whether Threepenny-worth of Truth and Sense is not more worth their purchasing than all the Rubbish and Nonsense of the Week, which will cost them twenty times as much. In other Words, Is it not better to give their Understanding an Entertainment once a Week, than to surcharge it every Day with coarse and homely Fare?

I shall conclude the whole in the Words of the fair and honest Tradesman: Gentlemen, upon my Word and Honour, I can afford it no cheaper; and I believe there is no Shop in Town will use you better for the Price.[2]

that weekly by the 'Beauty' of his print and paper, the quantity and quality of the matter in it, and the great learning of the writer (i. 136). Fielding's *Champion*, appearing three times a week, sold for three half-pence a copy, and his *Jacobite's Journal*, another weekly, for two pence a copy, the low price of the latter possibly indicating a government subsidy.

[1] A mechnic was a low or vulgar person (*OED*, which cites Fielding's *Intriguing Chambermaid*, ii. ix). See also 'An Essay on Conversation', *Miscellanies* (1743), i. 138. The term melds social and literary inferiorities, and Fielding may not be entirely playful in wishing to distinguish himself from the hack writer of no social standing. See above, p. 108, *n.* 1.

[2] Locke, p. 44, says that Fielding gives 'the sentiment but not the exact wording' of Defoe's 'Of Honesty in Dealing', *Complete English Tradesman* (London, 1726), Letter xvii. But the resemblance is slight, and there is no evidence that the 'source' is other than colloquial.

OBSERVATIONS

ON THE

PRESENT REBELLION.

The Rebellion is at present so seriously the Concern of every sensible Man, who wishes well to the Religion and Liberties of his Country, and the Zeal which all the different Sects of Protestants have discovered on this Occasion, is so hearty and unanimous, that it would be lost Labour to endeavour at inflaming the Minds of my Countrymen on this Occasion.

On the contrary, it is rather the Business of a good Public Writer, in some Measure, to moderate and direct this Spirit, which now so gloriously animates us. Cool and temperate Councils will be of singular Use at this Time, when the Rashness of inconsiderate, tho' well-meaning Men, may do Injury to that Cause which they desire to support with their All, and on which THEIR ALL depends.

Of this kind is that indiscriminate Censure which some over-hot Men are at this Season too apt to vent on the whole Body of the *Scottish* Nation. True it is, that the Rebellion with which we are threatned, broke out in that Corner of *Great Britain*: A Circumstance very unfortunate for the Honest and Loyal, whose Persons and Fortunes have been exposed to the most horrid Insults and Depredations.

But let us consider of what Persons this rebellious Rabble consists; and we shall find them to be the savage Inhabitants of Wilds and Mountains, who are almost a distinct Body from the rest of their Country. Some Thousands of them are Outlaws, Robbers, and Cut-throats, who live in a constant State of War, or rather Robbery, with the civilized Part of *Scotland*. The Estates of this Part have been always pillaged by the Thefts of these Ruffians, by whom they are now openly plundered.

And how greatly is it to the Honour of the Nobility and Gentry of *North Britain*, that they have rather chose to submit to this Alternative than join or countenance a Rebellion, which hath hitherto been carried on in their Country with such a Torrent of Success. This is a Fact so true, that except Outlaws, and *one* or *two* profligate younger Brothers,[1]

---

[1] Fitting this somewhat derisive category were Lord George Murray (1694–1760), younger brother to the duke of Athol, who joined the YP at Perth *c.* 5 September and became one of his principal military advisers; Hon. William Murray (1696–1756), third earl of Dunmore (1752), younger brother of John Murray, second earl of Dunmore, who joined at the same time; David Wemyss (1721–87), styled Lord Elcho, son of the fourth earl of Wemyss, who joined on 16 September; Lord Lewis Gordon (d. 1754), younger brother of the third duke of Gordon, who joined on 15 October with 300 men; and James Drummond (1713–46), titular third duke of Perth, who joined at Perth on 4 September and was reported (erroneously) by some London papers to have been killed at Prestonpans. See *Yale Walpole*, xix. 102, 104; Blaikie, *Itinerary*, pp. 11, 17.

there is not a SINGLE MAN OF ANY NAME in the Kingdom, who hath given Sanction to the Pretender's Cause. And what other Step could Loyalty and Honesty dictate to the best affected, when their Clans are disarmed by Act of Parliament,[1] than what they have taken, of securing their Persons by Flight, and abandoning that Property which they could no longer defend.

Why did not the young Invader, who, with such admirable Policy, issued forth a formal Summons of Parliament,[2] proceed in the Execution of his Scheme, but because he could not procure a Number to obey these Summons, which would be sufficient to defend the Assembly from Ridicule and Contempt? Was *Scotland*, or the major Part of it, unanimous in his Cause, what prevents his Father's being King of *Scotland*, not only supported by Force, but acknowledged by their Law? A Consequence which would make this Rebellion of a very different Consideration from what it is at present.

Have not the *Scotch* Clergy behaved with the utmost Spirit which Loyalty could dictate, or Courage execute? It is their Interest and their Duty so to do; they knew their Interest, and have fulfilled their Duty. They prayed for his Majesty King GEORGE, in the midst of his Enemies; and when they were unable, from Violence, to discharge this Duty, they scorned the Popish pitiful Evasion which was dictated to them, and deserted their Churches. But let the Behaviour of the Synod of *Glasgow*, which deserves every Epithet of both Good and Great, speak the Temper of those People; who, within ten Days of the Battle of *Preston Pans*, when the Pretender was absolutely victorious, when his Numbers were greatly increasing, when all *Scotland* was in Confusion; when the *Highland* Banditti, animated with Success, breathed nothing but Fury against their Enemies, and Part of this Army was within their Walls, demanding Contributions for the Support of the Rebellion, did, at this Season, with the most admirable Courage, persevere in their Loyalty, prayed for and preached their true King, addressed him, and with the heartiest Zeal avowed and set about to promote his Cause.[3]

---

[1] As a result of the 'Fifteen', by 1 Geo. I, stat. 2 (1715), c. 54, sec. 1; and 11 Geo. I (1724), c. 26. The whig duke of Argyll, who was reputed to be able to put more men in the field than all the government forces in Scotland put together, based his refusal of government arms on the existence of such legislation: 'it is not lawful for any person in the Highlands to defend the Government, or his own Home, family or goods, though attacked by Robbers or Rebels'; SP Scot. 25/61 and 62, as quoted in Jarvis, i. 104.

[2] So reported in the London papers—*DA* of 27 September 1745 cites 'an order for the Parliament of Scotland to meet . . . the 7th of October' in Edinburgh—but the report was unfounded. The YP in fact called a council on 22 September, which met daily at Holyrood; Blaikie, *Itinerary*, p. 17. See no. 10 (7 January 1746), below, p. 172 and *n*.

[3] The 'Memorial and Admonition of the Reverend Synod of Glasgow' was reprinted in the London papers (e.g. *General Advertiser* of 22 October 1745), often with the comment that it had been

The common People of the Lowlands in *Scotland* are as well affected to his Majesty as any of his Subjects. Indeed they can have no Motive to be otherwise. They are rigid Presbyterians, and have tasted too much the Spirit of Persecution under a *Stuart*, who was, or pretended to be, a Protestant, ever to trust a known and avowed Papist of the same Family. The least Degree of common Honesty is not required to preserve the Loyalty of these People, the lowest Portion of common Sense will be sufficient. They must be Fools or Madmen, should they endeavour to set this Popish Pretender on the Throne: But they have endeavoured at no such thing; and as the Nature of the Case gives us no Suspicion, so neither have their Actions given us any. They are Fellow-Protestants and Fellow-Sufferers with ourselves; nay, they are hitherto much greater Sufferers, and have seen and felt that Devastation which we are to expect.

Let us not therefore entertain or vent any Suspicion of these People, who will most assuredly, in their several Stations, exert that Courage for which they are, in common with us, renowned over *Europe*, in Defence of that Religion and Liberty which in common with us, they enjoy. Let us remember the Behaviour of the gallant Earl of *Loudoun* and his *Scotch* Followers,[1] the only Soldiers on our Side who rallied at the late Battle, and the glorious Death of Colonel *Gardiner*, who being born a *Scotchman*, fell in the Cause of Liberty with the Spirit of a *Roman*.[2]

(*To be continued.*)

TUESDAY, NOVEMBER 12, 1745.   NUMB. 2.

Fallit enim vitium specie virtutis et umbra.

JUVENAL.[3]

The Title of a Work being often of no less Consequence to its Success

composed and published on 1 October, under conditions such as are described here. The 'Memorial' closed with a prayer on behalf of George II. *General Advertiser* of 1 November 1745 reprinted the 'Address' of the synod directly to the king, over the signature of James Stirling, the moderator, and transmitted by the duke of Argyll.

[1] John Campbell (1705–82), fourth earl of Loudoun (1731), governor of Stirling Castle (1741–63), had raised in June 1745 a regiment of Highlanders, consisting of twelve companies. Their comportment during the battle at Prestonpans was generally conceded to have been better than that of Cope's 'English' forces. Loudoun (Loudon) is also mentioned commendatorily in *History*, above, p. 65.

[2] For Colonel James Gardiner, commander of one of the two regiments of dragoons with Cope at Prestonpans and one of the few 'heroes' on the English side, see *History*, above, p. 65 and *nn*.

[3] *Satires*, xiv. 109: 'For that vice has a deceptive appearance and semblance of virtue' (Loeb). Juvenal is describing avarice. The line is also used as the motto of *Champion* of 4 March 1740, where it is erroneously attributed to Horace; i. 328.

than the Name of the Author, I had it long under Deliberation before I fixed on that Title which now appears at the Head of my Paper.

But though I was at last determined in my Choice, by Considerations which appeared to me of great Moment, I had the Misfortune, however, to find it opposed by many of my Friends; one of whom, a pretty Free-speaker, advised me rather to appear under the Character of *The Pick-pocket*. A Title, he said, which would as effectually recommend me to my Country as that which I have chosen.

It must be confess'd, indeed, that this Word *Patriot* hath of late Years been very scandalously abused by some Persons, who, from their Actions as well public as private, appear to have a much juster Claim to that Appellation which my humorous Friend above recommended. Ambition, Avarice, Revenge, Envy, Malice, every bad Passion in the Mind of Man, have cloaked themselves under this amiable Character, and have misrepresented Persons and Things in unjust Colours to the Public. We have now Men among us, who have stiled themselves Patriots, while they have pushed their own Preferment, and the Ruin of their Enemies, at the manifest Hazard of the Ruin of their Country.[1]

I shall not expatiate on this disagreeable Subject, at such a Season; nay, I should have declined mentioning it at all, had it not been necessary to give my Reader a very early Information, that this Paper is not writ on the Principles, or with the Purposes, of modern Patriotism;[2] it being my sincere Intention to calm and heal, not to blow up and inflame any Party-Divisions. Another Consequence which I hope may follow from the bare Mention of false Patriotism, at this Time, is, that all Persons conscious of having acted any such Part, would manifest an extraordinary and particular Zeal in endeavouring to put out those Coals which they may perhaps have had some Share in the kindling, tho' they have not intended to raise the Flame which now threatens this Nation.[3]

[1] The first of many references to the opposition of 1745–6, led by Granville and Bath, both of whom had at one time been in the coalitions against Walpole and hence entitled to be called 'patriots'. For a summary of their 'misrepresentations' of the rebellion, as well as of their aggressive foreign policy, see *TP* no. 26 (22–9 April 1746), below, pp. 274–5; for the larger political background of the opposition to the Pelhams, see 'General Introduction', above, pp. lxii–lxxxix.

[2] The broad-bottom coalition of November 1744 included some, but by no means all, of the so-called patriot opposition. From the standpoint of those who were included—that is, the standpoint of Fielding's political mentors and of the *TP* itself—'modern' or false patriotism abandons the fundamental antifactionalism of former times, in the interest of getting into place and ultimately into power. See 'General Introduction', above, pp. lxxviii–lxxxv.

[3] To judge from shifts in the tone of opposition journalism at this juncture, some quarters were beginning to concede that playing down the significance of the rebellion and obstructing ministerial efforts to deal more vigorously with it had contributed alarmingly to its success. See, for example, the letter signed 'Agricola' in *OE* of 9 November 1745, which claims that nothing has aided the rebel cause so much as 'the common idle reports spread about from among our common news-papers'; reprinted in *GM*, xv (1745), 588–9.

But, however the Word *Patriot* hath been abused, or whatever Odium it may have thence contracted among the honest Part of Mankind, the Word itself, so far from deserving Contempt and Abhorrence, doth certainly set before us the most amiable Character in human Nature: For what less is meant by Patriotism, than the Love of one's Country carried into Action? A Virtue by which not only particular Men, but Nations have been ambitious of distinguishing themselves, and by which alone they have risen to the greatest Heights of human Glory and Power.

The Difficulty then is the same in this as in other Virtues, to distinguish Truth from Falshood and Pretence. This is indeed an Art, which requires so great Attention, as well as Penetration, that few (if qualified) will take Pains to arrive at or practise it.[1] Hence the Hypocrite finds it so easy to impose on Mankind. The thinnest Disguise is sufficient to hide the grossest Affectation; and Men have little more to do, than to declare they are what they desire to be thought.

As there is no Affectation of so dangerous a Nature to Society, so none seems so impudent, as this of Patriotism; and yet all Ages and Nations have produced Men who, without one Ingredient of this excellent Character in their Natures, have pretended to be Patriots, and under that Denomination have ruined their Country.

Instead of giving any ancient or modern Example of this Deceit at present, I shall endeavour to arm my Countrymen against it for the future, by lending them some Assistance to discover the true Patriot from the false. And here I shall lay down some negative Rules, by which they may be, at least, enabled to declare, that particular Persons do not, nor can, deserve this amiable Character.

First, It is certain that no Man can love his Country, who doth not love a single Person in it.[2] A morose surly ill-natured Fellow, who never smiled in his Life, (unless peradventure when he saw a Wretch tumble from a House and break his Neck) would make a good Inquisitor, but a very bad Patriot. If any Virtue requires Philanthropy, it is this; and *Brutus*, the great Exemplar of it, was as amiable in private as in public Life.[3] If such a Person as is above described, should presume to affect

---

[1] The difficulty of separating truth when it is blended with falsehood is similarly described in *JJ* no. 28 (11 June 1748), p. 304.

[2] Cf. Fielding's 'Essay on the Knowledge of the Characters of Men', *Miscellanies* (1743), i. 176: 'It is well said in one of Mr. *Pope's* Letters; "How shall a Man love five Millions, who could never love a single Person"'; an imperfect recollection of *Letters of Mr. Alexander Pope* (London, 1737), p. 95, where in a letter to Fielding's cousin Lady Mary Wortley Montagu (20 August 1716) Pope's figure is 'twenty thousand People'. See also *Correspondence of Alexander Pope*, ed. George Sherburn, i (Oxford, 1956), 357.

[3] Marcus Junius Brutus (?85–42 BC), the tyrannicide, impressed Cicero and other contemporaries with his moral earnestness and humane governance. Fielding mentions him often as an exemplar of

this Character, let us answer him in the sacred Words of Scripture: *If thou lovest not thy Brother whom thou hast seen, how canst thou love seven Millions whom thou hast not seen?*[1]

Secondly, The Man who is known to love a Guinea better than his Friend, or even his own Soul, can never deserve the Name of *Patriot*. One whose whole Life hath been a constant Course of tenacious as well as rapacious Avarice, who hath been guilty of the most flagitious Acts in acquiring immense Wealth, and the most sordid in retaining it.[2] It must argue the most absolute Want of Modesty in such a Man to affect the Character of a Patriot, and the most deplorable Want of Common-sense in those who can be imposed on by him. Can those Hands, which have pilfered his Neighbour's private Purse, be safely trusted in that of the Public? Is his Conscience so peculiarly tender, that he will plunder no Family but that of his Friend? Preposterous and absurd! If there be a self-evident Proposition, this is surely so; That the Man who will sell his Friend, will sell his Country.

Thirdly, No Man can love his Country who would set it on fire. The Motives to a private Incendiary are but two: A Desire of Revenge, or a Desire of Gain. The Motives to a public Incendiary are no other. And the latter attempt to throw their Country into Flames, with the same View as the former set fire to a House, either to destroy the Master, or to enrich themselves with the plundering it.[3] Destruction is a Consequence equally certain in both Instances. *Factiones fuere eruntque plurimis civitatibus exitium*; says the greatest of all the *Roman* Historians.[4] *Athens*,

the great and good man. See, for example, 'Preface' to the *Miscellanies* (1743), i. 12; 'Of the Remedy of Affliction for the Loss of Our Friends', *Miscellanies* (1743), i. 213; *Jonathan Wild*, i. i; *JJ* no. 8 (23 January 1748), p. 138, and no. 28 (11 June 1748), p. 306; *Tom Jones*, iv. iv. 163.

[1] Cf. 1 John 4: 20: for he that loveth not his brother whom he hath seen, how can he love God whom he hath not seen? It is not clear whether Fielding means his interpolated figure of 7 million to represent England and Wales only, or Scotland as well. Estimates of mid-century population for England and Wales put the figure at between 6 and 6.5 million; for Scotland, at 1.2 million; *Abstract of British Historical Studies*, ed. B. R. Mitchell (Cambridge, 1962), p. 5. In *TP* no. 7 (17 December 1745) Parson Adams estimates 12 million; see below, p. 153. A letter in *DA* of 26 September 1745 estimates 8 million in 'this Nation'.

[2] The portrait here is deliberately general; however, close readers of Fielding may feel he had Peter Walter in the back of his mind. For a jocular treatment of the latter's fondness for the guinea, see 'Some Papers Proper to be Read before the R——l Society, Concerning the Terrestrial Chrysipus, Golden-Foot or Guinea' (1742), in *Miscellanies* (1743), i. 191–204. The title-page of 'Some Papers' states that they were 'Collected by Petrus Gualterus'. In addition to being for his time the very 'type' of usurer, Walter seems also to have snapped up the farm properties (at East Stour) belonging to Fielding and his siblings until at least 1738; *Salisbury and Winchester Journal* of 11 September 1780, cited by Cross, i. 241. For evidence that Fielding and Walter were acquainted, see W. B. Coley, 'Fielding and the Two Walpoles', *PQ*, xlv (1966), 169–70.

[3] The incendiary metaphors resemble those used to describe James Ralph's editorship of the opposition *Remembrancer* in 1748; see *JJ* no. 17 (26 March 1748), p. 215.

[4] 'Factions have been and will be the downfall of many states.' Adapted from Livy, *Historia*, iv.

Sparta, and even *Rome* herself fell a Sacrifice to this Firebrand; and our own Country hath frequently experienced its fatal Mischiefs. The great *Boadicea*[1] told our Ancestors, they were not conquered by the *Romans*, but by their own Factions;[2] and *Galgacus*, their General, many years afterwards repeated the same Observation.[3] To these I will add the Words of a very sensible, tho' antient Writer, who tells us, *That the* Britons, *after the* Romans *had left them, were no less burdened with the* TUMUL- TOUS UPROARS OF THEIR OWN GREAT MEN, WHO STROVE FOR THE SUPREME GOVERNMENT, *than with the barbarous Nations*, &c.[4] I have chosen these Instances out of the remoter Ages, and purposely omit those modern Examples which might bear a nearer Resemblance to our own Days; my Design being to awaken my Reader's Remembrance, and, if possible, to caution him from any future Imposition, without inflaming his Resent- ment against the past.

I am aware, it may be objected, Are we not then in Times of Danger to alarm our Country against the Designs of her Enemies? Surely it is our Duty so to do; but the Disease ought to be great and certain, for the Remedy is violent and dangerous. A Convulsion in the whole political Œconomy must be the immediate Consequence; and this may be attended with its Dissolution before it can effect a Cure. There are some

ix. 3: *ex certamine factionum, quae fuerunt eruntque pluribus populis exitio*. In *TP* no. 8 (24 December 1745), below, p. 160, Fielding praises Livy for his use of circumstantial detail. See also ch. ix of 'A Journey from this World to the Next', *Miscellanies* (1743), ii. 73; *JJ* no. 15 (12 March 1748), p. 196.

[1] After the death (AD 60) of her husband Prasutagus, client-king of the Iceni tribe in East Anglia, Boudicca ('Boadicea') resisted the Roman dismantling of the kingdom and the outrages which accompanied it, by leading the forces of the tribal confederacy against detachments of the army of the military governor, Suetonius Paulinus. She gained victories at Colchester, London, and St Albans before the terminal loss to Suetonius in 61. See Donald R. Dudley and Graham Webster, *The Rebel- lion of Boudicca* (London, 1962), ch. 4.

[2] None of the classical sources (Tacitus, *Agricola*, lvi. 1–2, and *Annales*, xiv. 35; Dio Cassius, *Roman History*, lxii. 3–5) includes any statement about factions in their versions of Boudicca's speech. Field- ing's source would appear to be Bk. vi, ch. 7 of John Speed's *History of Great Britaine under the Conquests of the Romans*: 'Indeed overcome we are, but by our selves, our owne *factions* still giving way to *their* [Roman] *intrusions*. . . . Our *Dissensions* therefore have been their only rising, and our designes still weakened by home-bred *Conspirators*' (2nd ed. [London, 1627], p. 199). This attribution is strengthened by the fact that Speed appears to be the 'very sensible, tho' antient Writer' mentioned in the next sentence. See *n*. 4 below.

[3] A slip for Calcagus, *primus inter pares* of the tribal chieftains in the army which faced Agricola *ad montem Graupium* in AD 84. As given by Tacitus, *Agricola* xxxii, Calcagus' speech on that occasion began with a statement about factions: *nostris illi dissensionibus ac discordiis clari vitia hostium in gloriam exercitus sui vertunt* ('it is our dissensions and feuds that bring them fame: their enemy's mistake becomes their army's glory' [Loeb]).

[4] Cf. Speed, *History*, Bk. vii, ch. 1: 'The Britaines thus abandoned of all the *Roman Garrisons*, and emptied of *strengths* that should have supported her now *down-falling-estate*, lay prostrate to confusion and miserable calamities; no lesse burdened with the tumultuous uproares of her owne great men, who strove for the *supreme* Government, then of the Barbarous Nations' (ed. cit., p. 281). Baker, item no. 313, lists the 1650 edition among Fielding's books.

Imperfections perhaps innate in our Constitution,[1] and others too inveterate and established, to be eradicated; to these, wise and prudent Men will rather submit, than hazard shocking the Constitution itself by a rash Endeavour to remove them.

There are then some Occasions which not only justify, but require our having recourse to this dangerous Expedient. When the Disease attacks our Vitals, it must be expelled by the most immediate and efficacious Remedies. Nay, there may be some Evils attending the Politic as well as the Natural Body, which, tho' not in their Nature mortal, may however be so grievous and oppressive, and which would reduce us to so miserable and enervate a State, that it is worth our utmost Risque to relieve ourselves from them; but to sound this Alarm, when there is no real Danger, to misrepresent the best of Men as Enemies to the Public, and the most wholesome Schemes of Government as Snares for our Liberties, in order to animate the People to their Subversion; this is unwarrantable: This must proceed from the Motives I have above mentioned; from an Incendiary, not a Patriot.

Besides those and other general Symptoms, there is a particular one which deserves our Attention at this Time, and which will evidently distinguish the true from pretended Patriotism, at so critical a Juncture, when it is of the utmost Importance to us to know, with perfect Certainty, our Friends from our Foes.

As the preserving the present Royal Family on the Throne, is the only Way to preserve THE VERY BEING of this Nation, a true Patriot will use his most ardent Endeavours, even at the Hazard of his Life, to extinguish a Rebellion which so greatly threatens the Destruction of *Both*; nothing sure can prevail on such a Man to attempt, at this Season, to embarrass or distress the King and his Service, when the most perfect Unanimity is requisite to defeat the Designs of those powerful Enemies, who are allied with the utmost Unanimity against us.

It is with great Pleasure that I embrace the Opportunity which has been given me, at my first setting out as a Weekly Writer, of communicating to

---

[1] Here and in the next paragraph Fielding takes notice of the opposition tactic of claiming that there was a close connection between the success of the rebellion and the supposedly rotten state of the body politic at home. The price of having the opposition cooperate in defense measures was in effect a 'redress of grievances', constitutional reform, place bills, repeal of septennial parliaments, overhaul of the military and naval establishments. See, for example, the *Craftsman* of 5 and 12 October, 2 November, 1745; *Westminster Journal* of 9 November 1745; reprinted in *GM*, xv (1745), 545, 546–7, 586–7. Fielding's sensitivity to such issues may be owing in part to his having supported many of them when he was an opposition journalist during the last years of the Walpole administration. See 'General Introduction', above, p. civ.

the Public a Letter from a Lady upon a very interesting and important Subject, and one which, from the manly Sentiments it contains, I should rather have expected from one of my own Sex. Mr. *Addison*, in one of his Papers called the *Freeholder*, observes, (as I remember) *That the Women of our Island, who were the most eminent for Virtue and Good-sense, were in the Interest of the Government at the Time when he writ those Papers*, which was during the unnatural and unsuccessful Rebellion in the Year 1715.[1] And this early Specimen of Loyalty from one who, (if I am right in my Conjectures) is no less eminent for her Virtues than her Rank, will, I am persuaded, be looked upon as a Proof that the Women of this Age are no ways degenerated, but are disposed to exert their Endeavours to extinguish the present audacious Rebellion, no less than their Predecessors did in the Days of the *Freeholder*. But not to detain my Reader any longer from the Perusal of the Letter itself, it is as follows.

Sir,

Whether you are Lord *B——ke*, the B——p of *** or any other noble Person,[2] I neither know nor care: The Title of your Paper pleased me, and the Perusal of it proved that you are a Man of Sense, and consequently have Compassion. My Sex at this time particularly are Objects of it; many of them have their whole Fortunes in the Public Funds;[3] and I learn by their Conversation they have such dreadful Notions instilled into their tender, I do not say weak, Minds; that I apprehend many of them will let unreasonable Fears prevail so far as to injure themselves extremely. I am every Day amazed to hear Women, who upon all other Subjects speak rationally, talk of selling out of the Stocks, and drawing Money out of the Bank by way of securing it: When I have asked what they propose doing with a large Sum, one answered, she would dig a Hole and hide it; another, she would keep it in her Cabinet; with many other Schemes equally ridiculous. It is in vain that I have represented to them, that they run the Hazard of their own Lives as well as Fortunes, by such a Conduct; for I have used all the Arguments I am Mistress of, to convince them, that the Bank, South-Sea, and East-India Stock,[4] is the

[1] *Freeholder* no. 4 (2 January 1716) begins: 'It is with great Satisfaction I observe, that the Women of our Island, who are the most eminent for Virtue and good Sense, are in the Interest of the present Government.' Baker, item no. 22, lists the 1744 edition among Fielding's books.

[2] In the initial leader of the *TP* Fielding playfully (but pointedly) suggested that the author of the paper might be 'Lord *B——ke*' or 'the B——p of ****', that is, Bolingbroke and, probably, Benjamin Hoadly, Bishop of Winchester. See above, pp. 108–9, and *TP* no. 3 (19 November 1745), below, p. 129.

[3] The stock of the national debt, considered as a mode of investment (*OED*). See the next note, and the index to this volume, *s.v.* 'Funds, public' and 'Debt, National'.

[4] The three major joint-stock companies comprising the Funds, chartered by the crown and given monopoly privileges in their respective areas in return for loaning money to the government at

strongest Box they can put Money into; and that for my own Part I look upon selling to be so imprudent, that I think this a good time to purchase. Perhaps many other People may be of the same Mind. And from thence, as well as from the Pains that are taken by the Enemies of our Public Credit, may spring those Stories that are industriously insinuated to terrify the Females of this Nation;[1] of whose Taste I have so good an Opinion, that I imagine your Paper will be read by them with all due Attention; and possibly an Admonition upon that Point may have a better Effect than any thing that has been, or can be said, by your humble Servant,

An Old Gentlewoman.

In Compliance with the Request of my kind Correspondent, I shall here present the Reader with a few Reflections which occurred to me upon the Perusal of her Letter.

It is not to be wondered at, that the Proprietors of the Public Funds, and especially the Female Part of them, should be solicitous to provide for their own Security. But they would do well to consider, that there is no Passion so fatal to Individuals, as well as to the Community at large, as excessive and unseasonable Fear in Time of Danger. Too great Security may make us disregard or overlook impending Danger; but Despondency disarms us, and deprives us of the very Means of Safety. One may consider the Proprietors in the Funds at this time as a numerous Assembly of People, who have been suddenly alarmed with a Cry of Fire, and address himself to them in somewhat like the following Manner: "Gentlemen, it is true there is a Fire; but if you can bring yourselves to look calmly on your Danger, and unite your Endeavours heartily to encourage and support those whose Business it is to put out the Flames, there is no doubt but you will soon see the Fire happily extinguished, and long before it reaches you; but if, instead of uniting thus for the common Good, you should be all in a hurry to *get out*, you will not only run great Hazard of having your Pockets pick'd, but of being crushed to pieces in the Croud."

The Enemies of the present Government will no doubt be assiduous

perpetual, assured rates of interest and for assuming certain responsibilities in the management of the national debt. The public could buy shares in these companies and in doing so became in effect private owners of the public indebtedness, receiving in turn interest from their investment. See E. L. Hargreaves, *The National Debt* (London, 1930), ch. 1 and pp. 52–3.

[1] Cf. the letter from Sarah Butterfield to Lady Catherine Verney, 13 October 1745: 'I for my part am in no great frit [over the rebellion], what I am the most alarmd at is the Sheten oup of the Bank & great Disafeckshon to the King in generall'; *Verney Letters of the Eighteenth Century from the MSS at Claydon House*, ed. Margaret Maria Lady Verney, ii (London, 1930), 199.

in magnifying the Dangers which threaten us; since it is plain, that the reducing the Value of our National Securities would greatly help on their Designs. Nay, they may probably have a farther View in this than is at present apprehended; for should a Revolution in favour of a Popish Pretender ever take place in this Country, the giving an Opportunity to his needy Dependants to purchase the National Securities at low Prices might perhaps more effectually answer his Purposes, than could be done by wiping off the National Debt at once.[1]

I should not perform my Duty as a true Patriot, if I did not caution such of my Readers as have any Property in the Funds against selling out, at this time, for the following Reasons, among many others which my sensible Readers will be able to suggest to themselves on cool Reflection.

In the *first* Place, As selling out tends naturally to lower the Price of Stocks, the Man who does it, contributes, tho' perhaps inadvertently, to diminish the National Credit, and consequently to strengthen the Adversaries of his Country. It may be looked upon therefore as a Mark of Disloyalty.

Secondly, It is imprudent. To shew this, we need only make use of a familiar Instance: Suppose a Person possessed of a Mortgage should make it over to another, at a considerable Discount, only because some Body else had set up a pretended Title to the Estate, in prejudice of the right Owner;[2] would you say such a one acted like a prudent Man? But if this be the Case with regard to private Securities, it holds much stronger with respect to public ones; for as his Majesty's Title is at least as good as that which any Subject whatsoever has to his Estate, so his Power and Ability to support that Title, may, I think, fairly be allowed to be much greater than that of any Subject is, to maintain his own Property.

Thirdly, It would be highly dishonourable for us who are indebted to the present happy Establishment for all the Blessings we enjoy, to withhold our Assistance at this Time of Danger. But I need not expatiate on this Head; for, to the Honour of my Countrymen be it spoken, I believe there are very few amongst them who would not be willing to lay down their Lives and Fortunes in its Defence. And as for the other Sex, for whose Use these Reflections are principally intended, tho' they are not

---

[1] For the traditional charge that in the event of their restoration the Stuarts intended to disavow or 'wipe out' the national debt as having been contracted under an illegal government, see *Proper Answer* (1747), p. 80 and *n.*; *JJ* no. 20 (16 April 1748), p. 244, and no. 21 (23 April 1748), p. 249; and the index to the present volume, *s.v.* 'Sponge'.

[2] The analogy is to the case of a shareholder who, during the reign of the Hanoverian king ('the right Owner'), sells out disadvantageously in expectation of a Stuart pretender. For evidence that Fielding himself sold out his stocks at this time, see *TP* no. 11 (14 January 1746), below, p. 187 *n.* 1.

intitled to the Glory of fighting for their Country, nor can decently enter into Associations for the Support of the Government;[1] yet those of them whose Fortunes are in the Funds, may be intitled to some Share of Merit, by contributing all that lies in their Power to keep up the Credit of those Funds which were originally raised for its Support.

Fourthly, It is impossible to make your Money more secure than it is: If this Rebellion should be successless, your Property is not only safe, but will be more valuable than at present; if on the contrary, the Rebellion should have an Issue[2] which there is now (God be praised) no great reason to apprehend, your Money will be as insecure in your own Chests as in those of the Public.

Lastly, There is, I hope, not one among my fair Countrywomen, who, from the mean Consideration of a present Interest, would be contented to entail Poverty and Slavery upon her Posterity! For nothing else can reasonably be expected from a Government, compounded of *Highland* Rapine, *Italian* Bigotry, and *French* Tyranny.

OBSERVATIONS *on the* REBELLION, *continued.*

A *second* Instance of mistaken Zeal on this Occasion, is by expressing a violent Animosity against all the Roman Catholics in general. It is indeed impossible either to speak or write with too much Invective against this Religion at any Season, and the Remissness of many under whose Province it more immediately fell to animate Men against it, and to obviate the indefatigable Labours of Romish Priests, hath been highly blameable; yet we are to preserve the Temper of Protestants, while we are preaching against Popery; we must not imbibe her Spirit out of Abhorrence to her Doctrine.[3]

The Principles of this Religion, it is true, are to propagate her Doctrines, and to extirpate Heresy by all Methods whatever. These are the Means by which Pardon for all Sins is to be obtained, and the Omission of these is itself the greatest of Sins. This the Priests universally teach, and the Bigots will on all Opportunities practice. A sufficient Argument for opposing this Religion, and the Establishment of it under a Prince

---

[1] For the nature and political role of the military associations, see *Serious Address*, above, p. 31, and 'General Introduction', above, p. xliii.

[2] i.e., should come to a conclusion, in this case a negative or unfavorable one.

[3] The colophon of *TP* no. 3 (19 November 1745), Locke, p. [56], calls attention to this essay, entitling it 'An Apology for Roman Catholics'. Fielding himself refers to his tolerance in this matter, in his final leader: 'I did my utmost to dissuade the well-meaning but rash Part of my Countrymen from general and violent Attacks on whole Bodies of Men, even on the *Roman Catholicks* themselves.' See below, p. 307.

who is a known Bigot, with the utmost Force and most animated Resolution.

But some Members of this Church are, I hope, (in common with the Members of others) less bigotted. There are some surely so good, that their Religion cannot absolutely divest them of their social Passions, and others too wise to sacrifice their selfish Passions to such monstrous Tenets.

In the *first* Place, I am convinced many Roman Catholics in this Kingdom (I hope much the greater Part) could not be induced by any Persuasions of their Priests to assist in a Massacre,[1] nor would wish to see a Popish Prince introduced by any such Means; nay, I am assured there are many whose Zeal for their Religion will not animate them to attempt its Establishment by the Sacrifice of their Lives and Fortunes.

Secondly, I make no doubt but there are some, and that no inconsiderable Number, who, tho' educated in the Romish Faith, which perhaps rather Principles of Honour than of Religion inspire them to maintain, do not even wish well to a Cause, the Success of which must inevitably destroy their Civil Liberties. The Possession of Abbey Lands, and of Estates in the Funds,[2] are strong Arguments to others against contributing to, or desiring a Revolution.

Lastly, There is no Man of Sense, Property, Honour and Humanity, who can possibly hope to see his Religion introduced by a Banditti of Robbers and Cut-throats, who would certainly make his Country a Scene of Blood and Desolation.

I would not, however, be here understood to endeavour at slackening the Vigilance of the Government over ALL Persons of this Persuasion. The Tenets of this Religion are such that must render every Man who embraces them suspected; nor can too much Care be applied at this dangerous Season, in watching, disarming, and every way preventing them from lending Assistance to the Rebellion which threatens our total Ruin.

My Design is no other than to restrain violent Men from executing or denouncing Vengeance against the whole Body of Roman Catholics, while they remain in Peace and Submission to the Government. They

[1] Anti-jacobite propaganda reiterated the likelihood that a restoration of the Stuarts could only be effected by religious massacres resembling those of the 17th century. See *TP* no. 10 (7 January 1746), below, p. 172, and the index, *s.v.* 'Massacres'.

[2] Referring to the ecclesiastical lands appropriated to lay persons during the reign of Henry VIII, some of them presumably now owned by catholics, and to the public stock in the national debt, some of it presumably held by catholics in spite of anti-jacobite assertions that a Stuart restoration would 'wipe off' such claims on the government as having been contracted under a usurpation. See *TP* no. 4 (26 November 1745), below, p. 137, and *n.* 1; also the index, *s.v.* 'Abbey Lands' and 'Funds, public'.

have hitherto done so, and I hope will continue in this State; and while they do, I am satisfied they may always depend on a Continuance of the Indulgence they have so long enjoyed. But, on the contrary, should any considerable Number of these People lay hold on this Time of Danger, to disturb the Public, I should be no longer an Advocate for any Moderation towards them. Self-preservation would then justify the Protestants in exerting the Power which God hath placed in their Hand; and the uniting the Innocent with the Guilty in one common Vengeance, might be perhaps a hard, but would then become an unavoidable Necessity.

The *Third* Fault which I shall mention, and which is likewise the Effect of a warm and sanguine Temper, is treating the Force of our Enemies with Contempt. In a Case of this Kind, there can be no more room for extreme Confidence than Despair. OUR ALL is at Stake, and we should tremble for the Event, tho' we have never so great Odds on our Side: But in reality our Enemies are by no means the Object of Contempt. A Banditti of many Thousands (perhaps many more than they are represented or imagined) most of them well armed, bold, active, nimble, hardy, inured to Cold and Hunger. These are headed by a rash and desperate young Man, who is advised by many experienced Officers as well Foreigners as Natives: His Cause backed and supported by the United Crowns of *France* and *Spain*, who have already sent him Money, Arms, and Officers, and are now, we are told, actually watching an Opportunity to throw an Army into these Kingdoms. These surely seem no contemptible Object, especially when we consider for what we are to encounter them; such indeed is the Stake to be decided, that it is terrible to have a Chance against us.

Let us however still keep in our Remembrance, that the Odds are greatly on our Side; so greatly, that nothing but Contempt, Neglect, the most absurd Folly, or most abject Pusillanimity, can destroy us. *First,* In Numbers; for were the Number of our Enemies ten times as great as it possibly can be, it is still our own Fault if we are not ten to one against them. And 2*dly*, In the Spirit of our Cause; for tho' Necessity and Lust may animate these Ruffians with equal Violence to assail our Properties, our Wives and Daughters, as it can us to defend them; yet upon the whole, their Gain will not be equal to our Loss, and whatever Weight the Regard to Religion and Liberty can add, must be thrown into our Scale of Courage on this Occasion.

Upon the whole then, we are to be at once desperate and cautious. On the former Head I have nothing, nor I hope ever shall have to object; but can we as well be defended on the latter? What additional Strength have all our Associations produced in the Space of two Months?[1] Have we any Body of Men *yet raised* on whom we can place the least Dependence (our Army from *Flanders* only excepted)? Is this Army yet entirely brought over? Is it increased to its real Establishment? Can we not throw a Body of foreign Troops into the North of *Scotland*? Would not that Step bid the fairest to put a final End to this Rebellion? Are these, or any of these Measures expedient? Are they in our Power? Why are they not executed?

These Queries will be expatiated on in our next; but we hope the Hint will be immediately taken by those to whom it is chiefly intended.

TUESDAY, NOVEMBER 19, 1745.   NUMB. 3.

—— *Furit ensis et ignis*
Quique caret Flammâ scelerum est locus.

SILIUS ITALICUS.[2]

The Rebellion having long been the universal Subject of Conversation, in this Town, it is no Wonder that what so absolutely engages our waking Thoughts should attend us to the Pillow, and represent to us in Dreams or Visions those Ideas which Fear had before suggested to our Minds.[3]

It is natural, on all occasions, to have some little Attention to our private Welfare, nor do I ever honour the Patriot the less (I am sure I confide in him much the more) whose own Good is involved in that of the Public. I am not, therefore, ashamed to give the Public the following

---

[1] Somewhat equivocal answers to this and the following questions are provided in 'Observations on the Rebellion, *continued*', *TP* no. 3 (19 November 1745), below, pp. 351–2. The answers are contained in a letter, which is introduced editorially as 'from a Person of very high Eminence' and may not be Fielding's work. About this time the London papers were calling attention to the fact that the supposedly liberal subscriptions and associations had not in fact produced troops ready to serve; see, for example, *General Advertiser* of 13 November 1745.

[2] *Punica*, ii. 657–8: 'fire and sword run riot, | and any spot that is not burning is a scene of crime' (Loeb). The lines form part of what Fielding, later in this leader, calls the 'fine Picture drawn by *Silius Italicus*, in his second Book, where he describes the sacking of the brave City of *Saguntum* by a less savage Army'. The Carthaginians under Hannibal sacked and took Saguntum in 219 BC, thereby opening up the second Punic war.

[3] French, p. 213, compares *The Opposition: A Vision* (1742), p. [1]: 'Whatever makes a strong Impression on our waking Minds, either from it's Novelty, or any other Cause, is generally the Subject of our Dreams.' See also *Amelia*, IX. vi. 379; and *CGJ* no. 65 (7 October 1752), ii. 108–9, which attributes the general notion to Cicero, presumably *De Divinatione*, lxiii, or 'Somnium Scipionis', i. 4. For Fielding on the dream-vision tradition among English periodical writers, see *Champion* of 13 December 1739, i. 87–93.

Dream or Vision, tho' my own little Affairs, and the private Consequences, which the Success of this Rebellion would produce to myself,
form the principal Object: For, I believe, at the same time, there are few of
my Readers who will not find themselves interested in some Parts of it.

Methought, I was sitting in my Study,[1] meditating for the Good and
Entertainment of the Public, with my two little Children (as is my usual
Course to suffer them) playing near me; when I heard a very hard Knock
at my Door, and immediatgely afterwards several ill-looked Rascals
burst in upon me, one of whom seized me with great Violence, saying I
was his Prisoner, and must go with him. I asked him for what Offence.
Have you the Impudence to ask that, said he, when the Words *True
Patriot* lie now before you? I then bid him shew me his Warrant. He
answered, *there it is*, pointing to several Men, who were in Highland
Dresses, with broad Swords by their Sides. My Children then ran
towards me, and bursting into Tears, exprest their Concern for their
poor Papa. Upon which one of the Ruffians seized my little Boy,[2] and
pulling him from me, dashed him against the Ground; and all immediately hurried me away out of my Room and House, before I could be
sensible of the Effects of this Barbarity.

My Concern for my poor Children, from whom I had been torn in the
above Manner, prevented me from taking much notice of any Objects in
the Streets, through which I was dragg'd, with many Insults. Houses
burnt down, dead Bodies of Men, Women and Children, strewed every
where as we passed, and great Numbers of Highlanders, and Popish
Priests in their several Habits, made, however, too forcible an Impression on me to be unobserved.

My Guard now brought me to *Newgate*,[3] where they were informed
that Goal was too full to admit a single Person more. I was then conducted to a large Booth in *Smithfield*,[4] as I thought, where I was shut in

[1] Although the conventions of the dream-vision in no way require it, scholars persist in relating
details like this to the known facts of Fielding's biography. In 1745 Fielding was renting one of the
most expensive houses in Boswell Court, a favorite residential quarter for lawyers, located between
Carey Street and Butcher Row, on part of the site now occupied by the Royal Courts of Justice. See
J. Paul de Castro, 'Fielding at Boswell Court', *N&Q*, 12th series, i (1 April 1916), 264–5.

[2] Austin Dobson, *Fielding* (London, 1883), p. 110, cites this as evidence that in addition to the surviving daughter Harriet (1733–66) Fielding also had a son by his first wife, Charlotte (d. November
1744). T. C. Duncan Eaves and B. D. Kimpel, 'Henry Fielding's Son by His First Wife', *N&Q*, NS XV
(June 1968), 212, describe the 1750 burial record of a Henry Fielding, aged eight, 'from Cov.ᵗ Garding'.
In 1750 Fielding occupied a house in Bow Street, parish of St Paul's, Covent Garden, and was the
only person of that name listed in the rate books.

[3] The famous prison; see *TP* no. 10 (7 January 1746), below, p. 173.

[4] Site of the large cattle market northeast of the city, in Farrington Ward Without. During the
Forty-Five people often remembered its historical notoriety as the place of religious executions; see
TP no. 10 (7 January 1746), below, p. 176, and *General Evening Post* of 3–5 October 1745, where a letter
signed 'Montanus' refers to 'the Burnings in Smithfield, especially under *Queen Mary*'. The 'large

with a great Number of Prisoners, amongst whom were many of the most considerable Persons in this Kingdom. Two of these were in a very particular Manner reviled by the Highland Guards, (for all the Soldiers were in that Dress) and these two I presently recollected to be the A–chb–sh–p of *Y—k*,[1] and the B——p of *Win——r*.[2]

As there is great Inconsistency of Time and Place, in most Dreams, I now found myself, by an unaccountable Transition, in a Court which bore some Resemblance to the Court of King's Bench, only a great Cross was erected in the middle; and instead of those Officers of Justice who usually attend that Court, a Number of Highlanders, with drawn Swords, stood there as Centinels; the Judges too were Persons

Booth' here would appear to be one of the pens used to collect and shelter cattle, prominent features of the west side of the market place. Fielding may have been influenced in his choice of the term 'Booth' by the fact that each summer during Bartholomew Fair in Smithfield leading players from the London theatres set up booths there and put on continuous performances from early afternoon until late at night.

[1] Thomas Herring (1693–1757), bishop of Bangor 1732, archbishop of York 1743, Canterbury 1747. On 24 September 1745 Herring presided over a meeting of the gentry and nobility of the county of York, called for the purpose of raising a force to oppose the rebels; *DA* of 16 September 1745 prints the call. The archbishop's speech on that occasion had, in Walpole's words, 'as much true spirit, honesty and bravery in it: as ever was penned by an historian for an ancient hero'; to Mann, 4 October 1745, *Yale Walpole*, xix. 126. Far away in Florence Horace Mann read Herring's speech and wrote that it 'must procure him the love, esteem, and applause of all honest people'; to Walpole, 10 November 1745 NS, *Yale Walpole*, xix. 148. The Yorkshire association initiated at the meeting subscribed £40,000 towards maintaining the troops raised to fight the rebels; *GM*, xv (1745), 499. Herring was also rumored to have appeared in regimentals at the head of his clergy, which made him an even more convenient symbol of the church militant in the popular prints of the day. See Stephens, BM Catalogue, iii, items nos. 2634, 2635, 2658, 2675; and Coxe, *Memoirs of Horatio, Lord Walpole* (London, 1802), ch. 39, p. 437 *n*. Herring's speech, which was widely reprinted (e.g. in *DA* of 30 September 1745; *GM*, xv [1745], 471–2), emphasized that the jacobite rebellion was part of a larger plan by France and Spain to establish popery in England. For evidence that Herring's somewhat uncharacteristic militancy may have owed a good deal to Lord Hardwicke's promptings, see R. Garnett, 'Correspondence of Archbishop Herring and Lord Hardwicke during the Rebellion of 1745', *EHR*, xix (1904), 528–50, 719–42.

[2] Benjamin Hoadly (1676–1761), bishop of Bangor 1715, Hereford 1721, Salisbury 1723, Winchester 1734. An extreme latitudinarian and eminent controversialist, Hoadly was the leader of the low-church divines who maintained 'whig' or revolutionary principles against the high-church proponents of hereditary right and passive obedience. The compliment here is nostalgic and probably personal. Fielding may have known Hoadly and his two sons Benjamin and John from his own early days in Salisbury; see Cross, i. 112. The bishop's most active period came during the reigns of Anne and George I, notably in the so-called Bangorian controversy of 1717 and after, and by 1745 he was no longer in the limelight. However, Fielding praises him in 'Of True Greatness' (1741), v. 256, where he is said to 'blaze' among the divines; in *Joseph Andrews*, i. xvii. 83, where his *Plain Account of the Nature and End of the Sacrament of the Lord's Supper* (1735) is called 'a Book written . . . with the Pen of an Angel'; in *Tom Jones*, ii. vii. 105, which alludes to his 'great Reputation in the Science' of divinity. In the present context Fielding may have had in mind Hoadly's much-reprinted anti-jacobite sermon *The Happiness of the Present Establishment, and the Unhappiness of Absolute Monarchy* (1708), which has been suggested as the basis for the remarks on limited and absolute governments in *Tom Jones*, xx. xii. 671–2, and *n*. Hoadly appears to be the bishop praised in *TP* no. 1 (5 November 1745), above, p. 109, for his 'Zeal for the Protestant Religion'.

whose Faces I had never seen before.[1] I was obliged, I thought, to stand some time at the Bar, before my Trial came on, the Court being busied in a Cause where an Abbot was Plaintiff, in determining the Boundaries of some Abbey Land,[2] which they decided for the Plaintiff, the Chief Justice declaring, it was his Majesty's Pleasure, in all doubtful Cases, that Judgment should be in favour of the Church.

A Charge of High-Treason was then, I dream'd, exhibited against me, for having writ in Defence of his Present Majesty King GEORGE, and my Paper of the *True Patriot* was produced in Evidence against me.

Being called upon to make my Defence, I insisted entirely on the Statute of *Hen*. 7. by which all Persons are exempted from incurring the Penalties of Treason, in Defence of the King *de Facto*.[3] But the Chief Justice told me in broken *English*, that if I had no other Plea, they should presently over-rule that; for that his Majesty was resolved to make an Example of all who had any ways distinguished themselves, in Opposition to his Cause.

Methought I then reply'd, with a Resolution which I hope every *Englishman* would exert on such an Occasion, THAT THE LIFE OF NO MAN WAS WORTH PRESERVING LONGER THAN IT WAS TO BE DEFENDED BY THE KNOWN LAWS OF HIS COUNTRY; and that if the King's arbitrary Pleasure was to be that Law, I was indifferent what he determined concerning myself.

The Court having plut it to the Vote, (for no Jury, I thought, attended)[4] and unanimously agreed that I was guilty, proceeded to pass the Sentence usual in Cases of High-Treason, having first made many Elogiums on the Pope, the *Roman* Catholic Religion, and the King who was to support both, and be supported by them.

I was then delivered into the Hands of the Executioner, who stood ready, and was ordered to allow me only three Hours to confess myself and be reconciled to the Church of *Rome*. Upon which a Priest, whose Face I remember to have seen at a Place called an Oratory,[5] and who

---

[1] Cf. the 'imaginary Journal of Events', *TP* no. 10 (7 January 1746), below, p. 172: 'The twelve Judges removed, and twelve new ones appointed, some of whom had scarce ever been in *Westminster-Hall* before.' Implicit in the present vision is Fielding's familiarity with the eminent members of his profession.

[2] For the significance of this litigation, see *TP* no. 4 (26 November 1745), below, p. 137, and no. 10 (7 January 1746), below, p. 175.

[3] The statute 1495, 11 Henry VII, c. 1 (said by some writers to be only declaratory of the common law), was passed for the protection of all subjects who assisted and obeyed a king *de facto* (Jowitt, *Dictionary*). See *Statutes at Large*, iv. 55, and *Serious Address*, above, p. 30.

[4] In *A Charge to the Grand Jury* (1749) Fielding asserts that 'The Institution of Juries, Gentlemen, is a Privilege which distinguishes the Liberty of *Englishmen* from those of all other Nations' (p. 8).

[5] The identification of John ('Orator') Henley is secured by the further reference, in *TP* no. 10 (7 January 1746), below, p. 174, to 'Mr. *Mac-henly* the Ordinary'. Henley, the 'large black Ghost, who appeared in a horrible Shape on Sunday Evening last, at Half an Hour past six, near Clare-Market'

was, for his good Services, preferred to be the Ordinary of *Newgate*,[1] immediately advanced, and began to revile me, saying, I was the wickedest Heretic in the Kingdom, and had exerted myself with more Impudence against his Majesty and his Holiness than any other Person whatsoever: But he added, as I had the good Fortune to make some Atonement for my Impiety by being hanged, if I would embrace his Religion, confess myself and receive Absolution, I might possibly, after some Expiation in Purgatory, receive a final Pardon.

I was hence conducted into a Dungeon, where, by a glimmering Light, I saw many Wretches my Fellow-Prisoners, who for various Crimes were condemn'd to various Punishments.

Among these appeared one in a very ragged Plight, whom I very well knew, and who, the last time I saw him, appeared to live in great Affluence and Splendor. Upon my enquiring the Reason of his being detained in that Region of Horror, he very frankly told me it was for stealing a Loaf. He acknowledged the Fact; but said, he had been obliged to it for the Relief of his indigent Family. I see, continued he, your Surprize at this Change of my Fortune; but, you must know, my whole Estate was in the Funds, by the wiping out of which I was at once reduced to the Condition in which you now see me.[2] I rose in the Morning with 40000 *l.* I had a Wife whom I tenderly loved, and three blooming Daughters. The Eldest was within a Week of her Marriage, and I was to have paid down 10000 *l.* with her. At Noon I found a Royal Decree had reduced me to downright Beggary. My Daughter hath lost her Marriage, and is gone distracted. My Wife is dead of a broken Heart, and my poor Girls have neither Cloaths to cover them, nor Meat to feed them; so that I may truly say,

—— *Miser, O miser, omnia ademit*
Una dies infesta mihi tot præmia vitæ.[3]

Here, methought, he stopt, and a Flood of Tears gushed from his Eyes. I should perhaps have been a greater Sharer in his Sorrow, had not

('Apocrypha', *TP* no. 1 [5 November 1745], below, p. 338), advertised his place of preaching as 'The Oratory–British Chapel', which Fielding parodies as 'the Oratory-British-Spanish-Popist-Nonsense Chapel' in the 'Apocrypha' of nos. 2 and 3, below, pp. 345, 350. For Henley and Fielding, see 'General Introduction', above, pp. lvii–lix, and *Dialogue*, above, p. 98.

[1] The chaplain of that prison, whose duty it was to prepare condemned prisoners for death (*OED*). See *TP* no. 10 (7 January 1746), below, p. 174.

[2] On the wiping out or disavowing of the public debt represented by the Funds, see *Serious Address*, above, p. 30, where it is said to be one of the consequences of a jacobite takeover; see also index, *s.v.* 'Debt, National'.

[3] Adapted from Lucretius, *De Rerum Natura*, iii. 898–9: 'O wretched, wretched man, one fatal day has robbed me of so many of life's blessings.' The accepted text reads: '*misero misere,' aiunt, 'omnia ademit una dies infesta tibi tot praemia vitae.*'

the Consideration of his Childrens Ruin represented to me the Situation of my own. Good Gods! What were the Agonies I then felt, tho' in a Dream? Racks, Wheels, Gibbets, were no longer the Objects of Terror. My Children possessed my whole Mind, and my fearful Imagination run thro' every Scene of Horror which Villains can act on their Fellow-Creatures. Sometimes I saw their helpless Hands struggling for a moment with a barbarous Cut-throat. Here I saw my poor Boy, my whole Ambition, the Hopes and Prospect of my Age, sprawling on the Floor, and weltering in his Blood; there my Fancy painted my Daughter, the Object of all my Tenderness, prostituted even in her Infancy to the brutal Lust of a Ruffian, and then sacrificed to his Cruelty. Such were my Terrors, when I was relieved from them by the welcome Presence of the Executioner, who summoned me immediately forth, telling me since I had refused the Assistance of the Priest, he could grant me no longer Indulgence.

The first Sight which occurred[1] to me as I past through the Streets, (for common Objects totally escape the Observation of a Man in my present Temper of Mind) was a young Lady of Quality, and the greatest Beauty of this Age, in the Hands of two *Highlanders*, who were struggling with each other for their Booty. The lovely Prize, tho' her Hair was dishevelled and torn, her Eyes swollen with Tears, her Face all pale, and some Marks of Blood both on that and her Breast, which was all naked and exposed, retained still sufficient Charms to discover herself to me,[2] who have always beheld her with Wonder and Admiration. Indeed it may be questioned whether perfect Beauty loses or acquires Charms by Distress. This Sight was Matter of Entertainment to my Conductors, who, however, hurried me presently from it, as I wish they had also from her Screams, which reached my Ears to a great Distance.

After such a Spectacle as this, the dead Bodies which lay every where in the Streets (for there had been, I was told, a Massacre the Night before)[3] scarce made any Impression; nay, the very Fires in which Protestants were roasting, were, in my Sense, Objects of much less Horror; nay, such an Effect had this Sight wrought on my Mind, which hath been always full of the utmost Tenderness for that charming Sex, that for a moment it obliterated all Concern for my Children, from

---

[1] i.e., presented itself, appeared (*OED*).

[2] The 'young Lady of Quality' has not been identified, although the concluding clause implies that Fielding intended to compliment a particular person.

[3] Drawing on various 17th-century massacres of protestants, anti-jacobite writers during the Forty-Five often stressed the likelihood that such events would happen again if the rebellion was crowned with success. See *TP* no. 10 (7 January 1746), below, p. 172, and no. 12 (21 January 1746), below, p. 195; also *Dialogue*, above, p. 89.

whom I was to be hurried for ever without a Farewel, or without knowing in what Condition I left them; or indeed whether they had hitherto survived the Cruelty which now methought raged every where, with all the Fury which Rage, Zeal, Lust, and wanton Fierceness could inspire into the bloody Hearts of Popish Priests, Bigots and Barbarians. Of such a Scene my learned Reader may see a fine Picture drawn by *Silius Italicus*, in his second Book, where he describes the sacking the brave City of *Saguntum* by a less savage Army.[1]

I then overheard a Priest admonish the Executioner to exert the utmost Rigour of my Sentence towards me; after which the same Priest advancing forwards, and putting on a Look of Compassion, advised me, for the Sake of my Soul, to embrace the holy Communion. I gave him no Answer, and he turned his Back, thundering forth Curses against me.

At length I arrived at the fatal Place which promised me a speedy End to all my Sufferings. Here, methought, I saw a Man who by his Countenance and Actions exprest the highest Degree of Despair. He stamped with his Feet, beat his Face, tore his Hair, and uttered the most horrid Execrations. Upon enquiring into the Circumstances of this Person, I was informed by one of the Bystanders, that he was a Nonjuror,[2] who had lent considerable Assistance to the Pretender's Cause, out of Principle;[3] and was now lamenting the Consequences which the Success of it had brought on such honest Gentlemen as myself. My Informer added, with a Smile, The wise Man expected his Majesty would keep his Word with Heretics.[4]

The Executioner then attempted to put the Rope round my Neck, when my little Girl enter'd my Bed-chamber, and put an end to my

[1] See the motto of this leader, and the note thereon. Baker, item no. 262, lists Drakenborchius' edition of 1717 among Fielding's books.

[2] French, p. 223, suggests the identification of Thomas Deacon (1697–1753), nonjuring bishop (1733) and since 1744 the nominal leader of the nonjuring clergy in England. Deacon had a jacobite affiliation going back to the Fifteen and was about to become visibly active in the Forty-Five. But the identification seems unlikely. Deacon, whose Manchester communion went by the title of the 'True British Catholic Church', had been resident in that city since *c.* 1720, and his notoriety with respect to the Forty-Five does not appear to have been noticed in London until after the YP entered Manchester at the end of November (when Deacon's three sons enlisted in the YP's service); Henry Broxap, *A Biography of Thomas Deacon, the Manchester Non-Juror* (Manchester, 1911), pp. 99, 146, *et passim*; Walpole to Mann, 9 December 1745, *Yale Walpole*, xix. 179 and *n.* More likely Fielding's reference is to the nonjurors in general, between whom and the Stuarts negotiations were 'certainly conducted' before and during the rebellion, in part through the mediation of the jacobite historian Thomas Carte; Broxap, *The Later Non-Jurors* (Cambridge, 1924), pp. 217–21, 226–8, 276. For charges of jacobitism made against Deacon during and after the Forty-Five, see *Manchester Vindicated* (Chester, 1749); for Fielding and Carte, see *The Jacobite's Journal and Related Writings* (Oxford, 1974), index, *s.v.* 'Carte'.

[3] For a satirical version of the nonjurors' principles, see *TP* no. 24 (8–15 April 1746), below, p. 263.

[4] Alluding to the supposititious catholic tenet that faith was not to be kept with heretics; see index, *s.v.* 'Heretics'.

Dream, by pulling open my Eyes, and telling me, that the Taylor had brought home my Cloaths for his Majesty's Birth-day.[1]

The Sight of my dear Child, added to the Name of that gracious Prince, at once deprived me of every private and public Fear; and the Joy which now began to arise, being soon after heightned by Consideration of the Day, the Sound of Bells, and the Hurry which prevailed every where from the Eagerness of all Sorts of People to demonstrate their Loyalty at this Season, gave me altogether as delightful a Sensation as perhaps the Heart of Man is capable of feeling;[2] of which I have the Pleasure to know every Reader must partake, who hath had Good-Nature enough to sympathize with me in the foregoing Part of this Vision.

To CHARLES STUART, *Esq*;

Sir,

I received the Favour of yours by the Hands of the common Hangman,[3] a Gentleman who, if not known to yourself, will, I am convinced, be soon personally acquainted with most of your Friends.

I did at first intend to have sent you a very long and particular Answer to this Performance; but am prevented by the *Occasional Writer*,[4] who with great Spirit and Force of Reasoning hath taken your Manifesto, as you call it, to pieces, and given a very masterly Answer to every Part of it which he hath though worth considering.

[1] 'The Present History of Great Britain', *TP* no. 1 (5 November 1745) begins 'the Home Part of our History' with a description of the celebrations at court of George II's birthday on 30 October 1745: 'Nor was the Splendour of the Court less remarkable than the Number. Among the Ladies who filled a very large Room, there was scarce one dress'd in plain Silk'; below, p. 334.

[2] *TP* no. 4 (26 November 1745), below, p. 357, prints a letter signed 'Your Friend' and dated from White's, suggesting that among the reasons for the delightful sensation here described was the tailor's having brought the 'Patriot' a new suit.

[3] On 6 November 1745 the Lords resolved to condemn two manifestoes signed by the OP (dated 23 December 1743 NS) and four by the YP (16 May, 22 August, 9 and 10 October 1745). On 7 November the Commons was asked to concur and did. The resolution proposed that the manifestoes be 'burnt by the common Hangman, at the Royal Exchange, in *London*, on *Tuesday* the Twelfth Day of this instant *November*, at One of the Clock in the Afternoon'; *Journals of Commons*, xxv. 16. *GM*, xv (1745), 611, reported the burning. Walpole wrote Mann (15 November) that he concluded the ministry 'knew the danger was all over; for the Duke of Newcastle ventured to have the Pretender's declaration burnt at the Royal Exchange'; *Yale Walpole*, xix. 161.

[4] *The Occasional Writer: Containing an Answer to the Second Manifesto of the Pretender's Eldest Son: Which Bears Date at the Palace of Holy-Rood-House, the 10th Day of October, 1745*. A Cooper imprint, it is advertised as published (*DA* of 12 November 1745) at one shilling. The text is signed 'Britannicus' and dated, presumably for rhetorical effect, 5 November. For some reason it was of considerable interest to somebody associated with the *TP*. In addition to the reference here, it is advertised in this issue and referred to in no. 6 (10 December 1745), below, p. 148, and no. 7 (17 December 1745), the latter in a letter signed 'A.Z.' and probably not by Fielding; see Locke, p. [84]. An unsigned letter in *DA* of 18 December 1745 takes note of the *TP*'s 'peculiar and publick Recommendation' of the pamphlet and says the 'learned and very ingenious Gentleman' who is the 'Author' of a new weekly paper 'acted with perfect Impartiality in giving his Judgment of this Pamphlet, being utterly ignorant of the Name of the Author'. In the 'Advertisement by the Publisher' of the 'second edition' (1746) the *TP* notices are remarked and credited with creating the popularity which led to the 'second Impression'.

However, as you address yourself to us all, I shall be pardoned for taking this Opportunity of giving you my Sentiments on the Justice of your Cause, and of your Proceedings in it.

In the first Place, Sir, I am very sorry to see you, as well in your Father's Name as your own, disclaiming all Pretensions to absolute Power. Those who know any thing of your Father, and of your own Behaviour in *Scotland*, will, I am afraid, give little Credit to this Declaration.

But in Reality, is not this giving up your whole Title? Your Grandfather you know, nay you own, exercised arbitrary Power. Did he not therefore forfeit his Crown? To say a King hath no Right to be arbitrary, and yet may be so with Impunity, is idle and absurd; if not with Impunity, how can he be punished; or what other Redress have the People besides by removing him from the Throne, when he hath broken those Conditions on which he ascended it?

This was the Sense of our Ancestors at the Revolution. This is the Sense of all who have ever been Advocates for the Liberty of the People; and this must be your Sense too, if you are in Reality what you profess yourself to be, an Enemy to arbitrary Power.

For the further Explanation of this Doctrine, and the Consequences to be drawn from it, I refer you to that excellent Pamphlet abovementioned. The only Conclusion I shall here insist on is, that if this Doctrine be true, neither you nor your Father have any Right at all to the Crown of these Realms; but you are the Invader of the Right of another, and consequently the Blood of every Man which is spilt in this Cause lies at your Door!

And are you not guilty of further Prevarication, when you endeavour to insinuate your Reliance on the Subjects of this Realm? Had you not previously stipulated for an Assistance from *Spain*? Did you not set out from *France*, assisted with Money, Arms, and Men, from that Crown? With all which you had landed, had not the Chance of War, and the Bravery of our Seamen, by disabling the *Elizabeth*, prevented it.[1]

But in Reality, Sir, where did you land? And what were the Subjects on whom you relied, and now do rely? Did you not land in a Part of the Island inhabited by Wildmen and Savages? Have you not with an Army of these Barbarians, who are scarce subjected to any Prince, or to any Laws, invaded the civilized Part of this Kingdom? Have you in that civilized Part found any Number of Abettors considerable enough to give you any Hopes, or even worth your mentioning? How unfairly then do you pretend to represent your Cause as favoured by this Nation, when you know, was it to be decided by Election, you would

---

[1] For the circumstances of the YP's arrival in Scotland, see *History*, above, pp. [35]–9.

not have one Vote in a thousand from those who have any Vote for the Legislature?

As your Family have therefore no Pretence from Right, and as little from the Good-will of the People, to this Crown, let us now see how you have recommended your Cause to their Favour, in the Manner of your Enterprize, *First*, By taking advantage of our Distress in the midst of a dangerous and expensive War, and at the End of an unsuccessful Campaign. *Secondly*, By attacking us under the Protection and with the Assistance of those very Crowns with whom we are engaged in this War; a War not undertaken to satisfy the Wantonness, the Revenge, or the Ambition of a Court; but to support our Interest and Trade, and at the universal Desire of the People.

In what Light can you imagine you must appear to us in such an Undertaking? Or in what Light must we conceive you are seen by our Enemies, who, while their Fleets and Privateers are endeavouring to ruin our Trade, have generously thrown their Ports open to your Ships, if you have any. *I am, Sir*, &c.

The TRUE PATRIOT.

TUESDAY, NOVEMBER 26, 1745.   NUMB. 4.

> Ambubaiarum Collegia, Pharmacopolæ,
> *Mendici, Mimi, Balatrones; hoc Genus omne*
> *Mœstum et solicitum est.——*
>
> HORACE.[1]

The Author of the *Serious Address to the People of* Great-Britain, (a Pamphlet which ought to be in every Man's Hands at this Season)[2] hath incontestably shewn the Danger of this Rebellion to all who have any Regard for the Protestant Religion, or the Laws and Liberties of their Country.

We have further endeavoured in our last Paper, to give a lively Picture of the utter Misery and Desolation it would introduce, and the Insecurity of our Estates, Properties, Lives and Families under the Government

---

[1] *Satires*, i. ii. 1–3: 'The flute-girls' guilds, the drug-quacks, beggars, actresses, buffoons, and all that breed are in grief and mourning' (Loeb). The first two words by themselves form the motto of *JJ* no. 29 (18 June 1748), p. 308; the first two lines form the motto of *CGJ* no. 8 (28 January 1752), i. 181, where they are coupled with *Dunciad* (1728), Bk. ii, 17–18, as glosses on the theme of free-thinking.

[2] Fielding is the author of the *Serious Address*, which is reprinted in the present volume, above, pp. [3]–31. Advertisements of 'The Second Edition Corrected, with Additions', are in *TP* nos. 1, 4, and 9. Fielding refers to the *Serious Address* in his footnote to *A Proper Answer* (1747), p. 79, as 'published in the Time of the late Rebellion', adding that the two pamphlets are by the same author. The title-page of the *Proper Answer* (p. [61]) states that it is 'By the Author of the *Jacobite's Journal*'.

of an absolute Popish Prince, (for absolute he would plainly be) introduced by the conquering Arms of *France*, *Spain*, and the *Highlands*.

So that every good and worthy Protestant in this Nation, who is attached to his Religion and Liberties, or who hath any Estate or Property, either in Church-Lands[1] or in the Funds,[2] (which includes almost every Man who hath either Estate or Property in the Kingdom) is concerned, in the highest Degree, to oppose the present Rebellion.

I am however aware, that there yet remains a Party to be spoken to, who are not strictly concerned in Interest in any of the preceeding Lights; I mean those Gentlemen who have no Property, nor any Regard either for the Religion or Liberty of their Country.

Now if I can make it appear, that those Persons likewise are interested in opposing the Pretender's Cause, I think we may then justly conclude, he cannot have a single Partizan in this Nation (the most bigotted Roman Catholics excepted) who is sensible enough to know his own Good.

And first, the most noble Party of Free-Thinkers, who have no Religion,[3] are most heartily concerned to oppose the Introduction of Popery, which would obtrude one on them, one not only inconsistent with Free-Thinking, but indeed with any Thinking at all. How would a Man of Spirit, whose Principles are too elevated to worship the Great Creator of the Universe, submit to pay his Adoration to a Rabble of Saints, most of whom he would have been justly ashamed to have kept Company with while alive?

---

[1] Anti-Stuart polemic insisted that the church lands dispersed to lay persons during the reign of Henry VIII (a dispersion confirmed by 1 & 2 Phil. & Mary, c. 30) would be restored to the church if the Stuarts themselves were restored. See index, *s.v.* 'Church lands', and *JJ* no. 20 (16 April 1748), pp. 242–5.

[2] The national debt, in the form of stock issued to the public by the government at interest. It was a traditional argument of anti-Stuart polemic that if the Stuarts were restored, they would 'sponge' or wipe out the funded indebtedness as having been contracted under an unlawful government or usurpation. See, for example, Swift's *Examiner* no. 15 (16 November 1710), *Prose Works*, ed. Herbert Davis, iii (Oxford, 1941), 17. In 1745 the issue was raised in particular connection with the statement in the YP's second 'manifesto' (10 October 1745) that with respect to this unlawfully acquired indebtedness his father would 'take the Advice of his Parliament concerning it'. See index, *s.v.* 'Debt, National'. For fear of the 'Spunge' as a whig election slogan in the age of Anne, see Defoe, 'The Age of Wonders', *Poems on Affairs of State*, vol. vii (New Haven, 1975), 498 *n*.

[3] In *Amelia*, I. iii. 30, Robinson is described as 'what they call a Freethinker, that is to say, a Deist, or, perhaps, an Atheist; for tho' he did not absolutely deny the Existence of a God; yet he entirely denied his Providence'. Cf. *CGJ* no. 62 (16 September 1752), ii. 95, where 'Philomath' defines a free-thinker, with unconscious irony, as one who 'makes use of his Reason as a Guide, and will believe nothing contradictory to that or common Sense, and who does not put faith in Matters he does not comprehend'; also *Joseph Andrews*, III. iii. 212–13, and *CGJ* no. 8 (28 January 1752), i. 184–5. Fielding often lumps the free-thinkers with the 'Political Philosophers' such as Hobbes, Mandeville, La Rochefoucauld, and others; see *Champion* of 22 January 1740, i. 206–10; *Tom Jones*, VI. i. 268–9; and the 'late Philosopher of great Eminence', mentioned later in the present leader (see p. 139 *n*. 2).

But besides the slavish Doctrines which he must believe, or, at least, meanly pretend to believe, how would a Genius who cannot conform to the little Acts of Decency required by a Protestant Church, support the slavish Impositions of Auricular Confession, Pennance, Fasting, and all the tiresome Forms and Ceremonies exacted by the Church of *Rome*?

Lastly, whereas the said Free-Thinkers have long regarded it as an intolerable Grievance, that a certain Body of Men called *Parsons* should, for the useless Services of Praying, Preaching, Catechising and Instructing the People, receive a certain fixed Stipend from the Public, which the Law foolishly allows them to call their own:[1] How would these Men brook the Restoration of Abbey-Lands, Impropriations,[2] and the numberless Flowers which the Reformation hath lopped off from the Church, and which the Re-establishment of Popery would most infallibly restore to it?

Again, there are many worthy Persons who, tho' very little concerned for the true Liberty of their Country, have, however, the utmost Respect for what is by several mistaken for it, I mean Licentiousness, or a free Power of abusing the King, Ministry, and every Thing great, noble and solemn.

The Impunity with which this Liberty hath been of late Years practis'd,[3] must be acknowledged by every Man of the least Candour. Indeed to such a Degree, that Power and Government, instead of being Objects of Reverence and Terror, have been set up as the Butts of Ridicule and Buffoonry, as if they were only intended to be laughed at by the People.

Now this is a Liberty which hath only flourished under this Royal Family. His present Majesty, as he hath less deserved than his Predecessors to be the Object of it, so he hath supported it with more Dignity and Contempt than they have done:[4] But how impatient the Pretender will be under this Liberty, and how certainly he will abolish it may be concluded, not only from the absolute Power which he infallibly brings with him; but from the many Ears and Noses which his Family, without such Power, have, heretofore, sacrificed on these Occasions.

---

[1] Cf. *CGJ* no. 8 (28 January 1752), i. 182, where one of the Robinhoodian debaters argues: 'Besides, if we haf no Relidgin we shall haf no *Pairsuns*, and that will be a grate Savin to the Sosyaty; and it is a *Maksum* in Trayd, That a Penny sav'd is a Penny got.' On the pejorative implications of the term 'Parson' itself, see *TP* no. 14 (28 January–4 February 1746), below, p. 208.

[2] Annexation of a benefice or its revenues to a corporation or individuals, esp. a lay corporation or lay individual (*OED*).

[3] Under its more respectable heading, 'Liberty of the Press', this issue surfaced periodically among opposition journalists. See, for example, *Old England* of 29 January 1745, reprinted in *GM*, xv (1745), 41–4, and 12 October 1745.

[4] A similar connection between the liberty of the press and the mildness or lenity of the government is made in *JJ* no. 33 (16 July 1748), pp. 343–5.

And this is a Loss not only to be deplored by those Men of Genius, who have exerted and may exert their great Talents this Way. There are many who without the Capacity of Writing have that of Reading, and have done their utmost to support and encourage such Authors and their Works. These will lose their favourite Amusement, all those Laughs and Shrugs which they have formerly vented at the Expence of their Superiors.

But if these Concerns should appear chimerical, I come now to pecuniary Considerations; to a large Body of Men whose whole Trade would be ruined by this Man's Success. The Reader will be perhaps in doubt what Trade can be carried on by such Persons as I have described in the Beginning of this Paper: How much more will he be surprized to hear, that it is the principal Trade which of late Years hath been carried on in this Kingdom. To keep him therefore no longer in Suspence, I mean the honest Method of selling ourselves, which hath flourished so notably for a long time among us.[1] A Business which I have ventured to call honest, notwithstanding the Objections raised by weak and scrupulous People against it.

I know indeed many Answers have been given to these Objections by a late Philosopher of great Eminence,[2] and by the Followers of his School; such as, *That all Mankind are Rascals; That they are only to be governed by Corruption*, &c. But to say the Truth, there is no Occasion of having Recourse to these deep and obscure Doctrines for this purpose; there is a much fuller and plainer Answer to be given, and which is founded on Principles the very Reverse of those which were taught in this School, namely, the Principles of Common Sense and Common Honesty: for if it be granted, as surely it will be, that we are Freemen, we have certainly

[1] French, pp. 240–1, compares *The Crisis: A Sermon* (1741), a work frequently attributed to Fielding: 'We cannot absolutely sell ourselves. We cannot give an absolute Power over our own Lives to another; for this is a Power which the Almighty retains himself, and hath not entrusted us with' (p. 8). Writing of the Walpole period, Bolingbroke gives the latent political ideology its loftiest and most 'patriot' expression: 'The means of invading liberty more effectually by constitution of the revenue, than it ever had been invaded by prerogative, were not then grown up into strength. They are so now: and a bold and insolent use is made of them'; 'A Letter on the Spirit of Patriotism' (1736), *Works*, ed. Goldsmith, iv (London, 1809), 210.

[2] Possibly Bernard Mandeville (1670–1733), Part I of whose *Fable of the Bees* (1714; 1729) concludes with a restatement of 'the seeming Paradox . . . that Private Vices by the dextrous Management of a skilful Politician may be turned into Publick Benefits'; ed. F. B. Kaye (Oxford [1924]), i. 369. See Locke, p. 66. However, Fielding's references to this 'Philoso-Political School', as he calls it later in the leader, or to the 'Political Philosophers', as he calls them in the *Champion* of 22 January 1740 (i. 207), always seem ambiguous. The *sententiae* he attributes to them cannot be unequivocally derived from the original texts. Indeed, as Fielding phrases and identifies them, they seem curiously applicable to Sir Robert Walpole, between whose 'All these men have their price' politics and the 'private vices, public virtues' of the philosophers Fielding may have been hoping to suggest a connection. On the implications of this for 'patriot' politics, see 'General Introduction', above, pp. lxxiii–lxxiv; also *TP* no. 17 (18–25 February 1746), pp. 223–6.

a Right to ourselves; and whatever we have a Right to, we have also a Right to sell. And perhaps it was a Doubt in that great Philosopher, *whether we were Freemen or no*, that led him into those Doctrines I have mentioned.

Now this Trade, by which alone so many Thousands have got an honest Livelihood for themselves and Families, must be totally ruined; for if this Nation should be once enslaved, it would be impossible for an honest Man to carry on this Business any longer. A Freeman (as hath been proved) may justly sell himself, but a Slave cannot.

And if a Man would be so dishonourable and base as to offer at carrying on this Trade in an enslaved Country, contrary to all the Rules of Honesty, and all the most solemn Ties of Slavery, yet who would buy him? The Reasons against such a Purchase are too obvious to be mentioned. Indeed we may say in general, that as it is dishonest in a Slave to sell, so it is as foolish in a Slave to buy; for as the one hath no Property to part with, so neither can the other acquire any.

For these Reasons, I think it is visibly the Interest of all that Part of the Nation, to whom I have addressed myself in the Beginning of this Paper, to exclude Popery and arbitrary Power.

There is, however, one Objection which I foresee may and will be made to this Conclusion; and that is, whereas the Estates of all the Lords and Commons of this Kingdom will be forfeited, and at the Disposal of the Conqueror, and the personal Fortunes of all others will, in the Confusion at least, be liable to Plunder, that such honest Gentlemen may have a sufficient Chance abundantly to repair or compensate all their Losses.

I own there is something very plausible in this Argument, and it might perhaps have great Force, if the Pretender's Son had landed in *England*, as he did in *Scotland*; and had been pleased to place that Confidence in an *English* Rabble, with which he hath vouchsafed rather to honour these Highland Banditti. In this Case, I grant, no Man could justly have been blamed who had fixed the Eyes of his Affection on his Neighbour's Estate, Gardens, House, Purse, Wife, or Daughter, for joining the young Man's Cause, provided the Success of it had been probable: Such a Behaviour would then have been highly consistent with all the Rules taught in that School of Philosophy abovementioned, and none but a musty Moralist, for whose Doctrine great Men have doubtless an adequate Contempt, would have condemned it.

But the Fact is otherwise: The *Highlanders* are those to whom he must owe any Success he may attain; these are therefore to be served before you; and I easily refer to your own Consideration, when *Rome*, and

France, and *Spain*, are repaid their Demands, when a vast Army of hungry *Highlanders*, and a larger Army of as hungry Priests, are satisfied, how miserable a Pittance will remain to your Share? Indeed so small a one must this be, that the greatest Adept in our Philoso-Political School would think it scarce worth his while to sacrifice his Conscience to the Certainty of obtaining it.

These latter Considerations I earnestly recommend to the most serious Attention of the Gentlemen for whose Use this Paper is calculated; and I am certain that any Argument for the Pretender's Cause, drawn from the Hopes of plundering their Neighbours (with which perhaps some honest Men have too fondly flattered themselves) will have very little Weight with any Person. Nay I must remind them, that they will not be suffered to rifle the very Churches themselves, upon whose small Riches most probably the said Gentlemen have cast their Eyes.

It appears then that none will be, or can be Gainers by this Rebellion but Popish Priests and Highlanders; and I have too good an Opinion of my Country to apprehend that her Religion, Liberties and Properties, can ever be endangered by such Adversaries.

TUESDAY, DECEMBER 3, 1745.   NUMB. 5.

Odisti, et fugis, ut Drusonem Debitor Æris.

HORACE.[1]

A violent Storm obliged me, the other Day, to shelter myself under a certain Gate-way in this Town, where two Gentlemen at the same Time took Refuge. As this was the Place of their Meeting, they embraced and kissed each other with great Affection. Their Dress was so remarkable, that I could not help observing them. It had a Mixture in it of military and civil, of the Gentleman and the Footman, of the Smart[2] and the Man of Business. They had not been long together before they began to lament the Decay of Business, and to curse the Rebellion, which they declared, if it continued a few Months longer, would ruin them both:

[1] *Satires*, i. iii. 86, reading *Rusonem* for *Drusonem*: 'You hate him bitterly and shun him, as Ruso is shunned by his debtor' (Loeb). Ruso was a usurer with literary aspirations; he made his debtors listen to him read his own compositions. Just possibly Fielding had his mind turned to the subject of indebtedness by his deepening involvement (as legal adviser and surety) in an action for debt that had been brought against his friend Arthur Collier. See 'General Introduction', above, p. xxix, and below, p. 256 *n.* 2.
[2] One who affects smartness in dress, manners, or talk (*OED*). In *Spectator* no. 442 (28 July 1712) the Smarts seem to be grouped with the Beaux and the Rakes (iv. 53).

For, says one of them, *I have not executed a single Writ this Fortnight*. To which the other answer'd, He believed the Nation was utterly undone; for he had carried but one Man to Goal,[1] since the first Day of the Term.[2] They then proceeded to be witty on some Person, whose Name they did not mention, but by Signs and Tokens signified it to each other; and in conclusion, one laid the other a Wager, that he *nabbed* him in a Fortnight; the other answer'd, he'd be *d—n'd* if he did, for he was as *shy a Cock*,[3] as any in the whole Town.

When the Storm was over, I left my two Friends, being less pleased with the Oddity of the Dialogue, than concerned at the Inhumanity which can inspire Men to make not only a Livelihood, but a Jest of the Distresses of others. At my Return home, I found the following Letter on my Table, which comes from a Man who hath had the Misfortune to fall into the Hands of some of these Miscreants.

To the PATRIOT.

Sir,

I am as zealously affected to his Majesty King GEORGE, as any other Subject whatsoever, and have endeavoured to promote his Service at this Season in the most hearty Manner; surely, therefore, some ill-designing Persons must have represented me to that gracious Prince, or he would never have sent a Letter to his Sheriffs to take me up *for running up and down the Country*[4] with *one* JOHN DOE,[5] who is, I suppose, a *Highlander*, or disaffected Person, and utterly unknown to me. Now, Sir, so far am I from running up and down with this sorry Fellow, that I have

---

[1] These two gentlemen are bailiffs or under-officers of the sheriff, or perhaps of someone like the warden of the Fleet. Colloquially called 'Tipstaffs', they did their business in serving ('executing') writs for debt and, when the nature of the action required, arresting the persons named in the writs so as to ensure their appearance in court. The form and nature of the writ will become clear in the letter which follows.

[2] A term was that portion of the year, according to the ancient practice of the courts of common law, during which judicial business could be transacted. The term referred to here would be the Michaelmas term, running in effect through the month of November.

[3] Evidently a colloquialism among bailiffs; cf. *Amelia*, VIII. i. 309.

[4] The conventional language of a writ in English speaks of 'running' or 'lurking' in the 'County', that is, in the bailiwick of the sheriff responsible for executing the writ in question. Since the sheriff of Middlesex is alleged not to have been able to find his man, apparently a second, more generally directed writ has been issued to the 'Country' at large. Here and below, the use of italics and capitals for phrases, terms, or names indicates the legal and linguistic conventions of the writ itself.

[5] With 'Richard Roe', one of the fictitious names familiar to English law, particularly in actions of ejectment. In actions for debt these were the names customarily given to the sureties who were technically required to be named even at initial stages of the action. In the present instance, however, which appears to involve a writ of *Capias ad satisfaciendum*, the fiction appears to have a different purpose.

not been without my own Doors, except on a Sunday,[1] for these two Months last past. I am told, indeed, by a Friend of mine, a Lawyer, that his Majesty knows nothing of the matter, but that the *Plaintiff* (as they call him) and his Attorney have put his sacred Name to this Letter, which they call a *Rit*, without his Notice, tho' the Sheriff be ordered to keep me safe lock'd up for several Weeks, and then have MY BODY before the King himself at *Westminster*, to answer one *Thomas Johnson*; and that it is the usual Custom so to do. Sure such Insolence is incredible! But however this be, I was surprized in my House, and robb'd of my Liberty, under Pretence of this Letter, wherein there are many other Falshoods, particularly that the King had sent a Letter to the Sheriff of *Middlesex*, ordering to take me, and that the said Sheriff had *returned* an Answer that I was not to be found.[2] Whereas that Sheriff, with whom I am acquainted, knew very well where I lived, and hath since assured me he never had any such Letter, or returned any such Answer. The Truth is, I owe the *Plaintiff* 11 *l.*[3] which I should have paid him long since, had not this vile Rebellion, by putting an entire Stop to all Trade, and locking up all the little Money in the Kingdom in a few private Coffers, prevented me. This *Plaintiff* is a very rich Man, and would as little know what to do with the 11 *l.* I owe him, as I at present know where to procure it. As you have been pleased to say, in one of your Papers,[4] that no Man who doth not love his Friends and Neighbours can love his Country, be so kind to tell us whether one who would at this Season distress an honest Man, and deprive him of his Liberty, for Money which he himself does not want, and which he knows the other hath it not in his Power to pay, can be sincerely attached to the Liberties of Mankind? Your Thoughts on this Subject will greatly oblige

Your unhappy humble Servant,

TIMOTHY PAUPER.

From my Garret, 3 Pair of
   Stairs, at the Hand and
   Tipstaff, Gray's Inn Lane.[5]

---

[1] According to the provisions of 29 Car. II, c. 7, on Sundays debtors could not be arrested for debt. See 'To the Right Honourable Sir Robert Walpole', *Miscellanies* (1743), i. 57.

[2] When a sheriff could not find the person upon whom he was to execute the writ, he 'returned' the writ with the notation *non est inventus*.

[3] If the action was for a sworn debt of more than £10, then the person named could be arrested so as to ensure his appearance. See Giles Jacob, *Every Man His Own Lawyer*, 4th ed. (London, 1750), pp. 9–14.

[4] *TP* no. 2 (12 November 1745), above, p. 117, where it is said, 'no Man can love his Country, who doth not love a single Person in it'.

[5] A 'poor' address. Cf. *Tom Jones*, XIII. ii. 689: 'And as he happened to arrive first in a Quarter of Town, the Inhabitants of which have very little Intercourse with the Housholders of Hanover or Grosvenor Square, (for he entered through Grays-Inn Lane) so he rambled about some Time before he could even find his Way to those happy Mansions, where Fortune segregates from the Vulgar,

Notwithstanding the Air of Drollery which runs through the above Letter, and which seems to indicate a very philosophical Turn of Mind in the Writer, if he be really in the Circumstances he describes, the Matter of it is of very serious Consequence, and I shall readily comply with my Correspondent's Request, by throwing together such Thoughts as occur to me on the Occasion.[1]

How consistent it is with the Character of a true Christian to persecute an unhappy Man, to the Ruin of himself and his Family, for Debt, under any common Circumstances, at another Time, I shall not now debate. Sure I am that the Case must be of a very extraordinary Nature, to reconcile such a Conduct to the Doctrine and Precepts of that Religion which he professes.

Indeed there are two Kinds of Debts, very different from each other. The one contracted for vain Superfluities, misbecoming the Condition and Fortune of the Person, with Wantonness and Fraud, with a Consciousness of being unable to pay at present, and without any Design of ever paying hereafter. The other incurred for the real Necessaries, or at most the ordinary Conveniencies of Life, without Extravagance or Imposition, with a reasonable Probability of satisfying the Creditor, and with a fixed Intention of so doing. As the former of these falls little short of a Cheat, it is hard to deny the latter the Character of an honest Man, tho' unforeseen Accidents and Misfortunes should defeat the utmost Industry, and render him in the End insolvent.

Now different as these Cases are, it is perhaps impossible for the written Letter of Law to distinguish between their Punishment; but this is a Distinction which can seldom escape the Creditor himself. The Character and Situation of the Person, and the Manner in which the Debt was contracted, must generally demonstrate under which of these two Classes his Debtor is to be ranked; if under the latter, I think Humanity will not suffer him (Christianity certainly will not) to inflict one of the most grievous Punishments (for such is the Loss of Liberty) on an unhappy Man, and complete the Ruin of his Family.

And what doth he really gain by pursuing a Man in desperate Circumstances, but the Satisfaction of Malice, or Revenge for what in this favourable Case is but a supposed Injury. A Satisfaction, if his Mind be

those magnanimous Heroes'; also *Amelia*, VIII. i. 309, where the bailiff takes Booth to 'my House . . . in *Gray's-Inn-Lane*'. The particular house, probably a sponging house, has not been identified; the name suggests a satiric fiction, the coercive legal context.

[1] The harsh treatment accorded debtors in his day is a recurrent theme in Fielding's writing (and may have been in his life). A helpful gloss on the 'Thoughts' here, as well as on the letter which gives rise to them, is *Joseph Andrews*, III. iii. 218–20, where Mr Wilson illustrates the problem from his own experience, thereby provoking Parson Adams to thoughts not unlike those offered here.

so depraved to think it one, by obtaining which he must himself contract so bitter a Debt to the Justice of an avenging GOD.[1]

Nay further, he will often be a Loser by it, in a temporal Sense. An untimely Prosecution hath prevented many an honest Man from discharging his Debt. How foolish, as well as barbarous, is it to defeat the Purposes of Industry, when it labours probably for your own Good! How will a Man answer it to himself, any more than to his Neighbour or his GOD, who, by a hasty Arrest, is the only Means of preventing his Debtor from being just to him.

I have heard it said by one not extremely eminent for his Goodness,[2] that he never thought any Man owed him more than he was able to pay. It is a weak as well as rapacious Temper, which pushes us on to defraud ourselves, by ruining a Wretch who is labouring to be honest.

These are Arguments which may at all Times be used against this Practice; but they have a double Weight at this Season, when all Trade is at a Stand; when both the public and private Fountains of Wealth are in a manner dry'd up;[3] when Estates in Land, or in the Funds, yield little more than future Hopes to their Possessors; and when the utmost Industry, in any Kind of Business, will scarce provide the most Successful with Food for their Families: In a word, when War, both at Home and Abroad, seems to call in the Assistance of Pestilence[4] and Famine to destroy this miserable Nation.

In such a Time as this, can a Christian, nay can a human Being become a Minister of Wrath to his Fellow-Creatures? Will the Rich and Powerful, instead of endeavouring the Relief, Support and Consolation of the Distrest, add Chains to Poverty, and rob those of the Benefit of wholesome Air who have scarce any other Food or Comfort? What a Man, or rather what a Dæmon, must he be, who at this Season can tear a Husband from his Wife, or a Father from his Children, and by laying up the Master of a Family, to rot and starve in an unwholesome Goal,[5]

---

[1] Cf. *Champion* of 19 February 1740, i. 287–8: 'but let a Christian . . . remember that as surely as he forgives not his Neighbour his Trespasses, so surely will his Father in Heaven deny to forgive him his; nor do I know any Crime in this World which can appear to a finite Understanding to deserve infinite Punishment, so much as that cursed and rancorous Disposition which could bring a Man to cause the destruction of a Family, or the Confinement of a human Creature in Misery during his Life, for any Debt whatever, unless the contracting it be attended with great Circumstances of Villainy'.

[2] If 'Goodness' here can be taken to mean leniency in matters financial, the reference may just possibly be to Peter Walter. See *TP* no. 2 (12 November 1745), above, p. 118 and *n.* 2.

[3] This dismal view of the public finances was shared by members of the administration. See Pelham to Trevor, 11 December 1745, Coxe, *Pelham*, i. 283; and *TP* no. 11 (14 January 1746), below, p. 188.

[4] Referring to the distemper then raging among the horned cattle. See *TP* no. 7 (17 December 1745), below, p. 155, where the pestilence is again associated with famine.

[5] An acceptable spelling of 'Gaol'. On the matter of jailing debtors, see *Champion* of 16 February

deprive the rest of that Support which his Industry and Labour produced them.

Can such a Wretch as this expect the Assistance of an all-merciful and all-just Being, to protect his Possessions from the Rapine of *Highland* Robbers and Ruffians? Nay, hath he the Assurance to name those Banditti with Terms of Reproach and Detestation, when he acts from viler Principles, and is himself more barbarous and inhuman than the worst of them? He hath not the Plea of Necessity to lessen, and cold Blood, and the Relation of Countryman and Neighbour aggravate his Cruelty.

Should this Temper prevail at present, it would become the Wisdom of our Government to consider of enlarging the Places set apart for the Reception alike of the Unfortunate and the Guilty. But I hope the Gentlemen whom I mentioned in the Beginning of this Paper, will have still greater Reason to lament their Loss of Business; nay, that they will be compelled, like Pikes, to prey on each other. Indeed, could I think otherwise of the Temper of my Countrymen, I should almost be driven to wish, that the Legislature had itself taken from them the Power of exerting their Cruelty, and had suspended the Laws by which Men are arrested for Debt, at the same time when they suspended the *Habeas Corpus*.[1]

1740 and 19 February 1740, i. 277–9, 284–8. French, p. 249, compares 'Apocrypha' of *TP* no. 11 (14 January 1746), below, p. 404, which comments on a report that London authorities were being asked if they had room in their jails for the rebels taken at Carlisle: 'It is hoped these poor Wretches [the prisoners in the London jails], whom the Hardness of the Times, and the greater Hardness of their diabolical Condition, have confined in these Goals, will be obliged to make Room for those who so much better deserve their Places.' Fielding may have had more personal reasons for being sensitive to the issue. In 1741–2 he had himself been involved in an action for debt brought by one Joseph King; Cross, i. 375–7. In June 1745 Fielding and James Harris had gone surety for a £400 debt owed by their mutual friend Arthur Collier. As Collier's legal adviser, Fielding had, in November 1745, twice appealed to delay execution. Among the innumerable contemporary references to his financial difficulties is one which seems to place him in the Fleet prison for debt; see 'Verses to the injur'd Patriot, written in 1733', in *A Miscellaneous Collection of Original Poems... Written Chiefly on Political and Moral Subjects* (London, 1740), p. 206. In any event, debt and society's treatment of it are something of a topos running throughout his work. See *Pasquin* (1736), IV. i; *Champion* of 22 July and 19 August 1740; *Joseph Andrews* (1742), III. iii; *Jonathan Wild* (1743), I. iv; *Tom Jones* (1749), XIII. ix; *Amelia* (1751), VIII. i; *CGJ* no. 39 (16 May 1752).

[1] Despite considerable opposition grumbling about the liberties of Englishmen, the Commons voted on 18 October 1745 to suspend the *habeas corpus* act for a term of six months; on 19 October the Lords concurred, and the royal assent was given on 21 October; *Journals of Commons*, xxv. 6, 7, 8; also 19 Geo II, c. 1, *Statutes at Large*, v. 452.

Tuesday, December 10, 1745.   Numb. 6.

Quid statis? Nolint. Atqui licet esse beatis.

Horace.[1]

Notwithstanding the universal Desire of Happiness which Nature hath implanted in the Mind of every Man, such are the Mistakes both in Opinion and Practice, and so far are the Actions of the Generality of Mankind from having any visible Tendency towards their real Good, that one is sometimes tempted to predicate of the human Species, that Man is an Animal which industriously seeks his own Misery.

Here I shall omit all trite Observation on those most general as well as powerful Passions of Ambition, Avarice, &c. which may be considered as cruel Tyrants, imposing the severest Tasks on their Slaves, for the painful Performance of which they are to receive no Wages nor Enjoyment; but there is one Argument which I do not remember to have seen much insisted on in this Light, tho' it is otherwise obvious enough; I mean, that Fickleness or Inconstancy of Temper which renders us uneasy and discontented in the Possession of real Happiness, as if, like a too luscious Dainty, it had something sating and surfeiting in its Nature; whence certain Persons have concluded, I think a little too hastily, that there is no such thing as real Happiness in this World.

But without staying, at present, to obviate this Sentiment, we may most certainly affirm, (and that without Reference to the Brevity of Life itself) that there is no human Happiness *durable*, of which this very Fickleness and Inconstancy of our Temper is a sufficient Proof.

Numberless Instances of this Kind may be furnished by every Day's Experience. Nothing is more common than to see Men, as it were, over-loaded with Happiness, and groaning under its Weight. The Possession of the Object of our Love, or an unexpected Access of Fortune, have become intolerable Burdens. Spleen and Vapours inhabit Palaces, and are attired with Pomp and Splendor, while they shun Rags and Prisons. In a word, I have made it my Observation, that those Persons who seem to have Happiness the most in their Power, have it least in their Possession.

If these positive and domestic Blessings create in us so dull and indurable[2] a Happiness, it is less to be wondered at, that negative and

---

[1] *Satires*, I. i. 19: '"what are you standing around for?" They would refuse. And yet it is in their power to be happy' (adapted from Loeb). The question in quotes concludes a speech to a group of malcontents by a *deus ex machina* who has offered them a chance to change their places in life. The answer and the concluding observation are supplied by the satiric speaker.

[2] Not durable; not enduring or lasting (*OED*, which lists no usage between 1450 and 1899).

public Good, such as the Exemption from Slavery, should find us insensible to its Charms. The Excellence of a political Constitution is a Blessing aptly to be compared to the Health of a natural Body, which, tho' it be the Foundation of every other Enjoyment, gives us but little Enjoyment in itself. Hence is Health little valued by those who possess it; often wantonly sported away, sacrificed to Whim, and given in Exchange for the lightest Trifles. In the same Manner have Nations wantoned away their Liberties, have barter'd them for a worthless Price, or carelessly and idly suffered them to slip from their Hands.

As both these Blessings are justly to be esteem'd above Life, because without them Life is only a Punishment, an intolerable Burthen; so by an equal Fatality, are they seldom valued till they are to be lamented. Disease and Slavery teach us to remember their sweet Relish, when they are no longer to be tasted. They are both alike too often insensibly lost, and sometimes by the Few who esteem them the most, by too great a Caution to preserve them.

I am sorry to say, there is little Reason at present to search for Examples of this Kind. Here I would not be understood to insinuate, that there is a single *British Protestant* foolish, or mad, or wicked enough to desire the Destruction of *British* Liberty: But it is too manifest, that there are some simple enough to flatter themselves, that this Liberty might be safe under the Protection of a bigotted *Popish* Prince, educated in the highest Principles of absolute Power, coming in as a Conqueror, by the Assistance of the Arms of *France*.[1]

Now with such as these it is really absurd to argue at all; for what is it less than undertaking to prove a self-evident Proposition: But that they may be left without any Excuse, some have undertaken to evince them by reason of the Folly and Nonsense of their Tenets. Among those none hath deserved so well of his Country as the *Occasional Writer*, in his Answer to the Pretender's second Declaration.[2] A Pamphlet which some Administrations would have thought worth propagating by Authority.

[1] The language here resembles that of *Proper Answer* (1747), p. 80.

[2] *The Occasional Writer: Containing an Answer to the Second Manifesto of the Pretender's Eldest Son: Which Bears Date at the Palace of Holy-Rood-House, the 10th Day of October, 1745*. This shilling pamphlet of 54 pages is advertised as published in *DA* of 12 November 1745. It bears the imprint of M. Cooper, who advertised it in *TP* no. 3 (19 November 1745). There are further references to it in the letter 'To Charles Stuart, Esq;' in *TP* no. 3, above, p. 134, and in 'A Letter to the Jacobites', *TP* no. 7 (17 December 1745), Locke, p. [84]. An unsigned letter in *DA* of 18 December 1745 goes out of its way to assert that the author of the *TP* 'acted with perfect Impartiality in giving his Judgment of this Pamphlet, being utterly ignorant of the Name of the Author'. *The Occasional Writer* has been attributed to William Grant (Lord Prestongrange) and to Thomas Hollis. According to the 'Advertisement by the Publisher' (p. iii) of the titularly designated 'second' edition (1746), favorable critical notices, like those in the *TP*, led to that 'second Impression'.

There are others (and those a much larger Number) who are guilty of the Remissness I have above mentioned. Men who are not sanguine in their Hopes that this *Popish* Pretender would protect their Liberties, but are in Reality as little sanguine in their Defence; who either, from a deplorable Levity of Temper, have not duly considered the Value of what they are to lose; or from a more blameable Profligacy, are so wholly occupied in the Pursuit of Pleasure or Profit, that they cannot attend a Moment to the Cause of their Country; or lastly, from the basest Pusillanimity, the most contemptible Cowardice, can tamely submit to the Loss of every Thing which can render Life amiable, or even supportable, rather than bravely risque that Life itself in the Defence of those inestimable Blessings.

One of these Censures (let him chuse which he will) every Man deserves who shakes his Head, and expresses any Despair or even Doubt of our Success against these paultry Rebels. Admit their Numbers to be tenfold what they really are, admit they were doubled by the Troops of *France* or *Spain*, if we are unanimous, if we have the Courage of *Britons*, we may destroy them; if we would preserve our Religion and Liberties, we must; if we are worthy of those Blessings, we certainly shall.

When a base *Roman* proposed in Council to abandon his Country in the highest State of Danger, what did the brave *Scipio*, then a Youth? (*admodum Adolescens*, says *Livy*.)[1] He drew his Sword, and brandishing it over the Heads of several present, took the most solemn Oath, that he would never desert his Country, nor suffer any other *Roman* Citizen to desert it. What did the brave Prince of *Orange* (an Instance nearer to us in Time as well as Place) when the insolent *Frenchman*, who advised him to submit to the Conqueror, asked him, If he did not see that his Country was lost? Did he not answer him, I see indeed it is in great Danger, but there is a sure Way never to see it lost, by dying in the last Ditch.[2]

---

[1] *Historia*, XXII. liii. 3, where the accepted text reads *admodum adulescentem*. According to Livy, the 'base Roman' was Publius Furius Philus, son of an ex-consul, who after the Roman surrender to Hannibal at Canusium (216 BC) counseled flight from Italy. Scipio (236–184/3 BC), in his new role as supreme commander, repudiated Philus and forced the reluctant followers of Metellus to swear allegiance to Rome.

[2] The association of the so-called last Ditch speech with an 'insolent Frenchman' has not been identified. Burnet, who says the prince of Orange 'told me this himself', records this speech as an answer to the duke of Buckingham's assertion that Holland could not hold out against both England and France in 1672 and should therefore conciliate; *History of My Own Time* (London, 1724), i. 327. Burnet's association of the speech with Buckingham is the accepted one. Possibly Fielding is confusing the speech with the prince's response to the somewhat later French proposal that he be established as sovereign over the provinces, but under the protection of France and England. See Sir William Temple, 'Memoirs of What Passed in Christendom from the War begun 1672, to the Peace concluded 1679', *Works*, 2nd ed. (London, 1731), i. 381–2. After listing the features which constitute

I thank God, we are in a better Situation than either the *Romans* or the *Hollanders* were. We have seen no Battle of *Cannæ*,[1] no War in which the Flower of our People hath been cut off. We have no *Hannibal*, no King of *France* with immense Armies at our Gates. We have only a few ragged Ruffians to deal with, assisted at the worst with a Set of starved enslaved *Frenchmen*, whose Ancestors have always fled before us, and who at *Fontenoy* run from our Forces (tho' they were but a third of their Number) till their Cannon gave them a dishonourable Victory;[2] if they could be said to obtain any, over an Army which retreated in Order from the Attack, and which they durst not pursue.

Against these Rebels, and these their Assistants, we have an Army now in this Kingdom of upwards of sixty thousand Men,[3] exclusive of Marines, Invalids,[4] Train'd Bands[5] and Militia; and these backed by two millions of People (for so many at least may be supposed also to bear Arms)[6] among whom there is not, I hope, a single Protestant, capable of drawing his Sword, who would not unsheath it in Defence of his present

an object of universal hatred and contempt, the *Champion* of 15 January 1740 remarks, 'we have had no Person in whom all these Symptoms have met, since *Buckingham*, and I heartily hope we shall never see such another' (i. 191).

[1] The battle (216 BC) immediately preceding the Roman surrender at Canusium and the efforts made by the young Scipio to regroup. See above, p. 149 *n*. 1, and Livy, *Historia*, XXII. xliv–l.

[2] This tendentious account of the battle of Fontenoy (11 May 1745) squares with the popular view held by English contemporaries. Cf. *The Conduct of our Officers, as well General as Inferior, in the late Battle near Tournay* (London, 1745), p. 9: 'And when in the Account of this late Event we add to this superior Skill in War their Superiority in Numbers, the prodigious Force of their Artillery, and the Advantage of the Ground . . . let us no longer wonder that we were repulsed.'

[3] Fielding's source for this figure has not been identified. In 'Further Considerations concerning the Establishment of a Militia', *TP* no. 10 (7 January 1746), below, p. 181, the present strength of the army, 'including Invalids and Marines, (making about 14000)' is put at 74,000 men. Fielding appears to be the author of 'Further Considerations'. C. T. Atkinson, 'Jenkins' Ear, the Austrian Succession War and the "Forty-Five"', *Journal of the Society for Army Historical Research*, xxii (1943/4), 280–98, identifies the regular units on domestic service in December 1745 but does not give complete strength estimates; for the forces around London, see G. R. Miller, 'Hogarth's "March to Finchley"', *Journal of the Society for Army Historical Research*, xxvii (1949), 48–50.

[4] Soldiers or sailors disabled by illness or injury from active service; formerly often employed on garrison duty, or as a reserve force (*OED*).

[5] Also Train Bands. When distinguished, as here, from the regular militia, trained companies of citizen soldiery, organized in London and other parts in the 16th, 17th, and 18th centuries (*OED*). Traditionally, every householder worth £500 a year was required to furnish a horse and a horseman. Those worth £50 a year were required to raise a foot soldier. Much more of an 'occasional' force than the regular militia, the trained bands were activated mainly in local emergencies.

[6] The basis for this computation has not been identified. In an unsigned letter 'from a Person of *great Property*', as well as *great Abilities*', *TP* no. 9 (31 December 1745), Locke, p. [100], it is asserted that 'we have two Millions as capable [as the regular troops] of bearing Arms'. Legally, of course, catholics were not permitted to own arms, and the accumulating game-law legislation had severely restricted the right to own guns among those without a considerable property qualification. In *TP* no. 7 (17 December 1745) 'Parson Adams' estimates 'above a hundred thousand . . . have Arms in their Hands'. *DA* of 26 September 1745 prints a letter which asks, 'Is not one Million [armed citizens], which is one Hundred to one, able to conquer ten Thousand?'

Majesty, of his legal and mild Administration, and of the Religion, Laws, and Liberties of his Country.

Let us banish, therefore, all Despair, as well from our Brows as from our Hearts. Let us resolve to empty the last Farthing from our Purses, and drain the last Drop from our Hearts in this glorious Cause. Let us resolve to live Free Men, or die Brave Ones.

Should this be our Resolution, the Success of our Enemies is (humanly speaking) impossible; nay, the personal Danger to most of us is so inconsiderable, that those who bravely determine to attend his Majesty in the last Exigency, will most probably never be called for; but should unforeseen Accidents demand it, nothing but absolute Impotency from Age or Infirmity can excuse our Attendance. The Use of Arms is soon learned; and tho' we may not be expert Soldiers, if our Hearts are good, our Hands will be of Service.

To conclude, I hope there are but few of us, who are so simple to be sick of the Happiness they enjoy from Liberty, and are therefore desirous to part with it; or being desirous to retain it, base enough to decline its Defence, at any Risque whatsoever.

TUESDAY, DECEMBER 17, 1745. NUMB. 7.

To the TRUE PATRIOT.[1]

My Worthy Friend,

I received your Paper, intitled the *True Patriot*, Numbers one and two, inclosed in the Franks of my great and most honoured Patron,[2] for which I have the highest Thanks for you both. I am delighted, and that greatly, with many Passages in these Papers. The Moderation which you profess towards all Parties, perfectly becomes a Christian. Indeed I have always thought, that Moderation in the Shepherd was the best, if not only, Way

---

[1] No motto was printed at the head of this leader. However, the letter writer ('Abraham Adams') soon declares his admiration for the custom and later identifies the lines from Pythagoras as 'my Motto'. See p. 152 and *n.* 5, below.

[2] Locke, p. 85, conjectures Ralph Allen, and is supported by Benjamin Boyce, *The Benevolent Man: A Life of Ralph Allen of Bath* (Cambridge, Mass., 1967), p. 166 *n.* However, in view of two ensuing references to his life in 'the World' as dating from the publication of *Joseph Andrews*, the writer more likely means Squire Booby, husband of Pamela, nephew to the late Sir Thomas Booby, and donor, to Adams, of a living worth £130 a year; *Joseph Andrews*, IV. xvi. 344. If the nephew was heir to his uncle the baronet, as the novel implies, he might be imagined to have franking privileges. The case for fictionality seems strengthened by the fact that in his other letter to the *TP* Adams recounts an adventure with his 'good friend Mr. Wilson', the father of Joseph Andrews; see no. 13 (21–8 January 1746), below, p. 201.

to bring Home all the straggling Sheep to his Flock. I have intimated this at the Vestry, and even at Visitation before the Archdeacon:

Sed Cassandræ non creditum est.[1]

I like your Method of placing a Motto from the Classics at the Head of every Paper. It must give some Encouragement to your Readers, that the Author understands (at least) one Line of *Latin*, which is perhaps more than can be safely predicated of every Writer in this Age.

You desire me, Sir, to write you something proper to be seen, *et quidem*,[2] by the Public; as therefore a Subject worthy their most serious Attention now offers itself, *viz.* The ensuing Fast ordain'd by Authority,[3] I have communicated my Thoughts to you thereon, which you may suppress or publicate[4] as you think meet.

—— ἔϱχεν ἐπ᾽ ἔϱγον
Θεοῖσιν ἐπευξαμενος τελέσαι.

PYTHAGORAS.[5]

—— "Go upon the Work,
Having first prayed to the Gods for Success."

As it is impossible for any Man to reflect seriously on the Progress of the present unnatural Rebellion, without imputing such unparallel'd Success to some other Cause than has yet appeared, some other Strength than what any visible human Means hath placed in the Hands of the Rebels; so will it be extremely difficult to assign any adequate Cause whatsoever, without recurring to One, of whose great Efficacy we have frequent Examples in Sacred History. I mean the just Judgment of God against an offending People.

And that this is really so, we may conclude from these two Considerations: First, from the Rapidity of the Rebels Progress, so unaccountable from all human Means; for can History produce an Instance parallel to

---

[1] 'But Cassandra was not to be believed'. The tradition that Cassandra's prophecies were fated to be disbelieved is at least as old as Aeschylus (*Agamemnon*). By the time the tradition had hardened into Latin, it had become something of a tag. One exemplary text might have been Phaedrus, 'Fabularum Aesopiarum', III. x. ('Poeta'), [3]–4: *Hippolitus obiit, quia novercae creditum est;| Cassandrae quia non creditum, ruit Ilium.*

[2] 'Indeed'. Apparently a favorite with Adams; see *TP* no. 13 (21–8 January 1746), below, p. 203.

[3] Cf. 'Present History of Great Britain', *TP* no. 2 (12 November 1745) below, p. 341: 'His Majesty hath been pleased to order a Proclamation for a General Fast to be held on the 18th of December next.' The royal proclamation, dated Whitehall, 7 November, was first published in the *London Gazette* of 9 November 1745. Fielding dilates more generally on the significance of a fast-day in *Champion* of 8 January 1740, i. 165–70.

[4] 'Publish'. *OED* cites this passage.

[5] 'Aurea Carmina', vv. 48–9. The subjoined translation appears to be original.

this, of six or seven Men landing in a great and powerful Nation,[1] in opposition to the Inclination of the People, in defiance of a vast and mighty Army: (for tho' the greater Part of this Army was not then in the Kingdom, it was so nearly within Call, that every Man of them might, within the Compass of a few Days or Weeks at farthest, have been brought home and landed in any Part of it.)[2] If we consider, I say, this Handful of Men landing in the most desolate Corner, among a Sett of poor, naked, hungry, disarm'd Slaves, abiding there with Impunity, till they had, as it were, in the Face of a large Body of his Majesty's Troops, collected a kind of Army, or rather Rabble, together; if we view this Army intimidating the King's Forces from approaching them by their Situation; soon afterwards quitting that Situation, marching directly up to the Northern Capital, and entering it without Surprize or without a Blow.[3] If we again view this half-armed, half-disciplined Mob, without the Assistance of a single Piece of Artillery, march up to, attack, and *smite* a superior Number of the King's Regular Troops, with Cannon in their Front to defend them.[4] If we consider them returning from this complete Victory to the Capital, which they had before taken; there remaining, for near two Months, in contempt of twelve Millions of People,[5] above a hundred thousand of which have Arms in their Hands, and one half of these the best Troops in *Europe*. If we consider them afterwards, at the Approach of a large Army, under a General of great Experience and approved Merit,[6] bending their Course, tho' not in

---

[1] For the landing of the so-called 'seven men of Moidart' and the subsequent narrative of the rebellion, see *History*, above, pp. [35]–73.

[2] The parenthesis seems unduly digressive, even for Parson Adams. Perhaps he alludes, ironically, to the political squabbling within the Pelham ministry, which delayed considerably the latter's call for the units from Flanders. See 'General Introduction', above, pp. xxxi–xxxii.

[3] Edinburgh was entered, bloodlessly but not without some 'Surprize', on 17 September 1745; see Blaikie, *Itinerary*, p. 15. In *History*, above, p. 56, Fielding suggests that Edinburgh was betrayed by some of its officials.

[4] At Prestonpans, 21 September 1745, the first pitched battle of the rebellion. For a supposedly 'eyewitness' account of it, see *History*, above, pp. 63–6.

[5] 'Adams' apparently includes England, Wales, Scotland, and Ireland in this estimate, which even so is a million high. See *Abstract of British Historical Statistics*, ed. B. R. Mitchell (Cambridge, 1962), p. 5, where roughly contemporary estimates round off (in millions) as follows: England and Wales 6.5; Scotland 1.2; Ireland 3.2. *DA* of 26 September 1745 prints a letter which estimates the population 'of this Nation' at 8 million.

[6] George Wade (1673–1748), MP Bath 1722–48, field marshal 1743, had served with distinction in the wars of William III and Marlborough. In the 'Fifteen' he secured Bath, which was jacobite in tendency, for the government and began a long friendship with Ralph Allen, Fielding's friend and benefactor. Wade's Scottish experience included being commander-in-chief there from 1724 to 1740, during which time he built the famous roads and bridges which bear his name. In 1743 he had been made commander-in-chief in Flanders, but was not successful and resigned the command early in 1745. Following the outbreak of the rebellion in that year Wade was put in charge in Scotland once more and, after Cope's defeat at Prestonpans, took command of the 'northern' army in the field. French, p. 277, conjectures that Fielding may have known Wade personally, through Ralph

a direct Line, towards this Army; and then, by long and painful Marches, over almost inaccessible Mountains, through the worst of Roads, in the worst of Seasons; by those means, I say, slipping that Army, and leaving it behind them. If we view them next march on towards another Army still greater, under a young, brave, vigilant, and indefatigable Prince,[1] who were advancing in their Front to meet, as the others were in their Rear to pursue them. If we consider, I say, these Banditti not yet increased to full 6000, and above a third of these old Men and Boys, not to be depended on, proceeding without a Check through a long Track of Country, through many Towns and Cities, which they plundered, at least to a Degree, up within a few Miles of this third Army,[2] sent to oppose them; then, by the Advantage of a dark Night, passing by this Army likewise, and by a most incredible March getting between that and the Metropolis, into which they struck a Terror scarce to be credited. Tho' besides the two Armies at their Heels, there was still one in this very Metropolis infinitely superior to these Rebels, not only in Arms and Discipline, but in Numbers. Who, I say, can consider such Things as these, and retain the least Doubt, whether he shall impute them to a Judgment inflicted on this sinful Nation; especially when in the second Place, we must allow such Judgment to be most undoubtedly our Due.

To run through every Species of Crimes with which our *Sodom* abounds, would fill your whole Paper. Indeed, such monstrous Impieties and Iniquities have I both seen and heard of, within these three last Years,[3]

Allen. The conjecture is strengthened by an unpublished letter from Fielding to James Harris, dated 5 October 1745: 'but I believe as Mr Wade says we must trust to the Troops [the regular units, as opposed to those raised by the Associations] for the Extirpation of the Rebels, wch I doubt not they will be able to perform: for he will have within ten Days no less than 16000 with him.' Fielding may also have written Wade's obituary in *JJ* no. 16 (19 March 1748), p. 463: 'He was besides, in private life, a Gentleman of the highest Honour, Humanity and Generosity, and hath done more good and benevolent Actions than this whole Paper can contain.' Fielding had complimented Wade in his unpublished 'An Epistle to Mr. Lyttelton' (1733); see Isobel M. Grundy, 'New Verse by Henry Fielding', *PMLA*, lxxxvii (1972), 242.

[1] William duke of Cumberland, the king's second son, who had been recalled from Flanders in October to head the regular units being readied to fight the rebels. He arrived in London on 18 October and was appointed commander 'of the Army which is upon its March towards Lancashire' on November 23; *London Gazette* of 15–19 October and 19–23 November 1745. Cumberland took over actual field command from Sir John Ligonier at Lichfield on 27 November.

[2] A slip for 'second'. Wade's and Cumberland's are the only armies that could be said to be 'sent to oppose them'. The 'third' army is properly the one mentioned by 'Adams' in the next sentence. Assembled at Finchley Common and under the command of Lord Stair, it was supposed to defend the metropolis in case the rebels gave the duke the slip and made a march on London. The rebels never came 'within a few Miles' of this third army; they did come that close to Cumberland near Lichfield, before slipping round him to stop at Derby.

[3] Thus dating his fictional 'life' in the world from the publication of *Joseph Andrews*, which appeared on or about 22 February 1742. In the penultimate sentence of his letter 'Adams' refers to his 'four Years Knowledge of the World', a dating which is only two months out.

during my sojourning in what is called the World, particularly the last Winter, while I tarried in the Great City, that while I verily believe we are the silliest Nation under Heaven in every other Light, we are wiser than *Sodom* in Wickedness. If we would avoid, therefore, that final Judgment which was denounced against that City;[1] if we would avoid that total Destruction, with which we are threatned not remotely and at a Distance, but immediately and at hand; if we would pacify that Vengeance which hath already begun to operate by sending Rebels, foreign Enemies, Pestilence the Forerunner of Famine,[2] and Poverty among us; if we would pacify that Vengeance which seems already bent to our Destruction, by breathing the Breath of Folly, as well as Perfidy, into the Nostrils of the Great;[3] what have we to do, but to set about THE WORK recommended by the wise and pious, tho' Heathen Philosopher, in my Motto. And what is THIS WORK, but a thorough Amendment of our Lives, a perfect Alteration of our Ways? But before we begin this, let us, in obedience to the Rule of that Philosopher prescrib'd above, first apply ourselves by Fasting and Prayer to the Throne of offended Grace. My Lords the Bishops have wisely set apart a particular Day for this solemn Service.[4] A Day, which I hope will be kept universally thro' this Kingdom with all those Marks of true Piety and Repentance, which our present dreadful Situation demands.[5] Indeed the Wretch whose hard Heart is not seriously in earnest on this Occasion, deserves no more the Appellation of a good *Englishman*, than of a good Churchman, or a true

[1] Genesis 19: 24: Then the Lord rained upon Sodom and upon Gomorrah brimstone and fire from the Lord out of heaven.

[2] Cf. Psalms 91: 6: Nor for the pestilence that walketh in darkness; nor for the destruction that wasteth at noonday. 'Adams' alludes to the infectious 'distemper' or murrain that was currently raging among the horned cattle. In a similar litany of disasters attendant upon the rebellion Walpole wrote Mann (29 November 1745) that the distemper might possibly have 'fatal consequences', that 'we are not eat milk, butter, beef, nor anything from that species', and that the public rumor was, 'the Papists had empoisoned the pools'; *Yale Walpole*, xix. 174. The pestilence got worse, and on 17 January 1746 the commons considered a bill setting up regulations for preventing the spread of it; on 13 February 1746 the king gave the royal assent; *Journals of Commons*, xxv. 34, and *GM*, xvi (1746), 105. See also *TP* no. 5 (17 December 1745), above, p. 145, and the letter signed 'Rusticus' in the present issue, reprinted in Locke, p. [82].

[3] Alluding to the activities of the opposition under the direction of lords Bath and Granville. See 'General Introduction', above, pp. lxxxiii–lxxxix, and index, *s.v.* 'Opposition'.

[4] 'His Majesty hath been pleased to order a Proclamation for a General Fast to be held on the 18th of December next'; *TP* no. 2 (12 November 1745), below, p. 341. *TP* no. 6 (10 December 1745), below, p. 376, notes that 'We have likewise received a letter, or rather Sermon, on the ensuing Fast, from our Old Friend Mr. Abraham Adams.'

[5] On 18 December the Lords went to St Peter's, Westminster, to hear a sermon by Dr Lisle, the bishop of St Asaph; the Commons went to St Margaret's, Westminster, to hear Dr Newton, rector of St Mary-le-Bow. Both preachers spoke on the text from Revelations 2: 5: Remember therefore whence thou art fallen and repent; *GM*, xv (1745), 666. Locke, p. 86, suggests that Fielding 'must have had advance knowledge of the text to be used in the services', but the emphasis on 'Repentance' is surely commonplace.

Christian. All sober and wise Nations have, in Times of public Danger, instituted certain solemn Sacrifices to their Gods; now the Christian Sacrifices are those of Fasting and Prayer; and if ever these were in a more extraordinary manner necessary, it is surely now, when the least Reflection must convince us that we do in so eminent a Manner deserve the Judgment of God, and when we have so much Reason to apprehend it is coming upon us. I hope therefore, (I repeat it once more) that this Day will be kept by us ALL, in the most solemn Manner, and that not a Man will dare refuse complying with those Duties which the State requires of us: But I must, at the same Time, recommend to my Countrymen a Caution, that they would not mistake THE WORK itself for what is only the Beginning of, or Preface to it. Let them not vainly imagine, that when they have fasted and prayed for a Day; nay, even for an Age, that THE WORK is done. It is a total Amendment of Life, a total Change of Manners, which can bring THE WORK to a Conclusion, or produce any good Effects from it. Here again, to give particular Instances would be to enumerate all those Vices which I have already declin'd recounting, and would be too prolix. They are known, they are obvious; and few Men who resolve to amend their Lives, will, I believe, want any Assistance to discover what Parts of them stand in need of Amendment. I shall, however, point at two or three Particulars, which I the rather single out, because I have heard, that there are some who dispute whether they are really Vices or no, tho' every Polity as well as the Christian have agreed in condemning them as such. The first of these is Lying. The Devil himself is, in Scripture, said to be the Father of Lies;[1] and Liars are perhaps some of the vilest and wickedest Children he has. Nay, I think the Morals of all civilized Nations have denied even the Character of a Gentleman to a Liar. So heinous is this Vice, that it has not only stigmatized particular Persons, but whole Communities with Infamy. And yet have we not Persons, ay, and very great Persons too, so famous for it, that their Credit is a Jest, and their Words mere Wind?[2] I need not point them out, for they take sufficient Care to point out themselves. Luxury is a second Vice, which is so far from being acknowledged as criminal, that it is ostentatiously affected.[3] Now this is not only a Vice in itself, but it is in reality a Privation of all Virtue. For

---

[1] John 8: 44.

[2] Cf. Job 6: 26: Do ye imagine to reprove words, and the speeches of one that is desperate, which are as wind? There may be a covert allusion here to the supposed machinations of the Bath–Granville opposition.

[3] For Fielding on the *topos* of 'Luxury', see his *Charge Delivered to the Grand Jury* (1749), pp. 51–4; *Enquiry into the Causes of the late Increase of Robbers* (1751), pp. xi–xii, and sects. i–iii, pp. 3–30; also the index to the present volume, *s.v.*

first, in lower Fortunes it prevents Men from being honest; and, in higher Situations, it excludes that Virtue without which no Man can be a Christian, namely Charity. For as surely as Charity covereth a Multitude of Sins, so must a Multitude of Dishes, Pictures, Jewels, Houses, Horses, Servants, &c. cover all Charity. I remember Dining last Winter at a great Man's Table, where we had among many others one Dish, the Expence of which would have provided very liberally for a poor Family a whole Twelvemonth.[1] In short, I never saw, during my Abode in the Great City, a single Man who gave me Reason to think, that he would have enabled himself to be charitable, by retrenching the most idle Superfluity of his Expence. Perhaps the large Subscriptions which have prevailed all over the Kingdom at this Season, may be urged as an Instance of Charity. To this I answer, in the Words of a very great and generous Friend of mine, who disclaim'd all Merit from a very liberal Subscription, saying, "It was rather Sense than Goodness, to sacrifice a small Part for the Security of the Whole."[2] Now true Charity is of another Kind, it has no self-interested Motives, pursues no immediate Return nor worldly Good, well knowing that it is laying up a much surer and much greater Reward for itself. But, indeed, who wonders that Men are so backward in sacrificing any of their Wealth to their Consciences, who before had sacrificed their Consciences to the Acquisition of that very Wealth? Can we expect to find Charity in an Age, when scarce Any refuse to own the most profligate Rapaciousness? When no Man is ashamed of avowing the Pursuit of Riches through every dirty Road and Track? To speak out, in an Age when every thing is venal; and when there is scarce one among the Mighty who would not be equally ashamed at being thought not to set *some Price* on himself,[3] as he would at being imagin'd to set too low a one. This is an Assertion whose Truth is too well known. Indeed, my four Years Knowledge of the World hath scarce furnished me with Examples of any other Kind. I believe I have already exceeded my Portion of Hour-Glass; I shall therefore reserve what I have farther to say on this Subject to some other Opportunity.[4]

I am, &c.

Abraham Adams.

---

[1] Details, including place settings, of such an extravagant meal are provided by Romney Sedgwick, 'The Duke of Newcastle's Cook', *History Today*, v (1935), 308–16.

[2] Not identified. The quality of modest generosity suggests Ralph Allen, but perhaps there is no need to seek an 'original'.

[3] The 'every man has his price' *sententia* was and is commonly attributed to Sir Robert Walpole, often, it is held, by Fielding himself. Such an attribution traditionally assumes that the sentiment reflects more on its supposed author than on his times. It is worth noting that in describing the 'venal' age 'Adams' here reverses that emphasis and in fact does not raise the question of authorship at all. For the Walpole association, see *TP* no. 17 (18–25 February 1746), below, p. 223, and Locke, p. 157.

[4] See *TP* no. 13 (21–8 January 1746), below, pp. 201–7.

Quidque agat ignarus, stupet: et nec Fræna remittit,
Nec retinere valet ——.

OVID, *Metamorphoses*.[2]

I have often thought it one of the best Arguments to prove Man a Social Animal, that Nature hath severally endow'd us with Talents so different from each other. Men, indeed, in this Light, seem as regularly designed to form a Society, as the several Parts of a Machine to compose the whole.

This Variety in the human Capacity, is too obvious to have escaped the Notice of any one who hath ever reflected on his own Species. In some this Intention of Nature is so apparent, and the Disposition to this or that Purpose is so strong, that they may be said to be born Mathematicians, Poets, Painters, &c.

It is a trite Observation on this Head, that Nature very seldom bestows two or more of these Talents, in any Degree of Perfection, on the same Person: And tho' perhaps Instances may be found, where she hath given almost every one of them to a single Man, yet such are extremely rare; and may be either imputed to that Wantonness which she hath been noted sometimes to exert in all her Works; or perhaps more justly to an Intention of forming some very great Character, such as *Homer*, who appears to have (at least) known the Principles of every Art and Science which were discovered in his Time.[3]

---

[1] French, pp. 291–2, suggests, plausibly, that the aim of this leader is to urge the inclusion of Pitt in the Pelham administration. During November 1745 negotiations to this end were carried on between Hardwicke, Harrington, Newcastle, and Pelham, for the 'old' ministry, and Gower, Bedford, and (less forcibly) Cobham, for the 'new' allies; Basil Williams, *Life of William Pitt* (London, 1913), ii. 141–3; Owen, *Rise of the Pelhams*, pp. 289–92. Pitt, who in Walpole's words was 'ravenous for the place of secretary of war' (to Mann, 22 November 1745, *Yale Walpole*, xix. 168), was clearly impatient at the Pelhams' failure to carry their point against the king and Granville. In December 1745 Pitt opposed employment of the Hessians, and there are signs that contemporaries viewed him as politically volatile. From Ireland Chesterfield wrote Newcastle, 11 January 1746: 'I am astonished and grieved at the unaccountable conduct of Pitt; who I hear (but I don't know whether it is true) is reconnected with Young Master [the Prince of Wales]. And by your letter Young Master seems to announce opposition'; *Letters of Philip Dormer Stanhope, 4th Earl of Chesterfield*, ed. Bonamy Dobrée (London, 1932), iii. 717–18. Also Lodge, *Private Correspondence of Chesterfield and Newcastle 1744–46* (London, 1930), p. 100. For Pitt and Fielding and the residuals of the old 'patriot' opposition, see 'General Introduction', above, pp. lxxxv–lxxxvii.

[2] *Metamorphoses*, ii. 191–2: 'Dazed, he knows not what to do; he neither lets go the reins nor can he hold them' (Loeb). The lines describe Phaeton as he looks down from the apogee of his celestial journey.

[3] The tradition of Homer's learning is widespread, but given the explicit reference later in this leader, Fielding may have been put in mind of it by Sir William Temple, whose 'Of Poetry' asserts of Homer that 'the greatest Masters have found in his Works the best and truest Principles of all their Sciences or Arts'; *Works*, 2nd ed. (London, 1731), i. 237. See also *Joseph Andrews*, III. ii. 197; *Tom Jones*, IX. i. 492, and XIV. i. 740, where Homer is said to have been master of 'all the Learning' of his time. Baker, item no. 487, lists a 1693 edition of Temple's *Miscellanies* among Fielding's books.

But there is a second Observation which occurs to me, and which I do not remember to have met with, tho' it is the most evident Proof of this original Designation. I mean the consummate Wisdom with which these Talents are proportion'd, and distributed according to their Usefulness in Society: For as the laborious and servile Offices are much the more numerous, so the greater Part of Mankind are born with no other Capacity than what fits them for Labour. *Aristotle* in his Politics rightly stiles them, ὀργάνα ἔμψυχα[1] *animated Organs or Instruments*. In like manner we see Talents in the next Degrees distributed more liberally by Nature, than when we come to the highest and greatest Offices; for which it is sufficient, that a very few only at one Time should be qualified, whereas Society hath a larger Demand for the others. Sir *William Temple* accordingly remarks, That the World hath produced a thousand *Alexanders* to one *Homer*.[2] Indeed there are no Characters which are so seldom seen in their highest Perfection, as a great Poet, Lawgiver, and Statesman; as correcting the Morals, reforming the Laws, or regulating the Government of a Nation, are Works which as they demand the highest Talents, require but very few Persons.

If Men therefore be formed with those various Talents, severally disposed for the Purposes of Society, it follows that Society can never exist in a perfect and natural State, but when its several Members have those Offices alotted them, in this great Political Machine, for which they are formed and destin'd by Nature. A Republic, where the contrary Method is observed, may be considered as a Clock with its Wheels displaced, the greater Movements being put in the Room of those which are nicer and finer, in which Case the Clock would be unable to perform its Functions.

The very Imagination of such a Clock may appear absurd and impossible to some, who would not be equally shocked by this improper Disposition of the Members in a Commonwealth.

Let us, however, for Argument sake, suppose a Man in Possession of the Clock above described. It is certain, tho' he wind it up never so carefully, tho' he oyl every Part of it, tho' the Weights be never so exactly adapted, yet while the Wheels remain out of their proper Places, the Clock cannot perform its Operation. What will the Man then do, if he have any Understanding? Will he sit down, lament his Fortune, and

---

[1] *Politics*, I. ii. 4 (1253b. 29), where the accepted text reads ὀργάνων for Fielding's ὀργάνα.

[2] In *Champion* of 27 November 1739, i. 134, Fielding had also attributed the Homer–Alexander ratio to Temple, but in fact the latter is not so precise about the identities: 'I know not whether . . . for one Man that is born capable of making such a Poet as *Homer* or *Virgil*, there may not be a Thousand born capable of making as Great Generals of Armies or Ministers of State, as any the most Renowned in Story'; 'Of Poetry', ed. cit., i. 238.

curse his Stars? Will he spend his whole Time in adjusting the Pendulum, or his *whole Fortune* in buying Oyl? Would he not rather send for a judicious Clock-maker, who would immediately see where the Fault lay, and by replacing every Thing in its proper Order, would soon enable the Machine to perform its Functions in a regular Manner.

I believe no one will deny, but that sufficient Examples may be found in History of this disorderly and improper Collocation of the Members of a Commonwealth. And here the same Consequence will follow, with this Difference only, that as the Public is not reduced, like the Machine above described, to a State of Rest; but still goes on in a violent, tho' an irregular Motion, it will, by that Means, be in Danger of absolute Destruction.

I have always considered the Story of *Phaeton*, in the *Metamorphoses*, as a fine Fable, by which this Truth is meant to be illustrated. There are many beautiful Passages which may be applied to Men who affect,

> —— *Quæ non viribus istis*
> *Munera conveniunt*.[1]

The Historian *Livy*, before he recounts any Action, gives us so just a Detail of all the Circumstances that preceded and produced it, that it requires no extraordinary Penetration in his Reader to foresee the future Consequence. A little before he relates the Destruction of *Capua*, he hath these Words: *In magistratu autem erat, qui indignitate sua vim ac jus magistratui, quem gerebat demsisset*.[2] "There was a Person in Power, who had not thence derived any Honours to himself, but, by his weak Administration, had strip'd the Magistracy of all its Force and Authority." The Name of this Man was *Seppius Lesius*, whose Mother was (it seems) a better Politician than himself: For upon hearing it prophecy'd, that her Son should hereafter be at the Head of Affairs at *Capua*, she, who knew the Genius of the Lad, had Sense enough immediately to foretel the Ruin of her Country.[3]

Indeed all History is a kind of Comment on the Truth I have before

[1] *Metamorphoses*, ii. 54–5: 'rewards which do not befit thy powers'. The lines form part of Phoebus's speech to Phaeton after the latter has requested permission to drive the sun chariot for a day. Fielding makes the same quotation in *Amelia*, i. ii. 20.

[2] Derived from *Historia*, XXVI. xii. 8, where the full accepted text reads: 'In magistratu erat qui non sibi honorem adiecisset, sed indignitate sua vim ac ius magistratui quem gerebat dempsisset.' Although Fielding's Latin omits *non sibi honorem adiecisset, sed*, his translation presumes the presence of these words. See also *Amelia*, XI. ii. 462, where Dr Harrison makes a more generalized, but similar point, and attributes it to Livy.

[3] According to Livy, *Historia*, XXVI. vi. 13, Seppius Lesius (Loesius) was indeed the *medix tuticus*, or highest ranking magistrate, among the Campanians. The anecdote of his mother's prediction is in vi. 14–15. Fielding alludes to Livy's account of Capua just before its destruction, in *Amelia*, XI. ii. 462.

asserted. For, as the great Cardinal *Richlieu* maintain'd, Fortune or blind Chance doth not interfere so much in the great Affairs of this World, as her complaisant Votaries the Fools would persuade us.[1] What we call ill Luck, is generally ill Conduct. Generals and Ministers, who destroy their own Armies and Countries, and then lay the Blame on Fortune, talk as absurdly as the passionate bad Player at Chess, who swore he had lost the Game by one d—n'd unlucky Move, which exposed the King to Cheque-mate.[2] When the Machine is rightly made up, when all its Members are disposed in their due Order, it is then only capable of performing its regular Functions. When, on the contrary, every Thing is displaced, and all its Parts improperly ranged, it must either rust in a State of Inaction; or, if put into Motion, must soon run on to its own Dissolution.

And here it may not be improper to mention some of those Talents, which ought to constitute the principal Wheels of this our Political Machine.

I believe it will not be contended, but that a sound Judgment is one necessary Qualification for Offices of high Importance in every Government. Indeed a Man who is visibly defective in this Faculty, will be hardly allowed capable of undertaking any Trust, in the Execution of which he is not to be under the immediate Controul and Direction of some abler Person than himself. And yet, however necessary this Power may be, which is no other than the Distinction of Right from Wrong; or as Mr. *Lock* hath more accurately describ'd it, "The separating carefully Ideas wherein can be found the least Difference, thereby to avoid being misled by Similitude, and by Affinity to take one Thing for another."[3] Yet if we examine the Actions of Men, we shall not be apt to conclude, that Nature hath been over liberal of Judgment among us.

But this is not enough, he must have Sagacity likewise; this, says the

---

[1] Not located. In *Champion* of 6 December 1739, i. 64, it is said of Richelieu 'that it is well known he struck the Word *unfortunate* out of his Dictionary, affirming that every Man succeeded well or ill, according as his Conduct was right or wrong'. The *Champion* reference may derive from Pierre Bayle, *Dictionary*, v. 372–3, *s.n.* 'Timoleon', where it is stated that Richelieu held that 'imprudent' and 'unfortunate' are two words for the same thing. Bayle's note (Remark L) appears to credit 'this Particular' to Antoine Aubery, *L'Histoire du cardinal Mazarin* (Paris, 1688), i. 100, and goes on to quote from Richelieu's so-called 'Political Testament', but nothing in that work quite fits Fielding's sentence here. *Spectator* no. 293 (5 February 1712), iii. 42–3, appears to derive the saying from Bayle, without the detail of the *Dictionary*.

[2] Cf. *Amelia*, i. i. 16, where to blame Fortune in life is said to be as absurd as to blame bad luck in chess. However, Fielding's view of the matter may not have been consistent. In *Champion* of 6 December 1739, i. 64, he writes, 'Human Life appears to me to resemble the Game of *Hazard*, much more than that of Chess.' For more on the *topos*, see *Tom Jones*, XIV. viii. 770–1.

[3] Quoted somewhat inexactly from *Essay concerning Human Understanding* (1690), II. xi. 2, where Locke is defining 'Judgment'. Cf. *Tom Jones*, IX. i. 491.

last-mention'd Philosopher, is "A Quickness in the Mind to find out those intermediate Ideas, that discover the Agreement or Disagreement of any other, and to apply them right."[1] Now to adapt this to Politics. 'Tis by this that a Minister having found the Interest of Princes, will be equally Master of their Designs, and consequently enabled to obviate and circumvent them. In the same Manner a General will foresee the Stratagems of his Enemy. He does not want to be told that Cannon hath been carried to this Place, or an Ambuscade laid in that. It is sufficient that he knows they are proper for such Purposes; nor can he be deceived by every Feint of the Enemy, for Sagacity hath already acquainted him with the March or Action which he will certainly undertake. Of this we have a pregnant Instance in the Great Duke of *Marlborough*, who discovered the Designs of *Charles* XII. by observing the Attention with which he surveyed a Map of *Russia*.[2]

This Sagacity is above defined to be a *Quickness* of the Mind, without which Quality it would be of little Use. Our Adversaries will not allow the Time which a Blockhead requires to inspect their Actions. And After-thoughts are but of little Service to the Politician.

King *Augustus* recollected, that he had the King of *Sweden* in his Power after he was again out of it; and, as a General of the latter observed, held a Council to Day, to consider what he should have done Yesterday.[3] This Slowness of Penetration is as properly Stupidity as Slowness of Recollection, to which the Author whom I have already twice cited

---

[1] Op. cit., iv. ii. 3, where Locke is defining 'Sagacity'.

[2] The episode is found in Voltaire, *The History of Charles XII*, 2nd ed. (London 1732), p. 145: 'He [Marlborough] mentioned the Czar to him [Charles XII], and took Notice that his Eyes always kindled at his Name, notwithstanding the Moderation of the Conference; and he farther remarked, that a Map of *Muscovy* lay before him on the Table. He wanted no more to determine him in his Judgment, that the real Design of the King of *Sweden*, and his sole Ambition, were to dethrone the Czar, as he had already done the King of *Poland*.' Marlborough had been sent by Queen Anne as ambassador to Charles XII, to sound out the latter's intentions with respect to European affairs. The episode does not appear in Gustavus Adlerfeld's history of Charles XII, nor in the French translation of his father's work by C. M. E. Adlerfeld, nor in the English translation of the latter (1740), which Fielding seems to have had some sort of hand in. See Cross, i. 285–7, for Fielding and Adlerfeld. That Fielding was acquainted with the Voltaire translation seems clear from the 'Prolegomena' to *The Covent-Garden Tragedy* (1732), where he prints a letter supposed to be from 'some fine Gentleman, who plays the Critick for his Diversion' (p. [1], A2ʳ), in which the latter boasts that he has read 'several Pages in *The History of the King of Sweden*, which is translated into *English*' (p. [2], A2ᵛ). Noted by Locke, p. 94, in her edition.

[3] Augustus II (1670–1733), elective king of Poland 1697 and, as Frederick Augustus I, Elector of Saxony 1694, was defeated for a last time by Charles XII at Fraustadt in 1706 and resigned the throne. While on his way to Russia Charles paid an unarmed and unplanned visit to Augustus at Dresden and, after several hours spent in touring the fortifications and conversing with various of Augustus's court, rode away again to join his own forces. On the day after Charles had left, Augustus held the council here referred to, which elicited the remark, attributed by Voltaire, *History of Charles XII*, 2nd ed., book iii, p. 153, to Renchild (Rheinschild), one of Charles's generals. Adlerfeld, *Military History of Charles XII* (London, 1740), ii. 361 *n.*, attributes the remark to Baron Stralenheim, the Swedish Ambassador to the Court of Vienna.

assigns that Name, and says, "That he who, thro' this Default in his Memory, has not the Ideas that are really preserved there, ready at hand, when Need and Occasion calls for them, had almost as good be without them quite, since they serve him to little Purpose. The dull Man, who loses the Opportunity, whilst he is seeking in his Mind for those Ideas which should serve his Turn, is not much more happy in his Knowledge than one that is perfectly ignorant."[1]

These are the two principal Qualifications of a Statesman, without which it is a Phaetontic Rashness and Folly in any Person to aspire to that Office. There are other Qualities requisite; but Persons who have the two former, are seldom without them. Such as Alertness, for nothing assures Success so certain as Dispatch; Delays are always dangerous, and have defeated the greatest Designs. Steadiness is another Ingredient, without which no one is qualified to conduct any Business whatever. But indeed this naturally results from Judgment and Sagacity. For those who lay their Schemes on certain Foundations, are seldom likely to alter them, unless the Measures on which they are founded be themselves altered. On the contrary, where Men, for want of sure and sound Judgment, fluctuate every Hour in their Opinions, they must be subject to the same Mutabilities in their Conduct. Such Men give Orders to Day, contradict them to morrow, and renew them the next Day; the sure Consequence of which is, that they seldom do any thing right, and very often effect nothing at all.

As I cannot be supposed to have Room here for such a Picture at full length, I must leave out some Features, which my Readers Imagination will easily supply; such as Knowledge, &c. As to the Qualities of the Heart, the better and nobler they are in our Statesman, the greater Certainty will the People have for his upright Conduct; but, in reality, it can so rarely be the Interest of a Great Man to injure his Country, that our Apprehensions of that kind are often chimerical. Of this I am sure, that if we allow a Rogue may possibly, in some Situations, ruin his Country, we must grant that a Fool will do it in all. I have avoided making any Applications, during the Course of this Paper; I shall conclude with this General One, That if we have any Abilities left in this Country, I hope they will be now employ'd in those Stations to which they are adapted, since our present Situation requires their utmost and immediate Assistance. If we have a Man among us blest with all the Talents I have before described, (and such I know we have) GOD forbid that Pique, Envy, Jealousy, or any other Motive, should be able to exclude him from the Capacity of serving, I will say SAVING his Country.

[1] Locke, op. cit., II. x. 8.

Tuesday, December 31, 1745.   Numb. 9.

Non hoc ista sibi tempus spectacula poscit.

Virgil.[1]

The following Letter came attended with a small present of *Bologna* Sausages,[2] *Naples* Soap, *Florence* Oyl, and a Paper of Maccaroni.

Signior Sar,

"Me be inform, dat you be de Patriat, dat is to say, van Parson who take Part vor de Muny;[3] now, Sar, dat be Comodity me did forget to bring over vid me: But ven me ave got one two tousand Pound me sal send you sum;[4] me desire, darefor, dat you woud rite sumting to recomend de Opera, or begar me sal be oblige to go back to *Italy* like one Fool as me did cum,[5] and dey will laff at me for bring no Muny from an Country vich ave give so much Muny for Song.

Me be, Signior Sar,
Of Your Excellence, de most umble Sclave,

Giovani Cantilena.[6]

[1] *Aeneid*, vi. 37: 'Not sights like these does this hour demand!' (Loeb). Spoken by Deiphobe the Sibyl, daughter of Glaucus and priestess of Apollo and Hecate, to Aeneas, who has just come to the temple of Apollo at Cumae and is musing over its pictured gates. The Sibyl admonishes him to get on with the necessary prayers and sacrifices.

[2] Apparently delicacies of some rarity in England. Cf. *Tom Jones*, I. i. 32: 'In reality, true Nature is as difficult to be met with in Authors, as the *Bayonne* Ham or *Bologna* Sausage is to be found in the Shops.' See also the letter signed 'Heliogabalus' in *TP* no. 5 (3 December 1745), below, pp. 367–8, where 'Bologna Sausages' are listed among the delicacies not normally relished by the 'lowest Vulgar'.

[3] That is, who takes sides for money. The implied distinction between this sort of patriot and the 'true' patriot hits at those members of the formerly 'patriot' opposition who continue to oppose because they are not all included in the broad bottom—whose politics, in other words, are based not on patriotism, but on 'Muny'. Cf. *TP* no. 4 (26 November 1745), above, pp. 136–41.

[4] The basic contract for principal singers was probably about £1,000 and could be hugely supplemented by gifts at their benefits. In 1730 Senesino had been paid 1,400 guineas. What was paid by contract to Farinelli, who was even more popular, is not known, but it was estimated that the gifts at his benefit on 15 March 1735 would reach £2,000; *DA* of 22 March 1735. The basic annual salary roll for the singers as a group probably came to somewhat more than £4,000, although a defensive letter in *General Advertiser* of 4 January 1746 claims only £2,000 is 'carried out of the Kingdom'. See Deutsch, *Handel*, pp. 246, 258, 520–1; *London Stage*, Part 3: *1729–1747*, vol. i, pp. lxxi–lxxii.

[5] Not identified. However, *DA* of 24 September 1745 noted that 'Several Italian Singers arriv'd in Town on Saturday, having been hir'd at Venice and other Parts of Italy, to sing at the Operas in the Hay-Market this Winter.' Given the strong sentiment against the opera, as well as the doubtful financing of it, some defections must have occurred among those singers who did not believe the season would ever come to pass.

[6] A cantilena was the principal melody or 'air' in any composition. Charles Burney, *A General History of Music* (London, 1789), III. ii. 165, states that 'modern' composers gave the principal melody to the soprano or else the highest part. Fielding is attacking the popularity of the *castrati* or 'foreign Eunuchs'; see *TP* no. 13 (21–8 January 1746), below, p. 202; also no. 25 (15–22 April 1746), below, p. 269.

Though I by no means admit that Character of Patriotism which the Signior hath conceived, whether in *Italy* or *England* I will not determine, yet as I think it one Part of Integrity to dare oppose popular Clamour, I shall, in compliance with my good Friend, and in return for his kind Present, offer such Thoughts as occur to me in favour of a Diversion, against which so much Disgust seems to prevail at this Season.[1]

And in the first Place, I think it should be consider'd, that these poor *Italians*, whose Property is their Throats, did not come over of their own Accord; but were invited hither. Nor is the Rebellion a sufficient Excuse to send them back unrewarded, since the Poverty and Distress of this Nation, even before this Rebellion, occasioned by Debts, Wars, and almost every Public Calamity, must have deterred any Persons from such an Undertaking, who had not resolved to have an Opera at any Rate, and in any Situation.

But perhaps this melancholy Situation of our Affairs was a principal Reason for the Introduction of this Opera. Is any thing more proper to soften and compose the Mind in Misfortunes than Music? Hath it not always been found the most effectual Remedy in Grief? And was accordingly used as such by the Great *Nero*, to calm and compose the Agonies of his Mind, while his own City was in Flames;[2] and *Homer* informs us, that *Achilles* used to assuage the Wrath and Impetuosity of his Temper by the Music which old *Chiron* had taught him.[3] Nay, it hath been prescribed, by Physicians, as a Medicine for a diseased Mind; and we are told by *Josephus*, that "When *Saul* was agitated with Fits, like a Dæmoniac, his *Physicians not being able to give any natural or philosophical Account of the Distemper*, only advised the having some body about him

---

[1] Cf. *General Advertiser* of 4 January 1746: 'It being found that a Cabal was forming against Operas, under the Mask of publick Virtue, by Persons who have an Interest in opposing it; three Letters have been published in the *Daily Advertiser* ... But how have they been answer'd? Only with random Assertions, with Ridicule, or with Falsities.' See also *TP* no. 13 (21–8 January 1746), below, p. 202.

[2] A curious departure from the classical accounts, none of which attributes 'Agonies' to Nero. Suetonius, *Lives of the Caesars*, vi ('Nero'). xxxviii. 2, describes Nero as exulting in the beauty of the flames while singing a song of his own composition; Tacitus, *Annales*, xv. xxxix, mentions a report that 'at the very moment when Rome was aflame, he had mounted his private stage, and, typifying the ills of the present by the calamities of the past, had sung the destruction of Troy' (Loeb). Dio Cassius, *Roman History*, lxii. 18, reports similarly.

[3] *Iliad*, ix. 186–9, does not really sound the note of anger. Achilles, who is sulking in his tent when visited by Agamemnon's delegates, is described as 'delighting his soul with a clear-toned lyre' (Loeb). Locke, p. 102, notes that Pope's emphasis is closer to Fielding's: 'With this he soothes his angry Soul, and sings | Th'immortal Deeds of Heroes and of Kings' (*Iliad*, ix. 249–50). The identification of Chiron as Achilles' music teacher is not in Homer. Indeed the association of Chiron with music is a post-Homeric tradition. Locke, p. 102, suggests that Fielding's direct source for the entire example was Plutarch, *Moralia*, 1145 ('De Musica'), sec. 40: 'The employment of music that is fitting for a man may be learned from our noble Homer. To show that music is useful in many circumstances he gives us Achilles in the poem digesting his anger against Agamemnon by means of music, which he learned from the most wise Cheiron' (Loeb). Plutarch next quotes *Iliad*, ix. 186–9.

that could sing or play upon the Harp well, that might be ready at hand to give him the Diversion of an Hymn or an Air. This Advice was taken, and *David* sent for, who by his Voice and Harp cured the Patient."[1]

The great Power over the Passions, which the ancient Philosophers assigned to Music, is almost too well known to be mention'd. *Socrates* learned to sing, in his old Age.[2] *Plato* had so high an Opinion of Music, that he considered the Application of it to Amusement only, as a high Perversion of its Institution; for he imagin'd it given by the Gods to Men for much more divine and noble Purposes.[3] And *Pythagoras* (to mention no more) is known to have held, that Virtue, Peace, Health, and all other good Things, was nothing but Harmony.[4] Hence perhaps arose that Notion maintain'd by some of the *Greeks*, from observing the Sympathy between them, that the Soul of Man was something very like the Sound of a Fiddle.[5]

And this Power Music is not only capable of exercising to allay and compose, it is altogether as efficacious in rousing and animating the Passions. Thus *Xenophantus* is recorded to have incited *Alexander* to Arms with his Music.[6] And *Plutarch*, in his Laconic Apophthegms, tells us,

---

[1] Paraphrased and somewhat condensed from *Jewish Antiquities*, vi. 166–7 (viii. 2).

[2] The classical tradition stresses the instrumental, not the vocal aspects of Socrates' late musicality. In *Phaedo*, 4 (60–2), Socrates says that he took up verse writing while imprisoned, in response to a recurrent dream telling him to 'make music and work at it'. In *Euthydemus*, 272, responding to Crito's question, whether he be too old to learn disputation, Socrates denies he is, but adds: 'The only thing I am afraid of is that I may bring the same disgrace upon our two visitors as upon Connus, son of Metrobius, the harper, who is still trying to teach me the harp; so that the boys who go to his lessons with me make fun of me and call Connus "the gaffer's master"' (Loeb). In *Menexenus*, 235 E, Socrates again identifies Connus as his music teacher. Cf. also Cicero, *De Senectute*, viii. 26, which mentions Socrates on the lyre.

[3] Cf. *Laws*, ii, especially 653–5: 'Most people, however, assert that the value of music consists in its power of affording pleasure to the soul. But such an assertion is quite intolerable, and it is blasphemy even to utter it' (Loeb). According to Plato the divine and noble purposes were those of educating for the elevation of the public morals. Cf. also *Republic*, iii. 401–2.

[4] Given the earlier uses of Plutarch in this leader, probably *Moralia*, 1147 ('De Musica'): 'But in fact, my friends, the greatest consideration, one that particularly reveals music as most worthy of all reverence, has been omitted. It is that the revolution of the universe and the courses of the stars are said by Pythagoras, Archytas, Plato and the rest of the ancient philosophers not to come into being or to be maintained without the influence of music; for they assert that God has shaped all things in a framework based on harmony' (Loeb). See also Diogenes Laertius, *Lives of Eminent Philosophers*, viii ('Pythagoras'), 29, on the ratios of harmony.

[5] See Plato, *Phaedo*, 86, 92, where the soul is likened to a 'harmony made up of the elements that are strung like harpstrings in the body' (Loeb). In his 'Preface' to the *Increase of Robbers* (1751) Fielding cites *Phaedo* as the source of the notion that harmony in the soul results from κρᾶσις 'or composition of the parts of the body, when these were properly tempered together; as harmony doth from the proper composition of the several parts in a well-tuned instrument' (p. vi). The term κρᾶσις occurs in *Phaedo* 86 c.

[6] See Seneca, *De Ira*, II. ii. 6, where it is said that a song from Xenophantes would make Alexander take his sword in hand. The power of exciting martial reactions in Alexander is also credited to Antigenides (Plutarch, 'De Alexandri magni fortuna . . .', *Moralia*, 335 A), and Timotheus (Dio Chrysostom, 'First Discourse on Kingship', 1–2). For Xenophantes, see Plutarch, *Lives* ('Demetrius'), liii. 3.

that *Agesilaus* being asked why the *Spartans* marched (or rather danced) up to the Enemy to some Tune, answer'd, that Music discovered the brave Man from the Coward: For those same Notes which made the Eyes of the Valiant sparkle with Fire, overspread the timorous Face with Paleness, and every other Mark of Terror.[1]

This, therefore, is a second good Reason for an Opera at present, provided the Music be properly adapted to the Times, be chiefly martial, and consist mostly of Trumpets and Kettle-Drums. The Subject likewise of the Drama (tho' that is generally considered as a Matter of little Consequence in those Compositions) may lend some Assistance; as suppose, for Instance, the famous Opera in which the celebrated *Nicolini* formerly killed a Lion with so much Bravery, should be revived on this Occasion.[2] Such an Example would almost animate the Ladies, nay, even the Beaus, to take up Arms in defence of their Country.

And what are the Objections which our anti-musical Enemies make to this Entertainment?

First, I apprehend it hath been said, that the Softness of *Italian* Music is calculated to enervate the Mind. This hath been obviated already: But admitting the Objection true, where is its Validity, when we consider of what Persons the Audiences will be composed? For not only the common Soldiers, but all inferior Officers, are excluded by the Price.[3] Indeed the Audience at an Opera consists chiefly of fine Gentlemen, fine Ladies, and their Servants, and except a few General Officers, whose Courage we ought to imagine superior to the Power of a languishing Air, scarce a Person is ever present, who is likely to see a Camp, or handle a Musquet; unless the Opera, by being regulated as above, should inspire a martial Spirit into them.

Secondly, it is said, that the immoderate Expence of this Diversion, at

---

[1] *Apophthegmata Laconica*, *s.n.* 'Agesilaus', xxxv (211 A). Up to the colon in his rendering Fielding is paraphrasing somewhat freely; after the colon he goes beyond the laconic Plutarch to gloss the apophthegm, which may be translated, 'When everybody moves in cadence, it may be known who is brave and who a coward.' Agesilaus (444–360 BC) succeeded to the throne of Sparta in 399 and to the command in Asia Minor in 394.

[2] The opera was *Hydaspes* (*L'Idaspe fedele*) by Francesco Mancini, libretto probably by Giovanni Candi. It premiered in England at the Queen's (Haymarket) on 23 March 1710, and by the next season was one of the most popular operas in the repertory. It was also one of the first to be sung in England wholly in Italian. Nicolini (Nicola Grimaldi, 1673–1732) had come to England in 1708 and was soon popular. According to *Spectator* no. 314 (29 February 1712), ii. 415, Nicolini's first appearance roused the 'Trunkmaker' in the upper gallery to demolish 'three Benches in the Fury of his Applause'. The realism with which he strangled the 'lion' was widely celebrated. See *Spectator* no. 13 (15 March 1711), i. 55–9, and *nn*; Burney, *A General History of Music*, iv. 207–9, 212–13; *London Stage*, Part 2: *1700–1729*, vol. i, p. cvi.

[3] According to *DA* of 8 January 1746 the price of tickets to the first opera, Gluck's *La Caduta de Giganti*, was half a guinea each, the gallery seats being five shillings.

a Season when Poverty spreads its black Banner over the whole Nation, and when much the greater Part are reduced to the most miserable Degrees of Want and Necessity, is an Argument of most abandoned Extravagance, and indecent Profligacy, scarce to be equalled by any Example in History.

This, I conceive, is the Objection on which our Adversaries principally rely. I shall apply myself, therefore, in a very particular Manner, to answer it.

And here I must premise, that this Objection proceeds on a tacit Admission of what is by no means true, *viz.* That the Sums expended on an Opera Subscription would otherwise be employed in the Public Service of the Nation, or at least in private Charity, to some of the numberless Objects of it.

But this would certainly not be the Case: For the Person who could think of promoting such a Diversion, in the midst of so much Calamity, must have neither Heart nor Head good enough to feel the Distresses of a Fellow-Creature, much less to relieve them; and surely it cannot be supposed, that these People will advance any thing in Defence of his Majesty, when they fly in his sacred Face, by attempting an Opera, tho' he hath himself, (or I am grossly misinformed) been pleased to declare, It is not now a Time for Operas.[1]

We must therefore conclude, that this Money, if not exhausted for the present good Purpose, would either remain dormant in the Purse of its Owner, or would otherwise be sacrificed at Cards, or lavished on some less innocent Article of Luxury or Wantonness.

The Expence then of this Entertainment, however great it should be, will not injure the Public. On the contrary, such will be its Political Utility, that I question whether this Opera may not preserve the Nation.

For, in the first Place, can any thing tend more to raise the Public Credit abroad, or so effectually to refute the Slanders of those Enemies, who have endeavoured to represent us in a Bankrupt Condition, than this very Undertaking. It hath been esteem'd a Master-stroke of *Roman* Policy, as well as Greatness, that in their highest Distress, they endeavoured, by all Kinds of Art, to insinuate their great Strength, and assert their Independency; for which Purpose was that ever-memorable

[1] Not authenticated. However, *DA* of 29 October 1745 prints an unsigned letter which states that the opera is 'laid aside' and that the King has expressed his disapproval of it. Fielding probably would like to give the impression he has privileged intelligence of something that was, in fact, widely reported. In normal circumstances the king paid the opera an annual subsidy of £1,000, and it may be significant that no record of such payment appears in the calendar of treasury books and papers for 1745.

Puff, with which they refused the Presents of King *Hiero*, after the Battle of *Thrasimene*.[1]

I cannot help regarding our sending for a Troop of *Italian* Singers, in this Time of Distress, as a State Puff of the same kind. Indeed I am convinced it was done with this Design: For are not the very Persons who are the forwardest in promoting this Diversion Courtiers, and consequently Friends to the Present Establishment? Are they not People of Fortune, and therefore highly interested in the Preservation of National Credit? Nor can I help observing, as a Proof of the Policy of this Measure, another Piece of State Craft, tending to shew our great inward Strength and Security: For while we sent for this Troop of Singers into *England*, we left several Troops of our Soldiers abroad.[2] And in what Part of *Europe* could this Policy be played off with such Advantage as in *Italy*, where our principal Enemies reside, and where the Scheme of our Destruction is supposed to have been laid?[3] The Success with which this Scheme hath been attended, must have answered our Expectation, since it is apparent, by the Arrival of these Singers, that they are *fairly taken in*,[4] and imposed upon to believe we have still as much Money as ever.

In this Light then the Opera and those who encourage it will deserve our highest Encomiums, and the Subscription to it may be ranked with the other public Subscriptions at this Season.[5] And in this Light we ought to see the Intention of those who have promoted it, for the Reasons above-mentioned; to which I will add the humane Maxim, of always assigning the best Motive possible to the Actions of every one.

But, on the contrary, should we be so cruel to deny any such good

[1] According to Livy, *Historia*, xxii. xxxvii, after the Roman defeat at Thrasimene (217 BC) Hieron II (? 305–215 BC), ruler of Syracuse and ally of the Romans since 263 BC, was so grieved by the news that he sent a fleet bearing 'all those things with which good and faithful allies were wont to assist their friends in time of war' (Loeb). The 'things' included a golden statue representing Victory ('for the omen's sake'), wheat and barley, and 1,000 archers and slingers. The senate turned the latter pair of items over to the consuls, accepted the golden statue of Victory, but apparently did not accept a sum of gold that seems to have accompanied the itemized gifts (xxxvii. 11–12). Polybius, *Historia*, iii.75. 7, records Hiero's gifts but does not indicate that the Romans returned any.

[2] For the political infighting that led to the delay in recalling English troops from Flanders, see 'General Introduction', above, p. xxxii. The issue was still alive as late as 23 October, when Pitt, presumably as part of his strategy for getting into place, moved to address the king to recall all British troops still in Flanders. All except 2,000 cavalry were already under orders to return; Owen, *Rise of the Pelhams*, p. 284.

[3] Alluding to the fact that the OP was resident in that country, as well as to the support given the jacobite enterprise by the pope. See *Dialogue*, above, pp. 83–5.

[4] 'deceived'.

[5] Beginning in late November 1745 the London papers carried advertisements requesting that the subscribers to the opera make the last payment of their subscription to the treasurer at the opera office in the Haymarket; see, for example, *DA* of 26 November 1745. Similar ads ran steadily through December. For the 'other public Subscriptions', see *TP* no. 11 (14 January 1746), below, p. 188.

Purpose to be at the Bottom; nay, should we derive this Desire of an Opera at present from the most depraved Levity of Mind, an utter Insensibility of Public Good or Evil, yet we may still draw Advantages from our Opera, tho' I must own I could be scarce sanguine enough to derive them from Design. For could it be imagined of any Nation, at such a Season of Danger and Distress, (which I decline painting at length, as the Picture is disagreeable, and already sufficiently known) that considerable Numbers of the Inhabitants, instead of contributing all the Assistance in their several Capacities to the Public, should employ their Time and their Money in endeavouring to promote an expensive foreign Diversion, composed of all the Ingredients of Softness and Luxury, such a Nation would not be worth invading. No powerful Prince could look on such a People with any Eyes of Fear or Jealousy, nor no wise One would send his Subjects among them, for fear of enervating their Minds, and debauching their Morals.

Such a Nation could inspire no other Ideas into its Neighbours, than those of Contempt and Ridicule. We ought to be considered as the silly Swan, whose last Breath goes out in a Cantata.[1] And as nothing but wanton Cruelty could move any Power to attack us, so would the Conquest of us be no less infamous than barbarous; and we should, from the same Reason, be as safe in the Neighbourhood of *France*, as the little Commonwealth of *Lucca* was in that of her Great Sister of *Rome*.[2]

For all these Reasons I am for an Opera: But I must then insist on it, that we strike up immediately, otherwise I must desire that Ghost of an Advertisement, calling for latter Payment from the Subscribers, which hath haunted the Public Papers this Month,[3] without having (as it seems) been spoken to by any one,[4] to disappear immediately: For

---

[1] See *Phaedo*, 84 E–85 B, where Socrates, taking note of the dying swan tradition, says that the swans 'sing at other times also, but when they feel that they are to die, sing most and best in their joy that they are to go to the god whose servants they are. But men, because of their own fear of death, misrepresent the swans and say that they sing for sorrow, in mourning for their own death. . . . I believe they have prophetic vision, and because they have foreknowledge of the blessings in the other world they sing and rejoice on that day more than ever before' (Loeb). Cf. Emilia's speech, 'I will play the swan, | And die in music' (*Othello*, v. ii. 247).

[2] A Roman colony *c.* 174 BC, Lucca (Luca) became a *municipium* by the *Lex Julia municipalis* of 90 BC, then reverted to colonial status under the Empire. Historically most famous as the place where Caesar and Pompey met (56 BC) to revive the first triumvirate, Lucca owed its economic importance to its location on an extension of the Via Clodia, in what today is Tuscany, northeast of Pisa.

[3] The advertisements referred to in *n.* 5, above. For Fielding's use of the term 'Ghost' as applied to advertisements, see under the heading 'Appeared' in 'Apocrypha' of *TP* no. 1 (5 November 1745), below, p. 338, where note is taken of 'Several Ghosts in the News-Papers of this Week, in the Shape of Puffs'. See also *JJ* no. 40 (3 September 1748), pp. 380–4, for the term in a wider, more 'literary' context.

[4] Cf. *JJ* no. 40 (3 September 1748), pp. 381–2: 'these, like other Ghosts, appear no longer than 'till

I would by no means have all *Europe* imagine, that *we want nothing* to establish our Opera at present, *but Money*.[1]

TUESDAY, JANUARY 7, 1746.   NUMB. 10.

Tu, Jupiter, quem statorem hujus urbis atque Imperii vere nominamus: HUNC *et* HUJUS *socios a tuis aris ceterisque templis, a tectis urbis ac mœnibus, a vita fortunisque civium omnium arcebis: et omnes bonorum inimicos, hostes patriæ, latrones Italiæ, scelerum fœdere inter se ac nefaria societate conjunctos æternis suppliciis, vivos mortuosque mactabis.*

CICERO, *In L. Catilinam.*[2]

To the TRUE PATRIOT

Dear Sir,   *Dec.* 14, 1745.[3]

Tho' I live on a small Fortune, in great Obscurity, yet I cannot but be interested in our present Troubles. My Thoughts sometimes lead me to meditate, what we are likely to expect, should Success attend the present Ravagers of our Country. Nay, I have even gone so far as to suppose them actual Victors, and have in this Light framed an imaginary Journal of Events, with which I here present you, as with a waking Dream.

they are properly spoken to by the Person whom they haunt'. Fielding must have been fond of this popular superstition. It is referred to in the 'Apocrypha' of *TP* no. 1, cited in the preceding note; in *Tom Jones*, XI. ii. 572; and in *CGJ* no. 65 (7 October 1752), ii. 107, which may not be his.

[1] *DA* of 3 January 1746 prints a letter signed 'Linus', which takes an adversary view of the critics of the opera: 'A third [critic] combats it with a Weapon (*Humour*) by which he has deservedly gain'd great Reputation, and could not but have won the Victory, had he been on the right Side of the Question.' If, as seems likely, this is a reference to *TP* no. 9, it demonstrates that Fielding's authorship of the paper was known.

[2] *In Catilinam*, I. xiii. 33, omitting a relative clause modifying Jupiter: 'O Jupiter . . . rightly called by us the preserver of this city and empire, thou wilt repel him and his allies from thy temple and from the other temples, from the dwellings of this city and its walls, from the lives and fortunes of all the citizens, and these men, enemies of the upright, foes of the state, plunderers of Italy, who are united by bonds and crime in an abominable association, thou wilt punish living and dead with eternal punishments' (Loeb).

[3] In an unpublished letter to James Harris dated 2 January, 1745[6], a Thursday, Fielding writes of receiving some 'Wit' from Harris, with which 'the public will regale themselves next Tuesday seven night', that is, on Tuesday, 14 January. However, in a letter of 11 January Fielding asks Harris's pardon for 'publishing y^r Ltr a week sooner' than originally promised, and also for making 'the Alteration of Italian Judges'. This latter is almost certainly a reference to the 'Journal' entry of 2 Jan., below, where the new judges appointed by the Pretender are not Italians, but simply unfamiliar with the precincts of the English judiciary, an alteration consistent with the lawyer-editor's care not to risk offending his profession. The letter of 11 January further says that Harris's contribution was the first *TP* leader to have been reprinted by another 'News Writer'. A reprint of *TP* no. 10 is in *General Advertiser* of 11 January 1745[6]. Although Fielding may have done some other, less important editing here, the case for Harris's authorship seems compelling. See also above, pp. xcix–c and *nn*.

The Person of my Drama, or Journalist, I suppose to be an honest Tradesman, living in the busy Part of the City.

January 1, 1746.

This Day the supposed Conqueror was proclaimed at *Stocks Market,*[1] amidst the loud Acclamations of Highlanders and Friars. I was enabled, from my own Windows, to view this Ceremony; *Wallbrook* Church,[2] the Mansion-House,[3] and several others adjoining, having been burnt and razed in the Massacre of last Week.[4] Father *O-Blaze,* an *Irish* Dominican, read upon the Occasion a Speech out of a Paper, which he stiled an extempore Address. Melancholy as I was, I could not help smiling at one of his Expressions, when speaking of the New Year, he talked of *Janus's* Faces, each of which look'd both backward and forward.[5]

Jan. 2. A Proclamation issued for a *free* Parliament *(according to the Declaration)*[6] to meet the 20th Instant. The twelve Judges removed, and twelve new ones appointed, some of whom had scarce ever been in *Westminster-Hall* before.[7]

[1] The City market at the junction of Cornhill, Threadneedle Street, Lombard Street, and the Poultry, in Walbrook Ward. Originally for the sale of fish and flesh, it burned in the great fire of 1666 and when rebuilt was converted to a market for fruit and vegetables. In 1737 it was removed to the site of the present Farringdon Street to make room for the building of Mansion House. Its name is traditionally derived from the presence on this site of a pair of stocks for the punishment of City offenders. Fielding may have chosen it as the place where the 'supposed Conqueror was proclaimed' because in it stood statues of Charles I and Charles II.

[2] St Stephen's Church, Walbrook, one of Wren's most celebrated churches, was built in 1672–9 after its predecessor was destroyed in the fire of London. It was the third church of its name on that site, immediately behind the Mansion House.

[3] At the junction of the Poultry and Cornhill on the south side, it was erected 1739–52, from the designs of George Dance, as the residence of the lord mayor during his year in office. Hence, a symbol of the wealth and dignity of the City of London.

[4] As anticatholic feeling intensified during the Forty-Five, warmed-over 'histories' of the massacres of protestants by catholics in the 17th century, particularly those in Ireland and France, began to appear in great number, and polemicists argued loudly that a general massacre was the likely outcome of a Stuart restoration. Cf. 'Observations on the Rebellion', *TP* no. 2 (12 November 1745), above, p. 125, where it is hoped that most roman catholics in England could not be induced 'to assist in a Massacre'. See also the index, *s.v.* 'Massacres'.

[5] An 'Irish bull', an expression containing a manifest contradiction in terms or involving a ludicrous inconsistency unperceived by the speaker (*OED, s.v.* 'Bull', *sb*[4]). In this dream vision Harris is at some pains to insist upon the Irish, French, and Italian implications of the catholicism which he predicts will follow a jacobite victory.

[6] In his manifesto or 'Proclamation' dated from Rome, 23 December 1743 NS, the OP (as James VIII of Scotland) declared 'that we will with all convenient speed call a free parliament; that by the advice and assistance of such an assembly, we may be enabled to repair the breaches caused by so long an usurpation, to redress all grievances, and to free our people from . . . all other hardships and impositions which have been the consequences of the pretended union'; text from James Browne, *History of the Highlands,* iii. 21–2. See also *TP* no. 1 (5 November 1745), above, p. 114 and *n.*

[7] The seat of the superior courts of justice, namely, Chancery and the three so-called common-law courts (King's Bench, Common Pleas, and Exchequer); hence the symbolic locus of English law. The twelve judges are those of the three common-law courts. Cf. Sir John Dalrymple, *Memoirs of Great*

Jan. 3. Queen *Anne's* Statue in *St. Paul's* Church Yard taken away,[1] and a large Crucifix erected in its Room.

Jan. 4, 5, 6. The Cash, Transfer Books, &c. removed to the Tower, from the Bank, South Sea, and India Houses, which ('tis reported) are to be turned into Convents.[2]

Jan. 10. Three Anabaptists[3] committed to *Newgate*, for pulling down the Crucifix in *Paul's* Church Yard.

Jan. 12. Being the first Sunday after Epiphany, Father *Mac-Dagger*, the Royal Confessor, preach'd at *St. James's*—sworn afterwards of the Privy Council[4]—arrived the *French* Ambassador with a numerous Retinue.[5]

Jan. 20. The *free* Parliament opened—the Speech and Addresses filled with Sentiments of *civil* and *religious Liberty*.[6]—An Act of Grace proposed from the Crown, to pardon all Treasons committed under Pretext of any Office, *civil* or *military*, before *the first Declaration's being promulgated, which was in the Isle of Mull, about* 19 *Months ago*.[7] The Judges consulted, whether all Persons throughout *Great Britain* were intended

Britain and Ireland (London, 1790), ii. 70: 'A saying of Lord Justice Hales was everywhere repeated: "That the twelve red coats in Westminster-hall were able to do more mischief to the nation, than as many thousands in the field."'

[1] Sculpted by Francis Bird in 1712 and sited before the west front of the church, to mark the location of St Gregory's early church, the statue of the protestant Queen was described by Garth as 'the vast Bulk of that stupendous Frame' ('On Her Majesty's Statue in St. Paul's Church-Yard', v. 1).

[2] See *TP* no. 12 (21 January 1746), below, p. 195, where the Pope is said to be 'determined to establish immediately a very considerable Number' of convents.

[3] Conventionally perceived as among the most fiercely anticatholic of the dissenting sects, whose representatives they are here. The dissenters as a whole were thought of as a key group, and both Hanoverian and jacobite propaganda paid court to their interest. The dissenters had already proffered a resolution, dated 28 September 1745, in support of George II; see *General Evening Post* of 28 September–1 October 1745.

[4] The historical precedent being Edward Petre (1631–99), jesuit, clerk of the Royal Chapel, and confessor of James II, named in 1687 to the privy council. For Fielding's later use of this and a number of other supposititious parallels to the reign of James II, see *JJ* no. 3 (19 December 1747), pp. 103–9.

[5] Indicating resumption of the French connection. England and France had been at war since early 1744.

[6] According to the YP's manifesto dated Paris, 16 May 1745 NS, his father was resolved to 'maintain the Church of England by law established' and to secure all civil and ecclesiastical liberties; text in James Browne, *History of the Highlands*, iii. 65.

[7] The OP's manifesto of 23 December 1743 NS reads: 'We do therefore, by this our royal declaration, absolutely and effectually pardon and remit all treasons, and other crimes hitherto committed against our royal father [James II] or ourselves. From the benefit of which pardon we except none but such as shall, after the publication hereof, wilfully and maliciously oppose'; text from Browne, iii. 21–2. The YP's Paris manifesto of 16 May 1745 NS reiterates the pardon and its terms, the effective date now being that of the publication of his manifesto. Harris satirizes the impertinence of the dating by placing the YP's landing a year earlier than it actually occurred. In *History*, above, p. 37, Fielding follows the *London Gazette* of 13–17 August, which puts the YP's landing between the isles of Mull and Skye. But Newcastle wrote Argyll on 1 August 1745: 'There is one letter that says, the Pretender's son is absolutely landed in the Isle of Mull'; Coxe, *Pelham*, i. 255. Some of the early newspaper reports also cited Mull.

to be *bound* by this Promulgation, as being *privy* to it. 'Twas held they were, because *Ignorantia legis non excusat*.

Jan. 22. Three Members, to wit, Mr. *D——n*, Mr. *P——t*, and Mr. *L——n*,[1] were seized in their Houses, and sent to the Tower, by a Warrant from a Secretary of State. The same Day I heard another Great Man was dismissed from his Place, but his Name I could neither learn nor guess.

Jan. 23. His Highness sends a Message to the House, That he would make no further Removals, till he saw better Reason.

Jan. 24. A Great Court at *St. James's*, at which were present * and * and * and * and *, and all kissed Hands.

Jan. 24. The three Anabaptists above-mention'd tried for their Offence, and sentenced to be hang'd. Executed the same Day, attended by Mr. *Mac-henly* the Ordinary.[2] Their Teacher Mr. *Obadiah Washum*, the Currier,[3] was refused Access from their first Commitment.

Jan. 26. This Day the *Gazette* informs us, that *Portsmouth*, *Berwick* and *Plymouth*, were delivered into the Hands of *French* Commissaries, as *Cautionary* Towns;[4] and also twenty Ships of the Line, with their Guns and Rigging, pursuant to Treaty.

Jan. 27. *Tom Blatch*,[5] the old Small-Coal-Man, committed to the *Compter*,[6] for a violent Assault on Father *Mac-dagger* and three young Friars. 'Twas the Talk about Town, that they had attempted the Chastity of his Daughter *Kate*.

---

[1] Dodington, Pitt, and Lyttelton. For the first and last, see *TP* no. 1 (5 November 1745), above, p. 110; for Pitt see *TP* no. 8 (24 December 1745), above, p. 158; also 'General Introduction', above, pp. lxxxv–lxxxvii. Pitt, who had not as yet been given a place in the Pelham administration, is additionally complimented by his association here with two 'patriot' friends who were in place.

[2] See *TP* no. 3 (19 November 1745), above, p. 131, where John ('Orator') Henley 'was, for his good Services, preferred to be the Ordinary of Newgate'. For Henley, see also 'General Introduction', above, p. lxvii, and the letter signed 'Pertinax', *TP* no. 8 (24 December 1745), reprinted in Locke, p. [90].

[3] Alluding to the anabaptist practice of recruiting teachers from the lay ranks. His Hebrew name means 'servant of Yahweh', and his prophetic book in the Bible tells of the divine retribution to be visited upon Edom, and of the eventual restoration of Israel. His English name is a satirical reminder of the anabaptist belief in immersion.

[4] Towns delivered over, in this case to the French, as pledges of English good behavior towards that nation. Harris may have been put in mind of this item by *DA* of 11 December 1745, which printed what purported to be 'An extract of the articles of the late king *James* to the *French* king, in the year 1689, in consideration of that king's assistance for restoring king *James* to his lost dominions.' The sixth 'article' mandates the delivery of '*Dover* castle, *Plymouth*, and *Portsmouth*, to be garrison'd by *French* soldiers as cautionary towns for the security of performance'. Excerpted in *GM*, xv (1745), 636.

[5] *OED* lists no examples after 1607 of this obsolete verb ('blatch') meaning to smear with blacking or other black substance.

[6] Generically, the name of a prison, attached to a city court and under the supervision of the sheriffs, where debtors and petty disturbers of the peace were sent to await trial. At this time the two most notorious compters were those on the north side of the Poultry, in Cheap Ward, and at Wood Street, east side, in Cripplegate Ward.

Jan. 28. A Bill brought into the Commons, and twice read the same Day, to repeal the Act of Habeas Corpus,[1] and that by which the Writ *de Hæretico comburendo* was abolished.[2] A Mutiny the same Day among the Highland Soldiers—quelled by doubling their Pay.[3]

Jan. 31. The above Bill passed, and the Royal Assent given. A Motion made about the *Restoration of Abbey Lands*—rejected by the Lords, seven *English Roman Catholic* Peers being in the *Majority*.[4]

February 1. All Peerages declared void since the Revolution, and 24 new Peers created, without a Foot of Land in the Island. A second Mutiny among the Soldiery.

Feb. 2. *Long Acre* and *Covent Garden*[5] allotted out in Portions to the Highland Guards. Two Watermen and a Porter committed to the *Lollards* Tower at *Lambeth*,[6] for Heresy.

Feb. 3. Father *Poignardini*, an *Italian* Jesuit, made Privy Seal. A Bill proposed against the Liberty of the Press, and to place the Nomination of Jurors, *exempt from Challenge*, in the Crown. Several *Catholic* Lords and Gentlemen, being *English*, quit the Court, and retire into the Country. More Heretics sent to *Lambeth*.

[1] Which had in fact been suspended, over opposition objections, from 21 October 1745 until 19 April 1746, by 19 Geo. II, c. 1; *Statutes at Large*, v. 452; *Journals of Commons*, xxv. 7, 129, 194.

[2] 2 Charles II, c. 9, sec. 1 had abolished this common-law writ against a heretic, who having been convicted of heresy by a bishop, abjured it, and afterwards fell into the same again . . . and was thereupon delivered over to the secular power in order that he might be burnt to death (Jowitt, *Dictionary*, s.v. 'Haeretico comburendo').

[3] Home, *History of the Rebellion in 1745* (Edinburgh, 1822), p. 100: 'The pay of a captain in this army was half a crown a day; the pay of a lieutenant two shillings; the pay of an ensign one shilling and sixpence; and every private man received sixpence a day, without deductions'; cited by French, p. 319.

[4] The dispersion of church lands into lay hands during the reign of Henry VIII had been confirmed statutorily by 1 & 2 Phil. & Mary, c. 30; *Statutes at Large*, vi. 40. The implication of the negative vote here is that catholic peers had benefited from the dispersion and were not about to void it. Fielding will return to this issue in the 'Court of Criticism', *JJ* no. 20 (16 April 1748), pp. 242–4, and *JJ* no. 23 (7 May 1748), pp. 272–3. See also *Dialogue*, above, p. 91, and the index to the present volume, s.v. 'Church lands'.

[5] Long Acre was a spacious street running east-west between St Martin's Lane and Drury Lane; hence it was accessible to the theatre district and to all that implies. In addition it contained a proportionately large number of taverns, mug-houses, and bagnios. Covent Garden, the site of one of the two patent theatres, was once fashionable but had acquired by this time a reputation for immorality. In the 'Domestic News' of *JJ* no. 30 (25 June 1748), p. 476, a newspaper item about public nuisances in this area is annotated thus: 'I suppose the Writer means certain Ladies, who walk about there with Things that are a Nuisance.' The same department of *JJ* no. 5 (2 January 1748), p. 450, identifies Covent Garden as the appropriate place in which to school the military in various habits necessary to their profession. As a justice of the peace Fielding was to move to Bow Street, Covent Garden, and he named his last periodical (1752) after the area.

[6] The so-called Lollard's tower, at the west end of the chapel at Lambeth House (palace of the archbishops of Canterbury), was built by Archbishop Chicheley in 1434–45. At the top of the tower is a small room with rings set in its walls, presumed to have been a place of confinement for heretical persons and political prisoners. There was also a 'Lollard's Tower' in St Paul's, a notorious prison of the bishops of London, with which the Chicheley tower may have been confused in tradition.

Feb. 5. A Promotion of 18 General Officers, three only of which were *English*. Lord *John Drummond* made Colonel of the first Regiment of Foot Guards, the Duke of *Perth* of the Second, and Lord *George Murray* of the Third.[1]

Feb. 6. Various Grants passed the Privy Seal of Lands in various Counties to Generals, Ecclesiastics, and other Favourites, all *Foreigners*.

Feb. 9. A Petition from various Persons, Sufferers by the said Grants, setting forth their Fidelity to the Government, and that particularly in the late Troubles, tho' they had never enter'd into any Schemes in favour of his present Highness, yet they had *constantly declined* all Subscriptions, Associations, &c. to his Prejudice.[2] Father *Mac-dagger* brought them for Answer, that the Associators and Subscribers had at least shewn their Attachment to *some* Government, but that an Indifference to *all* Government deserved Favour from *none*, and that therefore their Petition was rejected.

Feb. 13. Four Heretics burnt in *Smithfield*[3]—Mr. *Mac-henly* attended them, assisted on this extraordinary Occasion by Father *O-Blaze*, the Dominican.

Feb. 19. Rumours of a Plot. More Heretics committed. The Judges declare the Power of the Crown to *suspend* Laws.[4] Father *Mac-dagger* made President of *Magdalen* College in *Oxford*.[5]

---

[1] Lord John Drummond (1714–47), titular fourth duke of Perth (1746), landed in Scotland on 22 November 1745 with about 800 men of the Royal Scots (a regiment in the French Service) and troops from six Irish regiments, also in the French service. On 2 December 1745 he sent General Wade a declaration that as chief of French forces in Scotland he had come under royal orders to make war on the Hanoverians; see *Scots Magazine*, vii (1745), 588, for a text; also Elcho, *Short Account*, p. 357. As of the date of this issue of the *TP* the titular duke of Perth was still James Drummond (1713–46), third duke, who joined the YP at Perth on 4 September 1745 and was made lt.-general; Elcho, *Short Account*, pp. 248–9. Walpole called him 'a silly race-horsing boy'; to Mann, 27 September 1745, *Yale Walpole*, xix. 118; also Murray of Broughton, *Memorials*, pp. 188–9. Lord George Murray (1694–1760) joined the YP at Perth about 5 September 1745, after having been rebuffed in his offer of service to George II. He had been 'out' in 1715 and in the opinion of many contemporaries was the most experienced and skilled of the YP's military advisers. Murray was lt.-general. For James Drummond and Murray, see also *History*, above, pp. 44, 45.

[2] Fielding will take up this theme in *TP* no. 11 (14 January 1746), below, p. 187.

[3] Famous in history as the place where many religious martyrs were burned or executed, especially during the Marian persecutions (*c*. 1555). Tradition has it that the first and the last person to be burned for heresy in England were burned at Smithfield. It was also the site of a cattle market and of Bartholomew Fair.

[4] By his two Declarations of Indulgence (1687, 1688) James II had generalized the dispensing power into a suspending power, whereby the laws themselves were remitted. The Declaration of Rights (1689) declared both the suspending power and the dispensing power to be illegal; the Declaration was embodied in the Bill of Rights (1 Will. & Mary, session 2, c. 2). See also *Proper Answer*, especially pp. 70–2.

[5] Upon the death of its president in 1687 Magdalen College, Oxford, was issued a *mandamus* from James II to appoint a particular successor. Although the Fellows disregarded the *mandamus* and elected one of their own, ultimately James II expelled the new president and installed Samuel Parker, who died shortly thereafter and was succeeded by Bonaventura Giffard, one of the four new vicars

Feb. 21. Four Lords and two Commoners taken into Custody for the Plot, all *English*, and two of them *Roman Catholics*. The Deanry of *Christ Church* given to Father *Poignardini*,[1] and the Bishoprics of *Winchester* and *Ely*, to the General of the Jesuits Order, *resident in Italy*.

Feb. 28. Six more Heretics burnt in *Smithfield*. A fresh Motion made *to restore the Abbey Lands*—carried in the Lords House, but rejected by the Commons. Several Members of the Lower House sent to the Tower by a Secretary of State's Warrant, and the next Day expelled, and fined by the Privy Council 1000 *l.* each.

March 1. The *French* Ambassador made a Duke, with Precedence. The Motion for restoring Abbey Lands carried, and an Address of both Houses prepared upon the Occasion. *Cape Breton* given back to the *French*,[2] and *Gibraltar* and *Portmahon* to the *Spaniards*.[3]

March 2. Seven more Heretics burnt. A Message from the Crown,

apostolic. Under Giffard's tenure Magdalen became almost altogether catholic; Hume, *History of England*, ch. lxx, *sub* 1687; *JJ* no. 25 (21 May 1748), p. 286, and no. 27 (4 June 1748), pp. 296–7; Charles Edward Mallet, *History of the University of Oxford* (London, 1924–7), ii. 452–56; J. R. Bloxham, *Magdalen College and King James II* (Oxford, 1886), pp. x–xxx, 242–71. *Westminster Journal* of 16 November 1745 extracts from a satirical letter from Oxford, which reports a *mandamus* from the YP to the fellows of Magdalen, requiring them to elect a certain Romish priest to their headship, now vacant on the death of Dr Butler. The 'Apocrypha' of *TP* no. 3 (19 November 1745), below, pp. 348–9, ridicules a similar (but perhaps 'serious') report in *St James's Evening Post*.

[1] John Massey (?1651–1715) became a catholic shortly after the accession of James II, and in October 1686 secured the deanery of Christ Church, Oxford, vacant after the death of Fell and in the royal gift. Massey's royal letter of appointment granted him a dispensation from the oaths and said expressly that Massey had not taken priest's orders. Burnet, who thought the deanery of Christ Church 'the most important post in the university', judged Massey's appointment to be the opening wedge of an attack on the universities; *A Supplement to Burnet's 'History of My Own Time'*, ed. H. C. Foxcroft (Oxford, 1902), pp. 215–16. James II also wanted to make Petre archbishop of York, but the Pope refused, on the grounds that such appointments were in opposition to the jesuit rules.

[2] Louisburg and with it Cape Breton Island fell in June 1745 to an army of New England colonials escorted by Commodore Peter Warren's ships. It was widely and wildly hailed by the public as the one unqualified success in the war with France. In *JJ* no. 14 (5 March 1748) 'Humphry Gubbins', contemplating the preliminaries to peace with France, took the popular posture: 'No, no, we will never part with *Cap Britton*—Tell um that.—We will never part with *Cap Britton*. As for all the rest we have a got by the War, they may have it again with all my Heart; but rather than part with *Cap Britown*, I woud gi my Vote to carry on the War to the End of the World' (pp. 183–4). In the peace negotiations already underway in 1746 the French were making its return an absolute condition, as Newcastle wrote Chesterfield, adding 'and who will dare to give it up, I know not'; 15 March 1746, in *Private Correspondence of Chesterfield and Newcastle 1744–46*, ed. Sir Richard Lodge (London, 1930), p. 128. See also Walpole to Mann, 16 May 1746, *Yale Walpole*, xix. 255, for a similar expression. The importance of Cape Breton and the manner of its capture are alluded to in '*Considerations* concerning the Establishment of a *Militia* continued', *TP* no. 11 (14 January 1746), below, p. 192.

[3] The preeminent British naval victories in the War of the Spanish Succession. In July 1704 a combined British–Dutch fleet took Gibraltar from Spain, and the British subsequently garrisoned it. In September 1708 Leake and Stanhope took Port Mahon, the principal harbor of Minorca, which at the time was garrisoned by the French. Like Gibraltar it was ceded to Great Britain by Spain in the Treaty of Utrecht (1713). Possession of the two ports established the British naval presence in the Mediterranean.

desiring the Advice of this *free* Parliament touching the *Funds*.[1] An humble Address immediately voted by way of Answer, praying that his Highness would take such Methods, as they might be effectually and speedily *annihilated*.

March 4. An eminent Physician fined 200 Marks in the *King's Bench*, for an Innuendo at *Batson's*,[2] that *Bath* Water was preferable to Holy Water. Three hundred Highlanders, of the opposite Party, with their Wives and Children, massacred in *Scotland*. The Pope's Nuncio arrived this evening at *Greenwich*.

March 7. The Pope's Nuncio makes his Public Entry—met at the *Royal Exchange* by my Lord Mayor (a *Frenchman*) with the Aldermen, who have all the Honour to kiss his Toe[3]—proceeds to *Paul's* Church Yard—met there by Father *O-Blaze*, who invites him, in the Name of the New Vicar-General and his Doctors, to a *Combustio Hæreticorum*, just then going to be celebrated. His Eminence accepts the Offer kindly, and attends them to *Smithfield*, where the Ordinary is introduced and well received—The Nuncio proceeds thence to St. *James's*, where he had been expected for five Hours—the Nobility and great Officers of State all admitted to kiss his Toe—A grand Office opened the same Night in *Drury Lane* for the Sale of Pardons and Indulgences.

March 9. My little Boy *Jacky* taken ill of the Itch. He had been on the Parade with his Godfather the Day before, to see the Life-Guards, and had just touched one of their Plaids.

March 12. His Highness sends a Message to the Commons, acquainting them with his Design of equipping a large Fleet for the Assistance of his good Brother of *France*, and for that Purpose demanding two Millions to be immediately raised by a Capitation.[4] A warm Debate thereon.

[1] The YP's second 'manifesto', dated 10 October 1745, states in part that with regard to the Funds and the public debt represented by them his father 'is resolved to take the Advice of his Parliament'; *The Edinburgh History of the Late Rebellion*, 4th ed. (London, 1752), p. 38; Browne, *History of the Highlands*, iii. 104–5. But anti-jacobite writers argued that the stress placed by this manifesto on the debt's having been contracted under an unlawful government indicated the OP meant to wipe out the debt. See *Proper Answer*, p. 80; also *JJ* no. 20 (16 April 1748), p. 244.

[2] 'Against the Royal Exchange in Cornhill', this busy coffee-house early in the century attracted the quacks of the time, many of whom advertised that their nostrums might be purchased at the house. However, it must have attracted more reputable members of the profession as well. The Sloane MSS, British Library, contain a 1732 letter 'To Dr. Mead, Batson's Coffee House'; Bryant Lillywhite, *London Coffee Houses* (London, 1963), p. 111. The waters of Bath were commonly prescribed, especially for certain muscular disorders of the kind often reported to have been cured by miracles of faith; see *Tom Jones*, VIII. xiii. 472–3, and *n*. The mark, in legal use in stating the amount of fines as late as 1770 (*OED*), was valued at 13*s*. 4*d*. or two-thirds of the £ sterling.

[3] *Champion* of 8 May 1740, ii. 193–4, compares the custom of kissing the Pope's toe with the even more debasing humilities of the Tartars. See also *Dialogue*, above, p. [77].

[4] The levy of a tax or charge by the head (*OED*, which cites this passage). Harris's choice of the term instead of the more native 'poll tax' emphasizes the French inspiration of the measure. In addition, head taxes were relied on much more by the French system of taxation than by the British.

His Highness goes to the House of Commons at 12 at Night, places himself in the Speaker's Chair,[1] and Introduces the *French* Ambassador. His
Excellency makes a long Speech, setting forth the many Services which
his Master had done this Nation, and the great Good-Will he had
always borne towards them, and concluding with many haughty
Menaces, in case they should prove ungrateful for all his Favours. He is
seconded by the Laird of *Keppoch*,[2] Chancellor of the Exchequer. The
Speaker stands up, and utters the Word *Privilege*,[3] upon which he is sent
to the Tower. Then Mr. Chancellor of the Exchequer moved, that the
Members against the Motion might have Leave to withdraw; and several
having left the House, the Question was put, and carried in the Affirmative, *nemine contradicente*.[4]

March 16. Lord C. J. *W——les*,[5] and Admiral *V——n*,[6] hang'd at

[1] A violation of the fundamental rights of the Commons, which guard against royal intrusion or
molestation of this preemptive kind. These rights are laid down by the Speaker himself at the
commencement of every parliament, and it is his duty to resist any invasion of these rights.

[2] Alexander Macdonald (Macdonell) of Keppoch (d. 1746), sixteenth laird of a notoriously
jacobite clan, was one of the first to declare for the YP. He commanded his clan at Prestonpans
(21 September 1745) and led 400 of them on the march into England; see Alexander Mackenzie,
History of the Macdonalds (Inverness, 1881), pp. 352, 430–1; Elcho, *Short Account*, pp. 241–5.

[3] That is, claims the 'privilege' of the house to be safeguarded against such a violation of space and
usurpation of power.

[4] A traditional term to signify the unanimous consent of the Commons to a vote or resolution. In a
like case in the Lords the term used is *nemine dissentiente*.

[5] Sir John Willes (1685–1761), MP West Looe 1727–37, Kt. 1737, chief justice of Common Pleas
from 1737, friend and supporter of Sir Robert Walpole, who preferred him to the justiceship. Some
time after Hardwicke got the lord chancellorship, the place Willes coveted, Willes abandoned
Walpole for Carteret (Granville), then the Pelhams briefly, and finally Pitt and the Leicester House
connection. His appearance in this leader is partly due to Harris's wish to praise the great men of the
opposition, and partly due to the fact that Willes had sought for and received a commission as colonel
of a regiment raised 'among the gentlemen of the Inns of Court' in December 1745; *DA* of 10 December 1745. Taking note of Willes in this capacity, Fielding characterizes him as 'a Gentleman who as
he hath from the highest Abilities, joined to the highest Integrity, done the greatest Honour to the
Law; so he is at the same time known to be possessed of all those Qualities which enable Men to
shine in the Profession of Arms'; 'Present History of Great Britain', *TP* no. 6 (10 December 1745),
below, p. 369. The regiment was not activated, and in less sympathetic quarters Willes' ambitions
seemed unduly political; see *The Political J——e; or He would be a Colonel* (London, 1745), listed among
the December books in *GM*, xv (1745), 672; also *GM*, xvi (1746), 44. In 1748 Willes became embroiled
with the Grenvilles over a bill to remove the summer assizes for the county of Buckingham, and
Fielding took the Grenvilles' side; see *JJ* no. 19 (9 April 1748), pp. 226–34, and *Yale Walpole*, xix.
470–1; xxvi. 27–8.

[6] Edward Vernon (1684–1757), contentious parliamentarian (MP Ipswich 1741–57) and career
naval officer, was promoted to vice-admiral in 1739 and put in command of the expedition to the
West Indies. He became hysterically popular at home after taking Porto Bello from the Spanish 'with
six Ships only', and his subsequent failures, at Cartagena (1741) and elsewhere, were popularly
blamed on the pacific incompetencies of the Walpole administration. Vernon's politics had been
those of an independent in opposition, and Fielding took advantage of that fact and of Vernon's continued popularity to write *The Vernoniad* (1741), an attack on the mercenary bases of Walpole's pacific
program. In August 1745 Vernon was named admiral of the White, commanding the fleet assembled
in the Downs to guard against the threatened invasion from France. But his differences with the
admiralty intensified, and in December 1745 he offered his resignation, which was accepted. He

Tyburn. Several others were reprieved on the Merit of having been Enemies to those two Great Men, and were only ordered to be whipt at the Cart's Tail.

March 17. Fresh Rumours of a Plot—a Riot in the City—a Rising in the North—a Descent in the West—Confusions, Uproars, Commitments, Hangings, Burnings, &c. &c.

——*verbum non amplius addam*.[1]

FURTHER CONSIDERATIONS concerning the Establishment of a MILITIA.

At a Time when the Rebellion, which certainly owes its Beginning and Encrease to the Absence of our Troops, and to the slender Force left in this Kingdom, hath grown to so formidable a Height; and when the Approach of these Rebels, together with the Apprehension of a Foreign Invasion hath infused such a Panic into this City, it wou'd be a most unpopular Attempt to offer at reviving any of those Arguments which have been formerly used against a standing Army.[2] An Endeavour at this Time to weaken our armed Force would be regarded, and justly too, as a Mark of Disaffection: nay, it would be thought no less than a manifest Design to betray the Nation into the Hands of its Enemies.

On the contrary, the Rebels having been so long able to maintain themselves in Defiance of this Army, tho' consisting I believe of the best Troops in the World; their March into the Heart of the Kingdom, nay, their daring, when they were almost in the Middle of three Bodies of Troops, every one of which was their Superior, to threaten the very Metropolis;[3] their Return with Impunity to join another large Body which have assembled themselves in *Scotland*; the immediate Apprehension of two great Invasions; and lastly, the Menaces which the King of *France* hath thundered aloud, of making this Kingdom the Seat of War in the ensuing Summer, seem all good Arguments for augmenting the

---

struck his flag on 2 January 1746 (*DA* of 4 January 1746), calling forth an encomium from Fielding, who then repeats a rumor that the recall and resignation were owing to Bedford, but suspends judgment as to who was at fault; 'Present History of Great Britain', *TP* no. 10 (7 January 1746), below, pp. 394–5. To vindicate himself Vernon published his correspondence with the admiralty, and in April 1746 his name was struck off the list of admirals. See *The Vernon Papers*, ed. B. McL. Ranft, Naval Records Society, xcix (n.p., 1958), 434–587; H. W. Richmond, *The Navy in the War of 1739–48*, ii (Cambridge, 1920), 182–6; Horace Walpole, *Memoirs of . . . George II*, i. 86 *n*.

[1] Horace, *Satires*, I. i. 121: 'Not a word more will I add' (Loeb). The concluding hemistich of Horace's satire, it is also used to conclude *CGJ* no. 72 (23 November 1752), the final issue of that paper. See also *Amelia*, x. i. 409.

[2] *TP* no. 9 (31 December 1745) printed an unsigned letter 'from a Person of *great Property*, as well as *great Abilities*', which raises some of the arguments against mercenary or standing armies and proposes instead the 'arming all the People of Property', i.e., a 'general Militia'. See Locke, p. [100].

[3] Cf. the wording of the 'Abraham Adams' account in no. 7 (17 December 1745), above, p. 154.

present Army, to double or treble its Numbers; nay, so forcible are these Arguments, that it is by no Means easy to give them an Answer.

For if the vast Expence be objected, I answer, nothing but an utter and absolute Incapacity should excuse us. Our All is at Stake, and therefore our All must be ventured, nay, given to support it. Was our Property only in Question, the preserving even the least Part would be more our Interest, than to abandon the Whole; but our Religion and Liberties are equally in Danger, and if we preserve these only by the Loss of every thing else we shall be Gainers. It may be replied, that this is only a temporary Expedient, for as it seems to admit, that we must be at last undone, and perhaps shortly too, we must at last submit to the Conqueror: I answer, it is still our Interest to hold out to the last; for to delay Final Ruin is the next Wisdom to the averting it.

Secondly, it may be objected, that if 74000 Men, of which Number our Army, including Invalids and Marines, (making about 14000) at present consists,[1] are not sufficient to secure us, neither will as many more, or indeed double that Number. Our Coasts are every where defenceless, and it will be impossible to canton such an Army so as to render them absolutely secure. For tho' indeed while we have, if that may be at present admitted, a Superiority at Sea, it will be hardly possible for any Power to throw in a Force sufficient absolutely to conquer such an Army as I have supposed above; yet they will always have a probable Chance of landing a Body of Men able to harrass and distress us, and to ravage some of our Towns and Cities from which they may retire with Impunity, and with Plunder enough to pay them for their Enterprize. But if we should once admit that a vast Debt, immense Expences, a general Decay of Trade, and in Consequence of these a totally weakened and impoverished State of the Public should entirely lose us this Dominion at Sea, and render us unable to look our Enemies in the Face in that Element, it will then be in their Power to attack us in our Island with a Force which we shall be unable to resist, and to make a perfect Conquest of this Kingdom; I answer, we must resist as long as we can; and if we cannot avert the whole Evil, we must employ our utmost Activity to avert a Part of it. And that, if it is not in our Power to preserve our Children from Slavery, we should, however, if we are able, preserve ourselves.

Indeed there is a Third Objection to the Augmentation of our standing Force, which, if it be attended with the Good it promises, is really

---

[1] Cf. the estimate in no. 6 (10 December 1745), above, p. 150, of 60,000 'exclusive of Marines, Invalids, Train'd Bands and Militia'. The source and authority of the estimate have not been identified.

unanswerable; and that is, that we have another Way to preserve ourselves; one, which, while it is attended with no Expence, would at the
same Time secure us not only from being conquered, but even from any
Danger of being invaded by our Enemies. Nay, which would make us
more formidable to their own Coast, would immediately increase our
Strength at Sea, and revive our Credit at Home; would, in Time, enable
us to discharge our national Debt; would again invigorate our Trade,
and once more circulate Wealth amongst the People; would secure the
Crown from any Apprehensions of a Rebellion; would free the People
from any Jealousies of the Crown; would spread the Terror of the *British*
Name farther than ever, and enable the King to hold the Balance of
Power, and be the uncontrouled Arbitrator of *Europe*.

I believe my Reader already sees that by this third Objection I mean
the Establishment of a well-disciplin'd National Militia. Indeed if he
can discover any other Scheme to effect half the Good which I have
above derived from this, he is a very bad Man if he conceals it.

* Before I enter into the Particulars of this Plan, or endeavour to
prove, as I hope to do demonstratively, that it would be attended with all
the public Advantages I have mentioned, I shall apply myself to answer
the several Objections which I have already heard made against a
Militia. Nor can this Method of considering Objections before I have
advanced my Plan be thought absurd, since these have been principally
made by Persons who have not considered, nor even known the Plan to
which they object; and indeed, most of them will upon Examination
appear to have arisen entirely from this Ignorance; and are only applicable to some Scheme in the Imagination of the Objectors, and not to the
Militia which we propose to establish.

First, they say it is not proper at this Time; the usual Answer to all

* *I have taken this Method to obviate the strong and unreasonable Prejudices which some Persons entertain
against this Scheme, from the Reasons which I here endeavour to answer; and which being once removed, I promise
myself a candid and impartial Examination of what I shall advance. But if any Persons are desirous to see the Plan
itself before they peruse these Objections and the Answers to them, they may be now supplied with the* Plan of a
National Militia, *&c. published by Mr.* Millar;[1] *This being the Scheme which, with some few Variations only, we
intend to embrace*.

[1] The date on its title-page notwithstanding, *A Plan for Establishing and Disciplining a National Militia
in Great Britain, Ireland, and in all the British Dominions of America* (London, 1745), seems to have been
first published by Millar in December 1744; see *Daily Gazetteer* of 7 December 1744, and *GM*, xiv
(1744), 680, which lists it among the December 1744 books. 'A New Edition, with a Preface suited to
the present State of Affairs', bearing a dateline of 1 October 1745 at the end of the preface, is advertised in *London Evening Post* of 26–9 October 1745. It is also advertised in *TP* no. 13 and, in a standing
advertisement of Millar books, in nos. 16–23. Fielding was evidently interested in the *Plan*. He
quotes from its 'Introduction' in no. 11 (14 January 1746), below, p. 190. He again appears to have his
eye on the 'Introduction' in no. 12 (21 January 1746), below, p. 197, and in nos. 13–15 he reprints *verbatim* segments of the main text (Locke, pp. [130], [135–6], [141–2]).

salutary Schemes; and which is always given when the Thing proposed is too reasonable to admit an absolute Refusal; but if ever this Answer was improper it is at present, when the national Force, tho' infinitely greater than we can support, is apparently and avowedly insufficient to protect the Nation from the Danger with which it is threatned.

Such of these Gentlemen as mean honestly, and with such only I argue, may probably conceive that the disciplining a Militia is a Work of long Time; but this is a Mistake; for whereas our Plan divides the Militia into two Bodies, the superior and inferior, the superior Part, which would consist entirely of Persons of Property, would immediately learn the Use of Arms; nor would the Inferior require above two or three Months at the most to bring them to such a Degree of Discipline, as must, if we consider their Numbers, above two Millions in the Whole,[1] make them a sufficient Bulwark for the Nation.

Secondly, these Gentlemen seem to dwell on the Inconvenience of disbanding or weakening the present standing Force; but no such Measure is intended. The present Army may be, and ought to be supported, till the Militia is thoroughly disciplined; which may be effected by Draughts from these of old and decrepit Soldiers, and by the Invalids, who are of very little Use as they are now employed.

Thirdly, it may appear to them not only impolitic but unjust to give any Offence to an Army which hath deserved so well of their Country, and done so much Honour to our National Bravery. Now so far from any Intention of doing an Act of Injustice to these Gentlemen who have suffered so many Hardships, and exposed themselves to so much Danger in the Service of the Public, their Interest is so effectually consulted, that whatever may be the Fate of our Plan, every Officer in the Army must necessarily be its Well-wisher; for it is proposed to incorporate them with the Militia, that every Officer shall reserve his Pay for Life, and that all shall rise to the highest Ranks of their Profession in their proper Turn. By which Means the only two Grievances which attend the Profession will be removed. First, the Injustice arising from Favour of preferring one Man over the Head of another, without any greater Regard to Merit than Precedency: Secondly, that which arises from Necessity of disbanding in Time of Peace, great Numbers of those to whose Dangers and Toils we owe that very State of Tranquillity, by which they are reduced to a very uncomfortable and beggarly Subsistence. Whereas, on the contrary, those who desire to establish a Militia propose to secure to the present Officers of the Army an improvable

---

[1] Evidently a canonical figure among proponents of a militia. See the unsigned letters in no. 9 (31 December 1745), Locke, p. [100], and no. 17 (18–25 February 1746), Locke, p. [156].

Annuity for Life, which they will be assured of possessing, not only with a Certainty of Rising to those who survive the longest, but most probably without any future Hazard or Fatigue. They may sit down under their own Vine,[1] and enjoy Affluence with Ease and Honour, in the Company of their Wives and Children, during the Residue of their Days.

(To be continued.)

TUESDAY, JANUARY 14, 1746.   NUMB. 11.

Τά χρημάτ' ἀνθρώποισιν τιμιώτατα
Δύναμίν τε πλείστην τῶν εν' ἀνθρώποις ἔχει.
EURIPIDES, *Phoenissae*.[2]

To the TRUE PATRIOT.

Sir,

I am a Citizen, a Haberdasher by Trade, and one of those Persons to whom the World allow the Epithets of wise and prudent. And I enjoy this Character the more, as I can fairly assure myself I deserve it; nor am indebted, on this Account, to any Thing but my own regular Conduct, unless to the good Instructions with which my Father launched me into the World, and upon which I formed this grand Principle, *That there is no real Value in any Thing but* Money.

The Truth of this Proposition may be argued from hence, that it is the only Thing in the Value of which Mankind are agreed: For, as to all other Matters, while they are held in high Estimation by some, they are disregarded and looked on as cheap and worthless by others. Nay, I believe it is difficult to find any two Persons, who place an equal Valuation on any Virtue, good or great Quality whatever.

Now having once established this Great Rule, I have, by Reference to it, been enabled to set a certain Value on every Thing else; in which I have governed myself by two Cautions, 1st. Never to purchase too dear; and 2dly, (which is a more uncommon Degree of Wisdom) Never to over-value what I am to sell; by which latter Misconduct I have observed many Persons guilty of great Imprudence.

---

[1] Cf. Micah 4: 4: But they shall sit every man under his vine and under his fig tree; and none shall make them afraid. There are other scriptural phrasings of this figure, but see *JJ* no. 33 (16 July 1748), pp. 340–1, where 'the figurative Language of the Prophet' is clearly identified.

[2] 'The Phoenician Maidens', vv. 439–40, where the lines are identified by Polyneices, who utters them, as an 'old saw': 'Wealth in men's eyes is honoured most of all, | And of all things on earth hath chiefest power' (Loeb).

It is not my Purpose to trouble you with Exemplifications of the fore-going Rule, in my ordinary Calling: I shall proceed to acquaint you with my Conduct concerning those Things which some silly People call invaluable, such as Reputation, Virtue, Sense, Beauty, &c. all which I have reduced to a certain Standard: For, as your Friend Mr. *Adams* says, in his Letter on the late Fast, I imagine every Man, Woman and Thing to have their Price.[1] His Astonishment at which Truth made me smile, as I dare swear it did you; it is, indeed, agreeable enough to the Simplicity of his Character.

But to proceed—In my Youth I fell violently in Love with a very pretty Woman. She had a good Fortune; but it was 500 *l.* less than I could with Justice demand, (I was heartily in Love with her, that's the Truth on it) I therefore took my Pen and Ink (for I do nothing without them) and set down the Particulars in the following Manner:

Mrs. *Amey Fairface* Debtor to *Stephen Grub*.

	l.	*s.*	*d.*
For Fortune, as *per* Marriage	5000	00	00

Per contra Creditor.

	l.	*s.*	*d.*
Imprimis, To Cash —	4500	00	00
Item, To Beauty (for she had a great deal, and I had a great Value for it)	100	00	00
Item, To Wit, as *per* Conversation	2	10	00
Item, To her Affection for me	30	00	00
Item, To good Housewifery, a sober chaste Education, and being a good Workwoman at her Needle, in all	50	00	00
Item, To her Skill in Music —	1	01	00
Item, To Dancing —	00	00	06
	4683	11	06
Mrs. *Amey* Debtor —	5000	00	00
Per contra Creditor —	4683	11	06
Due to Balance —	316	08	06

[1] See *TP* no. 7 (17 December 1745), above, p. 157 and *n.*, where 'Adams' observes that 'there is scarce one among the Mighty who would not be equally ashamed at being thought not to set *some Price* on himself'. For the common association of this saying with Sir Robert Walpole, see *TP* no. 17 (18–25 February 1746), below, p. 223 and *n.*

You see, Sir, I strained as hard as possible, and placed a higher Value (perhaps) on her several Perfections, than others would have done; but the Balance still remained against her, and I was reduced to the necessary Alternative of sacrificing that Sum for ever, or of quitting my Mistriss. You may easily guess on which a prudent Man would determine. Indeed, I had sufficient Reason to be afterwards pleased with my Prudence, as she proved to be a less valuable Woman than I imagined: For, two Years afterwards, having had a considerable Loss in Trade, by which the Balance above was satisfied, I renewed my Addresses, but the false-hearted Creature (forsooth) refused to see me.

A second Occasion which I had for my Pen and Ink, in this Way, was, when the Situation of my Affairs, after some Losses, was such, that I could clearly have put 1500 *l.* in my Pocket by breaking.[1] The Account then stood thus.

	l.	*s.*	*d.*
Stephen Grub, Debtor to Cash	1500	00	00
Per contra Creditor.			
To Danger to Soul as *per* Perjury	105	00	00
To Danger to Body as *per* Felony	1000	00	00
To Loss of Reputation —	500	00	00
To Conscience as *per* injuring others	0	02	06
To incidental Charges, Trouble, *&c.*	100	00	00

I am convinced you are so good a Master of Figures, that I need not cast up the Balance, which must so visibly have determined me to preserve the Character of an honest Man.

Not to trouble you with more Instances of a Life, of which you may easily guess the whole by this Specimen; for it hath been entirely *transacted* by my Golden Rule; I shall hasten to apply this Rule, by which I suppose many other Persons in this City conduct themselves, to the present Times.

And here, Sir, have we not Reason to suppose, that some good Men, for want of duly considering the Danger of their Property, *&c.* from the present Rebellion, and low State of Public Credit, have been too tenacious of their Money on the present Occasion: For, if we admit that the whole is in Danger, surely it is the Office of Prudence to be generous of the lesser Part, in order to secure the greater.[2]

---

[1] By 'declaring bankruptcy'.

[2] Cf. *TP* no. 7 (17 December 1745), above, p. 157, where 'Adams' quotes 'a very great and generous Friend of mine' to the same effect.

Let us see how this stands on Paper; for thus only we can argue with Certainty.

Suppose, then, the given Sum of your Property be 20000 *l.*

The Value of securing this will be more or less in Proportion to the Danger; for the Truth of which I need only appeal to the common Practice of Insurance.

If the Chance then be twenty to one, it follows that the Value of Insurance is at an Average with 1000 *l.*

And proportionally more or less, as the Danger is greater or less.

There are, besides, two other Articles, which I had like to have forgot, to which every Man almost affixes some Value. These are Religion and Liberty. Suppose therefore we set down

	l.	*s.*	*d.*
Religion at —	00	15	00
And Liberty at —	00	02	06

And I think none but a profligate Fellow can value them at a lower Rate; it follows, that to secure them from the same Proportion of Danger as above, is worth

l.	*s.*	*d.*
0	0	$10\frac{1}{2}$

Now this last Sum may be undoubtedly saved, as it would not be missed or called for, if Men would only seriously consider the Preservation of what is so infinitely more valuable, their Property; and advance their Money in its Defence, in due Proportion to the Degree of its Danger. And as there is nothing so pleasant as clear Gain, it must give some Satisfaction to every thinking Man, that while he risques his Money for the Preservation of his Property, his Religion and Liberty are tossed him into the Bargain.

You see, Sir, I have fairly ballanced between those hot-headed Zealots, who set these Conveniences above the Value of Money, and those profligate wicked People, who treat them as Matters of no Concern or Moment.

I have therefore been a little surprized at the Backwardness of some very prudent Men on this Occasion:[1] For it would be really doing them

---

[1] It was sometimes publicly intimated that the 'monied men' and other persons of substance were not entering wholeheartedly into the public subscriptions and associations in support of the military, preferring, it was charged, to play the stock market for their private ends. Walpole wrote Mann on 20 December 1745: 'The private rich are making immense fortunes out of the public distress: the dread of the French invasion has occasioned this'; *Yale Walpole*, xix. 187. On 28 November 1745

an Injury to suspect they do not set a just Value on Money, while every Action of their Lives demonstrates the contrary. I can therefore impute this Conduct only to a firm Persuasion that there will be foolish People enough found, who, from Loyalty to their King, Zeal for their Country, or some other ridiculous Principle, will subscribe sufficient Sums for the Defence of the Public; and so they might save their own Money, which will still encrease in Value, in Proportion to the Distress and Poverty of the Nation.

This would be certainly a wise and right Way of Reasoning; and such a Conduct must be highly commendable, if the Fact supposed was true; for as nothing is so truly great as to *turn the Penny*[1] while the World suspects your Ruin; so to convert the Misfortunes of a whole Community to your own Emolument must be a Thing highly eligible by every good Man, *i.e.* every *Plumb*.[2] But I am afraid this Rule will reach only private Persons at most, and cannot extend to those whose Examples, while they keep their own Purses shut, lock up the Purses of all their Neighbours.

A Fallacy of the same Kind I am afraid we fall into, when we refuse to lend our Money to the Government at a moderate Interest,[3] in Hopes of extorting more from the public Purse; with which Thought a very good Sort of Man, a Plumb, seemed Yesterday to hug himself in a Conversation which we had upon this Subject: But upon the nearest Computation I could make with my Pen, which I handled the Moment he left me, I find that this very Person, who proposed to gain 1 *per Cent.* in 20,000 *l.*

General Ligonier had written, 'Advise all your friends to buy stocks'; HMC, 10th Report, Appendix i (1885), p. 287, as cited by *Yale Walpole*, xix. 187 *n.* In an unpublished letter to James Harris, dated 5 October 1745, Fielding notes that the stocks were continuing to fall despite a lessening of public fear and congratulates himself for selling out 'in time'.

[1] To employ one's money profitably, to gain money (*OED*). Proverbial; see Tilley, *Dictionary of Proverbs in England in the Sixteenth and Seventeenth Centuries* (Ann Arbor, 1950), P211, p. 532.

[2] One who is possessed of £100,000 (*OED*). Cf. *CGJ* no. 33 (25 April 1752) i. 328, where the same figure is cited.

[3] Alluding to the separate financial problem of how to raise money for the supply, which had been occupying Pelham for some time. On 11 December 1745 he had written Trevor: 'nor can the hopes of gain, the most powerful influence that I know of amongst monied men, bring out the specie that is in the kingdom; but every one is locking up his own, and raking as much as he can into his own coffers'; Coxe, *Pelham*, i. 283. According to the 'Extract of a Letter to Sir J. B——d', 'a publick subscription ... was opened in the City at 4 *per Cent.* .... But notwithstanding all the endeavours used to support that subscription, it did not amount I think to more than 500,000 *l.* ... Under this difficulty application was immediately made to the bank of *England*, which, far from being in a condition to help the government, wanted assistance to support its own credit' (*GM*, xvi [1746], 193). The 'Extract' goes on to say that Pelham tried to get a cheaper contract than the one he was arranging with Gideon and others, but time ran out (p. 194). According to Egmont, the reason for rejecting Barnard's alternative was lack of confidence in the ability of his collaborators to raise the money; *Diary*, iii. 315. See also *Westminster Journal* of 29 March 1746, reprinted in *GM*, xvi (1746), 189–93.

would, by the consequential Effect on the public Credit, be a clear Loser of $2\frac{1}{2}$.[1]

In short, I am afraid certain Persons may at this Time run the Hazard of a Fate which too often attends very wise Men, who have not on all Occasions a Recourse to Figures, and may incur the Censure of an old Proverb *By being Penny wise and Pound foolish*. And since I may be involved, against my Will, in the Calamity, I shall be obliged to you if you will publish these Cautions, from,

Sir,
Your humble Servant,

STEPHEN GRUB.[2]

N.B. As your Paper supplies the Place of three Evening Posts, I save $1\frac{1}{2}d$. *per* Week by it; for which pray accept my Acknowledgment.[3]

CONSIDERATIONS concerning the Establishment of a MILITIA continued.

There are some who go farther, and absolutely object against the Establishment of a Militia. First, because they apprehend it would be of little or no Use, either against a foreign or domestic Enemy: And this they endeavour not only to prove, by the Experience of many Years, and particularly by the Behaviour of the Militia as well in the late as present Rebellion, but farther, to account for it from Reason, because this Militia is not subject to Martial Law.

Now it is plain, that the Objection drawn from Fact, *viz.* from the Behaviour of our Militia of late Years, can be applied only to such a Militia as is at present established, and such I readily give up to them; nay, I as readily abandon it to all the Ridicule with which it hath been treated, as well on the Stage as in Conversation; but surely such Ridicule was never aimed at a Militia in general; nor hath any Wit, I hope, had the Impudence to assert, that the present Establishment of Militia is the best Footing it can be put upon; or that the *Grecian*, *Roman*, or *Swiss* Militia, to which I will add that of our own Country in former Ages, were the Subjects of Ridicule, or under the same absurd Regulation as ours is at present.

And yet so dangerous a Weapon is this of Ridicule, and so apt are Men to confound Truth with Falshood, either from Want of sufficient

---

[1] Presumably because of the depressing effect on the stock market of a harder bargain driven with the government in the matter of the loan.

[2] 'Grub' here means primarily a money-grubber, but the word has other apposite resonances: a person of mean abilities, one who toils meanly for mean objectives, even a short, dwarfish person.

[3] For the basis of this calculation, see *TP* no. 1 (5 November 1745), above, pp. 111–12.

Capacity, or from not using sufficient Diligence, to separate one Idea from another, that much the greater Part of this Nation have no other Idea of a Militia, than of a drunken Country 'Squire who inherits the Title of Colonel, or Captain, from his Ancestors; and of a Set of awkward Country Louts with their Musquets on the wrong Shoulder; or, as the Author of the Plan terms them, *a Band of Porters (the Substitutes of Indolence) badly arm'd and not at all disciplin'd*:[1] Whence, as we derive our Notion of a National Militia, it is no Wonder we derive at the same Time a Contempt of its Institution.

The first Part of this Argument therefore either supposes our Militia is not capable of being put on a better Footing than it now is, which if it doth, supposes a manifest Falshood, as we shall prove hereafter; or it admits that it is capable of such Improvement, and then its Force is on our Side of the Question; and it joins with us in recommending some better and more effectual Method, by which these Bodies may be made more useful.

As to the latter Part of the Argument, which proceeds upon Reason, *viz.* That our Militia can never be made useful, because it is not subject to Martial Law,[2] I own it deserves more Consideration. It may be said as Fear is so predominant a Passion in some Minds that it can be subdued by no other, we may reasonably suspect that Men of this Kind, at the Approach of an Enemy, or in Time of Action, will not be deterr'd, either by pecuniary Mulcts, or the Dread of future Shame, from consulting their own Safety in Flight. And tho' it cannot be apprehended that our Army would be much lessen'd in Numbers by such Desertion, yet as these Examples would at least contribute to weaken the Courage and Confidence of the rest, they ought to be effectually provided against; which can be only done by Martial Law, and by inflicting the immediate Punishment of Death: For tho' this Desertion might be made Felony, (nay it is already so) yet the Form and Time required by Civil Judicature makes the Punishment come too late, and lessens its Terror when opposed to instant Danger.

This Objection hath, I confess, great Truth and Weight; but it is happily in our Power to remove all Occasion of making it: For as the Danger suggested is only when an Enemy is actually in the Land, whether Invaders or Rebels, it will be therefore sufficient that this Martial Law shall operate at that Time. From the Instant therefore of such actual

[1] 'Introduction', pp. xxxviii–xxxix, which takes notice of the ridicule traditionally heaped on the London militia. The author of the anonymous *Plan* is believed to be Samuel Martin; see J. R. Western, *The English Militia in the Eighteenth Century* (London, 1965), p. 106.

[2] In *TP* no. 9 (Locke, p. [100]), the unsigned letter on the militia addresses the same concern about martial law, evidently a staple of the argument over the militia.

Invasion or Rebellion, and Notice given of it by any Signal or Signals agreed on, Martial Law may become in Force, and again cease, when such Invasion or Rebellion is at an End.

Now it is apparent that such temporary Institution of Martial Law, in the Case of a Militia, would be adequate to this Purpose; nor would the maintaining it at other Times be in the least necessary; for all the Reasons which induce mercenary Soldiers to desert in Time of Peace; such as enlisting with a fraudulent View, long Absence from Home, being unable or unwilling to live on their Pay, ill Usage of their Officers, &c. would absolutely fail in the Case of a Militia. Nor can this temporary Allowance be fairly objected to by any: Surely not by those who, as Friends to a Standing Army, would allow the perpetual Exercise of it over a large Part of their Fellow Subjects; and indeed with as little Propriety by the Enemies to a Standing Army; since they are by this Means to be delivered from it; and this very Means appears so absolutely necessary to the establishing and substituting a Militia in its Stead.

And this Expedient of giving Force to Martial Law, only during the actual Attempts of an Enemy, is not without a Precedent. And here I shall not appeal to the dictatorial Power among the *Romans*, which was a temporary Institution of the same Nature; since it appears that this very Allowance of Martial Law in Time of War only, made a Part of our original excellent Constitution. "If a Lieutenant, (says Lord *Coke*, 3 *Instit. Fol.* 52) or other that hath Commission of Marshall Authority, in Time of Peace, hang, or otherwise execute any Man by Colour of Martial Law, this is Murder; for this is against *Mag. Charta*, cap. 29." It appears therefore, from this great Authority, that Martial Law was executed by our Ancestors over their Militia in Time of War. 2. That this Power of judging by Martial Law in Time of War was so established, that it was not taken away by the general Words of *Mag. Charta*, nay, of this very Chapter which hath been held as the principal Bulwark of our Liberties, by which we are exempted from any Trial or Punishment out of the ordinary Forms of Justice. 3. That this Martial Law was totally silent in Time of Peace. And accordingly we find in the 4 and 5 of *Philip* and *Mary*. When severe Penalties were enacted on Officers and Soldiers for divers Misdemeanours, and Jurisdiction given in the Act to several Civil Courts to enquire of and determine the said Offences, the following Clause is added: "Provided always, &c. that if any the Offences aforesaid, touching Captains, Petty Captains, or others having Charge of Men, shall be committed DURING THE TIME that any Army or Number of Men under a Lieutenant (*i.e.* of the County) shall be assembled and continue together, &c. That then, upon Complaint thereof, the Lord Lieutenant or Lord Warden, or OTHER CHIEFTAIN, during the Time of any his or their Commission, shall, and may, hear, order and determine the Offences BY HIS OR THEIR DISCRETION." 4 and 5 *Phil. &Ma.* cap. 3. S. 6. Instead of producing more needless Authorities to prove the antient Establishment of this Distinction among us, I shall proceed to a Country where it at present subsists, as this Country is under the Dominion of the Crown of *Great-Britain*. In some of our *American* Colonies Military Jurisdiction commences from the firing of Alarm Guns, the Signal of an Enemies Approach; and again ceases when the Enemy is vanquished or retired. From such Occasional Exercise of Martial Law, no Grievance or Oppression of public Notoriety ever happen'd in the Memory of Man; nor indeed can happen in the Institution proposed by our Plan. And therefore if the Martial Law shall be thought an Improvement, no wise Man will set himself against it. However, let it be remarked that the Conquest of *Cape Breton*[1] was made without Martial Law; without mercenary Soldiers, or regular bred Generals; and even without one Gun fired by our Ships of War: Yet that was a Conquest of great Difficulty, and of the utmost Importance to this Nation, as it commands the greatest Fishery of the World. Without doubt the brave Conquerors will be justly and amply rewarded; a civil Government established, and wisely administered; such as may induce great Numbers of our *American* Fellow-Subjects to settle there, sufficient to carry on the Fishery, and to secure so valuable a Possession against all the Attempts of our Enemies.

(To be continued.)

TUESDAY, JANUARY 21, 1746.   NUMB. 12.

Δεινὰ τυράννων λήματα, καὶ πῶς
Ὀλίγ᾽ ἀρχόμενοι, πολλὰ κρατοῦντες,
Χαλεπῶς ὀργὰς μεταβάλλουσι.

EURIPIDES, *Medea*.[2]

The following Letter having been found at *Penrith*,[3] in a Room which the Pretender's Son had just left in a Hurry on the Alarm of the Duke's Approach,[4] there can be no doubt of its being genuine.

---

[1] See *TP* no. 10 (7 January 1745), above, p. 177 and *n*.

[2] vv. 119–21: 'How terrible princes' moods are! | Long ruling, unschooled to obey, | Unforgiving, unsleeping their feuds are' (Loeb).

[3] In Cumberland, approximately eighteen miles south and slightly east of Carlisle. In his withdrawal from England the YP reached Penrith on either 17 or 18 December 1745; Blaikie, *Itinerary*, p. 31; Forbes, *Lyon in Mourning*, ii. 123, 194.

[4] In the evening of 18 December, after a day of alarms of imminent attack, Lord George Murray

To his Royal High——s Charles P—— of W—s, *at* St. James's, *or if he be not yet arrived there, at his Quarters somewhere in* England *or* Scotland.

J. R.[1]

Dear Son,

The News of your first Success in *Scotland*[2] was very grateful to us; and indeed it came seasonably enough: For as we had, by our last Disbursements on Account of your Enterprize, almost totally exhausted our Exchequer, several Tradesmen here began to grow clamorous; and, in particular, her Majesty's Mantua-maker was so saucy to declare, she could not make her any more Robes, till her Bill was discharged. *Paul Regnier* too, the Jew, was here for the Interest due on the last-advanced 40000 Crowns;[3] and we had nothing to content him but civil Words.

These Clamours have, I believe, been principally raised by some Emissaries of the Enemy, who have industriously reported, that you have not a Possibility of Success: For that the Heretic Nation are almost unanimous against you. However, your Victory hath contradicted them, and produced so good an Effect, that these Demands have entirely ceased, and our Court hath been more splendid than ever, no less than nineteen Persons having been at it in one Day.

You write us word, that you intend to set forward very shortly for *London*, and that you purpose to dine there on *Christmas* Day. We heartily wish you a good Journey, and shall say two thousand *Ave Marias* and one thousand *Pater Nosters* on that Account.[4] Do not fail writing as soon as you arrive: For we cannot conveniently set out from hence, till you either send us a Remittance, or some Account, which may enable us to borrow a larger Sum than is at present in our Power.

We are glad to hear your Army consists of such Ragamuffins as you

and the rear guard were in fact engaged by a body of Cumberland's cavalry and dismounted dragoons. In the resulting 'skirmish' at Clifton, Cumberland's forces were beaten off and the rebels made good their retreat to Carlisle. Cumberland spent the night of the 18th at Clifton, entering Penrith on the 19th and halting there till the main body could join him on the 20th; Blaikie, *Itinerary*, pp. 31–2. For a narrative of the rebels' retreat from Penrith, see 'Present History of Great Britain', *TP* no. 8 (24 December 1745) and no. 9 (31 December 1745), below, pp. 384–5, 388–9.

  [1] i.e., Jacobus Rex, the OP here assuming his putative title. The letter is of course fictitious, but James apparently did affect the title and in Rome was commonly known as the 'Re d'Inghilterra'; Walpole to Mann, 23 April 1740, *Yale Walpole*, xvi. 9 and *n.* 30.

  [2] The victory over Cope at Prestonpans on 21 September 1745. See *History*, above, pp. 63–6, for a supposedly 'eyewitness' account.

  [3] Neither the Jew nor his transaction has been identified; they are probably fictitious. The OP was resident in Italy and, according to Mann's informant, had been 'in person to ask the Pope for money for this holy undertaking' as early as August 1745; Mann to Walpole, 17 August 1745 NS, *Yale Walpole*, xix. 90. For other accounts of the OP's want of money, see *Yale Walpole*, xix. 94, 96, 170; also *Dialogue*, above, p. 84.

  [4] Cf. *Dialogue*, above, p. 82.

say. They are the fittest for our Purpose; and since not one in a hundred of them can read, we are convinced our good Friends the Priests must have reconciled them all: For Father *Sophisti* hath often lamented the Propagation of Reading among the Vulgar, as one of the most stubborn Causes of Heresy.

It surprizes me, that none of the *English* have yet dared to declare themselves in our Favour; but we shall have an Opportunity of being revenged, as well on our indolent Friends as our active Enemies;[1] and indeed it will be necessary for us to have all the Confiscation possible; for we shall have very high Demands from our good Brothers of *France* and *Spain*, who must not be out of Pocket in our Quarrel. His Holiness too, the other Day, lamented to us the Poverty of the Holy Coffers, and God forbid they should not be supplied. You may, however, make what Promises you please, for my Confessor says, they are all void.[2] As to any Claim of Merit in the *Highlanders*, it is absurd; for the most a Subject can do or suffer, in our Cause, is no more than a Discharge of his Duty. With regard to putting your Army hereafter into Breeches, as Decency seems to require it, and the Expence will be small, I shall have no Objection: But I see no Occasion of Shoes, since I am well inform'd, that near a third Part of the Subjects of our victorious and triumphant Brother of *France* are at present without them.

We very much approve your Intention of taking all the Public Money in your March into *England*, and all the Private Money in your Retreat, if you should be obliged to make a Retreat: For if you have no other Success in your Expedition than collecting a large Sum, that itself will make you very welcome to us at your Return. In doing this, you need not enquire whether the Persons plundered are Rebels or no, since a Subject can have no Property which doth not belong to his Prince.[3] This is a Tenet which we sucked in with our Milk, and which we have the Honour to hold in common with our two Royal Allies; and indeed it is sanctified by his Holiness himself: For, as to the sacred Goods of the Church, they are not the Property of a Subject.

As to burning the City of *London*, if you cannot easily make yourself

---

[1] Cf. the entry for 9 February in the 'honest' Tradesman's dream journal, *TP* no. 10 (7 January 1746), above, p. 176.

[2] See *Dialogue*, above, p. 86, and the index to the present volume, *s.v.* 'Heretics'. Hanoverian propaganda made much of this supposed tenet of catholicism, especially after the appearance of various jacobite 'manifestoes' declaring that religious and civil liberties would be preserved under the jacobite (Stuart) regime. In *JJ* no. 3 (19 Decmber 1747), pp. 104–5, Fielding quotes Thomas Cartwright, one of James II's Ecclesiastical Commissioners: 'The Promises of Princes are *Donatives*, and are not to be strictly examined or charged upon them'.

[3] Cf. 'Mystery *the* Third', *JJ* no. 3 (19 December 1747), p. 105, where it is said of a king's subjects that their 'Lives and Properties are all to be at his Disposal'.

Master of it, it would, as you say, be a glorious Exploit to purge that Sink of Heresy and Rebellion with Fire. But you will consider, that the great Treasures there are already our own, (in every respect, save only the Possession) use therefore your utmost Endeavours first to secure to us all its Wealth, at least the most precious Part, after which to set fire to the Shell may possibly be no unwholesome Expedient: For, I am informed by an *English* Father of the Society of *Jesus*, that there are very few Places fit for Convents, in the present Disposition of its Buildings, and of these his Holiness is determined to establish immediately a very considerable Number.[1]

You desire Instructions how to dispose of Rebels of Distinction, particularly of the Members of those two illegal Assemblies of L—ds and C——ns.[2] It is therefore our Will and Pleasure, if any such escape from the general Massacre,[3] which is to be executed by Authority on the Evening of your Arrival, that you take the Precaution of immediately securing their Persons in some Goal, where they are to attend our own final Judgment and Determination; we being inclin'd, notwithstanding so much Provocation, to exert the utmost Clemency, consistent with our own Dignity, to all those, who have never actually offended us, or opposed our Cause, provided they shall be willing to embrace our most holy Faith, and return to the Obedience of the Holy See.[4]

The Mischiefs which your Army may do to our trading Subjects are immaterial; for it will be totally inconsistent with those Engagements into which we have entered with *France*,[5] for us to support any kind of

[1] A project alluded to in the dream vision of *TP* no. 10 (7 January 1746), above, p. 173, where it is reported (entry for 4–6 January) that the Bank, the South Sea Company and India House are 'to be turned into Convents'. Cf. *JJ* no. 3 (19 December 1747), pp. 107–8, where James II is said to have 'erected Popish-Schools and Mass-Houses all over the Kingdom'.

[2] Lords and Commons. After George II issued an order convening Parliament on 17 October 1745, the *YP* in a proclamation of 9 October sought to prohibit all Scotch peers and commoners from attending any session or obeying any orders or resolutions published in the name of either house; James Browne, *History of the Highlands*, iii. 104. The 'Hanoverian' interpretation of the various manifestoes issued in the name of James or Charles held that the latter maintained the illegality of parliament, said parliament having been constituted and convened during the Hanoverian 'usurpation'. See, for example, the comment on the manifestoes in *GM*, xv (1745), 611, on the occasion of their burning at the hands of the public hangman on 12 November 1745.

[3] The likelihood of a general massacre if the rebels should take over is sounded frequently in the occasional literature of the period. See index, *s.v.* 'Massacres', for Fielding's sounding of this theme.

[4] Such a proviso contradicts the repeated assertions of religious liberty and toleration, made in the various jacobite manifestoes. See above, p. 194, *n.* 2.

[5] At Fontainebleau on 23 October 1745 NS, the French, with d'Argenson representing Louis XV, and the YP, represented by Colonel O'Brien, signed a 'treaty', the fifth clause of which stated that when peace was restored, the contracting parties should enter into 'un traité de commerce entre les sujets de part et d'autre, pour procurer tous les avantages mutuels qui peuvent tendre au bien réciproque des deux nations'; as printed in Browne, *History of the Highlands*, iii. 449. For other implications of the treaty, see Eveline Cruickshanks, *Political Untouchables: The Tories and the '45* (New York, 1979), pp. 82–3.

Trade in *England*. We are sensible this may be attended with some Inconvenience; but the Necessity of our Affairs hath forced us into these Engagements; and tho' our Promises to Subjects and Heretics are void, yet between Princes and Catholics Faith is sacred, and none but his Holiness can dissolve it.

We hope you continue constant at Confession, and persevere in all other Duties of Religion, and that you shew no Countenance to Heretical Worship: For, believe me, a Crown would be dearly bought by a bare Connivance at Rebellion against our Holy Mother. I know it is the Opinion of many Fathers of the Church, and of his Holiness himself, that our Royal Father was expelled out of his Kingdom, as a Punishment for his conniving at Heresy, even for a Time, tho' it was in order to its Extirpation.[1] However, you have his Holiness's Absolution for not pulling down their Churches, nor turning the Heretics out of them, till you have Possession of the Capital; as it might injure the Cause, and give those Heretic Dogs, who are our good Friends, some Suspicion that we shall not protect them in the future full Enjoyment of their Religion.

Nothing hath been omited here, which may contribute to your Success; besides private Prayers to the Saints, several Solemn Masses have been celebrated for that Purpose. Nothing, indeed, can equal the Zeal of his Holiness in our Cause. He hath sent *per* Bearer 50000 Pardons, and as many Indulgences, with positive Orders to allow them to your Friends at half the Price for which they are at present vended in the holy Markets of *Europe*. The Rev. Father who is charged with these, brings likewise with him 1000 Pair of each, to be distributed *gratis* among all those who have eminent Merit in the Service.[2]

This Father, whose Name is *O-Faggot*, was originally born our Subject; but hath been bred up under a *Spanish* Inquisitor.[3] His Holiness

---

[1] In his first speech to the privy council James II assured them of his support and defense of the Church of England, and his program of toleration was commemorated in the Declaration of Indulgence (1687), which granted pardon to 'all nonconformists, recusants, and other our loving subjects for all crimes ... contrary to the penal laws formerly made relating to religion'; text from *English Historical Documents 1660–1714*, ed. Andrew Browning (London, 1953), p. 397. See also Gilbert Burnet, *History of the Reign of King James the Second* (Oxford, 1852), p. 7; and David Ogg, *England in the Reigns of James II and William III* (Oxford, [1963]), p. 141. Louis XIV was reported, in 1689, to have attributed James II's downfall in part to 'being too mercifull to the Protestants'; HMC, Seventh Report, Part ii (London, 1879), Appendix (Marquis of Ormonde's MSS), p. 758. See also *Dialogue*, above, pp. 85–6.

[2] The entry for 7 March in the tradesman's journal, *TP* no. 10 (7 January 1746), above, p. 178, foretells that on the night of the reception for the papal nuncio at St James's a 'grand Office' was opened at Drury-Lane for the sale of pardons and indulgences. See also *Dialogue*, above, p. 84, and Mann to Walpole, 7 December 1745: 'The Pope has given the Pretender 50,000 crowns, and 100,000 indulgences, nay, to as many as will pray for the success [of the jacobite uprising]' (*Yale Walpole*, xix. 170).

[3] The name 'O-Faggot' emphasizes the considerable Irish presence in the services of France and Spain. For additional suggestions that an inquisition will follow a jacobite takeover, see index, *s.v.* 'Inquisition'.

hath been pleased to appoint him Inquisitor-General of *Great Britain*. Take Care, therefore, that he be received with great Honour and Respect, and be sure not to defer an Hour erecting that Court, and investing him in his Office, when it is in your Power.

You need not press us so earnestly to set out for *England*; for we are as desirous to be there, as it is possible for yourself to be to see us: But we shall not think of departing from hence, till we receive the Remittance above-mentioned, nor till we are positively assured, that there is not a single Regiment of our Enemies Troops unbroken. The Life of a King is sacred; and as it is the highest Crime in a Subject to attempt it, so is it the highest Offence in the King himself to be negligent in its Preservation. All other Men have four Duties, to God, their King, their Neighbour, and themselves; but we have only two, *viz.* the first and last of these: For, after assisting at Mass, and saying his Bead-Rolls, a Prince hath no other Obligation on him, but to take sufficient Care of himself, a Duty in which we purpose never to be defective: And so, after recommending you to the Care of *St. Thomas à Becket*, I subscribe myself, *&c.*

CONSIDERATIONS *concerning the Establishment of a National* MILITIA *continued.*

There are two more Objections against a National Militia, to which I am now to give an Answer, *viz.*

3. That it is an Innovation upon our Constitution of Government, and injurious to the Royal Prerogative.

4. That it is an impracticable Scheme.

As to the first of these Objections I wou'd intreat my Readers to consider, whether every new Act of Parliament may not with the same Propriety be called an Innovation: But no Act of the Legislature can be construed as such, which is conformable to the essential Principles of our Constitution; and I defy the Opposers of our Plan, to point out a single Instance of its Contrariety to the first Principles of the *British* Government. On the contrary it is notorious, that a general Militia was an essential Part of our antient Constitution; for then the feudal Law was in Force, and all the Lands of *England* were held either mediately or immediately of the King, upon the Tenure of yielding personal Military Service. Thus all the Landholders of *England* were formed into one great Body of Militia, by whose Valour our *Edwards* and *Henrys* atchieved many signal Victories in *France*, still renowned in History, which reflect Glory upon the present Generation.[1] From this Consideration only it is manifest, that a general

[1] The *Plan*, 'Introduction', p. xlii, also refers to the victories in France achieved by these kings. Here and elsewhere in this essay Fielding is following the argument of the *Plan*.

Militia was an essential Part of our antient Constitution. And our Histories teach us, that all those *British* Armies which fought so bravely abroad as well as at home, before the Restoration, were no other than a Militia. But as Luxury and Expence encreased, all these Personal Services were commuted for pecuniary Considerations; and of Course the Constitution of this Country became defective in the Means of public Defence. To supply that Defect, and at the same Time to answer better the sinister Purposes of self-interested Statesmen, mercenary Armies were established, and new Forms of arraying the Militia enacted, which continue down to this Day, in the Body of our Statutes. How then can such an Institution be called an Innovation upon our Constitution of Government?

It is true indeed, that all our Militia Acts since the Restoration, seem as if intended to defeat the true Purposes of public Defence, by obliging the People to confide only in mercenary Armies; for, by those Laws the Deputy Lieutenants are invested with discretionary, or rather, *absolute Power* to call forth a great Number of undisciplin'd useless People, at an enormous Expence of the landed Gentlemen. In this Respect our Plan is far preferable, because it enjoins impartially the personal Service of all Orders of Men;[1] proposes easy Methods of disciplining them, so as to become at least equal to any other Army whatsoever, at no Expence to the Public, nor to the poorest People, and at little Charge to the most opulent. This therefore is an Institution adequate to the Ends of public Defence, and perfectly suitable to the Constitution of a free Government, administer'd by regal Authority: For the Liberties of the People are not more regarded, than the Rights and Prerogatives of the Crown are preserved inviolate by the Appointment of General Officers for every County, under the sole Direction of the King. By the present Acts of Militia, the whole Appointment is left to the Discretion and Fidelity of one Man, the Lord Lieutenant of each County appointed by the King. In our Plan his Majesty not only appoints the Lord Lieutenant, or General in Chief, but all other subordinate General Officers, out of the best Men of each District, selected by the People.[2] In that Institution therefore the Royal Power cannot be abused, or disappointed, as in the other, but must be exercised for the public Benefit. This is properly Royal Prerogative, which in the Intention of our Law *is the King's Power to do all possible Good to his People*, without the Ability of doing wrong. A Power truly resembling that of the Deity, who is Almighty in Acts of Justice, Mercy, and Goodness, but under a moral Incapacity, by the Rectitude of his Nature, of doing Evil.

[1] See '*Proposition* 1' of the *Plan*, as reprinted in *TP* no. 13, Locke, p. [130].
[2] See '*Prop.* 4', Locke, p. [130].

But if any Man conceives the Prerogative of a *British* King to be a Power of acting capriciously, or to the Injury of his Subjects, he mistakes arbitrary Rule, or Tyranny, for Prerogative: A Power which no wise or good Man can wish for; a Power absolutely inconsistent with the Nature of a free Government, and derogating from the Honour of our lawful Sovereign, whose Glory, and Superiority over most other Kings in *Europe*, is that of ruling a Free People, while they tyrannize over abject Slaves. If there be any such in this Land of Freedom, let them retire to their Brethren of the North, from whence they may be driven to Destruction by those who deserve the Name of *Britons*; or forced to fly, with their Mock Prince, to the Regions of Oppression, where they may lick the Dust like Reptiles, and reap the Fruit of their Desire; the mighty Privilege of being voluntary Vassals; while the true Friends of Liberty concur in the Establishment of a National Militia, as the only infallible Means of defending our rightful Sovereign, and of preserving all those social Blessings, which are most dear and valuable to human Nature. I cannot quit this Head concerning the Prerogative, without making the following Observation.

That the King would have more Power over this Militia than any of his antient Predecessors had; for he will have the annual Appointment of every General Officer;[1] whereas the Barons, who were formerly the Commanders of the *British* Militia, were really independent on the Crown.

But the 4th Objection affirms, that an useful Militia is an impracticable Scheme.

Tho' a flat Denial is an Argument as good as a general Censure, yet I will deal more candidly with my Opposers, and endeavour to point out those Parts of our Plan which seem most exceptionable, however unnecessary this may be thought by those who have read the Plan with Attention.

In a former Paper I observed, that the Objection cannot be meant absolutely against the Practicability of a good Militia, because that would be to contradict the most notorious Facts of Antiquity, and even of the present Time; in which a Militia is the only Defence of all the Cantons of *Switzerland*, and of our North *American* Colonies. If therefore our Objectors have any Meaning, it must be against the Possibility of establishing a Militia suitable to a Nation of so great extent as this, consisting of many different Orders of Men, and adequate to all the purposes of Defence. Without Doubt there was no small Difficulty in

---

[1] Copy-text 'Officers' should perhaps be retained, but *OED* gives no examples of 'every' with a plural subordinate after 1671, and chiefly a defining word interposes.

accommodating a Scheme to all these different Circumstances; but if I am not mistaken the Plan now recommended is of that Sort: If not, it is very easy for so many great Politicians, and good Soldiers, as this Kingdom can furnish, to point out the Defects.

Perhaps the Objection of Impracticability may point at the Manner of electing military Officers by Ballot: But this will vanish upon a very transient View of our Plan, by which it will appear to be a Method less subject to wrangle and contention, more expeditious and easy, than our common Elections for parochial Officers: For it is observable, that no Election in our Plan extends to any greater Number than the People of a single Parish.[1]

The Ballot has been ever thought the most unbiassed, and the least invidious Manner of Election invented by the Art of Man. For that Reason one Branch of the *British* Legislature has frequently practised that Method in many great and important Cases. At *Venice* the Elections of Magistrates, State Councils, and all civil Officers are determined in the Way of Ballot; by which Means only that Government has ever been administer'd with the most Integrity of any in the World, as appears evidently by its Duration for so many Ages in the same exact civil Form; tho' its Constitution is nevertheless remarkably defective in the Want of a National Militia: For by that Defect only Venice has lost its most valuable Territories, and with them its Trade, Navigation, Riches and Power. May Heaven grant that the same Defect in the Constitution of this great and populous Government, shall not reduce it to the like state of Insignificance, or to a much more deplorable Condition, that of being a Province to *France*!

If there be any other Objections to our Plan, not founded upon the sinister Views of Faction,[2] I confess myself incapable of guessing at them: But whenever any such shall be offered to the Public, I promise a full and impartial Examination of them. In the mean Time it is the Duty of my Character, as a True Patriot, to press the Necessity of establishing a National Militia at this dangerous Crisis, when *France*, by only threatening Invasion, can oblige our Cruizers, and other Ships of War, to retire to our own Coasts for their Protection, leaving all the *British* Navigation defenceless, and a Prey to a few Privateers, as our excessive Losses for this Month past, evince beyond all Contradiction.

---

[1] See '*Prop*. 7', Locke, p. [130], and 'Sect. I. *The Form of establishing the Infantry of the Superior Militia*', in *TP* no. 14, Locke, p. [135].

[2] For the political ramifications of the various procedures for raising troops, see 'General Introduction', above, pp. xliii–xlv.

From TUESDAY, JANUARY 21, to TUESDAY, JANUARY 28,
1746.[1]   NUMB. 13.

Qui non recte instituunt atque erudiunt liberos, non solum liberis sed et Reipublicæ faciunt injuriam.

CICERO.[2]

Mr. *Adams* having favoured me with a second Letter,[3] I shall give it the Public without any Apology. If any Thing in it should at first a little shock those Readers who know the World better, I hope they will make Allowances for the Ignorance and Simplicity of the Writer.

To the TRUE PATRIOT.

My Worthy Friend,

I am concerned to find, by all our Public Accounts, that the Rebels still continue in the Land. In my last I evidently proved, that their Successes were owing to a Judgment denounced against our Sins, and concluded with some Exhortations for averting the Divine Anger, by the only Methods which suggested themselves to my Mind. These Exhortations, by the Event, I perceive have not had that Regard paid to them I had Reason to expect. Indeed I am the more confirmed in this Conjecture, by a Lad whom I lately met at a neighbouring Baronet's, where I sojourn'd the two last Days of the Year, with my good Friend Mr. *Wilson.*[4]

This Lad, whom I imagined to have been come from School to visit his Friends for the Holidays, (for tho' he is perhaps of sufficient Age, I found, on Examination, he was not yet qualified for the University) is, it seems, a Man *sui juris;*[5] and is, as I gather from the young Damsels Sir *John's* Daughters, a Member of the Society of *Bowes.*[6] I know not

---

[1] The formula of the unitary dateline is changed here and in all subsequent numbers.

[2] In *JJ* No. 22 (30 April 1748), p. 257, Fielding attributes the same passage to Cicero and translates it as follows: 'Those who do not rightly instruct and educate their Children, do not only an Injury to their Children, but to the Public.' The passage has not been located in Cicero, but cf. *Verrine Orations*, II. iii. 69 (161), which begins, 'Quibus in rebus non solum filio, Verres, sed etiam rei publicae fecisti iniuriam', and goes on to elaborate the theme.

[3] 'Adams's' first letter constitutes the leader of *TP* No. 7 (17 December 1745), above, pp. 151-7.

[4] Father of Joseph Andrews and, according to the novel (IV. xvi. 343), living in the same parish as his son. In *Joseph Andrews*, III. iii. 201-25, he relates his life history, some details of which seem apposite here.

[5] 'of his own right'. Applied to a person who is not a minor, nor insane, nor subject to any other disability (Jowitt, *Dictionary*).

[6] Beaux or Beaus.

whether I spell the Word right; for I am not ashamed to say, I neither understand its Etymology nor true Import, as it hath never once occurred in any Lexicon or Dictionary which I have yet perused.

Whatever this Society may be, either the Lad with whom I communed is an unworthy Member, or it would become the Government to put it down by Authority; for he utter'd many Things during our Discourse, for which I would have well scourged any of the Youth under my Care.

He had not long entered the Chamber before he acquainted the Damsels, that he and his Companions had carried the Opera,[1] in opposition to the Puts;[2] by which I afterwards learnt, he meant all sober and discreet Persons. And Fags![3] says he, (I am afraid tho' he made use of a worse Word) we expected the Bishops would have interfered;[4] but if they had, we should have silenced them. I then thought to myself, Stripling,[5] if I had you well-horsed[6] on the Back of another Lad, I would teach you more Reverence to their Lordships.

This Opera, I am informed, is a Diversion in which a prodigious Sum of Money,[7] more than is to be collected out of twenty Parishes, is lavish'd away on foreign Eunuchs and Papists, very scandalous to be suffered at any Time, especially at a Season when both War and Famine hang over our Heads.

During the whole Time of our Repast at Dinner, the Young Gentleman entertained us with an Account of several Drums and Routs, at

---

[1] Inasmuch as the 'Bowe', later in this leader, states that he left London on Christmas Day, the reference here cannot properly be to an actual performance. The opera did not open at the King's (Haymarket) till 7 January 1746. Instead the 'Bowe' must refer to a concerted backing of the opera in its deliberations over whether to open in such a time of crisis. Whatever the actual circumstances of the decision to open, it was apparently made before 2 December 1745, when Charles Wyndham wrote Hanbury Williams that the opera would come on despite the public phobia against catholics and Italians; Sir Charles Hanbury Williams MSS, lxviii, f. 47, as cited in *Yale Walpole*, xix. 177 *n.* For the social implications of backing the opera, see *TP* no. 9 (31 December 1745), above, pp. 167–71.

[2] A 'Put' is a stupid man, silly fellow, blockhead (*OED*). Cf. *CGJ* no. 33 (25 April 1752), i. 329, where the more conventional 'country Puts' is used. As the 'Bowe' uses it here, the term has class implications as well.

[3] An unmeaning substantive, alone or in exclamatory phrases, expressing asseveration or astonishment (*OED*). More commonly met with, perhaps, in such forms as 'Efags' or 'Ifacks', where it is a trivial oath amounting to a simple asseveration: In faith, by my faith (*OED*); see, for example, *Joseph Andrews*, i. xiv. 63, and ii. xiv. 167. It is also a favorite oath of Shamela's.

[4] Presumably to lend the weight of their moral disapprobation of such an 'unpatriotic' undertaking.

[5] Copy-text has 'Strippling', which *OED* records no later than the 17th century. The archaism may seem suitable to 'Adams', but the modern spelling occurs later in this same letter.

[6] To 'horse' is to elevate on a man's back, in order to be flogged; hence to flog (*OED*). In other contexts 'Adams' is less supportive of corporal punishment: 'I myself am now the Father of six, and have been of eleven, and I can say I never scourged a Child of my own, unless as his School-master, and then have felt every Stroke on my Posteriors'; *Joseph Andrews*, iii. iv. 226–7.

[7] *DA* of 6 January 1746 prints a letter defending the opera as an institution. The letter states that the cost of presenting operas for a season is £14,000, of which about £2,000 is paid to foreign singers and presumably taken out of the country. See also *TP* no. 9 (31 December 1745), above, pp. 167–9.

which he had been present. These are, it seems, large Congregations of Men and Women, who, instead of assembling together to hear something that is good; nay, or to divert themselves with Gambols, which might be allowed now and then in Holiday Times, meet for no other Purpose but that of Gaming, for a whole Guinea and much more at a Stake. At this married Women sit up all Night, nay sometimes till one or two in the Morning, neglect their Families, lose their Money, and some, Mr. *Wilson* says, have been suspected of doing even worse than that. Yet this is suffered in a Christian Kingdom; nay, *(quod prorsus incredibile est)*[1] the Holy Sabbath is, it seems, prostituted to these wicked Revellings; and Card-Playing goes on as publickly then, as on any other Day; nor this only among the young Lads and Damsels, who might be supposed to know no better, but Men advanced in Years, and grave Matrons, are not ashamed of being caught at the same Pastime. *O Tempora! O Mores!*[2]

When Grace was said after Meat, and the Damsels departed, the Lad began to grow more wicked. Sir *John*, who is an honest *Englishman*, hath no other Wine but that of *Portugal*. This our *Bowe* could not drink; and when Sir *John* very nobly declared he scorned to indulge his Palate with Rarities, for which he must furnish the Foe with Money to carry on a War with the Nation,[3] the Stripling replied, Rat the Nation, (God forgive me for repeating such Words) I had rather live under *French* Government, than be debarred from *French* Wine. Oho, my Youth! if I had you horsed, thinks I again.—But, indeed, Sir *John* well scourged him with his Tongue for that Expression, and I should have hoped he had made him ashamed, had not his subsequent Behaviour shewn him totally void of Grace. For when Sir *John* asked him for a Toast, which you know is another Word for drinking the Health of one's Friend or Wife, or some Person of Public Eminence, he named the Health of a married Woman, filled out a Bumper of Wine, swore he would drink her Health in Vinegar, and at last openly profest he would commit Adultery with her if he could. *Proh Pudor!*[4] Nay, and if such a Sin might admit of any Aggravation, she is, it seems, a Lady of very high Degree, *et quidem*[5] the Wife of a Lord.

---

[1] 'Which is utterly unbelievable'.   [2] From Cicero, *In Catilinam*, i. 2.

[3] In 1745–6 England was at war with France, and 'loyalists' would presumably refuse to buy from a belligerent. 'Port was patriotic and Whig and woolen; claret was Francophile and Jacobite—patriotic only in Scotland'; George Macaulay Trevelyan, *England under Queen Anne: Blenheim* (London, 1930), p. 301. Portuguese wines were also cheaper, which may partly account for the snobbery of the 'Bowe' in the matter. By the terms of the so-called Methuen treaty of 1703 Portuguese wines imported to England paid markedly lower duties than French wines, and despite subsequent tinkerings with the system of duties, the preference remained throughout the century.

[4] Martial, *Epigrams*, VIII. lxxviii. 4: 'What modesty!' (Loeb).

[5] 'Indeed', 'in fact'.

Et dies et charta deficerent si omnia vellem percurrere, multa quidem impura et impudica quæ memorare nefas, recitavit.[1] Nor is this Youth, it seems, a Monster or Prodigy in the Age he lives; on the contrary, I am told he is an Exemplar only of all the rest.

But I now proceed to what must surprize you. After he had spent an Hour in rehearsing all the Vices to which Youth have been ever too much addicted, and shewn us that he was possessed of them all. *Ut qui impudicus, adulter, Ganeo, Aleca, manu, ventre pene, bona Patria laceraverat,*[2] he began to enter upon Politics:

O Proceres censore opus an haruspice nobis.[3]

This Stripling, this Bowe, this Rake, discovered likewise all the Wickedness peculiar to Age, and that he had not with those Vices which proceed from the Warmth of Youth, one of the Virtues which we should naturally expect from the same sanguine Disposition. He shewed us, that grey Hairs could add nothing but Hypocrisy to him; for he avowed public Prostitution, laughed at all Honour, Public Spirit and Patriotism; and gave convincing Proofs, that the most phlegmatic old Miser upon Earth could not be sooner tempted with Gold to perpetrate the most horrid Iniquities than himself.

Whether this Youth be (*quod vix credo*)[4] concerned himself in the Public Weal, or whether he have his Information from others, I hope he greatly exceeded the Truth in what he delivered on this Subject: For was he to be believed, the Conclusion we must draw would be, that the only Concern of our great Men, even at this Time, was for Places and Pensions; that instead of applying themselves to renovate and restore our sick and drooping Common Weal, they were struggling to get closest to her Heart, and, like Leeches, to suck her last Drop of vital Blood.

---

[1] 'Both time and paper would run out if I wanted to run through all the things, indeed, the many rude and shameful things which, horrible to relate, he recited.' Cf. Cicero, *De Natura Deorum*, III. xxxii. 81: *Dies deficiat si velim enumerare quibus bonis male evenerit.* . . . Whether the departures from the Ciceronian original are owing to faulty memory or the presence of an intervening text (perhaps a school text) is not clear. Fielding was fond of quoting or englishing the passage, either in part or more or less whole. See the recently attributed 'Mum Budget' letter in *Common Sense* of 13 May 1738; *Champion* of 21 February and 1 March 1740; 'Some Papers Proper to be Read before the R—l Society', *Miscellanies* (1743), i. 203 (perhaps only a faint echo); and *CGJ* of 7 January 1752.

[2] Sallust, 'The War with Catiline', xiv. 2: 'As what wanton, adulterer, glutton, or gamester had wasted his patrimony in the hand [play], the belly [feasting] or the penis [debauchery]'. The text is corrupt in this place, but symmetry would appear to require that *manu*, *ventre*, and *pene* have as antecedents three (nor four) practitioners. 'Adams' or his text has added *adulter* and the printer may be responsible for what reads like *Aleca* (the type is very faint here) instead of the more customary *aleo* or *aleator*. In addition, the authoritative *Nam quicumque* with which the original opens has been altered (*ut qui*), apparently to fit better with the grammar of the ensuing main clause in English.

[3] Juvenal, *Satires*, ii. 121: 'O ye nobles of Rome, [is it] a soothsayer that we need, or a Censor?' (Loeb).

[4] 'Which I scarcely believe'.

I hope, however, better Things, and that this Lad deserves a good Rod, as well for lying as for all his other Iniquity; and if his Parents do not take Care to have it well laid on, I can assure them they have much to answer for.

Mr. *Wilson* now found me grow very uneasy, as indeed I had been from the Beginning, nor could any thing but Respect to the Company have prevented me from correcting the Boy long before; he therefore endeavoured to turn the Discourse, and asked our Spark, when he left *London*? To which he answer'd, the *Wednesday* before. How, Sir, said I, travel on *Christmas* Day? Was it so, says he, fags! that's more than I knew; but why not travel on *Christmas* Day as well as any other? Why not, said I, lifting my Voice; for I had lost all Patience. Was you not brought up in the Christian Religion? Did you never learn your Catechism? He then burst out into an unmannerly Laugh, and so provoked me, that I should certainly have smote him, had I not laid my Crabstick down in the Window, and had not Mr. *Wilson* been fortunately placed between us. Odso, Mr. Parson, says he, are you there? I wonder I had not smoked you before.[1] Smoke me! answered I, and at the same Time leap'd from my Chair, my Wrath being highly kindled. At which Instant a Jackanapes, who sat on my Left Hand, whipt my Peruke from my Head, which I no sooner perceived, than I porrected[2] him a Remembrance[3] over the Face, which laid him sprawling on the Floor. I was afterwards concerned at the Blow, tho' the Consequence was only a bloody Nose, and the Lad, who was a Companion of the others, and had uttered many wicked Things, which I pretermitted in my Narrative, very well deserved Correction.

A Bustle now arose, not worth recounting, which ended in my Departure with Mr. *Wilson*, tho' we had purposed to tarry there that Night.

In our Way home, we both lamented the peculiar Hardiness of this Country, which seems bent on its own Destruction, nor will take Warning by any Visitation, till the utmost Wrath of Divine Vengeance overtakes it.

In discoursing upon this Subject, we imputed much of the present Profligacy to the notorious Want of Care in Parents in the Education of Youth, who, as my Friend informs me, with very little School Learning,

---

[1] To 'smoke', meaning to observe, take note of, 'twig' (*OED*), often with implications of detecting an identity or occupation previously concealed or unnoticed, is frequently applied to Parson Adams. See, for example, *Joseph Andrews*, II. vii. 131, and xi. 146.

[2] To 'porrect' means, humorously, to tender, deal out (*OED*, citing only this example from the *TP*).

[3] A reminder given by some thing or fact; a thing or fact serving to remind one of something (*OED*). Cf. 'something to remember [me] by'.

and not at all instructed (*ne minime quidem imbuti*)[1] in any Principles of Religion, Virtue and Morality, are brought to the Great City, or sent to travel to other Great Cities abroad, before they are twenty Years of Age; where they become their own Masters, and enervate both their Bodies and Minds with all Sorts of Diseases and Vices, before they are adult.

After we were returned to Mr. *Wilson's* House, he presented me with two Sermons, on the Subject of educating Youth, lately preached by the Reverend Mr. *Dalton*, at the University of *Oxford*.[2] As these contain much excellent Doctrine, and very full Instructions to Parents upon this Head, you will do great Service to your Country by earnestly recommending them to the Public.

I shall conclude with a Passage in *Aristotle's Politics*, Lib. VIII. Cap. 1. Ὅτι μὲν οὖν τῷ νομοθέτῃ μάλιστα πραγματευτέον περὶ τὴν τῶν νέων παιδείαν, οὐδεὶς ἂν ἀμφισβητήσειε. καὶ γὰρ ἐν ταῖς πόλεσιν οὐ γιγνόμενον τοῦτο. βλάπτει τὰς πολιτείας. Which, for the Sake of Women, and those few Gentlemen who do not understand *Greek*, I have rendered somewhat paraphrastically in the *Vernacular*. "No Man can doubt but that the Education of Youth ought to be the principal Care of every Legislator; by the Neglect of which, great Mischief accrues to the Civil Polity in every City."[3]

---

[1] 'And not the least imbued', more or less translating the English phrase immediately preceding the parenthesis.

[2] *Two Sermons Preached before the University of Oxford, At St. Mary's, On Sept. 15ᵗʰ, and Oct. 20ᵗʰ, 1745. And now Publish'd for the Use of the Younger Students in the Two Universities. By John Dalton, M.A. and Fellow of Queen's College in Oxford* (Oxford, 1745). The dedication to the students reads in part: 'Preach'd and Publish'd in order to contribute, in some Degree, towards guarding them against the fashionable Prevalence of Irreligion, Prophaneness, and Impiety, and the consequent Disregard to the Authority of the just Government and happy Constitution of these Kingdoms, the fatal Effects of which are now so sensibly experienc'd.' Dalton (1709–63), versifier and adapter of Milton's *Comus* for the stage, had a long-standing Somerset connection and may have been known to Fielding. According to Walpole, Dalton and Lady Luxborough 'rhymed together till they chimed together' and had an illegitimate child as a result; to Lady Ossory, 3 August and 20 December 1775, *Yale Walpole*, xxxii. 243–4, 283. In the letter of 20 December Walpole adds the gossip that 'the seraphic Duchess [of Somerset, earlier Hertford], her friend, was suspected to have *chassé sur les même terres*, and so it is no wonder they were intimate, as they agreed *in eodem tertio*'. The countess of Hertford was among the privileged readers who received prepublication copies of *Tom Jones*, and she had read the first two volumes by 20 November 1748; Thomas Hull (ed.), *Select Letters between the Late Duchess of Somerset, Lady Luxborough . . . and Others*, i (London, 1778), 85. Given this connection, it is probably John Dalton who is the 'Mr. Dalton' Thomas Birch refers to as having also read the first two volumes and 'is loud in his commendation of it'; letter to Philip Yorke of 15 October 1748, BL Hardwicke Papers, Add. MSS 35397. M. C. and R. R. Battestin, 'Fielding, Bedford, and the Westminster Election of 1749', *Eighteenth-Century Studies*, ii (1977–8), 145 n., conjecture Richard Dalton (1715–91), architectural draughtsman, antiquary, and librarian to the prince of Wales, but the more 'literary' nature of the evidence in favor of John Dalton seems telling. Cross, ii. 223, thinks the latter was 'the Rev. Mr. Dalton', a robbery victim in one of the first cases brought before Fielding in Bow Street in 1748; citing *St James's Evening Post* of 8–10 December 1748.

[3] VIII. i (1337ª 11–13). In *JJ* no. 22 (30 April 1748), p. 257, Fielding cites this passage again and offers a very similar translation.

I am, while you write like an honest Man, and a good Christian,

Your hearty Friend and Well-wisher,

ABRAHAM ADAMS.[1]

CONSIDERATIONS *concerning the Establishment of a National*
MILITIA *continued.*

Having cleared away those Objections which inconsiderate Men have
made to the Establishment of a National Militia, which however weak
they have been proved to be, have filled some with Dislike to our Plan,
and many more with Despair of seeing it established, I now proceed to
lay the Plan itself before my Reader in as concise a Manner as possible.
Those who value their Country at two Shillings may for that Price purchase this Plan at large; in which they will find all the Propositions here
laid down enforced with the strongest and most convincing Reasons.[2]

From TUESDAY, JANUARY 28, to TUESDAY, FEBRUARY 4,
1746.   NUMB. 14.

*Mihi quidem, tamet si haudquaquam par gloria sequatur scriptorem et auctorem rerum;
tamen in primis arduum videtur res gestas scribere: primum quod factis dicta sunt
exæquanda: dehinc, quia plerique, quæ delicta reprehenderis, malevolentia et invidia dicta
putant.*

SALLUST, *Bellum Catilinarium.*[3]

There is no Practice more unfair, than to ascribe the Faults of particular
Members of a Profession to the Profession itself, and thence to derive
Ridicule and Contempt on the whole.[4]

[1] Perhaps sensing that this leader merited a push, Mrs Cooper took out advertisements for it in at
least two London papers, *General Advertiser* of 27 January and *London Evening Post* of 25–7 January
1746.

[2] After this hortatory, not to say mercenary, 'puff' Fielding begins quoting *verbatim* extracts from
the *Plan*: from pp. 1–20 in this number, from pp. 23–35 in no. 14, and from 35–49 in no. 15, after which
the series breaks off. See Locke, pp. [130], [135–6], [141–2].

[3] 'The War with Catiline', iii. 2, where modern texts read *sequitur* (for *sequatur*), *actorem* (for
auctorem), *facta dictis* (for *factis dicta*): 'For myself, although I am well aware that by no means equal
repute attends the narrator and the doer of deeds, yet I regard the writing of history as one of the most
difficult of tasks: first, because the style and diction must be equal to the deeds recorded; and in the
second place, because such criticisms as you make of others' shortcomings are thought by most men
to be due to malice and envy' (Loeb).

[4] Cf. *Champion* of 12 February 1740, i. 259: 'Nothing is greater Proof of the general Fondness in
Mankind for Scandal, than their Readiness to extend any Censure which may be justly incur'd by a
particular Member of a Profession to the Profession itself.' And for the contrary tendency, that of the
profession's appearing to ennoble the practitioner, see *Champion* of 29 March 1740, ii. 45.

Physicians and Lawyers have very sorely experienced this Temper in Mankind; nay, the Clergy themselves have felt its Bitterness, to the no small Advancement of Irreligion and Immorality, by lessening that Awe and Respect which we ought to bear towards a Body of Men, who are particularly appointed to instruct us in the Ways of true Piety and Virtue, and who generally deserve the utmost Regard from us.

The Method in which these Slanderers have proceeded is artful enough. They at first instituted a Cant Word, by which they pretended to denote Insufficiency and Demerit in the several Professions; and having at length sufficiently affixed those bad Ideas to the Words, they applied them indiscriminately to the Professions themselves: And thus Quack, Pettyfogger and Parson,[1] have at length come to represent the serious Characters of a Physician, Lawyer, and Minister of the Gospel.

There is still another Body of Men who have tasted this Injustice, and who, tho' they are not allowed the Honour of stiling themselves of a Profession, have however deserved well of Mankind. I mean those Gentlemen who, by their Writings, have either improved the Understanding, corrected the Will, or entertained the Imagination; such especially as have blended these three Talents together, who have temper'd Instruction and Correction with Humour, and have led Men pleased and smiling thro' the Paths of Knowledge and Virtue.

Now as this hath been attempted by some Men of mean and inadequate Capacities, while others have perverted great Talents to darken and corrupt the Minds of Men, by dressing up Falshood in the Colours of Truth, and Vice in those of Virtue, such Writers have justly raised the Contempt and Indignation of the Wise and Good, and have been stigmatized with the Appellation of *Scriblers*;[2] a Name which from the Persons on whom it was properly fixed, hath contracted much Scorn and Abhorrence.

This Appellation likewise hath been applied with great Indifference and Impropriety; and Fools, who are always the Ecchoes of Knaves,[3] have drivelled it out against some of the best and worthiest Members of Society: Those especially who apply their Talents to expose the Vices

---

[1] Cf. *TP* no. 28 (6–13 May 1746), below, p. 288, where 'Tom Skipton', the footman, desires not to be considered 'a Pimp of a Parson (as my master calls them)'; also *TP* no. 13 (21–8 January 1746), above, p. 205, where the 'Bowe' uses the appellation derogatorily to address 'Abraham Adams'. In *Joseph Andrews*, I. xv. 68, and IV. xvi. 342–3, 'Introduction' to 'A Journey from this World to the Next', *Miscellanies* (1743), ii. 4, and *JJ* no. 30 (25 June 1748), p. 316, 'Adams' is called 'Parson' in an apparently neutral way.

[2] A petty author; a writer without worth (Johnson); a mean or pitiful Writer (Bailey); a mean or bad writer both in character and composition (Dyche–Pardon).

[3] See *TP* no. 17 (18–25 February 1746), below, p. 224 and *n*. Seven paragraphs further on in the present leader Fielding will call the heads of political parties 'Knaves' and their followers 'Fools'.

and Follies which reign in their Age and Country, are most certain of incurring this Censure. For as there is no Minister of Vengeance whom great wicked Men both hate and fear equally with a good Writer, there is none whom they will so earnestly labour to ruin and depreciate. They have Ways enough to avoid all other Courts of Justice; but no Method is left them to escape from their Arraignment here, unless this of taking all Credit from the Tribunal.

But of all Writers, there is none so much exposed to this ungenerous Treatment, as those who meddle with Politics. Ministers of State, who are generally the worst and wickedest of Men, no sooner hear a Political Writer hath made his Appearance in the World, than they are alarm'd, even as a Thief would be, by one coming to awaken the Family while he was robbing the House. The Word is immediately given to all the Gang. Every Method is practised to *vilify* and decry the Writer and his Works, and *Scribler* resounds through all the Coffee-houses in Town.[1]

Such Arts have been practised in former Ages, nay within the Memory of Man; but I will do a great Man of the present Age the Justice to acknowledge, I have apprehended no such Treatment from him, nor, I believe, received it at his Hands. Those who have the Honour to know him better than myself, assure me he hath the utmost Indifference for all Writers, and the greatest Contempt for any Good or Harm which they can do him.[2]

This may proceed from a Consciousness of his own Rectitude, and I presume doth so; but in worse Men, and more corrupt Nations, such Contempt might have been derived from a Contempt of the whole People; from imagining them so sunk in Vice and Baseness, that they have neither Fears to be alarmed, nor Spirit to be roused; that the Cause of their Country could not awaken their Attention; but that they would *refuse to listen to the Voice of the Charmer* on that Subject, *charm'd he never so wisely*.[3]

Such, I am convinced, cannot be the Motive of our Great Man; such, I am as well convinced, is not the Character of this Nation: The Reader,

---

[1] Cf. 'Apocrypha', *TP* no. 11 (14 January 1746), below, p. 402: 'We hear several Masters of Coffee-houses have lost some of their best Customers, because they refused to take in the *True Patriot*.' The leader to this point is reprinted, without the motto, in *London Magazine*, xv (1746), 75–6.

[2] The 'great Man' of this paragraph is Henry Pelham; the witnesses to his contempt for political writers might include Fielding's friends in or close to the administration—Lyttelton, Pitt, Dodington. In 1748 Fielding animadverted on the Pelhams' refusal to buy off his colleague James Ralph, and in 1753 Pelham did express his contempt for Ralph 'while in pay'; see *JJ* no. 17 (26 March 1748), p. 214 and *n*. Whatever his private feelings about the profession of political writer, Pelham does appear to have spent far less for journalistic propaganda than did his predecessor and mentor, Sir Robert Walpole. See 'General Introduction', above, p. lxviii.

[3] Cf. Psalms 58: 5: Which will not hearken to the voice of charmers, charming never so wisely.

therefore, will pardon me, if I for once only speak, and that with Reluctance, of Myself, and endeavour to recommend the *True Patriot* to his Regard and serious Attention, from the following Considerations:

First, That this Paper was begun in a Time when this Nation was apprehended, by All, to be in a State of the utmost Danger; when a victorious Army of Rebels was actually in Possession of one Part of our Island, and preparing to attack the other; nay the 5th Paper,[1] which was designed to animate my Countrymen to the Defence of their Religion and Liberty, at the last Extremity, was actually writ on that memorable Day when the Rebels having, as it was thought, slipt the Duke's Army, were feared to be approaching this City by hasty Marches; and when this Apprehension, joined to that of an immediate Invasion from *France*, had thrown all Men into the most dreadful Consternation.

2dly, That this Paper was begun upon the true Principles of Liberty, and hath been, I hope, carried on in open Opposition to the Designs of Papists, Jacobites, and factious Malecontents, who would overturn our Religion and all our civil Liberties, on the one hand; and to Ministerial Slaves and Hirelings, who would corrupt, enervate, and betray us, on the other.

3dly, That its Author hath not sought the Protection of any Party, by adhering rigidly to the Principles of any, farther than is consistent with the true Interest of his Country, which no Party, it will be found, hath effectually consulted at all Times. Indeed this absurd and irrational Distinction of Parties hath principally contributed to poison our Constitution; and hath given wicked Ministers an Opportunity, by corrupting the Heads of Parties, who are generally Knaves, to cajole their Followers, who are always Fools.

It seems, therefore, difficult to impute the Original of this Paper to any of those corrupt Motives which have often given birth to Political Writings: For as the Hirelings of a Minister have sometimes counterfeited Public Spirit, while they have attempted to gloss over and defend the most flagitious Schemes, so have others as falsely pretended to that glorious Incentive, while Disappointment, Rage or Envy have prompted

---

[1] French, pp. 259, 262, argues that Fielding means his sixth leader (10 December 1745) above, pp. 147–51. *TP* no. 5 (3 December 1745) is mainly about money. It attacks financial ruthlessness in a time of crisis and prints a letter from 'Timothy Pauper' to show the pathos of indebtedness under such conditions. Furthermore, its date of composition could not have been later than the day it was published (3 December 1745), a bad time certainly, but hardly 'Black Friday' (6 December), the day London heard of the rebel penetration as far as Derby, the day of 'most dreadful Consternation'. *TP* no. 6, on the other hand, is entirely hortatory, emphasizing religion and liberty, and its date of composition presents no problems.

them to misrepresent Measures really justifiable, or to raise impertinent Clamours against such as the Necessities of the Times have demanded. By such Means clogging the Wheels of Government with needless Opposition, and raising dangerous Factions in the Community, when no actual Danger hath threatned it.

But a little Candour will be sufficient to prevent any Person from casting such Imputations on this Paper. Few Words are at present, I hope, necessary, and fewer will be hereafter, to skreen the Author from the Scandal of being the Tool of a Ministry. They must know little of Courts and Courtiers, who can imagine themselves making way to court Favours, by spending their Breath, or even their Blood, in Defence of their Sovereign. Kings hear not of such Merit, nor do Ministers acknowledge it. The Fate of such Persons is only Neglect from the Party they espouse, and sometimes Hanging from that which they oppose. It is the Flattery of Ministers, and the Support of their iniquitous Measures, which recommends to their Countenance. It is the *brevibus Gyaris et carcere dignum*,[1] which promotes Men to Places, Pensions and Rewards.

Nor can a Writer who disdains to enlist under the Banner of any Party, be with greater Fairness suspected of any Designs of Faction or determined Opposition. No Man who hath ever entertained Views of this Kind, hath been so wretched a Politician as to decline strengthening himself with the Friendship and Assistance of those who are embark'd in the same Scheme. Whereas I again declare, and I presume my Writings will bear the same Testimony, that I am engaged in no Party, nor in the support of any, unless of such as are truely and sincerely attached to the true Interest of their Country, and who are resolved to hazard all Things in its Preservation.[2]

This is, I hope, the largest and strongest of all Parties; for the Support of which the *True Patriot* was undertaken. To these alone he addresses his Writings, and from them he promises himself Encouragement and Attention, at a Time when the most Sanguine must confess this Nation is in real Danger, and if not in a desperate, is at least in a deplorable Situation, a Situation from whence to deliver us requires very great Abilities, as well as the highest Integrity.[3]

[1] Juvenal, *Satires*, i. 73: '[what merits] narrow Gyara or a gaol' (Loeb). Gyara (Gyaros), one of the Cyclades, is a small island southwest of Andros. Under the Roman empire it was used as a place of banishment and was one of the most dreaded places used for that purpose. Cf. Tacitus, *Annales*, iii. 68, 69; iv. 30.

[2] This paragraph and the one following are summarized in *London Magazine*, xv (1746), 76.

[3] The phrasing here resembles that of the letter in 'Observations on the Rebellion', *TP* no. 3 (19 November 1745), below, p. 352, where the difficulties of the crisis are seen as so great 'that nothing less than the highest Abilities, joined to the highest Integrity, can surmount them'. Cf. also *JJ* no. 43 (24 September 1748), p. 398.

From TUESDAY, FEBRUARY 4, to TUESDAY, FEBRUARY 11, 1746.   NUMB. 15.

> ——*Lucri bonus est Odor ex re*
> *Qualibet.*

JUVENAL.[1]

Evil be thou my Good, says the Devil, in *Milton.*[2] But tho' the Poet hath put this Sentiment into so bad a Mouth, it is capable of an Interpretation which might not misbecome a much better Being: For to convert Evil into Good, or to work the latter by great Art and Dexterity out of the former, is the Business of a good and great Man; it is, indeed, the highest Praise of the Politician, and may be often executed by him with much Facility. Numerous and heavy Taxes are a grievous Sore in every Government, and yet even these may be sometimes used to good Purposes, by being imposed on Luxury;[3] by which means they will contribute to extirpate, or at least lessen, that Pest and Bane of Society, which, according to the *Roman* Poet,[4] was a crueller Mischief to the *Romans*, than all their Wars had been, and avenged all the Injuries which that People had done to those Countries which they conquered, and from whence they brought Home this Pestilence.

The great Progress which Luxury hath made in this Nation of late Years, and the Poverty and Corruption which it hath introduced, have more need of being lamented than proved. If therefore the present Exigencies of the State may be made a means of eradicating, or at least of diminishing this Evil, I have no Doubt but our Governors will pursue so salutary a Measure.

And here my fair Readers must pardon me if I begin with them, or rather with their Dress, as one of the most obvious, and, if I may so say, strutting Articles of Luxury. I am sure they will presently suspect I mean their Hoop-Petticoats, which have of late grown to so very enormous, and indeed portentous a Size, that should they increase as they have done within these last ten Years, our Houses must be soon

---

[1] *Satires*, xiv. 204–5: 'The smell of gain is good whatever the thing from which it comes' (Loeb).

[2] *Paradise Lost*, iv. 110. '*Satan*, now in prospect of *Eden* . . . falls into many doubts with himself . . . but at length confirms himself in evil' ('Argument' of Book iv).

[3] Here and elsewhere 'Luxury' is a Fielding *topos*. See index, *s.v.*, and for its possible connection to the ideology of 'patriot' politics, see 'General Introduction' above, pp. lxiii–lxiv.

[4] Juvenal, *Satires*, vi. 292–300. In his 'Part of Juvenal's Sixth Satire, Modernized in Burlesque Verse', *Miscellanies*, i. 115, 117, Fielding makes the application to Britain: 'Severer Luxury abounds, | Avenging *France* of all her Wounds. | When our old *British* Plainness left us, | Of ev'ry Virtue it bereft us: | And we've imported from all Climes, | All sorts of Wickedness and Crimes.'

pulled down, and built with great Gates instead of Doors to admit them.

But as I have the utmost Tenderness for this dear Part of the Creation, whom I regard as the Dispensers to us of the highest human Happiness, I shall not venture to speak against any thing which long Habit may have persuaded some of them is a real Necessary of Life, without giving my Reasons for thinking otherwise, and at the same time endeavouring to answer all the Arguments which I conceive may be fairly urged in their Defence; for if it be not an absolute Superfluity, it is by no means an Article of Luxury, and cannot deserve to be taxed as such.

I will therefore begin with fully stating all which hath been, and may be, said in Defence of the Hoop-Petticoat, with my Answer to each Argument.

First, I know it is generally believed by my fair Countrywomen to be a Guard to what is dearer to them than Life, their Honour, to which it serves as a Sort of Fortification; a Woman being as it were intrenched in her Hoop, and the Assailer kept at a Distance; and therefore the higher and nobler the Honour of every Woman is, the larger and wider is her Hoop; that of a Right Honourable being generally of four times the Extent above the Hoop of the inferior Part of the Sex.

To this I answer, that there is nothing so fatal as to trust to Outworks of insufficient Strength; and tho' Beaus and Petit-Maitres[1] (who are generally Cowards in the Fields of *Venus*) may be deterred from making their Approaches by this Circumvallation,[2] yet when attacked by braver Assailants, I am afraid it will be tenable a very short time. And whenever these Works are *blown up*, as often happens, they discover too much the Nakedness of the Place, and thereby animate the Assailant. To which I will add, that a Woman by depending fatally on the Strength of this *Whalebone Work*, may neglect those Precautions which will most infallibly preserve her: And this is, I doubt not, the Reason that Ladies in the largest Hoops are apt to deride that moral and religious Assistance, in which lesser Hoops place their whole Trust.

A second Argument in Favour of the Hoop is, that it tends much to preserve the Superiority of the fair Sex over ours; for, that half a dozen Men, in the Company of as many behoop'd Ladies, look like so many Jackanapes, or like Lilliputians compared to the Inhabitants of *Brobdingnag*. That besides the Gracefulness which this adds to every Woman, it

---

[1] An effeminate man; a dandy, fop, coxcomb (*OED*).

[2] Cf. *Spectator* no. 127 (26 July 1711), ii. 6: 'It is most certain that a Woman's Honour cannot be better entrenched than after this manner, in Circle within Circle, amidst such a Variety of Outwork and Lines of Circumvallation.'

cannot fail of inspiring her Husband with Ideas of his Wife's superior Dignity, and may at least keep him at a proper Distance from her.

I own there is something plausible in this; but when it is considered, that it concludes to[1] the Husband, in whose Eyes a Woman is chiefly concerned to preserve her Dignity, and before whom *many* Wives are obliged to appear without their Hoops, she may possibly lose more Dignity than she gains by it. May not such a Woman appear as a skinned Rabbit, compared to one in the Warren; or like a Silk-worm when the Silk is wound off, and the little Grub appears at the Bottom? Lastly, may not an ignorant and innocent Bridegroom be apt to wonder what is become of ninety-nine Parts of what he espoused, and justly complain that he hath not above an hundredth Part so much Wife as he married?

The third and last Argument is in favour of Trade, That the Consumption of Silk, &c. would be greatly lessened, by the Reduction of Hoops; for that a Petticoat would not contain one fourth Part of what it now doth.

To this many Answers may be given; but I shall content myself with one, *viz.* That it is better for a Tradesman to sell one Yard of Silk for which he is paid, than many Yards for which he never will receive a Penny.[2]

Having thus fairly stated all those Reasons, which I imagine may be advanced on the Hoop-Petticoat Side, and given, I hope, satisfactory Answers to them all, I now proceed to those further Inconveniencies which attend this Fashion, and from which I apprehend no Colour of Good can be derived.

And first, tho' it might be reasonably imagined, that a Woman two Yards and a half wide, could never remove herself from the Room in which she is deposited, without breaking down the Walls, yet Experience teaches us, that they are able not only to convey themselves out of their own Houses, but likewise to crowd, sometimes four of them, into a Coach; for this Purpose, however, they are obliged to extend their several Hoops out of the Coach-windows. By this they probably intend to strike a Terror into the Beholders, from the Quantity of Whalebone with which they are fortified; but I assure them a very contrary Effect is produced, especially when a pretty Face is seen peeping over.

---

[1] The meaning is not absolutely certain; *OED* records no clear examples of this usage. Perhaps, to lead to a conclusion, to be conclusive. The 'plausible' argument is conclusive as far as the husband is concerned, but it is confined to him and his public anxieties. To the wife, with her more private responsibilities, the argument is neither so conclusive nor so confined.

[2] Alluding to the propensity of 'persons of quality' to put off paying their bills. Cf. *TP* no. 23 (1–8 April 1746), below, p. 258, where at the playhouse 'Every Joke on a Courtier's not paying his Debts, is sure to receive a thundering Applause from the Pit and Galleries.'

And as they are guilty of doing a public Injury by their Hoops in, or rather out, of their Coaches, so when they carry them to Places of Public Diversion, they do a private Mischief to the Proprietor. A Woman in six Yards of Hoop is dishonest if she doth not pay for three or four Places. Indeed a very few Ladies will shortly be able, in a literal Sense, to fill the Pit at the Opera. And thus those very Ladies who have, to their great Honour, established an Opera by their Interest, may destroy it with their Hoops.[1]

I omit the many domestic Inconveniencies which arise from Hoops, such as the Demolition of *China* and other brittle Ware, which, when two Hoops jostle together, may be, and often are, swept down from the Top of a Cabinet. The Use to which a Hoop may be applied, and for which indeed they might be thought originally intended, is abundantly sufficient to discourage any virtuous Woman from wearing them. I am far indeed from thinking they are often, if ever, made a hiding Place for a Gallant;[2] but as this is possible to be the Case, sure no Lady of Honour would give a Latitude to such a Suspicion in evil-minded Persons and censorious Prudes, who may pretend to have seen more Feet than two under a Petticoat.

Lastly, this preposterous Hoop is so far from being any Ornament to a Woman, that it makes her rather a monstrous and ridiculous Object; for as there can be no Beauty without Symmetry, how can we reconcile to this the Idea of a Creature who measures two Spans[3] round the Waste,[4] and six Yards round the Knees?[5] If it should be urged, that the Hoop being artfully lifted up, gives a Woman an Opportunity of shewing a Pair of handsome Legs, I answer, that may be done as well, and with more Ease to the Lady, by shortning her Petticoat one Foot, than by extending her Hoop twenty.

I therefore propose, that a Tax may be laid on this superfluous Piece of Apparel. What Number of Yards my Superiors will allow a Lady

---

[1] Faulkner's *Dublin Journal* of 10 April 1742 prints a request that 'the Ladies who honour this Performance [the première of Handel's *Messiah*, on 13 April 1742] with their Presence would be pleased to come without Hoops, as it will greatly increase the Charity, by making Room for more Company'; as quoted in Otto Erich Deutsch, *Handel* (New York, [n.d.]), p. 545. For Fielding's view of the so-called Opera of the Nobility, see *TP* no. 9 (31 December 1745), above, pp. 164–71.

[2] Cf. Swift, Letter xxxiv (3 November 1711), *Journal to Stella*, ed. Williams, ii. 409: 'Have you got the whalebone petticoats amongst you yet? I hate them; a woman here may hide a moderate gallant under them.'

[3] Approximately 18 inches, the distance from the tip of the thumb to the tip of the little finger of an extended palm being conventionally measured at 9 inches.

[4] The predominating 18th-century spelling of 'waist', which was rare until adopted in Johnson's *Dictionary* (1755) [*OED*].

[5] Cf. *CGJ* no. 37 (9 May 1752), i. 348, which notes the difficulty of cramming 'seven Yards of Hoop into a Hackney-Coach'.

gratis, must be submitted to them, as likewise the Sum they will assess on all above.

By these Means one Branch of Luxury will be abolished, or else made contributory to the Good of the Public.

From Tuesday, February 11, to Tuesday, February 18, 1746. Numb. 16.

> ———*Qui nimios optabat Honores*
> *Et nimias poscebat opes, Numerosa parabat*
> *Excelsæ Turris Tabulata, unde altior esset*
> *Casus, et impulsæ præceps immane Ruinæ.*
> *Quid Crassos, quid Pompeios evertit, et illum,*
> *Ad sua qui domitos deduxit flagra Quirites?*
> Summus nempe Locus nullo non* Marte petitus.
>
> Juvenal.[1]

Philosophers, as well as Divines, have treated of the Instability of Human Greatness, and have thence endeavoured gravely to dissuade Men from placing too high a Value on its Possession, or from being too eager in its Pursuit. Their Argument hath been, that it is hardly worth our while to risque our own Ease, Safety and Conscience, and to destroy Cities, Countries, and thousands of our Fellow-Creatures, from the Prospect of a Reward, which we can never be sure of maintaining the Possession of during half an Hour.

Other Writers have, from this Instability, taken Occasion to represent all worldly Greatness, as the Object of Ridicule and Contempt; have considered it as a mere Rattle; a worthless, trifling, childish Bauble, which none but Madmen or Fools could think worth their Pursuit, or even their Desire.

* Alii, *nulla non arte* sed perperam.[2]

---

[1] *Satires*, x. 104–10, with one emendation, as indicated in the next note, and typographical emphasis added: 'in coveting excessive honours, and seeking excessive wealth, he was but building up the many stories of a lofty tower whence the fall would be the greater, and the crash of headlong ruin more terrific. What was it that overthrew the Crassi, and the Pompeii, and him who brought the conquered Quirites under his lash? What but lust for the highest place pursued by every kind of [conflict]?' (Loeb).

[2] 'Others read *nulla non arte* but incorrectly'. The emendation from *arte* ('means') to *marte* ('conflict') stresses and particularizes the factionalism which Fielding attributes to Bath and Granville.

Greatness (says a Burlesque Writer) *is a lac'd Coat*
      from Monmouth Street,[1]
   Which Fortune lends us for a Day to wear;
   To-morrow puts it on another's Back.[2]

Shakespeare, in the following Lines, hath given us a fine Picture of this short-lived Happiness.

Life's but a walking Shadow, a poor Player,
THAT STRUTS AND FRETS HIS HOUR UPON THE STAGE,
AND THEN IS HEARD NO MORE. *It is a Farce*
Play'd by an Idiot, full of Sound and Fury,
Signifying Nothing.[3]

By Life here, is meant the Life of a Great Man. This appears as well by the Tenor of the Play, the Moral of which is levelled at Ambition, as by the Poet's putting this Sentiment into the Mouth of *Macbaeth**, in whose Person he characterizes the Vanity and Misery of this restless Passion.

The two Lines which immediately precede those I have quoted, when restored to their true Reading, farther illustrate the Drift of the Poet in this Speech. In Mr. *Theobald's* Edition, they stand thus.

And all our Yesterdays have lighted Fools
The Way to dusty Death; out, out, brief Candle.[4]

* This is the true Reading.[5]

---

[1] It extended from St Giles southwest to the end of Grafton Street and in the 18th century was notorious for the sale of second-hand clothing. Cf. Gay, *Trivia*, ii. 548–9: '*Thames-street* gives cheeses; *Covent-garden* fruits; | *Moorfields* old books, and *Monmouth-street* old suits.'

[2] The 'Burlesque Writer' is Fielding; the passage is from *The Tragedy of Tragedies; or the Life and Death of Tom Thumb the Great* (London, 1731), I. iv. 3–5.

[3] Emended from *Macbeth*, v. v. 24–8. Fielding's emendation of 'Farce Play'd' from the original 'Tale Told' permits yet another allusion to the farcical aspects of the Bath–Granville takeover of 10–12 February 1746. See 'General Introduction', above, pp. xcv–xcvi. Possibly the second of Fielding's own footnotes should have been placed here to call out the otherwise silent emendation, but his unauthorized spelling *Macbaeth*, to which that footnote now refers, is repeated and presumably intentional. See the next editorial footnote, below. In *Tom Jones*, VII. i. 324, Fielding calls quotations of this passage 'hackneyed'.

[4] *The Works of Shakespeare. In Seven Volumes. Collated with the oldest Copies and corrected; with Notes, Explanatory, and Critical: By Mr. Theobald* (London, 1733–4), v. 466. Lewis Theobald (1688–1744), dramatist, translator, and editor, was the 'hero' of the three-book *Dunciad* and the 'piddling Tibbald' of the *Epistle to Dr. Arbuthnot*. Fielding subscribed to Theobald's edition of Shakespeare, but seems to have been willing to charge him with editorial pedantry. See *Plutus* (1742): 'Mr. Theobald, who being a Critic of great Nicety himself, and great Diligence in correcting Mistakes in others, cannot be offended at the same Treatment' (p. xiii). Fielding further mocks his editorial pedantry in *A Journey from this World to the Next* (1743; I. viii); his 'wit' in 'Advice to the Nymphs of New S—m' (1730), as printed in *Miscellanies* (1743), i. 69; and his plays, in the *Tragedy of Tragedies* (1731), *passim*. For Fielding on the more general question of editing Shakespeare, see *Tom Jones*, x. i. [523], and *CGJ* no. 31 (18 April 1752), i. 315–20.

[5] Given the fact that this leader is devoted to satirizing the 'brief Cabal' of Bath and Granville, the

Dusty Death! says Mr. *Theobald*, *i.e.* Death which reduces to Dust and Ashes;[1] a Construction which, according to the usual Custom of Commentators, reduces the Author's Meaning to nothing. Thus they should be undoubtedly read.

> *And all our Yesterdays have lifted Tools*
> *The Way to dusty Death. Out, out, brief Cabal.*

Dusty here is not, as the above-mention'd Commentator would have it, an idle Epithet to Death, like yellow to Gold, cold to Ice, or any other such Botch, for which a School-boy would be whipt. On the contrary, it is intended to distinguish the Death of these *Tools of Ambition*, from that of other Men. *A dusty Death* is Death in a dusty Place, as for instance in a High-way, where a Crowd of Attendants raise a Dust; and this the Word *lifted* further indicates, as it points out the Vehicle in which those Tools *ought* to travel through this Way.[2]

The next Correction which I shall offer of *Cabal* for *Candle* puts the Matter beyond Dispute. *Macbaeth* having ruminated on what is to happen,

> *To Morrow,*[3] *to Morrow, and to Morrow;*

and, by reflecting on the Dusty Death which hath constantly attended such Tools as himself, having foretold, as it were, their Fate, fairly gives up his Schemes. Then addressing himself to his *brief Cabal*, (where by the by, the Word *brief* may be either apply'd to the Paucity of their Number, or to the Brevity of their Duration)[4] he says, *Out, Out, i.e.*

'true Reading' is probably intended to make the name *Macbeth* sound more like that of Lord Bath, titular leader of the 'forty-eight-hour' ministry. In the 'Present History of Great Britain' of this number Fielding refers to Bath by his satirical sobriquet of 'Will Waddle' and retails a witty anecdote of his political machinations: see below, pp. 418–19.

[1] *Works*, v. 466 n. 45, which comments on the alternative reading 'study Death': 'This Reading is as old as the 2d Edition in *folio*; but, surely, it is paying too great a Compliment to the Capacities of Fools. It would much better sort with the Character of wise Men, to study how to die from the Experience of past Times. I have restor'd the Reading of the first *Folio*, which Mr. *Pope* has thrown out of his text.

> *The way to dusty Death*

i.e. Death, which reduces us to Dust and Ashes.'

[2] The hangman's cart, by means of which those sentenced to die by hanging were transported through the streets to the place of public execution. In *TP* no. 20 (11–18 March 1746), below, p. 244, the Opposition is urged to deliver themselves into the hands of 'the Great Officer of Justice', the hangman; and in *TP* no. 26 (22–9 April 1746), below, p. 276, sentence of 'Dissection' is passed upon them, to be implemented, presumably, after they have been hanged.

[3] The omission of the particle ('and') seems unintentional. It is unauthoritative, and seemingly unsatirical.

[4] Referring to the inability of the Bath–Granville 'ministry' to fill even the essential cabinet posts and to sustain their tenure beyond two days. 'Cabal' is again applied to their adherents in *TP* no. 26 (22–9 April 1746), below, p. 274.

resign, go out before ye are kicked out, and brought to that *Dusty Death*, &c. He then proceeds very naturally to illustrate the Life of *such Tools* by a Player, who puts on a false Appearance on the Stage, being indeed the very Reverse of what he seems, and who, after having strutted a few Hours in the Habit and Character of a great Man, reverts again to his primitive State, and becomes an inconsiderable Member of the Community. And here perhaps the Poet intended to insinuate, that none but an Ideot, or very silly Fellow, would be desirous of acting such a *strutting, fretting, sounding, furious, insignificant* Part.[1]

But the most striking Ridicule of all worldly Greatness drawn from its Instability, is in the Duke of *Buckingham's* inimitable *Rehearsal*;[2] where the Gentleman Usher and Physician dethrone the two Kings of *Brentford* by a Whisper. The Scene is so excellent and natural that I cannot help transribing a Part of it.[3]

Physician.   If they heard us whisper, they'll turn us out, and no Body else will take us.

Smith.   Not for Politicians I dare answer for it.

Physician.   Let's then no more ourselves in vain bemoan;
We are not safe unless we them dethrone.

Usher.   'Tis right:
And since Occasion now seems debonair,
I'll seize on this, and you shall take that Chair.

[*They draw their Swords, and sit in the two great Chairs on the Stage.*

Bayes.   There's now an odd Surprize, *the whole State's turned quite Topsy-turvy*, without any Pother or stir in the whole World i'gad.

Johnson.   *A very silent Change of Government, truly, as ever I heard of.*

Bayes.   It is so: And yet you shall see me bring 'em in again, by and by, in as odd a Way every Jot.

[The Usurpers *march out flourishing*, &c.

---

[1] The leader to this point is reprinted in *London Magazine* xv (1746), 84–5, under the heading 'Ridicule on the Vanity of Human Greatness'.

[2] Fielding refers frequently to this play (1671) by George Villiers, second duke of Buckingham. From it he borrowed the name of his editorial *persona* in *CGJ* ('Sir Alexander Drawcansir'), and the 'old and new' Kings of Brentford in *The Author's Farce* (1730) derive from the same source. See also *The Tragedy of Tragedies* (II. iii), ed. James T. Hillhouse (New Haven, 1918), p. 109; and the 'Introduction' of *The Journal of a Voyage to Lisbon* (1755).

[3] II. iv. Fielding's transcription is not entirely exact; furthermore, he has used italics and capitals so as to point up the applicability of the lines to Bath and Granville. French, p. 381, refers to a supposititious letter of Chesterfield's, dated 5 March 1746, presumably from Dublin: 'Our two Great Departed Statesmen seiz'd on power with no more prospect of maintaining it, or foundation to support it, than King Phys and King Ush in the Rehearsal'; from John Robinson, 'A Letter of Lord Chesterfield on the Change of Ministry in 1746', *EHR*, iv (1889), 750. Cf. Henry Seymour Conway to Walpole, 19 February 1746: 'I would have given something . . . to have met our two ministers of Brentford coming down the backstairs'; *Yale Walpole*, xxxvii. 221.

Enter *Shirly*.

Shirly.   Hey ho! hey ho! *What a Change is here?*
                Hey ho, hey day!
                I know not what to do, or what to say!

Johnson.   Mr. *Bayes*, in my Opinion, now, that Gentleman might have said a little more upon this Occasion.[1]

Bayes.   No Sir, not at all; for I underwrit his Part on Purpose to set off the rest.

Johnson.   Cry you Mercy, Sir.

Smith.   But pray, Sir, how came they to depose the two Kings so easily?

Bayes.   Why, Sir, you must know, THEY HAD A DESIGN TO DO IT BEFORE, BUT NEVER COULD PUT IT IN PRACTICE TILL NOW. And to tell you the Truth, that's the Reason I made them whisper so.

But the Play doth not end here: For had Mr. *Bayes* left *two such Fellows* in Possession of their great Chairs, his Piece would have been deservedly hiss'd off the Stage. These two Usurpers therefore, who are always personated by *two very ridiculous Actors*, having sat a little while in their Places, to the great Diversion of the Spectators, *sneak off* as comically and as absurdly as they enter'd. Nothing indeed can be imagined more absurd and ridiculous, nor better calculated to inspire the Audience with Contempt than their *Exit*. For upon hearing of the Approach of the two whose Chairs they filled, without any Thing having happened which they must not have foreseen, one of the Usurpers addresses the other,

K. Usher.   Then, Brother *Phys*. 'tis Time we should be gone. *(Upon which they both steal out from their Chairs and run away.)*[2] No human Wit can ever bring Greatness to a more farcical End.

I cannot help mentioning one Piece of Ridicule more, as I apprehend it hath escaped common Observation; I mean that fine Raillery upon Greatness of Punchinello in a Puppet-shew, which hath been of late Years, for I know not what Reason, laid aside.[3]

Whoever hath been present at such Exhibitions, must remember that when the Emperor of *Muscovy*, or any other great Personage, hath

---

[1] This speech and the next two, constituting an exchange of comments on Shirly's short speech, were first printed in the 'third' or quarto edition of 1675.

[2] v. i, where the stage direction reads, 'The two Usurpers steal out of the Throne, and go away.' The next sentence of the leader is the *TP*'s editorial comment.

[3] For evidence that in 1748 Fielding brought back the puppet show, to the stage of 'Madam de la Nash's' theatre in Panton Street, see Martin C. Battestin, 'Fielding and Master Punch in Panton Street', *PQ*, xlv (1966), 191–208.

appeared in all his Splendor, to the great Admiration and Delight of the Spectators, the ingenious Conductor of the Piece took Care to introduce Mr. Punch and his Man Gudgeon, who with great Familiarity seat themselves on each Side the Emperor. Upon this the *Russian* Nobility immediately quit the Stage, and Mr. Punch and his Man being left alone, the Devil or some Monster enters, and carries them both off.[1] Then the Gentleman who plays on the Fiddle, and who performs the Part of the ancient Chorus in this Drama, winds up the whole with moral Animadversions on the Impudence of Punchinello, and the Justice of his Punishment.

I intended, at the Beginning of this Paper, to have followed so laudable an Example; and to have concluded with some wholesome Reflections on Ambition, and the comical as well as tragical Events which it produces; but I shall reserve them for some future Paper, the rather as I doubt whether my Reader may not be in too risible a Humour at present to attend willingly to any thing serious.[2]

From TUESDAY, FEBRUARY 18, to TUESDAY, FEBRUARY 25, 1746. NUMB. 17.

Whereas we have been informed by several Persons, that they have not been able to procure the TRUE PATRIOT *at any Rate: And we have great Reason to believe that many malicious and base Endeavours have been used to suppress the Sale of this Paper, by some who are concerned in imposing on the Public, by propagating Lies and Nonsense, which we have endeavoured to detect and expose. If any Hawkers, or others, will acquaint Mr.* A. Millar,[3] *Bookseller, opposite* Katharine-Street *in the* Strand, *with the Name of any Person who has bribed, or offered to bribe them to refuse delivering out the* TRUE PATRIOT *to their Customers, they shall be well rewarded, and their Names, if they desire it, concealed.*

[1] A conventional ending of the old puppet shows; see *Tom Jones*, XII. vi. 641 and *n.*; also George Speaight, *The History of the English Puppet Theatre* (London, 1955), p. 171. Apparently the emperor or czar of Muscovy was a conventional representative of the great figure brought low; in *Champion* of 8 May 1740, ii. 188, the raree-showman makes the czar dance at his command; also *Jonathan Wild*, III. xi.

[2] No future paper contains 'wholesome Reflections on Ambition, and the comical as well as tragical Events which it produces'.

[3] Andrew Millar (1706–68), a Scot, publisher of Thomson, Hume, and Johnson's *Dictionary*, had already published *Joseph Andrews* (1742), the *Miscellanies* (1743), and would publish *Tom Jones* (1749) and other Fielding works. The Strahan ledgers list billings to him for the printing of a number of Fielding pamphlets of the 1740s (including the three in the present volume) which appeared with the Cooper imprint, an arrangement which suggests that Millar held copyright and was in fact Fielding's primary publisher from 1742 on. For his personal relationship with Fielding, to two of whose sons he left legacies, see Austin Dobson, 'Fielding and Andrew Millar', *The Library*, third series, vii (1916), 177–90; and for the possible significance of his name in this headnote, 'General Introduction', above, pp. lxv–lxx.

Gentlemen and Ladies may be furnished with this Paper, by sending their Names and Habitations to Mrs. A. Dodd[1] *without* Temple-Bar; *to Mr.* Chappelle[2] *in* Grosvenor-Street; *or to* M. Cooper[3] *in* Pater-Noster-Row: *By whom Hawkers,* &c. *may be constantly supplied with them.*[4]

—— PETIMUS STULTITIA.
HORACE.[5]

[1] Ann Dodd (1716-*post* 1756), daughter of the better-known Ann (Barnes) Dodd and Nathaniel Dodd (d. 1723), inherited her mother's shop on the latter's death (1739) and during the '40s and '50s seems to have functioned as a kind of 'super' mercury for the West End of London. Her name is on the imprints of *Shamela* (1741) and *The Crisis: A Sermon* (1741; with E. Nutt and Henry Chappelle) as 'publisher'; as 'seller' it is on the imprint of *Ovid's Art of Love Paraphrased* (1747; with M. Cooper and Woodfall, Millar being listed only in the advertisements). According to the colophon of the *CGJ* (1752), it was 'Printed and Sold by Mrs. Dodd, at the *Peacock, Temple-Bar*'. Her busy shop is briefly described in *CGJ* no. 6 (21 January 1752), i. 171. For more on Cooper, Dodd, and the evidence of the imprint as to the copyright holder and the subordinate distributor, see Michael Treadwell, 'London Trade Publishers 1675–1750', *The Library*, sixth series, iv, no. 2 (June 1982), 99–134, but especially pp. 111, 115–16, and 123–5. The evidence suggests that the 'real' publisher was often someone other than the person named in the imprint.

[2] Henry Chappelle or Chapelle, bookseller and stationer, was one of the partners in the *Champion* conger, and his name appears on the imprint of the so-called second edition (1743) of the collected *Champion* reprint. He shares the imprint (with Ann Dodd and E. Nutt) of *The Crisis: A Sermon* (1741), a work commonly attributed to Fielding. There is no evidence which permits assigning Chappelle a larger role in the *TP* than that of distributor, as indicated in the headnote. See G. M. Godden, *Henry Fielding* (London, 1903), pp. 100, 115, 138–9; Cross, ii. 250.

[3] See 'General Introduction', above, pp. lxv–lxx, and *TP* no. 1 (5 November 1745), above, p. 106. Cooper's name appears on the imprint of all three of the pamphlets printed in the present volume, and her name on the colophon of all numbers of the *TP* indicates she had a more important role than either Dodd or Chappelle in the newspaper's undertaking.

[4] This headnote appears only in nos. 17 and 18. For its possible significance as an indicator of the *TP*'s fortunes, see 'General Introduction', above, pp. lxvi–lxvii. The lead item in the 'Apocrypha' of *TP* no. 11 (14 January 1746), below, p. 402, reads: 'We hear several Masters of Coffee-houses have lost some of their best Customers, because they refused to take in the TRUE PATRIOT. T.P. *We mention this purely that the rest of their Brethren may not suffer in like Manner for the same Fault.*' In the leader of *TP* no. 18 (25 February–4 March 1746), below, p. 234, Fielding claims, 'We have already received Advice of some Persons, who have ventured to nibble at our Paper, and in private Corners to whisper several disrespectful Matters against some of our most approved Performances, and against the Voice of the People.' Such claims have not been verified, and in view of the absence of any clear political hostility shown toward the *TP* in the published material of the time, it is tempting to view them as attention-getting strategies. In any event, they were commonplace. See, for example, *Champion* of 12 June 1740 (ii. 327), where it is claimed that coffee houses were asked 'not to take our Paper in, *dealing with* Hawkers not to spread it through the Town, and, if asked, to deny there was any such Paper extant'. See also the issues of 4 December 1739 (i. 57) and 5 June 1740 (ii. 305). Claims like those in the *Champion* and the *TP* may refer to the restrictive practices of bookseller shareholders in rival papers, who by the mid-1740s had a virtual monopoly of the London press and maintained it by bringing pressure to bear on the pamphlet shops, hawkers, and other means of distribution. See Michael Harris, 'The Management of the London Newspaper Press during the Eighteenth Century', *Publishing History*, iv (1978), 95–112, especially pp. 96–7, 107. However, the claims made in the *TP*, particularly in the leader of no. 18, do seem to have a more 'political' cast, which is reflected in the advertisements of the *History*: 'As the Facts told in this History put this young Invader in a true Light, the Enemies of our Constitution have used their utmost Endeavours to destroy and suppress it.' On balance, then, the *TP* is more likely to have provoked political resentment than it is to have threatened the booksellers' monopoly, but evidence for either is lacking.

[5] *Odes*, i. iii. 38: 'we seek in our folly' (Loeb). Fielding uses the completed clause (*caelum ipsum*

It was the Saying of a great Man, *That no one served the Public for nothing*.[1] I will venture to add, that if such a Man did really exist in a corrupt Country, the Public would deny him even the Honour he deserved, and would assign some interested Motive to his Actions.

In a Society where the Morals of its Members are totally depraved, (in *Newgate* for instance,[2] or any larger Community) it is a common Maxim not only to depreciate Virtue, but to deny its actual Existence, and to treat any Man as a Hypocrite who pretends to it. Every one who searches his own rotten Heart, and finds not a Grain of Goodness in it, very easily persuades himself, that there is none in any other.[3] This he proclaims aloud, and all those under the same Predicament as readily subscribe to his Opinion.

But, in Reality, what do these General Assertions presuppose less than, 1. That there is no Goodness in Human Nature. 2. That Honour, Praise and Glory are not sufficient Incentives to it in any Man. And 3. That the Pretence of a whole Nation to Christianity is an Imposture, and that no Man among us hath Faith enough in his Religion to be actuated by the strongest of its Precepts.

I am afraid there are too many among us, who are not incited to Good, or restrained from Evil, by any of these Principles. I believe there are some, and those far from being stigmatized, whose Profligacy hath no Bounds, and scarce any Cover over it; but I am as well assured this Rule is not universal. I myself know Exceptions to it, Men so far from desiring to make a Prey of their Country, or to fill themselves, like Bloodsuckers, with her vital Treasures, that they are ready to exhaust their own in her Defence.

petimus stultitia) in *Joseph Andrews*, II. xii. 152, and as the motto of *CGJ* no. 70 (11 November 1752), ii. 130, where it is englished, 'Our Folly would look into Heaven.'

[1] Whether or not its words ever actually crossed his lips, this 'Saying' and others like it were attributed by contemporaries to Sir Robert Walpole, of whom Coxe writes, 'It was a known Maxim with him, *That all Men were to be bought*, and, thro' his whole Administration he seems to have been govern'd, and to govern, by no other'; *Walpole*, ii. 80. Cf. *Enquiry into the Causes of the late Increase of Robbers* (1751), section vii: '... who, as a Great Man lately said, serves the Public for Nothing?' (p. 105). However, it would have been typical of the age to provide some sort of classical 'cover' for such sentiments, and in his annotation of Mammon's speech to Aeolus (''Tis not my way to ask a boon for nought'), in *The Vernoniad* (1741), Fielding cites Aulus Gellius, whose *Attic Nights*, XI. x. 2–4, says in effect that none of us comes here without pay, all of us are looking for something; Henley, xv. 50–1.

[2] Cf. the 'Preface' to the *Miscellanies* (1743), i. 10: 'But without considering *Newgate* as no other than Human Nature with its Mask off, which some very shameless Writers have done, a Thought which no Price should purchase me to entertain, I think we may be excused for suspecting, that the splendid Palaces of the Great are often no other than *Newgate* with the Mask on.'

[3] Cf. the 'Preface' to the *Miscellanies* (1743), i. 9: 'For my Part, I understand those Writers who describe Human Nature in this depraved Character, as speaking only of such Persons as *Wild* and his Gang; and I think it may be justly inferred, that they do not find in their own Bosoms any Deviation from the general Rule. Indeed it would be an insufferable Vanity in them to conceive themselves as the only Exception to it.' Cf. *Champion* of 11 December 1739 (i. 79), and *Tom Jones*, VI. i. 268–71, and VIII. xv. 484–5.

And what do such Men more than their Duty? What can any one do less who hath the Goodness of a Man, the Spirit of a *Roman*, or the Benevolence of a Christian? Nay, indeed, what is such Patriotism better than true Wisdom, and by what Action can we deserve the Appellation of *wise*, so justly as by using our utmost Endeavours to preserve our Properties, our Liberties, and our Religion?

The wicked Man in Scripture is called a Fool.[1] The sacred Writers, who penetrated into all the Depths of Human Nature by Inspiration, do not compliment such a Person with the Epithets of able, artful, cunning and politic; Titles which would satisfy many of us much better than those of good or virtuous; they declare openly and bluntly, that Wickedness is Folly, and that Knave and Fool are synonimous Terms.

Now if this be true in private Vices, as our Divines have abundantly proved, with regard as well to this World as to the next, how much more eminent Folly is Public Wickedness, where the Destruction is so much greater, and more irretrievable. In a religious Light, to sin against a whole Community must be surely of a deeper and more unpardonable Nature, than to commit an Offence against one or a few. This is therefore the highest Folly, in the literal Meaning of Scripture; and, in a worldly Sense, what Folly can equal the Ignorance and Blindness of a rich and great Man, (for no other can have it in his Power) who doth not perceive, that his own and his Family's Ruin are necessarily involved in the Ruin of his Country?

Whatever be the Price with which he is allured, or rather whatever be the Bait with which he is trapped, he is imposed on, bubbled, and made a Dupe of. His Conduct is indeed so diametrically opposite to his true Interest, that it is not easy to conceive what Reward he can propose to himself by a Bargain so silly, that the highest Marks of Profligacy in private Life will scarce serve to illustrate it. He who injures his Estate, by endeavouring to adorn it, or who weakens his Tenure, in order to increase his Land, are properly reputed Fools; but they are Fools in a less Degree. But he who ruins his Country, besides the Danger which he incurs from the Resentment of his Country, from which few have escaped; and their universal Hatred and Curses, from which none possibly can escape; he destroys his Soul, irretrievably

[1] Locke, p. 157, cites Psalms 14: 1, but no particular Scriptural text exactly makes the equation. That Fielding derives it from the exegetical tradition is clear from *Champion* of 11 March 1740 (i. 352): 'but others . . . assert that *Solomon* by the Word *Fool*, means every where a wicked Man or a Rogue; nay, they insist that the Words *Rogue* and *Fool* are convertible Terms'. Fielding was himself fond of their convertibility. See, for example, *TP* no. 14 (28 January–4 February 1746), above, p. 208: 'Fools, who are always the Ecchoes of Knaves'.

destroys it, and entitles himself to Infamy in this World, and Damnation in the next.

In short, this is a Folly of such stupendous Magnitude, that did not all Histories assure us of the contrary, it would be hard to conceive such a Fool had ever lived.

But if it be Folly in a great Man to ruin his Country for the Sake of the highest Degree of Power with which a Subject in a Monarchy, or a Citizen in a Commonwealth can be invested, what Degree of Idiotism must he possess, whom a trifling Reward, a vain Title of Honour, or a paltry Badge of Distinction can make a mean Hireling, a base Tool of Power, and an Under-actor in this absurd tho' deep Tragedy?

The Man described by *Seneca* the Tragedian in the following Lines is a Fool:

> *Cupit hic Regi proximus ipsi*
> *Clarusque latas ire per urbes:*
> *Urit miserum gloria Pectus.*
> *Cupit hic gazis implere famem.*
> *Colit hic Reges calcet ut omnes,*
> *Perdatque aliquos, nullumque levet*
> *Tantum ut noceat cupit esse potens.* [1]

This Man however, tho' he makes a simple Bargain, bargains nevertheless for a Price. He is courted, flattered, admired; he obtains Honour, Power, Riches, tho' I think he buys them too dear, by bartering for them his Country, his Fame, his Ease, his Safety, his Posterity, and his Soul.

But what shall we say of the Wretches who drudge on through Contempt and Infamy; who obey any Commands which Power dictates, bear any Burden it imposes, and undertake any dirty Office it appoints, rather than forego the most pitiful Offerings to Vanity or Luxury, or else be obliged to purchase these at the Expence of honest Industry and Labour? This is a Folly for which we want Words of adequate Contempt and Abhorrence. The penetrating Genius of *Sallust* hath describ'd these Men; *Inhonesta* (says he) *et perniciosa lubido tenet eos qui potentiæ paucorum decus atque libertatem suam gratificantur.* [2] "A most pernicious Longing

---

[1] *Hercules Oetaeus*, 618–21, 637–9: 'One man is eager to fare illustrious through broad towns next to the king himself; for greed of glory burns his wretched breast. Another longs with treasure to appease his hunger. . . . Another Man courts kings that he may trample all, may ruin many and establish none; he covets power only to harm therewith' (Loeb). Fielding uses the passage to point to the great influence Granville had with the king and to his misuse of that power in attempting the abortive ministry of 10–12 February 1746.

[2] Emended from 'The War with Jugurtha', III. iii: *inhonesta et perniciosa lubido tenet potentiae paucorum decus atque libertatem suam gratificari*. The source of the translation which follows in the next sentence has not been identified. It may be Fielding's.

possesses those who sacrifice their own Honour and Liberty to gratify the Power of a few." This he calls EXTREMEST MADNESS OR FOLLY. Tho' I have not cited the whole Sentence as it stands in the Original, the learned Reader knows I have done no Violence to the Meaning of my Author.[1]

There may be I confess some Situations, some Degrees of Poverty and Distress imagined, in which it might require rather divine than human Prudence, to adhere with Integrity to the Good of the Public. Necessity they say hath no Law, and I am afraid very little Honesty. To value the Liberty of a Country whose Laws deprive you of your own, or to consult the Prosperity of Millions while you are yourself starving. To prefer such Alternatives as these to Affluence with Dishonour, or with being accessary to pernicious Schemes would require the Benevolence of a *Socrates* or of a *Brutus*.[2]

But indeed such indigent Persons have it seldom in their Power to do Good or Harm. Countries are undone by those whose Worldly Interest (if they truly understood it) should prompt them to labour for their Preservation. Men childishly give away the most solid of Blessings for the lightest Baubles, and what they do not in the least want. A superfluous House, an additional Servant to the Chariot, or Dish to the Table, nay, a Title, or even a Feather, bribe Men out of their Honesty, and are often put in Competition with the Good of their Country. Such Men, I think, may in strict Propriety be called FOOLS.

And on what should I rather congratulate my Country than on a late memorable Instance, that these Fools are exceeding rare among us. Some such were indeed found, but their Number were so inconsiderable that they soon gave Room to public Virtue,[3] and to that glorious Body of Men who have shewn that the highest Dignity and Property in this Kingdom are accompany'd with the highest Honour; and that the Administration is in the Hands of Men who esteem Power and Preferment of no Value any longer than they can be preferred with a strict Adherence to the true Interest of their Country.

---

[1] *Frustra autem niti neque aliud se fatigando nisi odium quaerere, extremae dementiae est* (III. iii): 'Moreover, to struggle in vain and after wearisome exertion to gain nothing but hatred, is the height of folly' (Loeb).

[2] In *TP* no. 2 (12 November 1745), above, p. 117, Fielding cites Marcus Junius Brutus (? 78–42 BC) as 'the great Exemplar' of philanthropy and amiability, and he frequently links Brutus with Socrates as exemplars of virtue. Cf. 'Preface' to the *Miscellanies* (1743), i. 12; 'Of the Remedy of Affliction for the Loss of our Friends', *Miscellanies*, i. 213; and *JJ* no. 8 (23 January 1748), p. 138.

[3] Referring to the failure of the Bath–Granville takeover of 10–12 February 1746, in which the obvious lack of parliamentary support for the leadership prevented even the filling of essential cabinet posts.

The Present History *of* Great Britain.[1]

The Clouds which have so long hung over this Nation, and threatned us with the blackest Tempests, begin at length to disperse themselves. Our Fears of an Invasion are at an End, and the wicked Rebellion begun against the best of Princes, is, by the Bravery of his glorious Son, indeed by the very Terror of his Name, reduced to its primitive Insignificance. Not that this Fire can be yet considered as totally extinguish'd, at a time when we are told by Authority,[2] that the Rebels are compelling the Northern Inhabitants of Scotland to join them on Pain of Death, and when the Arch-Enemy of the Peace of Europe is yet sending more Troops to their Assistance.[3] The Vigilance of the Duke hath however put a Stop to the immediate Progress of this Rebellion, and so far dispersed its wicked Agents, that the Troops which are now in these Parts must be shortly able to drive them to take Refuge in small Parties in the Highlands, where the advancing Season will give us an Opportunity of destroying them, or at least of forcing them to abandon their Arms, and all farther Hopes of resuming their pernicious Enterprize.

But the most satisfactory Contemplation is, that the Administration of Affairs is now in the Hands of Men who have given such Proofs of their Integrity,[4] that have at once convinced us we are free Men, and may depend on being so under their Protection. It is indeed the rare Blessing of the Public, in the present Age, to be convinced that their Friends are

---

[1] French, pp. 394–5, remarks that beginning with this number the 'Present History' changes form. No longer either a narrative of the events of the rebellion or else *verbatim* reprintings from the *London Gazette* and *General Advertiser*, it now becomes a vehicle for editorial opinion. French assigns three reasons for this change in form and content: the diminished significance of the rebellion itself; the 'new' administration's need of ideological support and political unity; and the impending legal business of the Lenten assizes on the Western Circuit (to begin on 4 March at Southampton). French and Locke (p. 24) think Fielding continued to write the 'Present History', but left the collection of foreign and domestic news items to an assistant. The present editor, on the basis of the stylistic evidence, as well as that of tone and political content, considers the present essay to be Fielding's last contribution to the 'Present History'. See 'General Introduction', above, pp. lxii–lxiv.

[2] The *London Gazette* ('Published by Authority') does not make exactly this point in any of its regular issues; perhaps it appeared in one of the 'Extraordinary' issues. Cf. *DA* of 25 February 1746: 'the Rebels . . . commit the most enormous Excesses to increase it [their army in Aberdeenshire], putting all to Fire and Sword who refuse to join them'.

[3] As Walpole put it to Mann (6 March 1746), 'The French continually drop them [the rebels] a ship or two'; *Yale Walpole*, xix. 221–2. The present reference probably drives from the *London Gazette* of 18–22 February 1745[6], which prints extracts from 'a Letter from Commander Knowles in the Downes, dated February 21, 1745[6]', telling of the capture of two French ships from Ostend carrying the comte de Fitz-James, other 'Persons of Distinction', and 'about 5 or 600 of Fitzjames's regiment'. Knowles's letter is cited later in this instalment of the 'Present History' (below, p. 425), where it is said to have been taken from the account in the *General Advertiser* 'of Yesterday . . . being much clearer and better than the *Gazette's*'.

[4] That is, in the hands of the Pelhams after the aborted Bath–Granville takeover of 10–12 February 1746.

in Power; that the greatest Men in the Kingdom are at the same time the honestest; that the very Person to whose Councils it is to be attributed, that the Pretender hath not been long since in Possession of this City, is at the Head of the Ministry;[1] and that the greatest Enemies of the People are disabled from any longer hurting or oppressing them. Indeed it is now known in our Streets, to whom we owe the Preservation of this Kingdom, by the timely bringing our Troops from Flanders; and who they were who opposed and delayed that Measure.[2]

It is now therefore, that Opposition is really and truly Faction; that the Names of a Patriot and Courtier are not only compatible,but necessarily conjoined; and that none can be any longer Enemies to the Ministry, without being so to the Public.

All malicious and invidious Insinuations against such an Administration ought to be discouraged, and the Persons who forge or promote them, should be detested as the most dangerous Vermin to Society. Above all, we should be cautioned and guarded against those who make use of popular Topics, and endeavour to improve[3] popular Dislikes to particular Measures. Such, for instance, is a War on the Continent. As we have the utmost Reason to confide in our Ministry, as their Characters and Conduct have given us the highest Security, in the Power of Men, for their Integrity, we ought, from an Assurance of their upright Intention, to contract a strong Prepossession in favour of what they propose or undertake, and not violently to conclude, because wasting our Treasures in an unnecessary Continent War, carried on madly without Allies, or reasonable Views, is contrary to our Interest and true Policy, that therefore we should tamely suffer an ambitious, inveterate, and already too powerful Enemy to possess himself of all Flanders, Brabant and Holland, when, with the Assistance of Allies, who are jointly interested in the Cause, we may have a fair Probability of preventing them.

What Determinations of this Kind our Governors will think proper to make, I neither know nor will pretend to guess.[4] All that I would at

---

[1] Cf. the tone of this encomium on Henry Pelham with that of *TP* no. 14 (28 January–4 February 1746), above, p. 209.

[2] Yet another reference to the machinations of the Bath, Granville, Tweeddale connection in opposing any troop recall. See 'General Introduction', above, p. xxxii.

[3] To increase or augment (what is evil), to aggravate, make worse (*OED*).

[4] Cf. 'Present History' of *TP* no. 16 (11–18 February 1746), below, p. 420: 'Notwithstanding the Reports which have been spread of our sending 15000 Troops abroad, *we assure the Public no such Measure is as yet determined; nor will be, unless Affairs should take such a Turn, as must make every honest Man in Britain to desire their Embarkation*.' There was considerable disagreement both within the administration and without as to the appropriate posture to take with respect to the war with France. The ambivalence such an issue could effect in political hangers-on like Fielding may be seen by comparing the authoritative assurances above (concerning the troops for Europe) with the belligerence in his

present recommend to the Public is, an unanimous Resolution to adhere to, and support, those who have approved themselves their Friends. By these means they will effectually crush all that domestic Faction, which we must expect will arise from the Disappointment of the most detestable Views, and may at the same time discourage our foreign Enemies from persisting in Projects which are *visibly levied at the utter Ruin of this Kingdom*.

From TUESDAY, FEBRUARY 25, to TUESDAY, MARCH 4, 1746.
NUMB. 18.

Whereas we have been informed by several Persons, that they have not been able to procure the TRUE PATRIOT *at any Rate: And we have great Reason to believe that many malicious and base Endeavours have been used to suppress the Sale of this Paper, by some who are concerned in imposing on the Public, by propagating Lies and Nonsense, which we have endeavoured to detect and expose. If any Hawkers, or others, will acquaint Mr.* A. Millar, *Bookseller, opposite* Katharine-Street *in the* Strand, *with the Name of any Person who has bribed, or offered to bribe them to refuse delivering out the* TRUE PATRIOT *to their Customers, they shall be well rewarded, and their Names, if they desire it, concealed.*

Gentlemen and Ladies may be furnished with this Paper, by sending their Names and Habitations to Mrs. A. Dodd *without* Temple-Bar; *to Mr.* Chappelle *in* Grosvenor-Street; *or to* M. Cooper *in* Pater-Noster-Row: *By whom Hawkers, &c. may be constantly supplied with them.*

Majores nusquam Rhonchi juvenesque senesque
Et Pueri nasum Rhinocerotis habent.

MARTIAL.[1]

I was pleased the other Night with the ingenious Confession of a Gentleman, who sat by me at the Oratorio;[2] who, after having expressed a Dislike

further flattery of the duke of Bedford in the 'Present History' of no. 17: 'We are assured, by good Authority, that the Board of Admiralty, at the Head of which is a noble Peer, whose only Inducement to act in that Office is to promote the Good of his Country, have resolved to fit out a very formidable Fleet against our Enemies this Spring, by which means we hope to humble them in that Element, in which it is their greatest and deepest Design to rival us' (below, p. 425). To judge from this pair of comments Fielding at this time would appear to be siding, albeit cautiously, with those politicians (many of them 'patriots') who preferred a naval rather than a military emphasis.

[1] *Epigrammaton*, I. iii. 5–6. These lines are used for the motto of *CGJ* no. 3 (11 January 1752), i. 147, where they are englished, somewhat freely, as 'No Town can such a Gang of Critics shew, | Ev'n Boys turn up that Nose they cannot blow'. See also the title-page of *The Intriguing Chambermaid* (1734) and the motto of *Champion* of 27 November 1739, i. 32.

[2] Handel's 'A New Occasional Oratorio' was performed three times only, at Covent Garden on 14 February (Friday), 19 February (Wednesday), and 25 February 1745 (Tuesday); *London Stage*, Part 3, i. 1219, 1220, 1221. See 'Present History of Great Britain', *TP* no. 17 (18–25 February

to the Composition, and declared that the Opera was in his Opinion greatly its Superior, very shortly assured us all, that he had not the least Taste or Judgment in Music.

It might be wished, that several pretended Connoisseurs in other Sciences had the Grace to follow so good an Example: But, on the contrary, the more ignorant and incapable these are, the more self-sufficient we generally find them; the worst Judges, in Cases of this Nature, being the most rigid Asserters of their own Jurisdiction.

This is a dreadful Discouragement to all Men of true Genius, who are often contented to bury their Talents under a Bushel, rather than by producing them in Public, to trust the Decision of their Merit to a Tribunal, where Numbers, Noise and Power, too often carry the Question against Sense and Reason.

Painters as well as Musicians have complained, and not without Reason, of the Censure past on their Works by Men who have not the least Skill in their Art. Here, I am informed, the general Rule of judging, among ignorant Critics, is from the apparent Antiquity of the Piece. One celebrated Connoisseur in particular is said never to have given his Suffrage for a Picture, unless where the Colours were so sunk and faded, that no one could possibly discover what it was the Picture of.[1]

The Professors of Literature, Prose-writers as well as Poets, labour under this Calamity of being try'd by Judges who never read the Laws over which they preside. This is more particularly the Fate of Dramatic Authors. Every one hath heard of THE TOWN; a Name which the Play-House Critics gave their Body, and under which they sat many Years in

1746), below, p. 425, for remarks on Wednesday's performance; and for the rivalry between Handel and the Opera, *TP* no. 1 (5 November 1745), above, p. 104 and *n.*; Deutsch, *Handel*, pp. 602–10.

[1] The 'celebrated Connoisseur' has not been identified. Fielding is here satirizing the tenet of connoisseurship that 'Time' (with the assistance, if necessary, of tinted varnish) had a beneficent effect on color, by mellowing and softening it. *Spectator* no. 83 (5 June 1711), i. 356, affirms the tenet: 'I found his Pencil was so very light that it worked imperceptibly, and after a thousand Touches, scarce produced any visible effect in the Picture on which he was employ'd. However, as he busied himself incessantly, and repeated Touch after Touch without rest or intermission, he wore off insensibly every little disagreeable Gloss that hung upon a Figure. He also added such a beautiful Brown to the Shades, and Mellowness to the Colours, that he made every Picture appear more perfect than when it came fresh from the Master's Pencil. I could not forbear looking upon the Face of this ancient Workman, and immediately by the long Lock of Hair upon his Forehead discovered him to be TIME.' Fielding's friend Hogarth attacked this kind of connoisseurship in his 'Britophil' letter in *St James's Evening Post* of 7–9 June 1737, reprinted in *London Magazine*, vi (1737), 385–6; and his 'Time Smoking a Picture' (1761) presents the issue graphically. In his first two footnotes to ch. xiv of *The Analysis of Beauty* (1753), Hogarth disparages the 'deep rooted notion . . . that time is a great improver of good pictures'. The literary perspective on this essentially 'Ancients vs. Moderns' issue is provided by Pope's *The First Epistle of the Second Book of Horace, Imitated* ('To Augustus'), vv. 35–6: 'Authors, like Coins, grow dear as they grow old; | It is the rust we value, not the gold.'

Judgment on all Dramatic Pieces exhibited to the Public.[1] This Office of Criticism belonged formerly to another Body of Critics called THE PIT, so named from the Part of the Theatre which they occupied, whereas THE TOWN, their Successors, disposed themselves alike in all Parts of the Theatre, except the Boxes.

These Critics, like the Mohocs[2] of old, were long known only to the Members of their Society, and various were the Opinions concerning them. Some of the Ladies conceived, that this *Town* was a single Person who sat in the upper Gallery; for in that Part they always posted one of their Number, who was most remarkable for the Deepness of his Voice and the Shrillness of his Cat-call.[3] And according to this Opinion, I remember a young Fellow gave an Account of a Hiss at a Play about two Years ago.[4] "The Town (says he) was resolved the Play should not go on, and hissed. Then Mr. *Mills*[5] came forward, and offered to speak, and the

---

[1] Cf. *Tom Jones*, xv. ii. 785: 'when *Sophia* was thrown into that Consternation at the Play-house, by the Wit and Humour of a Set of young Gentlemen, who call themselves the Town'. *JJ* no. 7 (16 January 1748), pp. 133–4, prints 'A Petition from a small Body of Critics, signed THE TOWN', and a 'Counsellor Town' prosecutes the critics' case against *Amelia* in *CGJ* no. 7 (25 January 1752), i. 178–80, at the 'Court of Censorial Inquiry'.

[2] 'The name of a cruel nation of America given to ruffians who infested, or rather were imagined to infest the streets of London' (Johnson). Cf. Swift, 'Letter xliii' (8 March 1712), *Journal to Stella*, ed. Williams, ii. 508–9: 'Did I tell you of a race of Rakes called the Mohacks that play the devil about this Town [London] every Night, slit peoples noses, & beat them &c.' In the political tensions of 1712 this 'nocturnal Fraternity' was rumored to be part of a whig insurrection against the tory government, and the tories were frequently charged with trying to make political capital out of the matter. Many contemporaries, Chesterfield among them, doubted the very existence of the Mohocks; see *Spectator* no. 347 (8 April 1712). For a summary, see *Spectator* no. 324 (12 March 1712), iii. 186 n., and Robert J. Allen, *The Clubs of Augustan England*, Harvard Studies in English, vii (Cambridge, Mass., 1933), 105–18.

[3] A squeaky instrument, or kind of whistle, used especially in playhouses to express impatience or disapprobation (*OED*). *Spectator* no. 361 (24 April 1712), ii. 350–3, gives a satirical account of its supposed historical origins and applications in the playhouse. Cf. *CGJ* no. 71 (18 November 1752), ii. 140: 'They [the *Ninnies*] are armed with a dangerous Weapon called a Catcall, and attack with a most terrible Noise compounded of hissing, howling, yawning, groaning, shouting &c.'

[4] Plays appear to have been hissed on only two evenings in 1744: at Drury Lane on 17 November (*The Conscious Lovers* and *The Fortune Tellers*) and on 19 November (*The Provok'd Wife*); *London Stage*, Part 3, ii. 1130–1. Fielding's description more nearly fits Genest's account of the first night, when a performer did appear to 'excuse Fleetwood'; *Some Account of the English Stage*, iv (Bath, 1832), 137. See the next two notes. Horace Walpole, who was in the audience on the first night, rose up spontaneously and called Fleetwood 'an impudent rascal'; Walpole to Mann, 26 November 1744, *Yale Walpole*, xviii, 538–9.

[5] William ('Honest Billy') Mills (d. 1750), son of a more famous Drury Lane actor, John Mills (d. 1736), is not listed in the casts for either night of rioting in 1744. However, he may well have been the actor sent out by the manager to deal with the audience (see next note); his face was 'honest' and he was a great favorite of the 'Town'. No other account attempts an identification, but for a satirical version of what was said to the audience (by a 'Master *Knotty-Nob*'), see *The Disputes between the Director of D—y, and the Pit Potentates* (London, 1744), pp. 9–10. Mills, who acted in a number of Fielding's plays at Drury Lane, seems to have been an old friend. Fielding mentions him in *Joseph Andrews*, I. viii. 40; *Tom Jones*, VII. i. 329; and *JJ* no. 21 (23 April 1748), pp. 255–6. About this time in 1746 Mills was apparently in financial straits; he published an advertisement in *General Advertiser* of 12 February 1746 announcing 'a Benefit before my usual Time' and urging the public to help out.

Town cry'd, *Hear him, hear him*; but upon his offering to excuse *Fleet-wood*,[1] *the Town* presently took up an Apple and flung at his Head." From this Relation I at first concluded, that *the Town* was some impudent Rascal, who deserved to have been turned out of the House; but I afterwards found that *the Town* was *Nomen Collectivum*, and that the young Gentleman who told us the Story, was himself one of the Number meant by it.

Others imagined that *the Town* meant the Men of Learning and Taste; and others again concluded, that by *the Town* was understood every Man in the Town, at least all those who frequented such Entertainments, and that the Votes and Sentiments of all such were included in the Deter-minations made at the Play-House.

The Town ruled many Years with absolute Sway, till at last growing wanton with their Power, and insisting on a prescriptive Right to break the Heads of the Actors, and to pull down the House, or set it on fire, as often as they pleased; by which Means the Ladies and all others, except only *the Town*, were terrified from going to Plays, the Manager was obliged to take a List of *the Town*, in order to apply to a Court of Justice for Redress.[2] Which being done, *the Town* appeared to consist chiefly of young Gentlemen who were Apprentices to several Trades, mixed with some few who were *designed for* the Law,[3] and half a dozen young

---

[1] Charles Fleetwood (d. 1747), until December 1744 patentee of Drury Lane, had just come off the terrible season of 1743–4, during which he quarreled with and alienated many of his principal performers, notably Garrick and Macklin, who petitioned the lord chamberlain for permission to perform at the Haymarket rather than continue under Fleetwood's management. Although most of the actors capitulated before long, there was continued bad feeling on both sides, and a virulent pamphlet war. The playgoing public sided mostly with the actors, against Fleetwood in particular and managements in general. Fleetwood was forced to mortgage his patent, take a lien on the theatre's properties and costumes, and finally to raise the prices charged for pantomimes. At which point the audiences rioted twice, demolished the house so badly it had to be closed for repair, and in effect forced Fleetwood to sell out to the bankers; *London Stage*, Part 3, vol. i, pp. xciii–xcvi, and vol. ii, pp. 1130–3; *A Biographical Dictionary of Actors . . . in London, 1660–1800*, ed. Philip H. Highfill *et al.* (Southern Illinois Press, [1978]), v. 299–301. According to Genest, iv. 137, on 17 November the audience had first shouted for Fleetwood, who refused to appear but sent a performer to say that he would confer with any deputation in his office. Fleetwood's relations with Fielding appear to have been mixed. The largest single subscriber to the *Miscellanies* (he took twenty sets), he staged a number of Fielding's plays at Drury Lane. However, he seems to have 'prevented' *Don Quixote in England* from performance, and Fielding ridicules him in *Tumble-Down Dick*; see Cross, i. 206–7.

[2] Neither the manager in question nor his particular application for redress has been identified.

[3] A commonplace expression, applied, with irony, to those who were perceived to be going through the motions of preparing for a career in the law. Cf. *Tom Jones*, XI. i. 566–7: 'the greatest Number of Critics hath of late Years been found amongst the Lawyers. Many of these Gentlemen, from Despair, perhaps, of ever rising to the Bench in *Westminster-hall*, have placed themselves on the Benches at the Playhouse, where they have exerted their judicial Capacity, and have given Judgment, *i.e.* condemned without Mercy.' Abbé Le Blanc, 'Letter LXXXII', *Letters on the English and French Nations* (London, 1747), ii. 314, notes the power of 'these pretended professors' of the law and calls them the authors of most of the playhouse disturbances.

Members of the Army. Most of them being of that Age to which the Law assigns the Appellation of Infant.[1]

Upon this Discovery a Prosecution was commenced, on which it appearing that this prescriptive Right was not good in Law, *the Town* hath been since restrained within more moderate Bounds, and claim no Right of disturbing an Audience, except at a new Play, where they still maintain their ancient Privilege of Hissing, Cat-calling, *&c.*

It might be perhaps questioned, whether these young Gentlemen are all complete Judges of Dramatic Merit, and whether they do not some-times pass the Censure of vile Stuff and *lowe*,[2] (a Word in great Use in the Upper Gallery) a little improperly; but what is still worse, Corrup-tion as well as Ignorance prevails too often in this Court of Criticism, and the Cat-call is discharged not at the Play, but at its Author.

An Instance of this occurs to my Memory, at one of these Exhibitions, when I happened to sit next a Youth who was a most perfect Master of the Cat-call, and played upon it almost without Intermission. As the Performance did not, in my Opinion, deserve quite so severe a Treat-ment, I took an Occasion of remonstrating to my Neighbour, who with-out Hesitation swore he was resolved to damn the Play; for that the Author was in Possession of a very pretty Girl, for whom he had himself a violent Affection. Ay, damn him, says another who over-heard us, and who had hitherto accompanied the instrumental with very loud vocal Music, *I hate the Fellow, because he's a Whig*.

Without staying to comment on these mean Artifices of Revenge, the Baseness of which is sufficiently apparent, I cannot help observing, that some Persons have taken a Hint from *the Town*, and espouse and decry the Productions of Men of Learning, as the Author is or is not of their Party. This Method begins to prevail so much, that it will shortly be no more possible for a Man to gain Reputation in the Republic of Letters, without the Assistance of great Men, than it hath formerly been to procure a Place or Pension. Indeed, I think it will soon become no

---

[1] Cf. *Champion* of 27 November 1739, i. 37: 'That no Man under the Age of fourteen, should be entitled to give a Definitive Opinion (unless in the Play-house)'; and *CGJ* no. 3 (11 January 1752), i. 149–50: 'I shall not, for the future, admit any Males to the Office of Criticism till they be of the full Age of 18, that being the Age when the Laws allow them to have a Capacity of disposing personal Chattles'.

[2] Of inferior quality, character, or style; wanted in elevation, commonplace, mean (*OED*). *Champion* of 12 June 1740, ii. 328, annotates 'low' as 'A Word much used in the Theatre, but of such un-certain Signification, that I could never understand the Meaning of it.' In *Tom Jones*, v. i. 210, it is said to betray the agelastic critic, and in XI. i. 570, it is called 'a Word which becomes the Mouth of no Critic who is not RIGHT HONOURABLE'. For its place in the lexicon of disapprobation, see *Champion* of 24 November 1739, i. 24: 'Give me Leave, notwithstanding, Sir, to complain a little of your intro-ducing me to the Public with the Words *Damned Stuff*, *Low*, &c. in my Mouth, and with a *Cat-call* in my Hand'; also *CGJ* no. 3 (11 January 1752), i. 149, and no. 13 (15 February 1752), i. 215.

improper Application, to some of these, *Sir, I desire you will let me be a great Poet, or be pleased to let me have a great deal of Wit and Humour, in my Writings*.

As this is truly the Case, it certainly imports *The True Patriot* to warn his honest Readers against such Proceedings. A Man, who is determined to adhere to no Party longer than their Views are consistent with the Interest of his Country, and to oppose any who by their Principles or Practice are manifestly its Enemies, must necessarily expect that all Parties, who are guided by such base Politics, will unite in denying, or to borrow a Phrase from *the Town* abovementioned, on this Occasion, *in damning his* Writings.

We have indeed already received Advice of some Persons, who have ventured to nibble at our Paper, and in private Corners to whisper several disrespectful Matters against some of our most approved Performances, and against the Voice of the People.[1]

The Public, for whose Sake this Paper was instituted, and the more sensible Part of it, for whose Entertainment it is calculated, will not withdraw their Favour from our Endeavours, while we continue to deserve it. The Reason therefore of this Admonition is less intended for our own Sake, than to caution such Persons from persisting any longer in their base Purposes: For, however secretly they may imagine they have conducted their Malice, we assure them their Names are well known, and unless they immediately alter their Conduct towards us, they must shortly expect to find themselves gibbeted in our Paper, and exposed to the same universal Derision with the *Par nobile fratrum*,[2] whom we have lately hung forth as Objects of public Scorn and Contempt.

---

[1] Cf. 'the UNIVERSAL VOICE of the People', in 'Present History of Great Britain' in this issue, reprinted in Locke, p. [161], probably not by Fielding. And for the supposed attacks on the *TP* itself, see no. 17 (18–25 February 1746), above, p. 222 and *n*.

[2] Horace, *Satires*, II. iii. 243: 'a famous pair of brothers' (Loeb). Horace refers to the twin sons of Arrius and goes on to call them *nequitia et nugis, pravorum et amore gemellum* ('twins in wickedness, folly and perverted fancies' [Loeb]). Fielding is taking *nobile* also to mean 'noble', thus effecting a safe hit at Bath and Granville, twin leaders of the ill-fated ministry of 10–12 February 1746, who were both titled (i.e., noble) as well as famous or well known. Fielding's readers would have picked up the allusion to Bath and Granville, who were not related, and enjoyed an extra laugh, because Opposition writers habitually referred to Pelham and Newcastle, who really were siblings, as 'the two Brothers'.

From TUESDAY, MARCH 4, to TUESDAY, MARCH 11, 1746.
NUMB. 19.

An, cum Tibicines, iique qui Fidibus utuntur suo, non multitudinis, arbitrio, cantus modulantur; vir sapiens, multo arte majori præditus, non quid rectum sit, sed quid velit vulgus exquiret?

CICERO[1]

To the TRUE PATRIOT.

Sir,

I am greatly pleased with the Justness of your Observations in your last Paper. The Evil you there complain of, is certainly of a very pernicious Consequence to Society, as it is the highest Discouragement to Merit; and hath, I make no Doubt, deterred some Men of true Genius from exerting their Talents at all, and nipped many others in the Bud, who might have become very shining Lights in the Eyes of the Public.

The Instances you have produced of the Musician, the Painter, and the Writer, are extremely proper; to which give me Leave to add another, whom I suppose you must have omitted for Want of Room only, I mean the *Politician*, whose Talents are often misrepresented, and his honest Endeavours defeated, by total Want of Skill, and Weakness of Judgment, in those who take to themselves a Right of giving a definitive Sentence in Politics.

The Mischief arising from Incapacity in the Judge, in this last Instance, is on many Accounts the greatest, and particularly in this, as it is the most extensive: For, in all the Sciences you mention, though there are many who assume the Office of deciding, without any adequate Qualification, yet there are some who have the Modesty to confess their Ignorance; whereas, in Politics, every Man is an Adept;[2] and the lowest Mechanic delivers his Opinion, at his Club, upon the deepest Public Measures, with as much Dignity and Sufficiency as the highest Member of the Commonwealth.

---

[1] *Tusculan Disputations*, v. xxxvi. 104, reading *numerosque moderantur* for *modulantur*, and *verissimum* for *rectum*: 'Are flute players and harpists to follow their own tastes, not the tastes of the multitude in regulating the rhythm of music, and shall the wise man, gifted as he is with a far higher art, seek out not what is truest [right], but what is the pleasure of the populace?' (Loeb). The passage, with the same variant readings, is used as the motto of *JJ* no. 10 (6 February 1748), p. 147.

[2] 'It is, in its original signification, appropriate to the chymists, but is now extended to other artists' (Johnson). Animadverting on Cibber's reversal of its meaning in the first edition of his *Apology*, Fielding called it 'a Word which I apprehend no School-Boy hath ever wantonly employed, unless to signify the utmost Perfection'; *Champion* of 22 April 1740, ii. 132.

Now it is scarce probable that a Cobler, or indeed any other Man of Trade, nay not even the Country Squire himself, if he be a Sportsman, should find Time sufficient, from the Business of their several Callings, however well they may be qualified, to search much into the History and Policy of the several States of *Europe*; and thence to form an adequate and perfect Judgment of the true Interest of their own Country, as it stands connected with, or opposed to that of others. Hence therefore it may frequently happen, that the wisest and best Measures of a Ministry may not meet with the Approbation of a Two-penny Club,[1] or a Meeting of Fox-hunters.[2]

Besides, I am afraid there is sometimes as great a Mixture of Prejudice in the Judgments past here, as in those at the Play-House, which you mentioned in your last Paper. An additional Tax upon Leather, or any Discountenance given to an Act for the Preservation of the Game, would counterbalance the Merit of half a dozen Treaties, with the Gentlemen I have before named. Nay, I apprehend many who hiss at a Minister, might answer truly (if they had so much Honesty) with your Friend of the Town,[3] *Damn him, he is my Rival*: For Rivals for Power have seldom more Good-will to each other, than those who are Rivals for a Mistress.

I own, I apprehended it was the peculiar good Fortune of the present Ministry to have the whole People unanimous on their Side. That their Characters, Fortunes, and Conduct, had given such Security to the Public for their Integrity, that no Man would be audacious enough to attack them, at least whilst some late Transactions were fresh in every Memory.[4]

But I find my good Opinion of the Modesty of my Countrymen was a little too universal; for tho' it be certain, that no Administration had ever half the Popularity on its Side with the present, yet it seems there are some few who dare contradict the Sentiments of Lords, Commons, and almost the whole Nation.

This is so strange a Conduct, that I shall scarce quarrel with my Reader for disbelieving the following Story.

---

[1] According to *Spectator* no. 9 (10 March 1711), i. 42–3, a club for 'Artizans and Mechanicks', the 'Rules' of which, 'upon a Wall in a little Ale-house', give 'a pretty Picture of low Life'. The price in the title reflects the admission fee or quota.

[2] Drawing on the literary stereotype of the tory squire as a huntin'-fishin'-shootin' gentleman. For a vignette of the fox-hunter in a political context resembling that in which the *TP* was conceived, see *Freeholder* no. 2 (5 March 1716).

[3] The 'perfect Master of the Cat-call', in *TP* no. 18 (25 February–4 March 1746), above, p. 233, who damned a play because the author was his rival for the affections of a pretty girl.

[4] Yet another allusion to the Bath-Granville ministry of 10–12 February 1746.

Being a few Days since in a Place not far from *Westminster*,[1] I saw a small Knot of People, somewhat I believe above half a Score,[2] very earnestly discoursing together. As I knew none of their Faces, I had the Curiosity to enquire who and what they were, and was immediately answer'd with a Sneer, that they were THE OPPOSITION.

The Idea of such an Opposition as this to the Interest, and to the Inclination of a whole People, had something so ridiculous in it, that I should have doubted the Veracity of my Informer, had he not very seriously asserted the Truth of what he told me; and had not this again been corroborated by many Things which some of the Company uttered in so loud a Voice, that it appeared they intended to make no Secret of their Principles.

One of them, who was, it seems, a Knight or a Baronet,[3] and appeared to be regarded with much Respect and Reverence by the rest, very solemnly and loudly declared, *That the Nation was undone*; to which all the rest assented by shaking their Heads. The Knight then proceeded to shew, the "Many outrageous Acts which had been committed with Impunity, by entering into unlawful Subscriptions for preserving Religion and Liberty, which (he said) no People in the World, who had the least Remains of Liberty among them, would suffer. And then (continued he) to elapse[4] such a Time for securing our Liberties, when the

---

[1] Although formerly a whig stronghold, the City of London and the liberty of Westminster had by this time entered into strong opposition. In 1741 a tory–opposition whig affiliation calling itself 'the Independent Electors of Westminster' formed for the purpose of supporting antiministerial candidates in the Westminster elections of that year. The group continued to meet more or less regularly on the first Friday of each month. *DA* of 7 March 1746 had advertised one such: 'The Independent Electors of the City and Liberty of Westminster, are desired to meet this Evening at Seven o'Clock, at the *Crown and Anchor Tavern* in the *Strand*, to commemorate the Noble Struggle they so successfully made in Support of their Liberty and Independency.' Fielding's advertisements for his own *Gentleman & Alderman* (1747) state that the pamphlet was 'particularly' addressed to the Independent Electors; see 'General Introduction' to that volume, pp. xxxiii–xxxv. For evidence that during the Forty-Five the City was 'ready to receive the Prince [the Young Pretender] in its bosom', see *The House of Commons 1715–1754*, ed. Sedgwick, i. 283.

[2] The figure is of course satirical; it may also have been canonical. See the 'MS Parliamentary Journal' of Philip Yorke, reprinted in *Parliamentary History of England*, xiii. 1055, where Pitt is reported to have said, early in 1745, that Granville 'had not ten men in the nation that would follow him'.

[3] No exact identification is required. However, the further precision of 'Baronet' would have reminded knowledgeable contemporaries that several of the opposition leaders held this hereditary title, most notably perhaps Sir John Hynde Cotton (? 1688–1752), third baronet, and Sir Watkin Williams Wynne (? 1693–1749), third baronet, both of whom during the Forty-Five joined the appeal of English jacobites to the French government for a renewed expedition against England. In the speech which follows, the knight's emphasis on the unlawfulness of the military subscriptions and associations recalls parliamentary efforts to that effect by Sir John Philips (1701–64), sixth baronet, MP Carmarthen 1741–7, who in October 1745 had also tried to attach a clause to the royal address, demanding shorter parliaments and a diminution of government influence on elections; *Parliamentary History*, xiii. 1328.

[4] To suffer [time] to pass by (*OED*). This obsolete transitive use is nearly forty years later than *OED* records.

Rebels were in the Middle of the Kingdom, and madly to insist upon driving them out, before we entered upon Grievances.[1] Sir, I am afraid we shall never have such another Opportunity. What in the Devil's Name were they afraid of?" He then spoke a little lower, and I could only hear in a confused Jargon, the Words POPISH PRINCE; PROTESTANT RELIGION; HEREDITARY RIGHT; LIBERTY AND FREEDOM; with other such Inconsistencies, as made me a little doubt whether the honest Gentleman who uttered them was really in his right Senses. He had no sooner finished his Harangue, than a Gentleman, whom they called the Elderman or Alderman,[2] (for I could not rightly distinguish which) began in a violent Rage to assert, "That they should not have had a Penny. By G—, they (meaning, I at first supposed, some of his own Relations) should not have had a Penny, till they had complied with all he desired.[3] O my Country! my Country! I would have rather seen ten thousand Highlanders imbruing their Hands in thy Vitals, than thus see thee governed by a Set of Fellows, who pretend to reconcile the Interest of their" —— (He sunk that Word) "and Country together. Suppose this Pretender had succeeded, we should soon have kicked him out again, and then we might establish" ——[4] Here he spoke so low, I could not hear him

[1] A term with hallowed political resonances. Cf. Bill of Rights (1689), 1 Will. & Mar., session 2, c. 2, sec. 13: 'And that for redress of all grievances, and for the amending, strengthening and preserving of the laws . . .'; *Statutes at Large*, ix. 69.

[2] An unmistakable allusion to George Heathcote (1700–68), wealthy West India merchant and director of the South Sea Company, alderman of Walbrook ward (1739–49), sheriff of London (1739–40), lord mayor (1742), MP London (1741–7). A report to the Pretender dated 15 November 1745 stated that 'Alderman Heathcote . . . has been long a vigorous and bold opposer of the measures of the Hanoverian court, by which means he has been reckoned, especially since the base defection of Pulteney [Bath], the chief leader of the Patriot Whigs, not in the City of London only, but in the nation'; *The House of Commons 1715–1754*, ed. Sedgwick, ii. 122, citing Stuart MSS 227/155 and 271/3. Walpole wrote Mann (13 September 1745) that 'Alderman Heathcote proposed to petition for a redress of grievances, but not one man seconded him' at a City meeting to draw up the loyal address to the king; *Yale Walpole*, xix. 107.

[3] Probably referring to the offer of £3,000,000 which some of the underwriters or 'monied men' of the City, Heathcote's constituency, had arranged to advance Pelham toward the year's supply; Owen, *Rise of the Pelhams*, p. 296. The arrangement may have been reached in the hysterical days of December 1745 or in the relative tranquility of the end of January 1746; *Westminster Journal* of 29 March 1746, as reprinted in *GM*, xvi (1746), 189–93. It was withdrawn, according to Egmont (*Diary*, iii. 315), when Pelham left office during the Bath–Granville takeover of 10–12 February 1746. Sir John Barnard had a cheaper scheme, but 'it was not sure that the moneyed men of the city, who were to support this last, were able to raise the money proposed; whereas those who were engaged with Mr. Pelham were sure men'; Egmont, *Diary*, iii. 315. When the Pelham scheme was debated on 11 March 1746, it was opposed by the Prince of Wales's faction and Bath's, but supported by Granville and his adherents; Egmont, loc. cit. The opposition view of Pelham's scheme was that it was a ministerial 'job', a sentiment which accords with that of the 'Alderman' here.

[4] The unvoiced words here are probably 'a Republic'. As early as March 1731 Lord Egmont noted Heathcote's view that the power of kings must be limited, and concluded, 'His character is that of a republican Whig'; *Diary*, i. 27–8, 153. In his *Gentleman & Alderman* (1747) Fielding calls the 'Alderman', who seems to have been modeled on Heathcote, 'A Jacobite upon republican Principles'

distinctly, and the whole Company began to whisper for a Time. At last one of them broke forth, *A Circular, say you? Ay*, answered another. *An excellent Scheme, and must give the World an Idea of our Importance. Harkee* — (then he whispered) *will he be with us?* says the Baronet. *Never fear him, you know he is kicked out*, reply'd the other. *But will he not*, cry'd a third, *bring a Scandal on the Party?*[1] *We must not be nice in our Objections*, says the Baronet, *for if we are, we shall never increase in Numbers. And if we are not able to bring that about soon, we shall be laughed out of the World*. Then succeeded a long Whisper, after which several of them repeated the Word *Circular*, and so they departed.

A Friend of mine then joined me. He is a very grave Man, and of such deep Discernment, that he always sees further into a Thing than any other, and commonly discovers the highest *Machiavilian* Politics in the ordinary Occurrences of Life. He had, it seems, observed the Attention with which I had survey'd *the Opposition*, and perceiving me inclined to laugh, he reproved me very seriously, saying, he thought it was an unwarrantable Project of the Ministry to defeat the Purposes of all future Opposition, by hiring these Fellows to bring the Name into universal Odium and Contempt. I answered him freely, I thought he was mistaken, and that I believed the Gentlemen were really in earnest in their Schemes, however absurd or impossible they might appear. Ay, says he, you never look farther than the Surface of things; but can you really believe that any ten Men in their Senses, would set themselves in Opposition to the whole Kingdom, and *such Men* too? Very well, reply'd I, and do you think any Ministry in their Senses would employ *such Men* for any Purpose whatever?[2] My Friend staggered at that Objection to his profound Politics, and owned there was something in it worth further Consideration.

Upon my Return Home, I could not avoid several Reflections on what I had seen. First, I rejoiced extremely within myself, that the present just Administration of Power had reduced all Opposition to such a ridiculous Object, as I have here described; but could not, in the second Place, avoid feeling some Compassion for those Great Men, who while they refuse no Fatigue, from a Motive only of serving their Country, (as is

and makes him confess, 'I believe no King to have any Right at all, and therefore, whenever we have Grievances to redress, I would exchange him' (p. 9).

[1] The reference may be to Granville, whose loss of place ('he is kicked out') would seem to lead to opposition, but whose Hanoverian policies might 'bring Scandal on the Party'.

[2] Implicit here is the charge that some politicians either resumed opposition or went over to it simply because they had not been offered 'places'. In the shuffle that followed their resumption of power in February the Pelhams had to limit the number of places given to allies and potential opponents, for fear of offending those of the old corps also without office.

absolutely the Case of many now in Power) are liable to be traduced by such Wretches, at the same time, that I lamented the Weakness of Human Nature, which was capable of furnishing *a single Person* mean enough to admire or espouse SUCH AN OPPOSITION.

From TUESDAY, MARCH 11, to TUESDAY, MARCH 18, 1746.
NUMB. 20.

—— *Quod me manet stipendium?*
Essare, jussas cum Fide Pœnas luam,
Paratus expiare ——

HORACE.[1]

There are perhaps no Offices in a Commonwealth of more real Dignity, than those which are concerned in the Execution of Justice. And accordingly we see most of these in every Government arrayed with the highest Ensigns of Authority, and regarded with the greatest Marks of Honour.

There is one, however, which, tho' it be the most necessary of all, (being indeed the Consummation, and what completes and perfects the whole) is, by a strange Perversion, generally treated with the utmost Ridicule and Contempt; and the Person who officiates, is vilified and degraded as the lowest Member of the Society. My Reader must immediately guess I mean the *Hangman*, or, as he is called for Distinction-sake, the *Executioner*;[2] tho' it is certain, that without this GREAT OFFICER OF STATE, (for so in reality he is) Judges would soon be treated like Jack-puddings,[3] and Laws themselves become the Objects only of Scorn and Derision.

Mr. *Tournefort*, in his Voyages, tells us of a certain Island in the *Archipelago*, where the Inhabitants are so sensible of the Dignity of this Office, that it is justly reputed among them as the most honourable in the whole Commonwealth; and a Gentleman there, is as proud of

---

[1] *Epodes*, xvii. 36–8: 'What penalty awaits me? Speak out! The punishments commanded, I faithfully will pay, ready to make expiation' (Loeb).

[2] Cf. N. Bailey, *An Universal Etymological Dictionary*, 13th ed. (London, 1745), *s.v.* 'Hangman': an Executioner.

[3] A buffoon, clown, or merry-andrew, *esp.* one attending on a mountebank (*OED*). Cf. *JJ* no. 38 (20 August 1748), pp. 373–4, and *CGJ* no. 10 (4 February 1752), i. 193, both of which emphasize the function of the jackpudding to divert the public with laughter. See also *Spectator* no. 47 (24 April 1711).

reckoning a Hangman amongst his Ancestors, as in other Countries, Men are to derive their Stems from the Nobility themselves.[1]

And in however opprobrious a Light we ourselves may view this Office, our Forefathers clearly regarded it in a different Manner, at its original Institution. Nay, even at this Day, the High Sheriff of the County is properly the Executioner,[2] and must, if he can find no Deputy, tuck up[3] with his own Hands;[4] which is probably the Reason, that of late Years Persons of Great Fortune have declined this Office,[5] and little Men have been obliged to purchase the Honour at an Expence, which they have been hardly able to support.[6]

It may seem, therefore, somewhat difficult to account for the un-merited Contempt with which this High Officer is treated by most Nations. In *England*, indeed, where every Person and Thing is valued by Money, the low Salary or Fee which is annexed to his Office, to wit, Thirteen Pence Halfpenny *per* Head,[7] may be a sufficient Reason for

[1] Joseph Pitton de Tournefort, *Relation d'un Voyage du Levant* (Paris, 1717), ii. 311: 'Les bourreaux en Georgie sont fort riches, & les gens de qualité y exercent cette charge; bien loin qu-elle soit réputée infame, comme dans tout le reste du monde, c'est un titre glorieux en ce pays-là pour les familles.' Fielding's mistake of the 'Archipelago' for 'Georgia' suggests he was thinking of John Ozell's translation, *A Voyage into the Levant* (London, 1741), the running title of which reads 'Containing the ancient and modern State of the Islands of the Archipelago . . .'. There is no such designation in the Paris edition, the first volume of which does indeed deal with the Archipelago. Fielding makes the same geographical mistake in his *Enquiry into the Causes of the late Increase of Robbers* (London, 1751), section vii, p. 105. In a letter signed 'Jack Ketch', *Champion* of 26 April 1740, ii. 155, which is generally attributed to Ralph, the nobility of the hangman's office is located more accurately 'in the Neighbourhood of *Persia*'.

[2] Cf. *An Enquiry into the Causes of the late Increase of Robbers*, loc. cit.: 'Nay in this Kingdom [Britain] the Sheriff himself (who was one of the most considerable Persons in his County) is in Law the Hangman, and Mr. *Ketch* is only his Deputy.' As part of his duties to 'execute' the judgments handed down by the higher courts the sheriff had 'to take charge of all prisoners committed to the prison, and for [*sic*] the executions of felons and other persons condemned to die, which Sentence he is to see Executed'; Matthew Dalton, *Officium Vicecomitum: The Office and Authority of Sherifs* (London, 1670), cap. 98, p. 369. See also Matthew Hale, *History of the Pleas of the Crown*, Part I, ch. xlii.

[3] A slang term meaning to hang (a criminal).

[4] Cf. James Berry, *My Experiences as an Executioner*, ed. H. Snowden Ward, reprint ed. (Detroit, 1972), p. 123: 'In England the Sheriff is the officer appointed to carry out executions, and though he is allowed to employ a substitute if he can find one, it would fall to him to personally conduct the execution if no substitute could be obtained.' Berry's career dates from the later nineteenth century.

[5] Cf. *Spectator* no. 78 (30 May 1711), i. 335: 'It was pleasant to hear the several Excuses which were made, insomuch that some made as much Interest to be excused as they would from serving Sheriff.'

[6] Fielding may be thinking here of Alderman George Heathcote, who declined to stand for lord mayor of London in 1740 because 'he was just out of an expensive office (that of sheriff) and which had taken up so much of his time that he had not been able to attend to his own affairs'; as quoted in *The House of Commons 1715–1754*, ed. Romney Sedgwick (London, 1970), ii. 122. Heathcote's prominence in the opposition of 1745–6 is certainly alluded to in *TP* no. 19 (4–11 March 1746), above, p. 238, and he may well have served as a model for the 'Alderman' in Fielding's *Gentleman & Alderman* of 1747.

[7] No schedule of fees for the public hangmen of this period has been located. Horace Bleackley, *The Hangmen of England* (London, 1929), p. 10, assumes a combination of fixed annual salary and 'piece-work' and estimates (p. 11) that the job in London in 1715 was worth £40 a year, a figure which

the Dishonour affixed to it. But what shall we say of other Countries, where it is a Place of considerable Profit, and yet is held in no higher Esteem? In *France*, tho' the Hangman be usually as well dress'd a Man as any in the Kingdom, he is nevertheless infamous, nor can with Safety venture to mix in the Company of Gentlemen. In a certain Part of *Germany*, the Hangman is at present the richest Person in the whole Principality, and yet cannot marry a beautiful only Daughter to any Man in it. Nay, even the *Dutch*, whose God is Gold, agree to treat their Deity with Disrespect, in the Possession of the Executioner.[1]

To say the Truth, there seems to be somewhat of very deep and refined Policy at the Bottom of this: For by this Device of casting Infamy on the Hangman and his Office, Great Men have been principally enabled to escape from his Clutches.

Notwithstanding the Novelty of this my Conceit, let the Reader, before he rejects it, consider, *First*, Whether he can invent any other Argument against hanging a Great Man for the same Crime for which a little one suffers that Fate; but that this Death is base and infamous, and beneath the Quality of a Gentleman. *2dly*, Whence is the Infamy of this Death, but from the Infamy of him who inflicts it? Would it otherwise be more scandalous for a Man to be hang'd, than to be universally known to deserve it? Why else should the Infamy be transferred from the Crime to the Punishment, and that in those Punishments only which this Officer inflicts?

The Hangman, therefore, is excluded from all good Company, and his Office is represented as low and mean, in order to instil into the People a Persuasion, that the Objects of it are only the lowest Vulgar, and that Greatness and the Gallows are incompatible Ideas. An Opinion which hath prevailed so generally, that the Phrase is in every one's Mouth; *Such a one is* too great *to be hanged*.

I might corroborate the above Conjecture by another Maxim of Politics, which is to depress and expel out of Society any Person whom you have defrauded or injured, lest he should attain sufficient Power and Interest to do himself Justice. Now can any Man doubt, but that the Hangman is commonly the most injured in his Property of any Person whatever? Who doth not know, that whole Bodies of Men have been justly his Due, without his receiving one Individual of their Number?

is also in John Laurence, *A History of Capital Punishment* (London, [n.d.]), p. 99. See too Leon Radzinowicz, *A History of English Criminal Law and its Administration from 1750* (New York, 1948), p. 187 n.

[1] Cf. *An Enquiry into the Causes of the late Increase of Robbers*, section xi, p. 125: 'In *Holland*, the Executions (which are very rare) are incredibly solemn. They are performed in the Area before the Stadthouse, and attended by all the Magistrates.'

Can any Man conceive, that this could happen, or that he would sit tamely down contented with such Injustice, if he had that Access to, and Interest with the other Great Men in the Kingdom, to which the Dignity of his Office so well entitles him? Nay, Gentlemen would themselves be ashamed, when they looked on him as their Equal, to defraud him in so barefaced a Manner; for even the Greatest Persons do some Sort of Justice among themselves, and pay their Debts of Honour to each other. I have now a Great Man in my Eye,[1] who, if the Hangman had a proper Opportunity of fairly stating the Case to him, hath not, I am sure, sufficient Abilities to refute, nor, I believe, Impudence enough to deny the Justice of his Claim. I am indeed convinced, there are more Persons, who in such Case would be ashamed of not being hang'd, than ever were ashamed of being so.

In reality, the Scandal lies not in suffering, but in escaping from Punishment.[2] Nay, this purges the Offence, and the guilty Man, who hath undergone the Sentence alotted to his Crime, becomes again *rectus in Curia*.[3] On which Account some of the Civilians have very gravely and wisely recommended to Offenders to surrender themselves to the Magistrate, confess their Delinquencies, and, as my Schoolmaster used to say, take their Punishment quietly. Indeed, while Men are governed by Ambition, Vanity, Avarice, and other genteel Passions, it will be very difficult, if not impossible, for them to avoid the Comission of Crimes; but to be hang'd for them is in every Man's Power, if he be not a Slave to that Scoundrel Passion of Fear, whose Dominion no Gentleman will own.

And what Man of Honour can submit to the Baseness of Fearing, about a Life which is forfeited to the Hangman? Who can survey his Person with Pleasure in a Glass, however well drest or ornamented it may be, when he considers it is the Property of *Jack Ketch*,[4] if he be so

[1] French, p. 416, and Locke, p. 177, identify Granville, probably (but not certainly) correctly. Walpole wrote Mann (21 March 1746) that the Prince of Wales 'has lately erected a new opposition, by the councils of Lord Bath, who has got him from Lord Granville: the latter and his faction act with the court'; *Yale Walpole*, xix. 229. However, although Bath's adherents may have voted *en bloc* against the Pelhams after the February upheavals, Bath himself seems more or less to have retired from active politics; *The House of Commons 1715–1754*, ed. Sedgwick, ii. 376. Moreover, there were persistent rumors that Granville was down but not out; see, for example, *London Evening Post* of 10–12 April 1746: 'There is still a Report that the *great M*——*r*, whose last Ad——n continu'd almost the full Sum of *forty-eight Hours*, will soon take his Turn again at the Head of Aff——rs.' In any event Fielding tends to prefer him for the 'Great Man' type. See 'General Introduction', above, pp. xx, civ.

[2] Cf. *Champion* of 8 January 1740, i. 170: 'It is not being hanged, but deserving to be hanged, that is infamous ....' The entire *Champion* essay is relevant.

[3] 'right in the law', generally applied to one who stood at the bar of a court and no accusation was made against him (Jowitt, *Dictionary*). It was also, and more specially, applied to one whose outlawry had been reversed. Given the political context of *TP* no. 20, the latter application is more appropriate.

[4] The 17th-century executioner (d. 1686), who achieved notoriety in the exercise of his function during the turmoils of the later Restoration. Ketch executed Stephen College (1681), Lord Russell

low a Person as he is vulgarly reputed? On the contrary, if his Office intitle him to that Rank and Dignity which I have contended to be his Due, what Man of Honour is at Liberty to refuse a Gentleman, whom he hath injured, Satisfaction?

I intended, at the Conclusion of this Paper, to have recommended this Satisfaction, which the *French* call *Amende honorable*,[1] to some particular Persons; but as I have not Room for Half the Names and Titles which occur to me, I shall defer this to some other Opportunity. I shall therefore confine myself, at present, to one Sett of Men, whom I must earnestly desire to deliver themselves immediately into the Hands of the Great Officer of Justice abovementioned, as not only their own Honour, but the Good of the Public, absolutely requires it.[2]

I believe no honest Man can entertain the least Doubt, but that Persons who endeavour to embroil their Country in domestic Factions, at this Season, when it is not only in the utmost Danger from external Enemies, but a Flame actually subsists within her own Bowels; who misrepresent the Measures, clog the Wheels of Government, and oppose the best Friends which the Public have ever seen in Power; who, under a most impudent Pretence to a Zeal for Liberty, are clandestinely undermining her very Foundation, and attempting to introduce Popery and Arbitrary Power; I say, no Man can doubt, but that all such Persons deserve to be hanged.[3]

I do therefore most earnestly recommend to the PRESENT OPPOSITION to be tucked up instantly, which will be the first *Service* they have ever done their Country.[4]

(1683), Monmouth (1685), and flogged Titus Oates (1685). His name became the generic name for the common hangman or executioner even before the close of the 17th century. *DA* of 12 April 1746 refers to a volunteer who executed a sentence of whipping on a malefactor, 'in the Absence of Jack Ketch'.

[1] In French law a species of punishment to which offenders against public decency or morality were anciently condemned (Jowitt, *Dictionary*).

[2] Cf. *Champion* of 8 January 1740, i. 169: 'I do ... earnestly entreat any Person, who in his own Mind is convinced that he ought to be hanged, tho' the Law cannot reach him, to deliver himself immediately into the Hands of Justice, that speedy and due Methods of Execution may be taken.' The *Champion* reference here is to another 'Great Man', Sir Robert Walpole.

[3] The leader to this point is reprinted in John Hill's *The British Magazine for the Year MDCCXLVI* (London, 1746), pp. 19–22.

[4] In *TP* no. 26 (22–9 April 1746), below, p. 276, Fielding develops the recommendation that the opposition be hanged and passes 'Sentence of Dissection' upon them, by which their bodies will be used for anatomical purposes, like those of common criminals. For the increasing emphasis on the presence of an opposition, see 'General Introduction', above, p. lxxxvii, and 'Present History of Great Britain', *TP* no. 17 (18–25 February 1746), above, pp. 228–9.

From Tuesday, March 18, to Tuesday, March 25, 1746.
Numb. 21.[1]

> ———— *Quis talia fando,*
> *Myrmidonum, Dolopumve, aut duri miles Ulyssei,*
> *Temperet a lachrymis?*
>
> Virgil.[2]

At a Season when the whole Nation have the greatest Reason to be confident in the Integrity of those who have the Management of Public Affairs, I shall find much Opportunity to look into private Life, and to correct and expose the many Evils which infect the Domestic Œconomy; an Office which well becomes a *True Patriot*, the rather as most of the Mischiefs that grow up to threaten and destroy Commonwealths, spring originally from Seeds which first discover themselves in our own Families. This being with me a certain Maxim, That whoever is a bad Man in private Life, will never prove a good one in Public.

The following Letter is so truly pathetic, and seems so evidently to proceed from the Heart, that my Reader will make little Doubt whether it is genuine or no; and I am sure he who doth not sympathize with the Writer, must have a very bad Heart of his own.

Sir,

As my Situation at present admits neither of Relief or Comfort, I do not trouble you with this on my own Account, but in hopes that the Picture

---

[1] Both the introduction to the letter and the letter itself meet the *hath–doth* stylistic in so far as it applies, and Locke, p. 183, thinks it 'not unreasonable to assume that Fielding wrote the entire essay, using material already at hand'. Certainly this leader and the one which follows seem a bit eccentric to the main concerns of the *TP* as a whole, and Cross, ii. 40, followed, less certainly, by French, p. 420, suggests that the present letter was written by Sarah Fielding. In *TP* no. 16 (11–18 February 1746) an 'Advertisement' purportedly by 'The Author of *David Simple*' announces a deferment of *Familiar Letters* on the grounds that the rebellion prevented her friends from favoring her with their interest in the matter of subscriptions. Inasmuch as Sarah Fielding does not employ *hath* or *doth* in either *David Simple* or *Familiar Letters*, perhaps the present letter was one Fielding himself had designed originally as a contribution to the latter collection. The letter minus its introduction appeared in the *Penny London Post* of 26–8 March 1746, with the direction 'To the Printer', which may tell against Fielding's authorship. *GM*, xvi (1746), 118–19, and John Hill's *The British Magazine for the Year MDCCXLVI* (London, 1746), pp. 29–33, also reprint the letter.

[2] *Aeneid*, ii. 6–8: 'What Myrmidon or Dolopian, or soldier of stern Ulysses, could in telling such a tale refrain from tears?' (Loeb). An abbreviated quotation from the Latin appears in 'A Letter to the Jacobites', in *TP* no. 7 (17 December 1745), reprinted in Locke, p. [84]. French, p. 420, and Locke, p. 183, note that the motto as well as the subject of unhappy marriage may have been suggested by *Henry and Blanche: Or the Revengeful Marriage*, a Dodsley and Cooper book, advertised in *TP* no. 20 (11–18 March 1746) as 'A Tale: Taken from the French of Gil Blas', with the same motto from the *Aeneid*.

which I am about to draw, may be the means of preserving many Fathers from the Calamities that have fallen on me.

I am now in the fifty-sixth Year of my Age. I had the Misfortune at forty to lose an excellent Wife, who left me one only Daughter, an Infant four Years old.

My Love to my Wife was such, that I really believe nothing but the violent Affection I bore to this little Pledge, could have given me Resolution to bear up against, and support her Loss. Considerations of the Consequence which my Life was of to my Child, enabled me to struggle with and overcome that Grief, which I could otherwise with greater Pleasure have sunk under than survived.

Little *Fanny* (for that was her Name) was now become my only Care and Pleasure, and I enjoyed more and more of this latter every Day, as she grew more capable of being my Companion. I fancied I did not only trace in her the Features of my most-beloved Woman, but that I daily discover'd in her Mind a stronger Resemblance of that Goodness and Sweetness of Temper, which had distinguished her Mother from the greater Part of her Sex. She was always a Stranger to those Severities, which some Parents contend for, as necessary in the Education of Children, and perhaps they may be to a wicked and fierce Disposition; and therefore, instead of Fear, she contracted for me that Reverence which Love and Gratitude inspires into good and great Minds towards Superiors. In short, I had in my little *Fanny*, at fourteen Years old, a Companion and a Friend.

She was now the Mistress of my House, and studied my Humour in every Thing. Whatever I expressed a Satisfaction in, was sure to be continued; and even a Look of Disapprobation removed the Cause for ever. She often declared her highest Satisfaction was in pleasing me, and all her Actions confirmed it. When Business permitted me to be with her, no Engagement to any Company or Pleasure could force my *Fanny* from me; nor did she ever disobey me, unless by doing that which she knew would most please me, contrary to my own Request, as by sometimes sacrificing her innocent Diversions abroad to keep me Company at home.

On my Part, I had no Satisfaction but in what my Child was concerned. She was the Delight of my Eyes, and the Joy of my Heart. I became an absolute Slave to a very laborious Business, in order to raise her Fortune, and aggrandize her in the World. These Thoughts made the greatest Fatigues not only easy but pleasant; and I have walk'd a hundred Times through the Rain with great Chearfulness, comforting myself, that by these means my *Fanny* would hereafter ride in her Coach.

She was about eighteen Years of Age, when I began to observe some little Alteration in my *Fanny's* Temper. Her Chearfulness had now frequent Interruptions, and a Sigh would sometimes steal from her, which never escaped my Observation, though I believe it often escaped her own. I presently guessed the true Reason of this Change, and was soon after convinced not only that her Heart had received some Impressions of Love, but likewise who was the Object of her Affections.

This Man, whom I will call *Philander*, was on many Accounts so deserving, that I verily believe I should have been prevailed on to favour my Child's Inclinations, tho' his Fortune was greatly unequal to what I had a Right to demand for her, had not a young Gentleman, with a very large Estate, offered himself to my Choice. I was unable to resist such an Acquisition of Fortune and of Happiness, as I then thought, to my Daughter. I presently agreed to his Proposals, and introduced him to her as one whom I intended for her Husband.

As soon as his first Visit was ended, *Fanny* came to me, prostrated herself at my Knees, and begged me, as I tendered her future Happiness, never to mention this Match to her more, nor to insist on her receiving a second Visit from *Leontius*, (for so I will call this Gentleman, whom would to God I had never heard of.)

Now was the first Moment I uttered a harsh Word to my poor Child, who was bathed in Tears (as I am while I am writing.) I told her, in an angry Tone, that I was a better Judge of what would contribute to her future Happiness than herself; that she made me a very ungrateful Return for all the Cares and Labours I had undergone on her Account, to refuse me the first Command of Importance I had ever laid on her, especially as it was only to give me the Satisfaction of seeing her happy, and when I had agreed to leave myself a Beggar in order to accomplish it.

I then left her, as I had no Reason to expect an immediate Answer, to contemplate on what I said: But, at my Departure, told her, that if she expected to see me more, the Terms must be an absolute Compliance with my Commands, and that she should never afterwards ask me any thing in vain.

I saw her no more that Evening; and the next Morning early received a Message from her, that she could no longer endure my Absence, or the Apprehension of my Anger, and begged leave to attend me in my Dressing-Room. I immediately sent for her, and when she appeared, began: *Well, Fanny, I hope you have thoroughly considered the Matter, and will not make me miserable by Denial of this first* —— *No Papa,* answered she, *you shall never be miserable, if your poor Fanny can prevent it. I have considered, and am resolved to be obedient to you, whatever may be the Consequence to me*. I then caught her in my Arms, in an Agony of Passion, and Floods of Tears burst at once from both our Eyes.

The Eagerness of *Leontius* soon completed the Match, as there remained no Obstacle to it, and he became possessed of my All: For, besides my darling Child, my little Companion, my Friend, he carried from me almost every Farthing which I was worth in the World.

The Ceremony being over, the young Couple retired into the Country, and I had the Pleasure of seeing my *Fanny* run away in a Coach and Six of her own. Little did I then think, that it was the last unsullied Pleasure I was ever to derive from her Sight.

They returned at the End of a Month, tho' they had proposed to stay longer; and my Child, the Moment she arrived in Town, immediately sent me Word she would visit me early the next Morning.

I slept not a Wink that Night, from the Tumult which the Happiness I proposed to enjoy the next Day, had raised in my Mind; but what did I feel when the Morning came, and passed away, without bringing my Child to my Arms. After having expected her for some Hours, I repaired hastily to her Husband's House; but guess my Surprize, when a Servant told me, that neither his Master nor Lady were at home. I then returned back, thinking to have met with her at my own House, but all in vain. I now began to grow extremely uneasy at a Disappointment, which I had the more Reason to be troubled at, as I could not conceive she, who knew what I would feel from it, would give it me on any light Occasion. I went once more to her Husband's House, and received the same Answer as before. I then enquired for her Maid, who was at last produced to me, with her Eyes swollen with Tears, and from her I learnt, that the Villain *Leontius* had insisted on her not visiting me that Morning, had confined her to her own Room, and given a general Order to all the Servants when he went out, to carry no message or Letter from her till he returned.

I now flew up Stairs, and burst open the Door of the Room, which was locked. I there found my Child in a Situation which I am not able to describe any more than all the other Circumstances of our first Meeting. Such of your Readers as are capable of feeling a tender Sensation, will easily raise the tragical Picture to their own Eyes.

As soon as Passion permitted her Utterance, she spoke to me as follows: "Sir, I am undone; my Husband is jealous of me with a Man whom I have never seen since our Marriage. He accidentally found me reading a Letter I had formerly received from *Philander*, which I had foolishly preserved. He snatched it from me; indeed he might have commanded it from me, for I never have, nor never wou'd disobey him. This Letter having no Date, he fancied I had just receiv'd and hath treated me ever since with Inhumanity not to be described. When I have endeavoured to convince him of my Innocence, he hath spurned me from him with Indignation, and these poor Arms in Return to their tenderest Embraces, have many Marks of his Violence upon them." Here she sunk upon me.—Can Words paint my Affliction, or the Horrors I then felt? Should I attempt it, this Scene alone would fill your whole Paper. I will hasten therefore to the Conclusion.

Her Husband was at length convinced that she had received this Letter as she affirmed, and was outwardly reconciled: But Jealousy is a Distemper seldom to be totally eradicated, and her having preserved this Letter, and the reading it again, were Circumstances he could not forgive. He behaved to his Wife at best with Coldness, but oftner with Cruelty, insomuch that in half a Year, from a State of florid Health, she became pale and meagre. *Philander* who, I believe, really loved her to Distraction, took this Opportunity of renewing his Addresses to her; and her Husband's Barbarity, at length, drove her into his Arms, and one Evening they made their Escape together.

The Day after I had heard this News, I received from her the following Letter:

"*My dear Papa*,

I am not insensible of my Guilt: But to resist the sincere and tender Passion of *Philander* was no longer in my Power, and the good-natur'd World, when they oppose to this the cruellest Treatment from an injurious[1] Husband, to whom Duty and not Love had joined me, will perhaps pity your poor *Fanny*.

"But alas! these are trifling Considerations. The Anger of the best of Fathers, and the Concern which he may suffer on my Account, are the Objects of my Terror. Nor can I bear the Thoughts of never seeing you more. Believe me, it is this Apprehension alone which stands between me and Happiness, and was the last and hardest Struggle I had to overcome. I will therefore hope that I may be forgiven by him, that I may again be blest by paying my Duty to the kindest, tenderest of Fathers: For in that Hope consists my Being, *&c.*"

I will make but one Remark on this Letter, which is, That she never upbraids me with having undone her.

---

[1] wrongful; hurtful or prejudicial to the rights of another; wilfully inflicting injury or wrong (*OED*, which cites the opening sentence of Cibber's *The Careless Husband* [1704]: 'Was ever Woman's Spirit, by an injurious Husband, broke like mine?').

If you think my Story may be of Use to the Public, by cautioning Parents from thwarting the Affections of such Children as are capable of having any, it is at your Service.

I am, &c.

From TUESDAY, MARCH 25, to TUESDAY, APRIL 1, 1746.
NUMB. 22.[1]

To the TRUE PATRIOT

Sir,   *Crane-Court, March 25 1746.*[2]

I am one of those People to whom the World usually give the Title of *Virtuosi*.[3] And tho' I am very sensible that the Generality of Mankind are apt to entertain a low and contemptible Opinion of us, as an useless Sett of People, yet that they have little Reason for doing so, I hope will appear from what I am going to relate.

I have formerly been a very great Traveller, and when I was in *Germany*, some Years ago, I happened to make an Acquaintance with a celebrated Alchymist,[4] who had spent a great Part of his Life in search of the *Philosopher's Stone*. It has often happened, that altho' the Virtuosi of this Sort have failed in their principal Attempt; yet the accidental Discovery of some Secret, which they never aimed at, has fully recompensed them for the Labour of the Undertaking. This was the Case of

[1] This leader, which was reprinted in Hill's *British Magazine for the Year MDCCXLVI* (London, 1746), pp. 66–71, does not appear to be Fielding's. It does not meet the *hath–doth* stylistic, and the use of italic resembles that of material not written by him. The leader is the only one for which we have a primary text which omits a motto altogether, and this fact suggests a loosening of editorial responsibility. The publication date falls just at the close of the Western Circuit assizes, which Fielding may have attended. More impressionistically, the satire on the virtuosi of the Royal Society seems stiff and lacking in the wit which this subject usually calls forth from Fielding. See 'General Introduction', above, pp. lxii–lxiii.

[2] On the north side of Fleet Street, east of Fetter Lane, it had been since 1710 the meeting place of the Royal Society.

[3] For a commonplace satirical perspective, cf. 'Letter XL', which Fielding contributed to his sister's *Familiar Letters* (1747), ii. 299: 'The first great Corrupters of our Taste are the Virtuoso's. . . . These are a kind of burlesque natural Philosophers, whose Endeavours are not to discover the Beauties, but the Oddities and Frolicks of Nature. They are indeed a sort of natural Jugglers, whose Business it is to *elevate* and *surprize*, not to satisfy, inform, or entertain.' To compare Fielding's attitude toward the Royal Society, see Henry Knight Miller, *Essays on Fielding's 'Miscellanies'* (Princeton, 1961), pp. 315–31, especially pp. 329ff.

[4] Locke, p. 189, assumes the 'Alchymist' is based on the historical Galileo, who, though never in Germany, did devise a crude thermometer and just before he died invited the historical Torricelli to complete certain of his works. It should be noted, however, that the German location, the emphatic reference to '*untimely Death*', the references to alchemy and the philosopher's stone, require a heavy admixture of the Faustian.

my worthy Friend abovementioned. He was obliged, by an *untimely Death*, to leave the GREAT WORK unfinished; but it is owing to his Industry, that I am become a Master of a SECRET, of equal, if not of superior Importance.

My Acquaintance with this Gentleman commenced but a little before his Death; but he had taken such a Liking to me, in this short time, that by his last Will he bequeathed to me all his Books and Curiosities. It would be tedious to give an Account of all the *Rarities* which I thus became Master of; but amongst the rest was a curious Machine, which at first sight I took to be a *Thermometer*. It was constructed in the usual Form, but very small, the Glass Tube being not above three Inches long. This Tube was filled with a red transparent Liquor, and behind it was an Ivory Scale, upon which the Degrees of *Heat and Cold* (as I then thought) were delineated with the greatest Nicety; but there was no Inscription upon it to point out the Changes of the Air, as is usually done on the common Thermometers, by the Words *Hot, Temperate*, &c. I took this Instrument home with me, and placed it on the Table in my Study. That Night the Weather changed, as it does frequently in that Climate, from temperate to very cold. I was eager to see my Thermometer the next Morning, in Expectation that it would have very exactly shewn this Change; but I had no sooner cast my Eye upon it, but I saw that the *Spirits* stood exactly where they had done the Day before. I could not tell what to make of this; however, I had a Mind to make a farther Trial of it, and therefore placed it on my Table, near the Fire, to see if the Heat would make the *Spirits* rise. It is my constant Custom, in a Morning, while my Breakfast is getting ready, to entertain myself with a Book; and I generally take up one or other of the Classic Authors for this Purpose. That Morning I happened to take up a *Virgil*. I had no sooner began to read, but I saw the *Spirits* mount up suddenly in the Thermometer, from whence I concluded, that there must have been a very sudden Alteration in the Air; but upon laying the Book aside, to observe the Instrument more exactly, the *Spirits* immediately subsided to their former Pitch. This Accident surprized me pretty much; but I had greater Reason for Admiration when I observ'd, that the Moment I began to read on, the *Spirits* began to ascend again, and that they sunk as soon as ever I left off. I imagined, at first, that my Breath was the Cause of this sudden Change; but I soon laid aside that Thought, as I observ'd, that there was the same Appearance, whether I read aloud or to myself; and whether I was near to, or at a Distance from the *Glass*. Whilst I was in this Perplexity, I took up the first Book which came to hand, which happen'd to be a Volume of Sermons, which had been given me by an Eminent

Divine, when I first went abroad. I had scarcely dipp'd into it, when I saw, to my great Astonishment, that the Liquor, instead of rising, sunk down of a sudden to the very Bottom of the Tube, and ascended again as suddenly, upon my laying the Book aside. Most People, had they been in my Place, would have attributed this *Phænomenon* to *Magic*. And for my own Part, I must freely own, that I do not comprehend what secret properties this Liquor has, nor how it is prepared, but must leave that Matter to be discuss'd by the Philosophers and Naturalists of the Age; all I can say to it is, that by making a great many Experiments of the like kind, I always found, that the *Spirits* in the Tube rose or fell, in proportion to *Altitude* or *Depression* of the Author's Genius.[1]

As most great Inventions have been owing originally to Chance, so I may be said, by mere Accident, to have found out the Use of an *Instrument*, which may properly be stiled, *The Test of Understanding*; or, *The Weather-Glass of Wit*:[2] As it shews the Degree of *Heat* or *Coldness* in the *Understanding*, with as much Certainty, as the Common Thermometers do that of the Atmosphere. And, by the exactest Observations I have been able to make, it appears, that the different Degrees of *Sense* are ranged according to the ensuing Scale, which, for that Reason, I have affix'd to the *Thermometer*.

MADNESS.

WILDNESS.

TRUE WIT, or FIRE.

VIVACITY.

GOOD-SENSE.

GRAVITY.

PERTNESS.

DULLNESS.

STUPIDITY, or FOLLY.

If any Objection should be made to my placing the different Degrees of Understanding at equal Distances from each other, I must acquaint

[1] Similar applications of the 'weather glass' concept may be found in *Tatler* no. 214 (19–22 August 1710), where the glass is political; in *Tatler* no. 220 (2–5 September 1710), where it is ecclesiastical; in *Spectator* no. 281 (22 January 1712), where it tests people for humor and seriousness.

[2] Although the invention of the thermometer is generally credited to Galileo, the derivation known as the weather glass or barometer seems to have been credited to Torricelli; cf. *Tatler* no. 220 (2–5 September 1710): 'It is well known, that Torricellius, the Inventor of the common Weather-glass, made the Experiment in a long Tube which held Thirty-two Feet of Water.' *Tatler* no. 220 provides an ecclesiastical calibration for its glass that resembles the 'witty' one of this *TP* leader.

the Objector, that it did not proceed from my own Invention, but that it was the Result of several long and careful Experiments, which I made of the rising and falling of the *Spirits* in my Thermometer. Whenever I read a plain sensible Production of any Author, I always observed that the *Spirits* kept exactly to the *middle Point*. If Good-Sense was mix'd with here and there a lively Stroke, they rose to *Vivacity*. A Degree more of *Heat* raises the Thermometer to *Fire*; which is always the more laudable Quality in an Author, the more steadily and equably it burns. Too great a Degree of Fire degenerates into *Wildness*, or Extravagance, which last is but one Degree below *Madness*, or the *raving* Point. The lower part of the Scale points out the different Degrees of *Coldness* in the Understanding. *Good-Sense*, by a farther Degree of Cold, is *condensed* into *Gravity*: Gravity, as appears from my Glass, falling just as much short of Good-Sense, as Vivacity does of true Wit, or Fire; and, as they are but one Degree distant from each other, this may probably be the Reason why the Man of *Vivacity* is often mistaken for a *Wit*, and the *grave Man* for a *Man of Sense*. The next Degree below *Gravity* is *Pertness*: This Quality of the Mind is oftentimes called *Wit*; and indeed they appear, by my Scale, to be equally distant from Good-Sense; but with this Difference, that as true Wit is two Degrees above, so Pertness is just as many below that Point; for the witty Writer borders upon Extravagance, but the *pert* one is but one Degree above being *dull*.[1]

I may, perhaps, hereafter communicate to you the Observations which I have made, from Time to Time, upon different Kinds of Writers, by the help of my Thermometer; for I have brought it to so great a Degree of Exactness, that I can tell, to the *Twelfth Part of an Inch*, how much Wit there is in any Author. But I shall wave this Point at present, to acquaint you, That I seldom go into Company without taking my Glass along with me; and whilst others are employ'd in gazing upon it, and observing the Inscription, which is in a Character of my own Invention, somewhat resembling the *Chinese*, I have an Opportunity of examining the *Height* or *Depth* of their Capacities.

Give me Leave now to mention some of the many Advantages which the Public may reap from the Use of this *Machine*, and which may intitle the Inventor to your Encouragement, as a *True Patriot*. It will readily be allowed me, I presume, that my Thermometer may be rendered of the

---

[1] For Fielding's view of this quality, see also *CGJ* no. 40 (19 May 1752), i. 360–3, which prints '"Peri Tharsus", a Treatise on the Confident and Pert'; and *CGJ* no. 46 (9 June 1752), ii. 18–22, which like the earlier essay asserts the quality to be a peculiarly 'modern' one. As does Pope, *Peri Bathous*, ch. xii.

utmost Use to the Managers of the two Theatres,[1] by furnishing them with a certain Rule, by which they may judge of the Merit of new *Dramatic* Performances. I humbly hope, therefore, that those Gentlemen will constitute me *Surveyor-General* of Plays: And I submit to their Discretion, Whether it would not be proper, upon the first Night of a new Play, to give out *Bills*, in which the Quantity of Wit contain'd in each Scene should be marked down. For by this Means the Audience would be enabled to *clap* or *hiss* in the proper Place. And I believe most Authors, who have written for the Stage, will agree with me, that this is a Thing which is very much wanted at this Time, and which would greatly tend to promote a good Harmony between the *Poet* and the *Pitt*.

My *Thermometer* may still be of further Use, by enabling Readers of all Kinds, *gentle* as well as *simple*, to judge of the Merit of new Books, as well as of new Plays.—I have oftentimes secretly lamented, that the Generality of Readers have no certain Rule of doing this; and at the same Time pitied the Fate of young Authors, whose Works, for Want of some such Rule, have many Times been stifled, as one may say, at their very Birth.—The common Way of judging of new Performances, I know, is to cast an Eye upon the Title-page, to see what *capital* Letters are added at the End of the Author's Name: For the more or fewer there are of these, the greater or less is the Merit of the Work.—I have sometimes known the whole Impression of a Book sold off, in a few Days Time, by the Help of a *D.D.* and *F.R.S.* or *C.M.L.S.*[2] in the Title-page, when it would, perhaps, have lain upon the Bookseller's Hands for Years together, nay, and perhaps have been sent to the *Pastry Cooks* at last,[3] if it had wanted this Addition. There is another Way of judging of the Excellency of a Book, *viz.* by observing whom it is dedicated to: And it can hardly be imagined what an Effect a Dedication to his Grace of —,[4] my Lord *C*——,[5] or Dr. *M*——,[6] *&c.* has sometimes had, in filling the

---

[1] The two theatres holding a royal patent, Drury Lane and Covent Garden. In 1746 John Rich was manager of the latter, and Drury Lane was managed by James Lacy, who had been appointed during the 1744–5 season by the bankers who bought out Fleetwood. See *TP* no. 18 (25 February–4 March 1746), above, p. 232 *n.* 1.

[2] Not identified.

[3] Pastry cooks used waste paper, notably superfluous sheets of printed matter, to wrap their pies in, a practice which provided a convenient emblem for the destiny of unwanted art. Cf. Dryden, *Mac Flecknoe*, vv. 100–1: 'From dusty shops neglected Authors come, | Martyrs of Pies, and Reliques of the Bum.' Fielding dilates upon the matter in *CGJ* no. 6 (21 January 1752), i. 169–70. See also *JJ* no. 7 (16 January 1748), pp. 134–5.

[4] The omission of any identifying marks beyond the courtesy title requires the reader to think of nothing more than the efficacy of a dedication to a duke.

[5] Although again no identification is necessary, the contemporary reader would probably have thought of the earl of Chesterfield, who enjoyed a reputation as a patron and a man of letters.

[6] Probably Dr Richard Mead (1673–1754), eminent physician and bibliophile, of whom Warburton wrote to Birch (15 December 1739) that he was 'a man to whom all people that pretend to letters

Bookseller's *Pocket*, and inhancing the *Reputation* of the Author. There is a third Way of determining the Worth of a Book, which I prefer to either of the former, namely, by observing whom it is printed for. A very ingenious Friend of mine, whom I was lately talking with about the Character of a new Pamphlet, assured me, that it must be a very good one, because it was printed for *J.* and *P. K*——,[1] in *L*——*te Street*.—And this is the general Way of judging of all anonymous Pieces whatever. Now, although I allow each of these Methods to have its Use, yet, in my humble Opinion, the Value of Books may be more certainly ascertained by Means of my Thermometer, than by any of the three.

From what I have said of the Properties of my Weather-glass, you will perceive, that no Body is better qualified than myself, to carry into Execution a Project which wou'd be of universal Benefit, and which, for a long Time past, I have had in my Thoughts; *viz.* To erect *an Office for assaying Wit*, or trying whether it be *Standard*. I intend to take the Office of *Assay Master* on myself, and do hereby advertise all Booksellers, Publishers, &c. who deal in *Literary Wares*, that, by applying to my Office, they may have the *Metal*, which they traffic in, *assayed*, for a small Gratuity, in order to discover whether it be *true* or *counterfeit*. As you have profess'd yourself a *True Patriot*, I hope you will give Encouragement to my Scheme, by recommending it to the Public; and, in Return for the Favour, I shall be ready, at any Time, to *assay* your *Paper*, *gratis*; and to give you any farther Assistance which is in my Power. And I flatter myself that my Assistance will not be thought inconsiderable; since, by taking my Glass along with me into all Companies, from the Ministers *Levée* down to the City Club,[2] I have found out the Means of

ought to pay their tribute on account of his great eminence in them and patronage of them' (*DNB*). Fielding himself alludes to the great size of Mead's library in the 'Preface' to the *Journal of a Voyage to Lisbon* (1755) and again under the date 26 June 1754. Mead was the dedicatee of numerous works and he subscribed to most of the important historical and learned books which appeared in his time. French, p. 429, and Locke, p. 189, conjecture Dr Misaubin, the well-known empiric, to whom Fielding dedicated, ironically, *The Mock Doctor*, but Misaubin is an unlikely candidate, having died in 1734. See also Ioan Williams, *The Criticism of Henry Fielding* (New York, 1970), p. 353.

[1] John and Paul Knapton, London booksellers, at the Crown in Ludgate Street (1735–70), brothers to James Knapton (1687–1736) and successors to his business. The firm was in fact eminent and was associated with a number of the important publishing projects of the time. John Knapton was Master of the Stationers' Company in 1742, 1743, and 1745. See Plomer, *Dictionary*, p. 148. There is a friendly allusion to the Knaptons in the 'Index to the Times', *Champion* of 17 June 1740 (ii. 349), and possibly (and obliquely) in *Tom Jones*, XVIII. vi. 937.

[2] Apparently a generic name for a club composed of persons whose occupation kept them in the City. If the inclusion of its members among 'most of the considerable Persons in this Kingdom' is not ironic, then perhaps a merchants' club is meant; if, on the other hand, the city club is placed at the opposite end ('down') of the social and political spectrum from the ministerial *levée*, then perhaps it resembles the 'Two-penny Club' of the cobbler and other political 'Adepts' of his social standing; see

penetrating into the true Characters and Abilities of most of the considerable Persons in this Kingdom; and can, at any Time, furnish you with an exact Calculation of the Quantity of Wisdom and Folly which is to be found in this Metropolis.

> *I am*, &c.
> TORRICELLI, Jun[r].

From TUESDAY, APRIL 1, to TUESDAY, APRIL 8, 1746.
NUMB. 23.

> —— *Insanus paucis videatur eo quod*
> *Maxima pars hominum morbo jactatur eodem.*
>
> HORACE.[1]

I have heard of a Man who believed there was no real Existence in the World but himself; and that whatever he saw without him was mere Phantom and Illusion.

This Philosopher,[2] I imagine, hath not had many Followers in Theory; and yet if we were to derive the Principles of Mankind from their Practice, we should be almost persuaded that somewhat like this Madness had possessed not only particular Men, but their several orders and Professions. For tho' they do not absolutely deny all

TP no. 19 (4–11 March 1746), above, p. 235. In *Rape upon Rape* (1730) Fielding describes a city club as a place 'where Men drink out of Thimbles, that the Fancy may be heightened by the Wine' (I. vii; Henley, ix. 86).

[1] *Satires*, II. iii. 120–1: 'few [doubtless] would think him mad, because the mass of men toss about in the same kind of fever' (Loeb).

[2] The later implication that this 'Philosopher' is both dead and unrecognized suggests the reference is to Arthur Collier (1680–1732), metaphysician and divine, the running title of whose *Clavis Universalis* (1713) reads: 'Being a Demonstration of the Non-Existence, or Improbability, of an External World'. Collier's earliest biographer says of *Clavis Universalis* that it was unpurchased and unread and the author of it scarcely known beyond the limits of his own village; Robert Benson, *Memoirs of the Life and Writings of the Rev. Arthur Collier, M.A.* (London, 1837), p. 20. For material reasons Collier moved to Salisbury in his later years, where his children seem to have become acquainted with the Fieldings. Collier's son Arthur, a friend of Fielding's and a subscriber to his *Miscellanies* (1743) had in 1746 a case pending against him for a defaulted debt of £400. Fielding and James Harris, another friend from Salisbury, had pledged surety for Collier and the former apparently acted as Collier's legal counsel. In June 1746 the final judgment was adverse to Collier, who refused to pay, whereupon execution for the full amount plus damages was taken out, apparently against Fielding alone; see J. Paul de Castro, 'Fielding and the Collier Family', *N&Q*, twelfth series, ii (5 August 1916), 104–6, where it is conjectured (p. 105) that 'The adverse judgment rang the death-knell of *The True Patriot*'. But see 'General Introduction', above, pp. civ–cv. Cross, ii. 12, implies that during Fielding's residence in the commodious home in Old Boswell Court (1744–7) the metaphysician's daughter Margaret may have resided with Henry and his sister Sarah.

Existence to other Persons and Things, yet it is certain they hold them of no Consequence, and little worth their Consideration, unless they *trench*[1] somewhat towards their own Order or Calling.

As an Instance of this, let us observe three or four Members of any Profession met together in a general Company, though it be never so large, they make no Scruple of engrossing the whole Conversation, and turning it to their own Profession, without the least Consideration of all the other Persons present.

Another Example of the same Temper may be seen in the monopolizing particular Words, and confining their Meaning to their own Purposes, as if the rest of the World had in reality no Right to their Application. A signal Instance of which is in the Adjective Good.[2] A Word which of all others Mankind would least wish to be debarred from the Use of, or from appropriating to themselves and their Friends.

Now when the Divine, the Free-Thinker, the Citizen, the Whig, the Tory, *&c.* pronounce such an Individual to be a good Man, it is plain that they have all so many different Meanings; and he may be a very good Man in the Opinion of one in the Company, who would be a very bad one in that of all the others.

I remember to have supped last Winter at a Surgeon's, where were present some others of the Faculty. The Gentleman of the House declared he had a very good Subject above in the Garret. As the Gentleman who said this was, I knew, himself as good a Subject as any in the Kingdom, I could not avoid Surprize at his chusing to confine such a Person in a cold Night, in such a Place: But I soon found my Mistake, and that this good Subject had been hanged the Day before for a most heinous Felony.[3]

An Error of the same Kind once happened to me amongst some Gentlemen of the Army, who all agreed that one Mr. *Thunderson* was the best Man in *England*. I own I was somewhat staggered when I heard he

---

[1] In vaguer use, to come in thought, speech or action close upon (something); to border closely upon, to verge upon . . . hence, to have a bearing upon or reference to (something) [*OED*, which cites this passage].

[2] *CGJ* no. 4 (14 January 1752), i. 156, glosses 'Good' as 'A Word of as many different Senses as the Greek word Ἔχω or as the Latin *Ago*: for which Reason it is but little used by the Polite.' See also the 'Preface' to the *Miscellanies*, i. 10–12.

[3] For the practice of obtaining the bodies of executed malefactors for use in dissection, see *TP* no. 26 (22–9 April 1746), below, p. 276. Cf. *Spectator* no. 504 (8 October 1712), iv. 290: 'It is a Superstition with some Surgeons, who beg the Bodies of condemn'd Malefactors, to go to the Goal, and bargain for the Carkass with the Criminal himself.' On the 'Subjects' of dissection, cf. 'Apocrypha', *TP* no. 7 (17 December 1745), below, p. 379: 'Several Gentlemen, who are Surgeons, are set out for the Duke of Cumberland's Army, having enter'd themselves Voluntiers to serve under his Royal Highness as Occasion may require. D.A. *We hope these Gentlemen will make* good Subjects *of some of the Rebels.*' The italicized comment originated with the *TP* and is probably Fielding's.

was a Corporal of Grenadiers: But how much more was I astonished when I found that he had half a dozen Wives, and was the wickedest Fellow in the whole Regiment.

I cannot quit this Head without remarking that much Inconvenience may arise from these Mistakes; and one indeed happened in the last-mentioned Instance; for a grave wealthy Widow, of above 40, in the Town where the Regiment was quarter'd, having doubtless heard the same Character of this Man from his Officers, and misunderstanding them, as I myself had done before their Explanation, fell in Love with his Goodness and married him.

A third Example may be drawn from the Attention of the Readers of Books, or the Spectators at Plays. I have somewhere heard of a Geographer who received no other Pleasure from the *Æneid* of *Virgil*, than by tracing out the Voyage of *Æneas* in the Map.[1] To which I may add a certain Coach-maker, who having sufficient *Latin* to read the Story of *Phaeton* in the *Metamorphosis*,[2] shook his Head that so fine a Genius for making Chariots as *Ovid* had, was thrown away on making Poems.

This selfish Attention (if I may so call it) in the Spectators at our Theatres must be evident to all who have ever frequented them. Every Joke on a Courtier's not paying his Debts, is sure to receive a thundering Applause from the Pit and Galleries. This Debt is, however, paid by the Boxes, on the first facetious Allusion to Horns, or any other Symbol of Cuckoldom.[3] Indeed the whole House are seldom unanimous in their Claps, unless when the Ridicule is against the Ministry, the Law, or the Clergy; whence, I suppose, that as Government, Law, and Religion are looked upon as the great Grievances of the Nation, the whole Audience think themselves alike interested in their Demolition.

I knew a Gentleman, who had great Delight in observing the Humours of the Vulgar, and for that Purpose used frequently to mount into the Upper Gallery. Here, as he told me, he once seated himself

---

[1] Cf. *Spectator* no. 409 (19 June 1712), ii. 529: 'One of the most eminent Mathematicians of the Age has assured me, that the greatest Pleasure he took in reading *Virgil*, was in examining *Aeneas* his Voyage by the Map.'

[2] The description of Phoebus's chariot, designed for him by Vulcan, is to be found in *Metamorphoses*, ii. 107–10.

[3] The 'class structure' implicit in the seating arrangements of 18th-century theatrical audiences found the tradespeople, the professionals, and other middle-class habitués in the pit and lower gallery; the footmen and servant class in the galleries, particularly the upper gallery. Hence the knowledgeable applause from these locations for jokes at the expense of courtiers or persons of quality. The latter were generally seated in the boxes, from which they could signify approval of the allusions to cuckoldom, which in plays was traditionally effected by the courtier class upon the 'cits' of the middle class. For another perspective of the same distribution, see *TP* no. 18 (25 February–4 March 1746), above, p. 231.

between two Persons, one of whom he soon discovered to be a broken[1] Taylor; and the other, a Servant in a Country Family, just arrived in Town. The Play was *Henry the Eighth*, with that august Representation of the Coronation.[2] The former of these, instead of admiring the great Magnificence exhibited in that Ceremony, observed with a Sigh, "That he believed very few of these Cloaths were paid for." And the latter being ask'd how he liked the Play, (being the first he had ever seen) answered, "It was all very fine; but nothing came up, in his Opinion, to the Ingenuity of snuffing the Candles."

I cannot omit the following Story, which I think a very strong Example of the Temper I have above remarked. I remember to have been present at a certain Religious Assembly of the People called *Methodists*,[3] where the Preacher named the following Text: *It is reported, that Fornication is among you*.[4] The whole Congregation, as well as myself, expected, I believe, a wholesome Dissertation on all criminal Converse between the Sexes; and some, who laboured under Suspicions of that kind, began to express much Apprehension and Uneasiness in their Countenances: But, to our great Surprize, the Sermon was entirely confin'd to the former Part of the Text, and we were only instructed in the Nature and various kinds of *Reports*. This gave me some Curiosity to enquire into the Character of so extraordinary a Preacher; and I found, to my perfect Satisfaction, that he had got his living many Years by collecting Articles of News for one of the Public Papers.[5]

If we reflect seriously on this Disposition of Mankind, so universally exerted in private Life, it will lead us to account for the Behaviour of Men and Parties in Public; and we shall lose much of that Surprize, which might otherwise naturally enough affect us, from observing the

[1] failed in business, bankrupt.

[2] Act IV, scene i. Beginning in January 1744 advertisements for *Henry VIII* regularly called attention to the lavish staging accorded this scene. The play was performed at Drury Lane on 22 November and 26 December 1745, and 1 January 1746; *London Stage*, Part 3, ii. 1195, 1205, 1206.

[3] 'The People called Methodists' was a denomination much used by the Methodists themselves; e.g., John Wesley, *Advice to the People called Methodists* (n.p., 1745); George Whitefield, *A Brief Account of the Occasion . . . Between Some of the People call'd 'Methodists', Plaintiffs, and Certain Persons of the Town* (London, 1744). Whitefield's title suggests that the denomination may have derived from legal terminology in actions involving Methodists. In *DA* of 7 September 1745 Wesley published a letter entitled 'To the Part of the People called Methodists who are commonly styled the Moravian Brethren'. See also Wesley's *Journal*, ed. Nehemiah Curnock, iii (London, n.d.), 40, 120.

[4] From 1 Corinthians 5: 1. The same anecdote does service in *Champion* of 31 May 1740 (ii. 279–80), but with no application to the Methodists and no suggestion that the author was in the congregation. For Fielding's habit of associating Methodists with sexual license, see *Tom Jones*, I. x. 63 and note. The paradigm case is, of course, Parson Williams in *Shamela*. Not surprisingly, no published sermons on this particular text are listed in Samson Letsome's *The Preacher's Assistant* (London, n.d.) or his *Index to the Sermons Published Since the Restoration* (London, 1751).

[5] Alluding to the Methodists' practice of choosing members from the ranks to be local and itinerant preachers.

rigid Adherence which Men of no dishonest Characters preserve to their own Party and their own Schemes. Hence it is, that Men become more the Subjects of our Consideration than Measures; and hence it hath sometimes happened, that Men (and those not the worst of Men neither) have been more intent on advancing their own Schemes, than on advancing the Good of the Public, and would have risqued the Preservation of the latter, rather than have given up the Pursuit of the former. *I have said it*; *I have invented it*; *I have writ upon it*; are as substantial Arguments with some Politicians, as they are with the Doctor in *Gil Blas*, who had writ on the Virtues of Hot Water, and therefore refused to agree with those who prescribed cold.[1] To say the truth, this Partiality to ourselves, our own Opinions, and our own Party, hath introduced many dangerous Evils into Commonwealths. It is this Humour which keeps up the Name of *Jacobitism* in this Kingdom; and it is this Humour only, from which his present Majesty or his Administration can derive a single Enemy within it. The OPPOSITION (if a handful of Men, and those for the most part totally insignificant, as well in Fortune as Abilities, are worthy that Name) would I believe be puzzled to give any better Reason for their Conduct than the aforesaid Doctor, or than Parson *Adams* hath done for them,[2] who says, That *Opposition* is derived from the Verb *oppono*, and that the *English* of the Verb *oppono* is *to oppose*.

From TUESDAY, APRIL 8, to TUESDAY, APRIL 15, 1746.
NUMB. 24.

—— *Medici mediam pertundite venam.*

JUVENAL.[3]

[1] An inexact recollection of Le Sage, *The History of Gil Blas of Santillane*, 4th ed. (London, 1737), Bk. II, chs. iii–iv (I. 134, 136), where the doctor's differences with his professional colleagues are nowhere said to involve temperature. Fielding describes the staples of Sangrado's regimen, in *Joseph Andrews*, III. i. 187: 'Dr. *Sangrado* ... used his Patients as a Vintner doth his Wine-Vessels, by letting out their Blood, and filling them up with Water.'

[2] Adams's two previous appearances, in *TP* no. 7 (17 December 1745) and no. 13 (21–8 January 1746), above, pp. 151–7, 201–7, concerned the general social wickedness of the time and the political situation as a judgment upon that, without any marked distinction reserved for the parliamentary opposition.

[3] *Satires*, vi. 46. Fielding had earlier rendered it 'And Surgeons ope his middle Vein'; 'Part of Juvenal's Sixth Satire, Modernized in Burlesque Verse', *Miscellanies*, i. 91. Modern texts read *nimiam* for *mediam*, but Fielding's probable source, the Delphin edition of Juvenal and Persius, edited by Ludovicus Proteus, reads *mediam*. Baker, item no. 67, lists a 1722 London Delphin edition among Fielding's books. Cf. Dryden's rendering (1693), 'Run for the Surgeon; breathe the middle Vein'; *Poems*, ed. James Kinsley, ii (Oxford, 1958), 697.

I have heard it often objected to the Friends of the Government, when they have expressed their Apprehensions of a *Jacobite* Party in this Kingdom, that these Fears were counterfeited in order to form an Argument for the Support of a standing Army,[1] or to excuse some other Ministerial Schemes; for that, in reality, the very Seeds of *Jacobitism* were destroyed, and rooted out from the Minds of every Protestant *British* Subject.

I am not ashamed to own myself to have been one of the many who were imposed on by these Suggestions; I am much more concerned to see that this was an Imposition, and that Experience should at last have convinced every Man, that there are still some Persons, (an inconsiderable Party indeed, when compared to the Number of Loyal Subjects)[2] who profess the Protestant Religion, while they wish well to the Designs of a Popish Pretender.

The principal Motive which induced me to hold my former Opinion, was the Reasonableness of it. I disbelieved the Existence of Protestant Jacobitism, from the same Principles which inspire me to deny our Assent to many of these strange Relations which certain Voyage-Writers recount to us. I looked upon such an Animal as a greater Monster, than the most romantic of these Writers have ever described, and was therefore easily persuaded to credit those who very solemnly assured us, there was no such to be found in the Land.

I have hitherto avoided any Contest with these Sort of Gentlemen, not from the Contempt of so poor a Victory; for I should think my Labours well bestowed, in bringing the weakest of them over to the Cause of Truth; but in plain fact, they are the last Persons with whom I would willingly enter the Lists of Disputation, from absolute Despair of Success: For what is so difficult to answer as nothing, or what more impossible to be evinced, than the Light of the Sun to him who hath not Eyes to discern it. I have therefore greatly admired the Patriotism of those Heroes, who have formerly wasted much of their Time to prove, that Millions were not intended by an All-good Being, for the Use and

---

[1] With the inevitable power that such an establishment would confer upon the crown and the central government. For the political implications, see J. R. Western, *The English Militia in the Eighteenth Century* (London, 1965), chs. iv–v. One of the reasons the government was slow to respond to the jacobite threat in 1745 was the squabbling over the politically appropriate method of raising troops. See 'General Introduction', above, pp. xliii–xlv.

[2] *TP* no. 19 (4–11 March 1746), above, p. 239, concludes with the assertion that 'the present just Administration of Power had reduced all Opposition to such a ridiculous Object, as I have here described'. See also 'Present History of Great Britain' (probably not by Fielding) in *TP* no. 18 (25 February–4 March 1746), where it is said that with the recent restoration of the Pelhams 'Faction is no more, that Party Animosities are extinct, and that there is not the least Probability of *reviving* them' (Locke, p. [161]).

wanton Disposition of one Man;[1] that a Protestant Church was not absolutely secure under the Protection of a Prince who looks on himself as bound by his Religion, and that on Pain of Damnation, to destroy it;[2] that a Magistrate attempting to destroy those Laws and Constitutions which he was sworn and obliged to defend, forfeited that Power which he so entirely perverted,[3] with numberless other Propositions equally plain and demonstrable, or rather indeed self-evident. So that if the Absurdity of their Tenets was not of itself sufficiently apparent, and did not glare them in the Face, it hath been so irrefragably proved by the Labours of those good Men, who have undertaken the Defence of the Revolution, that the *Jacobites* of this Age have no other Excuse left, but that of not being able to read.

This is an Excuse which I am sensible may be fairly pleaded by many, and those none the least considerable Pillars of the Party. There have been, however, some who have not only read, but have endeavoured to answer these Writers; and have very modestly attempted to oppose the Common Sense of Mankind, in a Point wherein their highest Interest is concerned.

As such Performances are seldom long-lived, few of them have reached our Days: But the following Letter, which I look upon as a very curious Piece, and which was written in the Reign of the late King *William*,[4] contains, I believe, the Sum of all those Arguments which have been ever used on the Behalf of *Jacobitism*; I shall therefore give it the Reader, after having premised, that it was written by a Nonjuror[5] to his Son at *Oxford*.[6]

---

[1] Cf. 'Mystery the Third', *JJ* no. 3 (19 December 1747), p. 105: '. . . an Article of Jacobitical Faith, founded on long Tradition, and infinitely above all Reason, *viz.* That God hath been graciously pleased to create many Millions of People for the sole Use and Advantage, nay, for the Diversion of One.' Similar sentiments are in *Jonathan Wild*, I. xiv and II. iv.

[2] Cf. 'Mystery the Fourth', *JJ* no. 3, pp. 107–8: 'That a Popish Prince may be the Defender of a Protestant Church'. The *JJ* leader as a whole provides a useful satirical gloss on this paragraph of *TP* no. 24.

[3] Cf. 'Mystery the Second', *JJ* no. 3, p. 104: 'But the King of *England* is not absolute, but ought to govern by Law; but if he breaks the Law never so often, nay, if he attempts to subvert both the Law and the Constitution, as King *James* II. *of blessed Memory*, did in a thousand Instances, he is neither to be resisted, nor call'd to any Account for it.'

[4] Technically, William III ruled alone and in his own name from the death of his wife Mary on 27 December 1694, until his own death on 8 March 1702. However, both the 'curious Piece' and the dating are satiric fictions.

[5] Originally, one of the beneficed clergy who refused to take the oath of allegiance in 1689 to William and Mary (*OED*). By extension, as here, any person refusing the oaths of allegiance, supremacy, and abjuration. Fielding's nonjuror refuses the oaths, not because he belongs to a dissenting sect, but because he does not concede the validity of the legislation imposing these oaths, such legislation having been passed by a parliament and a monarch whom he does not recognize.

[6] Under the chancellorship of Ormonde's brother, Lord Arran, Oxford retained an aura of emotional jacobitism, which Fielding will exploit more fully in *JJ* no. 24 (14 May 1748) and no. 27 (4 June 1748), pp. 278–81, 295–8; see also 'General Introduction' to that volume, pp. lxiv, lxvi–lxvii.

Dear Son,

"I received yours of the 4th past, and am so well satisfied with your Conduct on the Birth-Day of that old Rump Rogue with an Orange,[1] that I have sent you a Draught on your Tutor, according to your Desires. As long as my Son preserves his Principles sound, I shall not be angry at any Frolicks of Youth. Provided therefore you never get drunk but on Holidays, (as the Government are pleased to call them) and in toasting the Damnation of the Rump,[2] and Confusion to the Day, &c. you may confess yourself freely, without fear of incurring my Displeasure. I approve the Company you keep much. Be sure not to herd with the Sons of Courtiers; for there is no Conscience nor Honesty in them; nor will the Nation ever thrive till the King enjoys his own again;[3] a Health which I never fail to drink every Day of my Life in a Bumper, and I hope you do the like. I shall never think I can remind you often enough of these Matters; for I had rather see you hanged for your true King, than enjoying a Place under this Orange Rascal, who has undone the Nation. Our Family have always, I thank God, been of the same Kidney, and I hope will remain so to all Posterity. It is the true old Cause, and we will live and die by it, Boy. Damn the Rump: That is my Motto. Old *England* will never see any good Days, 'till it is thoroughly roasted.[4] Your Godfather, Sir *John*, dined with me Yesterday, he asked kindly after you. We drank 9 Bottles a-piece of Stum,[5] and talked over all Matters. We scarce uttered a Word for which the rascally Whigs would not have hanged us; but I desire no better from Fellows who would pull down the Church, if they had it in their Power. I fear not, however, that it will be able to stand in Spite of all their Malice, and that I shall drink Church and King as long as I live. You know what King I mean. God remove him from that

---

[1] Before his translation to England, William had been prince of Orange. His birthday fell on November 4.

[2] The 'independent' remnant of the Long Parliament, from the time of Pride's Purge (December 1648) to its dissolution (or 'interruption') by Cromwell in April 1653. The Rump passed the ordinance creating a court of commissioners to try Charles I; it abolished the monarchy and the house of Lords (1649); and it tended toward the disestablishment of the Church. The nonjuror's association of the Rump with William expresses his conviction that the parliamentary action whereby William was invited to the British throne derives directly from the earlier usurpation of the prerogative by the Rump.

[3] A jacobite health or toast, referring to the hoped-for restitution of his English throne to the Stuart Pretender. See *JJ* no. 34 (23 July 1748), p. 352 and *n.*; also *Tom Jones*, VI. xiv. 321.

[4] The metaphor of 'roasting' the Rump for Old England's sake may have been popular, but Fielding could have been put in mind of it by the title and words of 'The Roast Beef of Old England', a nostalgic and patriotic popular song, of uncertain origin and variable text. Fielding included versions of it in *The Grub-Street Opera* (1731) and *Don Quixote in England* (1734), airs xlv and v, respectively.

[5] Vapid wine renewed by the mixture of stum (*OED*, which cites this passage). The admixture here is probably unfermented or partly fermented apple or grape juice. The beverage and the amount drunk bespeak a lack of fastidiousness.

Side of the Water on which he now is.[1] Let every Man have his own, I say, and I am sure that is the Sentiment of an honest Man; and of one who abhors these persecuting Rascals, who make Men pay for their Consciences.[2] But do thou, my Boy, rather submit to their Power than court their Favour; for Right is Right; and tho' Might may overcome it, it can never be abolished. If Kings derive their Power from Heaven, Men can have no just Pretence to deprive them of it. *Orange* hath no such Right. We know he was made by Men, and consequently his Title cannot be deduced from Heaven. Your Tutor informs me you have been in great Apprehension for the Church at *Oxford*, and we in the Country agree it is in Danger:[3] But let her Enemies do what they can, honest Hearts will continue to drink to her Preservation; and while the Whigs see the unalterable Determination of our Party, they will always be afraid of executing their wicked Purposes. As to Taxes, we must expect them, while the Government is in such Hands, and the true King in Banishment. A Whig Justice of Peace at the Sessions the other Day, had the Impudence to tell me they were imposed by Parliament: But how can that be a Parliament which wants one Part in three of its Constituents; nay, and that the Head? Is not the Head superior to the Body? And consequently, hath not the King a better Right to impose Taxes, than Lords and Commons without a King? Let Right take Place, say I, and then we will pay without grumbling; but to be taxed by a Rump, a Set of Whigs and Presbyterians,[4] and Fellows with an Orange in their Mouths; I will

[1] The OP was resident in Italy. For the jacobite toast to the king, in which 'each man having a glass of water on the left hand, and waving the glass of wine over the water' drinks in effect to James III in exile across the Channel, see *GM*, xvii (1747), 150. It is referred to in *JJ* no. 1 (5 December 1747), p. 92, and in *Tom Jones*, VII. iv. 338, where it is said to be a convention at Western's table.

[2] In conscience a strict nonjuror would refuse to take the various oaths required of most offices. See 'A Letter from a Jacobite ... to his Quondam Tutor', *JJ* no. 21 (23 April 1748), pp. 246–7. The 'Jacobite', who has been offered a 'Place' in the Customs, pleads his conscience: 'I am informed, that I must take a Sacrament-Oath (before I can be admitted to Business) that I believe G—— has a true Title to the Crown of *England*, as well *de jure* as *de facto*; which ... I can't do without Perjury.' The advice from the tutor is to take the oath.

[3] In *Gentleman & Alderman* (1747) the 'Gentleman' refers to 'that ever-memorable Cant Phrase of the Church being in Danger' (pp. 16–17). It was a rallying cry of high churchmen and tories whenever the religious establishment seemed threatened, either by 'whig' political adjustments or the encroachments of nonconformists and dissenters. See *Joseph Andrews*, II. vii. 133.

[4] Although the failure of the Restoration to settle the religious question on the basis of toleration much diminished their power and spirit, the Presbyterians' success in forcing on Charles I a temporary 'interruption' of the episcopacy nourished the conviction that they continued to be the most serious threat to the religious establishment. And Presbyterian doctrine (subordinating regnal to religious power) and modes of self-government (by elders chosen by a membership of equals) made it easy for high-church opponents like the nonjuror to envision them in league with their secular counterparts, the whigs. Even 'Parson Adams' is hostile: 'I had rather he should be a Blockhead than an Atheist or a Presbyterian'; *Joseph Andrews*, IV. v. 230. In addition, they had acquired the kind of kill-joy reputation which in some quarters gets attached to 'puritans': in *Tom Jones*, XII, vii. 647, the Puppet-show Man calls them 'Enemies to Puppet-shows'.

drink Confusion to them as long as I can stand. However, I hope soon to see better Times, and that we may change our Healths, and drink to our Friends openly; for we are assured here by some Roman Catholic Priests, who are honester Fellows than Whigs, and may be brought over to go to Church in Time, that the *French* King will do his utmost to restore us again to our Liberties and Properties: For which Reason we always drink his Health and Success, immediately after Church and King, and Confusion to the Rump. I hope you will do the same at your Club at *Oxford*; for take it from me as I have it from others, that all the Hopes this Nation have of being preserved is from that Quarter. Indeed there wants no other Reason for our drinking him, than that the Whigs are his Enemies; for nothing can ever be good for this Nation which those Rascals wish well to do. I am sure no one ever suspected me of wishing well to the Pope, and yet I would drink his Health sooner than I would that of a Presbyterian. I hope you will never converse with any such, but when you can't find true Church-of-*England*-Men, rather chuse Papists; for they are less Enemies to our Church;[1] and that they wou'd destroy it must be a Lie because the Whigs say it: But Confusion to them! and may the King enjoy his own again, will always be the Toast of, &c.

From TUESDAY, APRIL 15, to TUESDAY, APRIL 22, 1746.
NUMB. 25.[2]

Ita cuique eveniat, ut de republica quisque mereatur.
CICERO, *Philippics*, II.[3]

To the TRUE PATRIOT.

Sir,   *March* 27, 1746.

The Title of your Paper naturally leads me to submit the following Reflections to your superior Judgment, that you may give them a Place, if you think fit, and with such Alterations as you shall judge necessary.

---

[1] The notion held by some high-churchmen that it might be possible to find common cause with the catholics (*la cabale des accommodeurs*) lingered on well into the 1670s; Sir George Clark, *The Later Stuarts*, 2nd ed. (Oxford, 1961), pp. 18–19. In the 'country' the notion seems to have died even harder.

[2] This leader does not seem to be by Fielding. See 'General Introduction', above, p. ciii, and Appendix VI, below. Locke, p. 207, is 'inclined to think' that it was 'either written or suggested by Fielding during a time of absorption in legal concerns'.

[3] *Philippics*, II. xlvi. 119: 'each man's fortune may be according to his deserts toward the state' (Loeb). It is the concluding line of the peroration of the speech against Marcus Antonius.

Man is universally allowed to have been created a Social Animal, and intended for a Life of Society; we find therefore that he has implanted in his Nature several Passions and Affections, which tend to prompt him to the Practice of Benevolence, and the Exercise of the other Social Virtues: And as he was likewise designed for Happiness, his All-wise Creator thought proper also to place in him the Passion of Self-love, in order to excite him to the Pursuit of his own real Good. But Man (as he has done by many other of Nature's Gifts) has most shamefully perverted this necessary Principle of Action to the most vile Purposes, and made that which was intended by the Author of his Being as a Spur to noble Pursuits, as an Incentive to a laudable Emulation of every thing amiable and excellent, become a Bane, a Curse to him, and productive of the most base ignoble Actions. For, by indulging this Passion to Excess, and mistaking imaginary for real Happiness, Men have run into the most pernicious of all Vices, *Selfishness*; which (whenever it takes place) destroys all those godlike generous Virtues, for the Practice of which, as Social Beings, Men were peculiarly designed and adapted.

This narrow selfish Spirit, which pursues only an imaginary self-centred Happiness, has been the Cause of the most detestable Vices; such as Pride, Envy, Malice, Avarice, and Ambition. It is this that prompts us to invade our Neighbour's Rights, defile his Bed, and blast his Character; this has been the accurs'd Source of those Monsters, Lust and Ambition, which have laid waste so many Countries, depopulated the most fertile Lands, and spread Slavery and Misery over great Part of this our Globe; it is this that makes the Rebel bold and venturesome, and bids him, for the sake of private Gain, even sheath his Sword in the Bowels of his Native Country; this, with the Help of Flattery and *Jus Divinum*, makes Kings become Tyrants; and from this Root also spring Bribery and Corruption, which, like an infectious Contagion, spread an inactive Languor through the whole Community in which they prevail, and destroy that Integrity and Public Spirit, which are as it were the Vitals of every flourishing Constitution.

Every Man has it in his Power to be of some Service to his Country; and as far as the Ploughman does all he can in his low Situation in Life for the Public Good, he at least, in some measure, as justly deserves the Name of a Patriot, as the most active eloquent Senator, and more so, in case his Views are more upright and disinterested than the Other's; and he only is the *true Patriot*, who always does what is in his Power for his Country's Service, without any selfish Views, or Regard to private Interest.

The merely selfish Man, if he may be allowed the Name of Man, is neither fit for Earth nor Heaven. He thinks himself independent of the Community, and therefore deserves not to be considered as a Member of it; and as he grudges to do any thing for the Service of Society, he is not intitled to the Benefits of it. For though the transpiring Liberties, the Peace and Happiness of that Country in which he first drew Breath, press for his Aid, and call loudly for his Assistance; if he grants it, he'll go no further than his own Ease permits, and the least Inconvenience or Trouble to himself stops his helping Hand: Such a Man, as far as Words will go, may be at his Country's Service; but if Money be necessary to this Service, he cannot be brought to open his Purse, unless he's absolutely sure of getting some personal Advantage to himself from it.

It may perhaps by some be asked, What all this signifies? And it may be said, whatever the Case may have been, that Selfishness can have no Place among us now, since the whole Kingdom have shewn their Loyalty and Public Spirit, not only in their Addresses, but by their Subscriptions. This is easily said, but I am afraid not so easily proved. I confess there have been lately several eminent Instances of Patriotism and Public Spirit among us, and in none more conspicuous than in that Example which has been set us by the brave Duke of *Cumberland*, who has been the chief Instrument, in the Hands of Providence, of our Deliverance from our late Fears.1 But as I have neither Abilities nor Room to enlarge upon his Merit, I shall return to my Subject. I confess, I say, that there may be many who shewed their Zeal for their Country's Service; yet were there not also many among us, who have not even said any thing; and a much greater Number, who tho' in Words and Addresses they professed much, yet did nothing, and to whom what *Turnus* says to *Drancus* may be too justly applied.

> *Larga quidem semper, Drance, tibi Copia fandi,*
> *Tunc cum bella manus poscunt, patribusque vocatis*
> *Primus ades; sed non replenda est curia verbis.* 2

Has not this Selfishness together with its Companion Corruption spread itself thro' all Ranks and Degrees of Men, from the greatest

---

1 If the dateline of this letter is a true indication of the date of composition, this compliment to the commander of the forces in England must refer generally to the improvement in the military situation which followed upon his taking command and, with the aid of troops from the continental theatre, pursuing the rebels back into Scotland. On 16 April 1746 Cumberland had beaten the jacobites at Culloden, in what was the deciding battle of the rebellion. Unofficial news of this victory might just have had time to reach London by the publication date of this number of the *TP*, but authorized reports of the victory came one day later, and in any event there is no notice of Culloden here or elsewhere in this number.

2 *Aeneid*, xi. 378–80, where 'Drances' is the accepted denomination: 'Plenteous indeed, Drances, ever is thy stream of speech in the hour when battle calls for hands; and when the senate is summoned, thou art first to appear! But we need not fill the council-house with words' (Loeb).

Men at Court even down to the Pr——r of our Extraordinary *G—z—tte*?[1] Whence is it, that so many of our modern pretending Patriots, who learnedly and eloquently harangued in the Senate, and seemed deeply concerned for the Welfare of their Country, and were loud and strenuous Advocates for its Rights, and Defenders of its Liberties; whence is it, I say, that many of these have often of a sudden, and as it were instantaneously changed their Notes, and become fawning suppliant Courtiers? Is it not Self-Interest, that so suddenly and effectually breaks the opposing Tempest, and makes the former boisterous Northern Gales subside in a calm Southern Breeze? Do not our Parties, our foolish imaginary Distinctions proceed from this Source? Does not every one seem fond of ranking himself under some one particular party Banner? And does he not strictly, nay, nicely adhere to it, whether right or wrong?

To what else but this National Selfishness can we ascribe the late Success of that miscreant despicable Crew, who endeavoured to destroy our Laws, our Liberties, and our Constitution? Could our Ancestors rise out of their Graves, and see the Actions of us their degenerate Sons, would they not charge us with Selfishness and Cowardice, despise us for our Degeneracy, and blush to own us for their Posterity? What will our Neighbours say? What will our Children say? Unless they prove worse than ourselves, will they not justly brand us with the Name of Selfish, when they shall be told, or read it in our Annals, that this Rabble Rout, this rude and half unarm'd Banditti of Ruffians and Plunderers, not exceeding 6000 in all, were suffered, un-opposed, to lay waste all before them for several hundred Miles, and even to march, un-opposed, into the very Heart of a well-peopled Country; and that they might have reached even our Capital City, if our regular Forces had not providentially interposed.

Whence was it, that at this Time of imminent Danger the Miser's Coffers were still locked, and that those who had received most Benefit

---

[1] Conceivably the first 'disemvowelled' word might be 'Proprietor', that is, the holder of the life patent as *Gazette* writer. At this time the holder was Edward Weston (1703–70), an undersecretary in the northern department, later in 1746 to be the chief secretary for Ireland. Weston, whose patent was worth £300 a year, paid a deputy £30 to run the *Gazette*; P. M. Handover, *A History of the London Gazette 1665–1965* (London, 1965), pp. 54–5. According to HMC, Tenth Report, iv ('Weston Papers'), 200, Weston was 'sometimes styled by his contemporaries "The Gazeteer"'. However, in a letter signed 'A.B.' in *TP* no. 8 (24 December 1745), Locke, p. [91], the writer recommends 'Correction' for the persons responsible for the bad condition of the *Gazette*, and claims 'it is only some of the *Underlings* who are guilty in this Affair'. In the 'Apocrypha' of *TP* no. 6 (10 December 1745), below, p. 374, notice is taken of 'an Extraordinary Ghost' which appeared in Amen Corner. According to its colophon at this time the printer of the *Gazette* was E. [Edward] Owen of Amen Corner, a London printer of little note other than in this connection. His paper was frequently attacked for tardy publication, bad writing, and trivial content. See, for example, *London Evening Post* of 23–5 January 1746, and Handover, p. 55. Probably the present reference is to the 'Printer', Owen.

from the Government contributed least to its Defence? Or that any should then publickly declare, that those were the wisest who gave least, and did nothing for the Publick? 'Tis true, *Clodio*[1] did then subscribe, and as he says, as much as he could afford, but was it really all he could afford? No, surely not; for does he not still loll at Ease in his Gaudy Chariot? Does he not keep the same Number of idle Attendants, useless prancing Nags, and hungry Hounds as he did before? Does he not frequent the same costly Entertainments, and pursue the same extravagant Pleasures? Or has he retrenched one Farthing of his unnecessary Expences? No! Where then is his publick Spirit? He gave no more than what he did not know how to make Use of. Is this the Patriot? Surely not. Is not this far short of the noble Conduct of *Cato*, which the Poet thus describes?

> —— *Hi Mores, hæc duri immota Catonis*
> *Secta fuit, servare modum, finemque tenere,*
> *Naturamque sequi*, patriæque impendere vitam, *&c.*[2]

In a Word, whence is it, that we see the *Italian* Proverb too much verify'd among us, *Chi serve al Comme non serve a nissimo*;[3] "He that serves the Publick obliges no Body"?

Among the ancient *Romans* it was accounted *dulce et decorum pro patria mori*;[4] and our own Ancestors have shewn their Opinions the same by their noble Actions; but our modern fine Gentlemen have refined upon the Virtue of the Ancients, and think it much more *dulce et decorum* to have no Concern for their Country, and to keep out of Harm's Way; and whatever happens, to take Care to gratify their own Inclinations; and *mori pro patria* has too harsh a Sound in their fine Ears, who much more admire the charming, soft, engaging Notes of a foreign W—re,[5] or an *Italian* Eunuch, than the Grand, the Noble Majesty of Martial Music. In short, public Service is a Pill that seems very hard to be swallowed unless it is gilded, and then it goes down much better.

[1] The satirical *persona* is that of P. Clodius Pulcher, the corrupt and lecherous politician of republican Rome. In the early editions of his 'Epistle to Cobham' Pope had used the name to cover his satire of Philip, duke of Wharton (1698–1731). In the present case no identification has been made.

[2] Lucan, *De Bello Civili* ('Pharsalia'), ii. 380–2: 'Such was the character, such the inflexible rule of austere Cato—to observe moderation and hold fast to the limit, to follow nature, to give his life for his country' (Loeb).

[3] More correctly, 'Chi serve al comune, serve nessuno', which is consistent with the translation which follows.

[4] Adjusted, perhaps to fit the grammar, from Horace, *Odes*, III. ii. 13: ''Tis sweet and glorious to die for [the] fatherland' (Loeb).

[5] Alluding to the frequency with which female opera singers from abroad became the mistresses of the noblemen who were underwriting the opera in competition with Handel. See *TP* no. 9 (31 December 1745), above, p. 167.

Are not these Facts, and do they not loudly proclaim our Selfishness? All indeed are not thus contracted in their Views, but are we not generally addicted to it? Would I could say we were not; but the Thing speaks itself, and daily Experience shews we are. Let us not then deny or palliate, but confess and reform it; for unless we do, we must never expect to see our native Country re-assume her ancient Glory, or even escape the present threatning Dangers. Let us endeavour to revive Public Spirit and True Patriotism among us. Let us discard all Selfish Views, and from the highest to the lowest, scorn Corruption, practise Integrity, become true Friends to our Country, and resolve, notwithstanding private Interest, Party Cavils, or any other Obstacles, that in us, as in *Brutus* of old, *Vincit amor patriæ*.[1]

PHILANDER.

From TUESDAY, APRIL 22, to TUESDAY, APRIL 29, 1746.
NUMB. 26.

—— *Sui memores alios fecere merendo.*

VIRGIL.[2]

Whoever will cast his Eyes a few Months backwards, and attentively consider the Situation in which the Public then stood,[3] will, when he compares it with our present Condition, be obliged to own, that no Nation hath ever emerged so suddenly from the very Brink of Ruin, to a State of present Safety, and to the fairest Prospect of future Felicity.

How short an Interval hath past, since we saw at one and the same time the King of *Prussia* worrying our Allies in *Germany*;[4] the United

[1] *Aeneid*, vi. 823, where the accepted text reads *vincet*: 'Love of country shall prevail' (Loeb). Anchises is foretelling the glories of Rome, among them the patriotism of Lucius Julius Brutus, who put his two sons to death for conspiring to restore the tyranny of the Tarquins which he himself had overthrown.

[2] *Aeneid*, vi. 664: 'they [who] by service have won remembrance among men' (Loeb). Aeneas and the Sibyl have just emerged from the Plains of Grief, a region of darkness and misery, to Elysium, a region bathed in light, where all is happiness. The line which forms the motto describes the happy reward of people who have served the state.

[3] The subsequent reference to the threat posed by the jacobite penetration as far as Derby would imply a date in early December 1745 for this retrospective. For the formula, cf. *JJ* no. 24 (14 May 1748), p. 273: 'Whoever will be pleased to cast his Eye backward for one Month only . . .'; also *JJ* no. 45 (8 October 1748), p. 406.

[4] The Anglo-Prussian convention signed at Hanover in August 1745 bound Frederick II of Prussia to come to an accommodation with Maria Theresa upon the foot of the Treaty of Breslau (1742). Infuriated by Frederick's insistence on retaining Silesia, the queen refused to conclude. With Saxony, and in hopes of Russian intervention, she resumed offensive measures and maintained them

Armies of our Enemies having almost totally subdued the King of *Sardinia* in *Italy*;[1] the King of *France* just about to become Master not only of *Flanders*[2] and *Brabant*,[3] but of *Holland*;[4] a dangerous successful Rebellion in the very Heart of our own Country, threatning the Metropolis itself with immediate Plunder and Desolation;[5] great Part of our Forces abroad;[6] those which were returned lessened and harrassed by the

even after the defeat at Soor [Bohemia] on 30 September 1745 NS. Frederick invaded Saxony again, where on 15 December NS Leopold, Prince of Anhalt, defeated the Saxon army under Rutowsky at Kesseldorf and then took possession of Dresden itself. This 'worrying' forced Maria Theresa and Saxony to sign the treaty of Dresden (25 December 1745 NS), thereby ending the second Silesian war. For the *TP*'s view of the situation in early December 1745, see 'Present History of Europe', *TP* no. 5 (3 December 1745), Locke, p. [70].

[1] By the end of the Italian campaign of 1745 the French and Italian armies had overrun eastern Piedmont, taken key towns in Lombardy (Parma, Piacenza, Milan), and by the investiture of Alessandria were threatening Turin itself, Charles Emmanuel's capitol. For the English perception that Maria Theresa's failure to send reinforcements to Sardinia, as per treaty, would drive the latter to negotiate with France, see 'Present History of Europe', *TP* no. 5 (3 December 1745), Locke, p. [70]. On 26 December 1745 NS a 'mémoire' intended to form the basis of a treaty between Charles Emmanuel and France was signed but not ratified. On 17 February 1746 NS the two powers in fact signed an armistice, but France delayed implementation and Charles Emmanuel thereupon repudiated it.

[2] 'The Province . . . of *Flanders*, in its proper and limited Sense, (for the Name is sometimes used to signify all the Ten Provinces) is bounded towards the North by the Sea and that Branch of the *Scheld* call'd the *Hout*, which separates it from *Zealand*; by *Brabant* and Part of *Hainault* and *Artois* towards the South; and by the Sea and Part of *Artois* towards the West'; *Flanders Delineated; or, A View of the Austrian and French Netherlands* (Reading, 1745), p. 22. Many of the chief places in Flanders (Tournai, Ghent, Bruges, Ostend, Nieuport) had been taken by the French during the summer and autumn of 1745.

[3] 'Bounded on the East by the Bishoprick of *Liège*, on the West by *Flanders* and *Zealand*, on the North by *Holland* and *Guelderland*, and on the South by *Namur* and *Hainault*'; *Flanders Delineated*, p. 91. Roughly speaking, Brabant was that part of the Austrian Netherlands centering on Brussels. Cf. *GM*, xv (1745), 671: 'Since the recall of the *English* forces, the *French* have made great preparations on the *Scheld*, and at *Dendermond*, which seem to threaten *Antwerp*, or *Brussels* itself, where they keep a double guard.' Brussels did not fall until 2 February 1746 NS; Antwerp, on 31 May 1746 NS.

[4] One of the seven 'United Provinces' of the Netherlands (Holland, Zeeland, Utrecht, Friesland, Gelderland, Groningen, Overijssel). However, in English it was common to use 'Holland' to refer to the group as a whole. See *Gentleman & Alderman* (1747), p. 39, and *JJ* no. 48 (29 October 1748), p. 420, for Fielding's use of it in that looser sense. The loss of the barrier fortresses in Flanders had left the United Provinces vulnerable to French attack, and by January 1746 there was diplomatic speculation that France would declare war on the Dutch; *DA* of 13 January 1746.

[5] On 4 December 1745, 'having given the Slip' to Cumberland's army in Staffordshire, the rebel forces reached Derby, the point of their deepest penetration into England. The news of this advance reached the 'Metropolis' on December 6 ('Black Friday'), creating, in Parson Adams's words, 'a Terror scarce to be credited'; *TP* no. 7 (17 December 1745), above, p. 154. See also 'Present History of Great Britain', *TP* no. 6 (10 December 1745), below, p. 368.

[5] At the beginning of the 1745 campaign on the continent British troops allotted for service in Flanders were raised to a strength of 25,000, with a consequent reduction of the garrison in Great Britain to 15,000; Fortescue, *History*, ii. 108. By July 1745, however, Walpole estimated that there were 'not five thousand men in the island', a figure which agreed roughly with the projections of French intelligence; Walpole to Mann, 26 July 1745, *Yale Walpole*, xix. 79; and d'Aulnay to d'Argenson, 24 May 1745 NS, cited by H. W. Richmond, *The Navy in the War of 1739–48*, ii. 161. On 10 September 1745 Pelham wrote Trevor, 'We have scarce any regular troops in the country'; HMC, Fourteenth Report, Appendix, Part IX, p. 131, as cited in John W. Wilkes, *A Whig in Power* (Northwestern

Losses and Fatigues of an unhappy Campaign;[1] our Coasts, which constantly apprehended a formidable Invasion,[2] being obliged to trust to the uncertain Protection of Ships that could hardly keep the Seas;[3] all Trade at a stand;[4] Public Credit daily sinking almost to Desperation;[5] and the whole People struck with an universal Terror and Panic.

University Press, 1964), p. 153. During the king's summer absence in Hanover the lords justices ordered the recall of four regiments from the continent; Coxe, *Pelham*, i. 243, 258. And on his return the king with great reluctance ordered the recall of the remainder. Ten battalions under Sir John Ligonier arrived on 23 September 1745 and other elements continued to arrive until December; Blaikie, *Itinerary*, p. 22; Hardwicke to Herring, 12 September 1745, in George Harris, *Life of Hardwicke*, ii (London, 1847), 159; Coxe, *Pelham*, i. 243–5. 'Observations on the Rebellion', *TP* no. 3 (19 November 1745), below, p. 351, says of the English troops in Flanders, 'The Whole are now sent for' and praises the perseverance of the Pelhams against the obstructionist tactics of Granville, Tweeddale, and others.

[1] In 'Observations on the Rebellion', *TP* no. 2 (12 November 1745), above, p. 127, the question is asked, 'Is it [the army recalled from Flanders] increased to its real Establishment?' The question is answered in 'Observations on the Rebellion', *TP* no. 3 (19 November 1745), below, p. 351: 'I answer, every Endeavour hath been set on foot to bring it up to that Establishment'. Beginning with the serious loss at Fontenoy (11 May 1745 NS) the campaign in Flanders had been a series of setbacks for the British and Dutch, and Cumberland himself referred to the Fontenoy battalions which were recalled as essentially 'broken' battalions, seasoned but weakened; C. T. Atkinson, 'Jenkins' Ear, the Austrian Succession War, and the "Forty-Five"', *Journal of the Society for Army Historical Research*, xxii (Autumn 1944), 282–5. An additional factor was the practice of drafting from regiments at home so as to strengthen those in combat abroad. Cope's dragoons and infantry were under strength for this reason; Atkinson, loc. cit.

[2] For the panic on 13 December 1745, occasioned by rumors that a French fleet was essaying a landing on the Suffolk coast, see 'Present History of Great Britain', *TP* no. 7 (17 December 1745), below, p. 378. In early December the papers carried reports that the French were ready to embark 12,000 men at Dunkirk and Ostend; *DA* of 4, 6, 23 December 1745; Walpole to Mann, 9 December 1745, *Yale Walpole*, xix. 179; 'Present History of Great Britain', *TP* no. 6 (10 December 1745), below, p. 369. On 19 December 1745 Pelham found the invasion scare useful in his request for parliamentary aid in hiring mercenaries to replace the Dutch troops unwilling to fight against rebel forces, with their contingent of French.

[3] In view of Fielding's developing admiration for the duke of Bedford, first lord of the admiralty, this is probably not a reference to the very real disarray in the regular navy. *DA* of 14 December 1745 reported that the government had hired 'upwards of sixty vessels . . . which are manned to cruise and prevent any enemies landing'. 'Present History of Great Britain', *TP* no. 6 (10 December 1745), Locke, p. [76], reports that 'all the Sea Lieutenants were ordered on board such small Smacks as could be instantly procured, in which they might be very capable of giving great Annoyance to the smaller Vessels designed for this [French] Embarkation'. The use of such small ships outside of the regular establishment had been anticipated by Vernon's employment of Folkestone cutters as scouts to 'prevent Surprises in the Night'; *Seasonable Advice from an Honest Sailor* (London, 1746), p. 18. Vernon had complained to Sir John Philipps, the opposition tory, about want of provisions for them; Walpole to Mann, 22 November 1745, *Yale Walpole*, xix. 168.

[4] Cf. *TP* no. 5 (3 December 1745), above, p. 145: 'at this Season, when all Trade is at a Stand; when both the public and private Fountains of Wealth are in a manner dry'd up; when Estates in Land, or in the Funds, yield little more than future Hopes to their Possessors'.

[5] Cf. Pelham to Trevor, 11 December 1745: 'The terrible part to us, therefore, is, that whilst this race is running, our own troops are dwindling every day; our credit is in a manner totally stopped'; Coxe, *Pelham*, i. 283. On 12 December 1745 the directors of the Bank of England decided to call in 20 per cent from those who had subscribed to the last subscription for circulating Exchequer bills, and about this time there had been a run on the Bank, supposedly averted by paying all withdrawals in sixpences; W. Marston Acres, *The Bank of England from Within* (Oxford, 1931), i. 181; Sir John Clapham, *The Bank of England* (Cambridge, 1945), i. 233–4.

On the contrary, what is the Scene at present? The King of *Prussia* is at Peace with our Allies,[1] by which means the Emperor hath been enabled to send such a Force to the King of *Sardinia's* Assistance,[2] as hath already made that brave Prince superior to his Enemies, and hath given us a fair Prospect of seeing the *Spanish* Queen obliged to abandon her Projects in *Italy*, and by that means disunited from *France*,[3] to whom she is held in Alliance by those Views only. In *Flanders* we again see an Army gathering together,[4] (a Circumstance totally owing to the Peace of *Dresden*) which promises at least to check the Progress of the *French* King, while it draws his whole Force to that Quarter. At home the Rebellion is driven to the very Extremities of the Island, and there almost totally subdued and exterminated.[5] Our Army is recruited, restored, and, together with our Fleet, likely to carry Terror to the Coasts of our Enemies; our Trade begins again to flourish; Public

[1] As of the treaty of Dresden (25 December 1745 NS), an abridgment of which is given in 'Foreign History', *TP* no. 13 (21–8 January 1746), reprinted in Locke, p. [128]. The treaty secured for Frederick his acquisition of Silesia and required Augustus III of Saxony to renounce any claims for compensation out of the Prussian dominions of Brandenburg.

[2] In fact the co-signatory at Dresden was not Francis I, holy Roman emperor (1745–65) and grand duke of Tuscany (1737), who had been elected on 13 September 1745 NS and crowned 4 October NS, but his wife, Maria Theresa, who in the French text of the treaty is referred to as 'Sa Majesté l'Impératrice, Reine d'Hongrie'. For a full text, see F. A. G. Wenck, *Codex Juris Gentium Recentissimi*, ii (Lipsiae, 1787), 194–202; and for the text of Frederick's treaty with Augustus III of Poland and Saxony, ii. 207–15. The peace achieved at Dresden enabled Maria Theresa to send 30,000 troops under Graf von Brown from Bohemia to the Italian theatre. The Spanish army raised its siege of the castle of Milan and withdrew to Pavia, then Parma, and finally into Tuscany. On 7 March 1746 NS the Sardinians took Asti and its French garrison, and by 5 April 1746 NS Mann could write Walpole, 'Are you not amazed at the great change of affairs in Lombardy?'; *Yale Walpole*, xix. 230.

[3] The so-called Second Family Pact, signed by France and Spain at Fontainebleau on 25 October 1743 NS, obligated France to assist Elizabeth Farnese in her 'projects' of establishing the Infant Don Philip in Lombardy and guaranteeing the kingdoms of Naples and Sicily to the Infant Don Carlos. France was also to assist Spain in recovering Minorca and Gibraltar from England. For a text (in Spanish), see *The Consolidated Treaty Series*, ed. Clive Parry, xxxvii (Dobbs Ferry, NY, 1969), 211–15. For an English assessment of Spain's position at this time, see 'Foreign History' in *TP* no. 23 (1–8 April 1746) and no. 26 (22–9 April 1746), Locke, pp. [191–2, 209–10].

[4] Field Marshal von Waldeck's request for an army of 95,000 for Flanders was approved by George II, the approval being conveyed to Boetslaer by Harrington on 3 January 1746; *Journal of Commons*, xxv. 119–20. The king also agreed to continue 8,000 Hanoverians in Flanders, to return the 6,000 Hessians from England as soon as practicable, to share with the Dutch the expenses of 10,000 Saxon mercenaries, and to subsidize Maria Theresa (now at peace with Prussia) so that she might increase her contribution to 30,000 troops. The States General were to furnish 40,000. Waldeck shortly increased his requirements to 109,000; *Journal of Commons*, xxv. 121; 'Foreign History', *TP* no. 25 (15–22 April 1746), Locke, pp. [204–5]. Public estimates of what might actually be forthcoming tended to be lower; see *DA* of 17 March 1746, which, under dateline The Hague, 22 March NS, notes that England will have 'in pay in Brabant' 70,000 men 'without including any English'. Cf. Walpole to Mann, 15 April 1746, *Yale Walpole* xix. 240, where similar notice is taken of the reservation of English troops; also Coxe, *Pelham*, i. 285–6, 304–9, 316.

[5] After Culloden (16 April 1746) the surviving rebels were told by their chiefs to disperse and shift for themselves; Blaikie, *Itinerary*, p. 45. The YP himself was at this time shifting around the Hebrides, trying to get taken off by ship to France. Cf. 'Present History of Great Britain', *TP* no. 26 (22–9 April 1746), Locke, pp. [205–6].

Credit revives, and Chearfulness, Joy and Triumph, overspread the Countenance of every true *Englishman*.

Is it possible to contemplate these Things, with an honest Heart, without being filled with Sentiments of Gratitude to the Authors of such Blessings? who doth not overflow, on this Occasion, with Piety towards GOD, the Deliverer of Nations; and in the next Place, with the Praises of those glorious Men whom it hath pleased him to make the Instruments of our Preservation?

And will any Man doubt to whom these Praises are due, when he is told, in the first Place, *who it was* that advised and promoted the Treaty of *Dresden*?[1] A Treaty to which the very Safety of *Europe* is strictly owing; and when it is publickly known that this truly great and political Negotiation was steadily and laboriously pursued *in Opposition* to the Cabals of some Persons, who did not scruple to avow Schemes of a very contrary kind, and to denounce[2] Vengeance against the King of *Prussia*,[3] tho' it was as impracticable as impolitic to execute it.[4]

Now, as to this Treaty alone, wholly accomplished, in spite of the highest Difficulties, by our present Ministry, is justly to be ascribed the Preservation of *Europe*, and the whole Turn of Affairs abroad; let us enquire, in the next Place, to whom we owe our present Safety, and the Defeat of the Enemies of our Religion and Liberties at home.

And here we shall find the same glorious Persons pursuing the same salutary Councils in Opposition to the same Cabal. While this Cabal was endeavouring to lessen the Numbers and Force of the Rebels,[5] it was our present Ministry that advised and insisted on bringing home

[1] Alluding to the Pelham initiatives in the convention at Hanover (26 August 1745 NS), which formed the basis for the treaty. In this promotion the Pelhams had to overcome the lingering influence of Granville's anti-Prussian foreign policy, as well as George II's very real aversion to Frederick. See Coxe, *Pelham*, i. 247–8, and *n.* 3, below.

[2] To announce or proclaim in the manner of a threat or warning (punishment, vengeance, a curse, etc.) [*OED*].

[3] For the ministerial infighting which surrounded the signing of the convention, see Owen, *Rise of the Pelhams*, pp. 278–9. Fielding alludes here to the well-known anti-Prussian program of Granville and his adherents, but as Owen shows, the difficulties arose from other quarters as well, the king even going so far as to propose noncompliance. For Granville's policies, see Sir Richard Lodge, *Great Britain and Prussia in the Eighteenth Century* (Oxford, 1923), ch. ii.

[4] The anti-Prussian position held that Frederick had broken the terms of the treaty of Breslau (1742) as well as the Pragmatic Sanction by his belligerencies of 1744 and 1745. Any British 'vengeance' by force of arms against Prussia would have violated the defensive alliance he signed with the maritime powers at Westminster (September 1742), by which England guaranteed Frederick security from attack in his own dominions, to say nothing of the convention of Hanover itself. For Frederick and Granville against the background of Pelham hostility to the latter, see Basil Williams, *Carteret and Newcastle* (Cambridge, 1943), chs. viii–ix.

[5] Cf. Walpole to Mann, 20 September 1745, *Yale Walpole*, xix. 109: 'Lord Granville and his faction persist in persuading the King 'tis an affair of no consequence.' See also 'General Introduction', above, pp. xxxi–xxxii.

our Army from *Flanders* to secure us.[1] A Measure treated with the utmost Contempt and Ridicule by the Cabal, and pursued and carried, *in Defiance of that Contempt and Ridicule*, by that Ministry, to whose Wisdom and Integrity it is wholly owing, *that after the Defeat at Preston-Pans, we had a second Army in England to encounter the victorious Rebels*,[2] who might otherwise have marched without Opposition to the Capital, have placed their Popish Pretender on the Throne of these Realms, and at one Blow have extirpated our Religion and Liberties for ever.

These are the Men who by Degrees brought over the rest of our Troops from *Flanders*, and that as fast as it was in their Power; for every Step was opposed by the Cabal. By their means those Armies were afterwards formed in this Nation which preserved us; and by their Councils the Glorious Duke of CUMBERLAND, that *Fulmen Belli*,[3] was sent first to expel these desperate Banditti from this Part of the Island, and afterwards to extirpate them in the other.

These are Facts, known, undeniable Facts: And they are Panegyrics which no Rhetoric nor Oratory can amplify. They reflect a Praise almost incapable of Addition; and yet Truth itself forces me to *point at one Instance more*, as it is a Proof of Integrity unparallel'd in History, and by which we may be convinced that Power hath no longer Charms in the Eyes of those great Men, that while it can be exercised to their own real Honour, and for the true Interest of their Country.[4]

If the Facts I have here mentioned be true, can any Panegyric on their Authors be called Flattery? Will any Man be ashamed of giving Praise to such Men? Or indeed will not any Man be ashamed of with-holding it from them? What can give a Foreigner so contemptible an Idea of this Nation, as to hear that when all these Things are recent in every Man's Memory; nay, when their Effects are before our Eyes, and *while we are*

---

[1] Cf. Fox to Hanbury Williams, 5 September 1745, on the rebels having given the slip to Cope's army: 'This news has at length forced the sending for ten battalions of English, which were sent for by express, last night: a counsel that has prevailed with the greatest difficulty, and is blamed by Granville, as it is opposed by Lord Tweeddale'; quoted in Coxe, *Pelham*, i. 264.

[2] After Cope's defeat Wade was appointed (24 September 1745) commander-in-chief of the king's forces in Great Britain. His army was in the north, centered on Newcastle. When the rebels slipped by Wade and entered England itself, a second army, gathered about London and under the command first of Ligonier and then Cumberland, marched north into Lancashire to intercept them. On 4 December 1745, this 'second' army, which was heavily made up of troops from the Flanders theatre, was estimated at 7,000 infantry, 1,500 horse; Blaikie, *Itinerary*, p. 94. For the 'Parson Adams' enumeration of the armies involved, see *TP* no. 7 (17 December 1745), above, p. 154.

[3] 'thunderbolt of war'; taken from Lucretius, *De Rerum Natura*, iii. 1034, where it is applied to the Scipios as heroic conquerors of the Carthaginians. Cf. Virgil, *Aeneid*, vi. 842–3: 'duo fulmina belli, Scipiadas'.

[4] Alluding to the resignation of the Pelhams on 10 February 1746, in an effort finally to displace Granville in the king's favor and to secure real power for themselves.

actually enjoying the Blessings procured by them, there should yet remain a Faction among us who dare avow an Opposition to such an Administration. I have mentioned a Foreigner; for as to ourselves, who know of how few and of what Persons this Opposition consists, it must surprize us very little to find there are some few silly enough to maintain the Principles of *Republicans* and *Jacobites*;[1] and others base enough to prefer their own private Views and Ambition to the true Interest of their Country.

In order to maintain therefore the Honour of our Nation in the Eyes of Foreigners (as we find this Paper is translated into *French* and printed abroad)[2] we shall very speedily acquaint the Public with the whole Nature and Constitution of this Opposition: But as all Executions and Punishments of *Malefactors* are deferred on Holidays and public Festivals, so we shall reprieve the Opposition during the present Time of Jubilee: But we assure them that Sentence of Dissection[3] is past, and will very speedily be executed upon them.

At present then I shall conclude with heartily congratulating my Reader on the late Success in *Scotland*,[4] so glorious to the young Hero[5] who accomplished it, and so happy to us all. The Rebellion may now be considered as at an End, as its shatter'd Remains must be easily and shortly extinguished. Instead therefore of trembling any longer for our Houses, our Families, our Religion, and our Liberties, it now becomes us to put on a decent Confidence, and Hope, of transferring some Part of those Terrors to our Enemies. We are once more strong, and our

---

[1] Fielding elaborates this connection in *Gentleman & Alderman* (1747), pp. 6–12, 57–8. There are also references to it in *TP* no. 19 (4–11 March 1746), above, p. 238, and no. 29 (13–20 May 1746), below, p. 290.

[2] This not entirely implausible assertion has not been verified.

[3] There is a pun on dissection as the action of separating anything into elementary or minute parts for the purpose of critical examination (*OED*) and dissection in its anatomical sense. By letters patent granted by Elizabeth I and renewed by Charles II, the Royal College of Physicians was allowed up to six bodies of executed persons per year within London, Middlesex, and Surrey, for purposes of dissection. The Company of Barber Surgeons was allowed four. Beyond this 'authorized' figure there was extremely competitive negotiation from the teaching hospitals and private medical schools; see Peter Linebaugh, 'The Tyburn Riot against the Surgeons', in *Albion's Fatal Tree*, ed. Douglas Hay *et al.* (New York, 1975), pp. 65–117, especially pp. 69–88. In *TP* no. 20 (11–18 March 1746), above, p. 244, Fielding had called for the hanging of the Opposition. See also *TP* no. 29 (13–20 May 1746), below, p. 290.

[4] Cumberland's crushing defeat of the rebels at Culloden (16 April 1746). 'Present History' of this number reprints the 'authorized' version of the battle; see Locke, p. [211]. Official news of the battle does not seem to have reached London before April 23; see *London Gazette Extraordinary* of that date, which records receipt of the news 'at Noon'. The 'authorized' account from the duke himself did not appear until the *London Gazette Extraordinary* of 26 April 1746.

[5] Among the news items reprinted without comment in *TP* no. 25 (15–22 April 1746) is the following: 'Tuesday last [15 April] being the Birth-Day [of] his Royal Highness William Duke of Cumberland, second Son to his Majesty, who then entered the 26th Year of his Age, the same was observed in a very extraordinary Manner' (Locke, p. [206]).

Strength will be conducted by Men whose known Integrity assures us they will omit no Opportunity of employing it for our Service, so from their Prudence we may confide it will not be wasted in wanton Acts of Folly and Quixotism. Let us preserve but Unanimity among ourselves, and banish all Murmur and Discontent from among us: For those alone can now be our Bane, and to sow those Seeds in the Nation is now the only Resource of our malicious Enemies.

We are not therefore to wonder at the Murmurs of *Jacobites* at this Season, when nothing but Disaffection and Malecontentment, nothing but secret Divisions and Repinings among ourselves, can prevent us from being a happy, a glorious, and a tremendous People.

From TUESDAY, APRIL 29, to TUESDAY, MAY 6, 1746.
NUMB. 27.[1]

> *Conamur, tenues Grandia —*
> *Laudes egregii Cæsaris. —*
>
> HORACE, *Carmina*, I. 6.[2]

As we have endeavoured during the late cursed Rebellion, in common with the rest of our loyal Fellow-Subjects, to lend all the Assistance in our Power to the Subversion of Traytors and Rebels, against the best King, and the best Constitution with which any People were ever bless'd; we hope it will not be deem'd an unpardonable Presumption in us, if we now venture to approach, with others, the Steps of the Royal Throne with Congratulation, and presume to offer up our little Salver of Incense, together with those who are truly sensible of the great Deliverance we owe to the Conduct and Courage of the victorious Duke of *Cumberland*.[3] In short, as we should certainly have been one of the first in the String of Loyalists, who would have had the Honour of being

---

[1] This panegyric on the royal family was widely reprinted. See *GM*, xvi (1746), 246–8; *London Magazine*, xv (1746), 236–8; *General London Evening Mercury* of 8–10 May 1746, which in acknowledgment lauded the *TP* as 'a Paper of much Spirit, that is published weekly'; *General Advertiser* of 8 May 1746, with similar acknowledgment.

[2] Extracted from *Odes*, I. vi. 9–11: 'Too feeble I for such lofty themes … noble Caesar's glory' (Loeb). The full text reads 'Conamur, tenues grandia, dum pudor | imbellisque lyrae Musa potens vetat | laudes egregii Caesaris et tuas | culpa deterre ingenii.'

[3] Commander of the royal forces at Culloden on 16 April 1746. For a description of the battle, taken from the 'authorized' account in the *London Gazette Extraordinary* of 26 April 1746, see *TP* no. 26 (22–9 April 1746), Locke, p. [211].

hanged had the Rebellion succeeded,[1] we shall at least be allowed some Place among those who triumph in its Defeat.

And here when we contemplate that sacred Person whose Throne was attacked by these impious Miscreants, we are struck with as profound an Awe and Reverence, as the greatest Eastern Monarchs inspire into the Minds of their lowest Subjects, when they approach them. Those Monarchs indeed owe all that Respect to the outward Splendor and Magnificence of their Thrones, while our Sovereign wants not that Pomp to add to the Respect commanded by his Princely Virtues; and it is not barely by being seen, but by being known, that he becomes the Object of Admiration and Reverence.

If Justice be a Quality of this Kind, there is no Man, however tinctured with the Principles of *Jacobitism*, but must be obliged to confess that his present Majesty possesses this Virtue in the most eminent Degree. His whole Reign cannot produce one single Instance of Injustice, which can be derived from the Throne against the Properties of the meanest Person in *Great Britain*,[2] nor indeed which hath been suffered or winked at by our Sacred Sovereign. When the Oppressed can once reach his Ears, they are certain of obtaining immediate Redress; and if any have failed of this, it hath been owing to others, and not to the King himself; indeed to that Misfortune inseparable from the Constitution of all Government, in large Countries, where the Way to the Throne can never possibly lie open to every Subject: But this I will averr, and I do it not only from many public Examples, but from the Relation of those who have had the Honour to live within the nearest Sight of their Sovereign, that no Monarch, nay, no Man hath ever been more inflexibly just, and that as well in the Distribution of Rewards as Punishments.

Again, if in the latter Instance, to temper the Rigour and Severity of Justice with Mercy, be most amiable in the Character of a Prince, as this is a Quality of all others, which it is in the Power of the human to imitate the divine Majesty, this is known to reside so absolutely in the Breast of our Royal Sovereign, that with Regard to military Punishments, which in this Kingdom can never be inflicted without the King's signing the Sentence, the Officers of the Army have been often known to lament this merciful Disposition, that makes it always difficult to obtain the Royal Warrant for inflicting Death on Deserters: But this is so apparent from

---

[1] In *TP* no. 3 (19 November 1745), above, p. 130, the editorial *persona* dreams he is about to be hanged by order of the court of the King's Bench, as illegally appointed by the triumphant jacobites.

[2] For similar terms of panegyric, see *Gentleman & Alderman* (1747), p. 15, and *Proper Answer* (1747), p. 83.

the very rare Examples of this Kind, that it was scarce necessary even to mention it.[1]

This is a Quality which can never exist separate from Benevolence, nay, in Fact, it is no other than a Branch of it, or may be perhaps more properly called Benevolence in Authority. We shall therefore not be surprized to find numberless other Marks of this excellent Temper in our Sovereign. But how effectually must it endear him to his whole People, when it is publickly known, that the late glorious Victory conveyed but little Joy to the Throne, compared with what flowed thither from the Contemplation of the great Delight with which it was received by all Ranks of People. To find the Safety of his Throne established by the Strength of his Arms must have given Satisfaction to our Sovereign; but it was to find it established in the Hearts of his Subjects which gave Raptures. How excellent must be the Mind of a Prince who could declare, *It was the greatest Happiness he ever felt, to find he was so belov'd by his People*.[2]

And as no Prince ever could more deserve this Happiness, so I am

---

[1] The emphasis here on the military particulars of George II's clemency may be in part owing to his reputation as a strict disciplinarian of his troops and in part to early reports of severities at Culloden. On 23 April 1746 five soldiers from the foot guards were shot in Hyde Park for desertion in Flanders and subsequent enlistment in the French services; *DA* of 24 April 1746. *An Epistle to O——r H—nl—y* (London, 1746), p. 12, states that Henley's Sunday sermon of 27 April 1746 animadverted severely on these punishments, and in extenuation it cites (p. 16) an earlier case (1743?) in which the king pardoned two of five soldiers sentenced to die for desertion. George Harris, *Life of Hardwicke*, ii. 145–6, notes that this earlier case caused considerable resentment among the military for its excess of mercy. Henley's own advertisement in *DA* of 26 April 1746 makes clear a link to Culloden: 'Another Battle in H. Park? Price of each Rebel settled?' Some of the early reports from Culloden were disquieting: 'We are assured, that the great Slaughter made of the Rebels in the last Battle, was owing not only to the Knowledge which the King's Forces had of the Pretender's Orders to the Rebels, not to give Quarter, but to the Obstinacy of the Rebels, who, as they lay wounded on the Ground, fired many Pistol Shot at the Soldiers, which they pass'd by them, which obliged the latter, for their own Security, to dispatch them out of the Way'; *DA* of 30 April 1746. Even before Culloden, however, opposition journals had made an issue of the government's supposed inhumanity toward the rebels. *Old England*, which is consistently anti-Cumberland during this period, had raised the issue as far back as 25 January 1746 and returned to it on 12 April 1746: 'Such are the Reasons why, at this Time, I never hear an *Englishman* breathing and foaming out Fire and Fury against the *Scots* in general, but I take him in his Heart to be a *Jacobite*.'

[2] As a rule Fielding uses italic for complete sentences or substantial fragments when he wishes to indicate direct quotation. It is possible that one of his friends in the ministry may have quoted such a royal declaration to him, but no such source has been identified. Moreover, in a similar context *Gentleman & Alderman* (1747), p. 57, uses italic in an otherwise roman passage merely for emphasis, describing George II as 'a King . . . *whom, if his whole People personally knew, they would all personally love*'. The king's published 'declarations' do not speak quite so clearly to the touchy subject of Hanoverian popularity in England. See, for example, *DA* of 5 May 1746, which reprints the king's reply to the address of the City of London, and *Journals of Commons*, xxv. 141, which reprints the king's reply to the parliamentary address. For the suggestion that in composing this panegyric Fielding may have been somewhat influenced by the 'idea' of a patriot king, see 'General Introduction', above, p. lxxiii, and Bolingbroke's *The Idea of a Patriot King* (London, [1743]), ch. x, p. 78: 'The true Image of a Free People governed by a Patriot King, is that of a patriarchal Family, where the Head and all the Members are united by one common Interest. . . .'

convinced none was ever more certain of maintaining it. Infinitely the greatest Part of us have long been sensible of the Blessings we enjoy under his Reign; and even the few whose Principles have been misled by Education and Prejudice, begin now to open their Eyes, to see through and abhor the Designs of their Enemies, and more and more universally to acknowledge, that the Preservation of the present Royal Family is the Preservation of every Thing dear to *Britons*.

His Majesty therefore, whose great and princely Qualities are here so faintly touched, is first truly happy in himself: I say faintly touched; for that Courage, of which he hath given so many Proofs, would alone furnish Instances sufficient to fill this Paper. I will mention but one, as it is the latest, and must be recent in the Memory of all who live within the Precincts of the Court. When that *Scotch* Banditti had, by their Approach to *Darby*,[1] filled this whole City and Suburbs with Terror, his Majesty alone maintained his Courage and Constancy, and spoke of them with that Contempt and Defiance which it now appears they deserved.[2]

In the next Place, His Majesty may be truly called happy in the Love of his People: A Love which, I believe, no Prince hath ever enjoyed in a greater Extent.

Thirdly, and what may indeed be considered as the highest Instance of human Felicity, our Sovereign may be truly said to be happy in his Royal Family, some Instances of which I shall slightly mention, with that Caution which becomes a Man who hath no other Apprehension but of doing Violence to a Subject so extremely delicate.

And here how joyful a Contemplation must it be to this sacred Person to observe all his Virtues descending to the eldest Branch of his Royal

[1] This spelling reflects the southern (not the local) pronunciation of 'Derby' (*OED*). The conventional spelling is used in the 'Present History of Great Britain' in *TP* no. 6 and no. 7, Locke, p. [76] and below, p. 377, and in *JJ* no. 37 (13 August 1748), p. 367. Derby was the point of deepest rebel penetration into England ('the very Heart of the Kingdom', according to *JJ* no. 37, p. 366, and *Gentleman & Alderman* [1747], p. 7) and was entered on 4 December 1745. The news reached London on December 6 and caused the panic of 'Black Friday'. See 'Present History of Great Britain', *TP* no. 6 (10 December 1745), below, p. 368.

[2] Fielding may be trying to counter rumors that as the rebels approached Derby, George II ordered the royal plate and other valuables to be packed up and his yacht readied for a quick exit. See George Harris, *Life of Hardwicke*, ii. 178–9; Sir George Young, *Poor Fred* (London, 1937), p. 190; J. D. Griffith Davies, *A King in Toils* (London, 1938), p. 237; and, for a contemporary 'jacobite' account, Chevalier de Johnstone, *Memoirs of the Rebellion in 1745 and 1746*, 2nd ed. (London, 1821), pp. 76–7, 78: '... the King had formed the resolution of embarking immediately in one of his yachts, and setting sail for Holland, in case the battle which was expected at Derby, had proved unfavourable to his son, the Duke of Cumberland.' The 'Present History of Great Britain', *TP* no. 6 (10 December 1745), below, p. 368, refers disparagingly to the terror manifested by 'several public-spirited Persons', who packed up their money, jewels, and plate and prepared to flee into the country. Lady Hardwicke wrote Philip Yorke on 28 September 1745 of similar rumors concerning Newcastle and Pelham after the news of Prestonpans; Harris, *Life of Lord Chancellor Hardwicke*, ii. 168.

House;[1] and to consider that People, for whom he hath so paternal an Affection, in the fairest Prospect of transmitting their own Freedom to their Posterity, under a Succession of Princes sprung from his own Royal Loins. His Royal Highness hath never yet had a single Opportunity of carrying any great political or martial Quality into act;[2] and I am justified in saying it is owing to the Want of such an Opportunity only that the World do not see the most shining Examples of both, when I speak first from the Testimony of those who have the Honour to be near his Person, and to be admitted to his Conversation;[3] and secondly, from his exemplary Conduct in his own Family, the Knowledge of which extends to all within what is called the polite Circle: For it is no more than the strictest Truth to aver, that whoever would discover in one Man an Example of the tenderest Husband, the fondest Father, the sincerest

[1] Frederick Louis (1707–51), prince of Wales (1729), was in fact profoundly resented by his father and publicly (and popularly) known to be so. Such was the inveteracy of the parental dislike of the prince that at one time George II proposed excluding Frederick from the crown of England in favor of his younger son William, duke of Cumberland; Sir George Young, *Poor Fred*, pp. 29–30. There were even rumors that Frederick was a supposititious child; *Poor Fred*, pp. 8–10. After his father expelled him from St James's in 1737, Frederick became the epicenter of the final opposition to Walpole and as such was cultivated by Bolingbroke, Chesterfield, Dodington, Lyttelton, and Pitt, many of whom Fielding was also cultivating, then and later. Although Frederick seems to have abstained from opposition (on dynastic grounds) during the invasion scare of 1744 and during the Forty-Five as well, Walpole wrote Mann on 21 March 1746 that the prince was raising a new opposition, 'by the councils of Lord Bath, who has got him from Lord Granville'; *Yale Walpole*, xix. 229. For a contrary view, see *Poor Fred*, p. 200. Fielding may have written the flattering notice of Frederick's 39th birthday, in the 'Present History' of *TP* no. 12 (21 January 1746), below, p. 407.

[2] George II refused to appoint Frederick regent during any of the frequent royal absences on the continent. In 1745, for example, he had been left out of the regency on the grounds that he was too 'jacobite' and hence dangerous; Young, *Poor Fred*, p. 177. In 1743 the prince also asked for a command in Flanders, but his father preferred Cumberland. During the Forty-Five he asked, perhaps twice, to be given a command against the rebels; again the king preferred Cumberland, detaching him from the forces in Flanders to do so. Cf. Horace Walpole, *Memoirs of . . . George II*, ch. iii: 'Indeed it was not his [Frederick's] fault if he had not distinguished himself by any warlike achievements. He had solicited the command of our Army in Scotland during the Last Rebellion; though that Ambition was ascribed rather to jealousy of his brother than to his courage.' See also *Poor Fred*, p. 190. Although Frederick was considered at this time to be partial to Granville, not the Pelhams, Fielding is careful to flatter him in the *TP*, perhaps because of the good old days in the anti-Walpole opposition, perhaps because Fielding, like Dodington, wished to hedge his political bets. Cf. 'Present History of Great Britain', *TP* no. 11 (14 January 1746), below, p. 401, where an encomiastic comment on the prince's gift of £500 to the Guildhall subscription—a comment almost certainly written by Fielding himself—calls attention to the prince's happy family life and to his solicitation 'for Leave to expose his Person to all the Dangers and Fatigues of a Winter Campaign, against those Savage Blood-Hounds, who have so long infested this Kingdom with Impunity'.

[3] Fielding could have learned intimate details from his friends and political mentors: Dodington (who helped launch the prince in active opposition in 1737 and served him as secretary), Lyttelton (who succeeded Dodington as secretary), Pitt (who had a place with the prince). By 1746 these men were active in the broad bottom and no longer in the princely orbit. See 'General Introduction', above, pp. xci–xcvi. In addition some of Fielding's more literary connections—Ralph, Thomson, Moore, Young, Warburton—had received favors or employment from Frederick. For a survey, with sources, see David Harrison Stevens, *Party Politics and English Journalism 1702–1742* (Menasha, Wisconsin, 1916), ch. viii; also *TP* no. 1 (5 November 1745), above, p. 110 and *n*.

Friend, and the kindest Master, may see those Characters all at once exemplified in this Royal person.[1]

Again, what Raptures must that blooming Hero[2] convey to the Heart of a Father, who hath already received from Fortune such Opportunities of shewing the greatest Martial Virtues, and hath so nobly improved them; that at an Age when few Princes have scarce seen an Army,[3] he hath acquired to himself the noblest Lawrels, and hath almost out-stripp'd all his Competitors for Glory, among the most warlike Princes in Europe. To omit the Fields of *Dettingen* and *Fontenoy*, where he shewed the most heroic Contempt of Danger, in the first of which our Soldiers saw him receive a dangerous Wound, and in the latter began almost to conclude him invulnerable;[4] let us survey him at home, fighting more immediately in the Protection of his Country; let us behold him braving Danger, and despising Fatigue; driving a most desperate Banditti like a Flock of Sheep before him; and at last, with the most exquisite Conduct teaching Forces, who had twice given way to the Fury of their Enemies,[5] to stand, to defy, and totally to subdue a superior Number,[6] with a Loss incredibly small on his own Side.[7]

[1] The prince did enjoy a considerable contemporary reputation as a family man. See Christopher Smart, 'A Solemn Dirge, Sacred to the Memory of his Royal Highness Frederic Prince of Wales' (1751): 'Father! Master! Husband! Brother! | Every blessed tender Name! | You must dye—till such another, | Call you back to Life and Fame'; *Collected Poems*, ed. Norman Callan (Cambridge, Mass., 1949), pp. 7–9; also *Poor Fred*, pp. 166–75. *CGJ* no. 28 (7 April 1752), i. 298–300, prints an 'Elegy on the late Prince of Wales', signed 'Cantabrigiensis', which is not by Fielding but may be a sign of his continued interest.

[2] William, duke of Cumberland, George II's second son and, most recently, victor at Culloden. For additional panegyric on Cumberland, see Fielding's *Ovid's Art of Love Paraphrased* (1747), the preface of which asserts (p. iii) that the reason for publishing a work begun 'many Years ago' was the passage 'so justly applicable to the Glorious Duke of Cumberland'. See also *JJ* no. 15 (12 March 1748), p. 193. The relative clause which comes next in the present essay modifies 'Hero', not 'Father'.

[3] Cumberland's 25th birthday fell on 15 April 1746. For the celebrations in London, see *TP* no. 25 (15–22 April 1746), Locke, p. [206]. According to Chevalier de Johnstone, *Memoirs*, 2nd ed., p. 72, some of the jacobite chiefs thought that Cumberland's army might be rendered less formidable from the celebratory effects, when they met the next day on the field at Culloden.

[4] At Dettingen (27 June 1743 NS) Cumberland was shot in the calf and later developed a serious fever. The wound was inflicted by Austrian soldiers, who mistook him for a French officer when his horse bolted with him toward the French lines. His behavior in battle was agreed to have been admirable; Charteris, p. 132; Walpole to Mann, 24 June 1743, *Yale Walpole*, xviii. 258; James Wolfe (later the hero of Quebec) to his father, 23 June 1743, as reprinted in Robin Reilly, *The Rest to Fortune* (London, 1960), p. 28. At Fontenoy (11 May 1745 NS) Cumberland, who was captain-general of his majesty's forces in Great Britain and Flanders, was defeated by Saxe, with much of the contemporary blame being placed on the behavior of the Dutch troops. Cumberland's battlefield presence, if not his tactics, was again applauded; *DA* of 6 and 21 May 1745; Walpole to Mann, 11 May 1745 and 24 May 1745, *Yale Walpole*, xix. 44, 52; Charteris, pp. 187, 193.

[5] Under Cope at Prestonpans (21 September 1745) and Hawley at Falkirk (17 January 1746). Fielding briefly alludes to the former in *History*, above, pp. 63–7; for Falkirk, see 'Present History of Great Britain', *TP* no. 13 (21–8 January 1746), Locke, p. [129].

[6] Cumberland's troops numbered about 8,800; Blaikie, *Itinerary*, p. 98; Charteris, p. 266; Elcho, *Short Account*, pp. 424–5. *DA* of 25 April 1746 estimated the rebel army at 'upwards of Eight

[*See opposite page for n. 6 cont. and n. 7.*]

If we were disposed to dishonour this brave victorious Prince, with a Comparison, where could we find a baser than that of his pitiful Adversary;[1] who, to say no worse of him, having the Prospect of a Crown in his View, and having obtained, (what it would have been Impudence to have asked of Fortune) an Opportunity of fighting on advantageous Terms,[2] did not dare expose his worthless Life to the least Hazard,[3] in order to improve the Opportunity. He saw before him one of our best Bodies of Troops, under our best and greatest General, in whom our whole Confidence was placed, and who, he well knew, would not fail on any Emergency to expose his most valuable Person to the greatest Danger. He saw this Body inferior in Number to his own, and yet basely (tho' his All was at Stake, and so fairly staked too) consulted not Victory, but his own Safety and Retreat from the Beginning, whilst the brave Duke of *Cumberland* forwardly pushed to that Place where the greatest Danger and Distress was apprehended. *Charles* stood an idle Spectator of the Battle, at a safe Distance, and took the first Occasion to preserve by Flight, a Life perhaps more worthless and miserable than that of the meanest of those Wretches who had been the Followers of his Fortune, and were now, at a great Distance, the Followers of his Flight.

Thus hath he given a better Evidence than hath yet been produc'd by any Writer in his Favour of his Legitimacy.[4] It seems indeed hard any

Thousand Men', but although there were this many on the rebel muster rolls at the time, Patullo, the muster-master, said fewer than 5,000 were in the field; Blaikie, *Itinerary*, p. 97. John Prebble, *Culloden* (London, 1961), p. 64, and Tomasson and Buist, *Battles of the '45* (London, 1962), p. 138, give slightly lower figures; Elcho, *Short Account*, pp. 422–4, estimates nearly 7,000. Actual participants in the battle on both sides have been estimated at fewer than 3,000; Tomasson and Buist, p. 203.

[7] See the 'Present History of Great Britain', *TP* no. 26 (22–9 April 1746), Locke, p. [211], reprinted from *London Gazette Extraordinary* of 26 April 1746. This account gives the rebel losses in the field and in pursuit at 2,000, and the killed, wounded, and missing of Cumberland's troops at 'above 300'. *DA* of 28 April 1746 gives 50 killed and 259 wounded for Cumberland. More recent estimates put the rebel dead at 1,500 and Cumberland's at 43; Charteris, p. 270.

[1] Charles Edward Stuart, the Young Pretender. See *History*, above, p. [35], and index, *s.n.*

[2] In addition to the unfavorable numerical odds against him, the YP was persuaded to do battle on terrain that was also unfavorable; Prebble, p. 56; Tomasson and Buist, pp. 147–8.

[3] Although his symbolic 'presence' required his participation, the need to preserve the YP so far as possible required that he be placed in a relatively unexposed position to the rear. Later, when he rode up toward the right wing, his horse was shot, which may have given rise to the false rumors that he was wounded; Blaikie, *Itinerary*, p. 100; Tomasson and Buist, pp. 164–5. Accounts of the YP's subsequent behavior vary considerably; Charteris, pp. 27–71, alludes to several. His retreat from the field may have been accomplished forcibly by his closest military advisers; Prebble, pp. 113–14, and Tomasson and Buist, pp. 193–4. For a friendly view that he was in fact too far removed from the front (and held there by his 'Irish' advisers), see Chevalier de Johnstone, *Memoirs*, 2nd ed., p. 191.

[4] As anti-jacobite feeling intensified during the 1740s, the question of Stuart legitimacy was resurrected in all its forms, including the durable and scurrilous hypothesis that the male child (James Francis Edward, the Old Pretender and father of Charles Edward Stuart) born to James II and Mary of Modena on 20 June 1688 was in fact supposititious, having been smuggled into the place of *accouchement* so as to ensure continuation of the hitherto childless Stuart line. Fielding will allude again to this unsubstantiated hypothesis in *JJ* no. 6 (9 January 1748) and no. 32 (9 July 1748), pp. 125, 333.

longer to deny that he is truly descended from *James* the IId, and is the Third of his Family who hath basely deserted his own Cause,[1] after having sacrificed the Blood of Thousands of deluded Wretches to support it. A Consideration which is alone sufficient to prevent any but the most obstinate Madman from ever hereafter engaging on his Side; especially when they reflect that under the Banner of these Poltrons[2] they are to oppose Princes of the BRAVE and ILLUSTRIOUS HOUSE OF HANOVER.

From TUESDAY, MAY 6, to TUESDAY, MAY 13, 1746.
NUMB. 28.

(Contendere noli)
Stultitiam patiuntur opes. Tibi parvula res est.

HORACE.[3]

Tho' the Fact which occasioned the following Letter hath been pretty much obliterated out of the Minds of Men, by an Event of such mighty Consequence as the late Victory in *Scotland*,[4] it is however so recent in our Memory, that it is scarce necessary to hint that this Letter owes its Birth to the Execution of *Matthew Henderson*;[5] and is an Address from a Footman in a great Family to his Brethren of the Cloth.

[1] His grandfather, James II, avoided direct confrontation with the forces of William of Orange by fleeing in disguise to France in December 1688; his father, the Old Pretender, came over somewhat belatedly to assist Mar with the uprising of 1715 in Scotland and, with Mar, abandoned the hopeless cause in February 1716.

[2] An acceptable spelling of 'poltroon', 16th–19th centuries (*OED*). Cf. 'poltron, or the lowest name of infamy', *Craftsman* of 2 November 1745, as reprinted in *GM*, xv (1745), 586. Just possibly the term may have had Hanoverian echoes; cf. Basil Williams, *Life of William Pitt* (London, 1913), i. 107: 'When the Duc d'Arenberg begged him [George II] not to expose himself to danger [at Dettingen], he replied, "What do you think I came here for? To be a poltroon?"'

[3] *Epistles*, i. xviii. 28–9: '(Don't try to rival me) [my] wealth allows of folly; your means are but trifling' (Loeb).

[4] Cumberland's victory over the rebels at Culloden (16 April 1746), official news of which reached London on April 23. See *TP* no. 26 (22–9 April 1746), above, p. 276.

[5] Henderson (1727–46), a Scots footman, was committed by Sir Thomas DeVeil to the Gatehouse, Westminster, on 25 March 1746 for the murder and robbery of Elizabeth (Hamilton) Dalrymple, wife of Henderson's employer, Captain William Dalrymple, aide-de-camp and nephew of Lord Stair. In the first accounts Mrs. Dalrymple was said to have received 'above 50 wounds' (*GM*, xvi [1746], 411–12), a figure which later escalated wildly. On 9 April Henderson pleaded guilty at the Old Bailey sessions and two days later received sentence of death. In the following week advertisements appeared in the London papers announcing publication of his 'solemn Declaration of every Circumstance relating to that cruel Murder and Robbery' (*Penny London Post* of 14–16 April 1746). The declaration, published by John Thompson ('in the Old Baily') was indeed circumstantial, lurid, and very widely quoted; the 'substance' of it is in *GM*, xvi (1746), 174–5. Owing to the sanguinary nature of the crime, the Scots connection, elements of sex and class, as well as Henderson's confused attempt to get at his own motives, the case aroused enormous public interest. On 28 March 1746

Gentlemen,

It was with great Sorrow that I Yesterday saw a young Man, who had the Honour to be of our Order, brought to the most condign Punishment,[1] for one of the most flagitious Crimes which it ever entered into the wicked Heart of Man to commit. And tho' the World hath been more merciful in this Instance than it generally is, by not casting any invidious Reflection on our Cloth for the Offence of one who wore it,[2] you will pardon me if I take this Occasion of offering some wholesome Advice to all my Brethren. I am far from thinking that there is a single Man among us capable of imitating the Wretch who hath so lately been made a just Example for his Sins, yet give me Leave to say, Immorality hath of late Years taken very large Strides in our Fraternity,[3] and if not speedily put a Stop to, it is to be feared may in Time produce among us such Vices as must end in the Destruction of many.

I have given myself some Pains to search into the true Cause and Original of this Evil, and I am much mistaken if it be any other than a Desire in us to imitate our Masters. A Folly in which we have made such a Progress, that whoever frequents the public Assemblies of this Town, must be obliged to confess, that we are very near as bad as *our Betters*;[4] and as those have done us the Honour, especially in their Morning Dress,[5] to imitate us, it may very often puzzle People to distinguish the Man from the Master.

Some of us, I know, who do not sufficiently see into the Bottom of

Walpole wrote Mann, 'one hears of nothing else wherever one goes'; *Yale Walpole*, xix. 235. *TP* no. 22 (25 March–1 April 1746) had reprinted, without comment, notices of Henderson's committal and Mrs Dalrymple's death (Locke, p. [188]).

[1] Henderson was hanged on 25 April 1746. According to *London Evening Post* of 24–6 April 1746, 'He was attended by a Clergyman of the Church of England, and another of the Church of Scotland, who pray'd with him near an Hour; he was very penitent, but seem'd greatly shock'd at Death, and trembled very much when he went out of the Cart up the ladder. After the Execution he was carried in the Cart and hung up in Chains near the five Mile Stone on the Edgeware-Road, where vast Crowds of People went to see him.' Cf. *DA* of 26 April 1746: 'There were so many People on a Scaffold near the Place of Execution, that it broke down, but happily no Persons receiv'd any Damage.'

[2] French, pp. 465–6, compares the opening paragraph of *TP* no. 14 (28 January–4 February 1746), above, p. 207, where Fielding cites the unfair practice of ascribing the faults of individual members of a profession to the profession as a whole.

[3] *DA* of 24 March 1746 records the committal to the Gatehouse, by DeVeil, of one John Bramston, footman to Jacob Houbloe, for stealing £23 from his lady, who had presaged such an event and had marked some of the coins which were found on his person.

[4] Cf. the cry of Betty, the Tow-wouses' maid, caught *in flagrante delicto*: 'my Be— Betters are wo— worse than me'; *Joseph Andrews*, I. xvii. 85. French, p. 466, compares *CGJ* no. 27 (4 April 1752), i. 293–8.

[5] Fielding may have had in mind Swift's *Directions to Servants* (London, 1745), ch. iii ('Directions to the Footman'): 'You are sometimes a Pattern of Dress to your Master, and sometimes he is so to you'; *Prose Works*, ed. Herbert Davis, vol. viii (Oxford, 1959), p. 33. See also p. 286 *n*. 4, below, for what may be another echo of Swift's *Directions*, a Dodsley and Cooper imprint of November 1745; *GM*, xv (1745), 616.

Things, and are consequently misled by an ill-judging Ambition, may flatter their Vanity with such Mistakes: But to be serious, there are few, I hope, among us, who, upon a fair State[1] of the Case, will be found to have any Reason for their Triumph; since, I think, we can envy our Masters little more than their Fortune.

Besides, we are to consider, that what may become one Station in Life may very ill suit with another. The Vices of our Masters sit as improperly on us as their Cloaths, and we shall be laughed at for what is admired in them.

But if nothing worse than being ridiculous was to happen to us from this Imitation, it might perhaps give us little Apprehension; nay, some of us might be advantaged by it, since Men may as reasonably chuse Buffoons for Servants, as for Friends, which we who live in great Families see happen every Day.

This therefore, is the least Misfortune that will accrue to us. If we lose our Characters, we shall lose our Places, and never after be received into any other Family. Herein our Situation differs from that of our Betters; against whom no Profligacy is any Objection. And if by Treachery they happen to be discarded in one Place, (for that is the only Crime they can be guilty of) they are nevertheless received with open Arms in another. How many Men of Fashion do we all know, whose Characters would prevent any Person from taking them into his Family as Footmen, who[2] are well received, caressed and promoted by the Great as Gentlemen? We see therefore how highly it imports[3] us, and us only, to preserve our Reputation, since our Bread depends upon it. And we must be honest or starve, unless we will venture on Actions which may prove the Words of a late wicked Wit true, *viz.* That Hanging is the natural Death of a Footman.[4]

For we are to consider that we live in a Nation where there are Laws provided against little Men making their Fortunes by Knavery and Thieving.[5] Another Circumstance which should deter us from walking

---

[1] A statement, account, description, report ('of a transaction, events, a legal case, etc.) [*OED*].

[2] This relative clause modifies 'Men of Fashion', not 'Footmen'.

[3] To be of consequence or importance to; to concern (*OED*). This verb also occurs in the 'Present History of Great Britain', *TP* no. 21, Locke, p. [181], and 'Foreign History', *TP* no. 22, Locke, p. [186], neither of which seems to be by Fielding.

[4] Swift, *Directions to Servants*, loc. cit.: 'The last Advice I shall give you, relates to your Behaviour when you are going to be hanged; which, either for robbing your Master, for House-breaking, or going upon the High-way, or in a drunken Quarrel, by killing the first Man you meet, may very probably be your lot'; *Prose Works*, xiii. 44.

[5] Cf. *Beggar's Opera*, II. i, Jemmy Twitcher's first speech at the meeting of the gang: 'Why are the Laws levell'd at us? are we more dishonest than the rest of Mankind?' That the *Beggar's Opera* was in Fielding's mind, perhaps even before his eye, during the writing of this leader is confirmed in the penultimate paragraph of the leader. French, p. 467, compares *CGJ* no. 27 (4 April 1752), i. 295.

in the Steps of our Betters, whom those Laws do not reach. We have but one Way to get a Livelihood with Safety, and if our bad Character exclude us from that, we have no Resource. As to the several Professions, (tho' our Sons have sometimes thrived very well in them) yet the Door is, *for the most Part*, shut on ourselves. And with Regard to the genteel Arts of living, such as Pimping, V——ing,[1] Gaming, &c. the first alone is open to the Gentlemen of our Cloth. And even here with how much Hazard, and how little Advantage do we carry on this Business compared to the Safety and Emoluments which attend our Betters, who engage in the same. Horse-Ponds, Duckings, and Blanketings[2] are what we are constantly liable to, and even when we succeed best, how paultry are our Rewards! Many of us have spent their whole Lives in this Calling, to less Profit than hath sometimes accrued to our Betters by assisting in a single Prostitution.

And though some of us have got a poor beggarly Livelihood this Way, yet when we reflect what Numbers of our Betters are of this Profession, it will appear too full to admit many of our Order, even to that pitiful Provision which *it affords* us. So that in Reality, there is no Way of living open to a Footman who hath lost his Character, but what directly leads to *Tyburn*;[3] which very few of us (except[4] our Relations have Interest in B——ghs)[5] will have Interest enough to escape, if the Law sentences us to it. There will be no hushing up the Matter in our Case; for no Man will concern himself to preserve the Honour of a Footman, when it is known he hath no Honesty.

These Considerations therefore ought to deter us from any longer following the Example, and imitating the Morals of *Men of Fashion*. We must content ourselves with being only what Gentlemen shou'd be, instead of copying what they are. As I was bred at a Charity-School,[6]

---

[1] Copy-text prints 'V——ing', perhaps a misprint for 'W——ing' ('Whoring'). However, given the sex and station of the correspondent, copy-text may have intended the sign-word for 'Cuckolding', the vulgar emblem of which was and is the sign made by clenching the middle three fingers of the hand while extending the thumb and little finger so as to represent the horns of the cornuted state. See John Farmer and W. E. Henley, *Slang and Its Analogues, Past and Present*, vii (n.p., 1904), 268, *s.v.* 'V'.

[2] The punishment of being tossed in a blanket. *OED* cites Fielding's *The Letter Writers: or, a New Way to Keep a Wife at Home* (1731), I. i: 'This Affair, Sir, may end in a Blanketing . . . .' Like the other punishments here noted, it was *infra dig*.

[3] The celebrated gallows or public place of execution for criminals convicted in the county of Middlesex, until 1759 a permanent structure located on Tyburn Road near what is now Marble Arch, that is, at the junction of Edgeware Road, Oxford Street, and Bayswater Road. Like 'Jack Ketch' Tyburn had acquired metonymic force and could refer to the place of execution wherever it might be.

[4] A conjunction, with the force of 'unless'.

[5] A borough was a town possessing a municipal corporation and special privileges conferred by royal charter, or also a town which sent representatives to parliament (*OED*). The reference here is to political influence which might be used to 'get off' a criminal by having his sentence lightened.

[6] An omnibus term covering all schools, whether endowed or subscription, which were set up to

I remember a Proverb which my Master used often to repeat to us: *It is not lawful for every one to go to* Corinth.[1] By which, as he explained to us, was meant, that the Vices of High Life would be the Ruin of Men in a low Condition. To which I will add another Proverb better known among you: *That it is safer for one Man to steal a Horse, than for another to look over the Hedge.*[2]

It is not my Intention in this Epistle to abuse our Masters, and there-fore, I shall not attempt to say the least in Discredit of their Morals. They may perhaps be very proper and becoming to Persons in their Situation; nay, if Religion be a Jest,[3] and Honour and Virtue only Words with which sensible People cheat and impose on the Vulgar, as I have often heard at my Master's Table, surely Gentlemen are in the Right not to sacrifice their Interest to such *chimerical Good*. And if we could with the same Safety and Advantage throw them off, I shou'd not have troubled you with writing in their Defence. You will not therefore con-sider me as a Pimp of a Parson, (as my Master calls them) nor as one who is canting to you about the Good of your Souls, since I am well per-suaded, you all believe, as well as your Masters, that you have none. Your worldly Interest is what I recommend to your Attention, and I would by this Application, dissuade you, my worthy Brethren, from imitating your Masters for this plain Reason only; *because you will certainly be hanged if you do*; for as it is very wisely said in the *Beggar's Opera*: *If little Men will have their Vices, as well as the Great*, THEY *will be punished for them*.[4]

Let us content ourselves with that low State of Life to which it hath

provide 'christian and useful' instruction for the children of the poor; M. G. Jones, *The Charity School Movement* (Cambridge, 1938), ch. i, especially p. 19. Cf. the complaint of the beggar who finds Sophia Western's pocketbook containing the £100 note but cannot make out the denomination of the note: 'For had they [his parents] . . . sent me to Charity-School to learn to write and read and cast Account, I should have known the Value of these Matters as well as other People'; *Tom Jones*, XII. iv. 635. During the immediately preceding Lenten season, as was the custom, a good many 'charity sermons' were preached for the benefit of these schools and their children, and the London papers carried notices of same.

[1] In the *Champion* of 28 February 1740 (i. 318) Fielding uses the proverb and cites Aulus Gellius, whose *Attic Nights*, I. viii. 1–6, refers to a book ('The Horn of Amaltheia') by a Peripatetic named Sotion, which derives this Greek proverb from the legendary high fees charged by the prostitute Lais of Corinth. The proverb gained literary currency from Horace, *Epistles*, I. xvii. 36: *Non cuivis homini contingit adire Corinthum*.
[2] An English proverb, apparently first collected in the 16th century; see Tilley, *Dictionary of the Proverbs in England in the Sixteenth and Seventeenth Centuries* (Ann Arbor, 1950), H692, p. 325. Fielding may have been put in mind of it by Matt of the Mint's speech, *Beggar's Opera*, III. iv: 'See the Partiality of Mankind!—One Man may steal a Horse, better than another look over a Hedge.'
[3] French, p. 469, compares the glossary in *CGJ* no. 4 (14 January 1752), especially its definition of Religion as 'A Word of no Meaning; but which serves as a Bugbear to frighten Children with' (i. 157).
[4] Fielding's recollection of the Beggar's speech, III. xvi, about the original ('unhappy') ending of the play: ''Twould have shown that the lower Sort of People have their Vices in a degree as well as the Rich: And that they are punish'd for them.'

pleased God to call us; and not conclude when we see our Masters grow great, high and honourable by their Rogueries, that it would succeed with us in the same Manner: For tho' I have heard my Master and his Company at Table often laugh at the old Maxim, Honesty is the best Policy, yet I am sure *this will always hold true in a* FOOTMAN.

> *I am,*
> > *Gentlemen,*
> > > *Your affectionate Brother and Servant*,

April 26, 1746. TOM SKIPTON.[1]

From TUESDAY, MAY 13, to TUESDAY, MAY 20, 1746.
NUMB. 29.

— Hoc animo semper sui, ut INVIDIAM VIRTUTE PARTAM GLORIAM, *non invidiam putarem. Quamquam nonnulli sunt in hoc ordine, qui aut ea, quæ imminent, non videant: aut ea, quæ vident, dissimulent:* QUI SPEM CATILINÆ MOLLIBUS SENTENTIIS ALUERUNT, CONJURA-TIONEMQUE NASCENTEM NON CREDENDO CORROBORAVERUNT.

CICERO, *In L. Catilinam, Oratio* I.[2]

This was the Day intended for the Dissection of the Opposition:[3] But as we are naturally inclined to Mercy, and as the said Opposition have thought proper to humble themselves before us, and not only to submit to our Authority, but likewise to apply *properly* to our Bookseller,[4] we

---

[1] A 'skip' is probably short for a 'skip-kennel', a footman, lackey, or manservant (*OED*). Cf. Swift, *Directions to Servants*, ch. iii, which states that ladies' maids are 'sometimes apt to call you [Footmen] Skipkennel'; *Prose Works*, xiii. 34. The letter proper (without the paragraph which introduces it) was reprinted in *GM*, xvi (1746), 254–5; *London Magazine*, xv (1746), 242–4; and in *Penny London Post* of 19–21 May 1746, with a different introductory paragraph. *General Advertiser* of 13 May 1746 carries an advertisement: '*In the* Patriot, *or, The* History of our own Times' *An Address from a Footman to his Brethren*, published at 3*d.* for Cooper. This is almost certainly an advertisement for the issue of the *TP* containing the 'Skipton' letter, not for a separate publication, but Cooper did advertise (*DA* of 3 May 1746) *The Ordinary of Newgate's Account of the Behaviour . . . of Matthew Henderson* ('This is the Ordinary's genuine Account'), and her interest in the Henderson market may have had something to do with Fielding's taking up the subject.

[2] *In Catilinam*, I. xii. 29–30 (emphasis added): 'I have always believed that unpopularity won by uprightness was glory and not unpopularity. And yet there are some in this body who either do not see the disasters which threaten us or pretend that they do not see them; these have fostered the hopes of Catiline by mild measures and they have strengthened the growing conspiracy by not believing in its existence' (Loeb).

[3] See *TP* no. 26 (22–9 April 1746), above, p. 276: 'But we assure them [the Opposition] that Sentence of Dissection is past, and will be very speedily executed upon them.'

[4] See 'Apocrypha', *TP* no. 10 (7 January 1746), below, p. 401: 'Persons who correspond with the Patriot are desired not to direct their Letters to Mrs. Cooper, but to the Patriot at Mrs. Coopers; by which Means they come to him unopened.' The colophon of the first eighteen numbers reads in part: 'Printed for Mrs. Cooper, at the *Globe* in *Pater-Noster-Row*; where Advertisements and Letters to the

have graciously condescended to grant them a Reprieve *sine die*, and shall proceed farther hereafter according to their Behaviour.

To his Highness, The Great Sole TRUE PATRIOT of Great Britain.

The humble Petition of the People calling themselves The Opposition,[1]

Humbly sheweth,

That your Petitioners are greatly alarmed by the dreadful Sentence of Dissection lately pronounced by your Honour against them, as they are truly sensible of their utter Incapacity to stand against the all-conquering Force of that victorious Pen which hath long made all *England* tremble.

They beg Leave therefore, with the utmost Humility, to represent to your Honour the following Considerations in their Favour, which they presume to hope may in some Degree excuse what they dare not pretend to justify.

First, They hope that some of their Chiefs or Leaders will be allowed a Privilege to which they conceive they have an indubitable Title, of not being accountable for any of their Actions, as they properly fall within the Description of that Class which the Law calls Persons of *Insane Memory*.[2]

Others hope that their Opposition shall not be derived from any particular Spleen or Animosity against his present Majesty; for whom they have as great an Affection as for any other Monarch: But being perfectly convinced of the Excellence of a Republican Government,[3] and how exactly it suits with the Genius of this incorrupt and virtuous Nation, they humbly presume their Adherence to those Principles will be

Author are taken in.' Beginning with no. 19, the colophon adds 'And Sold by George Woodfall, near *Craig's Court, Charing-Cross*'. For the involvement of booksellers in the *TP*, see 'General Introduction', above, pp. lxv–lxvii.

[1] For a similar format, see the petition signed 'John Pudding' in *JJ* no. 13 (27 February 1748), pp. 178–9.

[2] The legal Latin is *non sanae memoriae*. Giles Jacob, *A New Law-Dictionary*, 4th ed. (London, 1739), s.v. 'Non Sane Memory', defines the term as 'used in Law for an Exception to an Act . . . and the Effect of it is, that the Party that did that Act, was not well in his Senses when he did it'. Older law held there to be four types of *non compos mentis*: *ideota* (an idiot), who from his birth, by a perpetual infirmity, is *non compos mentis*; he who by sickness, grief, or other accident, wholly loses his memory and understanding; a lunatic who sometimes has his memory and sometimes not; and he who by his own vicious act for a time deprives himself of memory and understanding, as he who is drunken. See Coke, *First Part of the Institutes*, bk. iii, cap. 6, sect. 405, where Coke says that '*Littleton* speaketh generally of men of non sane memorie'.

[3] On the polemical strategy of associating the jacobites with the republicans as two fonts of opposition, see *TP* no. 19 (4–11 March 1746), above, p. 238, where the opposition Alderman threatens, *sotto voce*, to replace the monarchy with a republic. This useful association is represented graphically by the frontispiece of Fielding's next political paper, *The Jacobite's Journal* of 1747–8, in which Harrington's *Oceana* is shown fastened to the tail of the jacobite ass.

excused, especially as they cannot be arraigned of Hypocrisy, and are very open and ready to avow their Sentiments.

A third Body beg Leave to represent in their Favour the Prejudices of their Education. Their Fathers have told them, that the Doctrine of Hereditary Right is founded on Truth and Justice, and tho' they are incapable of examining it themselves, they look upon it as their Duty to believe what their Fathers (and some with many Oaths and Imprecations) have told them.[1] These therefore hope they shall not be too severely censured for refusing to concur with Men who have been always the most steady Maintainers of the present Establishment, and with Schemes which directly tend to subvert all future Designs in favour of him whom they imagine to have the same Right over their Persons and Properties as any owner hath over his Cattle, especially when it is considered that they have not ventured either in his Cause, and can be only convicted of speaking in his Favour, and wishing him well.

The fourth Part, which includes all the rest, humbly shew, that their Actions (or rather their Words) proceed from two Motives, the one of which hath been always thought noble and laudable, and the latter hath been held almost a Justification of any Act whatever. These are Ambition and Necessity. If the Government will please to satisfy these, it is very well known they are ready to become its humble Servants at any Time. They have no Quarrel either with Men or Measures; but can never agree that their Country is taken Care of, whilst they themselves, who are that Part of their Country which they love best, are neglected. They have no more Hatred of Power than a Pack of Hounds have of a Hare, who bellow after her only because she runs away from them, and they cannot overtake her. Places are what they desire, and many of them very moderate ones. If the Government therefore, which well knows this, will not satisfy their Demands, the Fault, they conceive, is on their Side. Perhaps it may be answered, we cannot oblige every one.[2] The Reply is, if you cannot you must content yourselves with an Opposition.

Hitherto your Petitioners have severed[3] in their Defence. They now beg Leave to represent themselves jointly as the Objects of your Honour's Compassion. Be pleased, Great Sir, in the first Place to

---

[1] Cf. the letter from a nonjuror to his son at Oxford, *TP* no. 24 (8–15 April 1746), above, p. 263; and, for Fielding's continued interest in the power of education in such matters, the letters from a 'Jacobite' and 'Philo-Sacheverel' in *JJ* no. 21 (23 April 1748), pp. 245–9.

[2] Something like this answer was in fact given by the Pelhams to the 'New Allies', who wanted more places in the cabinet shuffle following the death of Winnington on 23 April 1746. See Owen, *Rise of the Pelhams*, pp. 301–2.

[3] In law, used of two or more defendants: to plead independently, to sever their challenges, in their defense (*OED*).

consider the smallness of their Numbers;[1] so inconsiderable are they in this Light, that were any of them equal in Abilities to the Leaders of their Enemies, this alone would render them so little dangerous, that it would be mere Wantonness in your Honour to discharge your Wit against them. They hope therefore to be at worst only the Object of your Contempt, and not of your Indignation: And that your Honour will not stoop to expose Men who have so unfortunately exposed themslevees.

This Circumstance, they hope will plead something on their Behalf. If universal Ridicule and Contempt be Punishments, they humbly presume no Opposition hath ever suffered those Punishments in a higher Degree. They are already become a By-word among the People, and when any one hath a Desire to express his Scorn of another, it is become usual to say, *the poor Fellow looks as if he was in* THE OPPOSITION.

As therefore they have done no Harm, nor are likely to do any; as some few are engaged from the Principles abovementioned, and the rest from that natural Motive of Self-Interest; as they are inconsiderable both in Number and Abilities, and as they already labour under so much Contempt, they hope your Honour will be graciously pleased to remit that dreadful Sentence which you so lately denounced against them; at least, they hope that the Execution of it shall be respited till they have done something, which as yet, they humbly conceive, cannot be laid to their Charge.

> *And your Petitioners,*
> *As in Duty bound, shall ever pray.*

> THE OPPOSITION.

To the TRUE PATRIOT.

Mr. *Patriot*,

When first you begun your d——d Papers, I ordered my Bookseller to send them me, as they came out, not doubting by your Title, but that you was an honest Man, and that you and he would have stood in the Pillory long ago for the Good of your Country.

I was very well pleased with you for some time, while you only writ against *Jacobites*, whom I despise as much as you can: But what the Devil do you mean by calling yourself a Patriot, while you write in favour of a Ministry?

Sir, I hate a Minister, that is my Principle. And if I understand *what a*

---

[1] The numerical inferiority of the opposition is also emphasized in *TP* no. 19 (4–11 March 1746), above, p. 237, and no. 23 (1–8 April 1746), above, p. 260.

Patriot is, he is one who opposes the Ministry.[1] I have always opposed Ministers, and always will. They are all alike, and all Rogues, and any Man who votes on the Side of the Ministry, shall be opposed with the utmost of my Power at his Election.

I hate all Ministers as I hate the Devil. *Old England* will never see happy Days till they are all hanged. That is the Way to rid us of Taxes,[2] and Armies, and Fleets, and *H−n−r−ns*.[3] Then we shall have Liberty and Property, and no Excise,[4] and may sing, *Old Rose and burn the Bellows*.[5]

[1] Cf. the definitions in *TP* no. 2 (12 November 1745), above, pp. 116–19; no. 23 (1–8 April 1746), above, p. 260, and no. 30 (20–7 May 1746), below, p. 297. The stress in this letter on reflexive opposition is intended to distinguish the tories, who generally refused 'places' in the central administration, from other elements of the opposition who merely wanted 'in'. The charge was an old one; see *London Journal* of 15, 22, 29 September 1722: 'I know it may be said by some, that I have carried the matter too far, when I have talked as if the resolutions of any persons were stretched to that degree as to extend to a constant and determined opposition to ministry, and even to make that the strongest and most infallible note of a true patriot. . . . Yet this is the current shibboleth of dangerous malcontents who oppose his Majesty's interest'; as quoted in Archibald S. Foord, *His Majesty's Opposition 1714–1830* (Oxford, 1964), p. 105.

[2] Cf. the letter from the 'non-juror' to his son, *TP* no. 24 (8–15 April 1746), above, p. 264: 'As to Taxes, we must expect them while the Government is in such Hands, and the true King in Banishment'. For the stereotyped 'country' association of taxes with the war and with the hiring of mercenaries like the Hanoverians, see *Gentleman & Alderman*, p. 33; and *JJ* no. 11 (13 February 1748) and no. 14 (5 March 1748), pp. 156–8, 182–5.

[3] Hanoverians, the mercenaries from the Electorate then paid for by parliamentary subsidy. The list of opposition aversions given here is typical. During the period 1725–42, for example, the opposition had forced a division over military matters at least once every session, except in 1738; Archibald S. Foord, *His Majesty's Opposition*, p. 176. By late 1743 Fielding's connections—Pitt, Lyttelton, Dodington, and Chesterfield, all still in opposition—were inclined, despite their continuing aversion to the Hanoverians, to support the war in Flanders, probably as part of their scheme to oust Granville by forming a coalition with Pelham. But Cobham and the Grenvilles, on the other hand, had fixed on a condemnation of the continental war in the hope that by forcing its abandonment they could overturn the entire ministry; Owen, *Rise of the Pelhams*, p. 204; Glover, *Memoirs*, p. 19. More recently, on 11 April 1746, when Pelham moved in committee for a grant to maintain the Hanoverians for the ensuing year, the debate, then and later, on the report, although less acrimonious than usual for such an issue, found many of the tories expressing their dislike of both foreign mercenaries and England's involvement in a continental land war; Owen, p. 306 and *n*. 1. Cf. the letters from 'Humphry Gubbins' in *JJ* no. 11 (13 February 1748) and no. 14 (5 March 1748), pp. 156–8, 182–5; and *TP* no. 30 (20–7 May 1746), below, p. 297, where one of the 'very honest Politicians' in the stage coach argues that English trading concerns did not require any military involvement on the continent, particularly with France. Similar 'country' sentiments may be found in *Proper Answer*, p. 76, and *Tom Jones*, VI. xiv. 321.

[4] A political shibboleth dating from the turbulence which accompanied Walpole's attempts (1732–3) to impose duties by excise. Although Walpole's aim in part was to abolish the land-tax with no loss of revenue, and although the 'country' interest abhorred the land-tax, the latter joined with the trading interest to defeat the Excise Bill as inconsistent with 'the trade, interest and liberty of the nation'; *Parliamentary History*, viii. 1223–35, 1267–1327; ix. 3. Coxe, *Walpole*, ch. xli, tells that 'Bonfires were made, effigies burnt, cockades were generally worn, inscribed with the motto of *Liberty, Property*, and *no Excise*.'

[5] 'Old Rose' appears to be the title of an old song, possibly of patriotic origins, now lost. There are references to it in Walton, *Compleat Angler* (London, 1653), ch. ii, p. 44, and 'The Seaman's Kind Answer', *Roxburghe Ballads*, ed. J. Woodfall Ebsworth, ii (Hertford, 1893), 540. At some point the title was incorporated in a catch, the refrain of which is the line 'Oldcoat' prints here. According to the

Don't tell me that the Ministry are Men of known Integrity, that they have distinguished themselves as such, that they have already preserved us in Times of the utmost Danger, that nothing can tempt them to go one Step beyond the true Interest of their Country, and that they have shewn it to Demonstration, and such Stuff. I tell you all Ministers are alike, *and a Patriot is he who opposes the Ministry*.

Write like a true *Englishman*, and in favour of the Opposition, or I hope to see your Paper burnt by the Hand of the common Hangman. In hopes of your Amendment, I am yet

Yours,

Gloucestershire,[1]
May 15.

OLIVER OLDCOAT.[2]

From TUESDAY, MAY 20, to TUESDAY, MAY 27, 1746.
NUMB. 30.

Conscia mens recti famæ mendacia ridet;
Sed nos in vitium credula turba sumus.

OVID, *Fasti*.[3]

editor of *Roxburghe Ballads*, ii. 540, '"Sing Old Rose and burn the bellows!" is seldom heard now as it had been in the days of our fathers, who could be temperate when they chose without ostentatiously anathematizing every one who "followeth not with us".' In his edition of Walton Sir Harris Nicholas annotates the reference by copying the song from a text 'inserted in Dr. Harrington's Collection from a publication temp. Charles I'; *Complete Angler* (London, 1836), i. 88. For a conjecture about the association of 'Old Rose' with 'burn the Bellows', see *Brewer's Dictionary of Phrase and Fable*, rev. by Ivor H. Evans (New York, 1970), p. 935. The King James Version translates Jeremiah 6: 29 as 'The bellows are burned, the lead is consumed of the fire.'

[1] The siting of this tory or 'country' letter in Gloucestershire must have been intended to reflect that county's predominantly tory complexion. In 1746 Thomas Chester and Norborne Berkeley, both tories, were its parliamentary representatives. Bristol (home of the tory 'Steadfast Society' [1737]), Cirencester (controlled by two tory families, each returning one member), Gloucester itself (a whig corporation but a tory majority), all had records of tory success. See *The House of Commons 1715–1754*, ed. Romney Sedgwick (London, 1970), i. 243–8.

[2] The name implies nostalgia for the good old days, the 'old England' of the buff coat affected by 17th-century English soldiering men. 'Oliver' is of course usefully alliterative, but its echoes of Cromwell and the 'Good Old Cause' of republican England are consistent with Fielding's strategy of associating those whose nostalgia was for the 'old Constitution' which existed before the 'whig' settlement of 1689 and those whose nostalgia went further back and incorporated an antagonism to all centralized power, including that of kings of whatever house. For an unsympathetic (and later) definition of the 'old Constitution', see *Proper Answer*, pp. 68–70.

[3] *Fasti*, iv. 311–12, where modern texts read *risit* for *ridet*: 'Conscious of innocence she laughed at fame's untruths; but we of the multitude are prone to think the worst' (Loeb).

The Boy in the Ship, is a Proverb well known to all who have been conversant with Maritime Affairs;[1] but may want some Explanation to many of my Inland Readers, who have perhaps never seen a Ship, unless in a Picture.—They are to know, therefore, that every Ship hath one Boy aboard at least, who, among many other good Uses, serves to bear the Faults of the whole Crew. If any Mischief is done, if any thing is lost, mislaid, or stolen, it was the Boy did it; and of consequence, if he passes a Day without Correction for the Fault of some of the Sailors, the Boy looks on himself as very singularly happy. Nay, I have been told, that this long Habit of laying all Blame on the Boy hath sometimes operated so strongly on their Minds, that, not contented with accusing him for their own Rogueries, they sometimes impute the Perverseness of the Weather to him, and the Boy is often cursed and cuffed on account of an adverse Gale; nay, is sometimes whipt in a Calm, in order to raise a Wind.

Many Writers have treated of a Commonwealth, under the Allegory of a Ship; and if we consider it in this Light, I think we may very properly regard a Minister as *the Boy in this Ship*.

I have somewhere seen a Story of a Muletteer, who, in the Administration of Cardinal *Mazarine*, was driving a stumbling Mule on the Road between *Orleans* and *Paris*.[2] This Mule was laden with some brittle

---

[1] Fielding's source for this 'Proverb' has not been identified. His subsequent elaboration of it suggests he considered himself to be 'conversant with Maritime Affairs'. Although his biographers have never remarked on such a conversancy, except perhaps with respect to *The Journal of a Voyage to Lisbon* (1755), Fielding may well have had a deeper interest in maritime affairs, generally, and in the role of young boys in it, particularly, than has been suspected. William Julius Mickle (1735–88), Scottish poet and translator of *The Lusiad*, wrote Boswell on 28 October 1786: 'We were dining at Mr. Hoole's, Henry Fielding happened to be mentioned. The Doctor inveighed against his moral character. I said he had done good. The Dr. said he never could find it out. I mentioned his instituting the marine society. The Dr. "The worst thing he ever did"'; *The Correspondence and Other Papers of James Boswell Relating to the Making of the 'Life of Johnson'*, ed. Marshall Waingrow (NY n.d.), p. 177. Mickle may well be confusing Henry with his half-brother John, whose role in founding the society is well attested to. Certainly chronology is against him, the society having been formally incorporated in 1756, two years after Henry Fielding's death. However, Johnson often 'inveighed' against HF's moral character and there is no record of his having such opinions of JF. HF may have been involved in preliminary efforts to set up such a society; cf. his connection with the Foundling Hospital.

[2] The source of this 'mazarinade' has not been identified. Cf. *Mémoires du Cardinal Retz, de Guy Joli* (Paris, 1828), i. 30: 'Ce nom [Mazarin] même tomba dans une telle horreur que le menu peuple s'en servait comme d'une espèce d'imprécation contre les choses déplaisantes; et il était assez ordinaire d'entendre les charretiers dans les rues, en frappant leurs chevaux, les traiter de *B*[ougres] *de Mazarins*.' Baker, item no. 166, lists a 1718 Amsterdam edition of the *Mémoires de Joli*, in two volumes, among Fielding's books. But perhaps Bayle may be allowed the last word (in translation): 'There was not one story which people did not believe in France, when it defamed either cardinal Richelieu, or cardinal Mazarin. . . . Would an Historian act a prudent part to pick up such stories? To be able to do it without just reproach, one must be co-temporary: for then it might be possible to make instructive inquiries: but at the end of three or four generations there is no possibility of finding out the grounds of uncertain and vulgar reports, which no author thought worth their while to adopt'; *The Dictionary Historical and Critical of Mr. Peter Bayle*, 2nd ed., iv (London, 1737), 511, Remark D, *s.n.* Paul II. Baker, item no. 472, lists the 1734 Paris edition of Bayle's *Dictionnaire historique et critique* among Fielding's books.

Ware, on which the Cardinal had a little before imposed a new Tax. Whenever the Beast stumbled (which frequently happened) the Muletteer, instead of blaming either his Mule, or himself, for trusting his Ware to so unsafe a Carrier, constantly vented his Wrath against the Prime Minister, and damned the Cardinal. At last down fell the Mule, and great was the Havock occasioned by his Fall. A Passenger coming by, as the Creature lay upon the Ground, and perceiving the Mischief which was done, began to utter some Expressions of Pity towards the poor Muletteer, who stood fretting and fuming at his Misfortune: But observing at the same time that the Road was extremely plain and good, could not help adding, "Sure this Mule must be very unsure-footed, or he could never have fallen in this Place." But the Muletteer, instead of abusing or defending his Beast, answered sullenly, *D—n the Cardinal*,[1] *I say, he hath ruined all those of our Business*.

If an absolute Government could produce this Muletteer, we are not to wonder, that in Free States, where Men have much Liberty to censure with Impunity, this Temper of blaming our Superiors for every Calamity we suffer, should reign in a much higher Degree. As no Nation, therefore, under Heaven, hath ever enjoyed a purer Freedom than this, so hath none, I believe, discovered more of this Inclination than the People of our Island.

That this Nation is at present involved in a very expensive, and hitherto unsuccessful War, is a Fact which can be doubted by no Man: But that this War should be laid at the Door of the present Ministry, would scarce be believed by any who did not hear these Censures, and could not derive them from that Temper I have above-mentioned: And that for this plain Reason, viz. *That it was begun in the Time of a former Ministry*,[2] *nay, even that Ministry was forced into it by the Clamours of the People*.[3]

[1] Mazarin (1602–61), Italian born protegé and successor of Richelieu's, was enormously unpopular because of his prosecution of the Thirty Years' War, the deteriorating financial conditions resulting from the war, and his own reputed financial rapacity. During the civil uprising known as the Fronde (c. 1648–53), 'la haine contre ce ministre', in Voltaire's words, 'semblait alors le devoir essentiel d'un Français'; *Le Siècle de Louis XIV*, ch. v. Mazarin's utility as a 'type' of political scapegoat lingered on, even in England, where during Walpole's administration, opposition journalists were fond of drawing parallels between the two ministers. See, for example, *Craftsman* no. 168 (20 September 1729).

[2] His subsequent emphasis on the coercive power of popular opinion indicates that Fielding refers here to the so-called War of Jenkins' Ear, declared against Spain in October 1739 during the generally pacific administration of Sir Robert Walpole (see the next note). England and France were not technically at war till March 1744, that is, during an administration nominally Pelhamite but in foreign affairs largely under the direction of Granville. It is perhaps worth noting here that in his Pelhamite apologetics of 1747 Fielding defined 'the present Administration' as coming into power after Granville's resignation of November 1744, at which time Pelham revamped his ministry into the broad bottom. Defined in this special way, the Pelham administration could be said to have 'found the Nation already engaged' in the war with France; see *Gentleman & Alderman*, p. 34.

[3] Cf. *Gentleman & Alderman*, p. 33: 'as to the War with *Spain*, this was most certainly undertaken at the

I could not help therefore being a little surprized at finding our present Ministers arraigned on this account, by two very honest Politicians, with whom I lately rode a short Journey in a Stage-Coach.[1]—We had not been long together before the Discourse turned on Politics, and one of these Gentlemen informed the Company, in less than a Mile, of many deep political Secrets, which I, who have spent some time in that Study, had never been able to discover in my most earnest Enquiries: As that *we were not at all concerned in the Affairs of the Continent: That the Ballance of Power in* Europe *was a mere Jest: That our Trade did not in the least depend on the restraining* French *Conquests within certain Bounds*, &c. He then proceeded to shew the many Mischiefs which had attended the present War, and after having, with much excellent Argument, charged it on the Ministry, he made some rhetorical Flourishes on Power and Places, and at last very logically concluded in the Words of my Friend Mr. *Oldcoat, That Ministers were all alike*.[2]

He was seconded by a very grave Personage, his Friend; but as this imitated what I have known done by some great Speakers in other Places, and did little more than repeat what the learned Gentleman, who spoke first, had said, I shall not trouble the Reader with another Repetition.

When we came to the Inn at which we were to dine, we had a very bad Dinner, bad Wine, and a very large Bill, as is the usual Custom.[3] The Wine my Landlord justified, by assuring us, that all the Gentlemen who called at his House, liked it extremely; as for the Dinner, he was sorry we did not like it; and for his Bill, he excused it, by *the Badness of the Times*.[4] To which, he inferred, it was owing, that one who furnished his Guests

earnest Desire of the *British* Merchants . . . It will not be said by any Man living, that this was either a War of Ambition, or enter'd into upon any Motives of ministerial Interest, or from any other Cause than a Regard to the Voice of the People, after long and repeated Efforts to avoid it by amicable Means.' Cf. also *Proper Answer*, pp. 73–4: 'The then Ministry was forced into this War, against their Will, they declined it to the very last . . . and were at last compelled to undertake it, by the united loud Voice of the People, raised by the Trumpets of the Opposition, which had long blown nothing but War into the Ears of the Nation.' As editor of the *Champion* from 1739 till sometime in 1741 Fielding himself had been one of the opposition trumpets. By 1746, however, his friends in that earlier, belligerent opposition—Chesterfield, Pitt, Lyttelton, Dodington—were all in place in the Pelham administration.

[1] French, p. 479, conjectures, perhaps unnecessarily, that Fielding may have met 'Politicians' like these on his recent travels to the Lenten assizes of the Western Circuit in March. For the notice of these and the itinerary, see *TP* no. 16 (11–18 February 1746), Locke, p. [147].

[2] See his letter in *TP* no. 29 (13–20 May 1746), above, p. 294, where he writes, 'I tell you all Ministers are alike, *and a Patriot is he who opposes the Ministry*.'

[3] In *Tom Jones*, VIII. vii. 429, Fielding describes a similar instance of cheapened quality and overcharging as conforming to the 'Maxims, which Publicans hold to be the grand Mysteries of their Trade'.

[4] Cf. *Craftsman* of 19 February 1737: '*Country Gentlemen* and *Farmers* are apt to complain of the *Badness of the Times*, and the *Want of Money*'; as reprinted in *GM*, vii (1737), 104.

with such excellent Entertainment, was not able in a few Years to get an Estate.

The very Mention of the Times silenced all Complaints in my Fellow-Travellers, and they again fell very eagerly to Politics, in which my Landlord, who was invited to sit down, bore his Share. The Discourse now rolled on the declining State of Trade; and it was impossible to miss one Observation, that none of the Speakers had the least Regard to any other Trade but his own, to which he constantly endeavoured to apply whatever was said. I soon therefore discovered, that one of my Fellow-Travellers was a Lace-man,[1] and the other a Distiller.

I own I was a little surprized, that three Persons, who seemed to have no public Consideration but for the Prosperity of their own Business, should be such Enemies to War, when all three owe great Part of their Livelihood to Soldiers.[2] However, as they were of that Species of Reasoners, with whom a Man, who hath any Regard for his Breath, would always cautiously avoid a Controversy, I never proposed any Doubt or Question; but chose rather, as often as I was applied to, to give my Assent with a Nod, or, at most, a very concise Approbation.

But this my Wonder was greatly lessened before my Arrival in Town; for now having swallowed two Bottles of very bad Wine, in drinking Revival to Trade, and many other good Healths, we again set out on our Journey. And soon after, being obliged to stop half an Hour at the Door of an Ale-house, while the Coachman and some of his Friends were drinking a Bowl of Punch, a Fellow came to the Coach-door with a Basket of Apples. Upon my asking him the Price of some Nonpareils,[3] he answered, *They were two for Six-pence*. I replied, I thought they were very dear. *Sir*, said he, *I wish I could afford them cheaper*, BUT APPLES ARE DEAR SINCE THE WAR.

This seemed to explain the whole Secret, and that the War is a Cant

---

[1] A manufacturer or dealer in lace.

[2] Lace was used as ornamental braid on many uniforms. The distiller sold a good deal of liquor to inns and public houses for eventual retail to soldiers, who had a reputation for hard drinking. In addition, the annual statute against mutiny and desertion, the so-called Mutiny Act, required the proprietor of inns and ale-houses to provide food and lodging for the military at a *per diem* of 4*d.* for foot-soldiers and 1*s.* for officers below the rank of captain. See Theodore Barlow, *The Justice of the Peace* (London, 1745), *s.v.* 'Soldiers'. This requirement was not generally appreciated by the publican class. See *Tom Jones*, VIII. ii. 408, where the landlady commiserates with Jones on his experience with Northerton: 'I think it is great Pity that such a pretty young Gentleman should undervalue himself so, as to go about with these Soldier Fellows. They call themselves Gentlemen, I warrant you; but, as my first Husband used to say, they should remember it is we that pay them. And to be sure it is very hard upon us to be obliged to pay them, and to keep 'em too, as we Publicans are.' Coxe, *Pelham*, i. 312, notes that to raise the additional supplies for 1746 the duties on spiritous liquors had been raised. The royal assent had been given on 19 March 1746; *Journals of Commons*, xxv. 96.

[3] A kind of apple (Johnson). Philip Miller, *The Gardener's Dictionary*, 2nd ed. (London, 1733), *s.v.* 'Apple Tree', lists them among the apples 'proper for a Desert', as distinguished from kitchen apples.

Phrase made use of by some People, with no other Intention than to pick their Neighbours Pockets: Nor could I help reflecting, with Concern, on so horrid a Degree of Disingenuity, as to endeavour to aggravate the Misfortunes of the Public beyond what in Truth and Reality they are. *2dly*, To attempt to impute the Cause of them to the Innocent, and, at the same time, to trie,[1] by all the Means of Craft and Subtilty,[2] to convert them to our own Use. Now every Man, who endeavours to make an immense Fortune out of the Distresses of his Country, is as much a greater Rogue, as he is a greater Man, than this *Three-penny Apple-Merchant*.

From TUESDAY, MAY 27, to TUESDAY, JUNE 3, 1746.

NUMB. 31.

> *Terruit Gentes grave te rediret*
> *Sæculum.——*

HORACE.[3]

To believe contrary to the Dictates of Reason, is certainly a very high Mark of Folly; but to carry such Faith into Act, especially in Matters which highly concern our Interest, seems to denote a downright Idiot. And this I apprehend is the true Moral intended by *Æsop* in his first Fable of *the Countryman and Snake*:[4] For what would Reason dictate to any Man, to expect from a venemous[5] Animal, but that he should bite him the Moment it was in his Power?

There seems, however, to be one Degree of Idiotism even higher than this; and that is, when Men do not only fly in the Face of Reason but Experience; when they place a Confidence in those whose noxious

---

[1] Thus copy-text, but emendation may be called for. *OED* finds no such form beyond the 17th century.

[2] Cunning, craftiness, guile (*OED*). In the 18th century a distinct variant, with many of the meanings of 'subtlety'.

[3] *Odes*, I. ii. 5–6, where the accepted text has always read *ne* for *te*: '[he] has filled with fear the people, lest there should come again the gruesome age' (Loeb). The use of *te* hopelessly corrupts the sense and must be either Fielding's error or the printer's. This leader, including Melfort's letter, is reprinted in *London Magazine*, xv (1746), 295–6.

[4] 'Fable IX' in Sir Roger L'Estrange, *Fables, of Aesop and other Eminent Mythologists*, 4th ed. (London, 1704), pp. 9–10. The countryman sees a half-frozen snake under a hedge, takes it up and warms it in his bosom. When the snake revives, it bites him. The Aesopian moral, in L'Estrange's words: 'There are some Men like Snakes; 'Tis Natural to them to be doing Mischief; and the Greater the Benefit on the One side; the More implacable the Malice on the other.'

[5] An acceptable spelling in the 18th century, it occurs in the 1704 edition of L'Estrange's version of the fable of the countryman and the snake. See preceding note.

Nature has been already tried, and put it in the Power of Persons who have injured and betrayed them already, to do them the same Offices a second Time.[1] As if the Countryman should, after having been bit by the Serpent, again have received and cherished it in his Bosom. This is indeed a kind of Wantonness in Credulity, and scarce deserves our Compassion. Nay, such Men may be said to participate of[2] the Guilt to which they become the Objects. They are in a manner *Felo's de se*,[3] and may more properly be said to impose on themselves, than to be imposed on by others.

And yet is not this last and greatest Degree of Folly the Portion of a *Protestant Jacobite*[4] at this Day? Their Ancestors, who opposed the Exclusion of *James* the Second, while Duke of *York*, because he was a Papist, tho' they sinned against all the Lights of Reason, had not yet experienced those Evils which wiser Men foresaw must be the inevitable Consequence of placing a Papist on the Throne. Senseless and absurd as it was, to expect that a Protestant Church should remain in Safety under a Popish Protector, they had not seen nor felt the Impossibility of it; and they might have pleaded solemn Promises and sacred Vows as some Excuse for their Credulity.[5] But their Sons and Grandsons are left without this Excuse. They err with their Eyes open, against not only the Light of Reason, which is called the Guide of Wisdom, but even against the Conviction of Experience, which hath been held a sufficient Defence for Folly itself.

But if all those Cruelties which he acted whilst on the Throne,[6] if that Invasion of our civil and religious Rights, which he had not an Opportunity of bringing to full Success and Maturity, have not been able to make his Name terrible to us; I congratulate my Country that they are now likely to see the whole Designs of his Party brought effectually to

[1] Alluding to the Bath–Granville administration of 10–12 February 1746. See 'General Introduction', above, p. xcvi, and index, *s.n.* 'Bath, William, Pulteney'.

[2] In the 18th century commonly construed *with* a person, *of* a thing. Cf. 'partake of'.

[3] 'Felons [with respect] to themselves', the legal term for suicides. For the term in a similar context of protestant jacobites, see *Tom Jones*, VIII. xiv. 477, where the 'Man of the Hill' is incredulous of such an anomaly.

[4] For this seeming 'anomaly', see *TP* no. 24 (8–15 April 1746), above, p. 261; also *JJ* no. 2 (12 December 1747), pp. 103–9, where in an essay revealing the four esoteric 'Mysteries' of jacobitism, Fielding concludes by joining these two words, 'which, when joined together, make the profoundest Mystery . . . a Protestant Jacobite'.

[5] French, pp. 483–4, compares *Serious Address*, above, p. 6: 'When in spite of that Bill he ascended the Throne, he fully justified the Caution of Parliament, and of those worthy Patriots, in their Design of excluding him . . . and this in direct Contradiction to the strongest and most solemn Promises of maintaining both our Religion and Liberties. . . .'

[6] French, pp. 484–5, compares *Serious Address*, above, p. 7: 'Besides his avowed Design of establishing Popery, besides all those Acts of arbitrary Power, enumerated in the Declaration of Rights . . . there are many Instances of wanton Cruelty and inveterate Revenge. . . .'

Light, and to have before their Eyes all those dreadful Consequences which would have attended this miserable Nation, had King *James* been restored to the Crown.

These will evidently appear from the Register and Series of the Negotiations of *John Drummond* Earl of *Melfort*, who was Secretary of State to King *James* the Second, and afterwards his Ambassador, when at *St. Germains*, to the Pope;[1] which Work will shortly be published.[2]

The whole will consist of authentic Memoirs, and Letters between the principal Persons who were intrusted with the Management of that Prince's Affairs at that Time. Of which the following Letter from the Earl of *Melfort* to Queen *Mary*, when her Husband was in *Ireland*,[3] and as it was then reported, had gained a Victory over King *William*,[4] is offered as a Specimen.

August 12, 1690.[5]

To the QUEEN.

May it please your Majesty,

All that Concern, Anxiety, Joy, or Fear, can bring, being on me almost at once, at least by near succeeding Fits, your Majesty cannot blame me if

---

[1] John Drummond (? 1649–1714), first earl and titular duke of Melfort, was a power in Scotland during the reign of Charles II, becoming secretary of state thereof in 1684. After Charles's death Melfort converted to catholicism, was created earl (1686), and fled England in 1688, becoming a prominent adviser at James's court at St Germains. In 1689 Melfort accompanied James to Ireland but was sent back to France because he proved obnoxious to both the French and Irish. His continued officiousness at St Germains resulted in his being sent to Rome (1689), according to White Kennet, 'not so much in Hopes of getting Money from the Pope, as to please the *Irish*, who had at that Time monopoliz'd the King's Favour; his Expectation from their Assistance being greater than from both the other Kingdoms'; *A Complete History of England*, iii (London, 1719), 601 *n.*, citing *Secret History of Europe*, Part xi, p. 244.

[2] The projected publication has never been identified; it may not have been brought out. Henry Ellis, *Original Letters, Illustrative of English History*, second series (London, 1827), iv. 186–7, notes that this letter of Melfort's (which he prints) and several others from the same source 'are copied from the Earl of Melfort's Register of what he wrote to the Court of St Germains during his negotiation with the Pope, from March 8th to Dec. 13th, 1690, preserved in three Volumes in folio among the Lansdowne Manuscripts in the [British] Museum. These Volumes were bought at Paris in 1744 of the then Countess of Melfort, who had married the Earl's grandson, by Mr. Barbutt Secretary of the Post-Office. They afterwards became the property of Philip Carteret Webb, Esq. at whose decease they were purchased by the Marquess of Lansdowne at that time Earl of Shelburne.' Ellis's authority in these matters is supported by the fact that when he printed Melfort's letter, he was keeper of manuscripts at the Museum. The original is BL MS Lansdowne 1163, vol. ii, p. 225. Ellis, op. cit., iv. 191–7, reprints.

[3] Where he had gone in March 1689, with French support, as the first step in his project of returning as king of Britain.

[4] At the Battle of the Boyne on 1 July 1690. In fact, James himself quit the field and although his forces retreated in good order and William failed to prosecute matters vigorously, the victory belonged clearly to the latter. For the rise of rumors to the contrary, see p. 302 *n.* 1.

[5] The date here is NS, and the place of writing is Rome. The *TP* prints only paragraphs 1, 6, 7, 8, 9, 10–11 (as one), and 12 of the original MS letter.

I long to be freed of them, by a full Confirmation of the Success in *Ireland*, and the Death of the Prince of *Orange*;[1] that the King is safe, and your Majesty once again happy in seeing him,[2] and having so near a Prospect of *Whitehall*.

Hoping this will be soon with your Majesty, I cannot hinder myself from saying, that the first Steps on *English* Ground are most dangerous, and that therefore great Care is to be had how they are made as to Treaty, if that be absolutely necessary, which I hope in God it shall not; but if it is, all the Rocks we have split upon must be minded, so as that in Time coming we may not be in Danger of the same Fate. These Rocks are obvious. Besides the Oaths, and Penal Laws, against Dissenters from the Church of *England*, there is the Standing Army of Foreigners, the Power of Money, the exorbitant Usurpations of Parliament, the Trial of High-Treason, or other Crimes against the Crown by Juries, the *Habeas Corpus* Act, and such like, which if not regulated more advantageously for the Crown, or quite abolished, I can see no Comfort the King can have of his Crown, or Safety the Subjects can have from their own Follies.

There is a great Consideration of forming the Party the King will choose to govern by, for by a Party a factious State must still be master'd, endeavouring to use all equally in it, being a certain Way to lose all; and that your Majesty may well remember was an Opinion

---

[1] On the day before the battle proper William was hit glancingly on the shoulder as he was surveying the field. According to Burnet, *History of My Own Time*, ii (London, 1734), 50, when William dismounted to have his wound attended to, 'a Deserter had gone over to the Enemy with the news, which was carried quickly into *France*, where it was taken for granted that he could not out-live such a Wound'. Cf. James Ralph, *History of England*, ii (London, 1746), 319 *n.*: 'It was about Midnight that the Court (of *France*) receiv'd the News of King *William*'s Death (on the Report of one of King *James*'s Lackeys) yet tho' it is not usual to make Bonfires for the Death of an Enemy before he is defeated in Battle, the Emissaries nevertheless immediately ran about the Streets, awaking up the People of the City, and crying out to them, *Rise and make Bonfires*! So that in less than an Hour, all *Paris* was in a Blaze'; citing the '*State of* Europe *for* August, 1690', p. 31. See also Kennet, *Complete History*, iii. 599. That rumors of death were soon conflated with rumors of victory is indicated by the second paragraph (not reprinted in the *TP*) of Melfort's letter to Queen Mary, in which he writes, 'as soon as the happy news of the usurper's defeat and death was brought hither, I demanded an audience [with the Pope]'. Later in the same letter Melfort says that other people had received letters 'which brought News of the total defeat in Ireland of the King's [James's] forces, and his flight, which had broken my heart if that of the death of Orange had not come before'; Ellis, *Original Letters*, iv. 192, 196–7. Melfort had written Queen Mary from Rome on 2 May 1690, praying for speedy notification of the 'News of the Rising' and asking that 'the M. C. King [Louis XIV] . . . send an Express with it hither, that we may make the greater impression with it'; *Arraignment . . . of Sir Rich. Grahme, Bart.* (London, 1691), p. 137; another text is in 'Somers Tracts' 2nd ed., x (London, 1813), 553–4. It is a sign of Melfort's estrangement from the centers of power that over a month later than this letter of August 12 he is still expressing uncertainty in these matters.

[2] After the Battle of the Boyne James left Ireland and made his way to France, reaching Brest on 20 July NS, and St Germains before the end of that month; James Macpherson, *Original Papers; Containing the Secret History of Great Britain*, 2nd ed. (London, 1776), p. 231.

I have had of a long Time, and might have done good then, as Experience shews now.

This Party ought to be Men of try'd Loyalty, for with our Countrymen there is no trusting to new Men, nor to Probability; so corrupt our Blood is grown by hereditary Rebellion against God and the King.——Of this Party, greater Care is yet to be had of forming the Court, both in regard to the King's, and to your Majesty's Servants, that the Persons composing it may be such, as dart back the Beams of Glory they receive, that is, do Honour to your Majesty from whom they receive it; that they be of the best Blood, and prudentest, honestest, and loyalest Principles, such as may make others impatient and ambitious to come into the Number, not such as we have seen in some Times past.

Those amongst them, who are in Authority over others of them, be Men of Order, and have Qualifications as well as Quality, to get Respect, and to force Obedience, that Things may look with that Regularity, which becomes the Service of so great a Monarch; and it were to be wish'd that the Way of serving were put into a more modern Dress. Above all Things Care must be had, that such as have been active in the King's Service, in his Absence, be well rewarded, and all Advantages taken to punish such as have been the Authors or Promoters of this Rebellion, and if the King be forced to pardon, let it be as few of the Rogues as he can, and with a watchful Eye over them, remembering that King *David* pardoned *Shimei* at his Return to *Jerusalem*, but took Care that he would sooner or later feel the Smart of his Wickedness the first Failing he made.[1]

Such as are excepted, no Pardon should ever be allowed, and amongst these should be as many of those Families, where Father and Son both are engaged, or such as have been hereditarily disloyal, for from such, there is no more Loyalty to be expected than Religion from the Devils,— it is not in their Nature, and Rebellion is like the Sin of Witchcraft: Neither can repent. One Thing has brought another, and when I begin to consider, all this is plainly impertinent to your Majesties, who understand your Affairs infinitely better than any other; but it's the Nature of true Concern, to be anxious for every Interest of the Persons it regards, and though I err, yet it is well meant, and I know your Majesty's Goodness will pardon me; and though on this Subject I have much more to add, yet respectfully I shall make my Fault no greater at this Time, and at this Distance.

---

[1] See 2 Samuel 16: 5–14, where Shimei, son of Gera, curses David on the latter's flight from Jerusalem during the usurpation of Absalom; also 2 Samuel 19: 16–23, where on David's return after Absalom's death Shimei confesses his sin and abases himself. David's political situation was so precarious that he did not dare put such a man to death, but on his own deathbed he advises Solomon to follow the law and execute judgment on Shimei; 1 Kings 2: 8–9, 36–8.

If this comes safe to your Majesty's Hands before any new Orders be sent me, it will be more than Time to send them, for as soon as the Confirmation of this new *Herod*, the Prince of *Orange* his Death shall come, all that is to be expected from this will be immediately done.

From TUESDAY, JUNE 3, to TUESDAY, JUNE 10, 1746.

NUMB. 32.

Pascitur in vivis Livor, post Fata quiescit.

OVID.[1]

The Observation is common, that it is much more difficult for a real Lover to convince his Mistress of the Sincerity of his Passion, than for a Fortune-hunter to succeed by Pretences to an Affection which is entirely counterfeited.[2]

If this Observation be just, as I believe it is, the chief Reason seems to be, that the former is less careful than the latter to watch the several Turns in the Lady's Temper and to apply and accommodate himself to them. The former rather considers her Interest than her Humour, and is more busied in discovering her Merit than in acquainting her with it. He is contented with esteeming and loving her without contributing every Minute to her Esteem and Love of herself, and endeavours rather to assure her how much she hath engaged his Affection, than how much she deserves it.

The latter acts the contrary Part. He knows the Power which Vanity hath over his Mistress, and makes a Friend of this. Nor is he so assiduous in defeating any other Rival as her Looking-glass, being well assured, if he can once outdo her Glass, in representing her more amiable to herself than that, his Business is done. She will love him, and then there will remain very little Difficulty to assure her of his Love.

Something like this happens to Men in acquiring all other Characters, as well as that of a Lover. The World is a Mistress as giddy, as fickle, as ill-discerning, and as vain as any fine Lady whatever, and generally bestows its Favours in the same Manner, not on true Merit, but on the Pretences to it. I might indeed run a general Parallel between them, and shew that Fortune, Title, Outside, and Impudence, are alike the Recommendations to their Favour, and that real Worth is commonly overlooked by both with equal Neglect and Scorn.

---

[1] *Amores*, I. xv. 39: 'It is the living that Envy feeds upon; after doom it stirs no more' (Loeb).

[2] Fielding makes use of a very similar 'Observation' in *Champion* of 4 March 1740, i. 329.

The Success must be consequently the same: For Men in their Choice of Friends do more consider the Satisfaction of their own Passions (and not rarely of Vanity itself) than any true and real Merit in the Person chosen. Hence a Flatterer requires no great Art to persuade us of possessing those Qualities, which being believed to exist in him, give a Sweetness and a Savour to all his Praise of ourselves; while we as certainly want both Eyes and Ears to that Merit which exerts not its Tongue in our Favour. To speak plainly, there are few good enough to love great Virtue, or to esteem great Parts, for their own Worth and Beauty. We rather ask ourselves, *Cui bono meo?*[1] and are little pleased with the Merit of another, which no way redounds to our own Use.

But we are sometimes more than insensible to true Merit. Envy intervenes, and I am afraid it is too common to hate another only because he deserves to be loved. The same may happen between Men, which is I believe common between Beaus and fine Ladies, who instead of liking each other's Beauty, consider only their own, and contract a mutual Hatred, for want of that reciprocal Admiration which each expects from the other.

As the World therefore exactly imitates the fine Lady in the Beginning of my Paper, so if we compare the Conduct of truly great and good Men, we shall find it correspond with that of the real Lover, while the Fortune-hunters of Women and of the World (if I may so call them) act both alike.

In the first Place, there is nothing so oppugnant to True Virtue, and true Understanding, as Ostentation. The innate Dignity which always attends these, will not stoop to mean and laborious Arts to inform others of what they conceive must be sufficiently apparent to them. Cunning, on the contrary, is eternally teaching the Counterfeits of all three a thousand little painful Tricks, to represent Falsehood as Truth, and to gain a Belief and Admiration by Imposition.

Again the former, tho' not ostentatious, are in their Nature open and free; they are conscious of their Truth and Worth, and are not afraid of being looked into. As they have nothing either to hide or affect, so they cannot apprehend a Discovery. On the other hand, Hypocrites and Counterfeits are always close and reserved, shunning Men and the Light, unless when they have an Opportunity of displaying themselves in false Colours, and ever full of Caution and Circumspection, lest they should betray themselves and be detected by others.

And as true Virtue and Understanding are open-hearted without Ostentation, so is their Dignity consistent with proper Humility. Men possessed of these are ever backward to arrogate much to themselves,

[1] Colloquially rendered, 'what's in it for me?'

nor are they more ready to exult in the Vices and Follies of the World, than a Lover would in the Imperfections of his Mistress. Rally them indeed they may; but it is with Concern, Gentleness, and a Desire of Reforming. This Rallery[1] differs as much from Slander and Invective, as the Rod of a tender Parent doth from that of an Executioner. Whereas the Pretenders to these Excellencies are always puffed up and elated with their sham Merit; are constantly affecting Superiority and exacting Applause, and as eager to despise and decry all others.

Lastly, Modesty is a sure Concomitant of the former, as Impudence never fails to attend the latter. A Cause which is almost adequate of itself to the End contended for.

This being the Case, how can the Event be otherwise than as it generally happens to true Merit, whether it applies to a Mistress or to the World; especially when Falsehood, its Rival, is always present to defame and run it down?

This Art of blasting good and great Characters with Lies, is the highest and deepest Policy of Knaves and Blockheads; Men of true Virtue and Understanding, who are without Power, are treated by such Persons, as the right Heir, when out of Possession, is by an Usurper. They know they can no longer keep them down in the World's Opinion, than while by Falsehood they prevent their Title to it from being enquired into.

It is indeed a melancholy Consideration, that by such Means as I have here mentioned, Men of indifferent Parts, and very corrupt Morals, have often enjoyed much Reputation, while some of the ablest and best of Men have been seen, during their Lives, in a disadvantageous Light.

Posterity, indeed, when all the abovementioned Causes cease, seldom fails doing Justice to the Memory of such as reach her. And poor as this Consolation may seem to some, yet such is the Love of Fame in great Minds, that it hath afforded them no small Comfort and Contentment under the unjust Persecution of their own Times.

But what Amends can be made to their Cotemporaries, who have, by these Means, been deprived of the Benefit of Great Parts, and of the Influence of Great Virtues?[2]

---

[1] An acceptable spelling, representing the older pronunciation. *OED* cites Fielding's *The Fathers: or, The Good-Natur'd Man* (London, 1778), I. i. 6: 'Brother, I admit rallery.' According to the 'Advertisement' [A1ᵛ], this 'lost sheep' was in fact 'written by the late Henry Fielding some years before his death'. Fielding died in 1754. Modern editors emend to 'raillery' despite the appearance, in the preceding sentence, of the verb 'rally', to which it seems clearly related.

[2] Locke, p. 253, notes 'a marked decline in the style' of this leader, and French, p. 491, thinks that the choice of theme is in part personal, deriving from the disappearance of advertisements (beginning with no. 26) and other indications of waning usefulness. For a different emphasis, see 'General Introduction', above, pp. civ–cv.

True Patriot, June 17. N.º 33.[1]

Substance of the AUTHOR'S FAREWEL to his READERS.

As the Rebellion is now brought to a happy Conclusion by the victorious Arms of his Royal Highness the Duke of *Cumberland*,[2] it is a proper Time for this Paper, which was entirely occasioned by that Rebellion, to cease with it.

The Intention with which the *Patriot* was undertaken, was to alarm my Fellow Subjects with the Dangers which that Rebellion threatned to their Religion and Liberties, indeed to every Thing valuable which they possessed.[3] These appeared to me to be immediately attacked by the Followers of that Standard which a Popish Pretender had openly set up in these Kingdoms; and who was at that Time attended with an Appearance of Success that struck the whole Nation with a general Panick.

It is not my Purpose here to claim to myself any extraordinary Merit from the Undertaking. To do all that in us lies, at such a Time, to defend ourselves and our Country, is perhaps no more than we are strictly obliged to. However, I hope I shall be allowed to have hereby discharged my Duty as an *Englishman*, and as a loyal Subject to his present Majesty.

And whoever hath taken the Pains to read these Writings, must likewise own, that I have done this with as little Bitterness and Invective against those very Parties whose mistaken Tenets had, I am afraid, too much encouraged this Undertaking, and had flattered the Invader with too great Hopes of final Success. I did my utmost to dissuade the well-meaning but rash Part of my Countrymen from general and violent

[1] No original copies of any number of the *TP* after no. 32 are known to exist. Copy-text for this the concluding number is taken from *The London Magazine: and Monthly Chronologer*, xv (June 1746), 298–9, which reprints it (dateline June 17) with the heading 'Substance of the Author's Farewel to his Readers'. French, p. 495, on the basis of the average length of a *TP* leader, estimates that the *London Magazine* reprints 'little more than two-thirds' of the original leader. However, the concluding numbers of the *JJ* (no. 49 [5 November 1748], pp. 424–6) and *CGJ* (no. 72 [25 November 1752], ii. 141–2), are both markedly shorter than is usual for those journals. Fielding may have had a motto for *TP* no. 33, but *London Magazine* does not print one.

[2] Although the YP was not taken in battle and did not in fact leave Scotland for France until 20 September 1746, the consensus at the time was that Cumberland's victory at Culloden (16 April 1746) marked the end of the rebellion. See *TP* no. 26 (22–9 April 1746), above, p. 276, the first leader composed after official news of the battle reached London; also 'Present History of Great Britain' in the same number, Locke, pp. [211–12]; and Walpole to Mann (16 May 1746), *Yale Walpole*, xix. 254. At the time Fielding wrote this concluding number, Cumberland, who did not return to London till 25 July 1746, was pursuing the pacification measures which were to earn him the title of 'Butcher'.

[3] But compare the curiously deliberate tone of the first two numbers, written somewhat prior to the 'general Panick' referred to in the next sentence. And for a more narrowly 'political' intention, see 'General Introduction', above, pp. lxix–lxxi, cv.

Attacks on whole Bodies of Men, even on the *Roman Catholicks* them-selves,[1] while they retained the Duty of their Allegiance, and preserved that Peace which the Law requires. I endeavoured likewise to obviate, as far as I was able, that Disinclination which was arising among too many against the whole *Scotish* Nation,[2] which I thought was at once unjust and dangerous to the common Cause.

Another Instance of the Lenity of this Paper is, that I have been totally silent with Regard to the Punishment of those Wretches, whose Lives are become forfeited to Justice upon this Occasion.[3] If ever there was a Time when Incentives to Acts of Severity would be seasonable, it is the present, when we have the mildest Administration, under the best natur'd Prince in the World.[4] But whoever knows me at all, must know that Cruelty is most foreign from my own Disposition; I have therefore left these unhappy Men to that Mercy, which I am sure they will find, as far as the Prudence of Policy, and the Insolence of their Abettors will allow it to be extended. This they may expect from that great and glorious Man, who is at the Head of our Law,[5] and whose Goodness of Heart is no less conspicuous than those great Parts, which, both in the

[1] See in particular 'Observations on the Present Rebellion' of *TP* no. 2 (12 November 1745), above, pp. 124–7, which somebody thought well enough of to advertise in the colophon of *TP* no. 3, where it is denominated 'an Apology for Roman Catholics'. In two cases the paper took news items about individual catholics and amplified them into statements about the loyal behavior of catholics in general; see 'Apocrypha' of *TP* no. 4 (26 November 1745), below, p. 355, and 'Apocrypha' of *TP* no. 6 (10 December 1745), below, p. 369, dealing with Edward Weld and the duke and duchess of Norfolk, respectively.

[2] See 'Observations on the Present Rebellion' of *TP* no. 1 (5 November 1745), above, pp. 113–15, an essay which is advertised in the colophons of *TP* no. 2 and no. 3 as 'an Apology for Scotland'. See also the strong disapproval of a 'general Imputation' of rebelliousness to the Scots, in 'Apocrypha' of *TP* no. 7 (17 December 1745), below, p. 380.

[3] By 17 June 1746 a number of the 'principal Rebels' were already in custody and hence subject to the provisions of the act (19 Geo. II, c. 9) regulating their trials for treason. Most notorious were the three Scottish peers (Balmerino, Cromarty, Kilmarnock), official notice of whose trials would be posted on 30 June 1746. They had been ordered to the Tower on 27 May, and there was considerable public interest in them well before the date of this leader. The public was also interested in the impending trial and likely execution of Francis Townley, David Morgan, and seven others of the Manchester 'regiment' which had risen in support of the YP. Walpole wrote Montagu on 24 June 1746: 'All the inns about town are crowded with rebel prisoners; and people are making parties of pleasure . . . to hear their trials'; *Yale Walpole*, ix. 34. See also Walpole to Mann (16 May 1746), *Yale Walpole*, xix. 254, and *DA* of 1 July 1746.

[4] For similar praise of the mildness of the crown and the ministry *after* the judicial proceedings against the captured rebels, see *Gentleman & Alderman* (1747), pp. 15–16.

[5] Philip Yorke (1690–1764), cr. (1733) baron Hardwicke, was lord chancellor 1737–56. In this capacity he assumed the temporary commission of lord high steward with the responsibility of presiding over the trials of the rebel peers before the Lords. As chancellor, Hardwicke was also responsible for seeing that the provisions of the act (19 Geo. II, c. 9) for regulating the trials were carried out in lesser cases as well. He is singled out for special praise in 'Present History of Great Britain', *TP* no. 16 (11–18 February 1746), below, p. 418. As a lawyer Fielding was also attentive to Hardwicke in *JJ* no. 8 (23 January 1748) and no. 15 (12 March 1748), pp. 137, 199–200; and *Tom Jones*, IV. vi. 172. In 1751 he would dedicate his *Enquiry into . . . the late Increase of Robbers* to Hardwicke.

Character of a Statesman and a Lawyer, are at once the Honour and the Protection of his Country.

A Temper like this preserved in a Writer, will, I believe, seldom recommend him greatly to the Party he espouses;[1] but it should always bespeak from[2] that which he opposes, such Treatment as becomes Men to give a fair and honest Adversary. Such I may certainly call myself, since I exerted Vehemence against the Enemy, only then when he was arrayed against us; for the Paper principally intended to inflame this Nation against the Rebels, was writ whilst they were at *Derby*,[3] and in that Day of Confusion, which God will, I hope, never suffer to have its Equal in this Kingdom.

Whatever therefore may be my Fate, as I have discharged my Duty to my King and Country, and have, at the same Time, preserved even a Decency to those who have (erroneously, I hope) embraced a Cause in Opposition to both, I shall now retire with the secret Satisfaction which attends right Actions, tho' they fail of any great Reward from the one,[4] and are prosecuted with Curses and Vengeance from the other.[5]

---

[1] Cf. the tone of unrequitedness in *TP* no. 32 (3–10 June 1746), above, p. 306, and *TP* no. 14 (28 January–4 February 1746), above, p. 211: 'They must know little of Courts and Courtiers, who can imagine themselves making way to court Favours, by spending their Breath, or even their Blood, in Defence of their Sovereign. Kings hear not of such Merit, nor do Ministers acknowledge it.'

[2] Used in not quite any of the senses given by the *OED*; here it seems to mean 'call forth', elicit, with a contractual implication close to 'stipulate'.

[3] Cf. *TP* no. 14 (28 January–4 February 1746), above, p. 210: 'nay the 5th Paper, which was designed to animate my Countrymen to the Defence of their Religion and Liberty, at the last Extremity, was actually writ on that memorable Day when the Rebels . . . were feared to be approaching this City by hasty Marches'. For the argument that this description fits better *TP* no. 6, see above, p. 210 *n*.

[4] For the probable significance of these disgruntled remarks, see 'General Introduction', above, p. cv. In *TP* no. 14 (28 January–4 February 1746), above, p. 209, Fielding alludes to Pelham's reputation for being indifferent to writers and to his 'Contempt for any Good or Harm which they can do to him'. *TP* no. 14 goes on to recommend itself to Pelham's 'Regard and serious Attention'.

[5] A largely rhetorical posture. Neither the newspapers nor the political pamphlets of 1745–6 pay any particular negative attention to Fielding's tenure on the *TP*, perhaps because during the rebellion the opposition was keeping a low public profile. For the very different treatment accorded his labors on the *JJ* (1747–8), see *JJ* no. 20 (16 April 1748), p. 235, and the 'General Introduction' to that volume, pp. lxxiv–lxxxii.

APPENDICES

Before using those appendices which are textual, the reader should consult the 'Textual Introduction', especially part 2, 'The Apparatus', pp. cx–cxii, where the conventions of annotation are described. In these textual appendices roman numerals (I, II) have been used to designate true *editions*: the two of the *Serious Address* and the only edition of the *Dialogue*. In the case of the *History*, where there was probably only a single impression, interrupted to correct a turned letter, letters of the alphabet (*a*, *b*, *c*) have been used to designate the three different *states* of that pamphlet.

Other designations are as follows: W stands for the present Wesleyan Edition; TP for the British Library file of the *True Patriot*.

APPENDIX I

List of Substantive Emendations

SERIOUS ADDRESS

3. 7 encourag'd] II; advised I
3. 13 it. ¶] II; it. It is a Cause, Gentlemen, in which our All is concerned; our Religion, our Liberties, our Properties, every Blessing which can make Life dear to ourselves, or our Posterity, are at Stake. A Cause in which it would be more eligible for us and our Children to fall, than to survive the Success of our Enemies. ¶ I
3. 21 Destruction? ¶] W; ~! ¶ II; ~! Nay, the very Roman Catholicks themselves must be blinded with Bigotry to desire the Change; for they are to purchase the Re-establishment of their Religion at the Expence of their Liberties, and will introduce SPANISH and FRENCH TYRANNY, together with a SPANISH INQUISITION. ¶ I
7. 14 *Vide . . . p. 583.] II; omit I
10. 3 expose] II; venture I
11. 7 Arms?] W; ~! I-II
14. 21 confined] II; ~, or rather hid, I
15. 23 Jansenists] I; Jansenist II
16. 8 neglect till] II; neglect it till I
17. 7 hath] W; has I-II
17. 22 says] I; say II
19. 18 this] I; his II
20. 5 after?] W; ~. I-II
20. 20 Order] II; other I
23. 17–18 against . . . Agreements;] II; omit I
23. 18 in France] II; at Paris I

23. 19–24 the first of which . . . unhappy] II; where so many Thousands of miserable I
23. 27 *Thuanus . . . Whitlock.] II; omit I
24. 7 in] II; even in I
24. 10 Liberties?] W; ~. I-II
25. 4 Protestants!] W; ~? I-II
25. 7 Sovereign!] W; ~? I-II
25. 10 hath] W; has I-II
27. 13 Kingdoms?] W; ~! I-II
27. 26 Atridæ] II; Astridæ I
28. 6 since] II; omit I
28. 18 herself?] W; ~. I-II
30. 7 Stake] I; Sake II
31. 5 Inhabitants?] W; ~. I-II
31. 6–7 (if the . . . Rage)] II; omit I
31. 10 Force?] W; ~. I-II

HISTORY

41. 11 was] W; were a–b
48. 24 nor the] W; nor the the a–b
53. 1 rebuked] b; rebnked a
67. 9 Haldane] W; Holdane a–b
68. 12 Basil Cochran] W; ~, ~ a–b
68. 14 Hardwick] W; Hadwick a–b
69. 1 Haldane] W; Holden a–b
70. 14 Lochiel's] W; Lochel's a–b
72. 18 Scheme] W; Seheme a–b

DIALOGUE

88. 7 Indignation?] W; ~. I
92. 18 and] W; and and I
95. 27 persecute] W; per-|persecute I

TRUE PATRIOT

108. 4 Reader] W; Readers TP
110. 1 Mr. F—g] W; Mr. Mr. F—g TP

110. 1 Mr. *T—n*] W; *T—n* TP
114. 17 execute?] W; ~. TP
117. 6 Action?] W; ~. TP
117. 23 them] W; him TP
135. 8 Your] W; Year TP
135. 25 Door!] W; ~? TP
137. 24 alive?] W; ~! TP
138. 5 *Rome?*] W; ~! TP
140. 30 vouchsafed] W; vouchafed TP
143. 20 where] W; were TP
157. 21 Wealth?] W; ~. TP
188. 2 demonstrates] W; demonstrate TP
188. 14 Rule will reach +] W; Rule | Gentleman's Court consisted mostly of Ladies; that | will reach+ TP
190. 20 Passion in] W; Passionins TP
199. 21 Officer] W; Officers TP
214. 12 married?] W; ~. TP

215. 24 Knees?] W; ~. TP
224. 24 Country?] W; ~. TP
225. 30 Labour?] W; ~. TP
242. 3 Esteem?] W; ~. TP
242. 35 whatever?] W; ~! TP
242. 36 Number?] W; ~! TP
244. 4 Satisfaction?] W; ~. TP
248. 10 then] W; then then TP
251. 25 make] W; made TP
252. 11 to] W; to to TP
254. 3 I] W; I | I TP
262. 17 their] W; there TP
264. 19 Head?] W; ~. TP
268. 1 *G-z-tte?*] W; G-z-tte. TP
268. 8 Courtiers?] W; ~. TP
269. 3 Publick?] W; ~. TP
274. 8 Preservation?] W; ~! TP
286. 23 Gentlemen?] W; ~. TP
292. 17 and] W; ahd TP
296. 17 this] W; that this TP

APPENDIX II

List of Accidentals Emendations

SERIOUS ADDRESS

3. 6 *popish*] II; *Popish* I
4. 8 established] II; establish'd I
4. 17–18 *Shall we return like a Dog to his Vomit?*] II; Shall we return like a Dog to his Vomit? I
4. 22 *that we have been under an Usurpation these fifty Years*] II; that we have been under an Usurpation these fifty Years I
5. 3 *High-Treason*] II; ~ₐ~ I
5. 7 Catholic] II; Catholick I
5. 15 occasion'd] II; occasioned I
5. 23 *Warranto's*] II; *warrantos* I
6. 3 *against Law*] II; against Law I
6. 3 *by Form of Law*] W; by Form of Law I; *by Form of Eaw* II
7. 10 Torture*;] II; ~ₐ; I
7. 11 cold] II; Cold I
8. 4 Factsₐ] II; ~, I
8. 13–14 which, however,] II; ~ₐ ~ₐ I
9. 2 compleated] II; completed I
9. 6 mock] II; Mock I
9. 9 want;] II; ~, I
9. 13 passed] II; pass'd I
9. 14 paralleled] II; parallel'd I
9. 14 *Scotland,*] II; ~ₐ I
9. 16 Roman] II; *Roman* I
10. 6–7 themselves,] II; ~ₐ I
10. 10 Demeanour] II; Demeanor I
10. 11 (for indeed . . . Instance;)] II; ₐ~ ~ . . . ~;ₐ I
10. 12 theatrical] II; Theatrical I
11. 1 who,] II; ~ₐ I
11. 2 Principles,] II; ~ₐ I
11. 7 Whatₐ] II; ~, I
11. 12 conquer'd] II; conquered I

11. 15 stain'd] II; stained I
11. 16 parallel'd] II; parallell'd I
11. 19 Property,] II; ~ₐ I
11. 19 Means] I; means II
12. 2 Tyranny,] II; ~ₐ I
12. 2 practis'd] II; practised I
12. 15 certain,] II; ~ₐ I
13. 10 accus'd] II; accused I
14. 4 but] W; *but* I-II
14. 13 *rarely*] II; rarely I
14. 13 *high Exigencies of State*] II; high Exigencies of State I
14. 13–14 *against dangerous and traiterous Persons only*] II; against dangerous and traiterous Persons only I
14. 26 So] I; so II
15. 3 Abbés] II; Abbées I
15. 11 *Gascon*] II; *Gascogne* I
15. 16 *Gascon*] II; *Gascogne* I
16. 17 Borough] II; Burrough I
16. 26–7 *they have almost lost the human Countenance*] II; they have almost lost the human Countenance I
17. 22 Instances (says he)] W; ~, ~ ~, I; ~, say he, II
18. 20 that I] I; That I II
18. 22 Question] II; question I
18. 28 Hereticks] I; Heretics II
18. 31 Sort] I; sort II
19. 7 *à*] II; *a* I
19. 8 Perusal] II; perusal I
19. 19 Inquisitor,] II; ~ₐ I
19. 22 Means] I; means II
20. 4 Personsₐ] II; ~, I
20. 7 accus'd] II; accused I
20. 11 Recourse] I; recourse II
20. 14 premis'd] II; premised I

20. 31 perform'd] II; performed I
20. 32 though] II; tho' I
20. 34 stript] II; stripp'd I
21. 3 perform'd] II; performed I
21. 14 Torture,] II; ~∧ I
21. 15 Cruelty,] II; ~∧ I
21. 17 wooden] II; Wooden I
21. 18 wooden] II; Wooden I
21. 19 Length] II; length I
21. 20 plac'd;] II; placed, I
21. 28 Water,] II; ~∧ I
21. 33 Agonies,] II; ~∧ I
22. 1 tortur'd] II; tortured I
22. 7 revok'd] II; revoked I
22. 15 Burning] II; burning I
22. 21 Heretics:] II; Hereticks. I
22. 22 Heretics] II; Hereticks I
22. 22 Burning] II; burning I
22. 25 *Hereticks*] I; *Heretics* II
22. 25 *Heretick*] I; *Heretic* II
22. 30 Hereticks] I; Heretics II
22. 32 Hereticks] I; Heretics II
22. 32 who,] I; ~∧ II
23. 17 Manner,] II; ~; I
23. 26 *only**.*] II; ~∧. I
24. 1 Heretics] II; Hereticks I
24. 7 Catholics] II; Catholicks I
24. 14 from] II; From I
24. 20 Catholic] II; Catholick I
25. 4 thro'] II; through I
25. 11 popish] II; Popish I
26. 5 popish] II; Popish I
27. 30 *Britain*] I; *Britan* II
28. 13 destroyed] II; destroy'd I
29. 16 profess'd] II; profest I
30. 3 Interests:] II; ~; I
30. 4 Abbey] II; Abby I
30. 17 King] II; ~, I
31. 7 threatned∧] II; ~, I
31. 12 and,] II; ~∧ I
31. 21 Life,] II; ~∧ I

HISTORY

38. 18 *Heretics*] W; *Hereticks a–b*
39. 3 *Nosters*] W; *nosters a–b*
39. 3 *Mary's*] W; *Marys a–b*
39. 22 Arms,] W; ~∧ *a–b*
40. 12 Time] W; time *a–b*
41. 2 Lieutenant-General] W; ~∧~ *a–b*
43. 11 Rendezvous] W; rendezvous *a–b*
43. 13 22d,] W; ~∧ *a–b*
43. 15 *Pater Nosters*] W; ~–~ *a–b*
44. 11 Battalion] W; Battallion *a–b*
45. 2 Stirling] W; Sterling *a–b*
45. 14 Time] W; time *a–b*
46. 7 Catholics] W; Catholicks *a–b*
46. 8 Number] W; number *a–b*
53. 4 Time] W; time *a–b*
53. 4 9th,] W; ~. *a–b*
53. 15 People] W; people *a–b*
55. 17 Time] W; time *a–b*
59. 11 Means] W; means *a–b*
64. 6 Time] W; time *a–b*
65. 7 *Gardiner*] W; *Gardner a–b*
65. 12 *Loudon*] W; *Loudoun a–b*
66. 5 *Gardiner*] W; *Gardner a–b*
66. 12 *Gardiner's*] W; *Gardner's a–b*
70. 1 *Gardiner's*] W; *Gardner's a–b*
73. 10 concerned;] W; —, *a–b*

DIALOGUE

79. 6 *aside*∧] W; ~. I
79. 18 Common] W; common I
79. 26 DEVIL∧ [*eagerly*].] W; ~, (*eagerly*). I
81. 18 PRETENDER∧] W; ~, I
82. 17 DEVIL∧ [*aside*].] W; ~, (*aside*). I
83. 24 Part] W; part I
85. 17 [*speaking...Devil*]] W; (*speaking ...Devil*) I
86. 22 DEVIL∧ [aside].] W; ~, (*aside*). I
88. 8 DEVIL∧ [*pulling ... out.*]] W; ~, (*pulling ... out.*) I

89. 13 DEVIL∧ [*half . . . Pretender*.]] W;
~, (*half . . . Pretender*.)
89. 18 Throats;] W; ~, 1
90. 1 DEVIL∧ [*stretching . . . Foot*.]] W;
~, (*stretching . . . Foot*.) 1
90. 8 [*aside*]] W; (*aside*) 1
94. 22 Earnest] W; earnest 1
97. 25 Daughter;] W; ~, 1
98. 1 Profligacy] W; Proffligacy 1
98. 18 *Catholics*] W; *Catholicks* 1
100. 7 Reality] W; reality 1
100. 13 DEVIL∧ [*with a Sneer*].] W; ~,
(*with a Sneer*). 1
101. 15 —.] W; —∧ 1

TRUE PATRIOT

103. 8 Matters] W; matters TP
103. 11 Times] W; times TP
103. 14 Manner] W; manner TP
105. 11 Molière] W; Moliere TP
106. 7 *Body*] W; *body* TP
107. 17 Necessity] W; necessity TP
108. 3 Reason] W; reason TP
108. 5 Time] W; time TP
108. 18 Reader's] W; Readers TP
112. 15 Reason] W; reason TP
112. 20 Difficulty] W; difficulty TP
112. 26 Words] W; words TP
113. 10 Measure] W; measure TP
115. 13 Devastation] W; devastation
TP
116. 4 Misfortune] W; misfortune TP
116. 25 Mention] W; mention TP
116. 25 Time] W; time TP
119. 19 Œconomy] W; Oeconomy TP
121. 30 Hazard] W; hazard TP
122. 1 Part] W; part TP
122. 31 Hazard] W; hazard TP
124. 3 Share] W; share TP
124. 4 Power] W; power TP
127. 3 excepted)?] W; ~?) TP
128. 19 Barbarity] W; barbarity TP
128. 27 *Newgate*] W; Newgate TP
129. 3 Manner] W; manner TP

130. 24 Treason] W; Trreason TP
132. 5–6 Fellow-Creatures] W; ~∧~
TP
133. 12 Sake] W; sake TP
135. 17 Reality] W; reality TP
135. 32 Reality] W; reality TP
137. 16 Good.] W; ~∧ TP (*pointing
unclear*)
137. 17 Free-Thinkers] W; ~∧~ TP
139. 23 Recourse] W; recourse TP
141. 23 Time] W; time TP
148. 7 Manner] W; manner TP
149. 22 what] W; What TP
154. 11 Degree] W; degree TP
155. 2 Great] W; great TP
156. 4 Manner] W; manner TP
156. 5 Manner] W; manner TP
156. 8 Manner] W; manner TP
156. 10 Time] W; time TP
157. 16 Kind] W; kind TP
158. 14 Degree] W; degree TP
159. 11 Time] W; time TP
160. 1 Time] W; time TP
160. 4 Thing] W; thing TP
160. 5 Manner] W; manner TP
160. 13 *Metamorphoses*] W; Metamorphoses TP
161. 26 another."] W; ~.") TP
163. 23 all.] W; ~∧ TP (*pointing unclear*)
163. 24 Room] W; room TP
169. 17 Arrival] W; Arrrival TP
170. 28 For] W; for TP
175. 14 Privy Seal] W; ~-~ TP (*hyphen
unclear*)
177. 6 Lords] W; Lord's TP
181. 5 All] W; all TP
182. 32 Plan of a National Militia] W;
Plan of a National Militia TP
183. 21 it] W; It TP
184. 16 Thing] W; thing TP
184. 19 *Thing*] W; *thing* TP
184. 21 Thing] W; thing TP
185. 3 Things] W; things TP
186. 6 afterwards] W; aftewards TP

188. 23 Moment] W; Mement TP
189. 35 Falshood] W; Fashood TP
192. 14 *Cape*] W; Cape TP
194. 23 Private] W; private TP
197. 14 these:] W; ~_∧ TP (*pointing unclear*)
197. 17 *à*] W; *a* TP
197. 29 Constitution] W; Con-|tution TP
200. 1 Circumstances] W; circumstances TP
200. 7 View] W; view TP
201. 7 Thing] W; thing TP
202. 3 occurred] W; occured TP
202. 14 Stripling] W; Strippling TP
206. 15 πολιτειας.] W; ~_∧ TP
222. 3 Pater-Noster] W; ~_∧~ TP
223. 14 2.] W; 2_∧ TP
223. 24 Bloodsuckers] W;
                          Blood uckers TP
229. 20 Pater-Noster] W; ~_∧~ TP
231. 13 Town (says he)] W; ~, ~ ~, TP
232. 2 *the*] W; the TP
232. 5 *the Town*] W; the *Town* TP
232. 17 *the Town*] W; the *Town* TP
233. 4 *the Town*] W; the Town TP
233. 26 *the Town*] W; the Town TP
237. 19 (he said)] W; _∧~ ~_∧ TP
237. 20–1 (continued he)] W; , ~ ~, TP

239. 2 Circular,] W; ~_∧ TP
239. 12 Thing] W; thing TP
245. 5 *a*] W; *à* TP
251. 11 Form] W; form TP
251. 22 *Spirits*] W; Spirits TP
251. 25 *Spirits*] W; Spirits TP
252. 30 Distances] W; distances TP
253. 5–6 Good-Sense] W; ~_∧~ TP
253. 12 Good-Sense] W; ~_∧~ TP
254. 11 promote] W; prom te TP
255. 27 Levée] W; Levee TP
257. 20 Surgeon's] W; Surgeons TP
257. 30 somewhat] W; some what TP
258. 5–6 last-mentioned] W; ~_∧~ TP
258. 16 *Metamorphosis*] W; Metamorphosis TP
264. 5 Favour] W; favour TP
275. 18 itself_∧] W; ~; TP
276. 6 *Republicans*] W; Republicans TP
283. 5 Fortune)] W; ~,) TP
283. 14 *Cumberland*] W; Cumberland TP
287. 5 Door is,] W; ~, is_∧ TP
287. 26 of *Men of Fashion*] W; *of Men* of Fashion TP
288. 22 *Opera*:] W; ~; TP
293. 7 *H-n—r-ns*] W; *H-n_∧r-ns* TP
294. 13 OLDCOAT.] W; ~_∧ TP (*pointing unclear*)
305. 16 other's] W; others TP

APPENDIX III

Word-Division

1. *End-of-the-Line Hyphenation in the Wesleyan Edition*

[NOTE. No hyphenation of a possible compound at the end of the line in the Wesleyan text is present in the copy-text except for the following readings, which are hyphenated within the line in the copy-text. Hyphenated compounds in which both elements are capitalized are excluded.]

SERIOUS ADDRESS

20. 16–17 under-ground

HISTORY

[*none*]

DIALOGUE

[*none*]

TRUE PATRIOT

112. 14–15 above-mentioned
116. 5–6 Free-speaker
123. 30–1 with-hold
142. 19–20 ill-designing
240. 21–2 Distinction-sake
266. 18–19 self-centred
305. 21–2 Fortune-hunters
307. 24–5 well-meaning

2. *End-of-the-Line Hyphenation in the Copy-Text*

[NOTE. The following compounds, or possible compounds, are hyphenated at the end of the line in the copy-text. The form in which they have been transcribed in the Wesleyan text, listed below, represents the general practice of the copy-text in so far as that may be ascertained by other appearances or by parallels.]

SERIOUS ADDRESS

3. 13 *dishearten*
9. 17 Nonjuror
11. 21 Forefathers
26. 10 Highwayman

HISTORY

55. 4 Day-break
58. 10 whatever
59. 24 somewhat

DIALOGUE

87. 15 something
90. 5 sometimes

TRUE PATRIOT

112. 13 Bookseller
112. 24 Threepenny-worth
137. 12 likewise
152. 23 whatsoever (*i.e.*, what-|soever)
167. 16 anti-musical
178. 22 Godfather
190. 12 hereafter
198. 21 whatsoever
200. 12 unbiassed
200. 29 whenever
203. 6 sometimes
209. 15 Coffee-houses
212. 8 misbecome

214. 32 Coach-windows
218. 20 foretold
230. 6 self-sufficient
233. 16 Cat-call
234. 10 abovementioned
237. 2 somewhat
239. 27 something
241. 15 Halfpenny
242. 12 Hangman
243. 19 Schoolmaster
244. 11 abovementioned
246. 10 overcome
257. 3 somewhat
258. 15 Coach-maker

259. 21 extraordinary
259. 24 Mankind
260. 4 sometimes
262. 17 Mankind
266. 34 Ploughman
282. 8 warlike
287. 4 sometimes
292. 8 something
298. 25 Nonpareils
299. 18 downright
305. 38 open-hearted
306. 12 otherwise
306. 18 Understanding
307. 23 Undertaking

3. *Special Cases*

[NOTE. The following compounds, or possible compounds, are hyphenated at the end of the line in the copy-text and in the Wesleyan text.]

SERIOUS ADDRESS

14. 28–15. 1 FORTY-|EIGHT (i.e. FORTY-EIGHT)

DIALOGUE

[*none*]

TRUE PATRIOT

[*none*]

HISTORY

56. 3–4 Van-|guard (i.e. Van-guard)

APPENDIX IV

Bibliographical Descriptions

A SERIOUS ADDRESS

(I) THE FIRST EDITION (*c.* 3 October 1745)

Title-page: A facsimile of the title-page is found on page [cxiii].

Collation: 8°: *A1 [= G4?]* B–F⁴ G³; $2 signed; 24 leaves, pp. *i–ii* 1–45 *46*

Press Figures: (sig.-page-fig.) B-7-1, E-26-2, F-38-1, G-42-2

Contents: A1: title (verso blank); B1: HT '[*double rule*] A SERIOUS | ADDRESS | TO THE | PEOPLE of *GREAT BRITAIN*'. with text beginning 'GENTLEMEN, | T⁴HE . . .', ending on G3; below: '*FINIS*'. G3ᵛ blank

Notes: (1) Copies observed: British Library (1093. e. 7), Bodley (G. Pamphlets 1575), Bodley (G. Pamphlets 873), National Library of Scotland (Rosebery I. 5. 229), Manchester Central Library (B.R. 942.072 C. 14), Yale (Fielding Collection 745s), Harvard (*EC7. F460. 745s), New York Public Library (CP p.v. 6 [no. 4]).

(2) Rupert C. Jarvis, 'Fielding and the "Forty-Five"', *N&Q*, ccii (1957), 23*n.*, postulates an ideal copy with half-title and a blank leaf after G3, thus giving *A²* B–G⁴. However, the present editor has seen no copy with either of these features. Jarvis considers that the position of the watermark tells against the hypothesis that the title-page may be conjugate with G1 (see also *Collected Papers*, ii. 187–8).

(II) THE SECOND EDITION (*c.* 21 October 1745)

Title-page: A facsimile of the title-page is found on page [1].

Collation: 8°: A–F⁴ G²; $2 (− A1, G2) signed; 26 leaves, pp. *i–ii* 3–51 *52*

Press Figures: (sig.-page-fig.) B-10-1, C-18-2, D-31-1, E-39-2, F-46-2, G-50-1

Contents: A1: title (verso blank); A2: HT '[*double rule*] A SERIOUS ADDRESS | TO THE PEOPLE OF | *GREAT BRITAIN*'. with text beginning 'GENTLEMEN, | T⁴HE . . .', ending on E4ᵛ; below *cw* 'A'; F1: HT '*A* CALM ADDRESS *to all Parties in* | *Religion, whether* Protestant *or* Catholic, | *on the Score of the* Present REBELLION; | *being a brief and dispassionate Enquiry,* | *whether the Reign of the* Pretender *would* | *be advantageous to the Civil Interest and* | *Commerce of* Great Britain, supposing *that* | *he was to succeed in his present Attempts,* | *and* allowing *that he afterwards would con|duct himself according to the Principles of* | HONOUR *and* HONESTY'. and text (cap. 2) ending on G2ʳ with '*FINIS*'; G2ᵛ blank

Notes: (1) Copies observed: British Library (8132. c. 24), Rylands (R67094), Yale (Fielding Collection 745sb).

(2) This distinct state is a true edition, substantially reset, with numerous and, in some cases, extensive variants from both the substantives and the accidentals of the first edition. It is evidently the '2ᵈ Edit.' for which Strahan billed Andrew Millar. Strahan's ledgers record a printing of 1,000 copies on 3¼ sheets of paper and then a charge to Millar 'For overrunning a Sheet of Dᵒ for the 1st Impression, Nᵒ 500', as well as 'For half a Ream of Paper for Dᵒ' (BL Add. MS 48800, f. 51ᵛ [38ᵛ]). The significance of the two last charges is not entirely certain, but the charge for 3¼ sheets—the first-edition copies required only 3 sheets— may result from the association of Fielding's title with *A Calm Address*, a penny pamphlet which was published both by itself and with at least one other title. *A Calm Address* is printed on pp. 41–51 of the second edition. Strahan's ledgers record the month and year, but not the day, of his jobs. The entry for the '2ᵈ Edit.' follows that pertaining to the *Dialogue*, which was first heavily advertised *c.* 15 October 1745, and this fact strongly implies a later publication date. *A Calm Address* was itself first advertised as a separate publication, in the *London Evening Post* of 15 October. It seems likely that any association with another title would postdate separate publication, and *A Calm Address* is advertised in a 'New Edition', having added to it 'The Drapier's Letter to the Good People of Ireland', in *General Evening Post* of 19–21 October. The proximate date offered here (*c.* 21 October) for the second edition of *A Serious Address* takes into account the preceding facts but is also predicated upon the resumption of continuous advertising in the *General Advertiser* of 21 October after a hiatus of twelve days.

(3) It has been hypothesized that Strahan's charges for 'overrunning' a sheet for 'the 1st Impression' are the result of the two large and proximate editorial deletions made by the second edition of material present in the first. The hypothesis requires that Strahan meant by 'the 1st Impression' the first time the forme was impressed on the sheet in question, that is, on the recto. It further assumes that the editorial deletions came to the printing shop after 250 sheets had already been worked off on one side, that is, before perfecting. In half-sheet imposition these sheets could not now be perfected since the type had now to be changed. So they were set aside as waste, the gathering was printed with the resetting of type, and Millar was billed accordingly for editorial corrections at press which required not only resetting but also half a ream of paper to replace the wasted sheets. See Peter Harold Hemingson, 'Fielding and the '45: Henry Fielding's Anti-Jacobite Pamphlets' (unpublished dissertation: Columbia University, 1973), pp. 90–3.

(4) There is also a 'Third Edition Corrected with Additions'. It appeared over what purported to be Cooper's imprint at a price of 'Sixpence'. The date of first publication is not known. Strahan's ledgers record no third edition, and the physical features and styling of this pamphlet do not resemble those of Strahan's work for Cooper at this time. Cooper is hardly likely to have gone to another printer with a title that had already appeared in at least two earlier formats and at double the price. Nor is it likely that Millar, who undoubtedly

functioned as Fielding's publisher of first instance, would have countenanced such practices. Most telling of all, perhaps, the so-called 'Third Edition' introduces no 'Additions' of any substance, and its way with accidentals seems careless, not corrective. In the opinion of the present editor it is a piracy and without textual authority. Hemingson, p. 96, notes an advertisement for the 'Third Edition' in the *Edinburgh Evening Courant* of 8 November 1745, announcing publication 'on Monday next' (11 November), and, on the basis of a comparison of the type used in that paper and in the 'Third Edition', suggests the latter may have been printed by the printers of the paper, Robert Fleming and Alexander Kincaid. Copies observed: Bodley (Vet. A4. e. 2555), Aberdeen (MacBean Collection Pamphlet), National Library of Scotland (2 copies: Blaikie 677, Rosebery 1. 5. 253 [2]), New York Public Library (CK p.v. 304), Yale (Fielding Collection 745 sc).

(5) There is also a London piracy of 26 pages, apparently based on the authentic first edition and hence prior to the spurious 'Third Edition' described above. *Collation*: 8°: A² B–C⁴ D¹; $2 signed (−A1); 13 leaves, pp. *i–ii 3* 4–26. There are no press figures, and no price is given on the title page, which is here reproduced on page cxiv. Copies observed: Yale (Fielding Collection 745 sa), New York Public Library (CK p.v. 304 [no. 9]). See also 'General Introduction', above, pp. xxxviii–xxxix.

THE HISTORY

(1) THE FIRST EDITION (*c.* 7 October 1745)

State *a*

Title-page: A facsimile of the title-page is found on p. [34].

Collation: 8°: *A*² B–G⁴; $2 signed; 26 leaves, pp. *i–iv* 1–47 *48*

Press Figures: (sig.-page-fig.) B-6-1, C-10-1, D-21-1, E-26-1, F-40-2, G-45-1

Contents: *A*1: half-title '[line of type-orn.] | THE | HISTORY | OF THE | PRESENT REBELLION | IN | *SCOTLAND* | [line of type-orn.] | ⟨Price One Shilling.⟩'; A1ᵛ blank; A2: title (verso blank); B1: HT '[double ruled line] | THE | HISTORY | OF THE | PRESENT REBELLION | IN | *SCOTLAND*.' and text (cap. 4) ending on G4ʳ with 'FINIS.'; below: printer's orn; G4ᵛ: blank

Notes: (1) Copy observed: Yale (Fielding Collection 745h).

(2) This is the only copy the editor has observed with an uncorrected turned letter (rebnked) on line 3 of D4ᵛ and with the press figure D-21-1 for the more common D-21-2. All observed copies of Cooper's London imprint exhibit the same typographical eccentricities and were printed from the same type setting. Strahan records only one impression of the *History*. These facts strongly suggest that the Yale copy, with its failure to correct and with its one differing press figure, came from an earlier stage of what was a single impression than the other known copies.

State b

As in state <i>a</i> except: the press figure on D2ʳ is '2' (giving D-21-2) and the turned letter on line 3 of D4ᵛ has been corrected.

Note: Copies observed: Yale (College Pamphlets v. 1035), National Library of Scotland (Blaikie 348²), Rylands (18361. 3), British Library (601. e. 21). Aberdeen (McP. J2¹) and British Library (111. d. 1) lack A1. National Library of Scotland (1927. 14) lacks G4 and positions the title as A1 and the half-title as A2.

State c

As in state <i>b</i> except: lacks a press figure on E1ᵛ

Notes: (1) Copies observed: Bodley (Don. e. 323) and Aberdeen (McP. J2²).

(2) Inasmuch as the press figure on E1ᵛ prints very light in the Rylands copy (18361. 3), its apparent absence from the Bodley and Aberdeen copies under consideration here is possibly the product of type failure and not a sign of an interrupted impression which might constitute a separate state.

There were unauthoritative reprintings of the *History* in Dublin and Belfast.

Copies observed: Dublin: British Library (8142. b. 36), Bodley (Vet. A4 e. 962); Belfast: Aberdeen (McP. J2³). The *History* was also reprinted in New England. There are copies of Boston 'editions' in Harvard (*EC7. F460. 745hc. [A]), the Boston Athenaeum, and the Bowdoin College Library. See A. LeRoy Greason, Jr., 'Fielding's *The History of the Present Rebellion in Scotland*', *PQ*, xxxvii (1958), 121–3, and Hemingson, pp. 217–20.

DIALOGUE

(I) THE FIRST EDITION (*c.* 15 October 1745)

Title-page: A facsimile of the title-page is found on p. [76].

Collation: 8°: *A*² B–F⁴; $2 signed; 22 leaves, pp. *i–iv* 5–44

Press Figures: (sig.-page-fig.) B-6-2, C-19-1, D-27-1, E-34-1, F-43-1

Contents: *A*1: half-title: '[line of type orn.] A | DIALOGUE | BETWEEN | The DEVIL, the POPE, | AND THE | PRETENDER. | [line of type-orn.] | [Price One Shilling.]'; *A*1ᵛ: blank; *A*2: title (verso blank); B1: HT '[double ruled line] | A | DIALOGUE | BETWEEN | The DEVIL, the POPE | AND THE | PRETENDER.' with text 'DEVIL. Y⁴OUR . . .', ending on F4ᵛ with '*FINIS*'.

Notes: (1) Copies observed: British Library (8132. aa. 27), National Library of Scotland (Blaikie 526), Rylands (R66593), Harvard (*EC7. F460. 747da), Yale (Fielding Collection 745d¹). British Library (111. c. 66) and Yale (Fielding Collection 745d²) lack *A*1.

(2) The Strahan ledgers record only one printing job (500 copies) in connec-

tion with the *Dialogue*. All copies observed by the editor exhibit the same typographical features, and all have the same press figures. It may therefore be concluded that the first edition was the product of a single impression.

THE TRUE PATRIOT

Collation: (2°-form) 4°: A^2; 2 leaves, unnumbered

Contents: *A*1: title: 'Numb. 1. [*flush right*] | THE TRUE PATRIOT: | AND | The History of Our Own Times. | (To be Continued Every TUESDAY.) | [*rule*] | TUESDAY, November 5, 1745. | [*rule*] | ILLE EGO, *qui qondam*——'; and text: 'F⁹[*fact.*]ASHION . . .', in three columns with '[Price THREE-PENCE.]' centred below middle column; *A*1ᵛ: text in three columns; *A*2: text in three columns; *A*2ᵛ: text and advertisements, with rule below and colophon: '*LONDON:* Printed for M. COOPER, at the *Globe* in *Pater-Noster-Row*; where Advertisements and Letters to | [centred] the AUTHOR are taken in'.

Notes: (1) From the horizontal position of the chain lines and the size of the leaf it can be inferred that *The True Patriot* was printed on a double sheet of paper which was cut in half before printing, thereby creating a (2°-form) 4°.

(2) The first line of *A*1 ('Numb. 1.') varies with each issue, of which 32 of the original 33 are known to survive in at least one copy.

(3) Line 6 of *A*1, the dateline, likewise varies with each issue. Beginning with issue no. 13 the dateline assumes a new format: 'From TUESDAY, JANUARY 21, to TUESDAY, JANUARY 28, 1746'. This format is maintained through the last known original issue (no. 32).

(4) No. 7 (17 December 1745) and no. 22 (25 March–1 April 1746) omit the Latin motto customarily positioned on line 8 of *A*1.

(5) The colophon on *A*2ᵛ varies considerably. No. 2 adds: 'Where may be had, N⁰ 1. containing an *Introductory Essay*, an *Apology for Scotland*, | a *New Loyal Song*, the *History of Europe, Great Britain, &c.*' No. 3 retains the additions of no. 2 and adds to them: 'And N⁰ 11. containing *An Essay on Patriotism, an Apology for Roman Catholics, &c.*' Nos. 4–18 remove the additions found in nos. 2 and 3, and add instead: 'Where may be had the former Numbers'. No. 19 reads: '. . . *Pater-Noster-Row*; And Sold by GEORGE WOODFALL, near *Craig's Court, Charing-Cross*. At both which Places Advertisements, and Letters to the AUTHOR, are taken in. Where . . . Numbers'. This format remains unchanged through the rest of the known issues.

(6) Nos. 17–18 insert between line 7 [*rule*] of *A*1 and the three columns of text: '*Whereas we have been informed by several Persons, that they have not been able to procure the* TRUE PATRIOT *at any Rate:* | *And we have great Reason to believe that many malicious and base Endeavours have been used to suppress the Sale of this* | *Paper, by some who are concerned in imposing on the Public, by propagating Lies and Nonsense, which we have endeavoured* | *to detect and expose. If any Hawkers, or others, will acquaint Mr.* A. Millar, *Bookseller, opposite* Katharine-Street *in the* | Strand, *with the Name of any Person who has bribed, or offered to bribe them to refuse delivering out the* TRUE*

PATRIOT *to* | *their Customers, they shall be well rewarded, and their Names, if they desire it, concealed.* [¶] *Gentlemen and Ladies may be furnished with this Paper, by sending their Names and Habitations to Mrs.* A. Dodd *without* | Temple-Bar; *to Mr.* Chappelle *in* Grosvenor-Street; *or to* M. Cooper *in* Pater Noster-Row: | *By whom Hawkers, &c. may* | *be constantly supplied with them.* [*rule*]'. Lines 2–6 and 8–9 of this insertion are indented two spaces.

APPENDIX V

The 'Murphy' Editions

The editor of Fielding's published writings must usually deal with the problems presented by the so-called 'Murphy' editions. In April 1762 *The Works of Henry Fielding, Esq; With the Life of the Author* was published by Andrew Millar in two 'editions', apparently simultaneously—a quarto in four and an octavo in eight volumes respectively. Because the life of the author is by Arthur Murphy and because scholars have found increasing evidence that Murphy exercised editorial supervision of sorts over the printed texts, the 1762 *Works* has traditionally (if informally) been associated with his name.

Tradition has also conferred considerable *cachet* on the 'Murphy' editions as the only editions published by Fielding's friend and principal publisher with editorial supervision, however undistinguished, of a person who could have known Fielding personally and who did in fact have access to some texts marked or corrected by Fielding himself. Fielding's son Allen disputed the notion that Murphy had any first-hand knowledge of his author, but until recently the tradition has exercised uncommon power, both in the matter of attributions and, though perhaps less so, in the matter of the texts themselves. As regards the contents of the present volume of the Wesleyan Fielding, the 1762 *Works* does not print the three pamphlets; it does print ten leader essays from the *True Patriot*. In the opinion of the present editor none of the *Works* variants from the texts of the original issues of the *True Patriot*, with one faintly possible exception, is authoritative. They seem more plausibly to be the result of the messy process of rejustification and reimposition, a difference in house styling, and, least noticeably, compositorial initiatives, not editorial intervention. For the convenience of the interested reader, the variants (with some exceptions) will be listed below.

The text of the 1762 *Works* has not yet been examined as a whole, though beginnings have been made (see Hugh Amory, 'Andrew Millar and the First Recension of Fielding's *Works* (1762)', *Transactions of the Cambridge Bibliographical Society*, viii (1981), 57–78; and 'What Murphy Knew: His Interpolations in Fielding's *Works* (1762), and Fielding's Revision of *Amelia*', *PBSA*, lxxvii (1983), 133–66). The 1762 quarto and octavo were printed from the same setting of type, rejustified in the stick, and reimposed. The title-pages of some (but not all) of the octavo first volumes bear the designation 'The Second Edition' and, thus encouraged, students of the problem have, until recently, argued for the priority of the quarto. Of the four printers involved in the printing of 1762, two are known: William Strahan, who printed the first volume quarto and the first two volumes octavo; and William Bowyer, who printed the fourth volume quarto and the seventh and eighth volumes octavo. According to Amory, Strahan seems to have printed the quarto first, whereas the printer (unknown) of the materials which are contained in the third volume quarto and the sixth volume octavo, which is where the *TP* leaders are to be found, seems to have begun with the octavo. At the end of the third volume quarto and the sixth volume octavo there is a cancellation which extends those volumes with the ten *TP* leaders and two leaders of the *Jacobite's Journal*. Noting that the *TP* leaders are printed at the rate of forty-five or forty-six lines per page, as against the normal fifty, Amory hypothesizes that the cancellation removed a divisional title-page to the *Jacobite's Journal* in order to insert the ten leaders from the *TP*.

Inasmuch as the *TP* material does not seem to have been authorially revised by 1762, the present editor has not attempted to work out either the textual or the typographical complexities, except to list those variants which appear to go beyond matters of 'house style' in the typography. The list of variants given below is complete in that it covers everything 1762 printed of the *TP*. The list does not distinguish between substantives and accidentals. Excluded are variants in the use of emphasis capitals, italics, expansion of contractions (e. g. tho', thro', wou'd, ask'd, reply'd), and other conventions of house style. Variants which seem the result of either editorial or, more likely, compositorial initiative are included. Given first in each entry are the page and line numbers of the Wesleyan edition. Next, to the left of the bracket, is the reading of the Wesleyan edition. It may be taken as identical to that of the copy-text, that is, the original issues of the *TP*, unless otherwise indicated. If necessary, such an indication will be made immediately to the right of the bracket, with the designation TP. The entry concludes with the reading of both 'Murphy' editions, unless they are explicitly differentiated.

THE TRUE PATRIOT

Number 1

107. 26 Sign-Post] sign posts 4°; sign post 8°
107. 32 *Grubstreet*] Grub-street
108. 4 Reader] Readers TP; readers
108. 18 Reader's] Readers TP; readers
110. 1 Mr. *F——g*] Mr. | Mr. *F——g* TP; Mr. *F——g*
110. 1 Mr. *T——n*] *T——n* TP; *T——n*
112. 23 needless;] ~:

Number 3

130. 4 Abbey] abby

130. 24 High-Treason] High-Trreason TP; high∧ treason 8°
131. 27 them;] ~:
132. 5–6 Fellow-|Creatures] ~∧ ~ TP; ~∧ ~
132. 16 past] passed
133. 15 Countenance] Conntenance 4°
134. 10 Good-Nature] ~∧ ~

Number 4

137. 16 Good.] ~∧ TP; ~.
137. 24 alive?] ~! TP; ~!
138. 4 Pennance] pen-|ance 8°

138. 5 Rome?] ~! TP; ~!
138. 11 Abbey] abby
139. 26 Honesty:] ~;
140. 30 vouchsafed] vouchafed TP; vouchsafed

Number 7

153. 3 (for tho'] ∧for though 8°
153. 3 not∧ then] not, (then 8°
153. 4 Cell,] ~∧ 8°
153. 7 Sett] set
154. 6 advancing] advanced 4°
154. 10 Track] tract
154. 14 Metropolis] Motropolis 4°
154. 18 these,] ~∧ 8°
154. 23 Indeed,] ~∧
156. 21 at] out

Number 9

165. 12 every] every other 4°
169. 17 Arrival] Arrrival TP; arrival
170. 24 But I] but 4°

Number 10

171. 12 lead] leads 4°
172. 15 appointed,] ~∧ 8°
173. 1 *St. Paul's*∧ Church∧ | Yard] ~ ~-~-~
173. 7 *Paul's*∧ Church∧ Yard] St. Paul's-church-yard
173. 10 Privy∧ Council] ~-~
173. 17 *Great Britain*] ~-~
174. 19 Small-Coal-Man] ~∧ ~∧ ~ 4°; ~-~∧ ~ 8°
175. 11 *Long Acre*] ~-~
175. 11 *Covent Garden*] ~-~
175. 14 *Privy∧ Seal*] ~-~ TP; ~-~
177. 6 Lords] Lord's TP; lord's
178. 1 this] the
178. 5 *King's∧ Bench*] ~-~
178. 11 *Royal∧ Exchange*] ~-~
178. 12–13 *Paul's*∧ Church∧ Yard] ~-~-~
178. 20 *Drury∧ Lane*] ~-~

Number 11

185. 12 on] of 4°
186. 6 afterwards] aftewards TP; afterwards
187. 19 *l. s. d.*] *omit*
187. 20 0 0] *omit*
187. 29 ballanced] balanced 8°
188. 2 demonstrates] demonstrate TP; demonstrate
188. 14 Rule will] Rule | Gentleman's Court consisted mostly of Ladies; that | will TP; Gentleman's ... that *omit*
189. 6 *Penny wise*] pennywise 4°

Number 13

202. 3 occurred] occured TP; occurred
202. 14 Stripling] Strippling TP; strippling
203. 11 this] is this
203. 19 Nation,] ~∧
204. 8 *Aleca*] *Aleea*
204. 17 Proofs,] ~∧
204. 27 Leeches,] ~∧
205. 2 Rod,] ~∧
205. 9 answer'd,] ~∧
205. 10 *Christmas* Day] ~-~
205. 11 *Christmas* Day] ~-~
206. 3 Age;] ~,
206. 6–11 After ... Public] *omit*

Number 23

257. 20 Surgeon's] Surgeons TP; surgeon's
257. 29 Army,] ~∧ 8°
257. 30 somewhat] some what TP; somewhat
258. 5–6 last-|mentioned] last∧ mentioned TP] ~∧ ~
258. 15 Coach-maker] coachmaker
258. 22 however,] ~∧

259. 7 answer'd,] —$_\wedge$
259. 14 myself,] ~$_\wedge$
259. 15 wholesome] wholsome
259. 21 Preacher;] ~$_\wedge$ 8°
260. 11 prescribed] prescribe

Number 24

261. 18 Voyage-Writers] ~$_\wedge$ ~
262. 17 their] there TP; their
264. 19 Head?] ~. TP; ~.

Fielding's Use of *hath* and *doth*

In many cases of literary attribution the argument from 'style' has seemed either hopelessly impressionistic or lifelessly quantified. In the case of Fielding, however, one stylistic 'test' has commanded considerable respect for over a century. The 'test' involves the third-person singular forms of the verbs *have* and *do*. In writings known certainly to be Fielding's the not quite invariable forms are *hath* and *doth* instead of the more common *has* and *does*.

Credit for first calling attention to this mannerism has generally been given to Thomas Keightley, the nineteenth-century classicist, historian, and editor. Writing of Fielding's style, Keightley observed that 'His most remarkable peculiarity is the constant employment, no matter who is the speaker, of hath and doth for has and does' (*Fraser's Magazine*, lvii [1858], 217). Unfortunately Keightley went on to assert that Fielding's 'remarkable peculiarity' was to be found 'in no other writer of the eighteenth century', an assertion so preposterous it would seem hardly to need refutation. Even by 1750 *doth* and *hath*, while hardly the dominant forms, were not exactly rare either, a fact which limits their value as an automatic 'test' for Fielding's authorship.

Keightley gave no source for his observation on Fielding's style, and as a result it has generally been thought original with him (for example, by Locke, p. 17). It was not. In *An Examen of the History of Tom Jones, A Foundling* (London, 1750) the pseudonymous and somewhat unfriendly 'Orbilius' noted (p. 3) Fielding's 'own elegant Termination of *th* instead of *s* in the third Person Singular, as often as the auxiliary Verbs do and have shall occur' (first cited, by the present editor, in *PQ*, xxxvi [1957], 490*n*.). 'Orbilius's description is important because it shows that contemporaries noted Fielding's mannerism—'Orbilius' makes no claim it was unique in the period—as well as its elegance, which perhaps borders on the affectation so evident in Fielding's frequent attempts to draw distinctions of social 'quality' between himself and mere journalists or hacks.

'Orbilius' and Keightley notwithstanding, the *hath*–*doth* stylistic must be handled with care. Not only were those forms used by contemporaries, but some of Fielding's own published writing fails to exhibit them. As the Battestins have shown (*SB*, xxxiii [1980], 135), in one case at least (a 1738 contribution to the opposition journal *Common Sense*) Fielding's manuscript *hath* was systematically changed to *has*, perhaps by a compositor acting without editorial authority. What this means is that in writing over which Fielding did not have direct editorial control the presence of *has* and *does* cannot be taken to tell automatically against his authorship.

And in fact it has not always done so. Faced in such cases with other evidence of Fielding's hand, scholars have accounted for the presence of *does* and *has* by postulating that Fielding wished thereby to disguise his authorship. Telling against this, however, is the extent of his partiality for the 'elegant' forms, a partiality so reflexive that it led him to introduce them into literary quotations, prose *and* poetry, which did not originally contain them. Given this fact, it seems unnecessary to insist much on the argument from disguise.

In the case of writings like those in the present volume, writings over which Fielding did have direct editorial control (if he cared to exercise it), it seems safe to regard the predominating use of *hath* and *doth* as a presumptive, perhaps almost a necessary, test of Fielding's hand, but not a 'sufficient' or absolutely determinative one. The present editor, rejecting the argument from disguise, has at least questioned any writing that does not exhibit a tendency to use *hath* and *doth* instead of *has* and *does*. In the minority of cases where both sets of forms appear, the editor calls attention to the problem, which seems in the case of the *True Patriot* at least to be more likely the result of editorial revision of material originally by another hand. There is unpublished evidence in Fielding's letters to James Harris that such revision did take place in the *True Patriot*. Consequently, the hypothesis of 'inconsistent' or incomplete editorial revision seems more attractive than either that of 'disguise' or that of unauthorized compositorial tinkering. In such 'mixed' cases, as also in those where neither set of forms appears at all, other sorts of evidence must take the weight.

APPENDIX VII

Uncertain Attributions from the *True Patriot*

The materials from the *True Patriot* reprinted in this appendix fall into two categories. First, Fielding's reworking, usually into a more continuous narrative, of historical items taken or adapted (in the case of 'Europe') from the *London Gazette* and, later, the *General Advertiser*, as well as (in the case of domestic news) designated London papers. When there was little or no reworking of the original sources for the two historical departments, the material has been omitted. It may be read in Locke's facsimile. In the department called 'Apocrypha', which features commentary (either interpolated or terminal) on items from the 'public prints', enough of the original items is reprinted to make the point of the commentary clear. Excerpts and omissions are indicated in the conventional way.

The second category includes materials which seem to have originated with the *TP* and which also bear possible marks of Fielding's hand. The editor has found attribution in these cases somewhat doubtful but has reprinted them to facilitate informed judgment. Omitted altogether from this appendix is material which may have originated with the *TP* but which appears to the editor to bear no marks of Fielding's hand. This material may be read in Locke's facsimile.

The reader is reminded that explanatory annotation for this appendix material is relatively 'light', being limited to crucial identifications and to items which bear on Fielding's career or literary interests as expressed elsewhere in the *TP* or in his *œuvre*. Copy-text for this appendix has *not* been accorded the bibliographical analysis accorded texts unequivocally assigned to HF. Some impediments to meaning (e.g. misspellings) have been removed silently, but there has been no systematic attempt either to preserve or normalize the typographical idiosyncrasies of the originals.

THE TRUE PATRIOT, No. 1, Tuesday, November 5, 1745.

THE

PRESENT HISTORY of *EUROPE*.

ITALY

The King of Sardinia's Affairs begin to wear a little better Countenance, and his Army to recover from the Consternation into which the late Success of the Enemy had thrown them. On the 16th Instant, they were so advantageously posted near Casal, that the Infant Don Philip, instead of attacking them, hath thought proper to send large Detachments to cover Pavia. In the mean time, General Gage advances daily in the Milanese; but as the Citadel of Milan is in itself strong, and hath a Garrison of Austrians, who will probably defend it to the last Extremity, it is hoped the expected Succours from Germany may arrive before that Place can be taken, or the King of Sardinia forced to another Action; in which Case this brave Prince will be again in a Condition to check the Progress of the Allies in that Part of the World, where the English Fleet, which now lies on the Coast of Genoa, endeavours to lend him Assistance.

GERMANY,

In the Northern Parts, Winter comes attended with the usual Cessation of Arms. Their Imperial Majesties arrived on the 27th, N. S. at Vienna, and next day assisted at a solemn Te Deum. The King of Prussia having quartered his Army in Silesia, along the Frontiers of Bohemia and Moravia, came on the 2d of November to Berlin, where he was received with great Demonstrations of Joy by the Inhabitants. An Alliance between these two Crowns hath been long laboured by the Well-wishers to that Cause which Great Britain hath spilt so much Blood to maintain. It is indeed a Measure of all others most dreadful to France, who have employed all the Means of Policy to prevent it, in which the unfavourable Inclinations of the Queen of Hungary to his Prussian Majesty give them too likely a Prospect of Success. There are some Hopes however, that mutual Interest will produce mutual Concessions, and, by degrees, a Reconciliation between these Powers: An Event which would give a fair Prospect of crushing all the ambitious Views of France, who is now preparing to lay up her Arms in Winter Quarters, in order to bring them forth again next Spring, to the Disturbance of all Europe.

From *The* PRESENT HISTORY *of* GREAT BRITAIN.

We cannot begin the Home Part of our History with a more agreeable Article than the Birth-day of our Gracious Sovereign. This excellent Prince, on the 30th of October last, entered into the 63d Year of his Life, eighteen years of which he hath reigned over us. His People, truly sensible of the Happiness they enjoy under his just and mild Government, determined to shew extraordinary Marks of Loyalty on this Occasion. The Bells began to ring long before Day. At Noon there was the largest Assembly of the Nobility and Gentry ever seen at Court, to compliment his Majesty and the Royal Family. Nor was the Splendour of the Court less remarkable than the Number. Among the Ladies who filled a very large Room, there was scarce one dress'd in plain Silk. At two the Birth-day Ode, composed by the Laureat, was perform'd by the Chapel Royal. We would present our Readers with a Copy, if we imagin'd they had any Chance of understanding it.[1]

[1] A hit at Colley Cibber (1671–1757), actor, playwright, theatre manager, and at this time poet laureate. Formerly on working terms with Fielding—he staged and acted in Fielding's first play, *Love in Several Masques* (1728), at Drury Lane—by *c.* 1733–4 Cibber seems to have earned a permanent place on Fielding's hit list. For a summary of their relations, see *Joseph Andrews*, p. 18n. The 'Birth-Day Ode' in question here is reprinted in *General Advertiser* of 31 October, *General Evening Post* of 29–31

Several of the Nobility, *&c.* distinguished themselves by sumptuous Entertainments on this Day. In the Evening there was a Ball at Court, where the young Princes and Princess, the Children of their Royal Highnesses, danced in Public for the first time. And Bells, Bonfires and Illuminations over the whole Town (and particularly in the City) exprest the Affection of the whole Populace, to a Prince who may be justly stiled the Preserver of our Religion and Liberties.

Nor was this extraordinary Zeal confined to London only, many Parts of England having taken the same Opportunity to shew their Loyalty at this Season.

On the 31st Instant, the Right Honourable the Lord Mayor and Court of Aldermen waited on his Majesty to congratulate him on the Birth of a young Prince, and had that gracious Reception which the Magistrates of so loyal a City deserve. And the Honour of Knighthood was conferred on Sir Richard Hoare, Knt. the present Lord-Mayor, who had the Misfortune to receive a slight Wound in his Forehead, by the Fore-glass of his Coach, which was broke by a sudden Jolt in the Procession.

Notwithstanding the Friends of Justice were disappointed in their Desire of immediately enquiring into some late Miscarriages, we are well assured that such an Enquiry is only deferred, and not waved. A great Man speaking of it in Conversation, repeated that Line in Virgil,

QUOS EGO—*Sed motos præstat componere fluctus*.[1]

The English Troops which remain in Brabant, are only the Horse-Guards, two Regiments of Horse, and some Dragoons, making in all about 1400 Men.[2] A Number, which, as they cannot be missed in England, we have no Reason to complain at keeping abroad, when the Dutch, whose Territories are so greatly exposed, at this time, to the Designs of France, have lent us a much larger Number of their own Troops.

The new-raised Regiments, under the Command of the several Noblemen, are to be maintained for four Months certain; and their Officers are to have the Continuance of that Rank in the Army to which they are now promoted. The Number of these Troops will amount to 15000 Men, consisting of 13 Regiments of Foot, two of Horse, and 20 Independant Companies. They are most of them

October and *Penny London Post* of 1–4 November 1745. In the *Champion* of 25 December 1739 (i. 129), attacking the 'redundancy' of Cibber's learning, Fielding instances a 'Gentleman reading his Odes' and crying out, '*Why this is all Hebrew*'. The *Champion* of 22 April 1740 (ii. 130) refers to Cibber's poems as 'strange Lumps called Odes'. See also *The Historical Register* (1737), I. i.

[1] *Aeneid*, i. 135: 'Whom I —! But better it is to calm the troubled waves' (Loeb), spoken by Neptune to the winds which had scattered the Trojan fleet. The 'great Man' has not been identified. Fielding is alluding to Hume Campbell's motion in the Commons on 28 October 1745 (seconded by Pitt) that a select committee be formed to inquire into the causes of the rebellion. The motion, which provoked considerable strain between the ministry and its 'new allies', was defeated by 82 votes. See *Marchmont Papers*, i. 143–7; *Journal of Commons*, xxv. 12; *Parliamentary History*, xiii. 1363–82; and Owen, *Rise of the Pelhams*, p. 286.

[2] On 23 October 1745 Pitt had moved the recall of all British troops still in Flanders. On the division the government's margin was only 12 votes, with Dodington, Lyttelton, and George Grenville among the 'new allies' voting with Pitt. See earl of Shaftesbury to James Harris, 24 October 1745, *A Series of Letters of the First Earl of Malmesbury . . . from 1745 to 1820* (London, 1870), i. 7–8; also Owen, p. 285.

compleat, and great Diligence is used in disciplining and exercising them; so that when we consider the Spirit with which these Men have inlisted at such a Season, we may promise ourselves that these Troops will not be proper Subjects of that Ridicule which some ill-minded Men seem inclined to cast upon them; but, on the contrary, that they will be worthy of ranking in an Army, whose Courage in the last Campaign, however unsuccessful it was from other Causes, hath been the Honour of their Country, and the Admiration of all Europe.[1]

A Subscription for an Opera being lately mentioned to a Lady of Fashion, whose public Spirit is as amiable as her private Character, she answered, If she had any Money to spare in this Time of Distress, it should be given to buy Gin to comfort those brave Fellows, who are forced at this Season to lie on the cold Ground, in the Service of their Country, and not lavished on Foreigners, who first plunder and then laugh at us.[2]

A Hackney Coach, in which were four young Ladies, passing the other Night through Temple-Bar, was stopt by one of the Trained Bands on Duty there, who open'd the Coach-door, in order to see if any Arms were concealed in the Bottom. Upon his shutting it again, one of the Ladies said smiling, Well, Sir, do you see any *Arms?* No, Madam, answered the Centinel, I see nothing but *Legs.* . . .

A few Days since died in Ireland, Dr. Jonathan Swift, Dean of St. Patrick's in Dublin. A Genius who deserves to be ranked among the first whom the World ever saw. He possessed the Talents of a Lucian, a Rabelais, and a Cervantes, and in his Works exceeded them all. He employed his Wit to the noblest Purposes, in ridiculing as well Superstition in Religion as Infidelity, and the several Errors and Immoralities which sprung up from time to time in his Age; and lastly, in the Defence of his Country, against several pernicious Schemes of wicked Politicians. Nor was he only a Genius and a Patriot; he was in private Life a good and charitable Man, and frequently lent Sums of Money without Interest to the Poor and Industrious; by which means many Families were preserved from Destruction. The Loss of so excellent a Person would have been more to be lamented, had not a Disease that affected his Understanding, long since deprived him of the Enjoyment of Life, and his Country of the Benefit of his great Talents; But we hope this short and hasty Character will not be the last Piece of Gratitude paid by his Cotemporaries to such eminent Merit. . . .[3]

[1] For these regiments and the political contention they provoked, especially over the question of giving their officers rank on the establishment, see 'General Introduction', above, pp. xliii–xlvi. Fielding's extended praise of them here is a reflection of their endorsement by the leadership of the 'new allies', in particular the initiatives of the duke of Bedford, who formed and commanded a regiment of foot. Owen, pp. 287–9, provides detailed documentation of the politics. The issue of the new regiments, like those of the recall of British troops from Flanders and the proposal of an inquiry into the rebellion, appeared to many to presage the disintegration of the ministerial coalition, the broad bottom.

[2] The first of the *TP*'s persistent attacks on the luxury of opera during a time of financial uncertainty. See index, *s.v.* The 'Lady of Fashion' has not been identified.

[3] All but the first sentence of this obituary originates with the *TP* and is almost certainly Fielding's work. Cf. *Tom Jones*, XIII. i. 686 and *n.*; and *CGJ* no. 10 (4 February 1752), i. 194.

The Number of the Rebels who remain in their Camp, is variously reported; but the best Authority says they are about 6000. If this be true, it is surprising they should have no greater Encrease. Their Camp is situated between two Rivers, one being in their Front, and the other in their Flank. A Position which may not be attended with the Advantages they propose, as these Rivers are not at a sufficient Distance to secure them from the Reach of our Cannon. Some imagine they will not trust to the Strength of their Situation; but will endeavour to give Marshal Wade the Slip, and enter into England by the Way of Kelso, and so attempt to march over Cheviot Hills, where these Savages will have a great Advantage over Regular Troops: But those who understand the Nature of the Highlanders best, say it will be difficult to prevail with them to undertake a March by which they must certainly lose all Hopes of Retreat; and rather imagine they will retire into the Highlands at the Marshal's Approach, and take the Advantage of those Fastnesses, to harrass the King's Army with the intolerable Fatigue of a Winter's Campaign.

These are the various Sentiments of different Persons at this Time and on this Occasion; and a few Days will shew us which Opinion is the truest.

From APOCRYPHA.

Being a curious Collection of certain true and important WE HEARS *from the News-Papers.*

... Marshal Wade, who arrived some Days since at Newcastle, is now at the Head of 13000 Men, and will very speedily advance against the Enemy; who, if they were double the Number which they are reported to be, cannot be able to face such an Army, under such a General.[1] He hath with him the Lords Tyrawley and Albemarle, besides other General Officers. ...

The Regiment of Welch Fusileers, *according to some Authors*, is gone into Suffolk; *according to others* to the North. ...

COMMITTED.

A Printer of Grubstreet News *(Query which.)* ...

DEAD.

... William Avery, Esq; at Bath. *He was one of a Triumvirate of Beaus, who have flourished there these fifty Years.*[2]

---

[1] The interpolated praise of Wade originates with the *TP* and is the first of several laudatory references to him; see index, *s.n.* Wade, a friend of Ralph Allen's and long associated with Bath, may have been known personally to Fielding; see no. 7 (17 December 1745), p. 153 *n.* 6.

[2] Until it abandons commentary altogether, the *TP* often singles out persons with connections to country with which Fielding was familiar—Bath, Salisbury, Dorset.

APPEARED.

Several Ghosts in the News-Papers of this Week, in the Shape of Puffs.[1] A Gent. in a Silver Waistcoat at the Ball at Court, and a Voluntier, who twice appeared, once in the Streets, and the second time at Lord Mayor's Feast, to the great charming of Ladies, who want to be *spoke to*[2] by them. And a large black Ghost, who appeared in a horrible Shape on Sunday Evening last, at half an Hour past six, near Clare-Market, when he talked for a whole Hour what none of his Hearers understood.[3] Lately appeared in Scotland, the Ghost of a Print called *A Hint to the Wise*, which so frightned the Pretender's Son, that he fainted, and was not seen in Public for two Days.[4]

A Loyal SONG, *with a Chorus, to the Tune of* LILLIBULLERO, *proper to be sung at all merry Meetings.*[5]

I.

O Brother SAWNEY, hear you the News,
Twang 'em, we'll bang'em, and hang 'em up all.
An Army's just coming without any Shoes,
Twang 'em, we'll bang'em, and hang 'em up all.
To Arms, to Arms,
Brave Boys, to Arms!

[1] Undue or inflated praise or commendation, uttered or written to influence public estimation; an extravagantly laudatory advertisement or review of a book, a performer or performance (*OED*). As Fielding uses it in the *TP*, 'Ghost' refers to advertisements or other puffery of materials he considered to be without substance or merit. For an extended definition, see *JJ* no. 40 (3 September 1748), pp. 380–3.

[2] The use of italic implies a quotation, in this case probably an indirect one from *Hamlet*, I. i. For other references to the notion that ghosts cannot speak until spoken to, see *JJ* no. 40 (3 September 1748), pp. 381–2; *Tom Jones*, XI. ii. 572; and *CGJ* no. 65 (7 October 1752), ii. 107, which may not be by Fielding.

[3] The first of a number of hits in the *TP* at John 'Orator' Henley, whom Fielding had earlier savaged in the *Dialogue*, above, p. 98. See also 'General Introduction', above, p. lvii, and index *s.n.* Henley advertised his Sunday 'Lectures' regularly and provocatively.

[4] The print, which is advertised as early as 22 October 1745 (*Daily Post*), is the subject of a 'Puff' (*DA* of 5 November 1745) to the effect that the YP fainted upon seeing it and was not seen in public for two days, thus giving rise to rumors that he had left Scotland and stimulating new orders for the print. An earlier public source of this 'Ghost' has not been identified, but the *TP* notice clearly presumes one. The print itself, as described in Stephens, *Catalogue*, III. i. 536–7 (no. 2675), appears to fault the broad-bottom coalition for political flinching.

[5] Although no printing of this much reprinted song has been found earlier than this number of the *TP*, it is probably not Fielding's work. The use of *doth* seems more archaic and poetic than otherwise. *General Advertiser* of 23 November 1745, *London Magazine*, xiv (1745), 561, and *Scots Magazine*, vii (1745), 523, all reprint without citing a source, and French (pp. 125–6) finds the song with minor variations in Johnson and Stenhouse, *The Scots Musical Museum* (Edinburgh, 1853), xiv. 12, where it is said to have been 'excerpted from a MSS collection of loyal songs, composed for the use of the Revolution Club'. However, there was at least one contemporary effort to associate the song with Fielding: it is reprinted, over a dateline of 28 November, in *The Beau's Miscellany* (London, 1745), whose title-page declares it to be 'Printed by David Simple for Joseph Andrews at Tulliber's [*sic*] Head and Sold by Abraham Adams at the Aesculus and Crabtree'. Locke, p. 44, says, 'In the cleverness and pointedness of the satire, the song is characteristic of Fielding's own composition.'

A true English Cause for your Courage doth call,
    Court, Country and City,
    Against a Banditti.
Twang 'em, we'll bang'em, and hang 'em up all.

II.

The Pope sends us over a bonny brisk Lad,
    Twang 'em, *&c.*
Who to court English Favour wears a Scotch Plad.
    Twang 'em, *&c.*
        To Arms, *&c.*

III.

A Protestant Church from Rome doth advance,
    Twang 'em, *&c.*
And what is more rare, he brings Freedom from France.
    Twang 'em, *&c.*
        To Arms, *&c.*

IV.

If this should surprize, there is News stranger yet,
    Twang 'em, *&c.*
He brings Highland Money to pay England's Debt.
    Twang 'em, *&c.*
        To Arms, *&c.*

V.

You must take it in Coin which the Country affords,
    Twang 'em, *&c.*
Instead of broad Pieces, he pays with broad Swords.
    Twang 'em, *&c.*
        To Arms, *&c.*

VI.

And sure this is paying you in the best Ore,
    Twang 'em, *&c.*
For who once is thus paid will never want more.
    Twang 'em, *&c.*
        To Arms, to Arms,
        Brave Boys, to Arms!
A true English Cause, *&c.*

THE TRUE PATRIOT, No. 2, Tuesday, November 12, 1745.

From *The* PRESENT HISTORY *of* GREAT BRITAIN.[1]

We can say nothing very certain concerning the Rebels, either as to their Numbers or Motions. A Letter from Lord Tyrawley makes the Number of those Troops on whom they depend to be no more than 5600; but there are besides a very large Rabble, of some Thousands; and it is universally agreed they are marching Southward.

The Army of General Wade, who remains at Newcastle, is about 11,000 strong, and consists of the following Number of Battalions and Squadrons. . . . The Duke of Richmond serves as a Lieutenant General, as will several young Lords and Gentlemen as Volunteers; among whom is the only Son of Lord Malton, who goes at seventeen Years of Age, on his own earnest Request, by the Consent of his Father and *Mother*. An Example worthy of great Praise and Imitation.

Saturday last Mr. Carrington, one of his Majesty's Messengers, assisted by a Constable, took into Custody one Gordon, a Popish Priest. He was seized near Red-Lion Square, at a Taylor's, who at first denied him, but being threatned by the Messenger to be made himself a Prisoner, he at last discovered his Guest. This Priest hath resided here a long time, and hath been concerned in remitting the Collections made for the Use of the Pretender, as well before as since the breaking forth of the Rebellion. Some material Discoveries are said to have been made from his Papers.

A few Days since an Express arrived from Admiral Byng, with an Account, that a suspicious Fellow had lately been taken on Land, and brought before him. This Fellow had, when he was seized, a Letter in his Pocket, which he tore in many Pieces; he did not however so destroy it, but that on joining the Pieces together, it appeared to have been directed to C. P. W. R.[2] and signed by a fictitious Name. It contained an Account, that some Forces from France, particularly the Irish Brigade, were actually sailed from Dunkirk, under the Command of the Duke of Ormond, *&c.* and were intended to land in Cumberland. The Seizure of this Man, with such a Letter, is a Fact; but we rather imagine it a Design to keep up the Spirits of the Pretender's Party, than that there is really any such Force embarked. However if they are, we hope they will not escape the Vigilance of our Men of War.

Lord Cl-nc-rty hath certainly hoisted his Flag at Dunkirk on board a French Man of War in the Name of the Pretender.

A Gentleman of Fashion lately arrived from the North, tells the following

[1] The 'History of Europe' in this number is 'postponed'.

[2] Charles Prince of Wales Regent, that is, the Young Pretender, who was thus designated by his father's declarations of 1743. A reprinted item in the 'Present History of Great Britain' of no. 3 (19 November 1745) reports that the YP sent a letter to the mayor of Carlisle 'in which he stiled himself Prince of Wales, Regent of England'. See Locke, p. [54].

Story, which he averrs to be true. A certain Person at Edinburgh having assisted the Pretender's Son with Money, &c. but having at the same time declined waiting upon him, was by him appointed to come to Holyrood-house privately in the Evening. While they were in Conference together, two Officers of the Highlanders broke abruptly into the Room. They were both very drunk, and complained of some Hardships they suffered, which had not been redressed; upbraiding the young Gentleman with not having kept his Word with them; recounting to him what they had done in his Service, and swearing if they were not better used, they would *gang hame* about their Business. The Pretender's Son at last with kind Words prevailed with them to depart; but as soon as they were gone, declared, that a Crown itself would scarce compensate what he suffered from the Temper and Behaviour of these People. How little could their Commanders, if they desired it, restrain the unlicensed Plunder of these Barbarians in this opulent City, with the Hopes of which they are actually buoyed up in undertaking this desperate Enterprize; for the Gentleman who relates this Story, adds, that the common Toast is to a happy Meeting in Lombard-Street.[1]

His Majesty hath been pleased to order a Proclamation for a General Fast to be held on the 18th of December next.

A poor Soldier, who was crippled at the Battle of Fontenoy, having attended at the Horse-Guards in order to be admitted as a Pensioner of Chelsea Hospital, would have gone thither with his Wife by Water, but had not Money sufficient to pay what the Waterman demanded. Upon this another Waterman, knowing his Case, and taking Compassion on him, offered to carry him for nothing. A Gentleman present, who compassionated the Soldier, and was pleased with the Generosity of the Waterman, gave a Crown to be divided between them. This Story, which is literally true, pleased me so well that I could not help inserting it.

From APOCRYPHA.

Being a curious Collection of certain true and important WE HEARS *from the News-Papers.*[2]

Whitehall, Nov. 5. By Letters of the 3d Instant from Berwick, there are Accounts, that upon the 27th past, a Party of the Rebels had been at Glasgow to demand the old Subsidy for the Tobacco brought in seven Ships, and just then landed at Greenock, which amounted to 10,000 Pounds Sterling: That they had also demanded three Years Excise upon the Small Beer, which likewise

---

[1] Extending from Mansion House to Gracechurch Street, and inhabited principally by goldsmiths, bankers, merchants, and other monied men, a *locus* of City finance.

[2] Beginning with this number, the use of italic commentary, both interpolated (within parentheses) and terminal, intensifies. Unless otherwise indicated, such italic commentary may be taken as originating with the *TP*, and the roman material may be assumed to originate with the *London Gazette* or other sources, as designated by the dateline or a set of initials. The initials or 'Marks of the Historians cited in this Work' are identified at the beginning of the 'Apocrypha' of no. 3, below, p. 348.

amounts to 10,000 Pounds Sterling: That upon the 31st past, 200 small Carts, *(a large Number)* in which were six Field-Pieces, Ammunition, Small Arms, &c. lately landed at Montrose, and which came over the Firth at Hagen's Nook, passed by on the West Side of Edinburgh, and went to Dalkeith, attended by two considerable Bodies of the Rebels.... Those advanced Parties gave out, that their whole Army was to follow them the next Day: That the Pretender's Son was to set out from Dalkeith upon the 3d, and that they were to march through Annandale to Carlisle: That the better to disguise their Motions, *(tho' they seem just before and after very explicit in declaring them)* Billets for Quarters had been sent to Musselburgh, Fishcraw, Inverask, Preston-Pans, Tranent, Haddington, and other Villages upon the East Road to Berwick, while considerable Numbers were to march by Night to the Westward....

Whitehall, Nov. 8. By Advices from the North of the 5th Instant, there are Accounts, that the Rebels were marching Southwards towards Langton and Carlisle, as was supposed, *(why so supposed?)* in three different Columns, the Westermost of which was thought to be their main Body by the Pretender's Son being with them, who was to take his Quarters at Broughton near Peebles, being the House of Murray his Secretary.... The Number of the Rebels who were at Peebles upon the same Day amounted to between four and five thousand, with 150 Cart-Loads of Baggage and some Artillery. Other Letters *(If these Letters are true, those before-mentioned must be false)* mention, that the French Arms, Ammunition, and Baggage, &c. landed some Time since at Montrose, had been brought to Perth, from whence Horses had been pressed to carry it to Allowa on the 27th past, under Pain of military Execution....

A certain Knight, in the West of Scotland, concern'd in the last Rebellion, having been prevailed on, by his Lady, to join the young Pretender, her Ladyship resolved to pay the Chevalier a Visit with all the Grandeur she was capable: Accordingly she set forward with a Coach and Six; but just as she was within a few Miles of the Camp, she was met by a Party of the Rebels, who readily shew'd their Highland Civility: For this Purpose they tied the Coachman Neck and Heels, and then seized upon the Lady, pulled her out of the Coach, and robb'd, ravish'd, and abused her, in a Manner too shocking to relate. Her ladyship, highly disgusted at this Usage, order'd her Coachman to drive directly homeward; and her Husband, as soon as he heard of it, without waiting to seek Satisfaction for so gross an Insult on his Honour, slink'd off from the Rebels, and return'd home. *Query, if this Lady, by her quiet Return, had not what she came for? Query, likewise, how the Coachman, who was ty'd Neck and Heels, drove her back?*

The Horned Cattle in the Counties of Surrey and Middlesex, are now in good Health, occasioned by the Use of Tar-Water. *G. A. The* Horned Cattle *in this Town, by the Decrease in the Bills of Mortality, seem in as good Health.*

The Marshal Count de Saxe is again taken ill at Ghent, and three Surgeons have been sent for from Paris to tap him. *We wish, for the Repose of Europe, they may let out his Politics....*

The Academy Royal of Sciences, at Berlin, have proposed, for the Subject of their next Prize, in May 1746, to determine the Order and Laws to which the Wind would be subject, if the Earth was on all Sides surrounded by Ocean; so that the Direction and Swiftness of the Wind might be predicted for all Times, in any Part of the Globe. *Wind probably will have more Power over those Experiments, than they will obtain over that Vapour, in which the Experiments themselves will most likely evaporate.*

We hear a Court Martial will sit in a few days to enquire into the Affair at Preston Pans. *St. J. E. We hear this is not true.*

They write from Paris, that the Second Son of the Pretender was return'd to that City, and had appeared publickly in the Opera; and that the General Discourse was, that he would speedily set out for Dunkirk, in order to embark with the Troops which are to be employed in his Favour, under the Command of the Lord Clare. *St. J. E. These Troops will have but two Difficulties to encounter, viz. first to get hither, and Secondly to get back again.*

'Tis rumour'd that the King of Sweden is going to be married to a Daughter of Col. Horn, and he is said to have assigned to his future Consort 6000 Ducats per Annum, to be paid out of the Revenue of his Landgraviate. *St. J. E. Whether this is a very agreeable young Lady,* according to Custom, *I don't know; but by her Dowry she seems to want the other Qualification given by the News-Writers, viz. a considerable Fortune.*

We hear, that the thirteen Regiments of Foot now raising in different Parts of England will consist of 800 Men each. And the Regiments of Horse will consist of 500 Men each, besides Officers. *St. J. E.* WE KNOW *the Foot will consist of more, and the Horse of not much above half so many.*

We have *Advice* from Maryland, by Way of New England, that the Report of the Virginia Fleet being taken is without Foundation, great Part of the same being arrived, and others were coming daily into that Colony. *Idem. Its hoped this Author's* Advice *is truer than his* Hearsay.

On Friday it was reported, that a certain Commander of the Land Forces was put under Arrest by Order of his Majesty. *L. E. Other Authors mention this more positively; and some* hear, *that this Officer is lately arrived from the North; but* we hear, *from much better Authority, that the whole is a Fiction.*

There is, 'tis said, *(Query, only by whom?)* an Account from the North, that soon after the Rebels had quitted Edinburgh, General Guest had ordered the Gates of this City to be shut, and that the Magistrates and Ministers of the Gospel had resumed their respective Functions. *D. A.*

This Week two noted Attorneys at Law were order'd by the Court of Chancery to the Fleet-Prison, for Contempt of the Court. *These Attornies, whatever they were before, are certainly* noted *now.*

Yesterday it was currently reported, that an Express was arrived with an Account, that Lord Loudon had taken upwards of 300 of the Rebels, who had been in Argyleshire to demand the Money raised by the Officers of Excise.

We hear that 5000 more Forces will speedily be sent to join Marshal Wade. *D. G. Both these Paragraphs, I believe, came by the same Express.*

His Grace the Duke of Argyle is gone for Scotland. *He set out only in the* London Courant, *his Grace remaining in Person at his House in this Town.*

We are advised from Dunbar of the 3d Instant, that the Fraziers, M'Donalds, Monro's, and several other Clans, are now under Arms, and within a few Miles of each other; they are in Number about 6000, under the Command of my Lord Loudon; and when collected, which may be done in a few Days, they may be able to cut off the Retreat of the Rebels: Mr. Campbell, well known amongst the well-affected Clans by the Name of Jack Campbell, has been very active in raising these Men. *G.A. Query, How many of these are cloathed in Buckram?*[1]

From the LONDON COURANT.

Chapel le Frith, Nov. 1, 1745.

If any Credit be due to History, especially to the more ancient ones, we find Times of Public Calamity, and great Revolutions, have frequently been preceded by Prodigies, and uncommon Appearances in Nature; if what follows shall appear to be something of that Kind, you may depend upon the Truth of every Particular.

In a Church about three Miles distant from us, the indecent Custom still prevails, of burying the Dead in the Place set a-part for the Devotions of the Living; but, as the Parish is not exceeding populous, one would scarce imagine the Inhabitants of the Grave should be straitned for want of room, yet so it should seem; for, on the last Day of August, several hundreds of Bodies arose in the open Day out of the Grave there at once, to the great Astonishment and Terror of several Spectators, of unquestioned Veracity, from whose Mouths I had the Account.

They arose, as I said, out of the Grave, and immediately ascended towards Heaven, singing in concert as they mounted along. They had not any Winding-Sheets about them, yet did not appear quite naked. Their Vesture seem'd to be streaked with Gold, interlaced with Sable, and skirted with White, but exceeding light, as was judged by the Agility of their Motion, and the Swiftness of their Ascent. They left a most fragrant and delicious Odour behind them, but were quickly out of Sight; and what is become of them since, or in what distant Region of this vast Universe they have taken up their Abode, no Mortal can tell. *This is an old Riddle of a Wasp's Nest, which was built in a Grave, the Vesture streaked with Gold, &c. is a Description of these Insects. Tho' all my Readers may not know the Explanation of this Nonsense, they may all conceive the Design with which it is now re-published in this Manner: But I must tell this silly or wicked Author, that this Rebellion, instead of calling Men out of the Grave, will probably send a great Number of Wretches thither. . . .*

Dead. . . . Richard Edwin Venelles, *possessed of a plentiful Estate.* John Middleton, Esq; who never had an Acquaintance without a Friend. *It is no Wonder that the Name of a Man, who must have had so few Acquaintance, was so little known.* . . .

Appeared. Several Ghosts in the Shape of Puffs, as usual. Particularly, 1. Lottery-Mongers, who keep but one Office *out of Gratitude to the Public*, of

---

[1] Cf. *1 Henry IV*, II. iv. 175 *et seq.*

which several News-Writers *think it incumbent on themselves* to inform their Readers. 2. Fortune in the shape of Brokers, delivering out Tickets which are to be Prizes. 3. One sells 4 l. more for 20 l. than all the rest.[1] 4. Brandy Merchants *determined* to keep up their Brandy to its usual Goodness, which has for 10 Years *withstood all Contrivances in opposition to it.*[2] At the Oratory-British-French-Spanish-Popish-Nonsense Chapel, a large black Ghost, at six in the Evening, as usual, to the great Terror of those who saw him.[3] *N.B.* It is hoped he will shortly be laid—if not in the Red Sea, at least in the Black Hole.[4]

THE TRUE PATRIOT, No. 3, Tuesday, November 19, 1745.

ASIA

From Retsch the Capital of Chailan, we are informed, that Schach Nadir had ordered all the Great Men of his Kingdom to appear with the utmost Magnificence at his Nuptials. He hath resolved to marry in Form a Girl who hath made an entire Conquest of his Heart. Whether she be one of his Seraglio, or some other, is yet uncertain.

The present HISTORY *of* EUROPE.

ITALY

General Pertusati, Commander of the Austrians in the Cremonese, hath lately made great Preparations to pass the Po, in order to penetrate into the Parmesan and Placentia, and take Vengeance of those two Dutchies for the Affection which they have discovered to the Spaniards. With this Design he hath got together a great Number of Boats and other Materials necessary for throwing a Bridge over that River; at the same time, he hath raised Redoubts mounted with Cannon, to secure his Retreat into the Cremonese. The Marquis of Castellar being advertised of these Dispositions, hath advanced towards the Po with all

---

[1] Cf. *DA* of 2 November 1745: 'We think it incumbent on us to inform our Readers, that J. Berry and Company . . . have a particular Method of Dividing their Tickets, by which every Adventurer will be sure to gain in each Twenty-Pound Prize, Four Pound per Ticket on the Shares of Chances more than paid by any other Office.' See also *DA* of 11 November.

[2] Cf. *DA* of 9 November 1745: 'The Proprietors of the Original Raisin-Brandy-Warehouse . . . are determin'd to keep up their Brandy to its usual Goodness, which has withstood for the ten Years past the various Contrivances in Opposition to it.'

[3] 'Orator' Henley's advertisement in *DA* of 9 November 1745 gives the location of his lectures as 'the Oratory-British Chapel, the Corner of Lincoln's Inn Fields, near Clare-Market'. To judge from the advertisement Henley spoke on topics that were incendiary and seemingly disloyal. For other attacks on Henley, see index, *s.v.*

[4] A colloquialism for the punishment cell or place of close confinement in prison. *OED* cites no example prior to 1758.

the Troops he could assemble, and hath carried off Part of the Boats and Materials which General Pertusati had collected, and by these means prevented the Execution of his Project; and in order to prevent a second Attempt of that General, who is extremely attentive to every Opportunity, the Count hath disposed several Spanish Regiments along the Banks of the River. Since which General Pertusati hath been wholly occupied in preparing for the Defence of Adda, and in perfecting the new Works designed for augmenting the Fortifications of Pizzighitone. Count Grammont, at the Head of eight Battalions of French Troops, hath taken Possession of the City of Asti, and hath laid all the Country under Contribution home almost to the Suburbs of Turin. The Garrison of Valencia having escaped from thence in the Night between the 29th and 30th of October last N.S. the Spaniards entered the Place the next Day, and made themselves Masters of a large Quantity of Artillery and warlike Stores. Count Gages hath received Orders to proceed from hence to the Attack of the Citadel of Alexandria; and afterwards to that of Casal, if the Season should permit. Reinforcements to the Imperial Army of General Pertusati arrive daily; but that General is not yet strong enough to face the Enemy, who, notwithstanding their Losses by Desertion, Sickness, and Sieges, remain yet his Superiors. The Marquis de Mirepoix, who hath long threatned the Siege of Leva, for which he had received the necessary Artillery and Ammunition, hath defiled hastily with his whole Body towards Nice, before the Snows shut up the Passes.

From Rome they write, that the Consistory in which the Pope is to acknowledge the Emperor, was to be convened the second Week of this Month. This, says a foreign Historian, is no more than his own Glory and Honour demand of him towards the first Prince in Christendom; *but perhaps his Holiness acts by more politic Motives.* [1]

SPAIN.

Several Vessels have lately sailed from Ferrol, laden with Arms for the Service of the Pretender; and an Ordinance hath been published at Madrid, importing, that all English Vessels which have the Pretender's Passport shall be received in all the Ports of the Spanish Monarchy, as they were before the War was declared against Great Britain, and Orders have been accordingly dispatch'd to all the Governors of the Maritime Provinces.

GERMANY.

So far from any Prospect of that Peace between the Empress and the King of Prussia, which might oblige France to give Repose to Europe, the Court of Vienna seems entirely busied in Preparations for War. On the 2d of November, N.S. a grand Council was held in the Presence of their Imperial Majesties, on

---

[1] The italic comment here and later (in 'France') originates with the *TP*.

the Subject of an Express which arrived the Day before from the Field Marshal Count Traun, after the breaking up of which the said Courier was again remitted. The Troops detached from the Rhine, are destined for Saxony, and the better Part of those under Prince Charles are in full March, in order to penetrate through Lusace into the Electorate of Brandenburg, on the Side of the Oder; by which Diversion the King of Prussia will be obliged to fly to the Succour of his own Dominions. This was the News which was most probably brought to his Prussian Majesty, when he was at the Rehearsal of an Opera; and that occasioned the immediate Orders which he gave for the March of a large Body of Troops in Garrison at Berlin, Part of which proceeded towards Magdeburg the very next Day. At the same time, the Court of Vienna hath ordered a Reinforcement of Regular Troops to join General Keyl, who commands on the Territories of the Higher Silesia, and which will put him in a Condition of acting with Vigour. It is likewise certain, that the Empress of Russia hath actually given Orders to a Body of 12,000 Men, under General Lacy, to march into Saxony to the Assistance of the King of Poland.

FRANCE.

The Commander of the Mercury Man of War arrived on the 30th at Brest with three English Prizes; and the Elizabeth, which sailed a few Days before with an English *My Lord*, returned thither with a Prize of 30 Guns. In the Night between the 8th and 9th, the French Army withdrew their Picket from the Bridge at Philipsburg, and the next Morning early their whole Army decamped, taking the Rout of Landau and Weissenburg, having thus at last entirely evacuated the Empire, where they were no longer able to support themselves. The other Troops of this Crown are likewise retiring from these Parts into Winter-Quarters. His Most Christian Majesty was the other Day encounter'd by a wild Boar in the Forest of Fontainbleau, which wounded his Horse. *His Majesty was probably much frightned, having never been so near an Enemy before.* The Pretender's second Son is at Paris, and is there called Prince Henry; and very extravagant Reports are spread of the Assistance which the French King is to give to his Father's Cause. But it is confidently said, the King of Prussia's Minister hath very loudly remonstrated at this Court, against their granting any Supply either of Men, Money, or Arms, to this Adventurer.

HOLLAND.

An Augmentation of 30,000 Men is talked of in the Troops of the Republic, in order to give weight to the Remonstrances of the Ministers of the Republic in the Empire. These Troops will be all new raised, and will cost the Republic less than taking Strangers into their Service. Several of their principal Men have offered to raise these Troops on the same Conditions which the Republic have granted of late Years to those who have undertaken this Service.

From *The* PRESENT HISTORY *of* GREAT BRITAIN.

... As the Inclemency of the Season is one of the most dangerous Enemies with which our Army is to encounter, his Majesty hath been graciously pleased to order a very large Blanket for every Tent; besides which, Mr. John Hanbury, an eminent Merchant of this City, hath, in the Name of the People called Quakers (being one himself) offered to Sir William Yonge, to supply the whole Army, which is now marching against the Rebels, with Wastecoats of Flannel. This Offer hath been kindly accepted, and must be of great use in preserving the Health of those who are at present the most useful to the Public of all his Majesty's Subjects. ...

The following Story told me by a Party present, serves to evidence the Truth of some Observations made in our last Paper. A Gentleman dined with a Friend of his a Roman Catholic, and after Dinner these two were drinking in company with a Priest, who was Chaplain to the Family: Their Bottle being emptied, the Master of the House sent his Chaplain for a fresh Bottle. When he was gone, the other turning to his Friend, said, 'Do you really think I can wish well to this Rebellion? Why, if Popery was established in England, that Fellow would have sent me on the Message on which I have now sent him.'

From APOCRYPHA.

Being a curious Collection of certain true and important WE HEARS *from the News-Papers.*

MARKS of the Historians cited in this Work.

G. A. General Advertiser.	L. C. London Courant.
D. A. Daily Advertiser.	S. J. E. St. James's Evening Post.
D. G. Daily Gazetteer.	L. E. London Evening Post.
D. P. Daily Post.	G. E. General Evening Post.

... Last Sunday as a Boy who belongs to the Emley Galley, lately arrived from the West Indies, was going along Bishopsgate Street, he was deluded by three Women into a House in Hand-Alley in that Street, who robb'd him of forty-six Shillings; upon which he had the Courage to call the Watch, and three Women were taken up, and brought before the Sitting Alderman, who committed them to Newgate. *From this Account we may conclude, the Boy's Courage to have been equal to his Chastity.*

It is confidently reported here, that a Mandamus is come from the young Pretender in Scotland to the Fellows of Magdalen-College, requiring them to elect a certain Romish Priest into their Headship, now vacant by the Death of Dr. Butler; but that the present Fellows will behave with the same honest Bravery as their Predecessors did against the Proceedings of the late K. James. *S. J. E. The Bravery of these* Fellows *is not doubted; but how brave a* Fellow *must he be who brought this* Mandamus, *and how silly a* Fellow *must be the Pretender's Son who sent it? Or shall we rather suspect the Truth of the Story, and that the Author if it is a ly—ng* Fellow?[1]

Saturday died at Erith in Kent, Captain Massey of Ogilvie's Regiment of Foot. He was wounded in the late Battle of Fontenoy, where he behaved with extraordinary Bravery. G. A. *For which reason we have kept him out of the common Vault in our Paper, as a Mark of Distinction, tho' we never heard of him or his Colonel before. . . .*

A Troop of Life-Guards march'd to Brentford, to relieve a Regiment of Light-Horse, which march'd from thence to Lancashire. G. A. *This Regiment of Light-Horse was raised by the Historian himself.*

We are certainly informed from Ware in Hertfordshire, that from one united Collection made thro' the Town for the County-Association, there amounted 170 l. of which 110 l. were subscrib'd by the Protestant Dissenters. *The Dissenters are as good Subjects to King GEORGE, and as much concerned in the Protestant Cause, as any others; those, therefore, who endeavour to cultivate Dissentions between us at any time, must weaken that Cause, and we may consequently guess from what Quarter these Attempts come at present. . . .*

We hear, that a great deal of Money was found *in the Hands* of Gordon the Priest, lately arrested for treasonable Practices. *If so much Money was found* in his Hands, *I hope they search'd* his Pockets.

From *Apocryphal History of the Rebellion.*

. . . According to the Accounts of our Correspondents of the best Integrity, the Highland Army is not 8000 strong, and many of those old and feeble, not fit for Action or Service. Numbers of them are deserting every Day, since General Wade published his Proclamation, of hopes of his Majesty's Pardon to such as retired to their own Habitations, and lived as peaceable Subjects. G. A.

From all those Accounts we learn ooo, *or in other Words, that an Army of* 7000 *Men, of which* 2000 *deserted at one time,* 700 *at another, and which still continue deserting in great Numbers; of which* 100 *Men were killed and* 100 *taken at one time; many thousands defeated at a second, and great Numbers killed and taken at a third. I say, we learn, that this Army of* 7000 *Men, having had all these Disasters, doth not at present amount to* 8000. *So that by these Accounts put together, it is most certain, that the whole Army of Rebels which came from Scotland is destroyed, and consequently those before Carlisle can be no other than* GHOSTS.

Dead. Edward Galloway, Esq; *many Years a Justice of Peace.* Mr. Arthur Wight, *a Town Clerk.* Mr. William Chettle, *ditto.* —— Daise, Esq; *a Sugar-Baker,* born in Denmark. Mr. Thompson, *a Prothonotary.* Mr. George North; *he was joint Clerk*

---

[1] Although he properly disparages this attempt to fashion a parallel with James II's coercion of the Oxford college, Fielding will not be above alluding to the latter for his own anti-jacobitical purposes in 1748; see *JJ* no. 25 (21 May 1748), no. 26 (28 May 1748), and no. 27 (4 June 1748), pp. 286, 291, 297 and *n.*

with his Father to the Merchant Taylors Company; by his Death therefore Half that Place is vacant. Mr. Laythin, an eminent Ironmonger. The Rev. Mr. Trunk, *a School-master.* Mrs. Hind, *a Maid*; she was of an antient Family. Richard Witherston, Esq; *Barrister at Law*; he was aged 44, and by an early Application to the most polite and no less useful Parts of Literature, greatly improved those Abilities Nature had so liberally bestowed on him. Thirteen Cows belonging to a Dairyman in Oxford Road. William Meakyns, Esq; *advanced in Years.* Mr. Tilbury, *an eminent Scarlet-Dyer.* Mr. Bick, *an eminent Wax-Chandler.* The Rev. Mr. Strange, much esteemed by all that knew him. Mr. Samuel Russell, *an eminent Linnen-Draper.* Mr. Clayton, *a Scarlet-Dyer*; he was reckoned rich. Charles Foxhill, Esq; he had a large Estate. James Markham, Esq; he had a large Estate likewise. Thomas Tonkin of Polgar in Cornwal, Esq; universally lamented by his Acquaintance. Upwards of 40 Cows belonging to one at Tottenham Court, *universally lamented by all their Acquaintance.* Mr. Hill, *an Upholder*, wealthy.

N.B. If great Men and Cattle die so fast, we shall scarce have room to bury them in our Paper.

Appeared. The usual Ghosts: 1. Lottery-mongers, who sell Prizes in the last Lottery. 2. A vast Quantity of *Spirits* in Watlingstreet, which have withstood all Opposition for 20 Years. 3. The Black Ghost at the Oratory British-French-Spanish-Popish-Nonsense Chapel. Note *he hath lately pulled in his Horns.* [1] In several Papers there *hath appeared* this Week a Popish Priest, in the Shape of a Presbyterian on Horseback. *He hath vented 52 Pages of Nonsense against some of the best Friends which the Government hath found in the Time of their Distress.* [2] Seven thousand Danes in Scotland, or the Daily Advertiser, to the great Terror of Lottery Tickets, which *run off* very fast at their Appearance.

OBSERVATIONS *on the* REBELLION, *continued.*

We shall postpone any Thoughts of our own, in order to present the Public with the following Letter, which we have great reason to believe, came from a Person of very high Eminence. [3]

---

[1] Another hit at 'Orator' Henley, who is called 'a large Black Ghost' in the 'Apocrypha' of nos. 1 and 2, above, pp. 338, 345. The late pulling in of Henley's horns has not been identified, unless it is his early October denial of jacobitism. See *Dialogue*, above, p. 98, and 'General Introduction', above, pp. lvii–lix.

[2] This title is advertised among the November books in *GM*, xv (1745), 616, at 6*d*. It appears to be connected with a 1717 book, *A Presbyterian getting on Horse-back, or the Dissenters run mad in Politicks.* Fielding's characterization of the Dissenters as 'some of the best Friends' of the government indicates the importance he and others attributed to the loyalty of such groups during the rebellion. Cf. the treatment accorded to the nonjurors in the dream vision of jacobite victory, in the leader of this number of the *TP*, above, p. 133.

[3] The letter which follows exhibits mixed 'stylistic' features (*has* and *hath*), perhaps the result of editorial revision, and although it is devoted to answering the queries Fielding raised in the 'Observations' of no. 2, above, pp. 124–7, it is not clearly his work.

To the TRUE PATRIOT

SIR,

I have a very good Opinion of you and your Writings, and am particularly pleased with your New Paper, which you begin with that Spirit of true Patriotism you profess. Your Apology for *Scotland*, and for the Body of Roman Catholics, becomes a Man of Sense and Honour, and must have given universal Satisfaction to your Readers.

But I must own myself a little surprized at the Queries with which you conclude the Observations in your last; the rather as you say they are intended for a Hint to some Persons. Whom you mean, I know not; but as you promise to expatiate further on these Queries, give me leave to send you what I imagine a satisfactory Answer to them all. This may either prevent your giving yourself that Trouble, or be of some Assistance to you, if you should pursue it.

Your first Query is, *What additional Strength have all our Associations produced in the Space of two Months?* I answer, all which it is in the Nature or Power of an Association to produce. It has discovered our Unanimity, and has thrown a Spirit into all Degrees of Men, which we can scarce find the Parallel of in History.

You proceed: *Have we any Body of Men yet raised on whom we can place the least Dependance, (our Army from* Flanders *only excepted?)* Surely the Answer is in the Affirmative. Of the thirteen Regiments proposed to be raised by Noblemen, many are compleat; particularly those of the Duke of *Bedford*, Lord *Halifax*, and Lord *Gower*. They are cloathed and trained, and are as good as Troops can possibly be made without actual Service.

This Method of raising Men was approved of as being much more expeditious than any other way of recruiting, and much more efficacious than the ordinary Method of raising the Militia. It was therefore embraced by those Noblemen with great Alacrity, from a Desire of serving the Public only. Most of them will be very considerably out of pocket by it; and when their Country beholds such noble Persons (as it certainly will) exposing their Lives at the Head of their several Corps, it must silence all those invidious Insinuations, which it is no wonder our Enemies should industriously spread among us, tho' in Defiance of common Sense as well as Truth.

You ask, *If our Army is entirely brought over from Flanders?* I wish I could say it was; but I can with Certainty affirm, THE WHOLE ARE NOW SENT FOR. And if the Public confess (as I believe they do) that the Preservation of this Kingdom is owing to that Part of this Army which is already in *England*, I hope they will soon know and acknowledge TO WHOM they owe their Embarkation.

Is this Army, say you, *increased to its real Establishment?* I answer, every Endeavour hath been set on foot to bring it up to that Establishment; for which purpose, no more effectual or expeditious Means could possibly be invented, than that which was first begun by the Vestry of St. *Martin*'s, and which hath been since pursued by many other Parishes. By these means, a great Number of

Men have been already raised, and are now daily raising, who are incorporated in the several Regiments, and will, it is hoped, very soon compleat them.[1]

Your last material Query is, *Can we not throw a Body of Foreign Troops into the North of* Scotland, *and would not that Step bid the fairest to put a final End to this Rebellion?* I confess it would, and this Measure would have been perhaps much wholesomer some time since than it would be now; but, Sir, the very Name of Foreign Troops is odious to this Kingdom. We have contracted a violent (I will not say unreasonable) Antipathy to them. An Opposition to such Troops is always popular, and the sending for them would give too plausible a Handle to our secret Enemies to foment Jealousies and Ill-will among the People. It is true, that the Danger arising to this Nation from the Introduction of 10,000 Foreigners, is too chimerical and absurd to deserve an Answer; but Antipathy is neither governed by Reason or Experience; if it could be subdued by the latter, a very late Instance, in which we severely suffered by this very Antipathy, might have been sufficient to remove it.

Thus you see, Sir, I have answered some of your Queries in the Affirmative; and where I have been obliged to give negative Answers, I have endeavoured to account for them. The Truth is, The Public will be served in their own Way. In free Nations, they always entertain Jealousies of their Governors, and these Jealousies are often laid hold on by wicked and designing Persons to frustrate the Intentions of the best meaning Men for the public Good. Indeed such are the Difficulties with which those who desire to preserve us in this Time of Danger, must struggle, that nothing less than the highest Abilities, joined to the highest Integrity, can surmount them.[2]

Had I not thought your Design of serving your Country at this Season sincere, and your Capacity equal to the Task, I should not have given myself the Trouble of these Animadversions. Go on steadily in this noble Pursuit, and you shall have every Assistance in the Power of

Your unknown humble Servant.

[1] *General Evening Post* of 15–17 October 1745 carries a paid notice datelined from the Vestry-Room of the parish of St Martin's-in-the-Fields, 1 October 1745, announcing its effort to raise enlistment monies by means of a house-to-house collection throughout the parish. The scheme, which was distinct from that of the general association for the Liberty of Westminster, was adjudged to be successful. See *General Evening Post* of 5–7 November 1745: 'On Tuesday [5 November] near 200 Volunteers enter'd into his Majesty's Service, encouraged by the Bounty of the Subscription of the Inhabitants of St. Martin's in the Fields, and were sworn before a Magistrate, and ordered into their respective Regiments.'

[2] The characteristically 'patriot' emphasis on 'Abilities' and especially 'Integrity' in ministers is made elsewhere in the *TP*; see, for example, no. 14 (28 January–4 February 1746), above, p. 211; no. 19 (4–11 March 1746), above, p. 236; no. 26 (22–9 April 1746), above, p. 275; and no. 32 (3–10 June 1746), above, p. 305.

THE TRUE PATRIOT, No. 4, Tuesday, November 26, 1745.

From *The* PRESENT HISTORY *of* GREAT BRITAIN.[1]

... General Ligonier being at length recovered of his Indisposition, set out on Sunday last for the Army which is assembling near Coventry. This Army is now reinforced by three Battalions of Guards, and by Cobham's Dragoons. They will be commanded by the Duke in Person, who proposed to set out as this Day for Coventry. These three Battalions of Guards make 2100 Men, excluding officers, and are selected out of the whole Body of Guards; every Man who hath the least bodily Infirmity having been rejected. So that the Army now consists of 12 of those Battalions who have seen the *Fields of Fontenoy*; of one old Regiment of Horse, and two old Regiments of Dragoons; besides four Squadrons and five Battalions of new raised Troops, all headed by the Noblemen their Colonels. God be praised, this Army, which would have had no indifferent Chance against the Forces of Alexander, is to fight on the Side of our Liberties: Indeed I heard a General Officer of Good-Sense and Experience swear, he believed them able to drive the whole Kingdoms of England and Scotland before them.

The following Story came from very great Authority. Lord George Murray met at Carlisle with an old Acquaintance, who very frankly told him the desperate Situation in which he apprehended him to be. Lord George replied, he knew very well his Danger; he saw they were betrayed, and must be soon cut to pieces; but he had gone too far to retreat either with Safety or Honour. . . .

Friday last Fortune rode in Triumph through the Streets of this City, in a Triumphal Carr, vulgarly called a Lottery-Wheel, attended with three other Cars, Guards, &c. from Whitehall to Guildhall, where yesterday she began to distribute her Favours in a very sparing manner; several Persons who were intitled to the whole Sixteenth Part of a Fifty thousandth Part of her highest Marks of Affection, having waited all Day to no purpose.

There appeared this Week in one of the Daily Papers a Letter signed MARIA; in which the Females of Great Britain are called upon to enter into Subscription for the Defence of their Country. A Proposal very worthy to be embraced by them at a Time when we may justly say their ALL is in Danger. But we must take this Opportunity to do justice to a Lady who had not only the Loyalty but the Bravery to advise such a Subscription, at the very Time when we were alarmed by the Defeat of our Army at Preston-Pans. This was done in a Pamphlet, intitled, *An Epistle from a British Lady to her Countrywomen*; which we recommend to their Perusal, as we think it the only Address of this Kind, in which the Female Part of the Creation are considered as Persons endowed with Principles of Sense and Honour, instead of being represented as Creatures worthy only of administring to the loose Pleasures or menial Necessities of

---

[1] The 'History of Europe' for this number is 'postponed'.

Mankind.[1] *If such an Author as this should not meet with all Encouragement from her own Sex, it is plain she doth not deserve it; by being guilty of so gross a Mistake.*

Sometime since died of an Asthma at the Bath, the Rev. Dr. William Broome. This Gentleman was not unknown in the Learned World, tho' perhaps he had less Reputation in it than he deserved. He read over the whole Comment of Eustathius in Greek, in order to furnish Mr. Pope with Notes to his Iliad and Odyssey. Nay perhaps he had some share in the translating, at least in the *construing* those Poems, if we may believe Mr. Pope himself:

And POPE *translating three whole Years with* BROOME.[2]

Last Week died at his House in Cleveland-Row, Mr. John Robinson, Son of Mr. Robinson of Bath. He was a young Man, who had given very early Proofs of a great Genius in his Profession of Portrait Painting.[3]

From APOCRYPHA.

Being a curious Collection of certain true and important WE HEARS *from the News-Papers.*

... Yesterday the Royal Blue Incorporated Volunteers of the City of London, met at Blackwell's Coffee-house, and chose Mr. *Leader* Cox, an eminent Merchant of this City, for their Captain. G. A. *A good Name for a Commander.*

General Ligonier is recover'd. G. A. He is judged in a fair way of Recovery, D. A. He is perfectly recover'd. G. A. He is to set out To-morrow, being Thursday. He set out to Day, being Thursday. He set out Yesterday, being Thursday. *Several Papers.*

If the Foreigners have twelve Millions in our Funds, and would subscribe only Three-Halfpence in the Pound, it would amount to seventy-five thousand Pounds; a fine Sum to be laid out in Premiums and Rewards to those who enter

---

[1] A Cooper imprint at 6*d.*, it is advertised in the *General Advertiser* of 5 October 1745. The author suggests (pp. 16–17) that women contribute their jewels and other adornments: 'Nor do I doubt, that as we are unable to contribute personal Strength in Concert with the Men, we shall outdo them in Subscriptions on this Occasion' (p. 17), which is not quite the point Fielding makes here. Cf. the letter from 'An Old Gentlewoman' in no. 2 (12 November 1745), above, p. 121. The 'Maria' letter is in the *DA* of 20 November 1745.

[2] *Dunciad* (1729), iii. 328. The line and Pope's egregious and untruthful note upon it remained until 1736, when Pope altered the line ('And Pope's, ten years to comment and translate') and removed the note. See Pope, *The 'Iliad' of Homer, Books I–IX*, ed. Maynard Mack (London, 1967), pp. xlii–xlvi; *Correspondence of Alexander Pope*, ed. George Sherburn (Oxford, 1956), i. 266; ii. 3, 40, 121, *et passim*. In *Tom Jones*, viii. i. 396–7, Fielding alludes to Broome's 'Observations on the Tenth Book' of the *Odyssey*, attributing it to Pope. Broome's 'Share' in the *Odyssey* amounted to eight books and the notes for many more, a fact Pope at first concealed from the public, with Broome's collusion. Although not italicized, the editorial comment here appears to originate with the *TP*, as it does in the next annotated item, below, also about a resident of Bath.

[3] According to Horace Walpole, *Anecdotes of Painting in England*, ed. Ralph Wornum (London, 1876), ii. 320, Robinson was educated under Vanderbank, married a rich woman, and 'suddenly came into great business, though his colouring was faint and feeble'. Walpole estimates that Robinson was 'not above thirty' when he died.

themselves Soldiers, and behave well in Battle, and may make Dividends in as little Danger of being annihilated as Land. D. A. *Q. What is meant by annihilating Dividends?* ...

Last Thursday Edward Weld, Esq; arrived at his Seat in Dorsetshire, from London, being releas'd from his Confinement with Honour. When he approach'd his own Estate he was met by a Number of his Tenants, who conducted him with great Joy to his own House. *He is a Gentleman of universal good Character, and one of those many Roman Catholics, who have too much Honour to molest a Government which has never put into Execution any of those severe Laws that were formerly made against them.* ...[1]

A certain Officer of the Foot-Guards, who was lately tried by a Court-Martial for leaving his Command at the Siege of Ostend, and returning to England without Leave of his superior Officer, has received Sentence of Death to be shot for Desertion. S. J. E. *The Sentence of the Court Martial is not yet known, and therefore if the News-Writer was a Member of this Court, he would be guilty of a high Misdemeanor in publishing it; but as he was not, we believe he is only guilty of a F--lsh---d.*

Yesterday the Saddles, &c. for the Duke of Bedford's Regiment of Horse, set out of Town for the Place of Rendezvous. Idem. *As the Duke of Bedford hath only a Regiment of Foot, it is probable these Saddles, &c. will shortly* set out *on their Way home again.* ...

From *Apocryphal History of the* Rebellion.

JUXTA SE POSITA MAGIS ELUCESCUNT.[2]

... Last Friday in the Afternoon, as the Pretender's Army march'd from Moffat, in their way to Carlisle, Mr. John Kirkpatrick, Lieutenant of the Cumberland Light-Horse, who went out to reconnoitre the Enemy, ventur'd within a Quarter of a Mile of them, and took James Brand, Esq; Lieutenant and Quartermaster of Lord Kilmarnock's Squadron. He was brought to this Town on Monday last, and examin'd by General Wade, behav'd very insolently, and said he did not value if he was shot immediately. He was dressed in a Highland Plaid and Bonnet, on one side of which was a Plate Cockade; he had two Case of uncharg'd Pistols, and a Backsword, and had about him a very remarkable Cap, work'd round with Iron Chain, which also cover'd his Neck, Shoulders and Breast, and was a sufficient Fence against any Sword. After Examination he was committed to Newgate. G. A. *Another Historian tells us, that Mr. Kirkpatrick himself and four Light-Horse are taken Prisoners. D. A.* ....

---

[1] Another instance of Fielding's keeping up his 'country' connections. Weld (1705–61) of Lulworth Castle, Dorset, was the addressee of an anonymous letter dropped near Poole and adjudged to be treasonable. On 10 October he was examined before the Council at the Cockpit and committed to the custody of one of the king's messengers (*St. James's Evening Post* of 10–12 October 1745). The treasonable letter is printed in *GM*, xv (1745), 554.

[2] 'Placed next to each other, they shine more brightly.' Evidently not a classical quotation; *elucescunt* is a 'late' or nonclassical form.

Letter from Lancashire, Nov. 15.

Sir,

'When the Rebels retired from Carlisle, which was done after summoning it to surrender, without firing a Gun, the Garrison made a Sally upon the Rear, and took two Cart-loads of Targets and another of Bread. It is also reported, that three or four were killed by the great Guns from the Garrison, one of whom was a Person of Distinction, believed to be Lord George Murray.' G. A. *Another Historian believes him to be the Marquis of Tullibardine. Another Mr. Murray the Secretary.* . . .

They write from Newcastle, that General Wade, with the Troops under his Command, was arrived at Hexham; but other Letters say, that he was arrived at Brampton. *D. A.*

We hear that Marshal Wade is a Day's March behind the Rebels. *G. A.*

Extract from a Letter, Newcastle, Nov. 20, at Noon.

'The King's Forces, commanded by Marshal Wade, marched then to Hexham, from whence they will return hither To-morrow. The Rebels marched Yesterday from Penrith, but as yet I cannot say whither. A more severe Season has scarce been felt; the Winds are fierce and bleak, and we have Snow lying deep on the Ground: Miserable Weather for a Campaign!' *L. C. These several Letters give us the greatest Idea of Marshal Wade's Army, which, if they are all true, was in four different Places at once.* . . .

The Reader hath here a Collection of the Ingenuity of a whole Week, for so small a Price as 3d. which to have purchased of the Historians at large, would have cost him 4s. 10d.½, even if he had been so wise as to have left out the Gazette. And we hope he will make much of this Specimen; for he shall never have such another in this Paper.[1]

Casualties. A Man in an indifferent Dress killed *by Drinking.* G. A. A Man well-drest *drowned.* A Waggoner *run over by his Waggon*, ib. The Wife of a Tinman *found murdered; the only Suspicion* against her Husband is that he made off, and hath not been since heard of. S. J. E. The Son of a Mercer *cut his Throat*, ib. A Gravesend Boat *overset*, and several Passengers *drowned.*

Preferred. Thomas Neale to be a *Land Waiter* in London. Thomas Lambe, Esq; to be a *Cursitor.* Mr. Horne, *Surveyor of the New Buildings at Portsmouth.* Alderman Baker, to be *Colonel of the Orange Regiment*, in the Room of Alderman Perry, who hath resigned. Mr. Chapman an Apothecary, to be *Captain-Lieutenant of the Blue.*

Committed. Thomas Dyer for the *Murder of his Wife.* John Hunt, for *Felonies and Robberies.* Anne Gilbert, for the *Murder of her Son.* Patrick Hand, for *privately Stealing. This Fellow made an ill Use of his Name.* John Dean, *a notorious Thief; said by the Historians to be the remaining* CAPITAL *Person of the Black Bog-Alley Gang.*

---

[1] Although editorial excerption may obscure the fact, the comment here refers to the 'Apocrypha' up to this point, not to the collected items which follow. See the 'Heliogabalus' letter in no. 5 (3 December 1745), below, pp. 367–8, and, for a more complete 'Collection', Locke, pp. [62–4].

Married. A Gentleman aged 22, to a Widow Gentlewoman *aged upwards of* 80. Mr. Lee, to Mrs. Howard, a Relict, *agreeable with a handsome Fortune.* Mr. Robert to Miss Dickinson, *a young Lady of great Beauty, and a Fortune of* 10,000 *l.* Capt. Smallwood and Miss Beddington, *an agreeable young Lady with a Fortune of* 4000 *l.*

Dead. John Richardson, Esq; a young Gentleman of a large Estate near Bath. Mr. Townshend, Master of a Tavern. Rev. Mr. Henry Grove, aged near 90. Mark Carey, Esq; who had a large Estate. Mr. Emerton, *an eminent Colourman*; he died of a Dropsy. Capt. Tho. Proctor, a Commander in the Portugal Trade, much known and universally lamented by all that knew him. *If so, we are glad we were not of the Number of his Acquaintance.* Mr. Thomas Cross; he hath left his Estate to Mr. George Ormerod. Mr. John Hall, Master of an Eating-house. Miss Boddicoat, *Daughter of Mr. John Boddicoat*, an eminent Merchant. Richard Channon, Esq; *a Justice of Peace.* Mr. Brunker, *a Builder.* Capt. Dayle, *a brave and experienced Commander.* Mr. Renton, formerly *a noted Glazier.* John Elder, *Common Cryer of London; his Place is vacant.* Mr. Huff, a Coal Merchant, *wealthy.* Mrs. Maria Kemp, *a Maiden.* Mrs. Nevill. Rev. Mr. Wicket; he had a Living in Kent. *He was well known at the polite End of the Town; but I have often heard it doubted whether the last Letter of his Name was* d *or* t. Mr. Hill, *an Upholder, wealthy.* Two Sisters within a few Hours of each other, one Wife to a Merchant, the other to an eminent Attorney. Dr. Broom, Professor of Musick. Mrs. Porten, Sister to Col. John Porten, and Aunt to Mrs. Gibson, *D. A.* Mrs. Porteen, a Maiden Gentlewoman, Sister of the late Sir Francis Porteen, Knt. Alderman, who died in 1727. *L. C. (Query, If these Historians mean the same Person?)*

Appeared. All the Ghosts which haunted the Town last Week; and several Ghosts of Books and Prints, which, if they appear any more without a proper Licence, will be most certainly laid in this Paper.

OBSERVATIONS *on the* REBELLION,

Postponed, for a Reason which I need scarce hint to my sensible Readers.

As an Instance that we can take a Joke as well as give one, we shall publish the following Letter.

To the TRUE PATRIOT.

Dear Pat.
Among the many Circumstances which you say raised that agreeable Sensation you felt at the End of your last tragical Paper, do confess, if your Taylor's having brought you home a new Suit was not one. Strange and unexpected Events, if they have nothing unpleasing in them, furnish us with the most agreeable Sensations. That Success may attend you is the Wish of

Your Friend.

White's, Wednesday Evening.[1]

[1] This letter, with its interesting gloss of the leader of no. 3, may well not be Fielding's work. It may point, however, to an 'event' in his life. White's, a fashionable private club in St James's Street, was known at this time for gambling activities.

THE TRUE PATRIOT, No. 5, Tuesday, December 3, 1745.

From *The* Present History *of* Great Britain.[1]

The following Letter, which was communicated to me by a Person of high Distinction, and which I assure my Reader is Authentic, will give him a very perfect Account of the Number and Condition of the Rebels; who are decreased more by Desertion, since the Writing it, than they are increased by additional Numbers.

Sir,   *Penrith, Nov. 25, 1745.*

I had writ to you before, but the Highland Army, which we have had marching in and out all the last Week, prevented all Communication by Post. The Vanguard, which they call'd 2 Squadrons of Horse (tho' upon reckoning they did not exceed 100) came in this Day se'ennight. They kept marching in all the Day on Wednesday, but the most numerous Body on Friday. I had Persons posted at two Bridges near this Town, as a Check on each other; and we took an Account of their Number, such as may be depended upon.

Their whole Force (with all the Stragglers that have been passing since Saturday, when the main Body left us) will not exceed 5000.—They have a great Number of Boys amongst them.

I counted all their Pieces of Artillery and Carriages. They have 13 Field-pieces, 2 other little Pieces, and something else like a Mortar. By the Diameter of their Bore, the biggest can't carry 4 lb. the rest betwixt 2 and 3 lb. Carriages with Baggage were about 60, 20 of which returned to Carlisle on Saturday. They have left that Garrison with about 130 Men. No Alteration in the Fortifications that we hear of, nor any Force in that Part of the Country; tho' six of their Hussars have this Morning been demanding Billets for above 1000 against Tomorrow. Their Rout seems to be Lancashire, and we begin to be afraid, they'll endeavour to get back again, when they hear of General Ligonier's Army. All our Wish is, that Marshal Wade, who is still about Newcastle and Durham, would get behind them.

The Highlanders are a shabby, ill-looking Generation, and have nothing formidable in them, but their meagre, hungry Looks, and their Filthiness. By all the Observations I could make, from the Acquaintance I pick'd up with some of their Officers, there is a strong Dejection amongst them; but they say, *There's no looking back.* Some few Deserters are repassing this Way, &c.

This being most undoubtedly a true and exact Account of their present Situation in England, we can have no other Fear but of their Retreat, or rather Flight back into Scotland; by which means they would greatly harrass our Troops, nor

---

[1] The 'present History of Europe' in this number has been omitted as showing signs of another hand. For a text, see Locke, p. [70].

would it perhaps be in our Power totally to disperse them this Winter. However, as they have actually advanced as far as Manchester, this seems not to be their Design; or at least they may probably delay it too long; for Marshal Wade was Yesterday at Witherby with his whole Army, whence he is making all possible Haste towards Manchester, by the Way of Leeds and Halifax. Should the Rebels, therefore, waste a very little Time where they are, or should they attempt to pass the River Mersey, the Marshal will be able to cut off their Retreat; and either force them to a Battle under the most unequal and desperate Circumstances, or to a Flight, in which very few will be able to escape the Pursuit of the Cavalry.

On the other hand, should the Rebels endeavour to push forward to North Wales, his Royal Highness, who is now at Litchfield, where the last Division of his Army will arrive To-morrow, must be able, if not to stop them, at least, to get so close behind them, that their Rear will be exposed to the constant Execution of his Horse and Dragoons: Nay, should they by the utmost Expedition (which they are not likely to use at present) get 3 or 4 Days Marches of the Duke, in their Way to North Wales, they must inevitably be soon cooped up by both Armies, in a Place where they could not subsist, and from whence they could have no Hopes of escaping.

As to the vain Conceit of some Persons that these Highlanders can avoid the Army under his Royal Highness, and make their way to Town,[1] it is to be regarded as merely chimerical, and to be inspired by a Mixture of Panic and Ignorance into the Minds of Men who are totally unacquainted with the March of Armies, and the Consequence which must attend a Body of Foot, who endeavour to outrun Horse who are at their Heels.

Nothing can equal the Heartiness and Unanimity with which all Degrees of Men have exerted their Zeal, in those Parts through which the Duke and his Army have passed. His Royal Highness hath been received every where with universal Acclamations. This young Prince, who is an Englishman in his Nature, as well as his Birth, will soon become the Darling of a People, who have always paid the highest Regard to Bravery and Generosity, Virtues for which, among many others, he is greatly eminent.

People have, at the same time, vied with each other in manifesting the utmost Affection for the Soldiers under the Duke's Command, who have been received as the Guardians and Defenders of the Laws and Liberties of their Country. They have been treated in most of the Towns with the utmost Liberality, by which means the Fatigues of this Winter Campaign have been rendered much more supportable. The same Kindness hath been shewn by the Town of Newcastle to those Troops under Marshal Wade, at their Return from Hexham, in which near 200 of them perished. The Marshal himself, in a Letter, expresses 'The highest Sense of the Behaviour of these Citizens, whose Humanity, he says, cannot enough be commended; for they provided not only Food for the

---

[1] i.e. to London.

Hungry, and Cordials for the Sick and Fatigu'd, but Beds or Blankets for the whole Army.'

The following is a Letter from Staffordshire, of which I saw the Original, and which I the rather insert, as it doth Honour to a Sett of Gentlemen, who are often the Subjects of Abuse, without deserving it.[1]

Eccleshal, Staffordshire, Nov. 27.

'This is a small Market Town, not wealthy, having no Manufacture, yet free Quarter is given to all his Majesty's Troops that pass through it, the private Houses receiving them chearfully. Mr. Colclough, who has many years practised here as an Attorney at Law, and for his great Integrity and Skill in the Value of Land, is intrusted with receiving Rents to the Amount of thirty thousand Pounds per annum, for Noblemen and Gentlemen in this and the adjacent Counties, has, at his own Expence, provided Entertainment for forty Soldiers every Day.'. . .

The following is a true Story of the Pretender's Son: In a long March which he lately made in Lancashire, through very bad Roads, he wore a Hole in one of his Shoes. Upon his Arrival at a small Village, he sent for a Blacksmith, and ordered him to make a thin Plate of Iron, which was fastened to the Bottom of the Sole. Then paying him for his Labour, said, *My Lad, thou art the first Blacksmith that ever shoed the Son of a King.*

This young Gentleman having in his last Declaration expressed some Surprize that his Cause was not better seconded, considering the late Grumblings of the People at some former Ministerial Measures; a Lady of Quality applied the known Fable of the Nurse and Wolf on this Occasion.

As a Wolf was hunting up and down for his Supper, he passed by a Door where a little Child was bawling, and an old Woman chiding it; *Leave your Vixentricks*, says the Woman, *or I'll throw you to the Wolf.* The Wolf overheard her, and waited a pretty while, in hopes the Woman would be as good as her Word; but no Child coming, away goes the Wolf for that Bout. He took his Walk the same Way again towards the Evening, and the Nurse, he found, had changed her Note; for she was then muzzling and coaxing of it. *That's a good Dear*, says she, *if the Wolf comes for my Child, we'ell e'en beat his Brains out.* The Wolf went muttering away upon it. *There's no meddling with People*, says he, *that say one Thing and mean another.*

The Application by the Lady is much more ingenious than the elaborate Comment of Sir Roger Lestrange, who has really mistaken the true Meaning of the Fable.[2]

---

[1] Fielding's compliment to his professional colleagues in the law should be compared to his compliments to lord chancellor Hardwicke and chief justice Willes; see index, *s.v.*

[2] His 'Reflexion' on Fable ccxix ('The Nurse and the Wolf') begins: 'The Heart and Tongue of a Woman are commonly a Great way a-sunder. And it may bear Another Moral: which is, that 'tis with Froward Men, and Froward Factions too; as 'tis with Froward Children, They'll be sooner quieted by Fear and Rough Dealing, then [*sic*] by any Sense of Duty or Good Nature . . .' (*Fables, of Aesop and other Eminent Mythologists*, 4th ed. [London, 1709 4], p. 200).

Saturday last the Royal Society met at Crane-Court, according to annual Custom; where the Officers were chosen for the Year ensuing. And on Sunday met at the Star and Garter, the Honourable Society of the DILATANTE being a Society of Noblemen and Gentlemen who have traversed the Alps; when the learned and ingenious Mr. Harris was continued Treasurer for the Year ensuing. We are informed that this is the only Society now in England, which has more Money in Bank than they know what to do with. *As we are acquainted with several of the Honourable Members, we doubt not but they will understand* the Hint hereby *intended to be given them.* [1]

The young Lawyers and Students of the Temple being willing to defend as well as practice the Laws of their Country, have lately applied themselves to the Study of the Laws of Arms, in which Exercise they are daily attended in the several Inns of Court by Serjeants. *Quere, Whether these be Serjeants at Law, or of the Army?* . . .

On Sunday, the 24th Instant, died at his Lodgings in Golden Square, the Lord Wyndham. He had been many Years Lord Chancellor of the Kingdom of Ireland, which Post he resigned about 5 Years ago, and retired to Salisbury, where he led a private Life, till the Decay of his Health brought him to this Town, the latter End of last Summer, for the Advice of the best Physicians. He was a good-natured and an honest Man. In Public he always preserved his Integrity, and in private Life an inoffensive Chearfulness, which made him an amiable Companion. [2]

From APOCRYPHA.

Being a curious Collection of certain true and important WE HEARS *from the News-Papers.*

Early Monday Morning some Sharpers took the Opportunity, while the Chairmen at the Temple-Gate were in a Publick-House, to carry off a poor Man's Chair, notwithstanding they were within a few Yards of the Centry fixed at a Temple-Bar. L. C. *This strange Robbery could not have happened, if the Chairmen themselves had been at their Post.*

Yesterday (*Nov.* 25.) between 30 and 40 Transports, with the British Cavalry, arrived at Gravesend. L. C. Yesterday (*Nov.* 25.) it was reported the British

---

[1] At this time the society, membership in which required residence in Italy, included Dodington, Charles Hanbury Williams (an Eton contemporary of Fielding's), David Mallet, Richard Grenville, Charles Fielding, and the duke of Bedford, with some or all of whom Fielding was acquainted. See *History of the Society of Dilettanti*, comp. Lionel Cust, ed. Sidney Colvin (London, 1898), Appendix ('List of Members'), pp. 239–54. In its early days the society included a fair number of the prince of Wales's 'patriot' adherents.

[2] Thomas Wyndham (1681–1745), baron Wyndham of Finglass (1731), came from an influential Somerset family. He was appointed recorder of Sarum in 1706 and, as Cross notes (ii. 25–6), held that post when Fielding was a boy visiting the Goulds at Salisbury. Wyndham subscribed to Fielding's *Miscellanies* (1743). The notice here of his life and character originates with the *TP*.

Cavalry were arrived at Gravesend, but in the Evening it was contradicted. G. A. Yesterday (*Nov.* 25.) 20 Transports arrived at Gravesend from Williamstadt, with the Remainder of the Forces from Flanders, which are most Horse. D. A. Yesterday arrived in the River, from Williamstadt, 36 Sail of Transports, having on board 2500 Horse. D. G. *Non nostrum tantas componere lites.*[1] We shall therefore call in the Gazette for our Assistance, who gave us on Tuesday last the following Article from Williamstadt.

Williamstadt, Nov. 26. *N. S.* Yesterday in the Afternoon arrived here one of the Newcastle Transports; it was separated from the Fleet last Tuesday, which came in this Day; the *whole* consists of fourteen Sail, twelve of which will take in the two Troops of Ligonier's, and four Troops of General Hawley's: The Embarkation will begin on Sunday Morning, and it is hoped all will be on Board by Tuesday Night. The other two Transports, with one that was left behind of the last Embarkation, will take in about 500 Foot, which are now here from the Hospital, and returned Prisoners from France. *On this I make no Comment.*

The French Ambassador at Stockholm has profered to the Swedish Officers, that will enter into the Service of France, 2000 Livres for a Colonel, 1800 for a Lieutenant Colonel, 1600 for a Captain, and 600 for every Subaltern. He has remitted to him for this Purpose 50,000 Crowns, and a great many Gentlemen offer to engage. S. J. E. *These Fellows who sell themselves as mercenary Tools, to effect the Mischiefs of Princes, are not to be regarded as Men, but as Cattle, or Slaves which are no better than Cattle, and are like these Colonels to be purchased in a Market.*

Next Tuesday is appointed for the Election of a Common Crier in this City, in the room of Mr. Elderton, deceased. *Idem. I suppose this is an Office of great Importance; for the Death of the last Cryer, the Declaration of the Vacancy, and the proceeding to a new Election, have been* CRIED *every Day in the Papers of this Week.*

On Thursday a great Quantity of meazly Pork, which had been seized by the City Marshal, was burnt in Smithfield. L. C. *In most Countries they have* Magistrates of Health; *but in* England *the Care of our Health is trusted only to Physicians, who may be more properly called* Magistrates of Disease.

On Saturday, being St. Andrew's Day, was held the Anniversary Election of the Council, and other Officers, of the Royal Society, at which were present several of the Nobility. When, after an elegant and learned Speech upon the Occasion, the Gold Medal, the annual Prize, was given to Mr. William Watson, Fellow of the Royal Society, for his surprising Discoveries with regard to several of the Properties of Electricity. When the Business of the Day was over, the Society were entertain'd at the Crown and Anchor, opposite St. Clement's Church in the Strand. *D. A. Query, whether the Business of the Day was not more properly just begun at the very Time when the Historian says it was over?* . . .

---

[1] Cf. Virgil, *Eclogues*, iii. 108: *Non nostrum inter vos tantas componere lites*: 'It is not for me to settle so high a contest between you' (Loeb). The sentence which follows the Latin, although not in italics, originates with the *TP*.

Apocryphal History of the REBELLION.

Our Accounts from Carlisle take Notice of the many detestable and shocking Villainies of the Highlanders during their Possession of that City, for not content with stripping several Families, of all their valuable Effects, they scrupled not to make free with the Persons of several young Ladies there, particularly one writes Word: *That after being in a manner strip'd of every Thing, he had the Misery to see his three Daughters treated in such a manner that he could not bear to relate it.* What does not this wicked Crew deserve! G. A. *As much Credit, I believe, as this Historian.*

Among other Circumstances concerning the taking of Carlisle, they relate the following, *viz.* that as the Governor's Men were nailing up one of the Cannon on the Ramparts, it accidentally went off, and killed a Frenchman, the principal Engineer the Rebels had. G. A. *We hope Fortune will stand our Friend, seeing, that if there be any Truth in Proverbs, our Politics entitle us justly to her Favours.* [1]

Our Account of Yesterday, that two Spies were committed to Chester Goal, is confirm'd by Letters from that Place, with this Addition, that they had been to deliver a Letter at a Person of Distinction's House, who was not at home, and had received a disagreeable Answer from his Son; that thereupon one of them, who seem'd to be the Principal, said he knew nothing of the Contents, that he was a Grocer in Cumberland, and his Name Pattison, and went away to an Inn; where it being observed, that the Man who was with him, often inadvertently called him my Lord, they were both taken up and committed. As it is mentioned in some Letters that the Marquis of Tullibardine disappeared of a sudden, after the Taking of Carlisle, it is not impossible that his Lordship may be secured, in the Shape of the Grocer. G. A. *We hope his Lordship will not regain his Liberty as easily as he return'd to Life, after having been killed by the Historians of last Week.*

Some Letters say that Marshal Wade is marching Southwards from Newcastle (where he got back on the 20th) their Reason for saying so is, that the Horse and Dragoons of his Army lay at Durham the 21st at Night. G. A. *We wish the Historians never said any Thing with less Reason.*

We hear, that as soon as the Packet arrived at Harwich, with the Dutch Mails, two Persons were taken on board, by his Majesty's Messengers, and their Papers seized, which we hear are of the greatest Consequence. *Idem. A Paragraph with two* WE HEARS *in it is very suspicious: For as two Negatives make an Affirmative, two* WE HEARS, *I am afraid, amount to a Negative.*

It is said, that the Rebels expected to have Chester delivered to them at their Approach; but thank God they are disappointed. S. J. E. *Before they have approached it.*

It is very currently reported, that Admiral Martin's Squadron has intercepted 16 Transports, and a large French Man of War, who were bound with Forces for Liverpool for the Use of the Rebels. *Idem. These* current *Reports generally* outrun *Truth.*

---

[1] Presumably the proverb that Fortune favours fools.

Extract of a Letter from Appleby in Westmorland, dated Novemb. 22.

'For these several Days past we have had a Party of the Rebels, consisting of about 200 in Number, reconnoitring this Town and the Villages adjacent; they have plunder'd and robb'd all without Distinction, neither sparing Men, Women or Children. At Mrs. Sheldon's they killed about 20 Sheep, and carried them off; at Aspey, they seized upon 12 Young Fellows, a Part of our Militia, whom they obliged to swear never to act against the Chevalier on Pain of military Execution; in short, they appear to be nothing but a ragged Crew of Miscreants, who commit every Outrage, without regard to Law or Decency.' G. A. *If these are such a ragged Crew, as here represented, the greater Shame it is to the Militia of those Parts to suffer such Outrages to be commited by them, with Impunity.*

Last Saturday (*Nov.* 23.) General Ligonier, attended by several Persons of Distinction, arrived at Northampton (where they lay that Night) in their Way to the Army, that General is going to command. L. C.

N.B. *This is a Greek Figure,* [1] *well understood by the Learned, to express the quickest Dispatch; for the General did not set out from this Town till the Day following,* viz. *Nov.* 24.

Yesterday his Royal Highness the Duke of Cumberland set out from St. James's with a large Retinue, to take upon him the Command of the Army now assembling in the Counties of Cheshire and Lancashire. L. C. *There is no such Army.*

The two Troops of Horse-Grenadiers now in Town have Orders to march to Litchfield. D. A. *There is but one in Town, the other is in Flanders.*

We are assured, that the Rebels do not exceed 5000. G. A.

Extract of a Letter from Leeds, Nov. 25.

'A Merchant who went from hence to Kendal last Week, only to gain Advices of the Rebels, wrote Yesterday, that he saw them come into that Place; that they cannot be above 7000, Women and Children included; that he saw many Boys with Musquet, Target, Pistols and Sword, who he thinks were not as long as the Swords they carried; and several of the Women had Arms; that the Horses were in general very bad, many such as we here would not give Asses in exchange for, and even some of the best did not appear in extraordinary good Case.' G. A.

Extract of a Letter, &c.

As to the Strength of the Rebel Army, I can give you no Account; but the Well-affected reckon them 9000. S. J. E.

Extract of a Letter from Wigan, Nov. 25.
Sunday Night Nine o'Clock.

'Just now a Person that was sent to Lancaster, to observe the Motions of the Rebels is come back, and tells us, he saw their Vanguard come into Lancaster

---

[1] 'Prolepsis' (πρόληψις), the representation or taking of something future as already done or existing; anticipation (*OED*).

this Day at one o'Clock, to the Number of about 4000 Foot and 150 Horse, he counting them as they passed over Lancaster Bridge.' G. A. *These Rebels must be very formidable by this Time, if they increase as fast in the Field as in the News-Papers,* viz. *In Paragraphs the same Day, from* 5000 *a* 7000, *a* 9000, *a* 15000 *at least; for an Army whose Vanguard is* 4000 *cannot be supposed less.*

The Duke of Richmond's Regiment was yesterday at Litchfield. G. A. *N.B. The Duke hath no Regiment.*

A Fellow is taken up at Newcastle, who had brought Letters from the Duke of Perth to several Papists in Northumberland, whose Answers he was carrying back, with about 250 l. in Money, which he had collected amongst them for the Support of the Cause. These Circumstances render it sufficiently evident, that this Man has it in his Power to make great Discoveries, and it is said he has manifested a Disposition to make all that he can; so that this Accident is looked upon as a Matter of great Importance here. *S. J. E. This Matter of Importance is* looked on here *to want one Circumstance of great Importance,* viz. *Truth.*

Extract from a Letter from Durham.

'All Accounts in your News-Papers about Carlisle are false, (i.e. *the whole News in the Papers of last Week, and* we hear *that next Week we shall* hear *the same of the News of this*) 'and drawn up, as I am informed, by an Eye-witness to the whole, who was an Officer of the Militia'. *I am informed most of these Letters were drawn up in this Town.*

Extract of a Letter from Edinburgh, Nov. 21.

'Yesterday we had a very singular Instance of Honesty and Loyalty in a Farmer in this Neighbourhood, who was in the Field of Battle at Prestonpans, where seeing the King's Forces intirely put to the Route, amidst the Confusion he carried off two Waggons laden with Baggage belonging to Col. Gardiner's Regiment; which he put into the Heart of a Stack of Corn in his Stock-yard. The Highlanders afterwards got notice of his carrying off these two Waggons, but neither Promises nor Threats could prevail on him to tell where he had put them, tho' he had Parties sent to his House several times for that Purpose, who made all the Search they could, but in vain. As soon as the Country was quiet, and General Handasyd with four Regiments from Berwick was arrived in Town, this Man waited upon the General, to whom he communicated what he did, and desired the General to send a Party to guard the Baggage to Town. This you may be sure was readily granted, and I myself saw the Waggons brought into the Parliament Close yesterday Afternoon.—So much Steadiness and Loyalty as this ought by no means to pass unobserved. *G. A. This Story is more likely to pass unbelieved than unobserved.*

Yesterday (Nov. 29) Colonel Frampton's Regiment of Foot marched from their Quarters in the Borough of Southwark for Portsmouth, where we hear they are to go on board a Ship, on some Expedition. *G. A. Great Part of this Regiment hath been on board a long time; therefore we believe their March yesterday was as great a Secret as the Expedition they are going on.*

We are assured that the Earl of Loudon is now at the Head of 1400 Men well armed and equipped, and waits only for Arms to serve the rest of the Independent Companies, and his Lordship's own Regiment. *G. A. His Lordship, I suppose helps his own Regiment to Arms the last, by the true Rules of Politeness, as Men serve their most intimate Friends last at their Table.*

Yesterday (Sunday) Morning about Three o'Clock, the Transports arrived from Williamstadt, between Gravesend and the Nore, with the rest of the Horse. *L. C. G. A. D. G. Query, Are these the Horse which arrived the Beginning of the last Week in the News Papers, or are they those which are not yet embarked? . . .*

Ships lost. The Running Fox, Capt. Lune, on the Coast of Zealand. *L. C.* Holland, *D. A.* Several French Ships in Dunkirk Road. Three Ships on the Isle of Wight, laden with Cheshire Cheese. *D. A.* The Spy Privateer, the Parham, and a Dutch Vessel, *G. A.* —loaden with Butter, *L. C. This may perhaps figuratively mean Men, Dutch Flesh being made of no other Composition. . . .*

Casualties. On Saturday last as a poor Woman, who lived on Saffron-Hill, was pulling a Piece of Timber out of a Chimney to make a Fire with, the whole Stack fell in upon her, which killed her on the Spot. *L. C. If these foreign and domestic Wars continue, we shall be all forced to follow the Example of this poor Woman, and burn our Chimneys themselves, for want of other Fewel to burn in them.* A Man's Leg broke by a Dray. *D. G.* A Supervisor of the Excise *robbed.* Mrs. Johnson robbed of 7s. A Man not known at Hampstead, and another well known there, have both hanged themselves. *D. A.* Another at Barnet hanged himself for Love. A Sadler robbed of 18s. *G. A.* A Broker robbed, *Idem. Note, This Participle* Robbed *after the Substantive* Broker *hath generally an active Signification. . . .*

Married. Paul Harcombe, Esq; *with a large Estate*, to Miss Alice Brownell, *with a handsome Fortune*, S. J. E. Mr. Thomas Ashburnham, *aged* 90, to an agreeable young Woman, *aged* 23. It is very remarkable that she is his ninth Wife. *L. C.* It is more remarkable if he be, as the Historian says, *Master* of a Tenement in *Poppin's Alley.* Josias Farrer, Esq; to Miss Fuller, *a very agreeable Lady, with a considerable Fortune.* Mr. John Rayner, a Quaker, to Miss Cowper, *with a handsome Fortune, and every Accomplishment which can render a Lady agreeable.* D. A. *Friend* Rayner, *thou hast chosen well.* Rev. Mr. Cooper to Miss Woodham, *an agreeable young Gentlewoman with a handsome Fortune.* Messrs. John Feary, a Vestry Clerk, and Fenwick, an eminent Distiller, to the Misses Drew and Crow; the former a young Gentlewoman, and the latter a beautiful young Lady, with large Fortunes. *D. A.*

Dead. Mr. John Johnson, *a Ship-Corker.* He was aged 111, known by most Sea-faring Men in the Kingdom. *L. C. And by their Great Grandfathers. . . .* Mrs. Mary Tyrrington; she was the last of her Name. *G. E. She is the first of it I have ever heard of.*

To the T R U E P A T R I O T.[1]

Sir,   *Bury Street, Tuesday Evening.*

I am one of those Persons whom the morose Part of Mankind distinguish by the Name of *Epicures*, only because we are blessed with a more exquisite Sensation in our Palates than themselves.

This Evening at Eight, as our company had finished their Dinner, to which we seldom allow more than four Hours, a Gentleman pulled your last Paper out of his Pocket, and read it aloud to us; and greatly, I assure you, to the Satisfaction of us all; for we have some Taste besides that which is seated in the Palate, and are capable of *relishing* Wit as well as any other Dainty.

It was observed, that you had cooked up the Entertainment you *serve* to the Public with much Propriety: You give us first a Dish of substantial Food, when our Appetites are brisk and keen; you then *serve up* several *petit Plats* from the News Papers; and lastly, send us away with a *Bon Bouche* of your own.

A Gentleman of great Delicacy of Taste declared, that you had a most excellent Way of *ragooing* these several Articles which you take from the Historians, as you are pleased to term them; and tho' this is the second Time of Dressing, the *Italic* Sauce which you add by way of Remark, gives a *delicious Flavour* to what was at first *flat* and *insipid*.

It was however agreed, that in your last Number you had crowded your Table too full with *plain Dishes* of this kind, without any *Decoration* whatever. Your apocryphal History of the Rebellion was indeed a Sort of *Hotch-potch* very difficult to digest. I am glad you offered it only as a *Taste*, and have promised to give us no more such *Food*.[2]

If the Public can swallow these *Compositions*, it is an Evidence that their *Appetite* is totally *depraved*, and you will find it as difficult to bring them to like what is really good, as to persuade the lowest Vulgar to relish Venison, Ortelans, Vermicelli, Bologna Sausages, Parmesan Cheese, &c. However, as even this may be effected in Time, an Instance of which I have seen in my own Valet de Chambre, who is become almost as delicate in his Diet as myself; so you may hope by Perseverance to work the same Change, at least in the Generality of Readers. *Season* therefore up to the Taste of Men of Sense, and I will engage you will, in the End, get the better of all the Three-halfpenny *Ordinaries* in Town; for your Bookseller is surely in the right, that a *Pheasant*

---

[1] This letter is commonly attributed to Fielding on grounds of its witty style, employment of his favourite analogy between eating and writing, and a further reference to the historical 'Heliogabalus' in *Tom Jones*. See, for example, Locke, p. 73, and *Tom Jones*, I. i. 33 and *n.* Furthermore, this letter does provide a cunning exposition of the 'method' of the *TP*. But the elaborate use of italic, though clearly in the service of the analogy, is not so characteristic of Fielding at this time as it is of some other hand or hands in the *TP*.

[2] Cf. Fielding's remark to the same effect, in the 'Apocrypha' of no. 4 (26 November 1745), above, p. 356.

with Egg is cheap at double the Price of a Crow. Farewell, I love you as much as I do anything which I can't eat, and am yours, *&c.*

HELIOGABALUS.

THE TRUE PATRIOT, No. 6, Tuesday, December 10, 1745.

AFRICA.

The Dey of Algiers has resigned his Government to his Nephew. This Prince hath always acted with the utmost Amity to the British Nation. This Resignation is occasioned by his great Age and ill Health.

The HISTORY *of* EUROPE.

GERMANY.

The City of Dresden is providing to defend itself, at least for a short Time, against the Approach of the Prussians. And as the Saxon and Austrian Armies are assembling in that Neighbourhood, it is likely they will attempt its Relief, should the Prussians attack it. Which may occasion a decisive Action between those Powers. However, the Gazette Writer informs us, that there is a Probability of seeing the Dissentions between their Polish and Prussian Majesties decided in a more amicable Manner; his Prussian Majesty having sent for his Minister to the Army; *and we know that Ministers chuse the Decisions of Treaties rather than of Battles.* [1]

From *The* PRESENT HISTORY *of* GREAT BRITAIN.

On Friday last, the Alarm of the Rebels having given the Duke the Slip, and being in full March for this Town, together with the Express abovementioned from Admiral Vernon,[2] struck such a Terror into several public-spirited Persons, that, to prevent their Money, Jewels, Plate, &c. falling into Rebellious or French Hands, they immediately began to pack up and secure the same. And that they themselves might not be forced against their Wills into bad Company, they began to prepare for Journies into the Country; concluding, that the Plunder of what must remain behind in this City would satisfy the Victors, to prevent them at least for a long time from pursuing them.

While these fine Ladies, some of whom wear Breeches, and are vulgarly called Beaus, were thus taking care of themselves, another Spirit hath prevailed amongst the Men, particularly in the City of London, where many Persons of

---

[1] This italic comment originates with the *TP.*
[2] Reporting a large-scale French embarkation at Dunkirk; see Lock, p. [76].

good Fortune having provided themselves with the Uniform, were on Saturday last inlisted as Volunteers in the Guards. And on Sunday the Associated Independent Companies were reviewed in Hyde-Park by General Folliot. The Lawyers likewise having exercised themselves in Arms, have subscribed an Engagement to form themselves into a Regiment, for the Defence of his Majesty's sacred person and Government, under the Command of the Right Honourable Lord Chief Justice Willes;[1] a Gentleman who as he hath, from the highest Abilities, joined to the highest Integrity, done the greatest Honour to the Law; so he is at the same time known to be possessed of all those Qualities which enable Men to shine in the Profession of Arms, and hath always distinguished himself with the utmost Bravery and Constancy in the Cause of the present Royal Family and the true Interest of his Country. . . .

On Thursday died the Earl of Rockingham; he was a young Nobleman of a very ambiable Character, as well in public as in private Life.

Last Week the Duke and Dutchess of Norfolk waited upon his Majesty at St. James's, and were very graciously received. Their Graces are both Roman Catholics; and as they are at the Head of the Nobility of the Kingdom of England, the Season which they have chosen to express their Attachment to his present Majesty, should silence the Clamours of hot-headed Men, who cannot separate the Ideas of a Roman Catholic and a Rebel, tho' it be a notorious Truth, that not one single Man of Consequence, who is a Professor of that Religion, hath taken the Opportunity, of these Times of Danger and Confusion, to express any Marks of Disaffection to the Government, or to endeavour molesting it.[2]

It was reported to Day, but with no Authority, that three Transports, with French Troops on board, have been taken off Montrose in Scotland; and should the Embarkation from Dunkirk and Ostend really take place, we shall, with the Blessing of God, give them such a Reception both by Sea and Land, as may probably teach the Grand Monarque to confine his Views to the Continent.

I am assured by a Person of high Distinction, that there is no certain Account of more than two Ships from France being landed in Scotland.

The principal Person upon whom the Pretender's Son hath depended upon in this Expedition, is one Sullivan; he is by Birth an Irishman, and was educated in a Romish College abroad, where he entered into Priests Orders. He had afterwards the Fortune to be recommended to Marshal Maillebois, by whom he was retained as a domestic Tutor to his Son. The Marshal perceiving in him some Symptoms of a Genius better adapted to the Sword than to the Gown, encouraged him rather to apply himself to the former than the latter Profession, which he did with such Success, that having attended his Master to Corsica,

---

[1] For Willes, see *TP* no. 10 (7 January 1746), above, p. 179 and *n.*, where this prominent member of Fielding's profession is coupled with Admiral Vernon ('these two Great Men') as likely victims of a jacobite takeover.

[2] The comment on the news item here, as on the Rockingham obituary notice above, originates with the *TP*. Cf. the praise of the catholic Edward Weld in no. 4, above, p. 355.

when the French undertook to deprive those poor People of their Liberties, he acted as his Secretary. The Marshal, who was a *Bon Vivant*, and used constantly to get drunk every Day after Dinner, was almost incapable of Business the greater Part of the Twenty-four Hours; during all which Time the whole Power devolved on Sullivan, who executed it in such a manner as to do great Honour both to himself and his Master; having here gained a very high Military Reputation, as well as much Knowledge in what is called the Art of making irregular War. He afterwards served two Campaigns, one in Italy, and the other on the Rhine; in which latter Campaign a French General giving a Character of him, said, that he understood the irregular Art of War better than any Man in Europe; nor was his Knowledge in the Regular much inferior to that of the best General. To the Abilities of this Man we may justly attribute the Success with which a Handful of Banditti have so long been able to over-run and plunder a large Part of this opulent and powerful Nation.[1]

APOCRYPHA.

Hawley's Regiment of Dragoons, one Squadron of Sir Robert Rich's Regiment of Dragoons, and two Squadrons of General Ligonier's Horse, are arrived at Gravesend, from Williamstadt. D. A. *For Squadrons of General Ligonier's, read Troops.*

Yesterday came Advice, that the Boscawen Privateer, Capt. Walker, had had an Engagement with two French Men of War, in which she was much shatter'd, but escaped being taken. Soon after she met with a hard Gale of Wind off St. Ives in *Cornhill*, and was unfortunately lost. D. A. *This is the first Ship which was ever lost so near the Royal Exchange.*

His Majesty has been pleased to grant a Commission to eight of his Justices of the Peace for the County of Middlesex, to examine into the present State of the Horned Cattle in the said County, to prevent the spreading of the Contagion, and to allow forty Shillings to the Owner of every Beast that is infected with it, and are directly knocked on the Head, as well as for those that die of it, provided that they are immediately buried in a Hole ten Feet deep. L. C. *This Care for the Health of the Public, and Charity for the Distressed, bespeaks a King who is the Father of his People; and we doubt not but such paternal Goodness will meet with the most dutiful Return from them.*

Last Week a great Cause was tried before the Lord Chief Justice Willes at Westminster-Hall, between the Weavers Company and an eminent Linnen-Draper, for selling printed Calico contrary to Law, when the Company obtain'd a Verdict for the Penalty of 20 l. with Costs. This is the second Verdict the Company have obtain'd.

---

[1] The biographical information here given concerning Sullivan, one of the 'Seven Men of Moidart' who came over to Scotland with the YP, is fuller than that given in the public press elsewhere and may imply some 'inside' source. For Sullivan, more commonly O'Sullivan, see index, *s.n.*.

Yesterday came on in the Court of King's Bench at Westminster, a Trial between the incorporated Company of Horners, Plaintiffs, and an Inkhorn-Turner, Defendant, for following that Business, having no legal Right thereto, when a Verdict was given in favour of the Plaintiffs. G. A. *We suppose this Verdict was likewise with Costs; for the Company of* HORNERS *generally make the Citizens pay Costs of* SUIT.

Last Week a Servant Maid to a Person of Distinction at Petersham in Surrey, was delivered of a Bastard Child, which she concealed; but her Fellow-servants suspecting it, search'd the House, and found the Child on some Stairs leading to the Leads; on which she immediately got away,but was catch'd at Kingston, where the Child, which had been secretly convey'd and buried there, was taken up out of the Church-yard, and a Jury set upon it, and brought in their Verdict *Wilful Murder*; but, on a Midwife's making Oath, the Woman was not fit to be moved, she was suffered to stay at an Inn there, with a Person to watch her; but on Friday last, some People made the Watchman drunk, and the Woman escaped again, and tho' strict Search was presently made after her, she could not be found. G. A. *As the Fear of Shame tempts those poor Wretches to the Commission of such Barbarities, it is pity it was not either less scandalous in Women to be seduced, or less reputable in Men to seduce them.*

From *Apocryphal History of the* REBELLION.

Extract of a private Letter from Chester, Nov. 30.

'We have now compleated the Works about our Castle, which is in so good Condition, that we are no longer in any Pain about the Rebels; they may come when they will, and be sure of a warm Welcome. In digging about the Walls there were found fourteen Bullets, each of forty Pounds Weight, supposed to have lain there from the Time that our Castle was besieged by Oliver Cromwell, who, though he had 20,000 Men under his Command, spent twenty Weeks before it, when the Garrison consisted but of 800 Men. As to the Rebels, according to the best Accounts we have, they diminish daily; they are at present at Manchester, between the two Armies, that of the Duke being ten Miles nearer to them than Marshal Wade. They listed in Manchester about 9 Men in two Hours, the Children of People executed in the last Rebellion. (*Hanging is an Hereditary Distemper in some Families.*) Four Regiments of the Duke's Foot are to be at Macclesfield this Day; the whole Army is so disposed as to be able to join in six Hours; we are not therefore like to have any Rebels here, unless they are brought here to join about twenty of their Friends, whom we have in Prison. I hope a Week's Time will give me an Opportunity of writing you better News, though, as Times go, I look upon this to be pretty good.' *L. C.*

'. . . All the young Gentlemen Rebels that were in the Action at Lowther, we supose, made their Escape to Carlisle. *G. A. These two Historians differ in so many*

Circumstances of their Relation, that it may be much question'd whether they both intend the same Fact.

They write from Deal, that on Tuesday last in the Afternoon was brought on Shore there, the Person who stiles himself Lord Derwentwater, with the young Man he calls his Son, and several other Prisoners, which were taken by the Sheereness Man of War, and were to set out immediately for London. They will be in Town as this Day. *L. C.*

We hear that five of the principal Prisoners taken in the Soleil Privateer will be brought to the Tower Tomorrow. *D. A. The whole Number of these Prisoners, have been brought to Town by the Historians every Day since Saturday last.*

... By the latest Accounts we have from Staffordshire, 'tis certain, that on Monday Night the Rebels came to Newcastle under Line; and that his Royal Highness the Duke set out from Stafford on Monday late at Night, to put himself at the Head of his Army. Therefore we may hourly expect to hear of an Action. *G. A.*

Extract of a private Letter, Stone, Dec. 2.

'The Rebel Army were Yesterday at Macclesfield, and took Possession of Sir Peter Davenport's House there. There has been a small Party of the Rebels at Congleton. His Royal Highness the Duke came hither this Day, and is gone back to Stafford. Our Artillery is arrived; we have about 3000 Men in the Town, and Orders have been issued for providing Quarters for the like Number Tomorrow.' *L. C.*

Extract of a private Letter, Stafford, Dec. 2.

'We are certainly on the Eve of some great Event; his Royal Highness's Army march this Night for Stone; the Highland Rebels are at Stockport, so that if they have the Courage to look the King's Forces in the Face, in two or three Days a Battle must ensue, which will put an End to the Depredations of those desperate Invaders.' *L. C.*

Extract of a private Letter, Stone, Dec. 3. *One in the Morning.*

'His Royal Highness the Duke is at the head of 4000 Men in a large Field, not far from this Place, in Expectation of the Rebels, who, as we have certain Intelligence, are march'd into Newcastle under Line; it cannot certainly be long now before all our Troubles are over, and this disorderly Rabble dispersed.' *L. C.*

Extract of a Letter from Rudgly in Staffordshire, Dec. 2.

'The Rebels are to be at Stone this Night, which is but eleven Miles from hence. The Artillery arrived here Yesterday in very complete order. At eight this Morning an Express came from the Duke, with an Account that the three Battalions of Guards are on the Road hither. The Train has begun its March towards Stone, and all the Army is to join it on the Road. *D. A.*

From all these several Paragraphs which are extracted from the Historians of Thursday *last, in their own Words, it appears that his Royal Highness and his Army were at several*

Places at one and the same Time; and that a Battle was to be fought hourly and daily every Day in the Week. Nor do the Historians agree much better concerning Marshal Wade, *whose Horse and Dragoons are by some said to have quartered in* York *the same Night when others tell us they lay at* Leeds.

Cockermouth, Nov. 28. Mr. John Holme, of Holme Hill, Junr. exerted himself in an extraordinary Manner, during the late Siege of Carlisle; that he opened his Cellars to the Use of the Militia, and comforted and inspired them with Courage and Resolution to defend the City till the Siege was rais'd. *S. J. E. By the Courage it inspir'd we conclude, (at least hope) he gave them only* Small *Beer.*

Three Regiments more, *viz.* the Royal Irish, Hawley's, and Pennington's Infantry, are order'd to join the Army under his Royal Highness the Duke of Cumberland; and they began their March on Tuesday for the North *S. J. E.*

We hear that several Regiments will be quarter'd in the Suburbs of London, and Villages adjacent, and are to be under the Command of Field-Marshal Stair. S. J. E. *These Paragraphs being both equally false, they should have both been introduced with* We hear.

By a private Letter from Penrith, of good Authority, we have Advice, that whilst the Rebels were at that Place, the French Ambassador (as he called himself) who had a Coach and six, and Attendants, lodg'd at Alderman Fishan's two Nights, where he had a Bottle of French Wine, and other Accommodations suitable to his seeming Dignity; but he paid only 4*s.* for Eating, Drinking, Corn, Hay, *&c.* and when he went away, there was, by *Mistake*, some Shoes belonging to the Alderman carried off, for the Use of the Ambassador, or his Retinue. S. J. E. *As Mr. Alderman is, I suppose, a Shoemaker, it was hard to drink his Claret, and carry off his Shoes* to boot.

... The Train of Artillery which was to have gone for Enfield Yesterday, is countermanded; as are also the three Battalions of Foot Guards; but are ordered to be in Readiness at an Hour's Warning. D. G. *In these five Paragraphs there are more than as many Mistakes; but the Countermand is true, and may well be accounted for by the following, if that* EXTRACT OF A LETTER *should (contrary to Custom) have any Truth in it. ...*

We hear that the Rebels are very much afflicted with the Bloody Flux. D. A. *A Distemper which may probably increase upon them, if General Hawley should be able to come up with them.*

We hear that the Cripplegate Grenadiers have, in Support of his Majesty King George, unanimously agreed to march to Finchly Common, or any other Place where his Majesty shall think most convenient, to preserve our happy Constitution. *A Punster, on reading this Paragraph, observed, that the most convenient Place for* Cripplegate *Grenadiers to march to, is Chelsea Hospital.*

We hear that a certain Broker in Exchange Alley, who had a Prize in the present Lottery of 100 l. went to the Chamberlain's Office at Guildhall, and subscribed it: An Example worthy the Notice of all true Englishmen! *If this Story be true, it is an Example worthy the Notice of the Royal Society; but we doubt the Historian hath mistaken a Figure for a Nought, and that this Ticket was really drawn a Prize of* 000.

Casualties. Mr. Wilkins, *G. A.* (Watkinson, *D. A.*) killed by a Cart. Mr. Tankard robbed, *G. A.*—A Carpenter robbed of 4*s.* 6*d.* and his Coat, *G. A. Which was perhaps worth as much more.* A Fire broke out in Bond-Street by the Carelessness of the Workmen, *G. A. This is more probable than that it was the Carefulness of the Papists, as silly People insinuated at the Time. . . .*

Committed. Elizabeth Taylor for stealing Stockings. Thomas Sutton for stealing old Iron. *G. A. He will probably Experience the Danger* Hudibras *asserts there is in meddling with that Commodity. . . .*

Dead. Lieutenant Col. Philips, Muster-Master of the City of London. There are various Candidates for his Place. *G. A.* Mrs. Dean, who for many Years kept a Boarding-School. *For which likewise we suppose there are various Candidates.* Mrs. Bestruan Relict of Mr. Bestruan, Arts-Master of Bridewell, *S. J. E. We never heard Gentlemen took their Degrees there.* Mr. Spirinock, an eminent and wealthy Distiller, *S. J. E.* An eminent Player on the Hautboy in the Streets, in which he died, *ibid. probably not wealthy.* Mr. Rose, an eminent Malster, reckon'd rich, *G. A.* A Man, supposed to be a Pensioner of the late Dutchess of Marlborough, *G. A. He is supposed to have been poor.*[1]

Appeared. In the Papers of this Week several Ghosts of Poets repeating Bellman's Verses. On Thursday Evening last an EXTRAORDINARY Ghost appeared in *Amen Corner.* After which he was shown in a few Shops *for Two-pence* a-piece. As this Ghost had given Notice in the Morning that he intended to *be out* that Night, and bring Tidings with him concerning the Rebellion, several Persons sat up in order to see him, but were very much disappointed by his telling them no more than what they before knew; except a Piece of News from Scotland, which they have since heard was not true.[2]

On Friday Night the same EXTRAORDINARY Ghost appeared again at the same Places, but uttered little or nothing. Are we to conclude that the *Powers above* do in Reality know nothing of what is doing here on Earth, or that they keep their Knowledge to themselves, and send this Ghost abroad with such Tidings as must make us all cry out with *Horatio* in *Hamlet*,

> There needs no Ghost, my Lord, come from the Grave
> To tell us this.[3]

[1] This rather grumpy comment may help settle a minor point in Fielding's biography. The partisan and quarrelsome duchess (1660–1745) was active in the anti-Walpole opposition and had supported 'patriot' efforts to unseat him. When the authorized 'Account' of her 'Conduct' appeared in March 1742, it was immediately and severely attacked. Fielding, whose mother's family (the Goulds) was distantly related to the Churchills, came to the duchess's defense with his *Full Vindication of the Dutchess Dowager of Marlborough* (April 1742). In his 'Of Good Nature', *Miscellanies* (1743), i. 31–2, he praises the power of her wealth to save 'From Poverty, from Prisons, and the Grave' (v. 36); her 'Mass' of wealth is cited (v. 20), perhaps not unequivocally, in 'Written *Extempore*, on a Half-penny', *Miscellanies*, i. 60. Cross, in notes (and rejects) the traditional surmise that the duchess had paid Fielding liberally for his *Vindication*. The TP comment here suggests two things: that she did not, and that he expected her to and felt unrequited. In her will the duchess did leave £20,000 to Chesterfield and £10,000 to Pitt for their efforts in opposition.

[2] *The London Gazette Extraordinary* of 5 December 1745, an evening publication on that date, was advertised in the morning *General Advertiser*. The *Gazette*, whose colophon located it in Amen Corner, is a particular target of satire in the *TP*. See index, *s.v.* '*London Gazette*'. It is not clear which of the few items of Scottish news Fielding believed untrue.   [3] I. v. 125–6.

As we cannot help thinking that sufficient Measures are now taken by the People of this Nation to secure themselves against any Attacks of their Enemies; instead of offering them any Serious Advice at present, we shall endeavour to relieve them from all those gloomy Thoughts with which they have been for some Time frightned, by a News-Paper of our own composing, which contains as much Truth as those Papers generally do.

We shall begin our Paper, according to Custom, with a Paragraph of much Darkness, Wit and Humour, and which we doubt not will be liked by all those who understand it.

LONDON, *Dec.* 10.

Notwithstanding the Sagac—ty of s—me People w–o have lately as–ured the Pub— that the —— from —— would very shortly arrive in —— it is conjectur'd that —— said E——n may not at present be in so gr— a Forw–rdness; which if so we may say with H—m in the Rehearsal,

> If this Design appears,
> We'll lug them by the Ears
> Until we make 'em crack.[1]

Extract of a Letter from Chester, *dated* Dec. 1.

Yesterday it was currently reported that 10,000 French Forces were landed at Halifax in Yorkshire. The Rebels are somewhere between Carlisle and Derby. If they should make us a Visit here, we are prepared to receive them; being all in high Spirits over a Bowl of Punch, in which we drank your Health, *&c.*

Extract of a private Letter from ——, *dated* December 5.

We are in the utmost Confusion here, being hourly in Expectation of a Visit from the Rebels. On which Account the Drum beat to Arms this Day at Noon; upon which great Numbers of the Townsmen assembled, and a Council being called, it was unanimously agreed to march—away from the Enemy.

Extract of a Letter from Salisbury.

A Foreigner, who arrived here last Night very dirty from the West, brought an Account which greatly alarmed us, That he saw 200 Ships upon the Plain, not far from the Hut. This being so confidently attested by a Person of seeming Vivacity staggered the most Incredulous: Till a certain Attorney here having more closely examined him, it came out, that these 200 Ships were no other than 200 Sheep or *Sheeps* as he pronounced them; a Discovery which gave great Joy to the whole Town, who are at present in *high Spirits*.

We hear that the Rebels are marching to Suffolk, tho' others think, they

---

[1] II. ii. 10–12, spoken by the first King of Brentford.

rather intend for Wales; others imagine they design to return to Scotland by Way of Carlisle; others rather imagine they will whip away from Marshal Wade and go to Newcastle; and some think they will give the Slip to the Army under the Duke, and that assembling at Finchley, and make their direct Way to London; Which last we the rather believe, as some Accounts from Fleet-street on Sunday Night last, informed us they were to lodge that Evening at St. Albans.

Saturday last Mr. George Froth, an eminent Brewer, was married to Miss Henrietta Clarinda, Daughter of Mr. Paul Rogers, an eminent Watchman of St. Margaret's Parish; a young Lady of great Sense, Beauty, Merit and Fortune.— The same Day died Mr. Peter Moses, who many Years kept a noted Round House in this Town.

The same Day James Gudgeon was committed to Newgate, by Theophilus Gibbet, Esq; for picking of Pockets.

We think it incumbent on us to acquaint the Public, that 6006076, drawn last Tuesday a Prize of 3000 *l.* was sold at Johnson's State Lottery Office in Pall-Mall.

Now we do assure the Public, that there is no one Syllable of Truth, to our Knowledge, in any of the preceeding Paragraphs, which are here published with no other Design, than what we conceive to be a very good one, of cautioning our Readers against believing all the Reports, I might almost say any of the Reports, which they hear, as most of those have been lately spread with the very worst of Designs.

The Letter to the Jacobites is received for which we thank the Author, and shall insert it in our next.[1] We have likewise received a Letter, or rather Sermon, on the ensuing Fast, from our old Friend Mr. Abraham Adams, which we shall likewise give the Public at the same Time.

N.B. Mrs. Cooper the Publisher of this Paper is provided with several walking Licences for Ghosts, by our Authority; which she issues forth to the said Ghosts at various Prices, from Three Shillings to Half a Guinea, according to the Length and Breadth of the respective Ghosts;[2] and all Shadows which for the future shall venture to *appear* abroad in the Shape of Puffs or Advertisements, without such Licence, shall be instantly lay'd in this Paper.

---

[1] It does not appear to have been written by Fielding; for a text, see Locke, p. [84].

[2] Apparently the actual rates of payment (according to size) of advertisements in the *TP*. The note may also imply that the proprietors of the paper were concerned about an insufficiency in this department; see 'General Introduction', above, pp. lxv–lxvii.

THE TRUE PATRIOT, No. 7, Tuesday, December 17, 1745.

From *The* PRESENT HISTORY *of* GREAT BRITAIN.[1]

When the Rebels arrived at Derby, they called a Council of War, in which the Pretender's Son insisted vehemently on marching with the utmost Expedition towards London; but one Member only of the Council seconded him. The rest represented the Impossibility of its Success; that he had already passed through those Counties where he had the greatest Reason to expect fresh Succours, but had found none of sufficient Consequence to deserve mentioning; that it was plain the Zeal of the English Catholics was too cold to venture any Thing in his Cause; and that they (the Highland Chiefs) could have no longer Dependance upon them. They were ready, therefore, to attend him back to Scotland, where they would lose all their Blood in his Cause; but did not imagine their Duty compelled them to rush on Destruction, without any Probability of Success. A Resolution was in consequence taken, to retreat towards Scotland.

While the Rebels were at Derby, they exacted a very large Sum, besides all the Excise and Land Tax, and County Subscription, which was there lodged in the Hands of Mr. Heathcott and Mr. Crumpton. All those whom they could find were obliged to double the Sum they subscribed. The Rebels no sooner heard of their Retreat, than they behaved with great Insolence and Rudeness; particularly they went to the Church of All Saints at Derby, where they read Prayers, praying for the Pretender by the Name of K— James the Third, and his Son by the Name of Charles Prince of Wales. After which they forced the Organist to play the old Tune of *The King shall enjoy his own again.* . . .[2]

His Royal Highness has, in the present Instance, rival'd the greatest military Characters in Expedition, which is an Article in which Julius Cæsar placed the principal Merit of a General. The Duke's March from Merriden to Macclesfield, in three Days, is perhaps more (especially if we consider the Badness of the Roads) than hath been effected by any General at the Head of Regular Troops. Nor hath the Spirit of those Troops been ever exceeded; for when it was proposed to select a thousand Voluntiers from the Guards for this Expedition, the whole Brigade offered themselves universally. Nor can I omit here, while I am speaking of the Spirit of these Troops, the Story of a very young Officer, who was lamed at the late Battle of Fontenoy, for which Reason, when the Battalion to which he belonged was ordered to march from this Town, his Commanding Officer, out of Compassion to his Infirmity, appointed another to supply his Place. Upon hearing this, the young Gentleman immediately repaired to his Commander, and asked him, if he had misbehaved in any Part of his Duty. To which the other very readily answered in the Negative; nay, and with some Commendation. Then, Sir, reply'd the young Man, I desire I may not

---

[1] The 'Present History of Europe' is omitted in this number without remark.

[2] The popular Stuart or 'legitimist' song, referring to the expectations of a restoration. See *JJ* no. 34 (23 July 1748), p. 352 and *n*. Squire Western adapts this refrain, in *Tom Jones*, VI. xiv. 321.

be disgraced by being put by my Command. If his Majesty thinks my late Wound has disqualified me for his future Service, I desire I may obtain an honourable Dismission from it, and not receive my Pay when I cannot do my Duty. This Spirit was greatly commended by his superior Officer, and the young Gentleman went accordingly on the Expedition. . . .

On Friday Morning last a Pannic run thro' this Town, little inferior to that which had seized us the Friday before; this on Friday last was occasioned by an Express which came to the Secretary's Office, at four in the Morning, with an Account, that a large Fleet of French Transports was attempting to land on the Coast of Suffolk. With this News his Majesty was disturbed very early, and a Council summoned to meet at break of Day; but before eleven o'Clock a second Express quieted all our Fears, by bringing certain Accounts that this French Fleet consisted only of some Smugglers and Fishing-boats of our own. The same Morning, indeed, two French Transports did arrive at Dover; but they were in Company with two Privateers, who took them in their Way from Bologne to Dunkirk. They were in all eight Sail, having on board Cloaths and Bedding for Soldiers; and were, when taken, under the Convoy of a French Man of War, of Twenty-two Guns. . . .

On Saturday Night last Colonel Lyttelton, Adjutant-General, and Brother to the Right Honourable George Lyttelton, Esq; one of the Lords of the Treasury, was married to her Grace the Duchess of Bridgwater.

The Mob are at present so zealous on the Right Side, that the Guards had great Difficulty to preserve the Lives of the Prisoners lately taken by the Sheerness, in their Way to London. They even attempted to burn the Coach in which the Principal of them were placed, where they supposed, not without some Reason, that a Person of very high Note was included. They could not by any means be restrain'd from Insults, such as throwing Halters into the Coach, &c. . . .

APOCRYPHA.

Extract of a Letter from Plymouth, dated Dec. 2.

'Friday last arrived the Hampton-Court, who had an Engagement with the Defiance for half an Hour, some Days since, mistaking each other for French Men of War; but the Defiance having a Shot lodged in her Side, one of the Sailors took it out, and finding the King's Broad R upon it, discover'd their Mistake.' G. A. *This Story seems to deserve the Mark of a broad L— upon it.*

Our Connoisseurs in political Physiognomy will observe, if they survey with Accuracy the Jacobites, since the Flight of their invincible ragged Heroes the Rebels, that the forked Tongues of the former are surprisingly blunted, and tipp'd with Oil; their Lips ting'd with Blackberries; their Faces white-wash'd from Top to Bottom, and the Gnomons of them pucker'd up; their Eyes sunk a French Yard in their Heads; their Chins extended half a Spanish Ell; and their

Hearts (alas!) sneaked down, above a Roman Foot, in their Paunches. D. A. *Our Connoisseurs in Nonsense, if they survey with Accuracy this Paragraph, will observe,* &c.

From *Apocryphal History of the* REBELLION.

We have received very Authentic Advices from Nottingham, by a Letter dated Saturday Night past 10 o'Clock, that Part of Marshal Wade's Horse arrived there that Evening. G. A.

Last Sunday Night Marshal Wade, with his whole Army, march'd from Doncaster and Ferrybridge towards Lancashire, in order to cut off the Retreat of the Rebels, in case they design to march for Scotland. S. J. E.

We hear, that Orders are sent for General Bland's Regiment of Horse, and Lord Mark Kerr's Dragoons, to march to the Army assembling on Finchley-Common. G. A. Tuesday.

Extract of a Letter from Stafford, Dec. 9.

'I believe by this Time the Rebels are got into Lancashire. Just now came in the Lord Cobham's, Lieutenant-General Ligonier's, and the Duke of Kingston's Light Horse; and into Uttoxeter, *Lord Mark Kerr's and Bland's Regiments of Horse.* —On Saturday last a Barrister at Law was taken into Custody at Readford, about a Mile from this Place; and we hear, that great Discoveries have been made by his Confession, and the Papers found upon him.' G. A. Thursday. *Non bene conveniunt.* [1]

Several Gentlemen, who are Surgeons, are set out for the Duke of Cumberland's Army, having enter'd themselves Voluntiers to serve under his Royal Highness as Occasion may require. D. A. *We hope these Gentlemen will make* GOOD SUBJECTS *of some of the Rebels. . . .* [2]

We hear that in filling up the Trenches before Carlisle, more than 20 dead Bodies of the Rebels were discovered, which they left unburied at the Time of the Siege; and 'tis also said, that near 200 of the Rebels had been killed before that Place, in a thick Fog; the Town's People having heard the Bagpipes playing at a small Distance, to which they directed this [*sic*]Guns, and the Rebels not having discovered their Nearness to the Town, till they felt the Heat of their Fire.

We have certain Accounts by a Gentleman from Brampton, that upwards of 500 Highlanders, Deserters from the Pretender's Army, have passed by Carlisle, since the main Body of the Rebels left that Town, in their Way to Scotland. G. A. *These Deserters are probably the Ghosts of those Highlanders who were killed before the Walls of Carlisle.*

---

[1] 'They do not go well together.' Cf. Ovid, *Metamorphoses*, ii. 846–7: 'non bene conveniunt nec in una sede morantur | maiestas et amor'.

[2] That is, use the cadavers of the rebel dead for surgical investigations. Cf. the anecdote in no. 23 (1–8 April 1746), above, p. 257.

Extract of a Letter from Brouchtie, Nov. 29. 1745.

I received yours, in which you complain that we have not enter'd into Associations here, as they have done in England. At that Time it was not in our Power, on Account of the Grand Association, but as soon as the Rebels left this Country, I address'd myself to my Neighbours with Success; for I prevailed on the Provosts, the other Magistrates, and Inhabitants of Brouchtie, Banchoria, Peter Culter, Sandend, Dyce, Garcock, Inch, Oyne, Raine, Tarves, Newburgh, Skirduston, Strichen, Auchterless, Banes-hole, Tetter-letter, Daucot, Aberchirder, Gowkilones, and Dalquarchie. The above Parishes, one with another, can send 300 good stout brave Fellows each. They have provided Arms for themselves, and are to serve four Months on their own Expences; besides them there will be 300 Men from Metross Slate-Quarry, and as many from the Quarries of Culsamond. They will join the noble Earl of Loudon, and we hope will give a good Account of the Rebels at Perth. Our greatest Fear is, that they will march South to join their Fellow Rebels; but if they do, we shall take Care how they return. We are hopeful before this comes to your Hand, that the brave Duke of Cumberland has entirely routed the Rebel Army in England, and then Marshal Wade's Forces, and our loyal Associators will have the Perth Rebels betwixt two Fires. By what you write, I judge the English think all Scotchmen Rebels. God forbid; and as it is not so, I am sorry they should judge so uncharitably of a whole populous Kingdom, for a few misled and desperate Men, who have done us a Favour in leaving the Country.' G. A. *Either this Author's Correspondent is a Fool, or the Author himself is one, for drawing a false Conclusion from his Correspondent's Words. Sure I am that such an Opinion as is here charged on the whole People of* England *can with Justice be imputed to none, except some hot-headed simple Men, who are forced to confound Innocence and Guilt, for want of any Share of the distinguishing Faculty; it would be indeed as fair to charge the* English *Northern Counties, in which the Rebels have been, with Rebellion, as to lay such a general Imputation on* Scotland. *Indeed the same Reasons and Arguments might be used to support both Accusations.* [1]

We hear from Manchester, that the Mob rose and beat the Van-guard of the Rebels out of the Town; and they add, a Butcher and his Man of that Town had taken two of them, and secured them. L. C.

Extract of a Letter from Stockport, Dec. 10.

The Rebels got to Manchester last Night; thirty of their Horse march'd in at 2 o'Clock, which was some Hours before the Pretender and the Main Body arrived. The Horse were rudely received by some People, who threw Stones at them.—I apprehend this will cause some Persons to be ill used.—We have just now Advice, that about 8 this Morning they began to march out; and that the Pretender, attended by some Officers, with the Rear of the Army, went over

---

[1] Cf. the 'Reasons and Arguments' against wholesale condemnation of the Scots, in 'Observations on the Present Rebellion', *TP*, no. 1 (5 November 1745), above, pp. 113–15. In no. 2 the same department takes up similar condemnation of the catholics.

Sawford-Bridge, before the Messenger came away.—This Minute a Messenger is come, with Advice, that the Rebels have left 500 Men to pillage the Town, for the Insults committed on their Horse.' G. A.

A Party of the Watchmen near Manchester, in the Night hearing some People coming along, who did not answer, when challeng'd, they fir'd, and killed one of the Rebels, whereupon the rest retreated, and acquainted the Pretender therewith, who sent out a Party, that took five of the Watchmen; who are carried to Wigan.—The Rebels in their March give out, that they will not halt till they get to Edinburgh.' G. A. *Q. If these three Accounts do not point at one and the same Fact. And Q. if that be a true One. . . .*

Yesterday came an Account, that a French Ship, bound to Scotland, with sixty Pieces of Cannon on Board, had, by Stress of Weather, been obliged to put into Dublin, where she was seiz'd; but all the Men, except three, had made their Escapes on Shore. D. A. *These Cannon are probably sent over by the* French *Treasurer in Lieu of the Livres demanded of them by Monsieur the Ambassador.*

They write from Newcastle Under-Line, that on Saturday last the Rebels took a Justice of the Peace from his own House in that Neighbourhood, and after plundering him, sent him back again almost naked. S. J. E. *Yet naked Justice is methinks an Object, which these Rascals shou'd not care to look at.*

Last Monday the two new Regiments raised by the Nobility and Gentry in Hampshire, under the Command of the Duke of Bolton and Sir George Musgrave, Bart. marched from Winchester for the Sea-Coast, to be ready to oppose any Foreign Invaders. L. E. *The former of these marched sometime since to* Portsmouth. *The Latter is not marched at all.*

We hear that the Gentlemen and Farmers in the several Parts of the Country where the Rebels are expected, have ploughed up the common Roads, cut down Trees, and laid them cross the Highways, so as to render them almost impassable. L. E. *We hope there are some standing Trees, which will obstruct their Progress more effectually, than any which lie down in their Way.*

York, Dec. 10 By a Letter from Appleby, 'tis advised, that last Saturday Evening the principal People of Carlisle being desirous of keeping the Rebel Garrison which is in the Castle in tolerable good Temper, were in Company with the officers till about 11 o'Clock; but about one in the Morning, the Rebels sent and took the Gentlemen all out of their Beds, and carried them Prisoners to the Castle. S. J. E. *These Dogs, it seems, are not Honest even in their Cups. . . .*

Casualties. An old Man drank 3 half Pints of Geneva for a Wager, L. C. *by which he won his Wager and lost his Life. . . .*

Dead. . . . Mr. Mee, formerly half an Apothecary. Mr. Thomas Letheuillier, an eminent Factor. Henry Hodges, Esq; of an eminent large Fortune, G. A. Walwin Mees, Esq; L. C. *Quer. Whether this be Mr. Mee as above. . . .*

Appeared. In several Papers lately the Ghost of a Print intituled the *Manual Exercise of a Foot Soldier.* We have seen this Ghost several Times, but have omitted Laying him, as not apprehending any Mischief from him. But on Saturday last he had the Assurance to appear in that Rendezvous of Ghosts *The*

Daily Advertiser, roaring forth, 'I am the Sheet Print of the Manual Exercise of a Foot Soldier. The Rebels took me at *Derby*, and showed me to the young Pretender, who upon the first Sight of me ordered me to be burnt, saying, *I had been of great Service to his Enemies in forwarding them in their Discipline*.'[1]

To the PATRIOT.

Sir,

Be pleased to add to your next Collection of Ghosts, that of a Candle-Snuffer, who *departed* from Mr. *Rich*'s Playhouse in that Quality, and hath since *risen* in a higher Capacity in the other.[2] This Ghost had the Assurance on Friday last in the *London Courant*,[3] to spit Fire and Brimstone at a very pretty Woman, and an incomparable Actress, whose Generosity and Goodness charm us more than even *her* Beauty and Talents cou'd have done.[4] Be pleased likewise to inform

[1] Cf. *DA* of 14 December 1745: 'We hear from Derby, that the Rebels plunder'd that Place of all the Horses, Saddles, Shoes, Boots, Bed-Ticks, and almost every Thing they could lay hold on; and meeting with a Parcel of the Sheet Print of the Manual Exercise of a Foot Soldier, (dedicated to his Royal Highness the Duke of Cumberland) which they presently shewed to the young Pretender, upon Sight thereof he order'd them to be burnt, saying it had been of great Service to his Enemies, in forwarding them in their Discipline.' The print, in which Cooper seems to have had an interest, is advertised, in a first impression, in *DA* of 29 October 1745, and in a 'third', in *DA* of 27 November 1745. Additionally, the *DA* had given the print a number of 'Puffs' or 'We hears' during November and December. A dozen of the illustrative 'Postures' used to illustrate the manual are reproduced in *London Magazine*, xv (1746), 190–1.

[2] Probably James Lacy (d. 1774), a member of Fielding's company at the New Haymarket in the 1730s, later a promoter at Ranelagh. In the early 1740s Rich appointed Lacy undermanager ('Candle-Snuffer') at Covent Garden. See Benjamin Victor, *A History of the Theatres* (London, 1761), p. 66; *London Stage*, Part 3, vol. i, p. xcvii. When the bankers finally forced Fleetwood out of Drury Lane in late 1745, Lacy succeeded him as manager of that house. In *Champion* of 9 September 1740, contemplating what might have happened if Fleetwood's difficulties of the preceding season had resulted in his ouster, Fielding hypothesizes the coming to power of a 'Deputy Manager', whom he later calls 'a Candle-Snuffer, or one who is qualified for no higher an Office'.   [3] Not traced; but see next note.

[4] Susanna[h] Maria Cibber (1714–60), actress and opera singer, sister of Fielding's acquaintance Thomas Arne and separated from Fielding's old antagonist Theophilus Cibber. In *JJ* no. 10 (6 February 1748), p. 153, she is complimented as an exemplar of the 'natural' style of acting (there is a similar compliment in *Tom Jones*, IX. i. 493), and in *JJ* no. 13 (27 February 1748), p. 181, she is ordered to 'prepare a good warm Box at her Benefit, for the Reception of Ourself and our fair Peggy'. See also *Amelia* (1751), v. viii, and *CGJ* no. 3 (11 January 1752), i. 152. In *DA* of 7 December 1745 Mrs. Cibber ran an advertisement offering to play 'Polly' in the *Beggar's Opera* for three performances, *gratis*, at Drury Lane, all proceeds from the house to go to the Veteran's scheme at Guildhall. On 9 December she announced in the same paper that inasmuch as Drury Lane had not responded, she would accept Rich's counteroffer to have her play at Covent Garden instead, and would do so on 14, 16, and 17 December. In the same issue of the *DA* a letter signed 'A Veteran Protestant' characterized Mrs. Cibber's offer as 'a Jesuitical Stroke of a Papist Actress in Pursuit of Protestant Popularity'. In the *General Advertiser* of 10 December she replied to this hostile letter, saying the author of it was no stranger to her and was trying to injure her character as a player. She wrote Garrick she was told that Lacy, Macklin, and Giffard sent 'advertisements against me . . . to the printer's'; *Private Correspondence of David Garrick*, ed. James Boaden (London, 1831), i. 45–8 (dated 11 December 1746[5] and 19 December 1746[5]). With the cast also playing *gratis* and the candles contributed by the chandlers, Rich paid slightly more than £600 into the veterans' fund; see *General Advertiser* of 21 December 1745; *GM*, xv (1745), 667.

the said Ghost, that if he will venture to walk here, and own himself the same, he will be laid—across the Shoulders with a Faggot Stick,

A VOLUNTEER BLUE.

Tilt Yard,[1] Sunday Night.

Addenda to the Present History of GREAT BRITAIN.

The Highlanders are running away as fast as they can; they have got the Start of the Duke, having left Manchester 22 Hours before he got thither.—Ribble Bridge, near Preston, and Lancaster Bridge are both broke down, to retard their Retreat.—The Rebels are very much fatigued with their long Marches, and very much dispirited.

P.S. The Post-boy from Manchester just brings Word, that 50 of the Rear of the Highlanders are taken Prisoners, near Preston, and they hope soon to be up with the rest.

General Oglethorpe came into Preston a few Hours after the Rebels left it. He took there one Capt. Mackenzie, with two private Men.

** *These Particulars came by Yesterday's Post to a Person of Distinction, from Derbyshire, and were sent me late last Night.*

THE TRUE PATRIOT, No. 8, Tuesday, December 24, 1745.

The present HISTORY *of* EUROPE.

GERMANY.

The King of Prussia, after the total Overthrow of the Saxon Army at Whilstorff, joined the Body of Troops under the Prince of Anhault Dessau, and marched directly towards Prince Charles, to offer him Battle; but that Prince chose rather to retire towards Bohemia. His Prussian Majesty then turned towards Dresden, the Gates of which City were thrown open to him, and the Garrison surrender'd Prisoners of War. By the Contributions raised in Leipsick and Mersebourg, and other Cities in Saxony, his Prussian Majesty seems determin'd not to be out of Pocket by this Winter Campaign, into which he hath been forced. These have, however, fallen very heavy on the Conquered, even so as to reduce them to present Beggary. However, his Majesty hath made them some amends by extraordinary Acts of Complaisance; for he waited on the young Princes and Princesses of Poland, appointed them a Guard of his Grenadiers,

---

[1] At this time a street before Whitehall, but formerly an open space abutting the old Banqueting Hall, the traditional site of tourneys and jousts. Both the dateline and the signature of this letter are meant to recall not only the benefit to military recruitment of Mrs. Cibber's proposal but also the contentiousness it provoked and her need of a 'protector'. Cf. *Spectator* no. 109 (5 July 1711).

which he assured them should be as absolutely under their Command, as if they were the Troops of the King their Father. He hath likewise entertained the Ladies with several Concerts, Balls and Operas; but if these be Acts of mere Gallantry only, the Acceptance of the same Terms of Accommodation, at this Season, which he proposed some Months since, is an Instance of real Greatness. This he hath done, and accordingly a Peace is at length concluded and signed, under the Mediation of the King of Great Britain, between her Hungarian Majesty and the Kings of Poland and Prussia;[1] an Event of the utmost Consequence to Europe in general, and to this our Nation in particular, since it must give some Check to the Ambition of France; nay, in its Consequences, if rightly improved, may cause that turbulent Power, which now is said to threaten Hanover, Holland and Great Britain, with Invasions, to tremble in her own Territories.

In short, the Grandeur of this Kingdom, and the Cause of Liberty and the Protestant Religion, are the Stake.

The Game is far from being desperate; nay, I think it is in our Hands. To which I will add, that Fortune seems on our Side.

But it is a dangerous Game, and difficult to play. It requires the greatest Abilities in the Politician who is to manage it; and any Blunder, the Loss of an Opportunity, or affording one to the Enemy, must be irretrievably fatal.

May that Being, therefore, in whose Power is the Disposition of all Things, grant our Affairs at present may be placed in Hands capable of managing them rightly, at a Season when the Alternative is, our being the Greatest, or Lowest Nation in the Universe.

From *The* PRESENT HISTORY *of* GREAT BRITAIN.

The great Expedition with which his Royal Highness the Duke hath pursued the Rebels, must have certainly prevented much Mischief to the Northern Counties, by forcing them to retreat with such Celerity: For when we consider the Temper in which the Rebels left Derby, incensed at their Disappointment, and the Ill-will which the Pretender and their Chiefs must have borne to their English Friends, from whom they received so little Assistance, we must necessarily conclude, that had they had sufficient Leisure, they would not only have plundered every Place through which they passed, but have left the most terrible Marks of Cruelty behind them. In this Light, therefore, his Royal Highness must have highly endeared himself to every honest *Englishman*. Nothing indeed could be more truely heroic than the Alacrity with which this brave young Prince, instead of sending an inferior General, put himself at the Head of a Detachment from his Army, and with equal Contempt of Danger and Fatigue, determin'd to pursue a much superior Number of desperate Ruffians, well provided with Cannon, while he was obliged to leave all his own behind

---

[1] The Treaty of Dresden, 25 December 1745 N.S. An 'Abridgment' is published in *TP* no. 13 (21–8 January 1746), Locke, pp. [128–9].

him. . . . The Rebels must be greatly weakned with the long Marches they have been obliged to take; but we do not find that their Loss in Numbers hath been very considerable, or that they have left either Baggage or Cannon behind them; and it is to be feared, that enow of them will be able to return to Scotland, to increase their Brethren there to a very formidable Body. These are already about 5000, besides the Auxiliaries from France, under the Lord John Drummond, which consist of near 700. They have with them a Train of Battering Artillery, and must probably be superior to the Forces which his Majesty now hath in those Parts; but should a Body of *Danes*,[1] together with the English Horse now embarking at Williamstadt, be landed at Newcastle, and there join the Army under Marshal Wade, which by this time is arrived in that Town, we may yet expect to see a speedy End put to this Rebellion, which is an Object no longer to be trifled with. Indeed I think I may assure my Readers, that such Measures will be certainly taken, as, humanly speaking, they must be attended with certain Success. Nay, I could wish that the little Force under the Duke was added to this Army; for we shall still be too strong in the South to fear any Efforts of our Enemies, the Flame in the North is the only Danger which threatens us, and that we ought not to lose a Moment in using every Endeavour to extinguish.

At Sea Fortune seems to declare on our Side, and to be equally watchful with the brave and vigilant Admiral Vernon, for our Preservation: For, besides the Safety of our Coasts being so well guarded by the excellent Disposition of that truly great Man;[2] besides the many Successes of our Men of War and Privateers in the Channel, by which so many of the French Transports have been destroy'd; we had, last Week, an Account from Vice-Admiral Townshend, dated in Prince Rupert's Bay, the 18th of November 1745, That he had, between the 31st of October last and the 2d of November, taken, sunk, and destroy'd, 30 Sail of Martinico Ships; and had forced a-ground a French Man of War, of 80 Guns, which was the Commodore of their Convoy, and had done her considerable Damage. His Majesty's Ship the Pembroke had before, on the 3d of October, taken two Martinico Ships; and, on the 22d, the Vice-Admiral had sunk a French Privateer, and retaken an English Prize. The French have likewise lost a 36 Gun Ship, going into Porto Rico; and had but three Men of War left in those Seas, when these Letters came away.

For further Particulars of this Action, we refer the Reader to an Account published on Friday last, by Authority, (Price Two-pence) *if he can understand it.*

Last Week Baron Boetzlaer was introduced to his Majesty, in Quality of Envoy-Extraordinary, from the States General. *Whence we may conjecture, they have at least deferred signing the Neutrality, till further Notice.*

On Saturday Fortune, who had a long Time kept her Votaries in Suspence,

---

[1] In 'Present History' of *TP* no. 9 (31 December 1745), below, p. 390, the compiler corrects the identification to 'Hessian Auxiliaries (which were in our last called *Danes* by Mistake)'.

[2] For the pattern of compliment to Vernon and its significance, see 'Present History' of no. 9 (31 December 1745) and especially no. 10 (7 January 1746), below, pp. 390, 394–5.

put an End to their Solicitude, by disposing of the two great Prizes in the Lottery, with great Discernment; the one on certain Messieurs in Limestreet. Square, and the other on Mr. Cramond, an Apothecary, in Gracechurch Street. The former of these Tickets was inclosed in a *small* Bladder, which is one of Fortune's Emblems, and lost some time since. This will be a Prize of 50 l. to the Person who hath found it, that Reward having been advertised upon its being restored. . . .

Monday Evening. I am just informed, there is Advice come, that the Rebels, being close press'd by the Duke, and unable to pass the River Eden, which is greatly swollen with Rains, had taken Refuge in Carlisle, where they were besieged in Form by his Royal Highness; who had caused some Cannon to be brought to his Army from Cockermouth, and expected shortly a Reinforcement of Foot from Marshal Wade. If this be so, our Young Hero will have the sole Glory of putting a final Stop to the Ravages of these Miscreants.

From APOCRYPHA.

The Accounts which the Historians *have given us of the Rebels are such a Heap of Rubbish, Nonsense, Inconsistency, Confusion and Contradiction; that, as we have not sufficient Room to insert all, we shall only extract some of their most curious Articles under the general Head of Apocrypha, which, for the future, we shall distinguish by the Days of the Week.*

Wednesday. . . . Yesterday a Spy, said to be a Frenchman, was taken up at Barnet, and brought to the Tilt-yard Coffee-House in a Cart, in order to be examin'd by the Secretaries of State. He is an antient Man, with a long Beard, and his Face full of Wrinkles. D. A. *This Fellow ought not to have been taken into Custody, since the Historian has given so good an Account of him.*

A Gentleman of Halifax, who was three Days Prisoner with the Rebels, informs us, that while the Pretender was at Dinner at Derby, he was alarmed with a Report of the Duke of Cumberland's being very near him; upon which he dropt his Knife, and said, *I am betrayed! ruined and undone!* They burn all Writings, and what they call Heretic Books. Justice Duckenfield's favourite Bible was first thrown into the Fire with this Expression, *Damn all Heretic Books and those that read them.* L. C. *I know not what may be Justice Duckenfield's favourite Bible, but I never heard that the Bible was accounted a Heretic Book.* . . .

Yesterday a Person of Distinction was brought up to Town from Lancashire, and carried to a Messenger's House. D. A.

Yesterday in the Evening a Gentleman, whose Name is Morgan, was brought to London in a Coach and Six from Chester, escorted by a large Party of Horse Guards, and committed to the Custody of one of his Majesty's Messengers for Examination. L. C. *We suppose this Person of Distinction of* Lancashire, *and this Gentleman of* Chester *are one and the same. The Mistake of a County being a small Blunder in these modern Historians.* . . .

Penrith, Dec. 8. *Four o'Clock in the Morning.* The common Rebels at Carlisle have got a Notion, that the Pretender Charles has lost the Battle, and is killed, and their Chiefs cannot persuade them to the contrary.—No Obedience was paid to the Summons for Horses, but, on the contrary, all the Horses near Carlisle are removed to a greater Distance. The Rebels have eleven Horses; they were ordered last Night out of the City into the Castle. The City Gates were shut Yesterday at Four o'Clock in the Afternoon, and only two Men on the Walls last Night on the Irish Side. L. C.—We suppose these several Paragraphs of curious News come from that *self same Side.*

The Fishmongers Company have expressed their Attachment to his Majesty, and their Care for the Preservation of their Property, with that of others, by ordering 300 l. to be subscribed at Guildhall, for the better Relief, Support and Encouragement of the Soldiers, employed to suppress the present Rebellion. L. C. *We wish this Worshipful Company, of whose* Care for their Property *we have not the least Doubt, wou'd take some Care to lower the present exorbitant* Price of Fish, *or very few Persons will shortly have Property enough to have any Dealings with that Commodity.*

We hear, by a Letter to a Gentleman of Newcastle on Monday last, that three Twenty-Gun Ships had landed a great Number of Marines on the Islands of Mull and Sky, who had burnt or destroy'd all the Houses, Corn, Cattle, &c. of the Rebels there. S. J. E. *We believe one of these Ships might have carried off the Whole. . . .*

It may not be amiss to inform our Readers that by Wednesday's Post, we received several Letters from Chester, and other Places near it, containing an Account of the King's Troops coming up with the Highland Rebels, and their intrenching themselves at Preston; but as these Letters were dated the 16th, and as we had Letters from Preston directly dated the Evening before, which gave quite another Relation, and that the Rebels were actually marched towards Lancaster, we did not think proper to amuse our Readers with those Reports, and the foregoing Letter sufficiently proves that we formed a right Judgment in not publishing them, inasmuch as Preston lies Fifty Miles South of Penrith. L. C. *This Historian would shew his Judgment by omitting most of the Articles which he Prints. One Instance of which he would have given had he left out* the foregoing Letter.

'Tis said, in a Letter from Burton near Kendal, dated Dec. 17, that the Coach in which rode the young Pretender's Favourite, Miss Jenny Cameron, and Mrs. Murray, broke down near that Place, and that the Country People rose, and seiz'd the two Ladies, with some of the Rebels. G. A. *It was a great Neglect in the Pretender, either as a Lover or a General, to leave his* Baggage *with so slender a Guard. . . .*

We hear from Oxfordshire, that the Right. Hon. the Earl of Macclesfield has raised a Regiment of Foot, and Mr. Rudge a Troop of Horse, which they maintain at their own Expence, besides levying and sending in a great Number of Recruits into Lord Harcourt's Regiment. A Zeal and Generosity not to be equall'd in all these Troubles. L. E. *If our Conduct was equal to our Zeal this Nation wou'd be invincible. . . .*

Casualties. . . . A House in Princes Street, Covent Garden, broke open and robbed of Goods to a considerable Value, while Numbers of People were passing by the Door, G. A. *Many I suppose to help off the Goods.* . . .

Dead. . . . James Round, Esq; formerly an eminent Bookseller, a Gentleman greatly respected. *Q. If this Bookseller, Gent. and Esq; be all one Person.* . . . John Marlow, Esq; an eminent Grocer; he fined for Sheriff of this City, L. C. *By that he got the Title of Esq*; . . .

THE TRUE PATRIOT, No. 9, Tuesday, December 31, 1745.

The present HISTORY *of* EUROPE.

The Prospect in Italy hath been of late so gloomy, that it is with Reluctance we cast our Eyes that Way. A Glimpse of Light, however, seems to break in upon the King of Sardinia, who is determined to struggle to the last. Prince Lichtenstein, at the Head of a large Body of *Austrians*, and some Piedmontese Battalions, is strongly encamped on the Ticino. He hath with him a good Train of Artillery, and hath lately routed an advanced Body of near 1000 Spaniards. We may hope at least that the late Accommodation with the King of Prussia may enable the Queen of Hungary to send a Force into Italy, which may once more enable his Sardinian Majesty to look the common Enemy in the Face.

Our Accounts from France and Flanders are full of little besides Councils of War, which have been held at Paris, at Ghent, at Brussels, *&c.* By all their Preparations, the French seem to intend an Extension of their Conquests in Brabant, before the Allies are in the Field. A Pannic (which is at present a Word much in Use) hath greatly prevailed at Brussels; but hath had a better Effect than a Pannic generally produces, by putting the Generals there on the most immediate Means of strengthning and defending as well the City of Antwerp as of Brussels, against any Surprize. We seem to be at the Eve of some great Event, or of some great Attempt at least of the Crown whose restless Ambition is the Curse or evil Genius of Europe.

By the late Treaty between the Courts of Vienna, Berlin, and Dresden, it is stipulated, *inter alia*, 1. That the King of Prussia and Elector Palatine, who is to be included in the Treaty, shall acknowledge the Emperor; and 2. That the King of Poland shall pay to the King of Prussia, at the next Leipsic Fair, the Sum of one million of German Crowns, in order to defray the Expence of the War.

From *The* PRESENT HISTORY *of* GREAT BRITAIN.

. . . Thus are these Banditti arrived once more safe in their own Neighbourhood, after an Expedition which is not to be parallel'd in History. In which as the Loss they have suffered hath been much less than they could have reasonably promised themselves, so have the Cruelties they have committed fallen altogether as short of what might have been apprehended from such a Rabble, especially when incensed with Disappointment. And this, as I have already hinted, is entirely owing to the Vigour with which they have been pursued by his Royal Highness.

Among the several Accounts of their Plunder and Rapine, there are some which seem to have affected a Kind of Humour. One of these Fellows sold his Horse to a poor Countryman for 10s. which was not the 10th Part of its Value; but as soon as he had touched the Money, instead of delivering the Horse, he told the Purchaser he was a damn'd Rogue to take the Advantage of a poor Stranger's Ignorance in Horse-flesh, and immediately rode off with both Money and Beast. Another having sold his Plad for a Crown, told the Person who bought it, he should have Occasion to wear it in his Journey Home; but he would be sure to surrender it if ever he saw him in the Highlands. A third robbed his Landlord of his Purse, and said he did it out of Kindness to him; for it was treasonable Money, and wou'd be sufficient Proof to hang him if it was found in his Pocket. They seldom took any Thing without pretending to pay for it, which was commonly at the Rate of a Half-penny or Penny in the Pound. Their Officers behaved like Gentlemen for the most Part, and instead of begging or taking by Force, generally made Use of the Word *borrow*, some offering to draw Bills on their King's Treasurer that was to be, and others inviting their Hosts to come and see them in the Highlands, where they promised to return their Civility.

The few Outrages which they committed on our Women are to be wondered at. In Lancashire a small Party of them overtook a very pretty young Woman on Horseback, whom they robbed of her Money and Horse, without even offering to salute her.

The Nastiness of these Savages is scarce credible: They may indeed be compared to Hogs; the same Stye in which they eat and sleep, serving them for every other Occasion of Life.

These Wretches being now returned to Scotland, persist still in their Plunder. At Dumfries they demanded 2000 *l.* Contribution, 1000 whereof was paid down, and they have taken with them two of the principal Inhabitants as Hostages for the other.

General Hawley is appointed Commander in Chief of the Forces in Scotland, and his Royal Highness, Marshal Wade, and Lord Tyrawley are soon expected to return to Town.

Mr. Hawley is a brave experienced Officer, and every Way equal to his Command; yet the Recall of the Duke is much lamented, particularly by the Scotch, who promised themselves, under his Conduct, the immediate Period to this Rebellion: For his Name, which is so dear to every Well-wisher of his Country, is become no less formidable to the Rebels. However, as the Troops which advanced to Carlisle under the Duke, joined to those under Marshal

Wade, with the Hessian Auxiliaries, (which were in our last called *Danes* by Mistake) will form a very strong Army, *we may yet hope to see these Banditti demolished, before they have quite ruined one Part of the Kingdom, and are become a just Object of Terror to the other.*

Admiral Vernon sailed last Thursday with seven Men of War, and some small Shallops, from the Downs, and stood towards the Coast of France; with an Intent, as it is imagined, to come to an Anchor off Dungeness. Whether the known Vigilance of this Admiral, with the Precautions he hath taken, or whether the present Situation of our Armies on Shore, have deterred the French from their Enterprize; or whether this Embarkation be like some former ones, no more than a Gascognade, or be intended to cover some other Design, certain it is that their invincible Armada remains yet in their own Ports, and may possibly wait for better Weather before they will think proper to venture forth.

At a time when several simple People have declined purchasing either Beef or Veal for their Families, from an Apprehension that the Flesh of Oxen and Calves is infected and unwholesome, it may not be amiss to acquaint the Public, that at the Quarterly Meeting of the College of Physicians held last Week in Warwick-Lane, a very large Sirloin of Beef was served on the Table, of which most of the learned Members present, and the President in particular, declared their Approbation with their Teeth, as well as their Tongues.[1]

Saturday last at 10 in the Morning, Fortune, which had seen Company publickly for above a Month last past, at her Court at Guildhall, and had distributed her Favours to those whom she liked best, was pleased to retire again from publick View, to the great Disappointment of many of her Solicitors, who had attended her Levee every Morning with the same Expectations to which the Levees of great Men usually owe their Attendants, and with the same Success. It is hoped her Ladyship will now give some Ear to her Votaries of another kind, and do something for the Restoration of public Credit; for otherwise the next time she removes to Guildhall, very few Persons in the Kingdom will be able to purchase one of those Tickets by which they are admitted to her Court. . . .

Admiral Vernon is expected in Town in a Day or two, and Admiral Mayne is to succeed him.—We shall soon know the Meaning of this News, which at present causes great Consternation.[2]

---

[1] The gibe may smack of 'inside' information, but despite Fielding's frequent recourse to physicians there is nothing to connect him with the society itself at this time. In 1745 the president was Henry Plumptre; William Munk, *The Roll of the Royal College of Physicians of London* (London, 1878), ii. 24; iii. 342.

[2] Edward Vernon (1684–1757), hero of Porto Bello (1739), MP Ipswich 1741–57, had been given command of the western squadron in August 1745, assembled in the Downs with responsibility for coastal defense. Vernon's long-standing difficulties with the admiralty were well known to insiders. As early as 20 December 1745 Walpole wrote Mann that he had heard of Vernon's recall ('for his absurdities'); *Yale Walpole*, xix. 188n. For the outcome, see 'Present History', *TP* no. 10 (7 January 1746), below, p. 394 and *n*. The early newspaper reports had rear-admiral Perry Mayne (*c.* 1700–61) replacing Vernon; in the event, it was admiral William Martin (*c.* 1696–1756); *DA* of 4 January 1746; H. W. Richmond, *The Navy in the War of 1739–48* (Cambridge, 1920), ii. 184–6.

APOCRYPHA.

Or We Hear.

Wednesday. We are assured, that his Mock Highness the pretended P. of W. who promised his Friends that he would dine at St. James's on Christmas-Day, was so disgusted with the Treatment he met with on the Road, that he has hastily turn'd his Back on them, without appointing any other Time;—or even redressing their Grievances. G. A. *If any of his Friends* INVITED *him, he hath Reason to be disgusted with their making no better Preparation for his Entertainment.*

Thursday. The same Letters say, that a very civil Message having been sent to the House of a certain rich Papist, to provide Quarters for some of the Duke's Army; Answer was returned, That the Master was from home, and that the Servants could not take upon them to provide. The Troops, however, marching thither, found Thirty Beds ready made, a great Number of Sheep, Geese, Fowls and Ducks killed, with Plenty of Liquor—*Designed for other Company.* L. C. *This Gentleman had as much Reason to complain of his Mock Highness, as he had to complain of his Friends in the foregoing Paragraph.*

We hear all the Forts and Castles in the Kingdom are order'd to be double garrison'd, *either by his Majesty's Forces*, or the new-raised Regiments *in Default* of a sufficient Number of the former; and that a Magazine of Arms is to be established in each of the said Forts and Castles, in order to obviate the Inconveniency and Danger of waiting for Arms from the Tower of London on any sudden Emergency. G. E. *Whose Forces are the new raised Regiments?*

Extract of a Letter from Canterbury, Dec. 22.

This Morning about 300 of the Townsmen, headed by several Gentlemen, went from hence on Horseback, arm'd with Guns, Swords and Pistols, and six Pioneers, to meet the Country People at Swinfield Minis, 10 Miles from this Place, pursuant to an Advertisement in our Paper from Admiral Vernon and the Deputy Lieutenants of the County, to repulse the Enemy in case they should attempt to land. There are already 4000 Men at Swinfield Minis, with two Days Provisions. S. J. E. *Among other Weapons we wou'd advise a proper Number of Spades and Pickaxes, that the* French *Rascals may not breed a Contagion, but be buried like Dogs as they are.*

Friday. On Monday last an Affidavit was made before the Right Hon. the Lord Mayor, by Mr. William Page, Mr. John Lucey, and Mr. William Gifford, belonging to the Worshipful Company of Butchers, that they had seized on Monday last Week in Leadenhall Market, at a public Stall, two Hind-Quarters of a Cow, which were unwholsome, not fit for Human Food, and as they apprehended the Cow was sick when she was killed: Whereupon his Lordship ordered the City Marshals, and other proper Officers, forthwith to destroy the same, by burning or otherwise, so that it might not be eaten by any Thing.—And the Meat was Yesterday burnt in Smithfield accordingly.

We hear, that in order to deter People from bringing such Meat into the

Markets for the future, those who are caught will have *proper Posts* fixed up at their Stalls, to denote what Sort of a Commodity they chuse to deal in. G. A. *The proper Posts are* Gibbets, *and the Commodity in which the Hangman deals shou'd be exposed upon them.*

A Man coming last Night to St. Martin's Vestry-Room, to offer to enlist, it being discovered he had Corks conceal'd in the Feet of his Stockings, *to raise him* above an Inch, and to make him measure the Height required; and the Person who came with him as a Voucher, being an Irishman, and confessing he was privy thereto, and to have had Part of the Money, they were both committed to Bridewell by the Justices then present. D. A. This poor Fellow had ill Luck; for his Betters have used much worse Practices *to raise themselves high* in the Army with Success.

Saturday. We are assured, that the nominal Dr. Kirkham, well known at the Custom-house, and *Hark'e Hark'e*, of Water-Lane, were intituled to the 1000 *l.* Prize drawn Yesterday; to the general Joy of all their Acquaintance. G. A.

The Ticket No. 11,000, which was drawn a Prize of 1000 *l.* Yesterday, is the Property of a Victualler in Idle-Lane, who offered it to Sale the Night before at Jonathan's Coffee House in Exchange-Alley, but could not get a Purchaser. L. C. *Is Hark'e Hark'e, the* nominal *Dr. Kirkham, and the* unnominal *Victualler one Person, or divers?*

It is written from Stourbridge, that the Nailers, Colliers, Glassmen, Locksmiths, Gunsmiths, Buckle-makers, &c. of whom there are 200,000 in a Circuit of about 30 Miles, are so alarm'd at a foreign Invasion, and the Apprehensions of a French Government, that it is with Difficulty that they are restrained from rising to pull down the Mass houses in that Neighbourhood, and seizing some Priest and Papists, who have been very active in sending out Horsemen all the while the Army of his Royal Highness was about Litchfield and Stafford. G. E. *If these Papists gave any Assistance to the Rebels, it is Pity some more legal Magistrate than a Mob doth not call them to an Account; but if they have behaved like quiet and peaceable Subjects, they are, in common with others, under the Protection of the Law.*

We hear that the Hon. Mrs. Temple has paid 50 *l.* into the Chamber of London, towards the Relief, Support, and Encouragement of the Soldiers employed in suppressing the present Unnatural Rebellion; And we have the Pleasure of acquainting the Public, that that laudable Undertaking has been greatly advanced by the generous Contributions of many other well-disposed Ladies. G. E. *It is pity the Names of those well-disposed Ladies (especially if unmarried) was not made public; since so well-judged and public-spirited a Charity wou'd add to their Charms, in the Eyes of every sensible and true* Englishman.

From GALLIMATIAS.

Being a faithful Abstract of Rebellious History from last Week's Dunghill of Papers

ABBREVIATIONS.

G. GAZETTE

D. G.	Daily Gazetteer.	D. A.	Daily Advertiser.
D. P.	Daily Post.	L. E.	London Evening Post.
L. C.	London Courant.	S. J. E.	St. James's Evening.
G. A.	General Advertiser.	G. E.	General Evening.

... On Friday 150 of the better Sort of Rebels advanced toward the River Eden, but General Huske (*who was then at or near Newcastle*) being there with a large Body of Men, *&c.* obliged them to retreat to Carlisle, G. A. The Van of the Rebel Army getting Notice of the Defeat of their Rear (*they being by this Account* 50 *Miles distant from each other*) deserted, and about 300 of them were pursued and taken by a Regiment of Dragoons, &c. (*where there could be no such Regiment*) L. C. ...

Barnard Castle, Dec. 22. Yesterday the whole Body of the Rebels marched from Carlisle towards the River Eske, which is unpassable by the late Rains. They seemed in great Confusion. The Country People observing this, immediately attacked, and drove them back to Carlisle. The Duke was then at Penrith, but immediately marched towards Carlisle, and arrived before that Place last Night, and has actually surrounded it, L. C.

Extract from a private Letter. Penrith, Dec. 23.

'His Royal Highness left this Place on Saturday last, and is now at Blackwell, between two and three Miles from Carlisle, waiting for Cannon from Whitehaven, in order to attack the Rebel Garrison therein, which is said to consist of about 300 Men. We hope to be Masters of the Place in a Day or two, as four Pieces of the Cannon we waited for are just now arrived, and the other six, all 18 Pounders, are expected To-morrow. The main Body of the Rebels passed the Eske on Friday, with great Difficulty; several were drowned, the Water being very high, and they were to be at Moffat on Saturday Night, as some of them give out, in their Way for Edinburgh; but others say, with more Probability, they will turn Westward for the Highlands, L. C.

These two last Contradictions are in the same Paper the same Day.

We have taken some Pains to collect this Rubbish, in order to shew the Public on what they spend their Time and Money. After this,

Si Populus vult decipi, decipiatur.[1]

... *Dead. Tuesday.* Mr. Tillcock an eminent Stocking Presser in GRUB-STREET, D. A. *Wednesday.* Mr. Tillcock is not dead but in perfect Health. D. A. G. A. *It is unpardonable in these Historians to mistake in Matters of such Consequence*, especially in their own Neighbourhood. .... Mr. Davis, one of the most eminent Limners in England, *in the Opinion of the* London Evening. ...

Appeared. On Thursday Night last another *Extraordinary* Ghost. He was wrapt up in half a very small Sheet, but not a white one. He pretended to walk

[1] 'If the public wishes to be deceived, let it be deceived.'

by Authority from above. He spoke but a very few Words, and concluded with
Price Two-pence, E. O. N. Amen.[1]

*The Essay in our last hath produced us several Letters, which we shall insert the first
Opportunity.*

We shall be obliged to the Lady who stiles herself Clarinda, *(if she be really in earnest)
for a further Explanation of that Paragraph in her Letter, which begins with these Words,*
There is no such, &c. *We assure her, we have the same Sentiments with herself on the
Subject she writes, and shall think her Proposal an Honour greatly worth embracing.*

ADVERTISEMENT.

*Any Person who hath enough of real Christianity to preserve a large Family from Destruc-
tion by advancing the Sum of Two hundred Pounds, on a reasonable Prospect of its being
repaid, may hear further Particulars, by applying to Mr.* Millar, *Bookseller, opposite*
Katharine Street *in the* Strand.[2]

THE TRUE PATRIOT, No. 10, Tuesday, January 7, 1746.

FOREIGN HISTORY

The only Accounts of any Consequence from abroad, since our last, are the
Death of Hamet Caramally, late Bashaw of Tripoli, who is succeeded by his
youngest Son, with the general Consent of the Inhabitants. Since his Accession
a Conspiracy hath been discovered by the Kehia, who with his two Sons hath
been put to Death on that Account.

In Italy Prince Lichtenstein hath defeated 7000 Spaniards, who attempted to
destroy his Bridges over the Tessin; but on the Approach of Don Philip, at the
Head of his whole Army, he was obliged to retire, and for the present to
abandon his Design of passing that River. But if the Empress is really in
earnest, (as I think her own Interest must dictate to her) in sending a Reinforcement of 15000 Men to Italy, his Highness will soon be enabled to resume his
Purpose; and we may hope to see the King of Sardinia once more in a Condition
of giving a powerful Diversion to the common Enemy on that side.

From *The* PRESENT HISTORY *of* GREAT BRITAIN.

So universal a Concern prevails among all Sorts of People in this Metropolis, at
Admiral Vernon's having left the Fleet, that it may be said, when he struck his

---

[1] *The London Gazette Extraordinary* of 26 December 1745. The paper, whose colophon stated that it
was published by E. Owen ('E.O.N.') of Amen Corner, also bore the inscription 'Published by
Authority'. For the numerous other gibes at it in the *TP*, see index, *s.v.* 'London Gazette'.

[2] The wording of this advertisement bears one mark of Fielding's style ('hath') and may have been
composed by him. The 'Family' in distress has not been identified.

Flag, the Spirits of the Nation sunk with it.[1] Indeed it may be questioned, whether his own Country derives greater Confidence, or our Enemies greater Terror, from the Bravery and Vigilance of this truly great Man in his Profession; and both these are well founded, as must appear, if, besides the plain blunt English Honesty and Integrity of his Character, we consider his Conduct ever since the Beginning of this War. In the Indies, not to mention his more known Exploits, he so effectually supported our Trade with his Cruizers, that during his whole Abode in those Seas, our Navigation there was almost as safe as in a Time of profound Peace. Scarce any, I believe I might say not one, of our Ships having been taken. On the contrary, such was the Apprehensions and Terror of the Enemy, that they seldom durst appear at Sea in those Parts; and if ever they ventured, it was to their own Destruction; for of four Register Ships, three were taken, and even the fourth, if I mistake not, rack'd. Such was the Terror of his Name, that while our Admiral was posted at St. Jago de Cuba, de Torres, who lay with a superior Fleet on the other Side of the Island, durst not shew his Face without the Harbour. How he hath behaved in his present Command I shall not venture to say; since his Recall is ascribed to a noble Duke, whose Character ought to be dear, nay even sacred, to every Englishman, as he certainly deserves every Honour his Country can bestow on it.[2] In Cases of this Kind, the only safe Way is to suspend our Judgment, till Time and Enquiry have set all Facts in a true and certain Light.

 . . . Thus hath his Royal Highness, without any Loss, reduced this Garrison.[3] Indeed, it is not easy to account for the Conduct of the Rebels in leaving any there, since it was only sacrificing such a Number of their Party to certain Destruction. Perhaps they were apprehensive of being farther pursued by the Duke, and took this Method to prevent, or at least retard, such a Pursuit. Whatever was their Design, these Rebels are now at his Majesty's Mercy; and happy had it been for the Nation, if the River Eske had been able to have driven back the rest of their Friends to the same Shelter; by which means our heroic young Prince would have returned with that full Harvest of Laurels which he so well

[1] On 2 January 1746, after the admiralty board had taken him up on his offer to resign (*c.* 21 December 1745). Vernon published a vindication of his behavior in two anonymous pamphlets (*Some Seasonable Advice from an Honest Sailor* and *A Specimen of Naked Truth from a British Sailor*), which contained considerable of his correspondence with the admiralty. Horace Walpole, *Memoirs of the Last Ten Years of the Reign of George the Second* (London, 1822), i. 100*n.*, asserts that Vernon's publication of the letters he had received from the admiralty board 'betrayed our spies and intelligence to the French'. When Vernon refused to answer queries about his authorship, the board struck him off the admirals' list (10 April 1746). See Richmond, *The Navy in the War of 1739–48*, ii. 182–6, and *The Vernon Papers*, ed. B. McL. Ranft, Naval Records Society, xcix (n.p. 1958), pp. 434–587.

[2] Another compliment to the duke of Bedford, first lord of the admiralty, a leading member of the broad-bottom coalition and a future patron of Fielding's. Fielding, who shared the earlier 'patriot' admiration of Vernon's political independency and his belligerent preference for naval (not military) supremacy for England (he was thus useful in the 'war' against Sir Robert Walpole), had made him the eponymous hero of his *Vernoniad* (1741). In the present instance Fielding finds himself between a rock and a hard place, wishing neither to abandon precipitously an old 'idol' nor to alienate needlessly a potentially much more useful one.

[3] At Carlisle, which capitulated on 30 December 1745 after having been invested by the duke on 21 December.

deserves; in the Pursuit of which he hath shewn an equal Contempt of Fatigue and Danger, and hath endeared his Name to the whole Kingdom.

... The following is a genuine Letter from an honest Citizen of Glasgow, who was a forward promoter of the King's Service, to his Son, who is a Tradesman in this Town.

Dear Son,

Tho', in the present Confusion we are in, in this City, I am but little able to write, and now too when my old Distemper has return'd upon me, so that I can hardly hold my Pen, yet I was resolved to write to you, not knowing when I may get another Opportunity; for the Rebels, we are certainly inform'd, have escaped from the Duke of Cumberland, and are got back to Scotland, and intend to pay us a Visit here. The Zeal which this City has shewn for the King's Service, makes us hope to get little Favour from them; and no Man less than myself on that Account. But I do not repent of what I have done in Support of my King and my Religion; nor will I fear any Sufferings for doing my Duty, since I know God can and will reward me, and a better Life than mine, that old Age and many Infirmities makes little worth, will be well worth losing in his Service. All my Concern is, for your poor Sisters; for as the most of what I have is in Stock, I can secure but very little from them, if they should plunder the City, as we are afraid. Some think it hard, that nothing has been done for our Security, but we must submit to God's Pleasure. I recommend you, and your Brothers and Sisters, to his Care, &c.

The Piety, Loyalty and Goodness, mix'd with Simplicity, of this Letter, will, I am confident, make the same Impression on many of my Readers which it did on myself, and must convince the most inveterate Enemy to the Scots, that there is as honest a Man on the North Side of the Tweed, as can be found on the South.

Eight Battalions of the Army lately under Marshal Wade are marching for Scotland, and will be at Edinburgh in a few Days. I am afraid these Corps, reduced as they must be with their Winter Campaign, will not amount to 4000 Men, at the highest Computation. They will find, at their Arrival in that City, 2 Regiments of Foot, and 2 of Dragoons, at which Time our whole Regular Force there may be supposed to consist of about 5000; nor can the additional Strength from the Edinburgh Volunteers, and Militia of the neighbouring Counties be very considerable. As to the scattered Bodies under Lord Loudon, General Campbell, Monro, and others, they will have enough to do where they already are, to prevent further Rising, and the Junction of fresh Parties from the High-lands, to the main Body of the Rebels. On the other hand, the Number of the Rebels returned from England are full 6000, and when joined by those from Aberdeen and Perth, with Lord John Drummond's People, cannot, in the whole, amount to less than 10000 Men. It is to be hoped, therefore, our Army will receive a considerable Reinforcement either of Hessians, of Horse from

Flanders, or from the Body of Troops under his Royal Highness, or indeed from all three, before they come to an Action of such vast Importance; by which indeed the Fate of Scotland is so absolutely to be decided, that should the Rebels be victorious, Self-Preservation must force every Inhabitant of that Kingdom either to abandon his Country, or (however reluctantly) to declare on their Side. The Consequence of which must be a long, expensive, dangerous War, which may probably in the End effect the manifest Designs of France, and prove fatal to this whole Island.

The extinguishing this Rebellion in Scotland should be the principal, the first Object of our Endeavours, for which Purpose I wish one half of the Troops within 30 Miles of this Town were within the same Distance from Edinburgh; for our Coasts would still be secure from any Invasion, did France really intend it; but I am always doubtful of that Crown's being in earnest in any Design, when there is so much Pomp and Parade in the Preparation. Her Views on the Continent are apparent, and she well knows our Good-Will and Forwardness to send our Forces thither to oppose her. This she prevents by alarming us at home; nay, it is likely her immediate View may be to raise the Rebellion to a more formidable Height in Scotland, by diverting our Forces another Way, in which God forbid she should succeed; indeed it is certain she will not, since it appears by the following Account published in the Gazette of Saturday, that her Designs are at last seen through, and that we shall be no longer amused nor terrified by her Gasconades.

The following Letter has been received at the Admiralty from Commodore Knowles, who was sent to enquire into the true State of the Preparations making in France to invade England.

'Since my last I have been over to Boulogne and Calais, and had as distinct Views of what is in those Places, as it is possible, unless I had been a-shore in Person. At Boulogne I stood within half a Mile of the Pier Heads, that even a Privateer Sloop's Shot went over me: The Battery from the Pier Head (which consists but of five Guns) fired many Shot, but none did Execution. It was not possible to count the Vessels as they lay, not knowing how to distinguish those of two Masts, or those of one; but upon the Whole I am of Opinion, there is not sixty Vessels of all Kinds in the Harbour, (and my Brother Captains do not think there are so many:) The largest of these was a Galliot Hoy, whose very Gaff was much higher than any of the other Vessels Mastsheads; and there was not one single one which had a Top-sail-yard rigg'd aloft.

'This Morning about Eight o'Clock I was within two or three Miles of Calais Town, and saw three or four small Top-sail Vessels in the Pier, the rest were all Galliots and Fishing Boats, and did not exceed 30 in Number.

'By Captain Gregory's Account of the same Date, who was sent to take a View of the Preparations at Dunkirk, it appears there are but five or six Vessels in the Road, and a very few in the Harbour.'

This, it is probable, may be the true Reason of recalling Admiral Vernon; for if we are no longer under Apprehension of Danger, nothing can be more just and proper than to give that Great Man some Repose, after the almost insupportable Fatigues which he hath undergone for us.

At the same Time, that we may not fall into the other Excess of too much Confidence in our Security, abundant Care hath been taken to strengthen ourselves as much as possible at home; for our Troops are canton'd in such a Manner, that by Means of the Subscription for lending Horses, (a Scheme which we are told *the Duke of Newcastle highly approves and recommends*) a large Army may in a few Hours assemble, either in the Metropolis or within 20 Miles of it. And besides this, we are informed, that the Lord Lieutenant of Norfolk hath granted Commissions to 6 Gentlemen to raise independent Companies, and that 300 Arms for them have been purchased by Subscription: That a large Number of Arms have been sent from the Tower into Suffolk, to arm the Inhabitants of that Coast; that 300 more have been sent from the same Place into Lincolnshire for the same Purpose; and 6000 into Cornwall to arm the Tinners; and the new-raised Regiments of the Lord Edgecumb, Berkley, and others are to be cloathed and armed forthwith, and to march for the Defence of the Coasts; lastly, that 10,000 Men in Kent assembled together, 6000 of which were well armed, *tho' it was a wet Morning, and there was no real Alarm of the French*. Upon the whole, as we are so very strong where there seems at present no Danger, it cannot be doubted but that an able Administration will take effectual Care to secure us on that Side where real Danger threatens. For this Reason it is the universal Wish of all People, that his Royal Highness might proceed to Scotland,[1] with which some will yet flatter themselves, as it would put a new Spirit into all the well-affected Part of that Nation, and would with a competent Force be a most certain Method of putting an immediate End to this pernicious Rebellion.

The latter End of last Week the most Honourable the Marquiss of Tweeddale resigned his Place of Secretary of State for Scottish Affairs. This Office, after having been sunk a long Time, was revived four Years ago; and it is doubtful whether the Marquiss may have any immediate Successor.

A Copy of Verses was published in one of the Grubstreet Papers on Saturday last, said to have been written at the Rehearsal of a new Opera, the Subject of which Opera is, we are told, a Compliment to the Nation on the Expulsion of the Rebels out of *England*.[2] Such servile Flattery may possibly agree with the Nature of Italians; but must be despised by a British Heart. The Rebels have certainly afforded us no Cause of Triumph yet, and when they do, our English Theatres, which have given many Instances of their Loyalty this Winter, and

---

[1] The duke left Carlisle on 2 January 1746 for London, arriving there on 5 January (*DA* of 6 January 1746). He would not leave for Scotland until 25 January (*DA* of 27 January 1746).

[2] See *DA* of 4 January 1746. The verses are there said to have been 'Written during the Rehearsal of the new Italian Drama, entitled *La Caduti* [*sic*] *di Giganti*, composed in Honour of his Majesty and the Nation, on Occasion of the Expulsion of the Rebels'.

have had some Share in raising that popular Spirit which hath exerted itself in this Town on the Side of our Liberties, will be able to celebrate our Victory, without the Assistance of emasculated Italian Slaves.

A long Letter hath been likewise published in two of the same Papers, in Defence of this Diversion, as being adapted to the Taste of People of Quality,[1] who are, it seems, above relishing the Productions of their own Country; but I will tell these People of Quality, if there be any such, that they are the Occasion of bringing a Contempt on their Country abroad, and are themselves despised by all Men of Sense and Virtue at home. And I hope a restrictive Law (since it is plain nothing else can) will shortly make this high Taste conform to the Good of the Public, and not suffer them any longer, by their Dress, their Furniture, their Entertainments, and their Diversions, to contribute, some Share at least, to our Ruin. It is indeed reasonable to expect that *Persons who are good for nothing but to consume the Fruits of the Earth*,[2] should be contented to consume those of their own Country, or of such other Countries as live in a State of Amity with it, and with which we carry on a Trade beneficial to ourselves. Such a Spirit and such Measures alone can save this Nation.

It is with this View only we are Enemies to a foreign Opera, and not from taking Part in any mean Musical Contention; for we frankly own, that if immense Sums are to be sent out of the Nation into the Hands of our Enemies, for their Silks, Laces, Wines, &c. the Expence of an Opera will become a Matter of very trifling Consideration.

On Sunday last in the Morning his Royal Highness the Duke arrived at St. James's, in good Health, after all the Fatigues he hath undergone in the Service of his Country.   .   .   .

From APOCRYPHA; Or, WE HEAR.

Tuesday. Yesterday four Chairman, who were carrying Chairs round St. James's Park for a Wager, and had brought a great Number of Persons into the Park, were taken into Custody by a File of Musketeers, and committed to the Hole at Whitehall *for a Riot*. D. A. *Upon the State of this Evidence, and from* the Peace Officers *who arrested these Chairmen, I conclude this Commitment* for a Riot *was rather* military *than* civil.

Wednesday. Yesterday at Noon six *Coaches and six*, filled with Rebel Prisoners, were brought to London, escorted by a very large Party of Horse and Foot Guards. L. C. *They will probably go out of Town in a Vehicle better adapted to their Dignity*.

[1] In *DA* of 3 January and *General Advertiser* of 4 January 1746, over the signature 'Linus'. The letter defends, among other things, the right of 'Persons of Quality' to spend their money on whatever entertainment they prefer. Fielding's attention may have been caught by what appears to be a reference to his own satire on the opera (*TP* no. 9 [31 December 1745], above, pp. 164–71): 'A third [opponent of the opera] combats it with a Weapon (*Humour*) by which he has deservedly gain'd great Reputation, and could not but have won the Victory, had he been on the right Side of the Question.'

[2] The use of italics here would seem to indicate a quotation; it has not been identified.

The Coast being so well guarded by our Men of War, and arm'd Vessels, has not only hitherto prevented the landing of any Troops from France, in Favour of the Pretender; but it has also prevented the *pernicious* Practice of Smuggling; for we are assured that near 200 of them have been observed, within this Fortnight, to return from the Coasts of Sussex and Kent, without their usual Loading. G. A. *I suppose if this Practice was* pernicious, *an effectual Stop would have been put to it long ago.*

Thursday. They write from Abergavenny in Monmouthshire, that one Elizabeth Powel, *a noted Cheat*, was lately taken up there for defrauding several Persons, particularly Mrs. Papps, of the Sum of 89 *l.* and that while she was in Custody, she took an Opportunity to swallow a Quantity of Arsenick, and died soon after. L. C. *One would think* a noted Cheat *should not be able to defraud any one.*

Among the many *Falsehoods* industriously propagated to damp our Spirits, that of the *Recalling* a brave and vigilant Admiral for only executing his Charge with too much *Activity* and *Secrecy*, is universally *hoped*, and generally *believed*, by all *True Britons*, to be *one.* L. E. *That this Admiral is recalled is true, as the Historian, if he had any Intelligence, must have known a Week ago;*[1] *but it is hoped the Reasons which he modestly assigns for recalling him are false.*

Friday. Yesterday a great Number of Galleys came up the River, and pickt up a great many useful Fellows to serve his Majesty, who were immediately sent on board the Tenders at Blackwall and Deptford. G. A. *If these Press Gangs should venture to the polite End of the Town, we advise them rather to lay hold on* USELESS *Fellows, by which Means they may possibly mann the whole Fleet.*

Saturday.   *Letter from Warrington, Jan.* 1. 1746.

  Sir,

'We have been much surprized here, at an Account inserted in the public Papers, concerning our Neighbour, Mr. Jared Leigh, Master of the Red Lion Inn; which is, that he was sentenc'd by his Royal Highness the Duke to be hang'd as a Spy, when I assure you he is a Man of an unblemish'd Character in his Profession, and has given many Proofs of his Loyalty and Attachment to the present happy Establishment, and was Author of some Verses published in the *St. James's Evening Post*, of the 9th of November last, in Vindication of the same. G. A. *It would have been too severe to hang this poor Man* for writing a few *bad Verses; which, it seems by this Letter, was the only Crime he was really guilty of.* . . .

We hear, that a very considerable Quantity of Specie has been landed within these few Days from Holland. G. A. *We hope their Specie will be of more Service to us than their Troops have been.* . . .

Married. Wednesday. Henry Talbot, Esq; to Miss Gordon, an agreeable young Lady with a Fortune of 6000 *l.* L. C. — Lee, Esq; to Miss Wade, *ib.* Henry Mackworth Praed, Esq; to Lady Delves; and George Pitt, Esq; to Miss Atkins. *The two last are celebrated Beauties.* . . .

---

[1] See 'Present History of Great Britain' in no. 9 (31 December 1745), above, p. 390.

Note. To prevent giving Offence to the many eminent dead Persons, as well as to several young Ladies of great Beauty, Merit and Fortune, we shall for the future register all Marriages and Deaths as they come to Hand, and leave all Distinction to the Public; after having premised that every Word printed in *Italics* is our own, and of these, and these only we will be answerable for the Truth.

Persons who correspond with the Patriot are desired not to direct their Letters to Mrs. Cooper, but to the Patriot at Mrs. Coopers; by which Means they come to him unopened. And the Public are desired to take Notice that every Letter which is not inserted, or the Receipt of it acknowledged in the very next Patriot, must have miscarried, and never reached our Hands.

The Abstract from a Letter to a Member of Parliament will be inserted in our next.[1] We have received Letters signed *Oliver Cromwell, T. D.* and one anonymous. *Note.* We desire the Favour of our Correspondents to put some Name or Mark to their Letters, that we may be able to signify the Receipt of them.

THE TRUE PATRIOT, No. 11, Tuesday, January 14, 1746.

From *The* PRESENT HISTORY *of* GREAT BRITAIN.[2]

On Thursday last his Royal Highness the Prince of Wales was pleased to send a Bank Note of Five Hundred Pounds unto the Right Hon. the Lord Mayor, as a Contribution towards the Subscription now carrying on at Guildhall, for the Relief, Support and Encouragement of the Soldiers employ'd in suppressing the present Rebellion. *A Benefaction truly noble and generous. Indeed half the Virtues which this Prince exemplifies in the little Circle of his private Family (the only Sphere in which he hath yet had an Opportunity of exerting them)[3] would, if known, make him as much belov'd by the whole World as he is by his own Servants; most of whom rather look on him as their Father than their Master: Nor is it more than Justice to his Character to inform Mankind in general of the Heroic as well as other Virtues of his Royal Highness; for no Man hath ever been more solicitous for Ease and Safety than his Royal Highness* FREDERIC *Prince of* Wales *hath been for Leave to expose his Person to all the Dangers and Fatigues of a Winter Campaign, against those Savage Blood-Hounds, who have so long infested this Kingdom with Impunity.*

The extraordinary Pannic with which this City was struck during the March

[1] It does not appear to have been published, unless it is the letter signed 'Gravis', which makes no such point about its identity and does not appear to be an 'Abstract'; for a text, see Locke, pp. [116–17].   [2] 'Foreign History' is omitted from this number without remark.

[3] Later in the *TP* Fielding will return to the point that, because of parental animosity, the prince 'hath never yet had a single Opportunity of carrying out any great political or martial Quality into act'; see no. 27 (29 April–6 May 1746), above, p. 281. Frederick had asked, apparently more than once, to be given command of the armies sent against the rebels, but the king would not hear of it; *Marchmont Papers*, i. 110–11; Walpole, *Memoirs of . . . George the Second*, i. 62; Walpole, *MS Political Papers*, f. 28, as cited in *Yale Walpole*, xix. 174*n*. Fielding's image of the prince as acknowledged *pater-familias* was a commonplace; it was also consonant with the 'patriot king' metapolitics of his Leicester House circle. See 'General Introduction', pp. lxii–lxxiv.

of the Rebels Southward is entirely dissipated since their Expulsion out of England by his Royal Highness the Duke of Cumberland; but our Fellow-Subjects in North-Britain feel the dismal Effects of their bad Success and utter Disappointment on this Side the Tweed. Their Behaviour at Glasgow was such as might be expected from a Crew incensed by Opposition of every kind, and one of the most fatiguing Marches, or rather Flights, that has been known. When they enter'd that City they did not exceed 4000 Horse and Foot; (an inconsiderable Number to alarm a Country which can, upon an Occasion like this, in which every Thing valuable is concerned, raise almost a Thousand Times as many) and some of those were either unarmed, or unable to use Arms if they had them. . . .

Small Parties of the Rebels have marched Northward, whether with an Intention of deserting the Service, or to raise more of their Friends is not known. The many Outrages and Barbarities they have perpetrated have justly incensed the People against them to the last Degree. As for the Well-affected in the North, our Readers will easily be able to form an Idea of their Sufferings by considering what uncontroul'd Barbarians are capable of inflicting on Enemies whom they regard as a kind of false Brethren. . . .

Upon the whole then, I think we may reasonably conclude, that so small a Number of Miscreants, harrass'd, jaded and disappointed as they are, cannot possibly stand their Ground long, against the whole Force of these Kingdoms, without some Assistance from their declared Friends the French and Spaniards. As for the Spaniards, however well inclined they may be to send them Succours, or however resolved to embark in an Affair in which they have scarce a Possibility of Success, they will be hardly able to transport any Troops in due Time. And as for the French, notwithstanding all those pompous Preparations which that Crown knows very well how to parade with, when she is least in earnest, we cannot be persuaded that her Politics savour enough of the Spanish Disposition to make her really undertake an Enterprize of this Quixottish Kind. Indeed it is likely her utmost View in this Affair is to foment these Civil Commotions, in order to divert us from checking the ambitious Projects she has constantly in View upon the Continent. . . .[1]

From APOCRYPHA.

Or We Hear.

We hear several Masters of Coffee-houses have lost some of their best Customers, because they refused to take in the TRUE PATRIOT. T. P. *We mention this purely that the rest of their Brethren may not suffer in like manner for the same Fault.*[2]

[1] The careful emphasis here on French designs for the continent may reflect the similar disposition among the Pelhams and many of their 'new allies' to look more favorably upon some form of English military commitment there. See Owen, pp. 292–4.

[2] Cf. the headnote prefixed to nos. 17 and 18, above, pp. 221, 229.

His Majesty's Ship the Dragon is ordered to be rebuilt with all Expedition; for which Purpose she was Yesterday put out of Commission at the Pay-Office in Boast-street. D. G. *Q. Whether it would not be as proper sometimes to put Statesmen out of Commission too, if not to be* rebuilt, *to be at least* refitted?

Tuesday. We are assured that Commodore Knowles, with the Squadron under his Command, will sail into the Harbour of Boulogne, to burn all the Transports in that Port, *which News* is hourly expected in Town. L. C. *If this News be not arrived already, how comes it that the Historian is* assured of it?

Wednesday. The new Musical Italian Drama, entitled *La Caduta de i Giganti, or, The Fall of the Giants*, writ on Occasion of the Expulsion of the Rebels, was perform'd last Night at the King's Theatre in the Hay-market. The Performance was received and carried on with great Attention, Tranquility and Applause. D. A. *The Music was thought to sound better than usual, which is by most People imputed to the Emptiness of the House.*[1]

We are informed, that one Mr. Bromley, belonging to the Revenue in Staffordshire, having made himself *remarkable, by observing* the Behaviour of several Persons in that Part of the County where he lived, whom he suspected to be Traitors to the Government, was *so often attempted* to be assassinated in the Country, that he found himself under a Necessity of coming to London, in order to screen himself from their zealous Fury; but on Saturday Night last *he was again attempted, at the Place where he chose to conceal himself*; (the Villains having narrowly watched him to Town) but he had the good Fortune to escape from them; and is now taking proper Measures to bring them to Justice. G. A. *If he can* conceal *himself as well as he hath done his Meaning in this Paragraph, he is in little Danger.*

Thursday. Last Night Mr. Goodfellow play'd the Part of King Richard the Third, at the Theatre-Royal in Drury-lane, with uncommon Applause.—It is remarkable that this is the second King Richard that has greatly succeeded from Goodman's Fields. G. A. *It is* not *remarkable, that this is the second Puff within these few Days from Drury-Lane.*[2]

Saturday. As the Rebels are in Scotland, and increasing their Numbers, nothing would be more serviceable than the sending a sufficient Number of

[1] Cf. 'Present History' of no. 10 (7 January 1746), see above, p. 399, and, for *La Caduta de i Giganti*, which opened the opera season on 7 January, see 'Apocrypha' of *TP* no. 16 (11–18 February 1746), below, p. 422. The reprinting here from *DA* of 8 January tactfully omits its concluding clause: 'and not a little enliven'd by the Presence of his Royal Highness the Duke of Cumberland'; as cited in *London Stage*, Part 3, ii. 1209. A letter from 'An Old Gentlewoman' in *TP* no. 12 (21 January 1746), Locke, p. [123], applauds the point made here and goes on to satirize the affectations of the audience.

[2] The 'Puff' from the *General Advertiser* is in the issue of 9 January 1746; the 'first' one has not been identified. J. Goodfellow (1722–59) played the title role in Cibber's adaptation of *Richard III* on two successive nights (8 and 9 January 1746). During the 1744–5 season he had been at Goodman's Fields, where he played the role for the first time on 5 December 1744. According to Mrs. Cibber, Goodfellow was being touted by Lacy as a rival to Fielding's friend Garrick, whose own first London performance was a triumphant Richard at Goodman's Fields on 19 October 1741. See *A Biographical Dictionary of Actors . . .*, ed. Philip Highfill *et al.*, vol. vi (Southern Illinois University Press, 1978), pp. 255–6; Boaden, *Private Correspondence of David Garrick*, i. 49; *London Stage*, Part 3, ii. 935, 1209, 1212.

Soldiers, that they may divide themselves in several Parts of that Kingdom: As to defeat any Number of the Rebels, we cannot be too expedient in this; for in defeating of the Rebels, will defeat France's pretended Invasion. As for the landing in Kent or Sussex, it is a false Alarm: Reason. Will they venture their Fleet to come so near ours? No. LONDON COURANT. *This admirable Paragraph, from its Politics, Sense, Stile and Grammar, smells so strong of* the Oratory, *that it seems to point out who is the true Author of this Paper, which, in its* Chimes of the Times, *the last Week, published a virulent Letter in Favour of Foreigners, against the People of England, and last Saturday begged Pardon for it; this being the third time of begging Pardon within these two Months for Offences of the like Kind.*[1]

We hear that Letters have been sent to the Right Honourable the Lord Mayor, and the High Sheriff of the County of Surrey, to know what Number of Prisoners the Goals in London and Southwark can receive, and make Preparations accordingly; it is therefore supposed, that the Rebels taken in Carlisle, *&c.* will be immediately brought to Town. G. A. *It is hoped these poor Wretches, whom the Hardness of the Times, and the greater Hardness of their diabolical Condition, have confined in these Goals, will be obliged to make Room for those who so much better deserve their Places.* . . .

Casualties. . . . Friday last one Mrs. Trulove, aged eighty, and who has kept a Shop in Stony-Stratford upwards of fifty Years, hang'd herself in her Chamber, for fear of wanting, notwithstanding above 500 *l.* in Money was found in her Possession. *This old Hag was scarce worth hanging.* . . .

Appeared. Last Saturday about 11 at Night the most impudent silly Ghost that ever endeavoured to impose upon the Public, many of whom gave him Four Pence a-piece for informing them, that a Gentleman in the North was made a Baronet.[2]

The Letter signed SOPHRONIA is receiv'd, and shall be taken Notice of in our next.[3]

---

[1] Another hit at 'Orator' Henley. The file of the *London Courant* for this period is scanty, and it has not been possible to ascertain if the paper actually had a department called 'Chimes of the Times'. Henley regularly advertised this title in association with his own 'Oratory' lectures, but he is not known to have been a writer for the *London Courant*. The *TP* attribution here is almost certainly ironic. During the early months of the rebellion Henley's lecture topics engendered charges that he was jacobite, and he published disclaimers, which Fielding may have been put in mind of by the *London Courant*'s. See 'General Introduction', above, pp. lvii–lix.

[2] *London Gazette* of 7–11 January 1746: 'The King has been pleased to grant unto Henry Grey of Howick, in the County of Northumberland, Esq; the Dignity of a Baronet of the Kingdom of Great Britain.'

[3] No letter with this signature is ever printed. It might be the letter signed 'An Old Gentlewoman' in no. 12 (21 January 1746), Locke, p. [123].

THE TRUE PATRIOT, No. 12, January 21, 1746.

FOREIGN HISTORY.

ITALY.

The Spaniards seem resolved immediately to undertake the Siege of the Castle of Milan. They have already form'd Lines of Circumvallation for that Purpose, have raised several Redoubts, and some Batteries. Don Philip entered the City on the 19th Instant. At the same time the Baron de Leutrum, having possessed himself of the most advantageous Posts on the Side of Final, hath totally cut off all Communication between Provence and the French and Spanish Armies. Besides the Reinforcement destined for Italy, from the Army of Count Traun, consisting of 20 Battalions, 12 Companies of Grenadiers, 28 Squadrons of Cuirassiers, and sixteen of Hussars, the Court of Vienna have resolved to send another Body of 20000 Men thither, so that his Sardinian Majesty will be most probably soon superior to the Enemy, tho' several Bodies of fresh Troops are defiling that Way, as well from Spain as France. His Majesty hath lately signified the Reasons which induced him to take the Corsicans under his Protection. This Edict was signed some time ago; but the Publication of it deferred till the English Fleet had made the Reduction of that Island certain.

FRANCE.

The Court seem to abandon all Hopes of amusing us any longer with their pretended Embarkation, and are preparing in earnest for the Campaign in the Netherlands. His Majesty intends to put himself at the Head of the Army in March next (*if the Weather be not too cold.*) A Company of 40 Ladies are appointed to attend him. These may possibly form his Body-Guard, as they will be very proper to defend him from any Danger to which he intends to expose himself. A Company of Fidlers will, it is expected, be shortly named for the same Expedition. They affect here to speak with Certainty of an Accommodation with the States-General; but this seems inconsistent with the Declarations of their High-Mightinesses, who have promised to furnish a Body of 40000 Men immediately in Flanders, who are to be joined with an equal Number in British Pay, and to be augmented by the Emperor to 120000.

Profert in lucem omnia tempus. [1]

From *The* PRESENT HISTORY *of* GREAT BRITAIN.

Our Letters from Scotland are full of extraordinary Encomiums on the Establish'd Clergy there, who distinguish themselves with an almost inimitable Zeal in the Service of the government. Many of them are not contented with exerting

[1] 'Time brings all [things] to light.'

their Abilities in their proper Functions only, but are also remarkably assiduous in raising Recruits for the Defence of their Country; and, to shew the People a good Example, serve as Volunteers themselves with great Chearfulness and Alacrity.—One of the Ministers of Edinburgh, as well known for his invincible Integrity, and strong Attachment to the present happy Constitution, as for his happy Talents in the Pulpit, has, by his excellent Discourses on this Occasion, done such eminent Service, that several of the *Jacobites* there have been heard to say, that they verily believed their Party was at least 6000 Men the weaker for his Preaching.

All Accounts from the North agree, that the Rebels are far from being formidable. On the contrary, their Numbers on both Sides the Forth, by the best Intelligence, do not exceed 6000; and the Parties of those who are in Arms for the Government in the North, hamper and harrass them in such a Manner, that there is scarce a Possibility of their increasing. The Defeat of a Party of Lord Loudon's Forces turns out, as we conjectured in our last, but an *inconsiderable Skirmish*: For the Loss on our Side was only seven Men killed and fifteen wounded and made Prisoners; while the Rebels are believed to have lost many more, tho' they were greatly superior in Number, *viz.* 1200 against 300. . . .

We own ourselves at a Loss to comprehend what can induce the Rebels, in their present distress'd Condition, and without the least Prospect of Success, to delay their dispersing and shifting for themselves one Moment, especially since they can have no Hope of receiving any additional Strength. Perhaps they are terrified by the Difficulties which must attend their Escape; but these will every Day encrease, and in a little time become altogether insurmountable: For the Troops in the King's Service, in that Part of the United Kingdom, are already double their Number, and must soon inevitably destroy them, unless they can preserve themselves by Flight. But how dreadful is the Condition of every loyal Subject in those Parts! Every Body knows that Scotland is by no means the most plentiful Spot of the Island, and that in many Places, particularly beyond the Forth, the Produce of the Ground, in Times of Peace and Plenty, is barely sufficient for the scanty Subsistance of the Inhabitants. What then must be the Condition of many thousands who are robb'd and plunder'd of the little they have; of those who are compelled to leave their Habitations at this Season of the Year, for fear of being forced into the Service of these Banditti; and of that immense Number of poor Creatures who are totally deprived of the means of their daily Sustenance, by the entire Stagnation of all manner of Trade and Business!— Their Case is indeed truly deplorable, and worthy the Consideration and Benevolence of their wealthier and happier Fellow-Subjects.

The Contributions the Pretender's Son hath demanded in Scotland wherever he hath come, have been so very great, and exacted with such uncommon and unheard-of Rigour, that some of his very sanguine Adherents there are highly disgusted at it, and have left his Party; and many of his Followers have actually been heard to say of late, that all is in vain, for they plainly see the Hearts of the People are utterly bent against their Prince as they are pleased to call him.

Nothing is more impertinent than the discoursing on Subjects in which we have no Knowledge; of this the Dabblers in Politics are usually guilty, in the most extraordinary manner. Witness their Assertions this Winter. First it was confidently said, that we were to engage no longer in a War on the Continent. Afterwards they changed their Opinion, and were for maintaining a foreign War, at least one Campaign longer, as the King of Prussia was to enter into it heartily, and the Dutch were to declare War against France, both which they were confident would happen. But it appears now that these wise Heads are mistaken in both: For we are to take t'other Bout on the Continent, tho' neither of those Circumstances are to be Conditions precedent.

Yesterday was the Birth-Day of his Royal Highness FREDERIC Prince of Wales, who then enter'd into his 40th Year.[1] His Majesty and their Royal Highnesses received the Compliments of the Nobility on this Occasion, and the Day was celebrated with Ringing of Bells, Bonfires, and other Demonstrations of Loyalty. The Birth-Day of a Prince, who, by so numerous a Progeny, hath assured the Preservation of our Religion and Liberties under the same Royal Line, to our distant Posterity, must give joyous Ideas to every Briton, who truly understands the Value of those Blessings, and how absolutely they depend on the maintaining the present Royal Family on the Throne.

The Mortality which hath raged so fatally among the Cattle, in the Neighbourhood of this Town, hath begun to shew itself in some other Parts of the Kingdom; but we hope it will not spread far, nor have any long Continuance. However, strict Orders have been given to prevent any Exportation of Cattle, for which there is a great Demand on the Continent, and the Legislature have at present this Matter, which seems to threaten with such dreadful Consequences, very properly under their Consideration. . . .

We hear that Advice came to the Government on Saturday last, of the Troops being dis-embark'd at Boulogne, on Account of their being very sickly.—*Perhaps it was thought convenient also for their Safety.*

On Friday last six Fireships went into the Downs, from Sheerness, and immediately Admiral Martin sailed in the Yarmouth, together with the Monmouth, Weazle Sloop, Swift Privateer, and the Fireships. And on Saturday last the Admiral, with the Monmouth returned to the Downs; but the others, we suppose, are gone on the Expedition for which they were intended, and are probably join'd by some Men of War in the Channel.

On Saturday Morning last an Express arrived at the Secretary's Office, from the North of England; and at 9 o'Clock at Night an Express arrived from Edinburgh, the Contents of which are not yet made public: But we hear, that General

---

[1] Although the compliment soon modulates into general support for the Hanoverian succession, here and elsewhere in the *TP* Fielding is careful to mete out appropriate praise to the prince of Wales, perhaps to hedge his political bets, perhaps in recognition of the former 'patriot' connection. Moreover, in early 1746 there is testimony to the effect that Frederic was uniting with his family in support of the ministerial coalition; *Marchmont Papers*, i. 166. See also 'Present History' of no. 11 (14 January 1746), above, p. 401; 'General Introduction', above, pp. lxxii–lxxviii; and index, *s.n.* 'Frederic Louis, prince of Wales'.

Hawley is marched towards the Rebels; and that Lord Elcho has left them. *These 4 last Paragraphs, which are all material, we have taken from the General Advertiser of Yesterday, the only Paper which contains either a Word of Truth or Common Sense.* [1]

An anonymous Letter directed to Sir Bourchier Wrey, Bart. at Exeter, and dated Moorfields, was about the End of last Month received by the said Gentleman, threatening him for promoting an Association of his Majesty's Subjects for the Public Defence; in order to discover and bring to Justice the Person and Persons, who wrote the said Letter, his Majesty has been pleased to promise his most gracious Pardon to any one of them, who shall discover his Accomplices, so as they may be apprehended and convicted thereof. As a further Encouragement a Reward of One Hundred Pounds is promis'd by the said Sir Bourchier Wrey. *All Attempts to discourage these Associations are as impudent as disloyal; but none carry so barefaced an Assurance as those which endeavour to represent them as illegal, and as Marks of Disaffection; of which Endeavour there have been some notorious Instances. . . .* [2]

From APOCRYPHA.

Wednesday. Extract of a private Letter, Northhampton, Jan. 13.

It is positively asserted by a Gentleman of undoubted Credit and Reputation, that the Inhabitants of Carlisle, Men, Women, and Children, were heard by the King's Forces to cry most lamentably in the Streets for Bread; and it is thought, that had not the Rebels taken the Liverpool Blues to be the Dutch Forces, and thereby conceived that the whole Army of Marshal Wade had joined the Duke's, this barbarous Banditti (whose White Flag for Capitulation was only a Piece of a ragged Shirt) would have compleated their Destruction, by starving them to Death, having ransack'd and taken most of the Provisions out of the Town into the Castle with them, as too plainly appeared at their Surrender, being well stored for a Five Weeks Siege, and in the Town little or no Sustenance was to be found.

By the same Gentleman 'tis assured, that the Duke of Perth was observed at

---

[1] An oblique slap at the *Gazette*, the only paper entitled to claim it was published 'by Authority'. Cf. 'Present History of Great Britain' in no. 15 (4–11 February 1746), below, p. 415, and no. 17 (18–25 February 1746), below, p. 425.

[2] For the political implications of associating to raise troops for 'the Public Defence' and for Fielding's earlier endorsement of associations, see 'General Introduction', above, pp. xliii–xlvi, and *Serious Address*, above, p. 31. Walpole, *Memoirs of . . . George the Second*, i. 98, notes that Sir John Philips had 'attempted during the last rebellion [the Forty-Five] to get the subscriptions and associations for the King declared illegal'. In the Commons the tory MP Humphrey Sydenham declared the subscriptions to be 'an encroachment upon the privileges of this House, and of such dangerous consequences to the liberties of the nation'; *Parliamentary History*, xiii. 1352. In London Alderman Heathcote tried to get the grand jury of Middlesex to present the associations and subscriptions as illegal, and in parliament he compared them to the Tudor benevolences; Eveline Cruickshanks, *Political Untouchables* (New York, 1979), pp. 84–5; L. Eardley-Simpson, *Derby and the Forty-Five* (London, 1933), p. 97. In addition a considerable pamphlet literature disputed their legality; see, for example, *The Folly and Danger of the Present Associations Demonstrated* (London, 1745), especially pp. 9–11.

Penrith to have carried off immense Sums; that himself was loaded in a Manner with Gold, as hardly to be able to walk; and also, that a Sumpter Horse laden with Money, died of its Burden on the Road between Penrith and Carlisle. LONDON COURANT. *We wish the Historian had named the Gentleman of undoubted Credit and Replutation; for at present the Truth of these silly Stories depends on the Relation of one whose Credit is very much doubted.*

We are credibly inform'd, that on Monday last, the Gentlemen of the Inquest of Walbrook Ward met according to Appointment, at the London-Stone Coffee-House, and at their own Expence dined together with the greatest Harmony. D. A. *We are as credibly informed that their Stomachs were equal to their Harmony.*

Thursday. Several Letters from the North say, the Pretender made such a precipitate Retreat from Carlisle, that he left his Military Chest behind him, in which were found several Sums of Money, and a Parcel of Papers of very great Consequence, L. C. *We believe these Papers were of as much Value as the Money.*

On Tuesday Night the Bodies of Mr. and Mrs Ward, who kept the Hercules Pillars in Bow-lane, Cheapside, were decently interr'd in Aldermary Church-yard, in the same Grave with her former Husband, who died in June last, and whose Corpse was taken up, and the Grave dug deep enough to receive them all. G. A. *To bury two Husbands in half a Year is indeed a Matter of great Decency.*

Last Monday Evening a Horse-Courser having sold two Horses of his Master's for 17*l.* 11*s.* went afterwards to Woodstreet Compter, to see a Woman Prisoner, where he stay'd all Night; but on his coming out the next Morning miss'd his Money; when the Keeper hearing the Complaint, made a diligent Search for it, but to no Purpose. D. G. *This Horse-Courser seems only to have been guilty of a small Mistake, by carrying the Money to his Mistress instead of his Master.*

Friday. Yesterday in the Afternoon Seven Waggons laden with Treasure, being the Second Division of the Treasure taken on board the French South Sea Ship which put into Cape Breton, was brought from Portsmouth to the Bank of England. D. G.

We hear the Rebels taken at Carlisle are coming to Town in forty-five Waggons, strongly guarded. D. A. *These Waggons are, I believe, laden with all the Treasure which their Companions left behind them.*

Saturday. The small Borough of Penryn in Cornwall has raised three hundred Guineas, which they have sent up to London to raise Men here for his Majesty's Service. D. A. *This small Borough is the only one, I believe, in the West of England which is better supplied with Money than Men.*

In the Gazette of this Day is the following Piece of Gallimatia, of which my Reader will make what he can.

Captain Faulkener, in the Vulture Sloop, being arrived at Inverkeithen Road, sent the Cutter and Boats before, who, upon their Arrival in Kincardin Road, saw a Brig come out of Airth, which the Rebels had seized in order to transport their Cannon from Allowa up the Firth, to batter Stirling Castle. . . .

Dead. . . . Mr. Gibson, an ingenious Carver and Guilder, and *what is much more to his Praise*, a Man of a good Character.[1]

THE TRUE PATRIOT, No. 13, From Tuesday, January 21, to Tuesday, January 28, 1746.

From *The* PRESENT HISTORY *of* GREAT BRITAIN.[2]

. . . All manner of Persons, as well English as Scots, express the highest Satisfaction at the Departure of his Royal Highness for Scotland. Those Persons who most earnestly wish to see this Rebellion extinguish'd, if they will do this Paper Justice, will allow us the Honour of having often prest the Necessity of sending an invincible Force to those Parts. There it is that the Fire which threatens this Nation rages, and consequently thither we should send our Engines and Firemen.

. . . A learned Gentleman publish'd a Dissertation Yesterday in one of the Grubstreet Papers, to prove it was better for the Proprietors to have 1 3 qrs. than 2 per Cent. and that every Man's Money would be safer in the Hands of the Company than in his own. . . .[3]

Dead. . . . William Meadows, Esq; aged 80. He had been a Justice of Peace upwards of 50 Years; *and I suppose was almost weary of the Office.*

THE TRUE PATRIOT, No. 14, From Tuesday, January 28, to Tuesday, February 4, 1746.

FOREIGN HISTORY.

It is reported from Durazzo, by the Way of Venice, that the Grand Signior is deposed, and that Osman Isbrahim, his Brother, is advanced to the Ottoman Throne in his Room.

Our Accounts from the Western Parts of Europe, are entirely filled with the

---

[1] The obituary of Peter Walter, the wealthy money-lender and Dorset landowner, is itemized without comment in this number; see Locke, p. [124]. Given Fielding's frequent satire of Walter and the likelihood that the two 'neighbours' were in fact acquainted, the absence of any comment is noteworthy. See W. B. Coley, 'Fielding and the Two Walpoles', *PQ*, xlv (1966), 169–70; *Champion* of 31 May 1740; *Miscellanies* (1743), i. 67, 130, 193, 199; and, for the tradition that Fielding's farm at East Stour came eventually into Walter's hands, *The Salisbury and Winchester Journal* of 11 September 1780.

[2] 'Foreign History' in this number is devoted to reprinting 'An Abridgment of the Treaties of Peace between the Emperor and the Kings of Poland and Prussia'; see Locke, pp. [128–9].

[3] See 'To the Proprietors of the South-Sea Stock', in *DA* of 27 January 1746. This 'Dissertation', which is signed 'A.B.', does not make its point quite so crudely as the *TP* here implies.

opening the ensuing Campaign, or Cock-Match, in the Low Countries. Several German Princes, or rather Farmers, who deal in Human-Fighting-Cocks, have fed considerable Numbers this Winter, which, they give out, they are now ready to march to the Market, where it is expected, that the English and Dutch Factors will attend to bid for them. It is supposed they will have them a Penny-worth, as no other will probably bid against them. Luckily for these Farmers, we are assured there will be a pretty high Demand; for one Lewis the Fifteenth, a great Cock-Merchant, threatens to bring above 200000 Head into the Pit, on the other Side. Very great Stakes are to be decided, and a large Piece of Ground called Europe, is deposited on the odd Battle. Some Ministers, who are considerable Gamesters, have high Bets depending, and one, it is reported, hath offered to lay his Head against a Sum of Money. As to the Prussian Gamesters, who have some of the best Cocks in Europe, it is generally believed they will not engage in this Match, unless a very extraordinary Price, for their Cocks, should induce them.

N.B. It is imagined most of the French are Shack-bags,[1] and only depend on the Superiority of their Numbers, as there are to be several Battles Royal.

From *The* PRESENT HISTORY *of* GREAT BRITAIN.

As the three *Gazettes*, since my last, have contained literally nothing, the Reader can expect no material Account in this Paper. The truth is, the History of the Rebellion, on which the Eyes of this Nation are properly fixed as the principal Object, is in a manner suspended, till the Duke is enabled to act against the Rebels in Scotland. This, we hope, he already is or soon will be, as some Regiments have joined the Forces at Edinburgh, since the Action,[2] and more are ordered to march that Way from the North of England. As to the Hessians, we are assured that they will not be able to arrive in Time enough to be of any Service. A General Action in Scotland must be of such vast Consequence, that the greatest Care which can now be taken, will undoubtedly be employ'd to send thither such a Force, as may leave the Rebels no Hopes of Success; for as a complete Victory over them must absolutely extinguish the Rebellion on the one Side, so will any Advantage which may arrive on their Side, be little less dreadful to us: For we must necessarily suppose they would improve it to the utmost against our Troops already there, and before we could send another Army against them, they must have an Opportunity to collect so formidable a Body, especially if they should have any Assistance from France or Spain, as must make the Conquest over them a Matter of infinitely more Difficulty than it

[1] Variant of 'shake-bag', a rogue, scoundrel (*OED*); from a 'cockpit' term meaning a cock turned out of a bag to fight another cock without the customary preliminaries. The present application of what was a fairly common metaphor appears to originate with the *TP*. Cf. 'Apocrypha' of no. 16 (11–18 February 1746), below, p. 422.

[2] The battle of Falkirk on 17 January 1746, in which the king's forces under Hawley were defeated. The 'Action' is reported, *via* the *Gazette* and other papers, in 'Present History' of *TP* no. 13 (21–8 January 1746), Locke, p. [129].

hath hitherto been; and may indeed make us apprehend[1] an Event to this Invasion begun by seven Men against a Nation, in which there are or should be upward of 70000 Soldiers, as horrible to be imagined, as it may seem ridiculous to be mentioned. . . .

We cannot help taking notice of the Behaviour of the worthy President and Governors of *Bridewell*, who have prevailed on several of the Youth committed to their Care and Correction, for disorderly Practices, to serve the King on board his Ships of War; for which Purpose, the Society hath cloathed them at their own Expence. *This may account for the Reason why Public Spirit hath been so difficult to be met with in other Parts of this Kingdom, since it now appears she is confined in Bridewell.* To which Place, it is probable, she hath been committed by some of our Great Men.[2]

Gallimatia concerning the late Battle.

Historians and their Marks.

G. A. General Advertiser.	D. G. Daily Gazetteer.
D. A. Daily Advertiser.	L. C. London Courant.

. . . While the Left Wing was on the long March, preceded by the Irish Dragoons about 200 Yards, the Dragoons were immediately attacked by the Rebels, and after standing one Fire, wheel'd upon the Glasgow Regiment, who were upon the long March before them, (i.e. *the Dragoons which preceded, retreated backwards, and by that means run upon those Foot who were before them*) treading some of them down, *&c.* One Regiment behaved well, L. C. . . .

From APOCRYPHA.

Tuesday. Saturday last in the Afternoon was committed to Newgate, at Bristol, John Barry, who kept the Harp and Star on the Key; 1. On a violent Suspicion of poisoning one James Barry, a Sailor, and an Officer of the Duke Privateer (whom he invited and got to his House, where he died in a short Time after:) 2. For forging his Will in Company with one P. Haynes, an Attorney, (whom he kept in his House for drawing Seamen's Wills, *&c.*) and a Servant Boy of his own: And 3. For Perjury, in swearing to the said Will himself.—It seems the Deceased was entitled to near 200 l. Prize Money.—Haynes and the Boy are both confined in Bridewell: Barry was taken out of his own House by the Sheriffs of the City in Person, attended by their Officers, where he had concealed himself under his Bed. L. C. *Murder, Forgery, and Perjury, are Crimes which shew some Genius in this honourable Gentleman, but when compared with those heroic Spirits who have destroyed their Country, he is but* a paultry Offender.

Thursday. Yesterday was held a General Court at the Bank of England, when

---

[1] To anticipate, look forward to, expect (*mostly* things adverse) [*OED*, which cites *Tom Jones*, III. iii. (127)].

[2] Like the italic sentence which precedes it, this roman sentence originates with the *TP*.

it was agreed to make a Call of 10 per Cent. on the Proprietors of their Stock, one half of the Money to be paid on or before the 23d of February, and the Remainder on or before the 28th Day of March next. The said 10 per Cent. is to be added to the Stock at Par. L. C. *Notwithstanding the wicked Attempts of some Persons, the Directors of the Bank have by their Management convinced the World that their Stock is good.*

By Letters from Edinburgh, we hear, that Mr. William Glover, Quarter-master of Lord Cobham's Regiment, Brother of Richard Glover, Esq; an eminent Merchant of this City, and Author of *Leonidas*, a Poem, was mortally wounded at the Battle of Falkirk, of which he languished two Days, when he died, universally lamented by all those Gentlemen who had the Pleasure of his Acquaintance. L. C. *If the Public did not know to whom they owe that excellent Poem,* [1] *the Historian would make it doubtful whether the Officer or the Merchant was its Author.*

Gloucester, Jan. 25. We hear from Chepstow in Monmouthshire, that early on Thursday Morning last they had a violent Tempest of Thunder and Lightning, by which a large Oak, near that Place, was torn up by the Roots, the Body of the Tree shatter'd (as it were) in ten thousand Pieces, and the Head left standing where the Tree grew, to the Admiration of all who have seen it. L. C. *And of all who have read it, if they can believe it.*

Newcastle, Jan. 25. On Monday last the Duke of Rutland's Regiment arrived here, (*The Duke of Rutland hath no Regiment*) they were reviewed Yesterday by Gen. Wentworth, and gave great Satisfaction.

On Tuesday the Duke of Bedford's Regiment arrived here, who are also in full Spirits. D. A. *I have heard hysterical Women talk of being in and out of Spirits: But I believe this Language was never applied to Soldiers till lately. Perhaps these Authors, who have imputed the ill Behaviour of Troops to a Pannic, might more properly have said,* The Army was out of Spirits.

A great many Cooks, &c. are set out for Scotland, in order to attend his Royal Highness the Duke of Cumberland at Holy-Rood House, where his Highness will stay for some Time. All Things are preparing there to receive him in such a Manner as is becoming his Dignity and Character. L. C. *By this* &c. *I suppose is meant Provisions; for otherwise the Cooks would I believe be very useless Officers in those Parts at present. Perhaps it is intended to let these Cooks fall into the Hands of the Enemy, which would be no bad Stratagem; for could we introduce some of our Luxury among them, we should soon find it a much easier Task to beat them.*

The Smugglers, who have lately committed great Outrages in the County of Sussex, dispersed on the first Approach of the regular Troops, and depend on

---

[1] *Leonidas* (1737), an epic poem in blank verse and nine books, seems to have been taken as something of a political manifesto by the 'patriot' faction among Sir Robert Walpole's enemies. It is extravagantly praised in *Common Sense* (9 April 1737, collected ed. [1738], i. 72–80), in the *Champion* (8 March 1740, i. 340), and in Fielding's 'A Journey from this World to the Next', *Miscellanies* (1743), ii. 63, where Glover is called 'a celebrated Poet of our Nation'. Richard Glover (1712–85), poet and politically active business leader, was instrumental in drawing up the merchants' petition of January 1742, which complained effectively of Walpole's inadequate protection of British commerce. At one time he had close 'patriot' connections with Lyttelton, Cobham, Dodington, and the prince of Wales.

Concealment only for their Security. L. C. *I'm glad they have no better Dependence.*

Last Monday Mr. John Florence, Riding-Officer at Wareham, seized at West-Lulworth, Twenty-five Casks of Brandy, which were all sent to his Majesty's Warehouse in the Port of Poole, in the County of Dorset. L. C. *If the Smugglers were once effectually demolished, these Seizures would be at an End.*

Saturday. We hear that the Commissioners of his Majesty's Court of Lieutenancy of this City are going to lay a Tax of Two-pence in the Pound on every House-keeper, in order to cause a sufficient Stock, by the Way of Trophy Money, to pay the several Commission and Non-Commission Officers, for the Days Marches, and Night Duties, which they have gone through since the Breaking out of the present Rebellion in Scotland. *If it be asked, what* Trophies *the Trained Bands have gained? The Answer will now be easy.*

We hear that the Worshipful Company of Surgeons are going to take a large Piece of Ground in the Old Bailey, to build a handsome Hall, and other Apartment, for the Use of the said Company; the Worshipful Company of Barbers (from whom they were lately separated by Act of Parliament) being to be left in the full Possession of their present fine Hall in Monkwell Street, near Cripplegate. L. C. *This Behaviour of the Gentlemen of the Lancet towards their quondam Brethren of the Razor, shews Generosity and Condescension; especially as the old Hall, being built at* Cripplegate, *seems to have been built by the Predecessors of the former Order.*

We hear, that Mr. Handel proposes to exhibit some Musical Entertainments on Wednesdays or Fridays the ensuing Lent, with Intent to make good to the Subscribers (that favoured him last Season) the Number of Performances he was not then able to compleat; in order thereto he is preparing a New Occasional Oratorio, which is design'd to be perform'd at the Theatre-Royal in Covent Garden. G. A. *If we must have public Entertainments at this Season, we hope the Merit of the Composers will be no Objection to them. If we cannot maintain the Virtue of Britons, it is hoped, we shall at least shew that we have the Taste of Italians.*[1]

We are certainly informed, that on Monday next, at the Theatre-Royal in Drury Lane, will be perform'd the Lying Valet, and that Mr. Stevens, at the particular Desire of some Persons of Quality, is to act the Part of Justice Guttle; in which Character he will devour twelve Pounds of Plumb-Cake at three Mouthfuls. D. A. *Such Stomachs should have been born in better Times.*[2]

On Wednesday last three Persons were apprehended at Hastings in Sussex,

---

[1] With this somewhat concessive flattery of Handel, cf. the compliment paid to the second performance of his oratorio in 'Present History' of *TP* no. 17 (18–25 February 1746), below, p. 425. Only three performances were given (Handel owed his subscribers eight nights from the truncated 1744–5 season), and Handel never again attempted a subscription for his performances; Deutsch, *Handel*, p. 629.

[2] No performance of Garrick's popular farce is recorded for Drury Lane between 11 January and 25 February 1746; *London Stage*, Part 3, ii. 1210, 1221. However, the performance at Goodman's Fields on 3 March advertises 'an additional Scene upon eating . . . never perform'd before'. Garrick himself was 'sitting out' the season in Dublin and when he returned late in the spring would work for Rich at Covent Garden.

on a strong Suspicion of being Spies; one appears like a Gentleman, another passes for his Servant, and the third is an old Man who owns himself a Papist, and pretends that he is Steward to some Gentleman of Distinction. They came about a Week since in a Boat to Boarne, which is eighteen Miles from Hastings, and are said to have offer'd ten Guineas at Hoo the Day before they were taken, for a Boat to carry them to France. It is hoped this will prove the Means of making great Discoveries. L. C. *We presume those who apprehended these Persons had some stronger Reasons for their Suspicion than this Historian hath been pleased to discover.* . . .

Dead. . . . Capt. Baxter, who presented the approved Scheme to the House of Commons to prevent the Running of Wool. *We wish it had been effectually executed as well as approved.* Dr. Copely a Physician in Covent Garden, *who was very eminent in York.* . . . Mr. Christopher Warren; he was many Years Collector of Excise, and *collected* a good Fortune, which he hath left to his Niece. Mr. Cox, an eminent Broker; he followed the Business many Years with great Reputation—*as a Pawnbroker.* . . . One Nowns, a Labourer, *most probably immensely poor, and yet as rich now as either of the two Preceding.* . . . Mrs. Lambert; her Brother in Law was an Alderman; her Husband kept the Bull Head; and her Father the Horn Tavern; *her Family seem to have much delighted* in Horns. . . .

THE TRUE PATRIOT, No. 15, From Tuesday, February 4, to Tuesday, February 11, 1746.

From *The* PRESENT HISTORY *of* GREAT BRITAIN.[1]

His Royal Highness the Duke having, with the most incredible Celerity, arrived in Scotland, and with an Expedition equal to any Thing in the Life of Cæsar, pursued the Rebels, they fled before him, and dispersed themselves even by the Terror of his Name; but his Royal Highness's own Words, in his Letters to the Duke of Newcastle and the Lord Justice Clerk, are so good an Account of the Matters of Fact, that I look upon the reprinting those Letters as the best Method of acquainting the Reader with the Particulars, since his Arrival in the North. . . .

The following Article is taken from the *General Advertiser* of Yesterday; a Paper whose Authority is very near as good as that of the *Gazette.* . . .[2]

[1] 'Foreign History' in this number is a declared reprinting from the *London Gazette* (8 February 1746).

[2] The irony at the expense of the *Gazette* is clear, but to read it also as telling against the *General Advertiser* is probably a misreading. See the praise of the latter in 'Present History' of *TP* no. 12 (21 January 1746), above, p. 408, and for another comparison with the *Gazette*, 'Present History' of no. 17 (18–25 February 1746), below, p. 425. There may have been some connection between the *TP*

From APOCRYPHA.

Tuesday. They write from Ratisbon, that a Marriage is on Foot between his Electoral Highness of Bavaria, and the eldest Daughter of his Royal Highness the Prince of Brazil, Heir apparent to the Crown of Portugal, tho' from Munich they write, that his Electoral Highness is on the Point of marrying a Princess of Saxony. L. C. *The Historian should have told us which to believe.*

Wednesday. The following is an exact List of his Majesty's Forces in Scotland, under the Command of the Duke of Cumberland, *viz.* Three Regiments of Horse, three of Dragoons, and nine of Foot, (being fifteen Regiments) all Veteran Troops, with the Glasgow and Aberdeen Regiments of Foot, and 1000 Volunteers of the Shire and City of Edinburgh, amounting in the whole to 16,7000 Men. L. C. *The above exact List is false in every Particular. There are no Horse in Scotland; four Regiments of Dragoons, and fifteen Regiments of Foot.*

Thursday. Yesterday Morning as the Henly Waggon was going along Hammersmith Road, between the Town and the Turnpike, run against another Waggon coming towards London, which broke the Axle-tree of the Henly Waggon, and overturned it in a Ditch, by which Accident a Woman Passenger was bruised to Death, by the Goods falling upon her. L. C. *Tho' this Paragraph is not English, the Story may probably be fact. Indeed the Insolence, Rudeness, Barbarity, Drunkenness, and Carelessness of Waggoners, Stage-Coachmen, &c. call aloud for the Notice of the Legislature.*

On Monday last one of the Pensioners of Chelsea Hospital, was turn'd out of the House, for Cursing his Majesty, and wishing the Pretender in his room. He had been admitted but a Fortnight, and when dismissed, had like to have been torn to Pieces by the Populace, when they heard the Cause of his Dismission. G. A. *The Judgments past at the Tribunal of the Populace, are generally hasty and severe; but seldom unjust. And it is with Pleasure we observe, that all Causes are at present decided by that Court in Favour of the Government.*

On Monday a large Sword, exactly resembling that carried by the Sword-bearer of the City of London before the Lord Mayor, was taken up by the Ballast-Men at Westminster New Bridge; the Blade was very much injur'd by Time; the Pomel and other Ornaments about it were of thick Silver, and several old Saxon Characters were about some of them, but not legible; the Scabbard seem'd to be scarlet Velvet; and it looked like a Sword of State, being inlayed and ornamented with Gold on the Blade, *&c.* D. A. *This Sword was probably lost on some Lord Mayor's Day, in the naval Procession, and the finding it betokens an ensuing Peace.*

and the *General Advertiser*, which reprints *TP* no. 10 in its issue of 11 January 1746 and advertises *TP* no. 13 in its issue of 27 January. At this time the *General Advertiser* was 'Printed for H. Woodfall, *jun.*' and its advertisements were taken in by, among others, George Woodfall, who appears as a seller of the *TP* in its colophons for nos. 19–32. More significantly perhaps, the *General Advertiser* had recently switched from 'straight' presentation of news items to the *TP*'s practice of commenting jocularly on them, and during the month of January, for example, it published poetical *encomia* on two 'patriot' figureheads, Bolingbroke and Chesterfield.

They write from Edinburgh, that two Captains, one Lieutenant, and six private Men of Hamilton's Regiment, are already sentenced to be shot for Cowardice, in the late Action near Falkirk. The Trial of an Officer, who had the Direction of the Artillery, came on last Thursday, but was not ended when the Letters came away. L. C. *For the Truth of this, we appeal to the same authentic Historian the very next Day, in the ensuing Paragraph.*

Friday. We are inform'd from unquestionable Authority, that notwithstanding what has been published to the contrary in the Papers, the Dragoons in general, and Hamilton's Regiment in particular, behaved very well in the Action at Falkirk, charging through the first Line of the Enemy before the Foot of the King's Army were formed; and so far is it from being true that either Officers or Men misbehaved in the least, that on the contrary their Courage and Conduct has been approved by their Generals; so that the invidious Reflections which have been propagated on this Subject, prove to be as groundless and false, as they are wicked and malicious, and it is with great Satisfaction we take this Opportunity of setting the World right in this Particular. L. C. *As the Historian had himself set the World wrong the Day before, it must be certainly a great Satisfaction to him to set them right, and avoid begging Pardon a 4th Time for injuring Reputation.*

Saturday. Berlin, Feb. 8. One of those who search after and pretend to find out Mysteries in Numbers, has remarked, that the Silesian War began in 1740, which includes 5 Times 348. That it continued 5 Years. That it has laid waste 5 Provinces, namely, Bohemia, Moravia, Silesia, Lusatia, and Saxony. That since its Commencement, 5 Battles have been fought, *viz.* Mollwitz, Chotusitz, Friedberg, Sorr, and Willsdorff. That the Battle of Mollwitz was fought the 10th of April, in which the Number 5 is contain'd twice, that of Sorr on the 30 of September, which includes 6 Times the same Number; the Peace was sign'd the 25th of December 1745, in which the Number 5 triumphs above every other, since there is not only just 5 Times the Number 349 in that of the Year, but also 5 Times in the Date of the Day, and that even the Month has taken its Name from the Number 10, which is twice 5; besides, the King had then reign'd just 5 Years, 5 Months, and 55 Days; from whence it may naturally be inferred, that his Prussian Majesty is an Adept at the Game of Fives. D. A. *There is 5 Times more Nonsense in this Paragraph than in all the 5 Morning Papers published on Wednesday last, which was the 5th Day of the Month; and within one of being the 5th Day of the Week.*

On Thursday Night some Persons found Means of getting into Westminster Abbey, and cut off the Gold Lace from the Figures in Wax-Work of King William and Queen Mary, Queen Anne, and the Duke of Buckingham, and broke and otherwise damaged the said Figures, and got out of the East Door undiscover'd with their Booty, by breaking the Stone Work where the Bolt goes into it. D. A. *Gold Lace is of more Service to a living Rogue, than a dead King.*

Yesterday Morning a Servant at the Py'd Bull in Islington, cut his Wife's Throat in Bed in such a Manner that her Head was almost separated from her Body. She was a Servant also in the said Inn, and they had been married about a Fortnight. When he came down he desired his Mistress to make him some

Punch, and whilst he was drinking it, his Wife was found murder'd, as above, wrapt up in the Blankets; whereupon he was immediately secured, D. A. *If this Story be true, the Man who did it was probably mad; if it be false, he who invented it is certainly a Fool.* . . .

Committed. Phillis Brocker for picking Pockets. George Edmunds for picking up Tobacco. Francis Otter for picking up Bread; *I hope not out of mere Necessity.* . . .[1]

Appeared. Grubstreet Poets without Number, singing to the Praise of Duke William; and Grubstreet Medallists trumpeting the Praises of their own Medals. A Soldier sold his Buckles to buy of one. Another will serve his Customers as soon as he is able, the Demand being very extraordinary. He makes Excuses, returns Thanks, *&c.*[2]

THE TRUE PATRIOT, No. 16, From Tuesday, February 11, to Tuesday, February 18, 1746.

From *The* PRESENT HISTORY *of* GREAT BRITAIN.[3]

. . . On Wednesday last, it being reported in Westminster-hall, that the Right Hon. the Lord Chancellor intended to resign the Great Seal, an universal Melancholy shewed itself in the Face of every Member of the Law. Indeed the Character which this Great Man hath supported through all the Ranks which he hath filled in his Profession, and the Ability, Clemency and Justice with which he hath administer'd the highest Offices in it, have made the inferior Branches to regard him in the Light of a Father. As such they lamented his apprehended Loss, and as such they rejoiced at his Restoration.[4]

A certain Wag, well known by the Name of *Will Waddle*,[5] played a comical

---

[1] In the 'Dead' section of news the obituary of 'The Hon. Charles Fielding [*sic*], Esq; Colonel in the Guards; Equerry to his Majesty, and Brother to the Earl of Denbigh' is given without comment.

[2] Like the poems, the commemorative medals celebrated the duke of Cumberland. Fielding seems to have had his eye on Christopher Pinchbeck's apologetic claim of excessive demand. The reference to the soldier selling his 'Buckles' has not been located. It may be the *TP*'s satiric adaptation of Pinchbeck's further claim that many common soldiers were buying the medals (*DA* of 6 February 1746).

[3] 'Foreign History' in this number is a declared reprinting from the *General Advertiser* (17 February 1746).

[4] Another in a continuing series of compliments to Philip Yorke (1690–1764), cr. baron Hardwicke (1733), lord chancellor (1737–56), titular head of Fielding's profession. See, for example, *Champion* of 9 September 1740 ('Thus our Law thrives under a *Hardwick*'); *TP* no. 33 (17 June 1746), above, p. 308; *JJ* nos. 8 (23 January 1748) and 11 (13 February 1748), pp. 137, 161; *Tom Jones*, IV. vi. 172; *A True Case of Bosavern Penlez* (1749); and the dedication of *An Enquiry into the Causes of the late Increase of Robbers* (1751). Hardwicke may have repaid Fielding's compliments by helping prepare the way for his entry into the judiciary; see Archibald Bolling Shepperson, 'Additions and Corrections to Facts about Fielding', *MP*, li (1954), 218.

[5] Referring to William Pulteney (1684–1764), earl of Bath (1742), former opposition whig and personal enemy of Sir Robert Walpole's. At this time Bath, who had deserted his 'patriot' colleagues in

unlucky Trick the other Day, with a Companion of his who is lately come from *Carlisle*.[1] *Will* told this Youth that he could procure him an *admirable* Place in the Family of a certain Great Man of his Acquaintance; and accordingly took the Youth, who had powder'd and bedress'd himself in a very extraordinary Manner, to the Gentleman's House. *Will* went in to the Gentleman, and left his Friend without to cool his Heels, as the Phrase is, in the Anti-chamber, having acquainted him that he should be soon called in, and hired. The *Carlisle* Lad waited a long Time expecting the Return of *Will*, who had slipt down a *Pair of Back Stairs* and departed; at last the House-Maid coming to sweep the Rooms, found this young Man walking backward and forward, and instead of getting his Place, he narrowly escaped being carry'd before Justice de Veil,[2] on Suspicion of having a felonious Design on the House.

We are inform'd, that a certain Person, who is well known to have been in an Opposition for many Years, and to owe to that all the Reputation he ever had, hath lately affected, in Public Coffee-houses, to decry all Opposition as unjust;[3] and in particular hath declared, that the Promotion of a Gentleman,[4] who hath exerted the highest Abilities, and most incorrupted Integrity, would give an Encouragement to young Men for the future to display their Talents the same Way.

the post-Walpole shuffles, was stage-managing the transfer of offices from the Pelham ministry (resigned) to the abortive Bath–Granville administration of 10–12 February 1746. See next note. Bath's corpulence and odd gait were often remarked by contemporary satirists. See, for example, Sir Charles Hanbury Williams, 'A New Ode' (1742): 'His step, his gait describe the man, | They paint him better than I can, | Waddling from side to side'; *Works* (London, 1822), i. 138; also *GM*, xii (1742), 441; *Yale Walpole*, xviii. 49.

[1] Henry Howard (1694–1758), fourth earl of Carlisle (1738), was active in the opposition to Walpole and later associated with Bath, who tried to place him as lord privy seal in the cabinet shuffles of late 1743. The *TP* anecdote here satirizes Bath's renewed attempts to procure the office for Carlisle as part of the aborted ministry of 10–12 February 1746. Carlisle's particular discomfiture was widely reported. See, for example, *Marchmont Papers*, i. 174; Walpole, *Memoires of . . . George the Second* (London, 1822), i. 151; *EHR*, iv (1889), 750–1, which reprints a supposititious letter of Chesterfield's, giving additional embarrassing detail. *The Foundling Hospital for Wit, Numb. iii* (1746), p. 60, reprints the *TP* anecdote, 'told by a tart Historian of the present Times', as if it were the first part of 'The Surprising History of a late long Administration' by 'Titus Livius, jun.' *GM*, xvi (1746), 332, lists this number of *The Foundling Hospital for Wit* among the June books.

[2] Thomas De Veil (*c.* 1684–1746), at this time justice of the peace for Westminster, the jurisdiction in question. De Veil had recently acquired a reputation for vigorous prosecutions against supposed 'jacobites', to go along with his even greater one as a trading justice who 'kept bad [i.e. low] people much in awe by the virulence of his practice'; *Memoires of the Life and Times of Sir Thomas Deveil, Knight* (London, 1748), pp. 64–5.

[3] Not identified. Possibly Bolingbroke, the apotheosis of opposition and in 1746 once again resident in England. Cf. 'Diary of Hugh Earl of Marchmont', *s.d.* 13 February 1746: 'Lord Bolingbroke told me, that Bath had resigned, and all was now over. He approved of what had been done, though he owned, that Walpole's faction had done what he had wrote, every king must expect, who nurses up a faction by governing by a party'; *Marchmont Papers*, i. 173; see also i. 70–5. However, the hostile tone and the siting of the 'Person' in public coffee-houses do not seem appropriate.

[4] Pitt, who would finally be given place (joint vice-treasurer of Ireland) on 22 February 1746. He wanted secretary at war, but the king refused to admit him to the closet, and the Pelhams decided to substitute some post not involving personal relations with the sovereign. See *Parliamentary History*, xiii. 1055–6; Owen, p. 301 *n.* 3; and, for Pitt's long exclusion from the broad bottom, 'General Introduction', above, pp. lxxiv–lxxxvii.

Amongst the many true Britons who have lately distinguished themselves as such, and have convinc'd us, we are a free People, a noble Earl deserves every Encomium which the noblest Spirit and truest Integrity can intitle him to. He hath indeed equall'd all that Heroic Ardour for the Public Weal which makes many British Peers, and particularly his own Great Ancestors, shine so bright in our Annals.[1]

All our Accounts from Scotland are full of the Gallantry of his Royal Highness the Duke; and the Respect which all Sorts of People (Rebels only excepted) ambitiously vie with each other in shewing him. During his short Abode at Edinburgh his Apartments, though he affected to have no Court, were crowded against his Will, and even by the Ladies, who wore Ribbons on their Breasts, in which his Name was embroider'd. The Clergy likewise waited on him in a Body, and returned extremely satisfied with their Reception....

The Hessians arrived on the 8th Instant at Leith, where they remain a-board in Attendance of the Duke's Order; but we hope that glorious Commander will now be able to put an End to this detestable Rebellion, without their Assistance.

Notwithstanding the Reports which have been spread of our sending 15000 Troops abroad, *we assure the Public no such Measure is as yet determined; nor will be, unless Affairs should take such a Turn, as must make every honest Man in Britain to desire their Embarkation....*

From APOCRYPHA.

Extract from a Letter, Newcastle, Feb. 10.

Tuesday. 'By Letters just arrived here by Express, of the 5th Instant, from Edinburgh, it is said, that a French Ship is arrived at Peterhead, with Ammunition for the Rebels, who had sent 40 of their Number to guard it; but *it is thought* she has fallen into the Hands of Lord Loudon's Men, who were much nearer that Town at the Time of her Arrival, than the Rebels were. *It is also hoped*, Cameron of Lockyel will be taken, as he was obliged to be carried off in a Litter; and *it is believed*, that Lord John Drummond is dead of his Wounds.' L. C. *There is no Truth in what is thought, what is hoped, nor what is believed.*

Our last Advices from Stirling assure us, that 350 Deserters from Lord John Drummond's Regiment were come into that Place; and that Jenny Cameron,

---

[1] Although at this time serving in Ireland (as lord lieutenant) and hence remote from the centers of power, Philip Dormer Stanhope (1694–1773), fourth earl of Chesterfield, must be meant. The compliment to his lineage could not accurately apply to William Stanhope, first earl of Harrington (1742), one of the secretaries of state and, as a Pelham loyalist, more of a prime mover in the shuffles of early 1746. Chesterfield's correspondence with Newcastle during this period reveals the ministry's interest in giving the 'noble Earl' a more active role, and Fielding's praise of him here, in addition to being self-serving, may also have been intended to encourage Chesterfield to fuller participation. Fielding will praise Chesterfield's lieutenancy in 'Letter XL. Valentine to David Simple', a contribution to Sarah Fielding's *Familiar Letters* (1747), ii. 295–6. The letter there is dated 20 December and may belong to 1746. Fielding also singles out the nobility of Chesterfield's birth in 'An Essay on Conversation', *Miscellanies* (1743), i. 126, 138.

who has been of late so much talk'd of, is actually a Prisoner there. L. C. *These Advices are thought and believed to assure with the same Degree of Truth as those above.*

Yesterday the Rebel Officers taken at Carlisle were brought to Town; Part of them were carried to New-Prison, and the rest, among whom were Hamilton, Governor of Carlisle, and the pretended Bishop of that See, were carried to Newgate, except those that were French, which were five in Number, *viz.* the French Engineer in a Coach, and four others, in a Waggon, who were carried to the Marshalsea prison. There were vast Numbers of People crowded to see them; and the Populace, to shew their Abhorrence of their *black* Designs, pelted them as they passed with Dirt, *&c.* D. A. *In order to make them and their Designs of the same Colour.*

Wednesday. It is assured, that the young Pretender, now that his Time of plundering is over, and being forsaken by his inferior Banditti, has gone on board the Hazard Sloop of War, (lately taken from us by the Rebels) in Company with Lord John Drummond, and some more of their Chiefs, in order to sail for France.

We hear that most of the Men, late under the Command of Lord John Drummond, have surrendered themselves Prisoners, and are coming to Edinburgh. L. C. *For the Truth of this* assured, *and* we hear, *see the two Paragraphs above.*

Thursday. One James Riddel was apprehended as a Spy at Stirling, and hang'd up; he had one of the Pretender's Passes in his Pocket. L. C. *This Pass conveyed him to the proper Place.*

Last Night above sixty Prisoners came under a strong Escort, and are confined here, amongst these is the celebrated Miss Jenny Cameron, with several young Gentlemen, that have been detained since the beginning of this Rebellion, in Stirling Castle. L. C. *This Historian hath so frequently mentioned this young Lady, that one would suspect she was rather a Mistress of his, than of the Pretender's; but however that be, I am well informed this celebrated Miss Jenny is Ætat.* 50. . . .

Last Week an uncommon Affair happened at Bradford in Wiltshire, *viz.* One Hannah Wilson was married three Years ago to one John Silk, who went from her about two Months after their Marriage; and she being inform'd, that he was gone to Sea, and since dead, she married again, but to her great Astonishment, her former Husband returned home from the East Indies, where he had been ever since he left her; on seeing him she directly left the House, and went into the Garden, and hang'd herself. G. A. *If her Husband hath any Grace, he will, within this Twelvemonth, be found hanging on the same Tree.*

It is said, that there will not be any British Troops sent abroad, till such Time as the Dutch declare War against France. D. A.

Friday. We hear now that 15000 of our Troops will be sent to Flanders this Summer. D. A. *As the Historian doth not tell us the Dutch will declare War, which Assertion are we to believe?*

By Letters from the North we have Advice, that the Lady of Lord Ogilvie, and several other Persons of Distinction, were actually taken; but as those Letters make no mention of any Engagement between his Majesty's Forces and the

Rebels, we may rest assured that those Reports are entirely without Foundation. L. C. *This poor Lady, who is, I believe, from her Attendance on her Husband, one of the best Wives in Europe, hath been often taken, and as often released by the Grubstreet Writers.*

The French Prisoners which were taken and brought into Hull some time since, by one of his Majesty's Ships of War, are all bringing to London, escorted by a strong Party of his Grace the Duke of Ancaster and Kevestan's Horse. L. C. *As there are no such Horse, possibly there may be no such Prisoners.*

They write from Rome, that the Pope hearing the Italian Singers were performing an Opera in London, called *La Rebellion* (*Ribellione* in *Italian*) *Punita*, (in Praise of the Duke of Cumberland, and to degrade the Pretender) he has excommunicated all the Roman Catholics belonging to the English Opera; and has caused a List of them to be hung upon the Pillars of St. Bartholomew's Church in Rome, with an Injunction, that if they are found in any Roman Catholic Country, they shall be put into the Inquisition. D. A. *They write in the same Letters, that his Holiness shed Tears on this Occasion; and that the Pretender, the Moment he heard it cry'd out,* Et Tu, *Lady,—and then fell into a Swoon: Upon his Recovery from which he immediately dispatched Letters of Revocation to his Son in* Scotland, *having given all for lost. From* Paris *they write, that Cardinal* Tencin *hath declared he fears the Opera called* The Fall of the Giants,[1] *may be ominous to the War in* Brabant, *and may portend the Fall of the* French. *It is added, that that Minister, speaking on that Subject concluded with a Sigh,* PLUS CANTIBUS ILLI, QUAM NOS ARMIS.[2]

Saturday. Yesterday Morning was fought a Duel in Hyde-Park, between a Surgeon of a Man of War, and a Gentleman of St. Ann's, Soho; they fell out at a Coffee-house in Holborn concerning a Gentlewoman: The latter took her Part, and wounded the former so, that his Life is despair'd of. D. A. *The Surgeon mistook his Business, which is to cure Wounds, and not to make them.*

We are inform'd, that on Monday last certain Dunghill Cocks, mistaking themselves for Game, were pitted at S—t Ja—s's; but next Day, being Shrove-Tuesday, the Error was discovered, and the Cocks so cruelly thrown at, with long Staves, that by Ash-Wednesday Morning they were reduced to a perfect State of Mortification, and took to their Heels with the little Life that was left in them. D. A. *This Paragraph of Cocks mistaking themselves, were pitted,* &c. *seems to be Nonsense; but perhaps it alludes to a Story of a Cock, which was heard crowing several Times in an upper Apartment near the Cockpit[3] one Night last Week, to the great*

[1] As the *TP* comment makes clear, all these reports are apocryphal, although the opera did commence its season, with *La Caduta de' Giganti*, music by Gluck, text by F. Vanneschi, on 7 January 1746 at the King's; *London Stage*, Part 3, ii. 1209. According to *DA* of 8 January 1746 this 'new musical Italian Drama . . . writ on the Occasion of the Expulsion of the Rebels was . . . not a little enliven'd by the Presence of his Royal Highness the Duke of Cumberland'.

[2] 'They [spend] more on song than we do on arms.'

[3] Apartments in Whitehall, looking out on St. James's, by this time used as an assembly room for meetings of the privy council and other political gatherings. See Walpole to Mann, 15 November 1742, *Yale Walpole*, xviii. 102 and *nn*. Although its details are by no means clear, the *TP*'s reworking of the trope from cockfighting appears to allude to the presumption and brevity of the Bath–Granville takeover.

Disturbance of the Neighbourhood, who resolved to twist his Neck, *but the next Morning, to their great Surprize, they found he was* got out *again as strangely as he* got in. *This silly People believe to have been a Ghost, as usual.*

... Our Soldiers have made a kind of military Auction, or Public Sale, of Houshold Goods, Cattle, Sheep, Hogs, *&c.* with what little Silver Plate they have been able to find, in the Houses of such Gentlemen as are with the Rebels.' L. C. *Most of the Cattle, I believe, may be brought away in their Bellies, and most of the Plate in their Fobs.*

Yesterday there was a very hot Press for Seamen below Bridge by several Men of War's Boats, in order to Man some of the Ships lying at Spithead and Chatham.

The present Frost being so intense has entirely froze up the Thames above Kingston Bridge, to the great Hindrance of Persons whose chief Dependance is on the Water-Carriages in those Parts. L. C. *These Persons should follow their Trade,* i.e. *the Water, to the Sea, where the preceding Paragraph shews us, they may find Business.*

Monday. Last Saturday a great Quantity of Apparel for the Foot-Guards were put on board a Vessel at the Tower, which is ordered to sail to Scotland with all Expedition. L. C. *Why the Foot-Guards who are all in London should send their Apparel to Scotland is not easy to guess, unless the Hessians are come over naked, and our Guards are so generous as to lend them their Cloaths.*

They write from Paris, that Major Brown, who arrived at Versailles with an Account of the Action at Falkirk, was made a Knight of the Order of St. Louis by the French King. D. A. *We suppose the Major hath the same Gift with this Historian: For had he given a* TRUE *Account of that Action, the French King would scarce have rewarded him for his News.*

The following Account from Mechlin, dated the 20th of February N.S. is handed about here.

'On Monday last the Garrison of Brussels made two successful Sallies, one out of the Schaarbeck, and the other out of the Leuven Gate, by which Means the Enemy lost above 200 Men, and nail'd up a Battery of Cannon without the Gate of Schaarbeck, and brought about fifty Prisoners into the Town. The 14th and 15th the Enemy endeavour'd to take Possession of the Flemish Gate, but was repulsed with great Loss. The 16th and 17th Instant, the Enemy threw a vast Number of Bombs and red-hot Bullets into the City of Brussels, by which Means a great many Houses were set on Fire. Yesterday and this Day the French did not fire one Shot.

'P.S. We are just now told, that the Prince of Waldeck, being joined by the first Division of Austrian Troops, consisting of 15000 Men, is with his whole Army in full March to attempt to raise the Siege.'

It was Yesterday reported, that Advices were received that Marshal Saxe had taken the City of Brussels, and made the Austrians and Hanoverians Prisoners of War; and it was stipulated that the Dutch should not serve against France for a certain Time. D. A. *As these Accounts seem contradictory, some Part may possibly be true, tho' they are in the Daily Advertiser. . . .*

Casualties. The Mistress of an Alehouse found dead in her Bed. L. C. *It is not mention'd whether she lay on the first or second Floor.* A Blacksmith smother'd in the Snow. *When he was found he was probably* a Whitesmith. . . . On Saturday last a Waiter at a noted Eating-house in Finch-lane, Cornhill, being in some Discontent of Mind, hang'd himself; when he was cut down there was a new Rope found in his Coat Pocket. *This Man as well as* Cato *was doubly* arm'd. . . .[1]

The *Gazette* Writer of Tuesday last is desired to explain the following Paragraph: At Crief the whole Rebel Army *disbanded, and marched in three separate Corps.* He is likewise desired to tell us, whether Capt. Norris took the Privateer, or only came up with her.

Saturday last a new Paper made its Appearance, the Author of which promised in a printed Advertisement, that he would publish no ingenious Conceits, *and he was as good as his Word. We expected he would likewise have kept his Promise in furnishing us with* Intelligence of his own, *i.e. like the* Daily Advertiser, of his own making: *But on the contrary, it was the most servile Transcript from the Morning Papers which was published that Evening.*[2]

The letter signed *Cato Britannicus* would have been inserted before this, had it not been unfortunately mislaid. If the Author will favour us with another Copy, it shall be inserted in our next.[3]

N.B. *The further Consideration of the Plan for a National Militia is postponed.*[4]

THE TRUE PATRIOT, No. 17, From Tuesday, February 18, to Tuesday, February 25, 1746.

From *The* PRESENT HISTORY *of* GREAT BRITAIN.[5]

. . . It is reported, and not without a Colour of Truth, that the King of Prussia hath represented to the Court of France, that if his most Unchristian Majesty

[1] A similar allusion in *Champion* of 20 March 1740 ('like *Cato* in the Play, we are like to be *doubly arm'd*; ii. 26) indicates that Addison's play ('Thus am I doubly arm'd: my death and life, | My bane and antidote, are both before me'), V. 21–2, not Plutarch, is to be recalled.

[2] *The Whitehall Evening Post; or, London Intelligencer* began publishing on 15 February 1746. According to a 'printed Advertisement' for it in the *Westminster Journal* of 15 February, 'This Paper will be supplied, for the most Part, with fresh Intelligence from Correspondents of its own, so as not to be a mere Transcript of others already published. . . . The Narrative will be plainly true, without the Interruptions of ingenious Conceits, or profound Speculations.' Fielding is here clearly responding to criticism of commentary like his own in the *TP*.

[3] The letter does not in fact appear until no. 19 (4–11 March 1746). For a text, see Locke, p. [169].

[4] It is never resumed.

[5] 'Foreign History' in this number is a declared reprinting from the *General Advertiser* (24 February 1746).

continues in fomenting the Troubles in England, and in extending his Conquests on the Continent, that he shall be obliged to assist the Common Cause with his whole Force.

We are assured, by good Authority, that the Board of Admiralty, at the Head of which is a noble Peer,[1] whose only Inducement to act in that Office is to promote the Good of his Country, have resolved to fit out a very formidable Fleet against our Enemies this Spring, by which Means we hope to humble them in that Element, in which it is their greatest and deepest Design to rival us.

The *General Advertiser* of Yesterday gives us the following Account of the French Ships taken by Commodore Knowles, which being much clearer and better than the *Gazette*'s, we shall transcribe from the former Historian.

Letter from Deal, Feb. 22.

'Commodore Knowles arrived here last Night, in his Majesty's Ship the Hastings, with the Tryton, Salamander, and Vulcan, who brought in two large French Ships, which they took off Ostend, bound to Scotland, having on board 500 Men, of Fitz-James's Regiment of Horse, in the Service of France, dismounted. The Persons of Distinction on board are,

Lord Fitz-James	A Marquis of France
The second Son of the	Sir Edward Butler
D. of Berwick	Sir Peter Nugent
Lord Tyrconnel	—— Nugent, Esq.;
Count de Ruth	Brigadier Cook

And several Officers, whose Names are not yet known, to the Number of 40 in the whole. One of these Ships has on board twelve Brass Cannon twenty-four Pounders, and a considerable Quantity of Money, 10,000 *l.* being, as we hear, already found.'

They write from Covent-Garden, that on Wednesday last there was at the Oratorio a great deal of excellent Music, and no Company;[2] and from the Haymarket on Saturday we are advised, that there was a great deal of Company there present, and no Music.

[1] The duke of Bedford, who succeeded Winchilsea as first lord in the cabinet formed on the 'broad bottom' of late 1744. He resigned with the Pelhams on 11 February 1746; Lord John Russell, *Correspondence of John, Fourth Duke of Bedford* (London, 1842), i. 62. The official notice of his reappointment is in the *London Gazette* of 24 February 1746. Fielding's compliment to Bedford, tacked on to an ordinary news item, is slanted to appeal to those readers, 'patriot' and otherwise, who preferred a naval to a military commitment in the war. Cf. *London Evening Post* of 25–7 February 1746: 'It is said no *British Troops* will be sent abroad this Campaign, but that the Strength of our Fleet will be exerted to the utmost.—Should this prove true, and all our *A——ls* [admirals] prove honest, we may at last give one Specimen of our *real* Power.'

[2] This oblique compliment to Handel refers to the second performance (19 February 1746) of his 'New Occasional Oratorio' and should be compared to the notice of the project in 'Apocrypha' of *TP* no. 14 (28 January–4 February 1746), above, p. 414. See also *London Stage*, Part 3, ii. 1219, 1220. The oratorio, with 'Words taken from Milton and Spenser', was part of Handel's scheme to make good to his subscribers his failure to mount the stipulated number of performances during the 1744–5 season.

An EPILOGUE,

Design'd to be spoken by Mrs. WOFFINGTON, *in the Character of a Volunteer.*[1]

Enter, reading a Gazette.

Curse on all Cowards, say I! Why, bless my Eyes—
No, no, it can't be true; this Gazette lies:
Our Men retreat before a scrub Banditti,
Who scarce cou'd fright the Buff-Coats of the City!
Well, if 'tis so, and that our Men can't stand,
'Tis Time we Women take the Thing in Hand.
Thus, in my Country's Cause, I now appear,
A bold, smart, Khevenhuller'd Volunteer.
And really, mark some Heroes in the Nation,
Ye'll think this no unnatural Transformation.
For if in Valour real Manhood lies,
All Cowards are but—Women in Disguise.
        They cry these Rebels are so stout and tall:
Ay, Lord, I'd lower the proudest of them all:
Try but my Mettle, place me in the Van,
And post me if I don't bring down my Man.
Had we an Army of such valorous Wenches,
What Men, d'ye think, would dare attack our Trenches?
Oh! how th'Artillery of our Eyes wou'd maul 'em!
But our mask'd Batteries! Lord, how they wou'd gall 'em!
No Rebel 'gainst such Force durst take the Field,
For, damme, but we'd die before we'd yield!
        Joking apart; we Women have strong Reason,
To stop the Progress of this Popish Treason;

[1] This widely reprinted *double entendre* is often attributed to Fielding (e.g. by Cross, iii. 338, and Locke, p. 158). However, it was published in *DA* of 24 February 1746, a day earlier than its publication in the *TP*, a fact which tells heavily against Fielding's authorship. A single-leaf printing (verso blank) of 'The Female Volunteer: or, An Attempt to make our Men *Stand*' prefaces a slightly variant text with an explanation that the epilogue was intended for Drury Lane, to be spoken by Woffington 'in the Habit of a Volunteer; upon reading the *Gazette Extraordinary*, containing an Account of the Battle of Falkirk'; see MacBean collection (Aberdeen), 'Pamphlets: Scottish Rebellion, Etc.', item no. 33. A 'Curious Print' entitled 'The Female Volunteer' is advertised at 6*d.* in *General Advertiser* of 26 February 1746, and *London Evening Post* of 1–4 March. The epilogue itself is also reprinted, with minor variations, in *Penny London Post* of 24–6 February; *The Foundling Hospital for Wit, Numb. iii* (London, 1746), pp. 24–5; *London Magazine*, xv (1746), 96. Woffington seems not to have delivered the 'New Occasional Epilogue' at Drury Lane until 13 March; *London Stage*, Part 3, ii. 1225. But an 'Epilogue in the Character of a Volunteer—Miss Harrison' was advertised for Goodman's Fields as early as 24 February; ibid., ii. 1221. John Doran, *London in the Jacobite Times* (London, 1877), ii. 150, offers an unsubstantiated and anachronistic account: 'One of these [bards], the Jacobites being defeated, wrote an epilogue . . . but the poem was not finished till interest in the matter had greatly evaporated, and the poet was told he was "too late". Of course, he shamed the rogues by printing his work'; cited by Locke, p. 158.

For now, when Female Liberty's at Stake,
All Women ought to bustle for its Sake.
Should these audacious Sons of *Rome* prevail,
Vows, Convents, and that Heathen Thing a Veil,
Must come in Fashion; and such Institutions
Would suit but oddly with our Constitutions:
What gay Coquet wou'd brook a Nun's Profession?
And I've some private Reasons 'gainst Confession.

    Besides, our good Men of the Church, they say,
(Who now, thank Heav'n, may Love as well as Pray)
Must then be only wed to cloyster'd Houses:
Stop,—there we're fobb'd of twenty thousand Spouses:
And, Faith, no bad ones, as I'm told; then judge ye,
Is't fit we lose our—Benefit of Clergy.

    In Freedom's Cause, ye Patriot-Fair, arise,
Exert the sacred Influence of your Eyes;
On valiant Merit deign alone to smile,
And vindicate the Glory of our Isle;
To no base Coward prostitute your Charms,
Disband the Lover who deserts his Arms:
So shall you fire each Hero to his Duty,
And British Rights be sav'd by British Beauty.

From APOCRYPHA.

... *Thursday.* The following is an exact List of the Privateers now fitting out at St. Malo's, *viz.* The St. Francis, 24 Guns; Felicite, 20 Guns; Cæsar, 26 Guns; Belarmine, 22 Guns; Royal, 26 Guns; Turk, 30 Guns; and tbe Belleisle, 28 Guns. The Eight following are said; *viz.* The Fortune, 24 Guns; St. Dennis, 22 Guns; Louis, 22 Guns; Deliverance, 26 Guns; Holy Cross, 24 Guns; Speedwell, 20 Guns; Soliel, 24 Guns; and the Vulcan, 20 Guns; besides two Men of War, 50 Guns each. D. G. *As we suppose the Historian keeps no Correspondence with the Enemy, it is strange how he gains such exact Intelligence.*

The Waistcoat of the Duke of Buckingham, which was taken among the rest of the Things from the Effigies in Westminster-Abby, has been found secreted behind a Seat in the Abby, where the Persons who shew them usually sit. D. G. *By this one would guess that the living Thief wanted a Waistcoat as little as the dead Duke. . . .*[1]

Yesterday it was reported, that the Person mentioned to be sent to the Bastile in Paris, is the Marshal Belleisle. D. A. *(Monday) If this be true, the Marshal may perhaps wish himself again in Windsor Castle.*[2]

[1] The original theft is noted and similarly commented on in 'Apocrypha' of no. 15 (4–11 February 1746), above, p. 417.

[2] Charles-Louis-Auguste Fouquet (1684–1761), comte de Belle-Isle, maréchal de France (1741), had been arrested on diplomatic business in Hanover on 20 December 1744 N.S., and brought to

All the Accounts from Scotland agree, that the Rebels are flying before the Duke of Cumberland *like hunted Hares*; that several are escaped out of Scotland; and that many of them are striving to come to Ireland, which will be a bad Asylum for them, as they will certainly be taken, and brought to condign Punishment. G. A. *By their taking the Water they may be more properly compared to hunted Stags.*

Yesterday was held at Bow Church in Cheapside, the Anniversary Meeting of the Society for propagating the Gospel in Foreign Parts; there were present his Grace the Archbishop of Canterbury, and several of the Bishops, the Right Hon. the Lord Mayor, Aldermen, *&c.* when an excellent Sermon was preached by the Right Rev. Dr. Matthew Hutton, Lord Bishop of Bangor, after which they were elegantly entertained by the Right Hon. the Lord Mayor, at Goldsmith's Hall in Forster Lane. L. C. *It is Pity some Method was not invented for the Propagation of the Gospel in Great Britain.*

The same Day an unhappy Accident happened to a Woman, Chambermaid to a Person of Reputation, that had, unknown to the Family she liv'd in, pawn'd her Mistress's Gold Watch, to the Pawnbroker lately burnt out in George's Court, who, on hearing of her Loss, went into her Chamber, and hang'd herself. L. C. *We mention this as a Warning to all Servants; that such who have imitated this Chambermaid in the Crime, may be incited to follow her Example in the Punishment.*

Monday. Last Friday came on a Trial at the Court of Common Pleas, Westminster, before the Lord Chief Justice Willes, in an Action of false Imprisonment, which was brought by George Fry, against Sir Chaloner Ogle, which lasted till two o'Clock on Saturday Morning, and then the Jury brought in a Verdict for the Plaintiff, and gave him a Thousand Pounds Damages. The Council for the Plaintiff were Mr. Serjeant Skinner, Mr. Serjeant Prime, and Mr. Serjeant Willes; and the Council for Sir Chaloner were Sir Thomas Bootle, Mr. Serjeant Birch, Mr. Serjeant Draper, Mr. Serjeant Bootle, Mr. Legg, and Mr. Mason. L. C. *Hence it appears that two to one is not as great Odds at Law as at Foot-Ball. . . .*[1]

Casualties. Several Persons have hanged and drowned themselves in the Papers; *but as their Names were never known (or perhaps heard of) while they were alive, we apprehend it would be to no Purpose to mention them now they are dead.*

Preferred. The Rev'd Mr. Charles Garth, to a Living. He was Author of several excellent Discourses on Christianity, D. G. *We are sorry we have never seen nor heard of any of these before.*

England in February 1745. His 'magnificently close' confinement at Windsor Castle provoked public comment on its costliness—Walpole wrote Mann (28 February 1745) that the cost was £100 per diem; *Yale Walpole*, xix. 18. In April 1745 Belle-Isle and his brother moved from Windsor to Frogmore House, which Belle-Isle had leased from the duchess of Northumberland for £600 for three years; *DA* of 12 April 1745, cited by *Yale Walpole*, loc. cit. Belle-Isle, who was suspected of being ready to assist the jacobite invasion, was formally released in July 1745 as part of the condition for freeing British prisoners held by the French. He left England on 13 August; *DA* of 16 August 1745.

[1] Fielding will state the odds similarly in *Tom Jones*, xii. ix. 655.

THE TRUE PATRIOT, No. 18, From Tuesday, February 25, to Tuesday, March 4, 1746.[1]

THE TRUE PATRIOT, No. 19, From Tuesday, March 4, to Tuesday, March 11, 1746.

From *The* PRESENT HISTORY *of* GREAT BRITAIN.

... *Marriages.* Captain Talbot to Miss Plunket, a beautiful Lady with a handsome Fortune. Symonds Steward, Esq; a Gentleman of a large Estate, to Miss Ruckland, a fine Lady and a good Fortune. Miss Turner, of Yorkshire, to a French Ensign in the Dutch Service. Mr. Winnington of Egremond in Cumberland, to Miss Towers, an agreeable Lady, with a handsome Fortune. Mr. Comber to Miss Petworth, a fine Lady, with a great Fortune. Mr. Turner, of Booth-Street, in Spittle-fields, to Mrs. Votier, of Spittle-Square. N.B. *None but happy Marriages get into the Papers.*[2]

Deaths. . . . Mr. Philpot, Summoner to the Commissioners of Sewers, to whose Place the D. A. has been pleased to recommend a *capable* and *deserving* Person. . . . Dr. Wright, an eminent *dissenting* Minister. Dr. Wright *not dead*, but only *reported* so. The Rev'd Mr. Conder. The same Gentleman *not dead*, but in a *fair Way* of *Recovery.* . . . Mr. Cowsmaker, a wealthy Brewer in Westminster. Henry Bull, Esq; he had a large Estate in Somersetshire. The Rev. Mr. Steer, a Yorkshire Clergyman of an excellent Character.

---

[1] Beginning with no. 18, 'Foreign History' ceases to rely mainly on reprintings from other papers and becomes much more editorial, announcing itself as 'a regular Series of History'. It also appears to be by another hand, possibly Ralph's. For texts, see Locke. 'Present History' also appears to be by another, more 'speculative' hand (Walpole applies this term to Ralph's work on *The Remembrancer*; *Memoirs of . . . George the Second*, i. 301). It defines 'the new Patriotism' rather than, as earlier, commenting on the rebellion. Beginning with no. 18 there is no 'Apocrypha' or organized commentary on news items from other papers. For the possible significance of these changes, see 'General Introduction', above, pp. lxii–lxiii. The Lenten assizes on the western circuit began 4 March 1746, and Fielding may have been away from his paper on that business.

[2] Given Fielding's likely absence from London on western circuit business, this comment and the others which follow probably should not be attributed to him. Furthermore, the mere italicizing of words and phrases from the original items, without further comment, differs from the practice of immediately preceding numbers and suggests that Fielding was no longer concerning himself with such matters. There is only one comment of any kind in no. 20 (Locke, p. [176]), and after that all commentary ceases.

INDEX OF NAMES, PLACES, AND TOPICS